A Glimpse Through Time:

Andronicus

ISBN 978-0-578-33696-1

Printed in the United States of America

Edited by Kevin Miller
Cover design by Fyra
Cover Images by Fyra / Adobe Stock

This book is dedicated to
Joseph DeMieri

What follows is a work of fantasy fiction. The world in this story is meant to be a reflection of our own, with many accurate similarities, while remaining a wholly fictional universe. While many different cultures' calendars are used throughout this story, all dates will only be referred to by the Christian calendar.

Act I
A True Spartan Warrior

Chapter 1
Andronicus

1

Three thousand years before the general would fulfill his destiny and wage the war between good and evil, he was a normal boy. He was born Andronicus in the kingdom of Sparta in the year 496 BC. He was born as all babies were born in Sparta at that time, delivered by a sort of midwife. His mother, Athenia, lay in the same bed in which he had been conceived, sweating and panting, clutching the sheets tight in her hands. Aristocles, her husband, stood silently in the doorway, watching anxiously, his fingers tapping restlessly against the sword still strapped to his side. The midwife instructed Athenia as she did all the mothers, and Athenia obeyed. She seemed to feel less pain than she had been told to expect. The midwife told her to push, and she did. She gave one hard push, accompanied by a yelp of pain, and Andronicus came into the world. He only cried a bit at first, and then he fell silent, taking in the new world around him.

As Athenia held him in her arms, he looked up into her soft green eyes. She was amazed at how green his eyes were; they almost seemed to glow. A moment later, Athenia felt Aristocles at her side.

"He is a fine baby," Aristocles proudly proclaimed, gazing down at his son. "He will make a fine warrior someday."

Athenia winced at the reminder that her child would only be hers for a few short years before entering a lifetime of soldiering. Nevertheless, they laughed and talked of the future, though perhaps not so very far ahead.

Andronicus was washed and coddled and placed on the bed between them. His parents noted right away what a calm, quiet baby he was. He didn't cry at all; he simply stared up at them with his bright green eyes. Athenia smiled down at her little boy with nothing but love, but Aristocles was unsettled by the way the boy just stared without making any noise. His little brothers had always cried when they were babies, although they had both died young.

2

Later that night, Aristocles went out walking through the small sea town of Gytheion. He wandered the empty streets, receiving a nod of approval from every guard he passed. He didn't need to wear his cloak; they all knew who he was.

He walked past the quiet houses and the empty market and up his favorite hill until he reached a cliff overlooking the sea. It was a quiet night, and he thought the moon looked bigger than it had in years. The stars appeared brighter too, covering the entire sky. There were no clouds, and the moon and the stars illuminated the land almost as if it were day.

In the distance Aristocles heard a wolf howl, quickly answered by its pack. He had always admired the wolves, the way they hunted, and the way they always had a leader. They reminded him of himself, and of Sparta.

As he walked along the cliff, Aristocles looked out over the vast Mediterranean Sea, the starlight flickered and danced across the lightly roving water. He stood there thinking of his new son and dreaming of what glorious battles might lay in his future. Aristocles was a great warrior, having fought against the Athenians in many battles over the years. He dreamed of little Andronicus growing up to be a mighty warrior someday, perhaps even a captain, as he was.

He stood there thinking large thoughts for his little boy when he felt something odd come over him, something he had never felt before. A kind of chill crept down his spine, and he suddenly had the distinct idea that something grand had begun that night. Something grander and greater than him or his wife, greater than any battle he might fight in, greater perhaps than Sparta itself.

This foreign thought frightened Aristocles. He was a great warrior, but he had never been much of a thinker. He had always followed orders and respected Spartan law above all. This new inkling of importance, of feeling a greater connection, disturbed Aristocles greatly. He believed in the gods as much as any man, and he feared their wrath, but he didn't think about them very often.

Aristocles had never liked thinking about the gods. Ideas like that, the kind of ideas that are the scariest, most important ideas, did nothing but frighten and confuse him. As far as he was concerned, matters of the gods, of sacrifices and offerings, and all the other holy garbage was better left to the priests and philosophers. The matter of defending Sparta, of killing anyone who stood against her, was better left to Aristocles and his kind.

The feeling that had come over him as he stood on the cliff frightened him more than any fight he had ever been in. It was more than a feeling; it was a kind of knowing, a cold assurance that his little boy would grow up to do more than Aristocles could possibly fathom.

He allowed these odd thoughts to linger for a while before he headed back home, more unsettled than he was before he left. As he walked, his mind returned to thoughts of battles his son might fight in one day, and the feeling he had on the cliff drifted away. By the time he stepped through his front door an hour later, he had forgotten it entirely.

3

While Aristocles was out contemplating things he had seldom thought of before, Athenia sat with Andronicus in her arms. She too thought of a grand future for their child. She imagined Andronicus growing up to be a handsome and gallant young man. Taking a wife and having children of his own. Being a peaceful man, a man who could convince others not to go to war. She even imagined him growing up to be a king someday, even though she knew that was impossible.

Just as Aristocles was feeling whatever it was

he was feeling while staring at the sea, Athenia felt something too, though not quite the same. Andronicus had been sleeping for almost an hour, and she had just been sitting there. One second she was nodding off, dreaming of her boy's future, and the next she was wide awake. She felt an odd feeling course through her body, and then the hairs on her neck slowly stood on end.

She looked down and almost screamed. Andronicus was looking up at her with wide eyes. He didn't make a sound or stir at all. He just lay there staring at her. If she had thought his eyes had glowed before, now his eyes seemed to burn with a green fire. In that moment she knew. She would forget soon after, but in that moment she knew who Andronicus would become. As she stared at his piercing green eyes, she thought she could almost see a light deep in his pupils. It was as if she could see a hint of white in the center of the black, shining with a brightness she had never seen before. His eyes seemed to draw her in, and for a moment she forgot where she was and who she was. All she knew was the light in Andronicus's little eyes.

Then it was gone. She blinked and looked down and saw Andronicus sleeping again, his little chest rising and falling and his eyes gently closed. She thought she must have dozed off and dreamed the light, and she forgot what she had seen almost immediately.

She heard Aristocles enter not long after, so she put Andronicus down in his little bed. When Aristocles entered, he looked rather pale.

"Are you alright?" She asked, smiling at him from their bed.

"Of course," he replied a little too abruptly. "I was just out thinking about the boy, and what a fine warrior he will make."

"Yes," Athenia agreed softly. In her mind's eye, she saw a flicker of bright light, and then it was gone in a flash. Aristocles slowly undressed and climbed into bed next to her.

"A fine warrior," she repeated as she dozed off-to sleep.

4

The first year of Andronicus's life passed quickly. While Aristocles spent the year away battling the Athenians, Athenia cherished her time with little Andronicus. She loved him more than anything. She had been scared and intimidated when she had been made to marry her husband, but also excited. She was only seventeen at the time, and Aristocles was twenty-four and already a renowned warrior. But her parents were gone, and she was eager to start her own family. She had grown to love Aristocles in short time, but it was nothing like the love she felt for her little Andronicus.

Andronicus was a very easy baby. He almost never cried, and Athenia would spend hours singing to him and staring out at the sea. Before Andronicus, Athenia had to wait for Aristocles's return alone, always fearing he would fall in battle, but now she had Andronicus to wait with her. It felt like she finally had something all to herself, even though she knew it wouldn't last long.

A little more than a year after Andronicus was born, Aristocles returned home for a short while. Not long after his return, Athenia became pregnant again. They spent a few months together as a family before Aristocles had to leave again.

Athenia spent most of her second pregnancy alone with Andronicus. Those first two years would always be special to Athenia, her years alone with her little boy. Andronicus learned to walk and soon after to talk. He ran everywhere, never crying when he fell. Even after he learned to talk, he was a quiet boy, only speaking when he was asked something or if he wanted to know something.

5

The night Androcles was born could not have been more different than the night Andronicus was born. A terrible storm had been lashing the area for three days and showed no signs of stopping. Thunder crashed outside, and the wind whistled through the small seaside town. Athenia was in much more pain this time. She screamed as the midwife coached her, just like before. Aristocles was still in Athens and would not return for a month, and her own parents had died when she was just a girl, so it was just her, the midwife, and Andronicus.

Andronicus sat in the corner, watching quietly as his mother screamed in pain. His young mind was confused by what he saw, but he sat there just as peaceful as ever. Athenia's labor took many hours, and after Androcles was born she looked terrible. She gazed upon him for a while, noting he had the same bright green eyes as his brother, before falling asleep. That night she dreamed more than she ever had before. She bounced from one dream to the next for what seemed an eternity, seeing things she didn't understand and didn't want to.

Athenia woke the next morning, as she would many mornings after, to the loud crying of Androcles. She could only remember a fragment of her dreams from the night before, and they started to fade quickly as she took Androcles out of his little bed. He was loud and restless, the polar opposite of Andronicus, but Athenia already loved him just the same.

When Aristocles returned the following month, he remarked on what a fine baby they had made, and announced his boys would both be great warriors someday. He never mentioned the dream he had the night Androcles was born. He hadn't even known it was the same night until a week later, and by then he had mostly forgotten it, but he could still recall a strange light and a dark figure that gave him chills whenever he thought of it.

6

They spent the next four years as a family. Aristocles spent most of his time away in battle, but when he was home he was a good father. He taught his boys how to fish and hunt before they were five years old. He even made them little wooden swords to practice fighting with. Aristocles always tried to teach both his boys the importance of loyalty and honor, but these lessons only got through to Andronicus, as Androcles was very little.

Aristocles died when Andronicus was six and Androcles only four. He died as he had always wanted, in battle. The Spartans thought of themselves as the greatest warriors in the world, and in Sparta there was no higher honor than to die a glorious death on the battlefield. Aristocles had spent most of his adult life fighting the Athenians and other Greek cities, but in the end he died fighting alongside the Athenians. A Persian army came to Greece, and men from every Greek city banded together to fight them.

Andronicus stood in the streets of the big city with his mother and brother, waiting excitedly for his father to ride in on his horse, like he always did. Andronicus loved seeing his father ride through the big archway with all the people cheering and applauding, though there didn't seem to be many people waiting this time. When the soldiers returned, there were far fewer of them than normal. Andronicus looked around for his father, but he didn't see him, and his little mind slowly started to understand.

A tall, somber-looking man approached Athenia and told her something, but Andronicus was still looking for his father. When Athenia turned to him, tears running down her face, and told him his father had died, Andronicus burst into tears for the first time she could remember. For the next few weeks Andronicus cried even more than his little brother. Andronicus was old enough to remember his father, but Androcles's only memory of their father was that of a fierce warrior.

7

Two months after his father died, Andronicus was sent off to begin his training in the city of Sparta. Sparta was a mighty nation, and its warriors were the finest Greece had to offer, perhaps the finest in the world, and they began their training young. Andronicus was one of eleven students under the teacher Archelaus. Archelaus had fought alongside Aristocles in the battles against Athens and the recent battle against the Persians, and he treated Andronicus differently than the other boys from the start.

Andronicus arrived at the camp a sad, lonely boy, still stricken with grief over his father's death. On his first day there, he met a boy named Euthymius, and they became friends almost instantly. By the second week, they were inseparable. Andronicus got along with almost all the boys in his class, but Euthymius quickly became his closest friend.

Andronicus showed superior fighting skill from the very beginning, beating every other student in his class. Most of the other boys seemed impressed with Andronicus, except for a boy named Lycus. Lycus was also the son of a great warrior; a great fallen warrior. Lycus always seemed jealous of the way Archelaus treated Andronicus, and the two boys constantly fought to be the best at anything and everything. They would fight each other often, and Archelaus would usually let them go until one was beaten, making them both stronger. Andronicus liked to think he had won more times, but he eventually lost count.

8

The boys trained every day from dawn to dusk. They ate three meals a day and ran five miles a day. By the time Androcles began training, two years later, Andronicus and his friends had become fit young fighters, ready to throw a blow at the slightest insult. Androcles had a different teacher, but the brothers got to see each other often enough. Andronicus gave his younger brother help and advice, and Androcles quickly became the best fighter in his class as well.

Androcles followed his older brother around whenever he could. Since he showed much the same promise, Andronicus's friends accepted him as part of their group. Androcles did have one friend, however, who was his own age, a boy named Theodotus. Androcles and Theodotus became friends much as Andronicus and Euthymius had. Theodotus was not a very strong boy, but he was probably the smartest of them all. Theodotus's father was a high priest in the temple of Apollo, and he made sure his son worshiped the gods fastidiously. Theodotus told them all kinds of stories about the gods, but only Androcles ever seemed to listen.

Over the next few years, Andronicus grew close with his band of friends and even with Lycus. Archelaus was strict and tough and drove the boys closer to each other through fear and exhaustion, and he made them strong. By the time Andronicus turned ten, he wanted nothing more in life than to be a great warrior like his father. He couldn't wait until the day he would fight in his first battle. He already knew he was a superior fighter, and he longed for the day he could finally prove himself. Andronicus wanted so desperately to prove himself as a great fighter, but not in his wildest dreams could he ever imagine just how much fighting he would have to do in his life.

Chapter 2
The First Test
1

Not long after Andronicus turned twelve, it was time for his first test, along with the rest of his class. They were all sent home for the night to see their families before they went off to face the mysterious trial.

Andronicus was surprised to see Androcles home as well. He was sick with a terrible cough and had been sent home to keep the other boys safe. Androcles tried asking him about the test, but Andronicus told him he had to concentrate.

Andronicus spent half the night lying in bed wide awake. He had spent months preparing for his first test, running and climbing and learning about the different plants and animals in the nearby woods. He didn't know what the test was going to be, but he guessed it would be something in the woods. The older boys had all said that Andronicus and his friends would be so scared, they would cry like girls.

Andronicus knew he could be brave, and yet he still could not fall asleep. He could hear Androcles's ragged snoring next to him. Androcles had had the bad cough all winter, and at night his breath sounded like stones grinding in a jar.

As he lay awake, Andronicus imagined the many different perils he might face the next day. His mind was full of monsters and demons. He knew that minotaurs didn't really exist, but he imagined fighting one with Lycus and Euthymius nonetheless. He knew there were wolves in the woods. He had heard them at night before, and he wondered if he would see one in his test.

He finally drifted off to sleep sometime later and awoke as the sun peeked through the window. He wasted no time getting dressed and ready for his big day. He was nervous and excited all at once, and more than anything he just wanted to get started. Androcles sat on his bed in the corner, coughing lightly every thirty seconds or so as Andronicus slid into his new sandals.

"What do you think you'll have to do?" Androcles asked.

Andronicus sighed deeply. "You know no one knows the test before they take it," he snapped, as if he hadn't been pondering the same question all night.

Andronicus turned around and saw his mother standing in the doorway, smiling at him. "You look wonderful, darling. Very tough," she said brightly. "Your brother looks tough, doesn't he, Androcles?"

"Oh, yes." Androcles perked up at being noticed. "He's the toughest in his whole class."

Andronicus was oblivious to his younger brother's admiration. When he had finished tying his belt, he marched out of his room with Androcles at his heels. Athenia bent down and gave Andronicus a quick kiss on the cheek, and he hurriedly wiped it off when Androcles started snickering.

Athenia and Androcles both wished him luck as he set off back to the city. As he rode back to Sparta in the back of a rickety oxcart, his mind jumped from one mad idea to the next, imagining things he knew wouldn't happen. He arrived at the compound thinking he was early, only to find Lycus and Nikopheros already waiting.

"Always just a step behind," Lycus said, to Niko's delight. Andronicus glared at them as they laughed.

"We'll see who's a step behind when the test is over," he replied, sneering. It looked like Lycus wanted to say something more, but at that moment a group of five boys walked up to join them, Euthymius amongst them. Thymi came over and stood next to Andronicus as they waited for the last few stragglers. The boys all spoke excitedly as they waited for the test to begin. Many of them claimed to have heard what the test was from their older brothers, but they all told a different story.

Andronicus and Thymi were listening intently to another boy's claim that they would be sent out to battle a group of Athenian boys when Archelaus emerged from his quarters. They all fell silent and scurried into line under Archelaus's fierce gaze. He looked them over silently, searching for any mistakes in their attire.

"You there," Archelaus barked, "your sandal is torn. Go home." The boy began to plead but stopped when he saw the menacing look on Archelaus's face. He turned and ran off, weeping loudly.

"Anyone else?" Archelaus asked. No one made so much as a peep.

"Good. Now line up behind me in two rows of five." The boys hurried into new lines as Archelaus spoke. "We are going to march through the old road and under the pass of Hermes. You will not speak to anyone. You will not wave to anyone. You will not so much as look at anyone, or I will send you home."

The boys all shuddered at the thought of Archelaus shouting their name in front of everyone and sending them away. They formed two perfectly straight lines and stood silently, awaiting instruction. Archelaus bellowed out his marching order, and the boys quickly fell to.

2

Andronicus marched at the head of his column of five. Their sandaled feet thudded against the old stones in perfect unison, as they had been practicing for months. The street was lined with women and young children watching the procession. Amongst the women, Andronicus saw a few men, the old and the wounded. The observers neither cheered nor waved; they simply watched the young phalanx march by. Andronicus remembered watching the older boys march off to their tests when he was a small child, and he felt immense pride at being one of those boys now.

Archelaus walked a few feet in front of the columns, leading them to their still unknown testing grounds. Andronicus didn't know what the test was going to be, but he was fairly confident he would pass it. He had risen to the top of the class quickly, and now, six years in, he was the natural group leader. The only other member of the class who could keep up with him was Lycus, who marched at his side, leading the other column.

As they marched in rhythm, some of the boys' mothers called to them or waved. Lycus's mother called out to him, and his pale skin flushed red when Andronicus looked over at him. Andronicus smirked to himself, knowing how much Lycus hated looking childish.

A few minutes later, Andronicus saw his own mother standing in the crowd, and he tensed up. She didn't wave, as some of the other mothers had; she simply smiled at him. He returned the smile and felt a warm assurance that he would pass his test, and pass it before Lycus.

Not long after that, Andronicus saw Androcles sitting with Theodotus. Androcles beamed and waved fiercely as Andronicus marched past. Andronicus smiled and gave his brother a quick wink before continuing down the path.

3

As they neared the end of the street, Andronicus felt his nerves start to rise again. He peered ahead but could not see any sign of a test. He looked over at Lycus and saw him searching around wildly for a clue of their test as well. When they finally reached the end of the stone path and passed under the high old archway of Hermes, Archelaus stopped and turned abruptly to face them. Andronicus and Lycus stopped in unison and blindly hoped the rest of the group would do likewise. Andronicus held his breath as Archelaus glared down at them with his scarred, angry face, waiting silently for his command.

"You may fall out of formation and walk the rest of the way from here," Archelaus said, finally breaking the tense silence. As soon as he said it, he turned and strode off down the dirt path leading toward the forest. Andronicus looked at Lycus and saw that he looked as puzzled as Andronicus felt. He looked behind him and saw Euthymius and Nikopheros looking at him for instruction. He turned back and saw Archelaus already fifty feet down the path. Andronicus sprinted after him and saw Lycus do the same out of the corner of his eye.

The two lead boys raced down the path, leaving the rest behind. Andronicus reached Archelaus's side two steps before Lycus.

"That's not fair!" Lycus shouted angrily. "You started first!" Andronicus laughed and flung his arms in the air, and Lycus lunged at him. Andronicus fell to the ground but pulled Lycus down with him. The boys wrestled in the dirt until Archelaus grabbed them both by the backs of their shirts and wrenched them apart. He threw them onto their backs in the dirt on opposing sides of the path.

"Enough!" Archelaus shouted ferociously. "I will have no nonsense on the day of your test." He glared down at Lycus, who shriveled away, trying but failing to hide his look of anger. "Any more of your outbursts, Lycus, and you can take your test with next year's class."

Archelaus turned and resumed his stoic march down the old road. Euthymius arrived a moment later and helped Andronicus to his feet. Nikopheros tried to help Lycus up, but Lycus swatted his hand away and scurried to his feet by himself. He glared at Andronicus before turning to follow Archelaus.

The boys walked in groups of twos and threes

down the path, with Archelaus in front. They whispered back and forth about what the mysterious test might be. Andronicus and Euthymius debated whether or not they would have to fight and, if so, what they would have to fight.

"They're not going to make us fight today, Thymi. We haven't even had that much training yet," Andronicus whispered. Euthymius still looked unconvinced as he nervously nipped at his fingernails.

"Yes, but everything is about fighting here," he replied. "It would be just like them to make us fight for our first test, to see if we can or not." Andronicus knew his friend could fight if he had to; he just didn't like it.

"I don't think it will be fighting, Thymi," Andronicus said, trying to reassure him. "I think it's going to be something about being strong and fast. Most of our training so far has been about being able to run a lot and be strong. The test is probably just that." Euthymius looked a little bit less worried, but Andronicus knew he was still quite scared.

"And besides," Andronicus continued, trying to reassure him, "even if it is fighting, you'll do just fine."

"Oh, I hate fighting," Euthymius whined. It was his favorite thing to say. "Everything is always about fighting." Andronicus shook his head and smiled, then continued walking toward the woods. It seemed more and more likely as they went that the test would be somewhere in the woods.

4

As the sun set in the west, Andronicus started wondering if the test would be in the dark, though he decided not to mention that thought to Thymi. He looked around and saw the other boys all walking with their heads down, all except Lycus. He was still shooting angry glances at Andronicus while grinding his teeth together. Andronicus liked beating Lycus, but he never really got that angry when he lost. Lycus, on the other hand, resented Andronicus for every single loss he had suffered over the years, and sometimes Andronicus worried about him.

The boys marched on, blindly following

Archelaus down the path. When the sun fell below the hills in the distance, the light began to fade. Soon the boys were marching through the dark night. The moon was barely a sliver, and a few dark clouds moved slowly across the starry sky. The boys huddled together and followed closely behind Archelaus, who hadn't said a word since they left the city.

The trees started to get thicker and denser as they went, and Andronicus realized they had entered the forest some time ago. He looked up and could no longer see the stars. He looked from side to side and could barely see the outline of the boys walking on either side of him. They kept walking through the dark for a while, a few of the boys stumbling along.

"Stop!" Archelaus's sturdy voice called out from ahead. Andronicus stopped immediately and felt the other boys do the same around him. Dark thoughts raced through Andronicus's mind as he stood there in the pitch dark, waiting for Archelaus to speak again. He wondered if this was the testing grounds, if they would have to spend the night there. Or perhaps Euthymius was right; maybe they would have to fight in the total darkness of the forest. Maybe Archelaus had stopped because he saw or heard something up ahead. He could have seen a wolf in the road, or a troop of Athenians sitting in the darkness, waiting for Spartans to come along so they could kill them. Andronicus's mind was full of all sorts of dark possibilities that might lay ahead.

"Your test begins now," Archelaus's menacing voice said softly from the darkness, and the boys all shrank back. "You will remain here in the forest."

Andronicus let out a small sigh of relief. Spending a night in the forest wouldn't be so bad.

"Until I return," Archelaus finished coldly.

A small chill went up Andronicus's spine as he heard Archelaus's heavy footfalls begin in the direction they had come from. Andronicus pondered the idea of being stuck out there for a week or more as Archelaus's footsteps faded away, but he tried not to think about it. The boys all remained silent until they couldn't hear Archelaus's steps anymore.

5

Andronicus crouched in the darkness, shivering lightly. He felt someone standing to either side of him, but he couldn't make out who they were. They all stood in silence, huddled together in the darkness, each contemplating what they might have to do before Archelaus returned.

"What do we do now?" Nikopheros asked, his voice finally breaking the tense silence.

"We wait, stupid," Lycus snapped, "and in the morning we hunt for food."

"Lycus is right," Andronicus agreed, trying to sound braver than he felt. He bent down and started feeling along the ground. "We can't see anything, so we might as well sleep here until morning."

A low chorus of sighs and groans greeted his recommendation, but the boys all spread out and found a spot to sleep for the night. It was slow going because none of them could see much of anything in the pitch black, but eventually they all got settled. Andronicus and Euthymius stayed up talking long after the others had fallen asleep.

"Living in the woods isn't so bad at all," Thymi said, sounding much calmer than he had been on the walk over, "I bet we could stay here for a week if we had to, even two."

"And what are we going to eat, knucklehead?" Andronicus asked. "Just because Lycus says he can hunt for us doesn't mean he can."

"Well, if he can't do it, then you'll have to," Thymi said. "We'll all try to help, but either you or him will have to do it." Andronicus fell silent as he considered that. He had always been the top of the class, but now it seemed he would truly have to be their leader.

"I know," he said after a long pause. They lay silently for some time before they drifted off to dream big dreams.

6

The boys rose with the sun, most of them

utterly confused at their strange surroundings. The trees were thick overhead, but bits of light shone through, lighting the forest floor. As they shook off their sleep and stretched their strained backs, they looked around at each other, no one knowing quite what to do.

"I guess it's time to get some food," Lycus said self-assuredly, looking at Andronicus.

"For now we should probably just look for berries," Andronicus suggested, "until we find something better."

"You can have berries for breakfast if you like," Lycus said with a laugh. "Me and Niko will be eating rabbit."

"And who will be catching this rabbit?" Andronicus asked with a smirk. Lycus turned a deep red and balled his hands into fists.

"I'm going to catch the rabbit," he said angrily, "I have caught plenty of rabbits before. Have you never caught a rabbit?" Some of the other boys snickered and looked at Andronicus nervously.

"I have killed many rabbits, "Andronicus replied coolly, staring back at Lycus, "but I have never caught a rabbit with my bare hands, and neither have you." All the boys' eyes got wide as they looked back to Lycus. He turned an even brighter shade of red and glared at Andronicus with fire in his eyes.

"Are you calling me a liar?" Lycus asked in a low, menacing voice.

Andronicus sighed in exasperation. "I'm not calling you anything, Lycus. I'm just saying that catching a rabbit is harder than you think. It will take you all day, if you can even do it at all. It's better if we find some berries for now and try to hunt for supper."

"Well, have fun with your berries then," Lycus teased. "Come on, Niko, we're going to get some real food." Niko looked uncertain as he glanced from Lycus's self-assured smirk to Andronicus's calm demeanor.

"Go on, Niko," Andronicus whispered, so Lycus couldn't hear. "I'll pick some extra berries for you just in case." Niko gave him a thankful smile and then turned to follow Lycus. Lycus glared at Andronicus before marching down the path.

As Lycus and Nikopheros crept through the woods looking for rabbits, Andronicus split the rest of the group in two, each group going a different way down the path, looking for berries. Archelaus had taught them about every berry that was in this forest, and Andronicus remembered all the poisonous ones. Kleitos claimed to remember all of the poisonous berries as well, so he led the second group.

Andronicus had only led his group about a hundred yards down the path when they found a short sword sticking straight out of the ground, its blade shoved deep into the dirt. Andronicus knew the sword must be from Archelaus, a test to see how they would handle it, and he was glad Lycus was not there at that moment.

Andronicus grasped the sword's hilt and tugged, but the thing wouldn't budge. He grabbed the hilt with both hands and planted his feet in the dirt. After taking a few quick, deep breaths, Andronicus pulled up with all his might. The dirt gave way, and the sword flew out, sending Andronicus tumbling backwards into the dirt. The boys all laughed as Andronicus got to his feet, dusting himself off and joining in the laughter.

"Well, now that we have a sword, we may actually be able to catch a rabbit or two," Andronicus said cheerily. "It's too bad Lycus isn't here to show us how." The boys all laughed cheerfully as they started back up the path.

7

When the sun reached its peak, Andronicus's little group had only found one small patch of berries. They split them up evenly until the bush was bare, and Andronicus set some aside for Niko and Lycus. He only hoped the other group had found some berries themselves. He had seen a couple of rabbits throughout the day, but the boys had been making so much noise that the animals had fled as soon as they were within earshot.

Andronicus turned his group back to meet up with the others, as they had agreed upon earlier. A few hours later, they found them not far from where they had spent the night. Kleitos's group had found three berry patches down their side of the path. After a quick discussion, they all agreed to spend the night by one of the patches down that way. They had begun to walk back down the path when Euthymius spoke up.

"Wait," he said, sounding alarmed. "What about Lycus and Niko? They won't know which way we went."

"Thymi's right," Andronicus said after a moment's thought. "I'll wait here for them. You boys follow Kleitos to the berry patch."

"I'll wait too then," Thymi said solemnly. "I'm the one who brought it up."

"Here," Andronicus said to Kleitos, holding out the sword, "you take it." Kleitos eyed the sword nervously. He was definitely smart, but he had never shown much skill with a blade.

"I think you should keep it," Kleitos said, trying to hide his red face. "There are more of us, so you two will need it." Andronicus shrugged his agreement, and Kleitos quickly turned away.

Andronicus and Euthymius found themselves a couple of nice trees to sit against as the rest of the group disappeared down the path.

"Do you think Lycus has caught any rabbits?" Thymi asked with a smirk. Andronicus burst into giggles, and Thymi joined him. They laughed for nearly twenty minutes, joking about Lycus trying to catch a rabbit with his bare hands.

"This is not such a bad test at all," Thymi said once they had settled down. "I actually kind of like being out here in the woods, eating berries and looking for rabbits." His grin faltered and then fell off completely. "It's a lot better than training to be a *great warrior* all day," he said mockingly.

"Training isn't so bad," Andronicus said. "You just don't like fighting is all."

"I don't like any of it," Thymi corrected him. "I don't like running or hunting or fishing, and I especially don't like fighting."

"So, what do you like, Thymi?" Andronicus asked in an exasperated tone.

"This," Thymi said, "just sitting around in the forest with nothing to do but watch the trees and the birds and the sky and talk."

"You would rather sit around in the forest all day than try to get better at fighting?" Andronicus asked, incredulous.

"Yes," Thymi answered seriously. He stared Andronicus in the eye. "I would much rather sit in the forest all day than be a great warrior."

Andronicus smiled at first, thinking Thymi was joking with him. Then he saw that Thymi truly meant what he had said. Andronicus couldn't fathom not wanting to be a great warrior. It was all he had ever wanted, but Thymi truly seemed to hate the idea of being a warrior.

The boys fell silent for a while, Andronicus struggling with the ideas Thymi had presented and Euthymius just sitting peacefully against his tree, a soft smile on his face.

8

About an hour later, Lycus and Niko came stumbling out of the trees. Both of them were covered in small cuts and scrapes, and Niko had a long deep red gash running across his left arm.

"Looks like you didn't have too much luck," Andronicus said with just a hint of teasing in his voice. "It turns out Archelaus left us a sword to hunt with."

Lycus looked up in outrage. Niko's face fell comically as he realized his day through the brush had been a total waste.

"So, have *you* caught any rabbits?" Lycus shot at him.

"Well, no," Andronicus admitted. "They all ran before I could get close."

Lycus's lips spread into a smirk. "Well, then I guess you won't mind if the next time we see one you let me take the sword," he taunted. Andronicus nodded reluctantly and then handed the sword to him.

The four boys set off down the path, trying to make as little noise as possible. Andronicus hated to think of Lycus coming back the hero, but if he really could catch a rabbit, it would be worth it. The berries would keep them alive, but his stomach was already yearning for a bit of meat.

9

They found no rabbits on the path before they came upon the rest of the group. Most of the other boys were sitting around eating berries and laughing when they arrived. The laughter quickly died when they saw Lycus's angry face.

"It will be getting dark in a couple of hours," Andronicus said to the group, "unless we want berries for breakfast, lunch, and dinner we better go catch a rabbit or two." Everyone nodded or grunted their agreement.

"I think me and Lycus should go," Andronicus said cautiously, looking over at Lycus. "We're the best hunters, and we'll have better luck if it's just the two of us." Lycus scowled at Andronicus. He looked to be somewhere between confusion and anger, as if he was unsure of Andronicus's intentions. No one protested, and Andronicus stared silently at Lycus, waiting for a response.

"Fine," Lycus finally spat, "but I get the sword first." Andronicus nodded and then rolled his eyes to Euthymius as Lycus turned his back. Euthymius held in his laughter as he watched the two of them walk off to their hunt.

They walked well down the path without saying a word to each other. Lycus still had his face all scrunched up in anger, and Andronicus didn't like the way he was gripping the sword.

Just then they heard a slight rustle to their left. Both boys instinctively dropped to the ground, neither making a sound. They crept to the nearest bush on the side of the path. Careful not to make a peep, they looked over the bush and saw a deer eating some grass about thirty yards away.

Andronicus turned to Lycus and motioned to

himself, pointed behind the deer, then motioned for Lycus to go wait in front of it. Lycus nodded curtly and then made his way around. Andronicus crept quietly through the dirt, trying to get as near to the doe as possible without spooking it. He was nearly behind the deer when he stepped on a small twig, sending a cracking noise echoing through the silent woods. The deer's head snapped up immediately. It stood perfectly still, one leg lifted as if it were about to flee, its head cocked around nearly all the way.

Andronicus held perfectly still, mimicking the deer. After a few seconds, the deer lowered its leg and then brought its head back down to the patch of grass. Andronicus crept a few feet closer and then stopped. He couldn't see Lycus, but he hoped he was in position. He could feel his heart racing as he waited for Lycus to give the signal. He started to worry the deer would leave before Lycus was ready.

Finally, he couldn't wait anymore; he just had to hope Lycus was in position. Andronicus jumped out from his hiding spot and shouted as loud as he could. The deer's initial flinch was quite comical. Andronicus startled it so badly, its feet slipped in the dirt before catching a grip. In an utter panic, the deer sprinted away.

Andronicus saw the sword before he saw Lycus. It spun through the air, glinting in the sun on each quick rotation. Andronicus watched in what felt like slow motion as the sword spun once, twice, and then plunged into the fleeing deer's side. The sword sank about halfway into the beast's hide, sending it into an awkward sideways gallop.

"Chase it!" Andronicus shouted, seeing Lycus already running after it. The boys ran after the deer as fast as they could, ducking and weaving around bushes. Even with the sword in its side, the deer was faster, but it stumbled awkwardly, leaving a thick trail of blood. They chased the poor beast for nearly half a mile before it finally collapsed. When they came upon it, it was still struggling to get up. Andronicus pulled the sword from its side and raised it over his head, when Lycus stopped him.

"Hold on," Lycus said between panting breaths, "it's my kill. I get to finish it." Lycus was right. Andronicus handed him the sword and stepped aside. Lycus quickly plunged the blade into the deer's neck. It struggled a second longer, its eyes filled with a wild, terrible fear, before keeling over.

Once the deer was dead, both boys took a step back and stared down at it.

"Good job, Lycus," Andronicus said softly without looking at him. "That was a perfect throw." Lycus didn't respond. Andronicus looked over at him and saw him staring down at the deer's face. For a moment it looked like Lycus was about to cry, but then it passed.

"How are we going to get it to the others?" Lycus finally asked. Andronicus hadn't thought about that. There was no way the two of them would be able to carry the carcass back to the group.

"I suppose I'll have to go and get them," Andronicus said, "and you wait here and guard it."

"I'll start on the deer then," Lycus said, kneeling beside his kill. "Try to find some good sticks for a fire on your way back."

Andronicus nodded and then headed back to the path. It wasn't hard to find because the deer had left such a thick trail of blood. Once he found the path, it didn't take him long to reach the group.

At first they didn't believe him when he said Lycus had killed a deer. He had to spend nearly ten minutes just convincing the group it wasn't a joke. Once he convinced them to at least come with him, they set out again.

10

When they reached Lycus, his arms and chest were covered in blood, and smears of blood were all over his pale face. He had already managed to skin the bottom half of the deer and was slowly working his way around the forelegs. It was an impressive sight as they walked up to him.

"Good work," Andronicus said, genuinely impressed with Lycus's quick progress. "Need any help?"

"Does it look like I need help?" Lycus smiled as he cut carefully through the deer's hide. Andronicus rolled his eyes as he turned to start the fire. They had gathered enough good sticks on the walk over, and they also found two stones that were perfect for starting a fire. Andronicus and Niko took turns trying to start the fire for nearly ten minutes before the flame finally took hold. By then Lycus had the deer's skin up over its back with just the head and front legs remaining.

"We should start cutting pieces off to cook," Andronicus suggested. Lycus nodded and started butchering the animal as he had been taught. He handed Andronicus several long strips of bloody red meat, and Andronicus stuck each strip of meat on a stick and started handing them out. Niko took the first piece and started cooking it over the fire.

It was slow work, and Lycus and Andronicus were the last to eat, but by the time it was fully dark, the boys had all eaten their fill of venison. They spread out and took places around the fire, preparing for another night in the forest. After a quick discussion, they decided someone should stay up to guard them, just in case a wolf came for their remaining meat. Niko wound up with the first watch as everyone else spread out for the night. Andronicus lay looking up at the stars until he dozed off to sleep.

11

Andronicus woke abruptly to the sound of shouting. He opened his eyes to see that it was still dark out, then turned to see what was going on. The fire they had built was just a smoldering pile of embers, but it gave just enough light for Andronicus to see Niko standing with the sword in his hands.

"Lycus! Andronicus!" Niko shouted. "Wake up! Wake up!"

"What is it?" Andronicus said in a sleepy voice, trying to see what Niko was afraid of.

"Wolves," Niko said, sounding terrified. "There are wolves out there. I can hear them."

"You probably just dozed off and had a dream," Lycus said from somewhere in the dark.

"No!" Niko shrieked, "I heard them. They're out there."

At that moment there was a loud rustling sound from somewhere in the dark, and all the boys fell silent. Andronicus scrambled to his feet and walked over to Niko, calmly taking the sword from Niko's shaking hands. Then they heard a low growl coming from somewhere in front of them. Andronicus knew Niko was right; he was sure the wolves had come for the deer meat. They should have known better than to sleep next to the carcass.

"Niko," Andronicus whispered, "try to get the fire going again." Niko bent down and began adding wood and blowing on the embers. Within a matter of seconds a small flame ignited.

"Everyone get away from the carcass," Lycus said as he helped Niko. "Come over here by the fire."

As the boys huddled together by the fire, Andronicus saw the first wolf come slinking toward them. It looked totally black as it crept forward out of the darkness, its head lowered in an intimidating stare. It stood almost as tall as Andronicus, baring its long white fangs. Andronicus stood his ground, the short sword gripped tightly in his hand. The rest of the boys all watched in dismay as Andronicus stepped forward, facing down the wolf.

The wolf waited a few seconds longer, perched on its haunches, growling at Andronicus. When the wolf leaped at him, Andronicus lunged with the sword. He felt the blade hit the wolf, then drive deep into the beast's chest. The wolf's jaws snapped shut inches from his face, and then he felt the claws hit his chest and dig in. Andronicus fell backward from the force of it, and the wolf landed on top of him. When Andronicus hit the dirt, he let out a heavy grunt and felt his lungs close.

As he gasped for air, he felt the wolf being lifted off him. When he was free, he rolled onto his side, still struggling to breathe. As he lay there, gasping for air, a loud howl rose up from the darkness, followed by a ferocious growl. Andronicus tried to scramble to his feet, still coughing and choking, but Lycus rushed forward and pulled the sword out of the dead wolf, waiting for the next one.

A second later another wolf came hurtling out of the darkness. It was much faster than the first one, and even though Lycus successfully plunged the sword into the beast, it hit him with its whole body, snapping its jaws at him and sending him flying backwards. The wolf's fang caught Lycus in the right cheek as it impaled itself, leaving a dark red gash. Lycus went flipping through the dirt, and the wolf collapsed into a dead heap. There was another wolf howl, followed by another, and then a whole chorus of them.

Andronicus grabbed the sword and then stepped forward, ready to face all the wolves, if necessary. Niko stepped up to his side, holding a rock in his hand, a determined look on his face. A moment later Thymi joined them, then Lycus, and then a few of the others. They all stood together, ready to fight the wolves to the death, when they heard a loud whistle.

Andronicus heard a wolf run at them from their left and then another from their right. He stood his ground, sword in hand, ready to fight to the very end. Then, out of nowhere, a large figure leapt in front of them. There was a flash of light as a sword was swung, and Andronicus heard one wolf go down and then the other. When the wolves were down, the dark figure turned to face the boys, who stared up at him in wonder.

"You did well today," Archelaus said from the darkness. Andronicus felt relief wash over him, and he heard several of the other boys let out nervous sighs. "You passed your test," Archelaus said. "I will take you home now."

"I thought we had to stay out here for a week," Niko said, his voice still shaking.

"You had to stay out here until you proved yourselves," Archelaus replied. "And you have done that."

"You were watching us," Andronicus said as the realization struck him. "You were watching us the whole time."

"Of course I was!" Archelaus barked. "You are children, but today you acted like men, like Spartans. Your fathers would be proud."

As they started back toward the city, the sun began to crest the horizon. The boys all walked in silence as the land brightened. Andronicus looked around and noticed that he and Lycus were both covered in wolf's blood and a bit of their own as well. Andronicus felt pride wash over him as he walked amongst his peers. He had saved them, and so had Lycus. They would be heroes. He hadn't known what to expect, but he left his test feeling prouder than he had ever felt before.

Chapter 3
A Thinker
1

The day after they returned from their test, Archelaus woke the boys earlier than usual. They got up slowly, stretching out the many aches in their necks and backs. After two days of sleeping on the ground in the woods, everyone was a little annoyed at being woken from their soft beds, but they knew better than to complain. Andronicus and Lycus dressed quickly while the others moped slowly along.

Once awake, the boys followed Archelaus out into the courtyard. Andronicus was sure he was going to make them begin training right away, and he felt ready. The boys all stopped and stared, totally baffled, as Archelaus walked right through the courtyard and out the main gate. They looked around nervously at each other, wondering if they were meant to follow.

"What are you waiting for?" Archelaus bellowed as he strode back through the gate. The boys all hurried along as Archelaus glared at them.

Once through the gate, Archelaus led the boys along a street going up the hill toward the temple of Apollo. Andronicus thought he saw people looking at them admiringly and wondered if everyone had heard how they had killed the wolves and defended themselves. He couldn't help but puff out his chest as they walked.

As they neared the temple, Archelaus turned up a narrow pathway that led farther up the hill. None of the boys had any clue as to where Archelaus was taking them, but they followed hurriedly nonetheless. The hill was steep, and all the boys but Andronicus and Lycus were panting heavily when they finally reached the top.

Andronicus looked around and was taken aback at the beauty of the place on top of the hill. He was not used to thinking of things as beautiful, but the grove that sat upon the hill couldn't be described any other way. There were tall green trees Andronicus had never seen before with strange, colorful fruit hanging from some of them. Beneath two of the biggest trees was a small blue pond surrounded by a circle of large round stones. The stones were positioned so that anyone sitting on them could look out over the Eurotas River for miles as it snaked through the countryside.

It wasn't until the rest of the group reached the top that Andronicus noticed the old man sitting on a large stone facing the others. He wore long white robes that matched his white hair and beard, which fell below his chest, and a golden rope wrapped around his collar. The man was dangling his feet in the water, an old pair of grey sandals sitting next to him.

"This is Philander," Archelaus said, pointing at the old man. "You will be spending the day with him." With that Archelaus turned and marched back down the path. The boys all looked around uncertainly at each other.

"Come now," the old man called in a soft voice. "Come and take a seat, each of you." Slowly, the boys made their way over to the pond and took a seat. Andronicus sat next to Euthymius and Kleitos. Once everyone was seated, they all looked at the old man expectantly. Philander looked at them one at a time, not saying a word.

"A strong group of boys you look like," he said finally. "Archelaus is turning you into fine young fighters, no doubt." The boys all nodded happily, pleased with the compliment.

"It is my duty to make sure you are thinkers as well," Philander said curtly, his voice cutting through the calm air. "Men like Archelaus think that a man is nothing if not a great warrior. I say that the philosopher is as important as the warrior. Perhaps one of you will become a great philosopher someday, like Anaximander or Pythagoras or Thales himself. Have you ever heard those names before?"

Everyone looked around nervously, hoping no one else knew the names either.

"But you have all heard of Achilles and Odysseus, no doubt." The old man was about to continue when Euthymius spoke up.

"Pythagoras was a mathematician," Euthymius said, almost too quietly to hear. "Thales was a philosopher, and Anaximander his pupil."

"Very good," Philander said, eyeing Euthymius with a wan smile, "at least one of you knows his histories. You, boy," Philander said, eyeing Andronicus coldly, "you do not like the idea of learning?"

"I want to learn how to fight," Andronicus said proudly. "I don't want to learn about old men and numbers." Lycus and Niko both held back their giggles, but Philander snorted laughter like he thought Andronicus had said the funniest thing he had ever heard. Andronicus glared at him. This old man was treating him like a stupid child even though he had led the boys though the forest and killed a wolf.

"You know the story of the Trojan War, boy?" Philander asked.

"Of course," Andronicus shot back. It was his favorite story, and Achilles was his favorite hero.

"Then you know that Agamemnon had the greatest army ever assembled and the greatest heroes who ever lived, and yet in twelve years he was not able to take the city with all his power and might. Do you know how Agamemnon took the city of Troy?"

"Odysseus tricked the Trojans," Andronicus said quickly. "He built a great wooden horse and gave it to them as an offering to Poseidon and hid in it with two dozen men."

"That is correct," Philander said, nodding and

smiling as he turned to the others. "So, what does this story teach us?"

"To trick our enemies?" Lycus said quickly.

"Mmm . . ." Philander looked gravely at Lycus. "I believe there is a better lesson than that."

"That two dozen good men can take down an army if they are stealthy enough," Andronicus said, knowing it was not the answer the old man sought.

"No," Philander said angrily, "that is not the lesson." He looked like he was about to scold Andronicus when Thymi spoke up.

"For twelve years the very best fighters failed. And when all the fighters failed, a single thinker succeeded." Everyone stared at Euthymius in surprise, each of them realizing the truth of his words. Philander smiled softly at Euthymius. He remained silent for a while, leaving the boys alone with their thoughts.

"When the best fighters failed, a single thinker succeeded," Philander said after a time, smiling softly. "You have a way with words, my young friend. What is your name?"

"Euthymius, but everyone calls me Thymi."

"You are a thinker, Thymi," Philander said. "Never let the fighters make you forget that." Thymi smiled proudly at the old man. Andronicus was thoroughly annoyed; he certainly knew why Archelaus had been in such a foul mood on the way up to see this old fool. Andronicus had wanted nothing but to be a great fighter since he was born, and now this old man favored Thymi for not wanting to fight. It was utterly maddening.

2

They spent the entire day with Philander, discussing everything Andronicus could imagine, from history to the stars to the gods themselves. When the sun went down, and Andronicus thought he could no longer listen to another word, Archelaus finally appeared at the steps.

"Here now!" Archelaus roared, snapping everyone out of their peaceful state. "Talking time is over." Andronicus leapt up and ran to Archelaus, Lycus and Niko at his heels.

"How was your day with the old thinker?" Archelaus asked mockingly.

"Old fool more like," Lycus said quietly. Andronicus and Niko both giggled quietly, and Archelaus's scarred face broke into a wicked grin. Andronicus looked over and saw Kleitos and Thymi frowning at them.

"Well, don't worry," Archelaus snarled. "I won't let the whole day go to waste. You are going to run before you sleep tonight."

"But it's dark," Kleitos said.

"Then I suggest you take care not to fall," Archelaus replied, already starting down the hill.

They walked slowly down the hill, careful of their footing, but once they reached the dirt road, they began to run. Archelaus turned them away from the courtyard and up an old road. As they ran, Andronicus thought he knew why Archelaus was making them run. He was punishing the ones who had enjoyed the day with Philander and giving the boys who had disliked it exactly what they wanted. Andronicus felt good for the first time all day as he ran ahead of the rest of the boys. He was back where he belonged, in the front.

When they finally reached the courtyard, Andronicus ran through the gate well before the group, with Lycus not far behind. When the others finally caught up, Andronicus expected them to congratulate him on winning again, like they normally did, but they didn't. They weren't even looking at him.

Kleitos and Thymi were debating who could name more star constellations, and the others were all listening in. For a moment Andronicus wanted to yell at them, to remind them that he was the fastest and the strongest. That he was the one who had killed the wolf and saved them. That constellations and math weren't going to win battles.

Thymi saw Andronicus glowering over at them and looked down. He told Kleitos that he couldn't remember any more and then walked over to Andronicus.

"Good race, Andy," Thymi said, smiling at him.

In that moment Andronicus felt shame wash over him. Thymi was his best friend. He had always been his best friend. Andronicus had always been the best at everything, and Thymi had never been the best. Now Thymi *was* the best at something, but did Andronicus congratulate him, as Thymi had always done for him? No, he was angry and jealous.

"I'm sorry, Thymi," Andronicus said, fighting back tears.

"For what?" Thymi asked, honestly taken aback.

"For acting like Lycus all day," he said, looking at his feet. "That old man Philander looks at you the way Archelaus looks at me. I guess I was jealous."

"You think I never get jealous of you?" Thymi asked. "You're the best at everything. But I think that's why we have two teachers, one a fighter and one a thinker, so we can learn both ways, and end up somewhere in the middle."

"Philander was right," Andronicus said, smiling, "you do have a way with words, Thymi. I'll give Philander a chance; I promise."

"Good," Thymi said as they started toward the others. "And I promise to do all the damned running Archelaus wants. With any luck we'll both end up a couple of true heroes."

Chapter 4
A Call to Duty
1

After their big test in the woods, everything began to fall into rhythm for Andronicus and his companions. The boys trained with Archelaus five days a week and studied with Philander on the other two days. Andronicus was always the best when it came to running and fighting, or almost anything physical. Lycus and Niko were the only two who could keep up with him, and it didn't take long before the three of them were facing down boys a few years older than them in fights, and winning. Andronicus and Lycus both gained reputations as fierce fighters by the age of thirteen.

When Andronicus turned fourteen, Androcles and Theodotus got moved up into the same group as him and his friends. At first Andronicus was worried that his brother would follow him around like a puppy, as he had when they were little. But Androcles had his own life and his own way. The two brothers lived separate lives, but they grew close nonetheless, as did their friends.

Over the years they became a strong group within the group: Andronicus, Androcles, Thymi, Theo, Niko, and Lycus. Lycus grew a bit less jealous with each passing year, though he still competed with Andronicus at every opportunity. Andronicus and Lycus even formed a special bond through their constant competition. They were the two fastest and strongest, and they continually pushed each other to be better.

During Philander's lessons, it was Thymi and Theodotus who shone. Thymi had a way with words and a way of thinking out problems that the rest of them couldn't. Theo, on the other hand, had a memory like an ocean. It was as if he never forgot a thing. The two of them would answer Philander's questions so often that the old man had to ask them to wait to see if anyone else could answer first.

Between their studies and their training, the boys grew into the warriors most of them had always dreamed of becoming. At sixteen, Andronicus had grown strong and tall. He stood over six feet and was covered in hard toned muscles. His shiny black hair had grown long and wavy, and he had even begun to sprout a few whiskers under his chin. His face had taken on a stoic demeanor, with a strong jaw and a stern brow, much like his father. The boys only got to see the young women of Sparta during festivals and marches, but even then Andronicus did quite well, as did Lycus.

Athenia and Archelaus both told Andronicus often how much he resembled his father. Androcles looked very much like Andronicus, and most people could tell they were brothers, but everyone who had known him said that Andronicus was the spitting image of Aristocles. His father had been a renowned warrior, and Andronicus had every intention to be even better. Archelaus told him he moved faster with a blade than anyone he had ever seen, but no matter how much Andronicus succeeded during training, it still wasn't the real thing.

When word of a second Persian invasion began to spread in the summer of 480 BC, Andronicus was the first to ask Archelaus to let him join the army. It was said that King Leonidas himself was leading a massive host of men from across the Greek cities to try and stop the Persian army before they reached Greece. At first Archelaus told him to stop being a foolish boy, that he was not ready for war. Andronicus argued that his father had gone to battle at seventeen, and Andronicus was only a few months shy of his seventeenth birthday, but still Archelaus refused.

Andronicus's frustration continued to grow. He wanted nothing more than to be able to fight the Persians, as his father had done. Not only would he finally be doing what he had spent his entire life training for, he would get to fight the very men who had killed his father. It didn't matter if it was actually the same men; to Andronicus, all of Persia was responsible for his father's death, and he intended to get his revenge on as many of them as possible.

2

Then one morning it finally happened. Archelaus lined the boys up in the courtyard as a thick fog spread around them. Everyone stood in dead silence, staring at Archelaus with cold sweat running down their backs, waiting for whatever terrible orders he had for them. Andronicus could tell everyone around him was nervous. He was not nervous though; he was exhilarated. He knew what was coming, and he knew he was going to be picked.

He looked to his right and saw Thymi looking like he was about to vomit. His face was a nasty pale green color, and he had one hand on his stomach. Andronicus turned to his left to see Lycus looking as eager as he felt, and he knew he would be coming as well. They stood in silence for a long moment, waiting breathlessly. The tension hung in the air like the mist around them.

"Andronicus!" Archelaus finally bellowed, making several boys jump slightly. Andronicus let out a huge sigh as relief and joy washed over him, leaving him feeling lightheaded. He was finally going to war. "Lycus," Archelaus continued. "Nikopheros. You three have been chosen to join the Spartan army under King Leonidas's command. They are marching north to defend against the Persian invaders. You are soldiers of Sparta now. Make sure you deserve it." Archelaus turned and marched off, leaving the three boys to say their goodbyes.

Andronicus saw Lycus and Niko embrace, smiling ear to ear. He turned around and saw Thymi and Androcles standing together with Theodotus behind them. Thymi looked nervous, relieved, happy and sad all at once, though he still looked like he might vomit. Androcles just looked scared.

"Don't worry, Droc," Andronicus said, calling his brother by the nickname only he used as he gripped him by the shoulders. "Thymi will watch out for you, and you have Theodotus as well."

"I'm not worried about me, Dron," Androcles replied with a worried frown. "You're going to war."

"This is what I wanted, what I've always wanted," Andronicus said happily, clapping Androcles on the back. "I'm finally going to war, just like Father."

"Father died," Androcles said angrily, shrugging Andronicus's hand off his shoulder. "He died fighting the same people you're going to fight. They say this Persian king has a host of over one hundred thousand men. King Leonidas is leading a host of just five thousand. You may think you're a great warrior like Father, but you're not ready, Dron." Andronicus felt hurt and angry at his little brother's doubts in him, and in their king.

"Andronicus is the best fighter any of us have ever seen," Thymi said, trying to reassure Androcles but sounding a bit unsure himself. "Besides, it's not like they're going to put him at the front of the vanguard. He'll be safe."

"Even if they do," Andronicus added quickly, "I'll be fine. I'll be with King Leonidas's personal guard, the best fighters in the world. And I'll have Lycus and Niko to watch my back. I'll be fine." Androcles looked none too convinced.

"Just promise me you won't try to be a hero," Androcles said, a worried look on his face. "You don't need to go charging into battle. Stand by the men next to you, and remember your lessons."

"*All* of your lessons," Thymi added quickly. "Philander's as well as Archelaus's."

"Be careful, brother," Androcles said solemnly before Andronicus could respond. "I need you to be there with me when I see my first battle."

Andronicus smiled and hugged Androcles, then Thymi. Andronicus stepped back and took one last look at his closest friends. Thymi gave him a reassuring grin, but Androcles just stared at him, fear and sadness etched across his face. Andronicus tried to give him a reassuring smile, like Thymi's, but knew his fell short. Then he turned and walked over to the gate. Lycus and Niko were already waiting anxiously, knowing Archelaus would return any minute.

While waiting, Andronicus felt an odd sense of loneliness, even though he was going with Lycus and Niko. Just before they left, Andronicus gazed around at the courtyard in which he had spent the last ten years training. He felt a cold assurance that, for better or worse, his days of training there were done.

3

An hour later, Andronicus, Lycus, and Niko were on the road, riding behind Archelaus. They were heading north to join Leonidas's army. Archelaus had come with them, but only until they found other soldiers going north. Leaving the city gave Andronicus an odd feeling. There was no crowd, no ceremonious procession as they marched off to war. They simply rode out of the city unnoticed, under the archway of Hermes, and down the old dirt road. The Greek army was amassing just west of the pass at Thermopylae, and Archelaus told them they would need to make the journey in less than two weeks.

The three young men and Archelaus set out from the city just after dawn and were well out of its sight by dusk. They had each been given a horse from the stables to take with them, free of charge, as they were riding off to fight for the king. The only things they had with them were a water bag, a bedroll, a small pan to cook in, a six-inch knife, and a sword and scabbard at their side. The swords were not particularly well made, but Andronicus knew he could kill with it.

Archelaus rode with them for a day and a half. On the second day, they met a small group from Tagea who were also heading north to join the army. Archelaus spoke with their commander and then came over to the boys.

"You're going to ride with these men for the rest of the way," he said. "They will make sure you're looked after."

Suddenly, Andronicus felt afraid. He had known Archelaus wasn't going to fight alongside them, but he wasn't ready for him to leave yet. All the confidence he had felt a moment ago seemed to be hanging by a single thread.

"You'll be okay," Archelaus said softly, as if he had read Andronicus's thoughts. Andronicus had never heard Archelaus sound that way before, and it made him feel even more afraid. "Just stick together, stay out of the front, and you'll be fine. You boys are three of the best fighters I have ever taught. You will become true Spartan warriors."

Lycus nodded slowly, looking uneasy. Niko looked like he was going to cry. Archelaus nodded to them, and they turned to join the new group. Andronicus began to turn as well, but Archelaus took him by the shoulder and pulled him back.

"Watch out for them, Andronicus," Archelaus whispered. "They need you."

With that Archelaus was gone, riding back the way they had come. Andronicus watched him go, not feeling at all like a soldier, then went to join the others.

None of the Tageans said so much as a word to them. Andronicus knew they were on their own now and that his friends would be looking to him for reassurance. Andronicus took a deep breath and tried to look as confident and commanding as he could, but he still felt afraid.

When their new group began riding again, they fell in at the back of the procession, trying not to look at any of the angry-looking men riding beside them.

4

They rode for a week and a half before they reached King Leonidas's army. They joined many other groups as they rode, so that when they finally arrived, they were riding with nearly two hundred men. They had become a small army from over a dozen cities and provinces and kept mostly in tight-knit bunches. A Tagean man had taken command of the group less than a week into the ride. He was tall and loud, and no one else seemed to want to challenge his rule.

The boys quickly found out they were the youngest riders in the group. Most of the men treated them like dogs because of it, even though they were Spartans. They were the last to eat at every meal, and they were forced to lay their bedrolls on the farthest side of the camp, where they would be the first victims of an ambush. Thankfully, no ambush came.

Andronicus was riding beside Lycus and Niko in the back of a long line of riders when he first saw the large encamped army. They were riding up a hill, and when they reached the top, they saw a vast sea of tents and fires spread out in the valley beneath them. The boys gazed in wonder at the army below as they began to tread down into the valley. Andronicus had never seen so many people in his entire life. He remembered hearing that the Persians had one hundred thousand men. As he gazed at the many Greek tents and fires, he was sure there were more than that in the Greek army.

When they reached the bottom of the hill, they were greeted by a man wearing a gold breastplate and helm and a red cloak over his shoulders. He had a

fierceness about him that none of the other men they
had encountered had, and Andronicus knew at once
that this man was a Spartan.

"Who are you?" the man demanded in a gruff,
impatient tone. "Where did you come from?"

"We are new recruits from Sparta," Andronicus
said, riding forward and bowing his head.

"Are you Archelaus's new boys?" the man
asked, raising his eyebrow slightly.

"Yes, sir," Andronicus answered, raising his
head to meet the man's eye. "Archelaus rode with us
until we joined the Tageans. Then he returned to
Sparta." The man nodded curtly, looking Andronicus
over.

"How many are you?" he asked, turning to the
others.

"Three, sir," Andronicus answered
apprehensively.

"Only three?" the man bellowed. He turned
away in anger for a moment, then turned back to
Andronicus. "Well, then I suppose you're the ones he
knows can handle themselves," he said with a sigh.

"Yes, sir," Lycus said, looking proud.

"Good," the man grunted. "Go to the back of
the camp. When you find the men with red cloaks, ask
for Perikles. He will be your captain."

With that the man turned away and went to
meet the next group coming in. The boys followed his
instructions, riding through the massive camp, all the
way to the back. They passed the tents of men from
nearly every Greek city that Andronicus knew of. They
passed tents of Corinthians and Mantineans, Thespians
and Thebans from the Peloponnese, Arcadians and
Phlians. There were a great number of tents from
Lacedaemon as well, the Spartans' kin. Andronicus
noted as they rode that there were no Athenian tents
among the army.

Finally, they came upon the men they had
been told about. In the back of the camp, closest to
the stream, was a cluster of large tents. The men
standing in front of them wore thick red cloaks. The
boys dismounted and walked over to the tents, not

looking directly at any of the fierce men glowering at them.

"Who in Ares' name are you?" a rough-looking man with a thick beard barked as he approached them.

"We're the new recruits," Andronicus said, trying not to sound like the little boy he felt like. "Archelaus sent us. We were told to report to Perikles." The bearded man glared at them for a moment, as if he wanted to swat them away like gnats. Then he turned and stormed off, leaving them standing there.

The two men left watching them were both tall and fierce looking. One had a dark scar running across his entire face, and the other had his arms crossed menacingly, showing the biggest forearms Andronicus had ever seen. Andronicus stood there with Lycus and Niko, feeling like a foolish child next to these men.

He had thought he was ready; he had felt ready for this for months, years even. But now, seeing the brutish warriors that made up the king's guard, he felt like a little boy. He turned to his right and saw Lycus and Niko looking exactly as he felt.

"You!" a voice shouted, snapping Andronicus out of his thoughts. "Are you Archelaus's lot?" The man striding toward them looked every bit as fierce as the others, but Andronicus saw kindness in his eyes as well. The man was tall and strong and had scars covering his arms and one across his left cheek, but his eyes said that he was a friend.

"Yes," Andronicus said nervously as the man approached.

"I am Perikles, your new captain," he said sternly. "And your names?"

"I am Andronicus, and this is Lycus and Nikopheros," Andronicus said, introducing the others. Perikles nodded curtly and then turned and walked off. They hurried after him. Perikles led them through the Spartans' camp to what appeared to be a blacksmith's tent.

"Karpos," Perikles called to a thin man sitting at a sharpening stone, "these are Archelaus's new boys. See that they are taken care of." Karpos sneered up at them from his seat with a mean, narrow face. He slowly got to his feet, dusting off his filthy jerkin, and stepped toward them.

"Let me see your blades," he said in a high, wheezy voice. Andronicus thought the man sounded the way a dog would sound if it could talk. He brought out his sword carefully, and Lycus and Niko did the same. Karpos took one look at their swords, then spat on them.

"Disgraceful," he said as he turned and went into the tent. A moment later he emerged carrying freshly forged swords, breastplates, and helmets, all jumbled together in his thin arms. He dropped the lot onto the table beside his stone.

The boys didn't even wait for permission; they dove right in. Andronicus picked up one of the fine bronze helmets first and held it up, looking at the perfect red plume on top. The sun reflected off the bronze, giving it a powerful look. Andronicus quickly put it on his head and then reached for the sword. Niko already had his breastplate strapped on, and Lycus was swinging his new sword about excitedly. Andronicus picked up his new sword and turned to Lycus.

He was about to challenge him when he saw the men standing around staring at them. Andronicus realized then how foolish they must look, a bunch of children getting to play at being soldiers. Andronicus set the sword down and quickly took the helmet off. Lycus seemed to notice the men staring as well because he stopped swinging the sword and walked back over to the table, his face bright red. They gathered their new belongings quickly and quietly, with Karpos and half a dozen other men eyeing them coldly, then returned to Perikles.

"Good," Perikles said when he saw they had their new armor. "Now there's one last thing you need before you can fight as a Spartan." Andronicus felt chills go down his spine; he knew exactly what it was. He had been waiting for the day he would receive his own Spartan cloak since the day he had watched his mother receive his father's cloak after his death. He had stopped and looked at that old cloak every single time he had been home since that day.

Perikles turned, and ducked into another tent, then reappeared a moment later with three bright red cloaks in his arms.

"Do you know why our cloaks are red?" Perikles asked as he walked over to them.

"So that when we use it to bind our wounds, our enemies cannot see our blood," Andronicus answered, just before Lycus.

"That is correct." Perikles nodded slowly as he handed out the cloaks. "When you see a Spartan whose cloak has grown short, you know he has seen many battles."

"Or he was very bad in one," Niko joked, then realized who he had said it to, but Perikles let out a long, hearty laugh.

"You boys wait here," he said, pointing to the tent he had just come out of. "And be ready for the call of battle. This is your tent. You will share it with Gaios, Diokles, and me. Welcome to King Leonidas's army, boys." Perikles let out a much more menacing laugh as he walked away. Andronicus glanced at Lycus and Niko and then entered the tent.

It was smaller inside than it had looked outside, and they were rather cramped by the time they had finally settled in. Gaios and Diokles were apparently elsewhere, so the boys returned to admiring their new armor and swords in the privacy of their tent.

5

Later that night Perikles led them to a large fire with a roasting boar above it. Men were sitting in small groups around the fire. Perikles led them to two men sitting close to the pig. They sat down on logs and rocks in a small circle. Perikles introduced the two men as Gaios and Diokles.

Gaios was tall and lean, and had a gaunt, wrinkled face and solemn eyes. He looked old, even though Andronicus could tell the man was no more than forty. He also looked oddly familiar, but Andronicus could not think of where he had seen him before.

Diokles was short, bald, and powerfully muscular. He had a thick black beard and an intense, menacing look about him. Andronicus pitied any man who had to face Diokles in battle. He looked down and noticed that Diokles was missing his little finger on his left hand. Then he saw that the bottom foot of his cloak was gone.

"So, you boys are the best Archelaus has to offer then?" Diokles goaded in a deep, scratchy voice.

"We are," Lycus answered defensively. Perikles chuckled as he cut a piece of meat from the boar's back. Lycus shot a nasty look at him, and Perikles stopped laughing.

"You think yourself a fighter then, boy?" Perikles asked in a joking tone.

"I do," Lycus said proudly, rising to his feet.

"And you think that means you're a killer, do you?" Diokles asked seriously.

"I am a killer," Lycus answered coldly. Perikles and Diokles both burst into laughter, but Gaios just frowned.

"And what have you ever killed?" Diokles managed to ask through his laughter. Lycus's face turned red as he realized his error.

"I killed a wolf when I was twelve," he proclaimed proudly, "and I have killed deer and rabbits." He tried to continue but was interrupted by a bellow from Diokles. The man sprayed pieces of chewed meat across the dirt as he roared with laughter.

"Killing a man is not the same as killing a beast," Gaios said quietly, "not even a wolf." Andronicus could barely hear him over Diokles's guffawing. Lycus scowled at Gaios, his face still red. Niko looked down at his feet, trying not to take a side, but Andronicus stared intently at Gaios. There was something eerily familiar about the man, something that fascinated Andronicus.

"It is not as if we will be killing Greek men," Andronicus said to Gaios, trying to defend his friend. "The Persians are beasts. Killing them will be no different than killing a wolf."

"You speak as though you hate the Persians," Perikles said as he took a bite of pork. "What have they ever done to you, boy?"

"They killed my father," Andronicus said gravely. All the laughter died down then. "In Darius's invasion ten years ago."

"Your father fought at Marathon?" Perikles asked seriously. Andronicus nodded slowly.

"What was his name?" Diokles asked. All the humor had left his face.

"Aristocles," Andronicus answered, wondering if these men had known his father.

"You're Aristocles's boy?" Gaios said, lifting his eyes from the fire. Then he nodded. "Yes, you look like him." He had a somber look on his face. Andronicus nodded again. All three men seemed to look at him differently now.

"Your father was one of the greatest fighters I have ever seen," Perikles said. Andronicus felt a sort of rush knowing that these men had not only known but also admired his father.

"Your father saved my life once," Gaios said, looking him dead in the eye as if studying his face. Andronicus didn't know how to respond. He met the man's eye and gave a small nod. Gaios stared at him a moment longer, then nodded and returned to eating his meat and staring into the fire.

"And what about you two?" Perikles asked Lycus and Niko. "Either of your fathers fight against the Persians?" Niko shook his head abashedly, but Lycus quickly perked up.

"My father was Lycurgus, son of Lycius," Lycus said with his chest puffed out. "He fought against the Persians at Marathon as well."

"Lycurgus," Diokles said with a dark expression, "never heard of him." Lycus glared at the man as he ripped a piece of meat off the bone with his teeth.

"I knew him," Gaios said placidly. Lycus looked eagerly at him, as if he expected him to say his father had saved his life too. Gaios didn't say anything more;

he simply chewed his meat and stared into the fire.

"My father was a great warrior as well," Lycus insisted. Gaios looked at Lycus. Andronicus couldn't tell what Gaios was thinking. He looked like he was about to say something, but then he simply turned back to the flames. Lycus looked like he was about to press the matter, but Andronicus interceded.

"When will the Persians land?" he asked, hoping Lycus would allow the change of topic.

"We don't know," Perikles said as he chewed his meat. "Could be any time now. It shouldn't be more than a week at most." The boys took this in silently, each of them contemplating the war they were now facing. Lycus left the matter of their fathers to rest, and they all ate in silence for a while, listening to the crackling fire and the men around them.

When they were done eating, they returned to the small tent that was meant to house the six of them. The older men got in first, taking their positions in the back of the tent, and the boys were left to cram themselves together in the corner. That first night Andronicus wasn't able to sleep a wink. All he could think about was his father and fighting the men who had killed him.

Chapter 5
The Battle of Thermopylae
1

The horns of war first blew on the morning of August twelfth, 480 BC. Andronicus and his friends dressed as quickly as possible, strapping on their shiny new armor as the horns blared outside their tent. Andronicus picked up his red cloak and held it in his hands for a moment, staring at it. He couldn't help but think of his father's old cloak, which still hung on his mother's wall.

The horn blew again, snapping him back to reality, and he swung the cloak over his shoulders. He strapped on his new sword in its thin leather scabbard, then picked up his lance and shield. Finally, he donned the great bronze helmet and stood, dressed for battle.

They left the tent and joined Diokles and Gaios

outside. Perikles came around the corner a moment later and hailed them all into line. The group ran through the mud to join the rest of the Spartan hoplites. They ran past men from every city until they reached the mass of red cloaks that had formed at the head of the camp. Andronicus felt small and foolish as he fell in line with the fierce men next to him.

He was standing in line, waiting nervously, when another horn rang out. A man came riding forward on the back of a great black horse, and everyone fell silent. The man looked fierce and weathered in equal measure. He had a thick black beard, but it was spotted with patches of grey. Andronicus had never seen him before, but he knew right away that it was the king.

Leonidas rode forward gracefully, every eye watching him as he went. Andronicus thought he looked every bit the great king he had imagined him to be. He held his head high as he met his armed guard, of which Andronicus was now a member. Leonidas looked out over his army solemnly as they waited silently for his word.

"Men!" Leonidas shouted (he even sounded a king). "Xerxes has returned to our shores," Leonidas said in a rough, deep voice that carried across the camp with ease, "with an army of savages at his back. He thinks his numbers will win him this war." Leonidas's voice grew more powerful with every word. Andronicus felt himself filling with confidence and pride, and he could see and feel the men around him felt the same.

"But he has yet to go to war with Sparta!" Leonidas shouted over the roaring men. "Look around you!" Leonidas bellowed. Andronicus looked to his right. Lycus and Niko were both staring awestruck at the mighty king. He turned to his left and saw Diokles and Perikles roaring wildly and pounding their shields. Gaios was standing next to Diokles, staring solemnly at the king. Again Andronicus was struck with how different Gaios was from the others.

"We are Spartans!" Leonidas shouted. An earth-shaking roar erupted from the men. Andronicus thought that the Persians would surely hear them. "We are the greatest fighters the world has ever known," the king continued. "Xerxes thinks his slaves will win his war, but the Persians fight out of fear, fear of their masters, the beasts that drive them to war. We fight for honor, for freedom, for Greece itself!" The vast army erupted into booming cheers again. The king's voice was drowned out for a moment by the thundering of five thousand spears pounding against five thousand shields.

"Set aside your differences," Leonidas continued, turning to the rest of the army. "Our cities have fought each other for a thousand years, but every man here is Greek. And every true Greek man would be damned before he let a Persian horde into his country." Again the army broke into uproar. Spears banged against shields and against the ground. Men bellowed war cries. The ground itself trembled under their thunderous clamor.

Andronicus had never felt so invigorated. It didn't matter how many men the Persians had; he knew they would beat them. Every man there knew they would beat them. How could they not, with a king as fierce as Leonidas?

2

The army marched east to the small mountain pass of Thermopylae. The Spartans rode at the head of the long column, Andronicus and his friends among them and King Leonidas at the very front. The rest of the Greek soldiers from the other cities marched behind the mounted Spartans. Perikles rode next to the boys, as did Gaios and Diokles; they had seemingly taken the boys under their wing.

About an hour into their ride, the king fell back next to Perikles. Andronicus couldn't help but stare at the powerful man. He looked as bold and ferocious as any man among them, and yet he also looked old and wise. Up close the grey in his hair was much more pronounced, and the wrinkles in his weathered face stood out clearly. His brown eyes looked like they had lived well beyond their years.

"Are these the new recruits?" the king asked, nodding toward the boys.

"Aye, my king. Archelaus picked them himself," Perikles answered courteously.

"You, boy," Leonidas looked right at Andronicus. For a moment he couldn't say anything; he just stared at the king, dumbfounded. "I know your face. Who is your father?"

"My name is Andronicus, my king," Andronicus tried not to let his voice tremble as he spoke. "My father was Aristocles." King Leonidas stopped his horse abruptly. The others around them also stopped, and then the entire army. The whole Greek army stood still, waiting for the king as he stared at Andronicus.

"You are Aristocles's boy, the older one?" Leonidas looked at Andronicus with a fierce concentration.

"Yes, my king," Andronicus said meekly, bowing his head, "he died fighting the—"

"I know how he died," Leonidas cut him off, staring intently at Andronicus. "I was there." For a moment Andronicus didn't know what to say. He felt both excited and nervous. He had never actually heard how his father died, just that he died fighting the Persians at Marathon.

"Your father was one of the bravest men I have ever known," Leonidas said. Then he turned forward and began riding again, and the entire host quickly followed suit. Andronicus wanted to hear more, but he was afraid to ask.

"What about the rest of you?" the king asked casually to Lycus and Niko, without looking back. "Either of your fathers fight in the wars?"

"My father fought with you," Lycus said eagerly. "Lycurgus. He was at the battle of Marathon as well." The king turned his head and eyed Lycus wearily for a moment.

"I knew him," Leonidas said bluntly, then spurred his horse forward, leaving the boys behind. Andronicus glanced over at Lycus as the king rode away and saw him staring down at his horse with a mixture of anger, shame, and confusion.

3

It took them five hours to reach the pass of Thermopylae. When they arrived, Andronicus was amazed. The pass itself was only fifty feet wide. Twenty-five men standing shoulder to shoulder would seal it entirely. The mountains to either side of the pass were steep and rocky, and it was clear no one would be able to climb them. Andronicus could not imagine how two armies could possibly fight in such a tight space.

The Persians were nowhere to be seen when they arrived. It seemed the Greeks had beaten them there by at least half a day. The Spartans dismounted and left their horses about a mile from the pass. The rest of the army was marching on foot, so they were still out of eyesight back down the road.

As the Spartans marched up to the pass, Andronicus noticed an old rock wall blocking the eastern side of the pass from invaders, though it had crumbled over the years. Leonidas ordered the men to begin rebuilding the wall. A second later Perikles was shouting at Andronicus and his friends, putting them to work.

4

The Spartans, with help from many of the other men as they continued to arrive, had the wall nearly back to its full strength by sundown. Earlier in the day, Niko had pointed out a small goat path behind the wall, leading up the face of the mountain. He asked Perikles about it, and Perikles said that the path was hidden on the other side and that someone could only find it if they knew just where to look, which only the Spartans did.

As the sun approached the horizon, Andronicus looked east, and saw a rider coming straight toward them. For a moment he thought it was a Persian scout, but then he recognized the man as one of the Spartans. He was not wearing his cloak, but Andronicus had seen him in line earlier. The man rode right up to Leonidas and then dismounted. They walked away from the rest of the men, apparently discussing what the scout had seen.

Andronicus stared longingly at them. He was fascinated by what the king might be saying and what battle plans he might be hatching. After several minutes Leonidas nodded to the scout, and the man mounted his horse and rode back toward the Persians. Andronicus watched as Leonidas walked over to where they were resting.

There were hot springs on the western side of the pass, and many of the men had stripped down and were bathing in the warm water. A great number of the Spartan warriors had taken their combs out and were casually flicking their hair. Andronicus and Lycus stared at their kin with a mixture of confusion and fascination. Diokles saw the look on their faces and laughed. "The Persian scouts are coming," he told them in his rough voice, "We're letting them know how we *fear* their great army."

Andronicus and Lycus joined in Diokles's laughter as understanding dawned on them. Andronicus had tucked a comb away in his belt; he knew it was customary for Spartan warriors to fix their hair before battle, though he had never been told why. He pulled it out and leaned against the rocks as he flicked his long black hair.

About ten minutes later, just as Diokles had said, a Persian escort came riding up to meet them. The man in front was dressed in luxurious yellow garments and rode on a big white horse. He had bright ornate robes that looked like they were made of pure silk. He had a black sash across his face and a shining gold necklace. The four men behind him were clearly soldiers. Each of them rode a plain brown horse and wore plain brown robes and had a long, thick sword at their side.

As they approached the Greek army, the man in front removed his sash. His face was a dark brown color that Andronicus had never seen before. He had a thin face with gaunt cheeks, a long nose, and a pointed little goatee. His dark, angry eyes roamed over the lounging men. Andronicus had never seen a

Persian before. He had hated them for as long as he could remember, but this was the first one he had ever seen. At first the man looked shocked, and then his shock turned to outrage.

King Leonidas stepped forward. Andronicus noticed no one was standing guard over the king, and that worried him for a moment. The king was completely exposed to the four Persian soldiers.

"I am Leonidas, son of the lion, descendant of Heracles, King of Sparta, and commander of the Greek armies. What have you to say to me?"

Andronicus was truly in awe of the mighty king as the thin man on the white horse glared down at Leonidas in contempt.

"I am here on behalf of Xerxes the Great," the gaunt man said with an odd accent, "King of Babylon, Emperor of the Great Persian Dynasty, King of Kings. He demands that your army surrender to him immediately."

"Tell your king of kings that no Spartan will ever surrender to him."

The men slowly stood up, one by one, many of them still in the water. Andronicus quickly got to his feet as well. The Persian looked around at the men, many of them were still naked.

"If you do not surrender to the great king of kings, you will be killed," he said, sneering down at Leonidas.

"King of kings be damned!" Leonidas bellowed, causing the Persian horses to retreat several steps away from his powerful roar. "If Xerxes the Great wants Greece, he can damn well try and take it from us."

"The great king of kings has one million men in his army!" the man shouted, astounded at Leonidas's gall. "If you do not kneel now, our arrows will blot out the sun, and you will be pierced one thousand times over."

"Let them come," Leonidas said with a menacing scowl. "We shall fight in the shade."

The Persian rider glared down at King Leonidas. A moment earlier Andronicus had feared for the king's safety. Now he feared the king would cut the five Persians in half before they could ride off. The Persian man seemed to share Andronicus's fear, because he quickly turned his horse around and rode away. The Spartans laughed boisterously and hailed their brave king as the Persian riders left.

Some of the men returned to the springs, but many of them started strapping on their armor. Andronicus thought of his brother's last words to him before he left and then quickly joined the men preparing for battle. Lycus and Niko went with him, and they all strapped on their armor in silence.

It wasn't until nearly an hour later that they caught their first glimpse of the Persian army. As the Persians crested the hill several miles to the north of them, Andronicus was amazed at how many of them there were. The line of soldiers seemed endless. More and more men marched over the horizon, straight toward them.

After ten minutes Andronicus was sure the Persian army covered over a mile. Ten minutes later he had lost nearly every bit of the confidence he had felt that morning. The Persian army was bigger than he would have thought possible. It already stretched over miles, and it showed no sign of stopping. Androcles had been right; the Persian army had to be one hundred thousand strong at least. The vast army marched down into the valley, filling it entirely.

Once the Persian army had filled the entire valley north of the mountain pass, horns began to blow, strange horns that Andronicus had never heard before bellowing from the massive horde. One called out and then another and another, answering each other across the valley. The front of the army started marching forward, and Andronicus prepared himself for the fight he had been anticipating for his entire life.

The small part of the Persian army marching toward them looked like it outnumbered the entire Greek army five to one, and it was still just a small part of the Persians' entire force. They marched slowly, banging war drums and letting their horns ring out.

The Spartans quickly fell into lines at the heart

of the pass, shoulder to shoulder, shield to shield, ready to defend against the oncoming army. The Persians stopped abruptly nearly a hundred yards short of them. The entire force halting at once made an impressive and intimidating sound that reverberated off the mountains. A thick silence hung over the Spartans for a moment that felt like a lifetime. Andronicus wondered why the Persians had stopped. They clearly had more men.

"Arrows!" Leonidas bellowed from somewhere to Andronicus's right. "Shields!" The men quickly got down on their knees, their shields covering their heads and backs. Andronicus knelt as well, Lycus and Niko beside him. They put their shields together, creating a larger shield to cover them all. Andronicus saw Perikles with Gaios and Diokles to his left. They all held like that for a moment longer, waiting. Andronicus could hear the heavy breathing of his friends and see the same fear he felt etched across their faces.

He heard the arrows first, whizzing high above them, and then the ground around them actually turned dark. The Persian rider had not lied; the arrows did blot out the sun. It sounded like nothing Andronicus had heard before, a thick whirring buzz, and then they were upon them. Thousands of arrows fell on them at once. Andronicus felt the pounding of every arrow that crashed against his shield and feared each one would be the one that pierced it and split his arm. But Karpos, it seemed, was a fine blacksmith indeed. None of the shields broke. The arrows splintered against their bronze and fell onto the dirt around them.

Andronicus heard someone cry out and turned to see a man with an arrow sticking out of the back of his calf. He had his eyes shut tight, but he didn't break his position; no one did. The Spartans held still as the arrows crashed upon them like rain.

The arrows fell for what seemed like an hour, though it was probably only a minute. When the barrage finally let up, voices began shouting to hold, to wait to see if the Persians were done. The men held a moment, looking around at the mass of black arrows sticking out of the dirt around them. Then the ground turned dark again, the whirring returned, and a moment later, the rain began again.

The Persians hit them with four barrages, each over a minute long. Andronicus thought they must have shot a million arrows at them at least, though he could not see a single dead man. Several men had been hit in the legs but none of them fatally. Andronicus's arms felt like they had taken a bad beating, but he held still; they all did. They held a moment longer until someone shouted that the archers were returning to the greater army.

The men slowly got to their feet, looking up to see the vast army marching back to join their cohort. The Spartans let out a loud war cry that echoed across the valley. Andronicus knew the Persians could hear them now.

"Perhaps they ran out of arrows!" someone shouted from behind Andronicus, and everyone broke into laughter. The Spartans marched back through the field of arrows until they reached their campground south of the pass. Lookouts were posted all along the pass, and the rest of the Spartans set down for the night as the last of the Greeks were arriving and finding their spots.

Andronicus walked slowly back to his horse with Lycus and Niko beside him. None of them spoke; they were all still rattled from seeing the size of the Persian army and getting pounded by hundreds of arrows. Their brand new shields were covered in small dents.

When they reached their horses, they took out their bedrolls and started back toward the front of the camp, where they found Gaios, Diokles, and Perikles. They had rabbits roasting over a fire, and the boys sat down to join them.

"You did well today," Perikles said to the newcomers.

"Not that you had to do very much," Diokles pointed out. "Just duck and cover, really. I expect tomorrow you'll see the real thing."

"He's right," Perikles said seriously. "Sleep well

tonight. Tomorrow you'll need your strength."

They ate mostly in silence. Andronicus heard a constant buzzing hum coming from the massive Persian army. He tried to count the number of fires burning across the valley and lost count somewhere after two hundred.

After eating, the boys laid down and tried to go to sleep. Andronicus had never had a harder time sleeping in his life. No matter what he tried to think of, his mind found its way back to the size of the Persian army. Every time his mind began down a new path, trying to escape the dark thoughts, the buzzing would wrench him back. He could hear a thousand distant voices speaking in a strange language, shouting war cries, and declaring themselves conquerors in their foreign tongue.

5

When dawn broke the next day, Andronicus rose with the rest of the men. He had not slept a wink the whole night. His mind had played a thousand games, all ending with a mass of dark-skinned men screaming and throwing themselves on him, stabbing him again and again.

Andronicus looked over at Lycus and Niko and could tell they hadn't slept either. They both had dark-red orbs under their bloodshot eyes. Andronicus wondered if he looked as bad as them.

"Gods, look at you!" Perikles exclaimed as he walked over to them. "You boys look like hell. I told you to get some sleep."

"We tried," Andronicus said in a hoarse voice. "We will be ready."

Perikles sighed. "Well, go get something to eat. You'll need your strength today." The boys went and ate with the other men as the sun rose. Then they went to put on their armor.

Not thirty minutes after dawn, the Greek army stood at attention in the heart of the pass, ready for battle. They waited for the Persians to attack for what seemed like forever before they finally walked back to the springs and rested.

Nearly an hour later, the Persian horns sounded. A massive Persian force began to march toward the pass. The Spartans quickly formed lines again and waited for the attack, but it never came. The Persians stopped far short of the actual pass. They stood there shouting war cries and waving their spears, but they never marched forward.

The Persians did this for nearly an hour before retreating. Andronicus couldn't understand why they had not attacked; their army was bigger than a city. He couldn't fathom how many men it actually was, millions if he had to guess. It looked like more men than he knew existed.

The Greeks waited all day for the Persians to attack, but they never did. They marched forward several times, showing off different legions of their army, but never pressed the attack.

When night fell the Spartans went back to their place behind the rocks, leaving several men on watch, and ate their supper in a joyous mood. That night Andronicus fell asleep like a baby. He still feared the massive Persian force, but now he believed they feared the Greeks as well.

6

The attack didn't come until the fifth day. The Persians spent four days showing their legions off one by one. Finally they seemed to realize the Greeks were not going to bow down in fear. Andronicus watched with the others as two massive forces started marching across the valley toward them.

The Spartans quickly formed lines across the narrowest part of the pass, next to the wall. The other Greek armies lay ready and waiting behind them.

At first Andronicus thought the Persians were just going to march out and stop, as all the others had done, but when they pressed far past the point the others had all stopped at, he knew the time had finally come.

Andronicus stood in the second wave of the Spartan defense; they would take the front when the first line tired. Lycus stood to his left and Diokles to his right, with Niko and Gaios standing behind them holding long spears. Andronicus could not see King Leonidas, but knew he was not far to their right.

"Medes and Cissians!" a voice shouted out from somewhere in the front. "Xerxes does not even honor us with his best fighters."

"If any man falls to these scum, I'll piss on his grave!" a voice shouted from Andronicus's left.

Andronicus watched the two armies march toward them with cold sweat running down the back of his neck. He was confident in his Spartan brethren, and he knew they had a clear tactical advantage, but the opposing army was still imposingly large. For a moment he held out hope that the armies would stop to taunt them once again, only from much closer this time. He felt his heart speeding up so much he feared it would start to make a noise as it banged against his breastplate.

When the Persians were less than a hundred feet away, they broke into a run. Thousands of screaming men raced toward them, swinging swords over their heads, and for a moment Andronicus remembered his waking dream from the first night. Fear filled him for a moment as the brown mass of soldiers drew nearer.

Then the Spartan war drums started pounding, the old drums he had trained to his whole life. As they banged louder and louder, Andronicus remembered his brother and his father. He remembered the many lessons from Archelaus and Philander. And he remembered the words of bold King Leonidas.

Andronicus planted his feet in the dirt and looked over at Lycus. Their eyes met for a moment, and Andronicus felt his confidence return. He took a deep breath as the screaming invaders closed the last few feet between them.

Then the Persians were on them at last. Their sprinting bodies crashed violently against the line of Spartan shields. Feeling the men in front of him getting pushed back into him, Andronicus planted his feet more firmly. The entire Spartan line pushed forward, resisting the force of the Persian horde.

Andronicus lost all sense of things for a moment. Drums pounded behind him, and horns bellowed before him. All around him a thousand men were screaming. He heard the Persians crying out in their foreign language. He couldn't understand the words, but he knew what they were saying. They were praying to their gods. Begging for their lives.

Andronicus watched, with his feet planted and his weight against the man in front of him, as the Mede and Cissian slaves crashed against their line. Spears flung forward all around him, ripping through Persian flesh. Many of the spears pierced the attackers' chests, and some even sank into their faces, tearing them away.

Andronicus had seen a thousand animals killed and gutted; he had done many of the deeds himself. He had hated these men since he was a child. He had waited his entire life for this moment. And yet now as he watched them being shoved forward, screaming helplessly until a spear ended their cries, he felt sick. These men were not the monsters he had thought them to be. He saw fear in their eyes. They didn't want to be there any more than he did, far less, in fact. Andronicus remembered the king saying the Persians were driven to war out of fear of their masters, and now he believed it.

Then it was suddenly his time to take the front. The Spartan lines slowly started swapping spots, keeping their shields firmly planted against the tide of Persians. Andronicus slipped between Lycus and the man falling back and fell hard against the shield in front of him. Instantly, he felt the weight of the Persian mass pushing him into the ground.

He pushed forward and felt something move under his foot. He looked down and saw a brown face covered in blood. There was a long red gash in the side of the bloody head, but its eyes were still open. They stared up at Andronicus, frozen with the terror they had died in. He yanked his foot back and planted it in the dirt.

As he held there, pushing against the shield, surrounded by the crashing of metal on metal, the banging of drums, and the foreign screams of dying men, he caught his first scent of it. At first it just smelled like flesh and dirt and sweat. Then he realized it was shit too. The dying men were defecating themselves as they screamed their way into death. Andronicus felt his stomach roll over, but he managed to keep from vomiting.

He looked up and saw Diokles shouting something down at him. He couldn't hear a word of it; all he could hear were drums and screams. He closed his eyes and shook his head, and when he opened them, he felt the world come crashing back.

"Use your damned spear, boy!" Diokles shouted. Andronicus looked up and realized the men crashing against his shield were swinging swords at him, and he was holding up the line. Without thinking, Andronicus raised his spear and thrust it forward. He felt the resistance of flesh as he drove his spear into an oncoming Persian. Andronicus heard the man let out a strangled cry as the blade plunged into his chest. He looked up and saw the man's eyes rolling madly as he died. They looked wild and scared, like a horse in a panic.

Andronicus jerked his spear back and watched the man collapse to the ground, dead, a thick red stain spreading down his body. He plunged the spear forward again, this time catching a man just above his collarbone. Blood gushed out of the man's neck as Andronicus wrenched his spear free.

He lost all sense of things then. Space and time mingled into a blind mass all around him. He had no idea how long he held the line or how many men he killed. He lost himself completely in the heat of battle. His arm thrust forward again and again, ending life after life. He knew that at some point he saw Lycus out of the corner of his eye, shouting wildly as he wrenched his spear free of a dead man's chest, but then it was back to the madness. He could neither see nor hear. The world had become a bottomless pit of whirring blackness, an endless tide of death and blood and drums, and under it all, the terrible wailing of the dying men.

It took Niko hammering on his back to bring him back to reality. Andronicus looked around and saw that the lines were swapping again. He stepped back, trying to keep the shield steady. As he stepped back, one of the Thespians took his spot. Once his weight was off the shield, he felt his legs turn to jelly.

Andronicus stumbled away from the battle like a drunkard. As soon as he was far enough away from the line, he dropped his spear, letting it clang against the rocks. He fell to his knees, cutting them both without noticing, his whole body trembling uncontrollably. He looked over and saw Lycus sitting on a rock a few feet away, a dazed look on his pale face. Niko was behind him, retching into the dirt.

"The smell of it," Niko said when he was done, standing up and wiping his mouth.

"Don't," Andronicus said, clenching his eyes tight, trying his best not to vomit as well.

"Their eyes," Lycus said softly. Andronicus could barely hear him over the racket behind them. "Did you see their eyes?"

"I saw them," Andronicus replied, still trying to stop his stomach from turning over.

"They were like cattle," Niko said as he sat down next to Lycus. "Did you see the ones in the back being whipped?"

"No," Andronicus answered dolefully as he stared down at the dirt. "I didn't see that."

"Oy!" a voice shouted behind them, snapping them out of their trance. Andronicus reached for his spear, but his hand fumbled and sent it rolling away. He heard the clanging of metal as Niko dropped his helmet. Lycus jumped to his feet and tried to draw his sword, but it caught in his scabbard.

"What in Ares' name do you think you're doing?" Diokles stood over them menacingly, his sword in his hand. Andronicus noticed both of his massive arms were covered to the elbows in blood, and there were splashes of blood across his face. "The battle is not over. Xerxes is going to send a second wave. Get off your asses."

Andronicus staggered to his feet, fumbling with

his helmet. When he looked back toward the battle, he saw that the Persians were retreating. Now he could see the men with the whips. They lashed at every man they could as the army fell back. In the distance, on a large platform across the valley, Andronicus saw King Xerxes. He was standing in front of his huge golden throne, shouting at the men around him.

As the Medes fell back into the Persian camp, surely to be whipped or killed for their insolence in surrender, the second Persian force began marching forward. Instantly, Andronicus could tell these men were different. As they got closer, marching in perfect formation, Andronicus saw their grandiose attire.

Each man wore ornate blue-and-gold robes with blue headdresses covering most of their faces. They each carried a small wicker shield in one hand and a short spear in the other. A long, curved sword hung at each of their sides and a dirk behind their backs. They also had bows and quivers slung across their left shoulders.

The Spartans retook their original positions next to the wall as the new force marched across the pass.

"The Persians' elite!" Leonidas shouted. "Now Xerxes honors us with his best warriors. We should return the favor in kind!" A fierce roar greeted the king's words.

Andronicus looked around and was astounded at the Spartan men beside him. They looked truly hungry for battle. Every spear tip Andronicus could see was soaked in blood, and many of the men themselves had blood splashed across their faces.

The men marching toward them looked like an imposing force. They had the reputation and the title, but they paled in comparison to the Spartans' ferocity. Some of the Persians stepped forward out of line and twirled their short spears around their arms and torso, showing off their skill. Andronicus saw the confidence on their faces as they marched.

As the Persian elites closed the distance between the two armies, Andronicus saw a few of the men in the front of the Persian line suddenly realize their folly. The Persian elites were renowned for their skill in combat. It was said that they had never truly lost a battle. But one look at the Spartan line waiting for them, and it was certain. The Spartans looked like bloodthirsty savages, fierce, hard, scarred bulls of men soaked in the blood of their enemies, and the Persians looked like fancy noblemen playing at war.

It was the eyes of the men standing beside him that Andronicus would remember. The Spartans looked like they truly wanted to kill the Persians, and not just kill them but maim and butcher them. Andronicus had thought he wanted to kill Persians, and in a childish sort of way he had, but not like the men he stood beside now. These men truly desired nothing more than to slaughter their enemies.

Andronicus watched with a sick feeling as the Persian elites came closer. The Medes had been scared of their masters and the Spartans. The elites looked not afraid in the least, except for a few in the front. They marched slowly and confidently, smirks on many of their faces. Andronicus knew what was going to happen though, even if they did not.

A dozen or so Spartans leapt over the stone wall that had been rebuilt, and charged at the elites, taking them by surprise. The few Persians that had been twirling their spears ran forward to meet the Spartans. The Spartans slaughtered the first attackers in mere seconds. Every Persian who charged was cut down with ease. Then the entire Persian line pressed forward. The dozen Spartans turned and ran back toward the sturdy line of their kin. Many of the men in the front of the Persian line ran forward with spears raised, breaking their own line in their eagerness to kill the retreating Spartans.

Then the long spears were thrust. The elites in front all fell as the Spartan line pushed forward. A split second later, the two lines met. The Persians fell against the Spartan shields, forced into them by the men behind them.

Once caught in the tight pass with the wall of fierce Spartans, the elite warriors fared no better than the slaves. They crashed against the shields and attempted to stab at the Spartans behind them. The Spartans, however, held the advantage. The men in front held the line, ducking down low to avoid the short spears, and the second line used their long spears to outreach the enemy.

Andronicus watched with a mixture of fascination and revulsion as the Spartans cut through the Persian elites. He had a long spear this time and would stand behind Niko and Diokles when their time came.

When it was his turn again, they stepped forward and swapped places with the first line, just as they had before.

Andronicus looked at the faces of the men leaving. Each one was covered in splashes of blood. Most of them looked nearly mad, a menacing mixture of triumph and hate etched under their bloody masks.

Then it was time. Andronicus saw Niko pushing against the shield in front of him, and he knew what he had to do.

Andronicus aimed his spear, ready to strike, and met the eyes of the Persian man stabbing at Niko. He had the same dark skin as the rest of them and a thick black beard under his headdress. Andronicus saw hate in the man's eyes. This was who he had come to fight. This man was the evil monster he had always dreamed the Persians to be. This was one of the men who had killed his father.

Andronicus thrust his spear forward as hard as he could. He watched as the blade sank into the man's chest. When he wrenched his spear free, a spout of blood poured down over Niko's head. Andronicus thrust his spear forward again, plunging it into another chest. He watched again and again as his spear pierced the Persians' unarmored bodies. After a while he realized it was far easier to yank his spear free of their necks than their chests, and he began aiming there.

Again Andronicus fell into a kind of stupor, only vaguely aware of his surroundings, though not as badly as before. During the first wave he had been pressed against a shield, his head down, his arm stabbing blindly. This time he faced his enemy on his feet and watched them each die. The sound became much the same as before, a deafening whir of drums and horns and cries, both in triumph and dismay. At one point Andronicus was sure he heard someone singing over the racket, but he couldn't make out the words.

Sometime later a man came up behind him and shouted that it was time to switch. Andronicus banged Niko and Diokles on the back and then fell back himself. The lines swapped seamlessly, and then they were free again. Andronicus plodded away from the battle, his ears still ringing loudly.

They fell back a ways and then turned to watch the fighting. Diokles was still holding the line, refusing to give up his spot, but Gaios sat down next to them, staring dejectedly at the slaughter before him. Andronicus turned to see Niko absolutely covered in blood. Lycus had blood splashed across his face and forearms, but Niko was drenched and looked like he might be sick again.

The battle lasted another twenty minutes, the Persian elites being massacred as they tried hopelessly to break the Greek line. Finally, they began to fall back. Again Andronicus saw the Great King Xerxes on his feet, shouting furiously at everyone around him. When the elites rejoined the mass army, no new legion marched forward. It seemed that the great king of kings had had enough for one day.

The Spartans and other Greeks let their war cries be heard by the retreating Persians. They shouted and banged on their shields before finally returning to the Greek camp. Andronicus and his friends tramped over to the hot springs and began washing the blood off their faces and arms. Many of the other men had the same idea, and soon the entire pool had an ominous crimson hue.

7

When they had the blood washed from their faces and arms and fresh clothes on, the boys walked over to where the fires were burning. They found Diokles, Gaios, and Perikles sitting around a fire, and they sat down slowly, wincing at the aches and pains they felt throughout their bodies. Andronicus never would have guessed actual war would be so much more physically demanding than training.

"You fought well today, boys," Perikles said proudly. "You are truly Spartan warriors now." Andronicus couldn't help but feel a twinge of pride at that.

"Aye," Diokles slurred drunkenly. Andronicus noticed he had a nearly empty wine pouch in his hand. "You did. Even you, boy." He pointed at Lycus, eyeing him coldly. "We all thought you would be a coward like your father, but you stood true."

Andronicus saw the anger on Lycus's face and knew he was about to do something stupid. Andronicus had heard whispers about Lycus's father before but nothing so direct as that.

"Take that back," Lycus demanded, jumping to his feet.

"Take what back?" Diokles asked, "I gave you a bloody compliment, boy."

"My father was not a coward," Lycus growled. "He died fighting for Sparta."

"He died as he lived," Diokles spat, "a craven fool with love for no one but himself." Lycus looked like he was going to step forward, but Niko grabbed him by the arm.

"He's drunk, Lycus," Niko whispered. "He doesn't know what he's saying." Lycus glared at Diokles a moment longer before storming off. Niko hurried after him. Andronicus stayed where he was, picking at the remainders of his charred coney. Diokles began shouting about how Lycus was being ungrateful, and Perikles quickly took him away. Only Gaios and Andronicus remained by the fire.

"He wasn't really a coward, was he?" Andronicus asked. "Lycus's father. I mean?" Gaios just continued to stare into the fire, like he always did.

"It is not my place to call a man craven," Gaios replied solemnly. "I have felt fear every single time I've gone into battle. Perhaps that makes me a coward."

"But why did Diokles say that?" Andronicus urged. "And why did the king look at Lycus like that when he told him his father's name?"

Gaios sighed. "It is better left in the past. Lycurgus has been dead for ten years, as has your father, and all the rest."

"What do you mean 'the rest'? What happened at Marathon? How did my father die?" Andronicus leaned forward, his face anxious.

"It is not my place to say," Gaios said, turning away.

"But you were there," Andronicus insisted. "You know what happened. I need to know. How did it happen? How did my father die?"

"Your father died fighting the Persians at Marathon," Gaios snapped. "He died a hero, saving others, and that is all you need to know." Andronicus had never seen Gaios angry before. Gaios also stormed off, leaving Andronicus alone by the fire.

Going to war had brought up questions Andronicus never even knew he needed answers to. He had always accepted that his father had died in battle. Now he felt like he had to know more. Something had happened at Marathon, and Lycus's father had been part of it.

Eventually, Andronicus walked over to their tent. Lycus and Niko were already asleep. Andronicus lay down next to them, but once again, he could not fall asleep. He knew he should be thinking of the battle he had fought that day and of the many men he had killed, but all he could think of was how his father might have died and how Lycus's father might have been involved.

8

When Andronicus woke, many of the men were already up and eating breakfast. Lycus was gone, but Niko still lay sleeping. He shook Niko awake and asked him where Lycus was. For a moment they both feared Lycus had gone to confront Diokles, but then Lycus came walking around the corner with bread in his arms.

They ate slowly, not talking at all, and then began dressing for battle. Andronicus noticed his helmet and breastplate had several dents that had not been there the previous morning.

The Persians didn't attack until nearly midday. Andronicus saw that Xerxes was sending forth his slaves again. They wore no armor and had no greater weapons than the day before. Andronicus could not understand why the Persian king was trying the same tactic again. The previous day he had lost thousands of men, and the Greeks had lost less than fifty; the Spartans had lost only seven men.

Andronicus fell in line with the others. He was not nervous this time around; he knew as well as everyone else that they would crush the Persian attack. The Persians charged again, and again they were slaughtered by the Greeks. The Persians pressed the attack until nearly all of them had fallen, and then they began falling back, once again into the whips of their masters.

The Persians sent forth three waves that second day, none of which had any success. By the end of the second day, the consensus was that Xerxes was the most foolish battle commander in the history of warfare. The men laughed at the very sound of his name. Throughout the camp the words "king of kings" were said with mocking fancy.

The boys ate with their new friends without any trouble. Diokles was sober, and no one brought up the battle of Marathon. Andronicus went to sleep that night feeling confident and proud. For the rest of his life he would be able to say that he stood by King Leonidas and defended Greece from the great Persian invasion, just like his father.

9

Andronicus snapped awake as someone shook him. He opened his eyes and saw that it was still dark out. He couldn't make out who was shaking him and quickly reached for his sword.

"It's me, boy," Gaios whispered through the blackness. "You have to leave. Now."

"What?" Andronicus said groggily. "What are you talking about?"

"We have been betrayed," Gaios said as he shook Niko awake. "The Persians will be here soon. You have to go."

"If they're coming, then we will fight them," Lycus said. "We are here to fight for Sparta."

"The rest of the Greeks are leaving," Gaios replied. "You have to go with them."

"No, Lycus is right," Andronicus said, getting to his feet. "We are part of the king's guard now. We will stay and fight until the last."

"No," Andronicus heard a deep voice say from behind him. He turned and saw King Leonidas standing there with a torch in hand. The orange light flickered on his weathered face, dancing across his thick beard. Andronicus would never forget the look on the king's face, sad and angry and defeated and yet filled with a fiery determination.

"You boys have fought bravely," Leonidas said, "but you are still boys. Every other man in my guard has a son to carry on his name. You boys were never meant to die with us. You have to go."

"We can't," Andronicus pleaded. "We're Spartans too, and we're here to fight."

"And fight you did," Leonidas said, giving Andronicus a solemn look. "But you are not here to die. The rest of us are. You have to go now."

"I won't leave," Lycus insisted. "If the Persians are coming then I will die fighting them, just as my father did." Leonidas looked at Lycus for a moment, as if he were really seeing him for the first time.

"We were wrong about you, Lycus, son of Lycurgus," the king said stoically. "You are as brave as any man here, and Sparta will need you in the wars to come. Sparta will need all three of you."

"My king," Andronicus pleaded, "we can't leave. We can't flee from a fight. We are Spartans; you said it yourself. And any Spartan would be damned to let a Persian horde kill his king." Andronicus tried to hold back the tears that were welling up in his eyes.

"You boys are true Spartans," Leonidas said,

nodding. "Archelaus did a fine job with you, but I will not let you die for me. I command you to leave this place, as your king."

Andronicus didn't know what to do. Leaving now would go against everything he believed in, everything he had ever been taught, everything that his father had died for. He tried to think of something else to say, of something that would make Leonidas let them stay and fight.

"The time for talking is over," Gaios said from behind him. "You have to leave now."

"Gaios is right," the king said. "Go, return to Sparta, and tell them what happened here."

"Please, my king," Andronicus pleaded, desperate now. "Let us follow you."

"You are not meant to follow, Andronicus, son of Aristocles. You are meant to lead. You will lead great armies into battle someday. You will not die this night. Now go." The king strode away, presumably to prepare for the oncoming attack. Andronicus turned back to Gaios.

"How did this happen?" Andronicus asked in shock.

"A traitor," Gaios answered as he helped them saddle their horses. "Some treasonous bastard named Ephialtes told Xerxes about the goat path. Within the hour we will be surrounded, which is why you must leave right now."

Andronicus sat on his horse, Lycus and Niko next to him. Most of the Greeks were already fleeing on foot. Gaios and Diokles stood next to each other, looking up at the boys.

"I am sorry I called your father craven," Diokles said to Lycus. "No matter what he was, you are a true Spartan." Lycus glared down at Diokles but gave him a curt nod, then turned to leave. Andronicus looked at Gaios, and the tears spilled from his eyes; he wasn't ready to say goodbye. There was so much he wanted to ask this man.

"Come with us," Andronicus said. "If we don't have to die then neither do you."

"We do," Gaios replied. "I have a son,

Andronicus. His name is Daios. Watch out for him for me." Then they turned and joined the massing Spartan force. Andronicus looked at Niko, and then they started away from the pass.

Andronicus turned back to take one last look at the soldiers who remained to fight. Three hundred of the greatest warriors on earth standing together, defiant, facing certain death head on. He saw King Leonidas standing with his torch, his face a mask of stone. Tears rolled down Andronicus's cheeks as he took his last look at them. Then he turned away and rode off with Niko and Lycus, never to see any of those brave men again.

Chapter 6
Coming Home
1

Their ride back south was dreary and sullen. At first they rode with the rest of the Greeks who had fled, but every day more men broke off from the large retreating force. Everyone but the Thespians and the Spartans had gotten out and were now headed back to their respective cities. The rumors were that the Thespians had chosen to stay behind as well, that they had said it would be an honor to die beside the Spartans in battle. This only added to the shame the three boys felt.

They barely spoke as they rode south with the scattered Greek forces. One by one groups of men broke off from the main bunch until they rode with less than a hundred men. Eventually, it was just the three of them, clad in their shining new Spartan armor, riding solemnly toward home. Each of them was silently trying to accept the shame of what they had done. They had been ordered to leave. Even though the king had commanded it, running from a fight was the most dishonorable thing any Spartan could do.

A week after they had left Thermopylae behind, the boys finally began to recognize the land again. They knew they were less than two days' ride from Sparta, and they began to get nervous. When they set up camp that night, there was a palpable tension in the air; they could all feel it.

"What are we going to tell them?" Lycus asked, finally breaking a long silence. Andronicus shot him a stony look.

"We're going to tell them the truth," he responded coldly as he began stacking wood for a fire, "all of it."

"They'll think we are cowards," Lycus insisted as he began to skin a hare. "They'll say we betrayed the king."

"The king ordered us to go," Andronicus shot back. "He said, 'I command you to leave.' What were we supposed to do?"

"We were supposed to stay," Niko said quietly, looking at his feet. It was the first thing he had said in days. "We were part of the king's guard. It was our duty to fight with him to the end."

Andronicus knew they had been smart to leave; they were just boys, and the king himself had commanded them to go. But in his heart he agreed with Niko. They should never have left their king or their friends.

During their journey back south, they had heard terrible stories about what had taken place at Thermopylae. Some said the Persians had surrounded the Spartans and rained down a million arrows, killing them all. Others said the Persians surrounded the Spartans and captured them and then flayed them all alive. Still others said the Persians surrounded the Spartans, and Xerxes himself had cut off Leonidas's head and waved it about for his whole army to see. The only thing everyone seemed to be clear on was that King Leonidas and all his men had been surrounded and killed.

"Everyone is going to think we're craven," Lycus said, clearly distressed by the thought.

"Why do you care what anyone thinks?" Andronicus asked. "The king commanded us to leave, and we did. If that makes everyone think we're cowards, then we probably are."

"It's not about being a coward or craven or any other stupid name. It's not about what anyone thinks of us at all," Niko had gotten to his feet, clearly outraged by the argument. "They all died," Niko said, tears forming in his eyes. "We left, and they all died."

"How could we have stayed?" Andronicus asked, wanting to believe they had done the right thing. "The king gave us a direct command."

"The Persians were not far," Niko said sadly, sitting back down. "All we had to do was stall for a few more minutes."

"For what?" Andronicus demanded, trying to convince himself as much as Niko. "So we could die with them? Gaios chose to save us. So did the king. If we had stayed, we would be dead right now. But we're not, because we left. We have a responsibility to tell the people back home what happened. We have a responsibility to fight again when Xerxes's army comes south."

Andronicus saw Niko's face change as he accepted the truth of Andronicus's words.

"You're right," Lycus said excitedly, perking up. "They'll be coming down south soon. We'll be able to show everyone we're not cowards." Andronicus was about to shout at Lycus again for being so conceited, but he saw Niko shaking his head, and let it go.

They finished eating in relative silence, then went to sleep. That night Andronicus had a terrible dream. He dreamed of their return and telling his brother they had fled. In his dream Androcles cursed him and called him a coward and shouted at Andronicus, saying he had betrayed their father.

There was something different about Androcles in this dream. Not just the fact that he was yelling at Andronicus; it was something else. It was hard to pinpoint, and Andronicus would forget almost as soon as he woke, but Androcles was older, a man full-grown. In the dream Androcles shouted something else at Andronicus, something much more important, but the next day Andronicus couldn't remember what it was.

2

In the morning Andronicus woke with a cold

sweat. He chose not to tell the others about his dream; it would only worry Lycus and anger Niko.

After a quick breakfast, they rode south toward Sparta, none of them talking. It wasn't until noon the next day that they first saw the city from afar. A rush of emotions hit Andronicus at the sight of his home, joy and relief but also sadness and regret, and beneath it all, a constant, overwhelming shame. Andronicus felt like crying; he had never felt so many emotions in his life.

As they approached the city, a small group of soldiers rode out to meet them. There were six of them, all dressed like the boys.

"Who are you?" one of the men demanded, reining his horse ahead of the others. The man was tall, even on his horse, and he had thick stalks for arms, covered in coarse black hair, and a big, bushy black beard.

"I am Andronicus, son of Aristocles. This is Lycus, son of Lycurgus, and Nikopheros, son of Nikomedes. We were at the pass at Thermopylae. We fought with the king, but he ordered us to leave when word of a sneak attack came." Andronicus waited anxiously to see if the man would believe him or not. They had no proof that they had not stolen their clothes from dead men.

"You are Archelaus's lot?" the man asked after what felt like a very long time.

"We are," Lycus replied from Andronicus's left.

"Did anyone else make it out?" the man asked, eyeing them carefully.

"Most of the other Greeks got out," Andronicus said, making sure to maintain eye contact. "Only the Spartans and the Thespians stayed behind to fight."

"We wanted to stay," Lycus added quickly, "but the king ordered us to leave." The man turned to Lycus, frowning at him.

"The *king* ordered you to go?" the man said in a mocking tone. A few of the men behind him laughed.

"He did, sir," Andronicus said as politely as possible. "He greeted us the first day. He said he liked to know every man in his personal guard. When word of the sneak attack came, one of our friends was telling us to leave. We wanted to stay, but the king told us to go. He said we were not meant to die with them." Andronicus looked down as he finished; he still couldn't help but feel ashamed as he spoke the words. "And we left. We have been riding south as fast as we could."

"Follow me inside the city," the man said, still frowning as he turned his horse around. "You will have to speak to the commander."

The boys followed him, the other soldiers surrounding them, through the great archway of Hermes. People everywhere stopped what they were doing and stared at them. Andronicus was confused; he had not expected a hero's welcome, but it looked like that was what they were going to get.

Just then another group of soldiers came down the path. "Who are these boys?" a lean, angry-looking man in front asked.

"Survivors of Thermopylae," the tall soldier who had first questioned them said. "They are Archelaus's boys. The king sent them home when they heard of the sneak attack." The new man shot the boys a furtive, bitter glance, then turned back to the tall man.

"Bring them with me," he barked, then turned to leave. As they rode up the street, the people began to cheer. Word that they were survivors of Thermopylae spread through the streets like wildfire. The boys were hailed as heroes all the way to the great stone temple atop the hill. Women and children cheered and waved, reaching out to touch their horses and their legs as they rode past.

Andronicus could not believe it; he remembered the day the men had come home from Marathon. He recalled sitting with Androcles and their mother, waiting excitedly for their father's return. Remembering the way the people had cheered that day, he wanted to shout at these people. Andronicus and his companions were not heroes, not like those men had been. Then it struck him that those men had likely felt the same way he did. Like as not, they had ridden home feeling the shame of every brother they had left behind.

He could still remember the way the sad-looking man had rode over to them and dismounted and the look of sorrow on his face as he told them Aristocles had fallen. As the old memory resurfaced, Andronicus suddenly realized who that man had been. His face had been younger, without the lines or the grey hair, and he had still had a thick mane atop his head, but it had been Gaios who had given them the news that day so long ago. Andronicus was sure of it.

As they rode through the deepening crowd, Andronicus let himself take it in. They might not be heroes, but perhaps that wasn't why the people were cheering. Perhaps they were simply cheering the fact that not all of the king's men had died, and he could live with that.

It took a long time to ride through the streets full of people, and the angry man who was leading them seemed to be getting more furious by the second. They were hailed as heroes all the way up to the great stone structure. As soon as they dismounted though, two men grabbed them each by the arms and pulled them inside.

They were shoved through dark passages, lit dimly by torches, until they reached a large room with a high stone ceiling. Inside was a big stone table, around which a group of men stood talking quietly. When the boys were brought in, the men turned around, and Andronicus saw that Archelaus was one of them. Archelaus stepped forward, and Andronicus wrenched himself free of the men holding him and ran into his arms.

"I feared you boys were dead," Archelaus said in his hard voice as he caught Andronicus. "How did you manage to escape?"

"The king ordered us to leave," Andronicus said, looking Archelaus in the eye. "A man named Gaios woke us. He saved us." Archelaus stared stoically at Andronicus for a moment and then nodded. Then Niko stepped forward and hugged Archelaus as well, and Lycus followed.

"So, the boys escaped because the king sent them away," an old man with a lean face and scraggly whiskers said from the table.

"Aye," Archelaus replied, daring anyone to challenge his word. "The king knew they were recruits. He would have sent them away if he could; they have no sons." Andronicus heard a soft buzz of chatter as the men around the table agreed.

"Very well," the old man said, "but they still need to provide answers for us." He stepped around the table and eyed them quizzically. "How did the Persians come to ambush the king? Do you know?"

"We were betrayed," Andronicus said, repeating what Gaios had told him. "A man named Ephialtes told Xerxes about the goat path that leads behind the wall at the pass. The Persians made for the path as soon as they could, but word had already gotten back of the betrayal. There was time for most of the Greeks to leave. Only the Spartans and the Thespians stayed behind."

"The Thespians should be rewarded for their loyalty," a large barrel-chested man grunted from the table.

"Yes," another said, "in time, but first we must deal with our enemies."

"You're sure the traitor was this man, Ephialtes?" the old man asked.

"No," Andronicus said. "That's just what Gaios told us as we left."

"If Gaios said it, it must be true," another man at the table said. Andronicus was surprised they knew who Gaios was.

"How many men did the Persians have?" the old man asked.

"Hundreds of thousands," Andronicus replied. "Maybe a million."

3

The council, or whoever they were, questioned the boys for hours before finally letting them go. When they were dismissed, Archelaus told them to go to their old barracks. They walked through the now-empty streets in silence. Andronicus didn't know what the others were thinking, but he was anxious and excited to see his brother and Thymi.

They arrived at the barracks after nightfall and let themselves in. A torch was burning in the courtyard, but other than that the place looked deserted.

Andronicus walked into the barracks with Niko and Lycus behind him, and there they were. Androcles, Theodotus, and Euthymius were all sitting up waiting for them. As soon as they heard them come in, Androcles jumped up and hugged his brother tightly. It had only been a little over two months since they had left, yet Androcles had grown nearly as tall as his older brother.

"We heard you were back," Thymi said, smiling excitedly. "Everyone in the city is talking about it. The boys who survived the slaughter." Thymi's smile faltered as he saw their faces. "What's wrong?" he asked. "You made it."

"We should have stayed," Niko said, looking at the floor.

Andronicus proceeded to tell them all about their adventures. They stayed up half the night talking. He told them about their journey north, about the Greek camps, about Gaios and Diokles, and about the mighty King Leonidas. He told them about almost everything—the battle, their escape, and their ride back south—everything except the bit about Lycus's father. It was well into the night when they finally went to sleep.

4

The next morning they woke at dawn and went out to the courtyard to meet Archelaus, just as they had always done. Andronicus was struck with how menial everything now seemed. After being part of an army and fighting in a real battle, their schoolyard training seemed childish. Nevertheless, they went about their usual routine as if nothing had happened. They practiced with wooden swords for over an hour. The whole time Andronicus couldn't help thinking that they would never need such a skill against a Persian horde.

After training they went for a run. Then they climbed the hill to see Philander. Andronicus couldn't believe it, but he was actually excited to see the old man. As they crested the hill and walked to the old pond, Andronicus expected to find Philander sitting serenely by the water, like he always was. Instead, Philander was on his feet, a grim expression of fear and worry on his face.

"I am very glad to see you boys again," he said to Andronicus, Lycus, and Niko. Andronicus knew they were probably his three least-favorite students, but he believed the old man meant the words nonetheless.

"We're glad to see you as well," Andronicus said, "but why do you look so worried?"

"I'm afraid dire news has come to Sparta," Philander said ominously. "Have a seat, boys. We have much to discuss this day." The boys all sat around the pond, looking anxiously at their normally calm teacher. Philander took his own seat, then breathed a heavy sigh before beginning.

"Xerxes has crossed the Hellespont, and now he travels south with his army. Boeotia and Attica have already fallen." Philander gave the boys a grave look. "The Greek fleet, led by Themistocles, held the Persians back at Artemisium at the same time that you boys were fighting beside the king. But after Leonidas fell at Thermopylae, Themistocles retreated the Athenian navy to Salamis. Now the council says there will be another battle, this time at the Straits of Salamis. I fear this time all of you will have to fight."

Andronicus was relieved at the news; he had wanted a chance to battle the Persians again, and it seemed he would get it much sooner than he expected. Perhaps if they were truly blessed, they might even get a chance to see this traitor Ephialtes. Andronicus looked around and realized that Lycus and Niko were the only other ones who felt the way he did. Everyone else looked terrified. The boys flicked nervous glances from one to another, shifting about uncomfortably.

"What of Athens?" Euthymius asked in a worried voice.

"They fled before the Persians arrived," Philander replied gravely. "The city belongs to Xerxes now, and I have heard rumors that Athens has been sacked. I know you boys are scared, but you must face your fears. Follow Andronicus, Lycus, and Niko. They fought alongside the king, and they will show you the way."

"We will," Andronicus said to the others. "We saw the Persian army. Other than their elites, they are an army of slaves. A good swordsman should fare well enough against them."

A few of the boys still looked worried, but Andronicus's words seemed to have reassured most of them. They spent the rest of the day talking about what was to come and what was happening in the north.

5

The next day the boys were all sent south to Andronicus's hometown of Gytheion, where the Spartan army was amassing to set sail for Salamis. Before going down to the docks with the rest, Andronicus snuck away and went to find his mother's home. When he got there, he found her sitting in her old chair, staring out at the sea, as she so often was. She looked up at the sound of his entering and immediately broke into tears. She rushed forward and hugged Andronicus so tightly he thought she would smother him. When she released him, they were both crying.

"I'm OK, Mother," Andronicus said, trying to sound stronger than he felt.

"They said the king and his men were all killed," Athenia sobbed. "I thought you had died."

"The king sent us away," Andronicus said sadly. "He told me we were not meant to die for him."

"Leonidas was always a good man," Athenia nodded. "Your father loved him like a brother."

"What happened to Father?" Andronicus asked. "How did he die? Did Gaios ever tell you? Did anyone ever tell you?"

"They told me he died fighting the Persians," Athenia said, apparently surprised by the question. "They told me he died saving others. Why do you ask? You never asked about that before."

"It doesn't matter," Andronicus lied. "That's all in the past now. I have to go again, Mother. The whole Spartan army is setting sail to fight again." Athenia nodded, her face lined with tears and fear.

"Don't worry though," Andronicus said, smiling. "I saw what the Persians have to offer, and they won't kill me."

Athenia did not look convinced, but she nodded and gave Andronicus another tight hug. Andronicus stayed and ate a quick meal with his mother, knowing in his heart that it could be their last. When he left again, he felt sorry for her, and he wished he didn't have to go.

Chapter 7
Dire Straits
1

Andronicus and his friends set sail from the port of Gytheion in the south of Sparta one week from the day they had returned. This time they were accompanied by the rest of their class, including Thymi. They were aboard one of sixteen Spartan ships that were sailing for the Straits of Salamis. Androcles and Theodotus had to stay behind because they were not yet of age to fight, and Andronicus once again had to bid a solemn farewell to his brother and mother as he sailed off to war.

All of the Greek cities were sending their navies to the Straits for one final attempt to stop Xerxes' invasion. Some of the other soldiers said that the Athenians were sending their entire army, which had refused to fight alongside Leonidas. Andronicus didn't like the thought of fighting next to Athenians, but he was curious to see what they could do.

Everyone knew that if the allied Greek forces failed to stop Xerxes at the Straits of Salamis, Greece would surely fall to the Persians. It was their last chance. If the Persians held Athens when winter came, they would be able to wait the winter out. But if the Greeks could defeat the Persian navy now, they could retake Athens and force Xerxes back to Asia for the winter.

Most of the new boys were anxious at the thought of battle. Andronicus knew that many of them were not ready, but there was no more time to prepare. Some of the boys asked Andronicus, Lycus, and Niko constant questions about Thermopylae, and they answered them as best they could. Inside, however, Andronicus knew that the battle to come would be far different and most likely far bloodier for the Greeks.

It took three days to reach the Straits. When they arrived the boys were all stunned into silence. More ships were huddled together than any of them had ever seen. Andronicus didn't even know so many Greek ships existed. Thymi started counting the Athenian ships and a long time later proclaimed there were just fewer than two hundred. There were also forty Corinthian ships, thirty Aegean ships, twenty Megarian ships, fifteen Sician ships, and a scattering of ships from the other smaller Greek cities. All told there were approximately 375 Greek ships to hold the Straits.

The ships slowly formed two great lines, from north to south, blocking the Straits entirely. By midday the Greek fleet was ready for battle. Then, as the sun began to set behind them, the Greeks caught their first glimpse of the Persian fleet, as it sailed in from the east. As more and more ships came into view, many of the boys started panicking.

"Relax," Andronicus told his nervous classmates, knowing the older soldiers were watching. "It doesn't matter how many ships they have. We have the pass blocked completely. They can't outnumber us if they don't have the room. It's exactly as we did at Thermopylae, force the fools into a tight pass, and fight them man to man."

"But they'll just keep coming," Kleitos said frantically. "Even if we do kill one of them, three more

will take his place. It's hopeless. We're doomed."
Andronicus looked at Kleitos with pity. He knew he
would likely die in this battle. He had always thought
that cowards had no place in war, but he had been
wrong. A coward's place in war is death.

"They will have to fight us one ship at a time,"
Andronicus said as calmly as he could manage. "We
can handle them. Just follow my lead, and remember
what Archelaus taught us."

"Follow *his* lead," Lycus said, motioning to
Andronicus, "but stay the hell away from me when the
fighting starts. Cowards do nothing but get men
killed." Andronicus frowned at Lycus, but he knew he
was right. He looked over at Thymi, who was sitting on
a barrel nervously chewing his fingernails, and walked
over to him.

"You'll be fine," Andronicus said as he sat down
next to his friend. "I'll make sure of it. Just don't leave
my side."

"I know," Thymi replied quietly. "I'm not like
Kleitos. I know what I have to do. That's what worries
me."

"What do you mean?" Andronicus asked,
raising an eyebrow.

"I know I'm going to have to kill a man,
probably many men," Thymi said dryly. "I know you
hate the Persians, Andy, and you're a great fighter,
and you probably enjoyed killing them. I'm not looking
forward to it though. If I had it my way, I would never
fight anyone."

Andronicus didn't say anything. He knew
Thymi had never liked fighting, but he was also wrong,
Andronicus had not enjoyed killing the Persians, not
even the elites. It had made him sick. He remembered
the way the Persian slaves had yelled and cried as they
were slaughtered, the way their eyes had ceased to
look human, the way they themselves had seemed to
turn into wild animals, trying desperately to live.
Andronicus had to close his eyes for a moment and
catch his breath; the memories still haunted him.

"I didn't," Andronicus finally said in a soft
voice. "I mean I don't, like killing Persians," he added

at Thymi's confused look. "I thought I would, but it isn't the same as killing an animal. Gaios was right about that." He stared out at the sea. "If I had it my way, I wouldn't want to fight either, but if we don't stop the Persians here, we'll spend the rest of our short lives fighting them until they kill us, if not in Salamis then at Corinth, Argos, or Tagea. Perhaps we'll even make it back to Sparta, but if we don't stop them here, we will die in Sparta, fighting the Persians."

"I know," Euthymius replied. "I'm not a coward. I'll fight with you until the end. But I still don't like it."

"Neither do I," Andronicus said with a sad smile.

2

Sometime after nightfall, Sophos, the captain of their ship, came down into the cabin. Sophos was a veteran sea captain, and Archelaus himself had chosen him to command the new recruits. He did not look anything like the Spartan warriors Andronicus had come to know. At Thermopylae the Spartans looked like they were made of steel and iron. The men of the Spartan navy looked very different, and Sophos was a prime example. He was short, much shorter than Andronicus, and large around the middle. He had massive arms that looked like they had spent the last twenty years rowing a ship and short, thick legs. He was bald, but he had a thick, wiry black beard that glistened with sea breeze.

"Gather around, men!" Sophos called. Andronicus could tell he was well practiced in speaking loud enough to be heard even over the ocean. Sophos waited until everyone in the cabin had gathered around. The boys looked pale and nervous next to the battle-hardened men. Andronicus tried to look hard and mean to make up for his peers, but all he saw were the older seafaring men scowling at them as if they were children.

"The Persians are going to attack soon," Sophos said in his raspy voice. "Themistocles of Athens sent a message to Xerxes that our fleet is cracking and that many of our ships have fled." Andronicus recognized the name "Themistocles." He was the Athenian general who had fought at Marathon and led the navy at Artemisium just a month ago. He was likely leading the Greek defenses since Leonidas's death.

"If Poseidon and Ares smile on us, Xerxes will take the bait and rush into our trap."

"And if he does not?" Kleitos asked in a panicked voice. Sophos shot him a cold look, and Kleitos seemed to wither like a leaf. Andronicus shook his head. He thought Kleitos would have been smarter than to ask the captain such a question, especially at a time like this.

"If he does not then he will likely take his army north, over the Straits, march into Salamis, surround us, and kill us all," Sophos said in a calm, angry tone. "So pray that the gods make Xerxes fall into the trap." Sophos shot Kleitos one last fiery look before storming back up to the deck.

"Fool," Lycus said to Kleitos as the group began to disband. "How stupid are you? To ask the captain a question like that."

"It was a good question," Kleitos said defensively, not meeting Lycus's angry stare. "If we are truly hanging all our hopes on this one lie, we should know it."

"This is not Philander's class," Andronicus said, no longer able to restrain his frustration. "This is wartime, and Sophos is our captain. You cannot speak out of turn like that, and you cannot ask him tactical questions in front of everyone when he is laying out our battle plans."

"I was just trying to be smart," Kleitos said, looking at his feet.

"Being smart will not help you here, Kleitos," Andronicus nearly shouted. "The time for talking is done. Xerxes *will* fall into this trap. I saw him at Thermopylae, and I saw the way he commands his army. This news of our retreat is just what he's been waiting for. He will rush forward, expecting to break us easily, and we'll be waiting for him. All we have to do

is wait, and they'll come to us. And then we fight."
Andronicus glared at Kleitos as he said this last part,
knowing full well that was exactly what Kleitos was
afraid of.

"Try to get some rest if you can, but be ready,"
Andronicus said to the rest of the boys who were still
gathered around listening. "Stay vigilant; the Persians
will be coming soon."

As the boys slumped off to their cots to try and
get some sleep, Lycus came and sat next to
Andronicus.

"He's not going to make it," Lycus said under
his breath, so only Andronicus could hear. "And he's
not the only one."

"Have faith in them, Lycus," Andronicus tried
to reassure him, even though he knew Lycus was
right. "They're our brothers; we've trained with them
for the last ten years."

"Which is how I know they're not going to
make it," Lycus said.

"They can," a voice said from behind them,
surprising them both. They turned to see Niko standing
there. "We have to help them. We have to try and
keep them alive. Remember what the king said to us."

"We can try to help them," Lycus whispered,
"but in the end they'll have to fight for themselves. Do
you really think Kleitos will live through an open battle
without an infantry line to hide behind? We're going to
have to fight them one on one this time, and the weak
are not going to make it."

"Perhaps not," Niko said with a sigh, "but we
still have to try."

"And we will," Andronicus said, looking at
Lycus. "They're going to look to us, and we have to
lead them." Lycus nodded slowly, meeting his friends'
stares. Then they made their way to their cots to rest
for the battle to come.

3

Andronicus was right; Xerxes fell for the bait
better than the Greeks had hoped. The great King of
Kings quickly readied his fleet, and at dawn sent the

whole Persian fleet west to break the remaining Greek ships and take the city of Salamis. When the Persian fleet came around the final bend, expecting to see a scattering of ships, they found two lines of Greek ships, each two hundred strong. The Greeks stood on the decks of their ships in full battle attire, shouting war cries across the water.

Andronicus and his troupe stood together on their ship with Sophos standing on the bow. All the boys were dressed in Spartan battle dress, though Andronicus, Lycus, and Niko clearly stood out from the others. The armor that Thymi and the other boys had gotten was either old and used or newly forged by a blacksmith clearly far below the skill that Karpos had possessed. Andronicus had thought little of Karpos at the time, thinking he was an angry, self-righteous little man, but now he knew why. Karpos's armor and swords were noticeably superior to the others, even those of the older veterans on the ship.

As they stood on the deck watching the looming mass of dark ships coming at them, several Persian ships tried to turn back, but it was too late. The Persian navy was too vast, and it had already fallen into the trap.

The Persian ships rushed toward the line of Greek ships. The Spartan ships held the rightmost end of the Greek line, and they knew they would be the first ones hit. The Athenians held the left and much of the middle, with the Corinthians taking most of the rest.

The Persian fleet surged forward in an unorganized mass. Orders rang out across the line of Greek ships, and oars began dropping into the water. The Greek fleet started moving slowly backward, feigning retreat but actually moving into a better position from which to defend the Straits. The ships slowly drifted back together, waiting for the moment to attack. Then from their left the Spartans saw many of the Corinthian ships break formation and start sailing north up the Straits.

"The Corinthians are abandoning us!" someone shouted from behind Andronicus.

"It's a ploy, you fool!" Sophos shouted. "Stay in line, and ready yourself for battle. The Persians are not expecting a fight, but we are."

As the Persian ships continued to approach, the wind finally picked up. Feeling a cool breeze against his back, Andronicus knew the time had come. From somewhere to their left a single Greek ship sailed forward, the wind pushing it toward the Persian fleet. Andronicus saw the men aboard the ship shouting wildly and waving their spears.

A moment later, Sophos yelled, and the sails fell above his head. Their ship jerked forward at the same time as the rest of the Greek line. The Greek ships formed a solid line as the Persians moved in awkwardly. Andronicus felt the ship swaying with the sea as it rushed toward a Persian ship, and he tried to steady his feet. He had a moment of doubt as the ships raced toward each other, fearing the Persian ship would ram them and sink them then and there, but he had confidence in the Spartan shipwrights. He had time to take one final breath and brace himself before the impact.

When the Spartan ship collided with one of the Persian ships, everyone flew forward; no one had expected such a violent impact. The Spartans just had time to regain their footing before the Persians rushed over the ship's bow. Many of the boys looked terrified, and for a moment Andronicus thought they would turn and flee.

Andronicus rushed forward, his shield raised and his sword ready to thrust. Many of the others did the same. Andronicus thrust his sword into one of the Persians and saw Niko kill a man beside him. When the first men were down, the boys stepped forward, moving on to the next. The Spartans pushed the Persians back easily, cutting through them with their superior swordsmanship.

When their ship was cleared, Sophos shouted a loud battle cry, and the Spartans followed him over the bow and onto the Persian ship. As the hundreds of ships came together in a tangled mess of wood and cloth, men began jumping and climbing from ship to ship. As Andronicus and the other Spartans climbed onto the Persian ship, they realized that many of the men from the Persian ships behind it had rushed forward to join the battle, and they met a much greater force than they had anticipated.

Andronicus rushed forward beside Lycus and Niko, the rest of the boys scattered about behind them. Andronicus and Niko worked together, killing one man after another, side by side. Thymi was behind them, fighting a man with a short spear. Andronicus tried to keep an eye on him, but he had to stay with Niko, as they held the vanguard of the attack.

The Persians ran forward, stabbing wildly at anything and everything. Andronicus watched as one Persian thrust his spear blindly into the back of one of his comrades, only to be cut down by Lycus. Andronicus held firm with Niko at his side, striking at one Persian and then another. Their feet began to slip as blood spread across the deck, and the fighting became even more hectic.

The battle became a wild, chaotic mass of men, fighting aimlessly and shouting their cries of death and glory. There were no battle drums this time, and far fewer horns blew. All they heard was shouting, screaming, the clashing of metal, and the creaking of many ships. The battle went on for some time, with the Spartans holding off wave after wave of Persians.

Finally, the Persians began to blow their horns of retreat. They stampeded over each other to get away from the Spartans. Many of the Spartans started after them, but Sophos quickly called them back. Andronicus did not know how the rest of the Greek ships had fared, but the Spartans he was with had massacred the Persians who had attacked them.

"Back to the ship!" Sophos shouted over the commotion. "Back to the ship now!" Andronicus ran toward their ship with Niko and Thymi at his side. He saw Lycus wrench his sword free of a man's chest and then turn and join them, a wild look in his eyes.

Then Andronicus saw Kleitos. His body lay on the blood-soaked deck, his dead eyes staring up at the sky. His throat had been cut open, and blood had turned his bronze breastplate a terrible shining red. Euthymius halted for a moment as well, staring down at his friend. Andronicus saw tears welling up in Thymi's eyes. Then he pushed him forward.

"There's no time," Andronicus said, turning away from Kleitos's haunting dead eyes. "We have to get back to the ship."

They left him there, lying dead amongst the many Persians they had slain, and returned to their ship.

Once the men had all boarded the ship, they grabbed the oars and started rowing as Sophos shouted orders. They made their way around the abandoned Persian ships into open water. Most of the Greek ships chased the Persian fleet all the way out of the Straits, shooting arrows at them as they went.

Dozens of ships had sunk in the battle, both Greek and Persian. The water was filled with hundreds of men trying to swim to shore and hundreds more floating dead. The normally crystal-blue Aegean Sea had turned an awful bloody red. As Andronicus stared down at the men in the water, he saw sharks swimming amongst them. Andronicus had seen sharks his whole life, growing up by the sea, but never like this. He and the other boys watched in horror as the sharks began ripping men to pieces.

The Greek fleet chased the Persians out of the Straits, sending them back across the Aegean and out of Greece, at least for the time being.

When the Persians were gone, a great cry of triumph rose from the many Greek ships. Andronicus saw Athenians and Spartans alike shouting together in victory. Aboard the Corinthian ships that had feigned retreat earlier, the men were covered in blood. Andronicus looked out over the mass of abandoned Persian ships and smiled. Many of them were on fire, and several had already sunk into the blood-filled water, but many of them would be able to serve the Greek navy now.

All in all, it was a great victory, one that could even change the tide of the war. If the Persians had suffered the kind of losses that Andronicus thought they had, it would greatly change the way Xerxes could use his navy. Andronicus knew he should feel joyful and relieved, but all he could think about was the way Kleitos's eyes had looked. It was far from the first person he had seen dead in battle, but it was the first dead person he had truly known.

None of the boys spoke as they sat down at the oars. Andronicus looked around and noticed that three others besides Kleitos had died. Only seven members of their class were left. Every one of them was covered in splashes of blood, and they all had a haunted look in their eyes. They sat in silence the whole night, taking turns rowing and sleeping as they headed back south to Sparta.

Chapter 8
The Battle of Plataea

1

After his defeat at Salamis, Xerxes The Great, King of Kings, ruler of the mighty Persian Empire, fled Greece in disgrace. He took the vast bulk of his army back to Asia with him but left behind sixty thousand handpicked men, much of them cavalry. They were led by a man named Mardonius, one of Xerxes' top generals, to finish the conquest for Persia. Mardonius took his new army north into Thessaly, leaving the burnt ruins of Athens to the Athenians.

Andronicus and his friends sailed back to Sparta with the rest of the Spartan fleet. Euthymius had grown sullen and quiet since the battle, and Andronicus knew he was still trying to accept what he had done. Meanwhile, Lycus, Niko, and Andronicus had gained something of a reputation. Everyone knew they had survived the battle of Thermopylae, and their bravery at Salamis had not gone unseen either. Everywhere they went around the ship, soldiers much older than them showed them a newfound respect.

When they arrived in Sparta, Andronicus went straight to the barracks to find his brother. Androcles was sitting with Theodotus, and he rushed over when he saw Andronicus.

"They say you and Lycus and Niko are the

fiercest warriors in the Spartan army," Androcles said as he hugged Andronicus.

"It's true," Theo said with a big grin. "Everyone is talking about it. How you three led the charge and slayed a hundred men each."

Andronicus let out a snort of laughter; he couldn't help it. "We could not have killed a hundred men between the three of us," he said. He broke into a fresh bout of laughter as he watched Androcles and Theodotus's expressions fall. "We did lead the charge," Andronicus added, "but only on our ship. One of the other ships really led the charge. We could not see if it was Spartan or Corinthian though."

"Well, regardless," Theo said, furrowing his brow and bending his lip in annoyance at Andronicus's correction, "the three of you have acquired a reputation as heroes."

"Archelaus says we'll be ready for battle soon enough," Androcles said excitedly. "Probably by this time next year."

"The war may be over by then," Andronicus said with a sigh as he sat down. "The war may even be over already." Androcles's face sank a bit at that, but Andronicus gave him an encouraging look. "But if the war is not over, you'll have to be ready to fight when your time comes. We all will."

When the others came in, everyone gathered around, and they all began telling stories of the battle. Almost everyone had something to say, some brave deed or another they had done in the heat of battle. Only Thymi stayed quiet. Andronicus could tell he was listening as the others told their stories, but he didn't say a word.

2

The next day the boys all reported for duty to Archelaus, as they always did. Archelaus walked through the courtyard in his usual curt fashion, looking them over one by one. He worked his way around to the front and then looked at Andronicus and his friends.

"You boys," Archelaus said in his rough voice.

"You who fought at Salamis, you have done me proud. You have done Sparta proud. Your time as children is finished. You are men now." Andronicus felt a rush of emotions but tried his best to hide it from the others. "You have finished your training," Archelaus continued, gazing proudly at them. "I have nothing more to teach you. You are to report to captain Sophos by sundown."

Andronicus didn't know what to say; he had not expected this. He had thought he would stay there another year at least. He looked to his right and saw that Euthymius was as shocked as he was.

"We will do you proud, Archelaus," Niko said. "Thank you for all you have taught us. You made us into warriors." Andronicus thought he saw Archelaus's mouth twitch for a moment, then it was gone. Archelaus stared at the boys, looking from one to the next.

"He is right," Andronicus added, trying not to let his voice break. "Thank you."

"Alright," Archelaus barked, scowling again, "enough of that. I taught you what I could, and you're welcome. Now go forth and defend Sparta." He turned to the other boys and started shouting orders, sending them scattering. Andronicus smiled to himself. He knew that was the most emotion Archelaus probably ever showed anyone.

3

The Spartans waited out the winter at home. Andronicus had never felt so bored or useless in his life. Everyone knew that Mardonius and his Persians were laying siege to Potidaea, far north of them, but the Spartans remained in Sparta. Andronicus's days consisted mainly of patrolling the streets of the city or rowing on one of Sophos's ships. Sophos had been given command of three ships after the Battle of Salamis, and the men under his command often spent weeks at sea.

When Andronicus wasn't out at sea, he got to live at home again with his mother. It was odd to live at home after so many years in the barracks, but Andronicus liked it. Androcles was still training under

Archelaus, so it was just Andronicus and Athenia for the first time since he was a baby. Like all women in Sparta, Athenia did her part, as a blacksmith's aid, but she and Andronicus would often have supper together.

With no real soldier's work to be done, Andronicus spent most of his free time sitting around with his friends. He, Thymi, Lycus, and Niko had all grown a very close bond after the battle, along with Androcles and Theodotus, though they were still in training most of the time. Andronicus visited his brother as often as he could, and Androcles would always talk about how he would be ready for battle soon as well.

Rumors of what was going on in the north came constantly throughout the long winter. There was word that the Athenians had demanded that the other Greek cities send their armies north to defeat Mardonius, but none had answered the call. The Athenians had fought bravely at the Battle of Salamis, but much of Greece still resented them for not standing with King Leonidas. The alliance that had been created in response to Xerxes' invasion seemed to be crumbling as quickly as it had formed.

Word came down that Mardonius had offered the Athenians peace; all they had to do was surrender the Straits and allow the Persians to enter the Peloponnesus. In return the Persians would allow the Athenians to keep their city and govern themselves as a part of Xerxes's great empire.

As winter turned to spring, the whispers grew darker. Mardonius had marched south again and retaken what remained of Athens. The Athenians still held the Straits but were said to be breaking. Everyone in Sparta knew that if the other Greek cities did not send aid soon, the Athenians would surrender the Straits to Mardonius, and Xerxes would be able to sail his entire army right back into Greece.

4

In July 479 BC, Andronicus and his friends finally left Sparta to face the Persians. They rode as part of a great army, heading north to defeat

Mardonius and his men. As Androcles had hoped, he and Theodotus had been allowed to go as well, even though they were both only fifteen. The army rode north in good spirits. It had been nearly a year since they had met the Persians in battle, and the Spartans were more than ready for another bout. Androcles in particular was invigorated at the notion of joining his brother and father as gloried Persian killers.

Word spread through the army as they traveled, that Mardonius had set fire to Athens again and fled north with his army. Whispers that the Persian cavalry would try to lure the Greeks into a trap quickly spread. Everyone seemed to expect the Persians to jump out of the woods and attack them at any moment. No attack came though, and the Greek army continued to grow as it moved north.

The number of Greeks that had joined the army was becoming something of legend. Men said it was the largest army Greece had ever amassed, greater even than Agamemnon's great army, which had sailed to Troy so long ago. No one was sure exactly how many men now marched north, but the consensus was that there were over sixty thousand.

As the Greek army entered Boeotia, the Persian cavalry finally showed itself, launching small attacks on the Greeks' outer lines as they marched. It was clear to everyone in the Greek army that Mardonius was trying to lure them into the attack they all feared, but they resisted. Whenever the Persians attacked, the Greeks would form a line and hold it as best they could, knowing the Persians wanted to lure the Greeks into an open field, but they held their lines firm.

5

One night one of the Persian cavalry commanders, a man named Mastisius, led a light cavalry assault on the Megarians' camp at the far left of the Greek army. They were successfully breaking the Megarians' line when an Athenian arrow took Mastisius down. When the Persian cavalry saw their commander fall, they fled. The Greek army knew that the rest of the Persians would likely attack at dawn, so they marched up a nearby hill and prepared for battle. The Spartans and Tageans held the right while the Athenians held the left.

Not long after the Greek army had taken up its position, the sun rising behind them, the Persian army appeared in the distance. Rather than attacking right away, the Persians seemed to be settling in themselves. The Greeks waited all day and into the night for the Persians to attack. When it became clear the attack would not come, they set up camp themselves.

The next day the tension throughout the Greek line was palpable as they stared out at the Persian army across the shallow valley. Andronicus tried to reassure the others by telling them they had waited five days at Thermopylae before attacking, but it seemed to do little good. The Athenian and Tagean tangents were beginning to show signs of panic. The Spartans stayed calm for the most part, knowing they would likely fare well in the battle to come, but the rest of the Greeks were far too nervous.

The men waited the whole day for an attack that never came, and the next day, and the next. Many more Greeks joined the vast army as they waited, each seeming to bring more dire news than the last.

After eight days of waiting, and staring at the army they would surely have to fight, word came down that Mardonius had begun to attack the convoys that were bringing supplies to the Greek army. The Persians had a steady supply line running from the north, and if the Greeks lost their own supply line, the Persians would surely be able to wait them out.

Two days later Mardonius hit the Greek supply line running from the Gargaphian spring, the army's only source of water. When the news spread, it created a panic. The food was already running low, and without water, the army would have to leave its tactically advantageous position.

Orders came down the line that the army would be falling back to a better position. In hopes of avoiding the Persian cavalry, the retreat was to be done at night.

Andronicus knew the plan was flawed from the start. Mardonius surely wanted them to do just that and would likely be waiting for them, but he also knew that they could not stay where they were. Andronicus saw the fear in his friends' eyes that night; even Lycus looked uneasy. He tried to console them, to tell them they would be fine, but he could hear the emptiness in his own words as he spoke them.

6

By the time night fell, men were fleeing everywhere Andronicus looked, Spartans and Athenians alike, running for their lives. If there had ever been a plan to make a deliberate, stealthy retreat, it was long gone. Andronicus watched throughout the night as the massive Greek army broke into a panicked escape. Someone shouted that the Athenians had already left and that the Persians would soon be upon them all.

At that very moment, Andronicus heard the first horn bellow. He felt his stomach drop. Even through the darkness he could see the Persian cavalry charging across the field toward them. Another horn blew and then another, and the Greek army slowly realized what was happening. Andronicus knew they had no time to flee; the Persian horses would surely run them down. He only had time for one thing.

"Everyone!" Andronicus shouted as loud as he could, and saw many men snap their necks toward him. "Spears!" Andronicus shouted. "Grab the long spears, now!" He raised his own spear and readied himself for the attack. To Andronicus's great surprise, nearly every man around him grabbed a spear and braced themselves.

When the Persian cavalry fell upon them, they were as ready as they could be. Andronicus had the base of his spear lodged in the dirt, the point ready for any oncoming horses, just as Archelaus had taught him. It was hard to make out the riders through the darkness, but Andronicus saw them just before they hit. The moment a horse came into his view, he moved his spear slightly to the left and watched in awe as the horse drove itself through his spear. He felt the wood snap and saw the end of the spear disappear into the horse's chest. Its eyes rolled as it fell to the ground, braying out its agony.

Out of the corner of his eye, Andronicus saw dozens of horses impaling themselves on spears. Riders flew forward all around him. The man whose horse Andronicus had killed fell with his horse on top of him. He let out a howl of pain, the horse having broken the rider's leg as they fell. Andronicus drew his sword and drove it into the man's chest before he could get up.

Andronicus looked up just in time to see a Persian sword swinging down at him. He ducked at the last second as the rider passed him. Another rider came right behind, aiming a spear at him. Andronicus raised his shield just in time. He heard a loud clang as the spear struck his bronze shield, sending him sprawling into the dirt.

Andronicus quickly scrambled back to his feet, and slashed at the rider's leg. His blade cut through the man's flesh, and blood sprayed over Andronicus's arm. The rider let go of his reins, reeling in pain, and grabbed his leg. Andronicus drove his sword up into the man's side and pulled him down off his horse.

He hoisted himself onto the dead man's horse and had a brief moment to look out over the battle. It was still dark, but he could see well enough. The Persian cavalry had attacked in full, but the Spartans and the Tageans had held their positions. Andronicus looked out over a sea of horses and men, fighting wildly and blindly in the blackness of the night.

Seconds later, another rider came rushing forward, having seen Andronicus atop his comrade's horse. The man screamed as he charged, thrusting his spear blindly. Andronicus raised his shield, and the spear banged against it. Then Andronicus lowered his shield and thrust his sword at the man. Again he hit his mark, driving his sword through the rider's thin armor and piercing his heart.

Andronicus wrenched his sword free and then looked around for his friends. He saw Lycus and Euthymius to his right, fighting side by side against a single rider. He looked to his left and saw Androcles in the distance engaged in single combat with a foot soldier. Niko and Theodotus were also nearby, each one fighting a soldier. Andronicus reared his horse and rode toward his brother.

On his way there, he became entangled with a new group of riders. Three Persians had taken it upon themselves to rid Andronicus of his horse. As he spun around, he could tell they were aiming to kill his horse before him. He removed one foot from its stirrup, and as one of the riders drove his spear down into his horse, Andronicus leapt at him, plunging his sword into the man's chest. He threw the man to the ground, pulled himself up into the saddle, and had just enough time to strike the second rider before the man realized what had happened.

With his companions dead and Andronicus still atop a horse, the third man tried to escape, but Andronicus struck him as he turned, slicing through the man's jerkin and into his back. He rode off, but Andronicus was sure he had wounded him fatally.

He turned back to look for his brother and was surprised to see Androcles prying his spear free of the man he had been fighting. As Andronicus rode forward, Androcles threw his spear, killing an oncoming rider. Finally, Andronicus reached his brother. A moment later, Niko and Theo were there as well.

"Stay behind me!" Andronicus yelled over the commotion around them. "We have to get to Thymi and Lycus. This way!" They all fell in behind Andronicus's horse. He rode forward, slashing at every Persian who came near, the others covering his rear.

The battle had become a complete mess. If Andronicus thought Salamis had been unorganized, it was nothing compared to the battle around him now. It was still too dark to really see what was happening, but everywhere he looked, he could see the half-moon's light shining off armor and swords alike. He could only make out the people just before him, all of them fighting blindly, but he could hear the rest of the battle clearly. The night rang with the clanging of metal and the shouts of both the victorious and the dying.

Andronicus saw Thymi and Lycus in the distance, fighting together, and was making his way to them when the arrows began to fall. At first he heard whizzing sounds go by him, like bees flying much too fast. Then he heard a man cry out, followed by another.

"Arrows!" someone shouted.

Andronicus's friends ducked behind his horse. He was attempting to dismount when he felt a sudden, sharp pain in his side. It felt as though something inside him had shifted, sending a jolt of fire up his back and down his leg. He jumped off the horse and fell to the ground. He felt the pain surge again as he tried to get up and fell back down. He looked down and felt his stomach turn.

A thin wooden arrow was sticking out of the top of his hip, just below his armor, buried deep in his flesh. As soon as he saw the arrow, the pain truly fell upon him. He could feel the skin where the arrow had pierced him and the flesh inside that it had cut through. He tried again to sit up and let out a sharp howl as the pain flared again.

"Stay down!" Niko shouted. "Just stay there! When the arrows are done, we'll get it out. Just stay down!"

Andronicus knew there was nothing he could do. He closed his eyes, covered his head, and waited for the barrage to end.

When the arrows finally stopped falling, he felt hands lifting him. He opened his eyes and saw Androcles and Niko pulling him up by the arms. Theodotus was sitting beside them, clutching at his left leg, which was covered in blood. Andronicus saw a bloody arrow lying next to him. Then he saw the hole it had made halfway up Theo's calf.

"Here," Niko said, handing Andronicus a clean arrow. "Bite down on this." Andronicus took it and bit down hard until he felt his teeth sink into the wood. He closed his eyes, and a moment later, he felt Niko pull the arrow free from his flesh. The pain was horrendous as he felt the arrow tearing through new flesh. He looked down and saw an alarming amount of blood spreading down his side into the dirt, then quickly looked away.

"Here," Niko said, shoving a rag against the wound. He took a piece of cloth off a dead rider and wrapped it around Andronicus's waist, pulling the rag tight against his wound.

"Stay down if you can't fight," Niko said, looking him in the eye, "but the battle is not over. Androcles, come with me now." Androcles looked at his older brother uncertainly, and Andronicus nodded to him.

"Go," Andronicus said in a raspy voice he barely recognized as his own. "Go find Thymi and Lycus." Androcles turned to leave when Andronicus reached out and pulled him back, wincing at the pain in his hip. "Stay by Niko's side," he added.

Androcles nodded, meeting Andronicus's eye. A moment later they were gone, fighting through the remaining Persians.

Andronicus turned to Theo, who was still clutching his bloody leg. "Can you stand?"

"I don't think so," Theo said through clenched teeth. Andronicus nodded slowly. He knew he could stay there with Theo, and no one would blame him, but he also knew that he could still fight.

"Stay down then," he said as he sat up, wincing in pain. "If the Persians come around, play dead. We'll find you when it's done." Theo nodded, looking scared, as Andronicus slowly got to his feet. The pain in his side was still bad, but he felt it less and less as he limped toward the nearest Persian, who was battling a Tagean man. When he reached them, he raised his sword high above his head and struck the man, feeling the blade sink deep into Persian flesh. The Tagean man didn't even stop to look at Andronicus; he just ran off in the direction of the retreat.

Dawn was not far off, and light had begun to

illuminate the battle. Everywhere Andronicus looked he saw dead and dying men. The dirt itself had become more red than brown. Andronicus looked around for any sign of his friends but saw nothing but the chaos of the battle. The Persian cavalry had all seemingly lost their horses, and Andronicus saw only a few score men still atop a mount.

The battle had become a gritty, face-to-face fight that had been more than a year in the making. There were no more special tactics, no way for one army to lure the other into a trap. The war had finally come to a head, the remaining Persian infantry against the remaining Greek infantry.

As the sun rose, and more light spread across the land, Andronicus could not believe his eyes. As far as he could see the ground was covered with dead men, both Greek and Persian. He looked around frantically for his friends, beginning to fear the worst as he took in the vast number of casualties.

Then he saw Lycus, covered in blood, with that wild look in his eyes. Thymi was right behind him, also covered in blood, looking utterly exhausted but apparently unharmed. Andronicus limped over to them.

"Lycus!" he shouted. Lycus turned at the sound of his name, and Andronicus saw the fire leave his eyes as recognition fell in.

"Andronicus," Lycus said, running over to him, Thymi right behind him, panting for breath. "You're wounded."

"An arrow," Andronicus said hoarsely. "Are you and Thymi alright?"

"We're fine," Lycus said, Thymi could only nod in agreement as he tried to catch his breath. "Have you seen the others?" Lycus asked, looking around.

"They were with me when I got hit," Andronicus said. "Niko and Androcles left to find you. Theo is hit in the leg. I left him back there."

"Well, if they're looking for us, the best thing we can do now is go to Theo and wait for them there," Lycus said. Andronicus nodded in agreement, then threw his arm over Lycus's shoulder. They walked slowly back to Theo, trying to avoid the battle, which had mostly moved down the field by then. They found Theo lying right where Andronicus had left him.

"OK," Lycus said when they were all settled, "you three stay here. I'll go find the others."

"Wait," Andronicus said. "I'm coming with you."

"No you're not," Lycus said. "You'll only slow me down and will be no help in a fight. You stay here, and I'll find your brother." Lycus didn't wait for Andronicus to argue, already running down the field to where the battle was still raging.

"I should go with him," Thymi said once he could breathe again.

"What?" Andronicus said in disbelief. "What are you talking about?"

"You and Theo are hurt," Thymi said, "I'm not. What kind of man would I be if I sat by and watched when I'm perfectly capable of fighting?"

"A living man," Andronicus said emphatically.

"A living man has to live with himself," Thymi said, looking gravely at Andronicus. "I may not be a great fighter, but I'm no coward." He rose to his feet, looking more like a man than Andronicus had ever seen him.

"I'll look for Androcles," Thymi said, "and we'll find you when it is done. Look after Theo." With that Thymi ran down the field as well. Andronicus was stuck sitting there with Theodotus. He had never wanted to be in a fight more. He had come to terms with killing over the past year. He still didn't like it, but he had accepted it. But now he wanted so badly to be able to stand by his friends and kill.

Andronicus waited for what felt like hours, watching what little of the battle he could see. He knew the fighting was taking place across the valley, likely covering miles. The sound of the battle had become distant and was slowly being drowned out by the wailing of dying men.

Those hours of waiting were the longest and darkest hours of Andronicus's life. The whole time his mind was filled with dark thoughts. He envisioned

Androcles and Thymi dying in a thousand terrible ways. He envisioned the Greek line failing and a Persian army racing up the hill toward him. Theo fell asleep at some point, but Andronicus just sat there watching and feeling guilty for not helping.

7

It was past midday when Andronicus finally saw his friends walking up the hill toward him.

"Theo," Andronicus said, shaking the boy awake, "they're back."

Theo sat up and rubbed his eyes. He and Andronicus watched as the four of them walked slowly up the hill. It was hard to tell if any of them had been wounded because they were all covered in blood.

"Are you wounded?" Andronicus called out as they approached.

"Not as bad as you!" Niko shouted. "A few cuts here and there. And Lycus lost part of his ear."

"Your ear?" Andronicus said in surprise, looking at Lycus. The left side of his face was indeed covered in blood. As they came closer, Andronicus saw the bottom half of Lycus's ear had been cut off. "How did you manage that?"

"Karpos makes a fine helmet," Lycus said, smiling. "The man had aimed his spear at my temple. I suppose losing half an ear isn't so bad. What about you? You were hit worse than me."

"Still hurts," Andronicus said. "I'm sure I'll be fine though. I take it we won the battle."

"As far as we can tell," Thymi said, panting heavily. "As long as the Athenians held the right, it should be over."

"I saw Mardonius die," Androcles said excitedly. "I saw a man cleave his head nearly in two."

"I doubt it was Mardonius, Droc," Andronicus said, rolling his eyes. "That was probably just some captain."

"No," Niko said as he helped Andronicus to his feet. "It was him. I saw it too. He was riding a big white horse, and he had his banner flying behind him. He was calling orders to his men when a great big

Spartan rode right up to him and bashed his head in."

"If Mardonius is dead, then . . ." Andronicus looked at the others with dawning excitement.

"It's not finished yet," Lycus said gloomily. "A few thousand infantry managed to fall back. They're still out there, but Mardonius's cavalry is done."

"Thank the gods," Andronicus said, sighing in relief. "I have had enough of fighting these Persians. I'm ready to go home."

"Had enough of fighting, have you?" Lycus said with a teasing smile. "I always knew you weren't cut out for war." The others all chuckled. Then the boys helped Andronicus and Theo down the hill in search of the remainder of the Greek army.

Chapter 9
Peacetime
1

After the victory at Plataea and the simultaneous victory that had happened at the sea battle of Mycale, across the Aegean, it seemed as if the war stopped all at once. Days after the battle ended, Captain Sophos came to the boys and told them they would be sailing back south with the rest of the Spartan army. The Athenians, along with many of the other Greeks, were going to stay and chase the remaining Persians back to Asia, but the Spartans wanted no part in it.

The news caused discord throughout the massive army. The Athenians thought the Spartans were cowards who only cared for their own land. The Spartans thought the Athenians were fools who were going to get themselves killed fighting a battle they had already won. The rest of the Greeks thought it best not to get between the two strongest cities.

The Spartans packed up their things as the rest of the army looked on sourly. Andronicus couldn't help feeling a bit guilty. They had been the ones to start the war. King Leonidas was the first to stand against Xerxes. Now that Xerxes had been sent back to Asia, his army in retreat, Andronicus knew it was time to go. And yet he still couldn't help feeling like they were leaving a job undone.

"We should finish this," Niko said uncertainly as they saddled their horses, echoing Andronicus's thoughts. "We should stay until all of them are dead. Then at least we can sleep knowing they won't come back for us someday." Andronicus agreed with Niko, but he remained silent, knowing he had to set a good example for his brother and his friends.

"We did what we came to do," Andronicus said, keeping loyal to his superiors despite his own reservations. "Sparta is safe from the Persians. It's not our job to protect the whole of Greece."

"Why not?" Thymi asked, looking out at the vast army they were leaving behind. "Why should we not protect them? We're strong enough. And are we not all Greeks?"

"No," Lycus answered coldly as he mounted his horse. "We're Spartans. Our duty is to protect Sparta and the people of Sparta, not march halfway across Asia trying to kill every last member of an army we have already beaten three times." Lycus rode off in a hurry before Thymi could respond.

"Lycus is right," Androcles said. Thymi and Niko looked at him in surprise. "The war is won," he said, meeting their surprised looks with a sad smile. "We're safe from the Persians, and if they should ever manage to amass a new army and attempt to march on our shores, we will come back and fight them again. But for now the fighting is done, and we should let it stay that way." No one said anything for a long while, letting Androcles's words hang in the air.

When the Spartan army was all saddled and mounted, they set off to the east, toward the sea, leaving the rest of the Greek army behind. Andronicus and his friends took one final look at the massive cluster of Greek soldiers. Even Lycus came riding back to get a final glimpse of the impressive Greek forces. They had all heard the rumors that this was the biggest Greek army in history, bigger even than that of King Agamemnon of old. There were tents and fires and groups of men standing and sitting about for miles. Andronicus looked east and west and wasn't able to see the end of the army in either direction. To the left it stretched out until a soft hill rose, and the army fell out of view. To the right the army stretched out of sight completely.

The six boys sat atop their horses, staring silently out at the tremendous army they had been a part of. Then the moment was gone. They turned their horses and headed south with the rest of their kin.

They rode all day, barely saying a word to each other. At dusk the Spartans halted and set up camp. The boys prepared a fire, and food was passed down the line.

They slept under the stars, dreaming of the battles they had won. Andronicus dreamed of King Leonidas, Gaios, and his father, hoping he was not dishonoring them by leaving.

When the sun rose, the army readied itself and was off again not long after. When they reached the sea, they boarded Sophos's ships and sailed south for Sparta.

2

When they entered the city through the old archway of Hermes, they were greeted with the biggest hero's welcome Andronicus had ever seen. Roughly eight thousand soldiers rode solemnly under the old stone archway to the sounds of cheers and sobbing. Men, women, and children lined the streets, waving and shouting. It was a larger and more energetic crowd than Andronicus had ever seen.

As he rode next to Androcles and Euthymius, looking out over all the people, he felt odd. He knew it should make him feel warm and welcome to be greeted by the people in such a way, but instead it made him feel cold and distant. He knew these people would be told stories of the war. The children he saw crying now would be told tales of their fathers, the way they had fought bravely and died as heroes. He thought of the stories he had been told about his own father, not only from his mother but also from the men he had fought with, and wondered how many of them were true.

Now that Andronicus had been to war himself, he knew that many of the stories may not be outright lies, but they were certainly romanticized. One couldn't tell a child that his father had died with a sword in his chest, screaming and crying and begging to the gods. Children had to be told that their fathers died fighting the bad people, and that they were heroes. Ever since Gaios and Diokles had spoken of his father, Andronicus desperately wanted to know what had really happened to him. Especially since even Leonidas had mentioned him.

They were riding slowly through the packed streets when, to Andronicus's surprise, his mother appeared. He didn't know where she had come from, but she walked slowly next to their horses. When she smiled up at Andronicus, he felt like bursting into tears, but he held it in.

When Androcles noticed her, he leapt down from his horse and hugged her tightly, letting his tears fall freely. Andronicus saw her whisper something in Androcles's ear, but he couldn't hear what it was.

Androcles stayed with her until Sophos came riding up behind them. He yelled at Androcles to get back on his horse, and Androcles quickly obeyed. They started moving again, but Athenia still walked next to them. Andronicus reached down, and took his mother's hand in his. That's when the tears began to fall. He couldn't hold them back any longer. It had been over a year since he had seen his mother's face, and seeing her again made him feel like he really was home. Athenia didn't say anything to Andronicus; she didn't need to. They simply held hands until the procession moved on.

Eventually, they left her behind, along with all the other spectators, as they rode up to the city barracks. When they arrived the boys were sent to a dark corner, where they all chose a bed. Nearly everyone was asleep in minutes. It had been months since they had slept in a bed under a roof. Andronicus lay there thinking about his battles. He tried to think of how he might tell his mother about them, but he fell asleep before he could decide.

After returning to Sparta, things got rather dull for Andronicus, the Spartans having chosen not to fight in the ongoing battles. Andronicus and his friends were all viewed as real soldiers now, and he, Lycus, and Niko were treated like heroes wherever they went. People already knew them as the boys who had survived Thermopylae, and since Plataea, they were treated more like old veterans than the teenagers they still were.

Andronicus didn't mind the attention. He had always wanted to be a great war hero like his father, and he supposed now he was. When he thought of his battles, he didn't feel like a hero or even much like a warrior. When things had gotten the bloodiest, he had lost control of himself completely. He had cut down more Persians than he could possibly hope to remember. He had killed slaves and elites and everyone else the Persians had offered. He had killed them all, and now he was a hero. However, being called a hero and treated like one felt different than he had expected.

Lycus seemed to love the attention. No one had ever called his father a hero except his mother, but that no longer mattered. It was as if he had righted his father's wrongs. Andronicus still didn't know what those wrongs were, but he wanted to. After fighting in his own war, he yearned to know what had happened at Marathon.

Niko hated being called a hero. His father was a simple blacksmith, and his mother was a kind, peaceful woman. The only reason Niko had become the fighter he had become was because of Lycus and Andronicus pushing him. Andronicus knew Niko would have followed in his father's footsteps if given the choice, but he had been given the role of soldier, and now he was a war hero, and he seemed to hate it. Where Andronicus and Lycus would often use their slight notoriety to their advantage with women, Niko wouldn't even talk to girls who knew who he was.

As time went on, without any wars to be

fought, many of the returned soldiers became restless. Andronicus felt conflicted in a way he didn't quite understand. He preferred not to have to fight if he didn't have to, but he was a soldier. He had trained his entire life to be a soldier, and he knew nothing else. A soldier had no place in peacetime, no place amongst the people he had fought to defend. Andronicus, like so many others, grew restless in the newfound peace and often found himself wishing a new war would come to Sparta just so he could have something to do.

Weeks turned into months, and eventually, months turned into years. Andronicus marched, he stood guard, and he sailed the Aegean with Sophos. Once a week he would go hunting with his friends in the old woods. They always talked about killing a wolf again, like they had when they were boys, but they never got the chance; they mostly just killed deer. At night Andronicus would go out with Lycus, strutting around as war heroes, looking for women or fights. He did these things for years, feeling more useless than he would have imagined possible, impatiently waiting for a chance to fight again.

4

Andronicus and his friends grew closer every year, and yet they also grew apart. Androcles and Theodotus kept themselves busy with the gods, thinking about them, talking about them, and worshiping them. They spent more time in the temples than they did in the barracks. Andronicus knew that Androcles wasn't the devout believer that Theo was, but he let it be. He knew his brother was happiest in the temples with Theo and the priests. Theo would almost surely become a high priest someday, like his father, and Andronicus often wondered if Androcles would follow him.

Thinking of Androcles as a priest seemed odd though. Theo already acted like a priest, but Androcles was a soldier, like his father and brother. Andronicus often wondered which god Androcles would choose to worship if he ever did become a priest, but he never could decide. Theo would become a priest of Apollo, like his father, but Androcles was always a mystery. Whenever Andronicus was alone with his brother, they never spoke of gods; they spoke of war, the one they had been in and the ones they would be in. Androcles could fool everyone else with his priestly act, but Andronicus knew his brother was like him and would leap at the first call for battle.

Euthymius, on the other hand, seemed to genuinely enjoy not having a war to fight. He spent his time reading. He was the only one of them who had mastered the skill, and he seemed intent on exercising it as often as possible. When he wasn't holed up in the old library or one of the temples, Thymi spent much of his time walking through the old woods outside the city or visiting with Philander. Sometimes Andronicus and Niko would join him. Philander had new students to teach, but he was always more than happy to talk with Euthymius, or any of them, for that matter. Thymi was the only one who truly seemed to relish the time of peace.

Niko married a beautiful young woman a few years after the war. Before long he had a son to look after, with another on the way. The others saw Niko less and less after his sons were born, but they understood. He still marched with them when it was time to march and stood guard where he was meant to stand guard, and he never missed their weekly hunts, but they knew his heart was with his family now. They were all a bit envious of him. By the time Andronicus was in his twenties, he would have gladly taken a wife like Niko's, if he could find one.

The years of peace and plenty were good to all of them, except perhaps Lycus. He wasn't cut out for peacetime at all. He had many of the same problems as Andronicus, only worse. He needed to use the skills he had honed for so many years, to use the muscles that had grown so strong.

When Lycus was twenty years old, he got caught stealing sacred wine from the temple. Captain Sophos wanted to cut off his arm to teach the rest of the men a lesson, but Andronicus and Niko were able to convince him not to do so. Instead, Sophos made

Lycus strip down to the nude and drink an entire cask of wine by himself in front of the battalion. Lycus sputtered and gagged down the wine for over an hour, sending most of it back into the dirt. By the end his pale skin was stained dark by the red wine.

When he was finished, wine and sweat and vomit covered the ground around him. After Sophos let him go, Lycus stumbled drunkenly to where his clothes lay and got dressed without looking at anyone. After that day he always seemed to be angry, like he blamed everyone who had witnessed his humiliation. Lycus had always had problems with his image, and Sophos's punishment did far more harm than good. Lycus never stole again as far as Andronicus knew, but he drank more and more and was always looking for a fight.

5

In 472 BC, when Andronicus was twenty-four, he was asked to marry the daughter of a powerful senator. Andronicus first heard about it from Sophos, who delivered the news as a warning. One night he was patrolling the docks at Gytheion, enjoying the cool sea breeze and the dancing light of the stars on the water, listening to the soft splashes of the waves against the boats, when Sophos came walking down the dock and told him to sit down on a barrel.

"What's this all about?" Andronicus asked, laughing nervously as Sophos gave him a funny look. "The Persians aren't back, are they?"

"No, no, nothing like that," Sophos said, waving his hand. "I have heard that Kyros from the high council is going to ask you to marry his daughter."

"What?" was all Andronicus could manage to say. He wanted to get married and have a family, but he had never thought he would be told whom to marry.

"This man, Kyros," Sophos continued, "his daughter has just turned sixteen, and he wishes for her to be married."

"But why me?" Andronicus asked, his head

reeling with shock and confusion.

"What do you mean?" Sophos asked. "You're a war hero, your father was a war hero, you come from a long line of noble Spartan warriors, going all the way back to the battle of Troy. You're also young, strong, and presumably virile. I guess Kyros has decided you would make a good husband for his daughter."

"But why doesn't he give her to another politician?" Andronicus asked. "I'm just a soldier, and I'll likely die in battle someday like my father and his father before him."

"We have been at peace for seven years now, and you'll not be dying anytime soon. Besides, perhaps he thinks *you* can be a politician someday." Sophos unleashed a hearty chuckle. "He'll let you remain in the army, but I bet he'll begin grooming you for office."

"He has the wrong man," Andronicus said, trying to convince his captain, who had no say in the matter. "I don't want to be a politician. I don't want to be anything but a soldier. Tell Kyros I'm not who he's looking for."

"I can't tell a senator that," Sophos laughed and clapped Andronicus on the back. "Besides, I'm not even supposed to know this. I'm just giving you a warning, so you're not completely unprepared when he comes to ask you."

"Can I say no?" Andronicus asked, clinging to the hope that he would not be forced to marry a sixteen-year-old girl he had never met.

"Of course you can. No man can force another man to marry." Sophos shrugged. "But if you do refuse, you'll never hold a command or be sent off to battle. You'll spend the rest of your days carrying out the worst duties he can think of."

Andronicus let out a long sigh and nodded. Sophos stayed a moment longer, just standing there, then turned and walked away.

Andronicus sat there contemplating how much his life was about to change. All he could hope was that his wife would be good. He also hoped she would be pretty and smart, but most of all he hoped she wouldn't be a child. Sixteen seemed so young to him now. He had gone to war at sixteen and killed men, but he had been trained for it. This girl was a senator's daughter, who was probably used to being waited on hand and foot. Andronicus spent what was meant to be a night of patrolling the docks sitting on a barrel, wondering about his wife and his life to be.

6

Less than a week later, Kyros came to visit Andronicus at his mother's home. Athenia answered the door and brought Kyros in to where Andronicus was waiting with a jug of wine. He had spent the last four days thinking of nothing else and in the end had decided to go through with it and take his chances with the girl.

When Athenia walked in with Kyros, Andronicus thought the man looked familiar. He was tall and thin and had a gaunt face with stern frown lines. Andronicus rose to greet him, and then they both took a seat.

"Do you remember me?" Kyros asked in a strong, sturdy voice. "I was there the day you returned from Thermopylae. You gave us some very useful information that day that may have even helped win the war, not to mention your contributions on the battlefield itself, which I hear were most copious."

"Thank you," Andronicus said nervously. "And yes, I do remember you. You were the one asking the questions that day, were you not?"

"Yes I was." Kyros nodded and smiled, a cold, intimidating smile. "You have a good memory. You're a smart young man in addition to being a war hero."

"So, is that why you want me to marry your daughter?" Andronicus asked, cutting to the chase. Kyros glared at him for a moment, apparently not used to being interrupted.

"Yes," Kyros said, eyeing Andronicus. "I wish for you to marry my daughter. You are known as a good man. I know you'll be kind to her, and you'll guarantee that my grandchildren will be great fighters, as all Spartans should be."

"Very well," Andronicus said, not wanting to pander to this man. "I'll gladly marry your daughter," he said, "although I would like to meet her first."

"Of course," Kyros said, his stern demeanor changing to pleasant surprise, as if he had expected more resistance. "You will come to my villa tomorrow then and meet Gaia, and we can begin discussing the marriage arrangements."

"Good," Andronicus said, getting to his feet. Kyros rose as well, and Andronicus walked him to the door. Just then Androcles stepped out of nowhere, loudly chewing an apple.

"Do you think it's right to sell your own daughter off like a whore?" Androcles asked the senator without a trace of apology in his voice.

"I'm sorry, Senator," Andronicus said quickly, stepping between Androcles and Kyros. "You'll have to ignore my brother. He does not have much sense when it comes to candor."

"He can't speak to me that way," Kyros spat. "He called my daughter, and your future wife, a whore!"

"You're giving her to my brother," Androcles said, tossing the apple core aside and giving the senator a dry smile. "You're demanding that she sleep with him and bear his children, and in exchange you'll give him wealth and a position of command. What would you call that, Senator?"

Andronicus stepped forward and hit Androcles hard in the face. He agreed with him, but he had to hit him, or the senator would do something much worse. Androcles took a step backward, looking shocked for a moment. Then he laughed and spat a wad of blood onto the floor. He smiled at the senator, who glared at him.

"I guess that's a good start," Androcles said casually, still laughing. "At least he's defending her honor. Too bad you're losing your own."

Androcles left before Andronicus or Kyros could reply. Kyros was seething. Andronicus considered trying to defend his brother but then thought better of it. Hitting him would have to do.

"I hope this doesn't change anything," Andronicus said, knowing that if the wedding got called off now, he would be even worse off than if he had simply said no in the first place.

"You will marry my daughter," Kyros said, his teeth still clenched in anger. "But that man will not be there, and you will never bring him around my daughter, ever."

"Of course," Andronicus said, already aware of how difficult Androcles had just made his life, and for nothing more than a good quip at a rich ponce.

"If he was not the son of Aristocles, I would have him hanged for that," Kyros said, more to himself than to Andronicus. "I'll see you at my villa tomorrow morning," he said, then stormed out of the house.

A moment later Athenia came into the room, looking worried and apologetic. Andronicus just looked at his mother. He didn't need to speak.

"You know how your brother can get," Athenia said softly.

Andronicus nodded. "I know. He just picked one hell of a bad time."

7

The next morning Andronicus walked up to the senator's villa feeling sick with anticipation. It was at the top of a hill overlooking most of the city of Sparta, and it looked bigger than any house Andronicus had ever seen.

A slave girl let him in, and he was struck immediately by the magnificent architecture of what seemed more like a palace than a villa. More than a dozen Helot slaves stood along the wall, waiting to be commanded.

"Andronicus!" Kyros bellowed as he came walking around the corner, his long white gown billowing in the breeze. "You're right on time. Gaia is just coming out now." Kyros turned, and a moment later a young girl stepped into the courtyard. She was also wearing a billowing white gown, her arms covering herself. She stared down at her feet, looking even more embarrassed than Andronicus felt.

"Come now," Kyros said to her in a stern voice. "Stand up straight, and look him in the eye, and lower your arms, girl."

"It's fine. She's perfect how she is," Andronicus said, smiling kindly and trying to make the poor girl relax. He was pleasantly surprised by her looks, but he still wanted to talk to her.

"How about we take a walk down to the gardens?" Kyros said, turning to Andronicus. "We can discuss the arrangements."

"Actually, sir," Andronicus said, meeting the old man's eye, "would you mind if we had some time alone first to get acquainted?"

"Fine," Kyros said, looking a little displeased, "but no funny business. Not until you're married."

"Of course." Andronicus nodded, and Kyros left. It still didn't feel much like they were alone, with a dozen slaves standing by with nothing to do but listen to them, but Andronicus figured they wouldn't say anything.

"Look," Andronicus said to Gaia once her father left, "I don't know how you feel about all of this, but I'm not going to make you do anything you don't want to."

"You mean," she said slowly, finally meeting his gaze, "you won't . . ."

"No," Andronicus said, cutting her off, "not until you want to." He smiled at her again, hoping she would lighten up a little, and she did. She smiled back, and her body relaxed. He was pleasantly surprised by her. She was definitely younger than he would have ever gone for, but he supposed it was not uncommon, especially with daughters of powerful men. His own mother had only been seventeen when she married his father. Gaia was quite pretty, more so than he had been expecting, and he knew someday she would grow into a real beauty. He decided he could wait for that day, if she could as well.

With the initial awkwardness out of the way, they spent the next hour asking each other questions. When Kyros returned, he brought them down to eat with him.

Andronicus spent the next two hours answering the senator's increasingly uncomfortable questions, with Gaia huddled in the corner, not daring to look her father's way. When he was finally done, Andronicus said a quick goodbye to Kyros and an even quicker goodbye to Gaia, then left in search of his friends.

8

The wedding took place a month later in the temple of Apollo. Theo's father led the ceremony. With Gaia being a senator's daughter, and Andronicus a renowned war hero, the large room was filled with important men and women from Sparta. Andronicus stood in front of his friends and family, with Thymi and his mother both crying openly. Androcles was not permitted to attend, but he wished Andronicus luck beforehand and even apologized for taunting the senator.

The wedding was a long and energetic celebration. Between the soldiers and the noblemen, more than a few casks of wine were finished. As expected, Lycus got far too drunk, and Niko finally had to pull him away and send him home. Even Theo drank with them. He would only drink wine in honor of Dionysus, and weddings counted. Andronicus had a wonderful time with his friends and comrades and with the noblemen, who all seemed to have advice of some kind, and even with his new wife. The celebrations were so hectic that he barely got to say a word to her, but he thought she was having fun as well.

It wasn't until later that evening that Andronicus was finally able to be alone with her. He had promised he wouldn't take advantage of her, but he was drunk, and she seemed to be enjoying herself. He started kissing her, and when she didn't resist, he took her over to their bed and laid her down. Andronicus had been with other women before, but nothing was like that first night with Gaia. Maybe it was because he knew she was his wife, and they would have children together, but it felt different. All of his reservations and fears about being married vanished, and they lost themselves in the heat of passion.

9

After the wedding, Andronicus moved with his new bride to a house in the city that Kyros gave to them. Andronicus was not used to being given things, but he was happy to be with Gaia.

Their first year together was perhaps the best year of his life. They spent most of their time together and spoke all the time about the children they would have. As time went on, and no children came, they began to spend less time together. They still tried often and would usually eat dinner together, but Andronicus went back to spending his time back in Gytheion or on patrol, and he went to sea every chance he got.

When he wasn't patrolling or sailing, he would try to find Lycus. Thymi had his books, Niko had his family, and Theo and Androcles had the gods, but Lycus was free of all those burdens. When Andronicus was angry, sad, or just bored, he would go see Lycus. Lycus spent his nights roaming the streets of Sparta looking for women but mostly finding men to fight. Andronicus missed fighting just as much as Lycus, and the two of them would often fight whole groups of men together for no reason. The men they fought were all Spartans, and soldiers more often than not, so the fights never went too far, but Andronicus would often come home bloody and bruised, terrifying his young wife.

On some level he did it to stop himself from thinking about the question that had been nagging him for ten years. As a boy he hadn't cared or even thought much about it, but since hearing about his father, he had become obsessed with finding out the truth of how he had died.

Andronicus felt like he had only half of the story. He knew that King Leonidas had led a small group of Spartans to fight with the Athenians at Marathon. Most of the men who had fought with Leonidas at Marathon had died with him at Thermopylae, like Gaios and Diokles. Aristocles was not the only Spartan to die at Marathon though. Lycurgus had died there too, as had at least fifty other men. Andronicus spent years looking for answers, for another survivor of Marathon, until he was sure only one remained: Archelaus.

10

Andronicus went to see his old teacher on a dark and stormy night. The wind howled, and rain poured down on him as he staggered drunkenly to Archelaus's door. The rain was so loud that he didn't even worry about waking the students he knew were sleeping close by. Andronicus pounded on the door, and a minute later Archelaus appeared, looking thoroughly irritated.

Andronicus could tell he had woken Archelaus, who stood in the doorway shirtless and rubbing his eyes. Andronicus saw a scar on Archelaus's stomach he had never noticed before, which he knew could only have come from a sword. Archelaus peered into the dark. When he saw that it was Andronicus standing in the rain, he reluctantly let him in.

"What in Hades' name do you want?" Archelaus barked as he pulled the stopper from a jug of wine on his table. "It's the middle of the night."

"I need answers," Andronicus said, the rain still dripping off him.

"Answers," Archelaus repeated irritably. "What are you talking about, boy?"

"My father," Andronicus said, looking at Archelaus with bloodshot eyes. "I need to know what happened." Archelaus's face turned to stone as he stared back at Andronicus. His lips were clenched tight, and for a moment Andronicus thought Archelaus might hit him.

"He died," Archelaus said, turning away and pouring himself a cup of wine.

"How?" Andronicus pleaded. "I need to know. How did it happen?"

"He died saving his brothers," Archelaus said, taking a long swig from the cup, "and that is all you need to know."

"And what about Lycus's father, Lycurgus?" Andronicus asked. "How did he die?"

Archelaus put his cup down and glared at him a moment longer. Andronicus dropped his gaze and shifted uncomfortably in his seat.

"Lycus is not his father," Archelaus said. "I made sure of that. I taught Lycus to be a true Spartan warrior, and that is what he is. Forget about his father. Everyone else has."

"Please, Archelaus," Andronicus pleaded, meeting his old teacher's stern gaze with desperation. "I need to know. I know something happened at Marathon; Gaios told me as much. But he died before I got the truth."

"Good," Archelaus said. "It's better that way. You think you want to know what happened, but you're wrong."

"I do," Andronicus nearly screamed, pounding his fist on the table. "I have to. I need to know Archelaus. Please."

"Fine." Archelaus sighed reluctantly, still glaring at Andronicus, only with pity now as well as anger. "You want to hear a story, I'll tell you a story." Archelaus finished off his cup and began pouring another.

"Once there was a young prince named Leonidas," Archelaus began, staring at the fire burning in the corner. "Leonidas was a fierce warrior, and he held honor above all else, as all true Spartan warriors do. When Leonidas heard the Persians had come to Greece, he knew he had to stop them, but his father ordered him to stay in Sparta. However, Leonidas disobeyed."

Archelaus smiled darkly. "He took a small party north with him to fight. He only took men he knew well and trusted with his life. I was one of those men, as were your father and Lycurgus. There were roughly one hundred of us all told."

Archelaus took a big gulp of wine as he stared into the fire. "We left the city in secret, not by the great archway but through a passage only the prince knew of. We traveled to Athens at night without being seen. We stayed off the roads, and kept to the forests."

Andronicus had marched those roads himself, and he imagined his father, Leonidas, and Gaios all marching through the woods, off to war together as young men.

"By the time we reached the Athenians, the battle had already begun." Archelaus's expression changed as he began to speak of the conflict itself. "Leonidas didn't waste any time with speeches or planning. He charged right into battle, and we all followed him. We were wearing Athenian armor, so no one knew we were Spartans. We joined the battle on the far right, where the Persian cavalry was."

Archelaus paused, and Andronicus waited anxiously for him to continue. Finally, Archelaus sighed deeply and then continued. "We helped fight the cavalry back, but then the elites came. You fought the elites at Thermopylae, did you not?" Archelaus asked Andronicus, finally looking away from the fire.

Andronicus nodded slowly, and Archelaus turned back to the fire. "Good," he said softly. "We fought the elites for over an hour. They killed at least thirty of us, but we killed at least two hundred of them. Your father killed more than any of us. I have never seen anyone fight the way your father fought that day. He cut through those Persian elites like Achilles himself."

Archelaus stopped talking again and stared into the fire for a long time.

"Then what happened?" Andronicus whispered, barely loud enough to hear over the rain. Archelaus looked over at him as if he wanted to tell him something, then turned back to the fire.

"Then Leonidas ordered us to retreat," Archelaus said, finishing off another cup of wine. "He shouted loud enough for us all to hear. He told us to gather around him. We slowly gathered together, and even more of us fell."

Andronicus could hardly breathe as he waited to hear what he had obsessed over for years.

"Once we were all together, Leonidas ordered

us to head up the hill we had come from. The Athenians were retreating to the south, but that hill was to the north. He knew we could not go with the Athenians, or we would be found out as Spartans, and that would not be good."

"We began moving north as a unit, cutting our way through the battle. The Athenians were pushing forward on the Persians, and we ran right through them. Then we hit another one of the elite contingents."

Archelaus paused again, pouring himself more wine. He was beginning to sway a bit in his chair as he spoke. He looked over at Andronicus, whose face was as white as a sheet, and handed him the jug. Andronicus filled his glass, took a large gulp of wine, then returned his gaze to Archelaus. He knew that this was it.

"We fought the elites, and another half dozen Spartans fell. We were nearly to the hill when Leonidas shouted for us to push forward again. We finally broke free of the main battle then. There were only a few dozen of us left. We raced toward the forest. More than half of us were badly wounded. I myself had a nice hole in my gut." Archelaus lifted his shirt he had put on once they were inside and pointed to the scar Andronicus had noticed earlier.

"We were nearly to the trees when a group of Persian riders came charging at us. There were maybe fifteen of them, but most of us could no longer fight. Leonidas ordered the six strongest men to stay back with him and fight while the rest of us broke for the woods. I ran to the woods with the other injured, as did Gaios. Your father stayed back to fight, as did Diokles, Lycurgus, and two others I can't remember.

"Just before we reached the woods, I saw your father take down two riders on the initial charge. I still don't know how he did that." Archelaus smiled faintly as he stared into the fire. Andronicus felt immense pride in hearing his father's last deeds, and tears began filling his eyes.

"That was when Lycurgus fled," Archelaus said coldly.

"What do you mean?" Andronicus asked, holding his breath.

"He ran," Archelaus said with a dark look on his face. "While the others were fighting, he took off running. The two men next to him were killed as soon as he left. The remaining Persians surrounded your father, Diokles, and the prince. There were still a half dozen mounted riders, and we watched as the three of them fought them off. Then your father shouted at Leonidas to run. We could hear him all the way from the woods. You definitely got your battle cry from your father." Archelaus laughed, a cold, flat laugh. Andronicus couldn't tell if he was remorseful or furious.

"What happened next?" Andronicus asked, leaning so far forward his chair was threatening to tip over. "How did my father die?"

"What more do you want me to tell you?" Archelaus asked, sounding exhausted. "Do you really not know how he died?" Andronicus didn't say anything, he couldn't. He was frozen solid. He did know what happened next, he didn't have to be told. But he couldn't speak, so Archelaus went on. "He died on his feet, with his sword in his hand," Archelaus said angrily. "Is that what you want to hear? Or do you need more detail than that?"

"No," Andronicus managed as he finally let the air out of his lungs. "That is enough."

"Is that all you came for then?" Archelaus asked angrily. "To bring up a dead man's story? Did you come here to find out what happened to your father or to Lycus's?"

"I had to know what happened," Andronicus said softly, staring at the wall, "and now I do."

"Are you going to tell Lycus?" Archelaus asked. "There's a reason I always kept that story to myself."

"No," Andronicus said, getting to his feet. "Lycus can never know. It would only do him harm."

"Good," Archelaus nodded and stood as well. "What about your brother, will you tell him?"

"I don't know," Andronicus said. "I was the one who needed to know. I think Androcles is fine just knowing our father died in battle."

"Then it's over," Archelaus said, walking Andronicus to the door. "You got what you came for, so let the past stay in the past, and let the dead stay dead."

Andronicus nodded slowly, then stumbled out into the rain.

11

Once Andronicus knew the truth, he hoped he would be able to rid himself of the obsession. Part of him had expected the tale to be more glorious and for Lycurgus's betrayal to be more dastardly. The way Diokles had spoken of him, Andronicus had thought he must have done something truly treacherous, but he had simply run. It was true that running from a fight was the most dishonorable thing any man could do, but it was not as if he had gotten Andronicus's father killed, as he had thought.

Andronicus wondered if Lycus knew any of that story. It was possible he had heard it from some other soldier over the years, which would explain Lycus's deep fear of being thought of as a coward. Part of Andronicus wanted to blame Lycus for what his father had done, but he knew he couldn't. Lycus was his friend, and no matter what his father had done, Lycus had fought with Andronicus in every battle he had ever been in. As he stumbled home that night, Andronicus finally felt like he could let go of the past and let his father rest.

12

Without the past to obsess over, Andronicus became even more restless than before. In truth, all of Sparta was becoming restless. They had reached the longest time of peace that Sparta had experienced in over a century. Before the Persians came, Sparta had been at war with Athens, but when the Persians attacked, Greece united itself. The peace was fragile, but it still held, and the Spartans had no one to fight, and so they waited.

Andronicus would go to sea a few times each year for a month or more at a time, rowing every day from dawn to dusk. When he wasn't at sea, he spent his days with Lycus and his nights with Gaia. She still had not gotten pregnant, and it made Andronicus feel inferior and weak, which made him want to fight even more. Of course he wanted there to be peace and for the people of Sparta to be safe, but he needed to fight again. It was what he had been trained for all his life. The war he had fought in as a teenager had felt important at the time to be sure, but he had never thought it would be his only war. He had thought he would fight in battle after battle throughout his life, like his father, but it had been ten years since the victory at Plataea. More than anything Andronicus just wanted to be able to prove to himself that he had not grown weak.

Chapter 10
The Cursed Journey
1

In 466 BC Andronicus finally got his long-awaited call to action. A small force of Persians had landed north of Sparta and begun burning crops and villages throughout the countryside, killing everyone they came across. A war council was formed and ordered a host be raised to destroy the small Persian troupe.

Andronicus was named captain almost instantly. Between his father's reputation, his own military success, and his senator father-in-law, he was an obvious choice. Andronicus could tell that Lycus was more than a little irked at him being given command so quickly, but thought it best not to broach the subject. Andronicus was given command of one hundred men and ordered not to return until every one of the Persian bandits was dead.

As soon as they heard Andronicus had been given command, his friends were the first to volunteer. Andronicus tried to tell Niko to stay behind with his family, but he would not hear of it. "Just because I have a family doesn't mean I don't miss it just as much as you and Lycus do," he told Andronicus after he had said goodbye to his wife and young sons.

Andronicus found that hard to believe, but he took Niko on anyway. It would be comforting to have Niko around; he had always been the most sure headed during battle.

Many of the men were soldiers whom Andronicus had fought with in the war. The rest were a spattering of new young soldiers who had been too young to fight back then. It was the first official command Andronicus had ever been given, and he felt nervous despite his confidence in himself. He wondered why they hadn't given command to Sophos or one of the other more experienced captains, but he didn't ask. He knew he could handle it, and he meant to prove himself once again.

Before they left the city, Andronicus went back home. As he strapped on his armor and felt his sword at his side again, he felt invigorated. It was when he threw his bright red cloak over his shoulders that it really hit him. He wasn't putting on his armor to go walk the docks, nodding at passersby. He didn't have his sword so he could wave it at passing ships. He wasn't wearing his cloak to show it off on patrol. He was dressed for battle, and he was finally going to war once again.

As he stepped out of his room Andronicus saw his mother standing there. She had moved to the city a few years before, and lived with Andronicus and Gaia in the large villa they had been given by Kyros. She had a sad smile on her face, and he could tell she was holding back tears. Gaia was standing behind her, looking pale and sick.

"Your father would be so proud," Athenia said as she stepped forward and hugged him. "He always wanted this for you."

"I know," Andronicus said, hugging her back. "I promise I'll honor him."

"Oh, you honor him every day, Andronicus," Athenia said as she stepped back to take in his striking resemblance to his father. "Just promise you'll keep your brother safe, and the others too."

"I will, Mother. Don't worry; these are only simple Persian pirates. We'll be back within a fortnight.

You make sure and take care of Gaia now."

Andronicus smiled confidently, hugged his mother one more time, then stepped over to his wife. Gaia had tears running down her face as well, and she looked like she might be sick. Andronicus took her in his arms and held her against his armored chest.

"I will be fine, Gaia," he assured her, then kissed her gently on the forehead. "I have trained all my life for this. Besides, I fought Persian armies that were in the thousands. This is only a few score pirates. I'll be back soon and unharmed. You need not worry."

"Promise me you will come back," Gaia said with trembling lips and tears in her eyes.

"I promise I'll come back," Andronicus said, then looked over at his mother as well, as if to make the same promise to her. Neither woman said anything; they simply wept, and let Andronicus go. He looked back at them both with a confident smile, then left to go command his men.

As Athenia watched him go, she couldn't help but weep. For a moment she had a terrible feeling that she would never see either of her boys again.

2

Andronicus looked at his mounted host before they set out. They were gathered together in a large courtyard, silently awaiting his orders.

"Men!" Andronicus shouted in his booming voice, snapping them all to attention. "The Persians have returned to our shores, but they are not part of Xerxes's army! He is not fool enough to test us again." A murmur of laughter swept through the men. "No! These men are simple pirates. Scoundrels come to burn and rape and pillage our people. We have been ordered by the king himself to chase down these pirates and kill every last one of them!" A roar went up, and one hundred spears thrust into the sky.

Andronicus looked out over his friends' faces and the faces of those now under his command. His men looked confident, if not inspired. He remembered the way Leonidas had brought his entire army into a bloodthirsty frenzy before battle and thought his own speech had fallen far short in comparison. He felt like he should end with a rallying cry of some kind, but he couldn't think of anything.

"Alright now, men," he shouted finally. "With me! Let's end these bastards!"

A chorus of grunts and shouts met his words, and he felt pleased enough.

Andronicus led his host out of the city, again hailed by a crowd as they made their way through the streets.

When they reached the gate, an armored guard was standing by to let them pass. They rode under the archway of Hermes as cheers and praises echoed behind them. For some reason Andronicus looked up at the old archway for a long time as they rode under it. For a moment he had the strangest feeling he would never see it again.

Once they were out of the city, they were able to spread out and move much faster. When night fell, they continued riding beneath the stars. Andronicus had been told that the bandits were three days' ride to the north of them, and he meant to make it there in two. They rode well into the night before he finally let his men stop.

They tied their horses down and ate quickly and quietly before dropping into sleep. They slept for five hours, and when the sun rose, they ate quickly and were off again. The second day they rode even harder, once again continuing well into the night.

On the third day, they woke knowing they would find the pirates that day. There was little talk amongst the men as they ate and prepared themselves for the ride and the eventual battle. As they rode north, Andronicus felt nervous and excited, not just at the prospect of leading men into battle but simply at the prospect of getting to fight the Persians again.

A few hours later, they began passing burnt fields and burnt houses as well, along with dozens of dead bodies. Andronicus looked north and saw nothing but destruction. He couldn't believe so few men could have done such damage.

"There," Lycus said, pointing to the west.

"Smoke. Do you see it?" Andronicus strained his eyes, but he couldn't see anything.

"Where?" he asked.

"I don't see anything either," Niko said.

"There," Lycus insisted, still pointing in the same direction.

"He's right!" Androcles shouted from nearby. "I see it too, to the west."

Andronicus strained his eyes again, and after a moment he saw it, a stream of black smoke, so far in the distance he couldn't believe Lycus had spotted it. Andronicus raised his spear and hailed the men to gallop toward the smoke.

It was much farther than Andronicus had thought. After twenty minutes of hard riding, the horses all began to tire, and they had to slow to a walk. The smoke became thicker and darker as they approached. Then they began to hear screaming in the distance.

Andronicus pressed forward again, charging through the smoke and hoping the Persians would be in front of them. Sure enough, when Andronicus and his men crested a small hill, they found the Persians spread out before them.

The bandits were all on horseback, and most of them were holding torches. Fires were burning all around them. Everywhere Andronicus looked he saw bright orange flames and thick black smoke that burned his eyes and his throat. The Persians had not seen them yet as they rode around setting fire to everything that was not already ablaze and killing anyone left alive.

Andronicus raised his sword and shouted across the field. The Spartans all charged at full gallop toward the pirates. Andronicus himself charged a group of three riders who were setting fire to a large hut. The Persians who took notice tried to charge the oncoming Spartans, but they were too late. Andronicus swung his sword at the first man and watched his head go flying as he slashed at the second man.

The Spartans cut down the Persian bandits in a matter of seconds. Only one Spartan died in the attack, a young man whom Andronicus barely knew. He tried to remember what the boy's name was but couldn't. Andronicus let out a victory whoop, and the others all cheered. For a moment he thought that they had completed their mission. Then he saw Lycus pointing north.

"There are more fires up there!" Lycus shouted, pointing up a hill. "There must be more of them."

Andronicus nodded and began shouting orders to the men. Within a few minutes the host was riding in formation again toward the fresh smoke.

It took them nearly two hours to reach the next burning village, but by then it was far too late. The ground was covered with the blackened, smoldering corpses of the Helot people who had lived there. The Spartans had sworn an oath to protect them, and they had failed every one of these poor souls.

They continued north in pursuit of the rest of the bandits, passing burnt homes and bodies the whole way. After another hour of riding through the decimation, they finally caught up to the Persians again. As Andronicus and his troupe crested a hill, they saw the bandits boarding a ship off the beach. The Spartans charged down the hill into the sand.

Some Persians were still on the beach when the Spartans reached them, and they were cut down instantly. Most of the bandits, however, had already made it aboard the ship. Lycus jumped off his horse, threw off his armor, and dove into the water, swimming after the ship. Several other Spartans dove in after him, but they were too late.

The oars lowered on either side of the ship, and a minute later, she was well out of swimming distance. Lycus and the others swam back, and then everyone looked at Andronicus. He knew they had already fouled up the mission; they were not supposed to let the pirates board their ship. He could not return to Sparta having let murderous Persian pirates escape. He realized they would have to chase them down, and they would need their own ships to do it.

"Lycus," Andronicus said, "you're the fastest rider here. Ride back and get us ships. The longer you take, the longer we'll have to chase them."

Lycus nodded, then jumped back on his horse and galloped away. Andronicus wasn't sure what to do with the rest of his men. He hadn't planned on having to wait on a beach for an unknown period of time. Eventually, he ordered some men to build a fire and others to hunt down some food. The rest of the troupe dismounted and spread out across the beach.

3

Andronicus and his men waited restlessly by the sea for Lycus's return. Every hour they waited was another three hours at least that they would have to chase the Persians. As night turned to day and day to night, Andronicus knew they were going to have to chase them for a long time.

The fires in the nearby villages had all been put out, and filthy, disheveled people came and went behind them as they waited.

On the second day, an old Helot woman came limping up to them. Right away Andronicus could see that she had been badly burnt. Her hair was all a strewn, and her eyes were an awful puffy red from sobbing. Thin tear lines tracked through the soot on her face. Awful red boils and blisters covered her entire left arm, making it look lewd and misshapen.

She began shouting at them in the language of her people, but none of Andronicus's men could understand it. He had always pitied the Helots. He had refused to accept Kyros's many offers of Helot slaves, even though Gaia had always owned them. He wondered what this woman was screaming at them, but thought he knew. She was cursing them for letting her burn and for whomever she may have lost.

"She says we're liars," Theo said gravely, making several men jump. Andronicus had forgotten that Theo knew the Helots' language. "She says we promised to keep them safe. That they would serve us, and we would never let anyone hurt them. That was the promise." Andronicus felt awful as he listened to Theo translate the woman's words, but he said nothing.

She was right; they had broken their promise. The Spartans treated the Helots like slaves in every sense of the word, but they were able to keep the Helots appeased with one simple promise: serve us, and we will always protect you. Andronicus looked at the dirty old woman—her hair wild, her clothes torn to shreds, the skin of her arm a terrible mess of hideous boiled red skin—and felt ashamed. If they had reached the pirates sooner, they may have been able to save more people.

The woman continued screaming at them in her horrible shrill voice. "We let them burn down her village," Theo continued dolefully, apparently not noticing the looks on the faces of the men around him. "They killed her father, her brother, and her son. She says the gods will make us pay for this betrayal. She says we'll be cursed until every last one of the men who slaughtered her family is dead. Our voyage will be blighted with death and misery."

"Enough!" Andronicus said. He didn't care how much the woman had lost; he would not allow someone to curse them before a long journey. The woman fell silent at Andronicus's shout. She scowled at them a moment longer, then whispered something under her breath and scurried off.

Andronicus looked out at his men and saw the disquiet he felt etched on their faces. He silently blamed Theo for giving voice to her terrible omens, though he supposed she was saying the words whether they understood them or not. He tried to reassure his men that it was all nonsense, heathen practices that the true gods laughed at, and he thought he saw relief on a few faces.

"I don't like this," Euthymius said to Andronicus when the others weren't listening. "Philander has told me stories of Helot curses. They're real."

"Enough," Andronicus hissed. "What am I supposed to do? The king ordered me to find and kill the bandits, and instead of chasing them down, you want me to tell him we can't go because a burnt slave woman cursed our voyage?" Euthymius didn't say anything, but Andronicus could tell he was not satisfied.

4

Lycus finally returned later that night. His cloak was dirty and wind battered, and his horse looked ready to keel over. Foam was curdling at the corners of the beast's mouth, and its eyes were reeling wildly. Lycus jumped down from the horse, and gave the reins to one of the men standing nearby. He walked straight to Andronicus and took him and Niko aside.

"I spoke with the king," Lycus said. "I told him the pirates have set sail and are likely heading north. He ordered Sophos to ready three ships. He's going to ferry us north as far as need be until we catch the bandits. The king says you still have command." The jealous tone in which Lycus said this was unmistakable, but Andronicus didn't say anything. "Sophos's word goes when it comes to the sea," Lycus finished. Andronicus and Niko nodded slowly.

"When will Sophos arrive?" Niko asked. Andronicus knew he could not be pleased about the long journey ahead of them and the prospect of being away from his family for so long.

"If it's three days' ride from Sparta to here, it should be two days' sail," Andronicus said. "With a favorable wind," he added as an afterthought.

"Which there is not," Lycus pointed out. "And it's a four-day ride, I managed it in three. Sophos should arrive after sunrise."

"He'd better," Niko said impatiently. "The pirates could be all the way to the Aegean by now. If they go to sea, we'll be chasing them for months." Andronicus hoped Niko was wrong, but he knew he was almost surely right. If the pirates were already in the Aegean when they set out after them, not only would they be two weeks behind, they would likely have to stop constantly to make sure the pirates hadn't changed course.

Andronicus and his close confidantes discussed

the voyage ahead at length, staying up half the night while the rest of the men slept.

As Lycus had predicted, not more than an hour after sunrise, three Spartan ships appeared on the horizon. At first they were heading up the coast, but Sophos must have seen their camp because all three ships turned and headed right toward them. The ships stopped not far off shore, and small boats made their way to the beach.

Andronicus saw his impatience mirrored on Niko and Lycus's faces as the men made their way into the boats and then off to the ships. By the time all one hundred men were safely on board, and the ships were headed north again, the sun was already high above them. Andronicus met with Sophos in his cabin, and they discussed the tactics they would use in following the long-departed pirate ship. They would have to stop at nearly every port along the coast to make sure they were still following the pirates, and Andronicus knew it could take months to catch them.

5

The ships made their way north much slower than Andronicus had hoped. The wind seemed to be constantly working against them, whether they sailed north or east. After only a week at sea, one of the three ships hit a large rock hidden under the water. The hull cracked, and water slowly started flowing in. The men evacuated to the other two boats, though several men drowned in the process. Once the two remaining ships were filled well past their intended capacity, they watched the ship sink beneath the water, then began sailing again, even slower than before.

The days turned to weeks as they sailed past Mycenae and Athens and through the pass at Karistos, then finally into the Aegean. It started raining more often as well, slowing them down even further. Andronicus could not remember a time when more rain fell for so many days in a row.

Their journey north grew slower and slower, until most of the men started thinking they weren't ever going to catch the pirates. Often Sophos would say the weather was too bad and sail both ships into a port or calm bay, where they would have to stay there until it was safe to sail again.

Whenever they came to land, Andronicus made sure to ask the locals if they had seen a Persian ship come through recently. From the answers he got, they were at least a few weeks behind them but still on their trail. He didn't know how long it was going to take to catch them, but he would not turn back until he did.

6

Sophos made them wait three whole days in port before he would set sail across the Aegean. They set out on a day as clear as any and sailed for two weeks into the Aegean without any trouble. Then a terrible storm hit. Andronicus had never been at sea during such a storm. The two long ships rode the massive waves through the pouring rain. There were three men on every oar instead of the usual two, and the rest of the men were either lying flat on the deck, holding on for dear life, or bundled together below deck, utterly helpless.

The wind roared, and the waves crashed over the ship every few seconds, making it impossible to see or hear anything. Andronicus tried to shout to his men, but even his loud voice was lost in the howling wind and water. He looked around at the men and saw terrified faces. Every man on those ships was a trained Spartan warrior, most of them battle tested, but it was clear they were all terrified of Poseidon's wrath.

The storm lasted the entire night. At one point Andronicus looked out and couldn't see the other ship. He got up and made his way over to where Sophos was steering. Sophos had such a look of determination on his face that Andronicus didn't want to disturb him. Eventually, there was a small break in the waves.

"The other ship!" Andronicus shouted over the howling wind. "Where's the other ship?"

Sophos turned to look at him, and Andronicus saw the battle rage in his eyes. "Gone!" Sophos shouted, turning back to the waves.

"Are you sure?" Andronicus replied. "Maybe we just lost them!"

"They're gone!" Sophos shouted, turning to Andronicus with a mad look in his eyes. "I saw it! They're all dead!" With that the captain returned to his fight against the storm.

Andronicus made his way back to his place in the bow. He looked around, making sure all his friends were still on board. He saw Lycus, Niko, and Theo all rowing hard, and behind them was Androcles. He knew Thymi was on the ship because he had seen him earlier, so he went to row next to Androcles.

"I had a dream about this storm!" Androcles shouted as Andronicus sat next to him.

"What are you talking about?" Andronicus replied, turning to look at his brother.

"A week ago, just after we set out into the Aegean!" Androcles yelled over the crashing waves and howling wind. "I had a dream about this very storm!"

"How do you know it was this storm?" Andronicus asked. "We've been at sea for two months. You probably dream about storms every night!"

"It was this storm!" Androcles shouted. He had an odd look in his eyes. "I saw that!" Androcles pointed at the sky. Andronicus looked up and saw a huge black cloud, much darker than all the rest, shaped like a bull. Every few seconds the darkness lit up, and the cloud shone blue as lightning struck inside. Andronicus turned back to Androcles and saw that he was already back to rowing. He didn't know what to say, so he just kept on rowing, but now he couldn't help but look up every few minutes and see the monstrous cloud Androcles had dreamed of.

7

When the storm finally cleared, there was no sign of the other ship. Andronicus tried to convince Sophos to search for it, but he refused, insisting he had seen it go down. Sophos sailed due east, making straight for the coast. After the terrifying storm and losing both of the other ships, every man aboard was eager to get back to land, and they all rowed tirelessly.

When they reached land again, most of the men wanted to disembark at once, but Sophos turned them north again, insisting they continue heading up the coast, looking for the pirate ship. Andronicus knew Sophos was eager to be rid of them and sail back to Greece. The other ship had held more than half of the provisions, and Sophos would almost surely leave Andronicus and the other soldiers as soon as the pirates were found.

After four more days up the coast, they finally found the Persian ship. It was washed ashore, tilted over on one side from the lack of tide. Sophos pulled his ship near to it, and Andronicus rowed out with two small boats.

Sophos said he thought they were near the city of Assos, north of Pergemon and south of old Troy.

When they investigated the abandoned ship, Andronicus could see that the pirates had gone north. The trails their sleds had made in the sand were still there. This gave him some hope that they might actually catch them. If they were pulling sleds, they couldn't be moving very fast.

Andronicus signaled back to the ship, and his remaining host of thirty-two men made their way to shore. By the time the host was ashore, and Sophos was sailing off with his last remaining ship, the sun had already set. They set up camp by the beach, knowing they would have to run like dogs come morning. Andronicus would have asked Sophos to stay and wait for them, but after losing two of his three ships and more than half of his crew, it was clear that Sophos wanted nothing more to do with this mission. Rumors had begun to spread that this mission was cursed, mostly because of the old woman who had literally cursed them, and Sophos and his men wanted to be rid of it all as soon as possible.

8

Andronicus led his small band of men east in pursuit of the remaining pirates. The Spartans had no horses, but they knew their prey didn't either. The tracks they were following were fresh enough that they could tell they were less than a week behind the Persians, and Andronicus pushed his men as hard as he could. They walked through the dry, hot desert panting like dogs. By the end of the third day most of the men were running dangerously low on water, and they had not seen any for two days.

On the fourth day, they didn't find any water, and four men died of thirst. That night Andronicus feared they all might die of thirst or starvation, but the next day they found a small creek and a few animals to eat. Lycus found signs that the pirates had also stopped at the creek, and the tracks still looked fresh.

Andronicus let his men rest by the creek for two hours. They ate and drank for the first time in two days and rested their tired legs. Then they filled their water bags and continued after the pirates. By nightfall they still hadn't caught up to them, but they knew they were close. At dawn they ate quickly and continued on.

It wasn't until well past noon that they finally found the pirates. Andronicus and his men came over a hill and saw a small village in the shadow of a mountain. Seconds after they saw the village, horns began blowing in the distance. Andronicus recognized the horns at once; they were the same horns he had heard the Persians use years before.

He expected the pirates to flee, as they had done at every turn so far, but to his surprise what looked like the entire village came charging toward them. There were at least a dozen men on horseback and twice as many on foot. Andronicus shouted for his men to get in line, and they quickly banded together. They had no spears, long or short, only their swords, and he knew that they couldn't stand against a cavalry charge like this. He shouted for his men to spread out, and they did as he ordered. He could see that most of his men were scared, and he knew many of them would likely die. But he could also see Lycus, who looked like he was alive for the first time in years, and thought he would at least make it out alive.

Once the Persian riders were within a hundred feet of them, Andronicus had to leave his men to their own devices and defend himself. He gripped his sword tightly and faced the man riding toward him. When the rider was ten feet away, Andronicus jumped to his right, just as Archelaus had taught him, and plunged his sword into the man's gut as he rode past. Andronicus' sword sent the man flying backward off his horse, which kept running.

Just as Andronicus pulled his sword free of the dead man, he saw another sword coming at him. He ducked just in time as another rider rode past him at full gallop. Before he had time to see where the rider had gone, the foot soldiers were on him. Three Persian men ran at Andronicus with their swords held high, screaming wildly.

Before the Persians realized he had come at them, Andronicus sliced one man's throat and stabbed another through the chest. The third man stopped running and stared at his dead companions in surprise. He looked like he wanted to say something, or at least turn and run, but before he could, Andronicus drove his sword through the man's gut.

Andronicus turned to see most of his men fighting the Persians. He saw at least three Spartans lying dead on the ground, and two more fell as he watched. Euthymius and Niko were surrounded by six foot soldiers, each fighting off three. Andronicus ran to them and cut down two men before they even saw him coming. Once they were down, Thymi and Niko were able to take care of the others.

The three of them moved together, working their way toward Androcles and Theodotus. As they went, Andronicus noticed more of his men lying in the dirt.

Once they reached Androcles and Theo, the five of them formed a small phalanx and started pushing forward. Almost all the riders had been killed, and they cut the remaining Persians down together. Andronicus saw Lycus in the distance, alone, covered in blood, with dead bodies all around him, his triumphant battle cry echoing across the valley.

When the Persians were down to a dozen men, they fled back to the village. Andronicus wanted to charge after them, but they had to regroup first. He shouted to his remaining host to gather around him. A minute later Andronicus and his eleven remaining men stood together. He could not believe they had become so few.

"We should leave this place," Thymi said through heavy breaths. "We should just go back to Sparta."

"Our mission is not complete yet," Andronicus said sternly. "We cannot go back."

"Thymi is right," Androcles urged his brother. "They're dead, and the ones who aren't dead have been driven all the way back to Persia. We can go back home now."

"Look around," Lycus said angrily, a wild look still in his eyes. "There were one hundred of us; now there are only twelve. They did that!"

"Poseidon took more of us than they did," Theodotus insisted.

"You think a magical old man who controls the sea is the reason those ships sank?" Lycus asked, glaring at Theodotus.

"Watch what you say," Theo replied menacingly. "We have had more than enough bad luck already. We don't need you cursing the gods."

"The gods have already cursed us," Niko said. "That old woman on the beach, the burnt woman, she was right. Everything she said would happen to us has happened."

"Do you remember how she ended her curse?" Andronicus asked. They all shook their heads, fearing the answer. "She said until every last one of the men who had burnt her village was dead, our voyage would be blighted with death and misery."

"So, we have to go after them," Lycus insisted. "We have to finish it."

"He's right," Theo said suddenly, his face a pale white. "The gods answered that woman's prayers. We have been cursed; there's no other explanation for our losses. We have to kill all of them, or none of us will ever make it back to Sparta."

"You really believe that?" Thymi asked softly.

Theo nodded slowly, staring down at the village. Shouts and screams were coming from down there, and Andronicus guessed they were preparing to flee again.

"Come on," Lycus insisted. "They're going to get away. We have to go after them now!"

"Fine," Andronicus said. "We'll kill them, and then we're leaving this terrible land." The twelve remaining Spartans ran down the hill to the village.

"There may be women and children down there!" Androcles shouted. "They have no part in this! Only kill the men!"

"He's right!" Andronicus agreed, and then they were there.

The Spartans ran into the village, and as expected, most of the remaining Persian men were preparing to ride away. Androcles ran toward the men loading the horses, a few Spartans behind him. Andronicus and Lycus charged at the men already on their horses, with Niko right behind them.

The Persians didn't even try to fight this time. As soon as they saw Andronicus and Lycus charging at them, the riders kicked at their horses. Andronicus and Lycus threw their swords simultaneously, and they both took down a rider. Niko took down another, but four other riders made it out. Andronicus pulled his sword free, and turned to see what was left. Androcles and the others had killed every man in the village, and the women and children were huddled together by a small hut.

"Four of them got away," Niko said as they walked over to the others.

"We have to go after them," Theo said quickly.

"Damn right we do," Lycus growled, walking over to one of the horses. "There are six horses here, and there were at least six horses still alive up the hill. We can ride after them."

"What do we do with them?" Androcles asked, pointing at the cowering women and children.

"We leave them," Andronicus said. He wasn't going to kill them just because they were Persian, but he certainly wasn't going to help them.

"Just leave them here to die?" Androcles said in shock. "With no men to hunt for them, they won't last a week."

"There are other villages they can go to," Lycus said angrily, "and if they die, so be it. They can join their murderous husbands and fathers."

Lycus turned his horse around, and rode up the hill. Niko quickly followed. It took them almost an hour to wrangle the remaining horses. By the time Andronicus and his small host began riding after the even smaller Persian host, they were at least two hours behind.

9

Andronicus and his raiding party rode for two days before they finally caught up to the Persians who had fled. Once they were in sight, it took another hour to catch them. The Persians fled to the very end. Once they were close enough, Andronicus and Lycus threw knives from their horses and took down two of the men. When the men fell, their horses stopped running, and then there were only two left. Androcles and Niko rode forward and took aim with their own knives. They each hit their mark. The one Androcles hit fell off his horse and hit the dirt, but the one Niko hit kept on riding with the knife sticking out of his back. Lycus spurred his horse forward. After a minute's hard ride, he flung his sword at the man, and he finally fell.

Andronicus and his host stopped riding once the last bandit had fallen. They looked at each other in joy and relief. It had been nearly a year since they had set out to kill the bandits, and now they were finally done.

"Oh, mighty Zeus!" Theo shouted to the sky, and everyone turned to listen to him. "We have finished our task. We have righted our wrong. Every last one of the men who betrayed your sovereignty is dead, just as the old woman bid it. Lift your curse. Call off your kin. Let Apollo guide our way back to the sea, and let Poseidon bless our voyage home. Let Hades take no more of our men, for we have done as you have asked."

"You think no more of us will die because of that?" Lycus asked once Theo fell silent. He believed less in the gods than anyone Andronicus knew. Everyone shot him angry and irritated looks in response, none of them wanting to upset the gods more than they already had, but Lycus persisted. "We're still in the middle of Persian country, we're at least a week's ride from the sea, and even then it will take months to find a ship again. Do you think that those were the only Persian bandits in this country? This is Persia! Just because you spoke some magic words, and your gods lifted their curse doesn't mean we won't still have to fight our way out of here. We're going to have to fight, and more of us are going to die."

"Enough!" Andronicus shouted, cutting off Lycus' rant. He knew what Lycus was saying was probably true, but the men didn't need to hear that.

"It's true, and you know it," Lycus said. "Pretending we're safe does no good for anyone."

"I'm not saying we're safe," Andronicus replied. "You're right; we're still in Persia, and it will take a long time to get home, but that doesn't mean more of us have to die. We don't have to chase anyone anymore, which means we can go at our own pace and go the safest way, not the way the bandits went. There are also fewer of us, which means we'll be harder to spot, and we can look after each other easier. We may not have to fight anyone at all."

"If you really think that then you're a fool," Lycus seethed, clenching his fists around his horse's reins.

"Perhaps I am," Andronicus replied, glaring back at Lycus. "But I'm still in command, and I say no more of this talk. We have completed our mission, and we can head home now."

"How do you suggest we do that?" Thymi asked suddenly, surprising Andronicus.

"What do you mean?" Andronicus asked, turning to him.

"Well, we sailed in from the south, but Sophos is gone, and we will not find a safe place to barter passage from the south for hundreds of miles. So, we'll have to go north, but that means we'll either have to go through the desert or go through heavily populated Persian lands."

"At least someone understands what kind of problem we have gotten ourselves into," Lycus said. "I would not have expected it to be you though."

"You can learn a thing or two from reading," Thymi said offhandedly to Lycus. "Like where in Persia is safe and where is not."

"Do you know a safe path we can take?" Andronicus asked, realizing only then that he was barely in command at that point and felt shame wash over him. He had left with one hundred men and had been expected to return home victorious within two weeks' time. Instead he had brought his men across the sea and into Persia, taking the better part of a year, and losing all but twelve of the men who had been entrusted to him. Andronicus knew that when he returned home it would be in disgrace, but that didn't matter anymore; he simply wanted to make it home with his friends and his brother still alive.

"I think so," Thymi said slowly, a look of concentration on his face. "If we go north through the desert of Mysia, past the old ruins of Troy, I think we may be able to avoid being seen. From there it will be much easier to find a Greek ship that we can take home."

"Do we have any other options than riding through a desert?" Androcles asked, voicing all of their doubts.

Thymi nodded. "Yes. We can try and ride past the city of Pergamon without being caught."

"We'll go through the desert," Andronicus said in as commanding a tone as he could manage. "If we're caught anywhere near Pergamon, we'll all die. In the desert we may yet live."

"Only a fool tries to cross a desert," Niko said ominously, sending a chill up Andronicus's spine. He had heard the words many times as a boy and always laughed at them, but he found no humor in them now. "Philander must have told us that a thousand times,"

Niko added eerily.

"Philander is a wise man and a kind man," Thymi said, "but he has never been to war, and he doesn't know how to stay alive. He may have said only a fool crosses a desert, but I say only a fool tries to sneak through a Persian city with twelve Greek men. Andronicus is right." His words were met by nervous laughter, and everyone seemed to relax a bit. It seemed settled that they would be taking the longer, safer path, and they all seemed glad to have come to a decision. They set off to the north, riding at a slow leisurely pace, knowing they would need to keep the horses alive for as long as possible.

10

It took three long, hot months to cross the desert of Mysia. They were down to eleven men when they finally entered the ancient lands of the forgotten Trojan empire. They had lost three of their horses and a young man named Tobias while crossing the desert. One day he had simply fallen off his horse, apparently from the heat, and he had never risen. Andronicus, Thymi and Niko all had a man sitting on their horse with them, and they were moving much slower than Andronicus would have liked.

One day they were making their way up a hill, hoping to see the sea from the top. They could smell the saltwater, and they knew they would find the sea soon. When they reached the top of the hill and looked down, instead of the sea, they saw a massive ruined city. They all dismounted and took a moment to admire the ancient wonder. No one spoke as they stared at the abandoned city of legend. Andronicus was struck by the size of Troy; it looked as though it had been nearly five times as big as Sparta. He sat down, thinking of all the old stories he had loved as a boy, the legends of Achilles and Odysseus and Hector, and could not believe they had all happened right down there.

"I can't believe it's still here," Theodotus said in rapt fascination. "All these years later. I would have thought it would be gone by now."

"It will be gone soon enough," Andronicus said with a sigh. "Someday the city of Troy will be nothing but a legend, just a bunch of stories to tell children."

"You don't really believe that, do you?" Androcles asked. "Troy is the most famous city there has ever been. How could people ever forget it?"

"With enough time people forget everything," Andronicus said sullenly. "The best you can hope for is that people will tell your story when you're gone."

"That's rather depressing," Thymi said, taking out a piece of dried meat to sup on. "And I think you're wrong. Troy will never be forgotten. Perhaps it will become the stuff of legend, and like it or not, that city will be dust one day, but I don't think it will be forgotten. And I don't think we'll be forgotten either," Thymi added as he took a bite of the meat. "Maybe our names will be, but not the battles we fought in. They will speak of those for centuries to come."

"And what about when those centuries have come, and gone again?" Andronicus said gloomily. "What about when the dust has all blown away, and the stories have all been forgotten? When our children's children have been dead a thousand years, what then? Like I said, in time people forget everything."

"I still think you're wrong," Thymi said stubbornly. "Besides, what does it matter what people remember a thousand years from now? It still happened."

11

After leaving the ancient ruins of Troy, Andronicus and his band of ten found the sea not far to the west. They walked along the sea until they found a fishing village blocking their way. They waited until nightfall, and then Lycus and Andronicus crept to the edge of the village. They were hoping to find Greek men there, but instead they found only Persians. They crept back to the others, then headed inland to avoid being seen in the morning. They rode for three hours through the night until they found a nice shadowy place under a large rock overhang, by the side of a mountain. They spread out and drifted off to sleep as the sun began to rise in the distance.

12

Andronicus was dreaming of a mountain in the middle of a storm. Wind and rain howled around him, and up ahead was some kind of strange light. It was as if it was coming out of the mountain itself. Andronicus started walking toward the light, shielding his eyes from the pounding rain.

As he got closer, the light got brighter. He could feel his heart racing, and he knew he was about to see where the light was coming from. A voice shouted out from the light, and Andronicus stopped moving. He cocked his head and listened, and the voice shouted again, louder this time.

Andronicus snapped awake and sat up. Lycus was on his feet, shouting at everyone to wake up. The rest of the men were just beginning to rise. Andronicus looked over to where Lycus was pointing and saw at least three dozen mounted riders charging toward them. Andronicus scrambled to his feet and grabbed his sword. He didn't have time to strap on his armor, so he ran to join Lycus bare chested. He could see that most of his men were awake, but a few were still asleep, including Androcles.

"Get up! Now!" Andronicus shouted. His voice echoed off the high mountain and then was drowned out by the shouts of the oncoming riders.

Andronicus and Lycus leaped onto their horses, then charged the oncoming riders without waiting for the others. They didn't look at each other, and they didn't need to; they both knew what to do.

Just before they met the riders, they turned their horses to the right. Just as they had hoped, the riders turned to follow them. They rode with the entire raiding party following them for a full minute and then turned again. Andronicus saw the rest of his men jumping on their horses with Niko already leading a small charge toward them.

Andronicus and Lycus each ducked a blow as the riders came upon them, and they slashed out with their swords, each taking a rider down. The two men fought alone against the horde of Persian riders for a full minute, which felt like an hour. They were completely surrounded by Persians, and then the others reached them. Andronicus heard Niko come crashing in with a loud shout and then saw Thymi fighting through as well.

There were at least two dozen Persians between him and the others, so he turned to fight with Lycus. Lycus didn't seem to need any help; all the Persians around him were falling in quick succession. Andronicus fought off the men around him while trying not to get hit, seeing as he wasn't wearing any armor.

At one point while he was cutting down the man in front of him, he felt a sharp pain down his back and turned to see a man pulling back his sword. Andronicus ducked the man's second blow and then took him down with a strong blow of his own. He reached around to feel his back, and his hand came away smeared with blood. He knew the cut was not deep, but it still hurt.

Andronicus turned back to see the battle was mostly over. Lycus was walking from one Persian to the next, driving his sword through their chests. Andronicus looked at his men, and felt his heart sink. Besides he and Lycus, only Androcles and Theo were on their feet. Andronicus quickly looked around for the others and saw Thymi on his knees. Andronicus rushed over, and then his stomach dropped out from under him. He fell to his own knees, unable to stop himself. Thymi was covered in blood, but it wasn't his. Niko lay in Thymi's arms, a big dark stain moving across his unarmored chest. His left arm was curled up, and Andronicus could see the blood leaking out of him. Euthymius was holding his head up and carefully bringing a water bag to his lips.

"Niko," was all Andronicus managed to say. Niko had been with him through everything. Every battle he had ever fought, Niko had been at his side. He tried to think how many times Niko had saved his life, not to mention Androcles's and Thymi's. Niko had always been the glue in their little group. He was the one who stopped the fights, the one who always had the right words, whether they hurt or not.

Andronicus felt tears fall down his face, and he let them come. A moment later the others were all gathered around Niko. His face was scrunched up, and his eyes were shut tight. Andronicus could see the pain his friend was in.

"Where are you hit?" Andronicus asked softly, hoping there was still a chance.

"It doesn't matter," Niko gasped. "I, am dying, Andronicus."

Andronicus's heart wrenched at the words. He felt powerless and weak as he watched his old friend bleed out in the dirt of this awful foreign land.

"We will never forget you, Nikopheros," Androcles said through his tears. "You were always the best of us."

"No, I was not." Niko coughed, opening his bloodshot eyes to look up at Androcles. "There is no best . . . and no worst. We . . . did it . . . together. That . . . is all . . . that matters."

"You're right," Euthymius said, his voice breaking on every word. "We did it together, always. You protected Sparta your entire life Niko. You're as true a Spartan as there ever was." Niko smiled softly, looking up at them all.

"Lycus," he said, coughing as he reached out to him. Lycus got down on his knees beside him. A tear rolled down his cheek as he took Niko's hand. It was the first time Andronicus had ever seen Lycus cry. Lycus bent his head down, and Niko whispered something in his ear, but Andronicus couldn't hear what it was. When Lycus pulled his head away, he had a look of stony determination on his face. He nodded slowly to Niko. Niko turned to the rest of them, a faint smile on his bloody lips.

"I . . . am . . . sorry," Niko said softly.

"Sorry for what?" Andronicus asked, tears running down his cheeks. "You have done nothing wrong, brother."

"I . . . am sorry . . . that I . . . will not . . . be . . . there with you," Niko said, barely loud enough for them to hear. Andronicus saw Niko's eyes beginning to drift, and he knew he didn't have long.

"That you will not be with us for what?" Andronicus asked, leaning forward.

"For . . . all of it," Niko said, and then he fell silent. His head drooped in Thymi's arms, and his eyes stared up into the sky without seeing.

None of them said anything for a long while. They just sat there, weeping over their fallen brother. In truth they had lost six brothers, but the others they barely knew. Niko had been a true brother to each of them.

Androcles finally got up, picked up one of the Persian swords, and began digging a hole. Theo joined him a moment later, as did the others.

13

They spent the rest of the day digging graves for their fallen. When all six of the dead Spartans were in the ground, the sun had nearly set. They all huddled around Niko's grave, and Theo said an old prayer of passing. Lycus had found a large flat stone and carved Niko's name into it with his knife. He laid the stone at the head of Niko's grave, then walked away. He hadn't spoken a word since Niko had died.

"We should leave his sword with him," Androcles said, looking down at the sword in his hands.

"No, he would not have wanted that," Andronicus said hoarsely. "That is one of the last swords of Karpos. He would want you to have it, Thymi."

"Me?" Thymi said, looking up in surprise, his eyes puffy and red from weeping. "No, let Androcles have it."

"It should be you," Androcles said, looking uncomfortable.

"No, I cannot," Thymi said, tears forming in his eyes again. "You take it."

"Take it, Androcles," Andronicus said. "We can give it to his sons when we return home." Androcles took the sword and looked down at it as if it held Niko inside of it.

"We'll have to look after his boys for him," Thymi said, staring at Niko's grave.

"We will," Andronicus promised. "We're going to make it back."

"There are only five of us left," Androcles said softly, lowering the sword. "Do you really think we can make it back to Greece?"

"I know we can," Andronicus replied, then turned and walked away. He knew there was almost no chance they would make it back, but he felt like he had to keep up the façade. Losing Niko made it all seem real, and he knew they could all die before they made it even close to home.

Chapter 11
A Glimpse Through Time
1

The harsh, dry lands they walked through had not seen rain for months, and yet every one of them could sense the storm that was to come. The sky was an ominous grey, covering the land in dark shadows, and they knew that the rain would fall soon. Andronicus led his four remaining friends west toward the nearest mountains in hopes of finding some shelter before the rain began. They had left the place where Niko died two weeks earlier and headed inland, avoiding any other villages.

They had killed and butchered their last horse three days earlier and were all on foot now. They needed to find shelter before the storm came, so Andronicus pushed them to move faster. They started to run as the first crash of thunder boomed across the land. Just as they reached the slope of the mountains, the rain began to fall. It came all at once, as if Poseidon himself had dropped the sea on top of them. They stumbled blindly up the hill, the dirt quickly turning to mud under their sandaled feet.

When they reached the top of the initial slope, they looked down and saw a pass running through the hill they had climbed and another. The water from both hills was quickly filling the pass, and rocks began to tumble down unpredictably.

"We can't go through that!" Theodotus shouted over the clamor of the pounding rain and booming thunder.

"We should climb the mountain!" Androcles shouted, pointing up the steep hill on their left. "Look for a cave!"

"Why would there be a cave up there?" Lycus asked irritably. Andronicus didn't think there would be a cave either, but he had no better idea.

"There will be no shelter down there!" Andronicus said pointing back down the way they had come. "And Theo is right; we can't go down there! Our best chance is to climb and look for a cave or at least some cover from the lightning!"

At that very moment, lightning struck an old dead tree not far to their right, splitting it in two and sending splinters flying everywhere. The old, rotten wood burst into angry flames that were quickly doused by the rain. A split second later the most deafening crash of thunder boomed down on them, and they all fell to the ground as the whole world seemed to shake around them.

"We have to get out of here!" Theo shouted. His face had turned as white as snow. Andronicus knew he was likely fearing some kind of awful "wrath of the gods" scenario. "Zeus has come to destroy these cursed lands!" Theo shouted, confirming Andronicus's suspicions. "We have to get to cover, or we will parish along with this foredoomed wasteland."

"I do not fear the gods!" Lycus shouted as if to challenge them himself. "But I do fear that damned lightning. Whatever we do, we need to do it now!"

"Come on!" Andronicus shouted. "Up the mountain. Spread out as far as we can without losing sight of each other. We want to cover as much ground as possible if we're looking for cover."

"Right!" Euthymius said. "Come on then."

The five of them started up the mountain, moving as fast as they could through the rain. The mud was beginning to run down the hill, and many of the rocks had lost their hold in the earth. All five of them slipped and stumbled their way up and across the hill.

"We have to go higher!" someone shouted to Andronicus's left. He couldn't see who it was, but the man was pointing up the hill, toward the mountain itself.

"There won't be any cover down here, just falling rocks," the shadowy figure said. "We have to go higher!"

"Androcles is right!" Euthymius called back from somewhere close by. "We have to go up!"

"Right!" Andronicus shouted, his voice booming above the rest, as always, even echoing back through the thick rain. "We need to move up the mountain. Keep your footing now!"

Andronicus started up the hill, only able to see Euthymius, but trusting that the others were still with them. He slipped constantly, seeming to slide back a step for every step he took. It was slow going, and the thunder and lightning crashed all around them, with the rain an ever-bearing presence, driving them down into the mud.

At one point a wicked blue fork of lightning crashed down far too close to them. Andronicus heard two of the others shout, and then the loudest, most terrible thunderous roar Andronicus had ever heard boomed right above them. The whole world shook from the force of it, and for a moment it felt like the mountain itself would crumble. When the thunder stopped, and the hill stopped shaking, Andronicus let out a shuddering sigh.

"Is anyone hit?" he yelled, praying he had not lost another friend.

"No!" Theodotus shouted back. "It just missed me!"

"Is everyone else alright?" Andronicus asked, looking around the black storm-covered hill for the others.

"Yes!" Thymi called out from somewhere up ahead.

"Aye! Keep moving!" Lycus shouted from somewhere close by.

"What about Androcles?" Andronicus shouted out, fearing for a second that his brother might have fallen.

"Up here!" Androcles shouted from high up the mountain, his voice barely carrying through the roaring storm. "Keep moving!"

Andronicus put his head down and continued up through the rocky mud. As he trudged, he wondered why the hell they had come this way in the first place. He couldn't remember whose idea it had been to take this path or to climb the hill.

When he finally reached the point where the hill met the mountain, Andronicus called out for the others again. It took nearly twenty minutes for them all to find each other.

"OK," Lycus said, "we climbed your damned hill, now someone please tell me why in Hades' name we're better off up here than we were down there!"

"Because there's a cave somewhere over there!" Androcles shouted, pointing deeper into the hills. "It's not far."

"How by the gods do you know that?" Lycus shouted angrily, throwing his arms up in exasperation. "You've never climbed these hills, and you can't see a thing."

"I don't know how I know," Androcles said, his voice sounding a bit funny to Andronicus. "I just know there is a cave over there."

"You just *know*?" Lycus asked, clearly outraged.

"The gods are in these lands this night," Theodotus said, ever the disciple. "Perhaps they sent Androcles the knowledge of this cave to save us from their wrath. They know we have no business here; we fulfilled our promise."

"Maybe your gods sent us this damned storm," Lycus said. "Did you ever think of that?"

"It doesn't matter," Thymi replied. "I believe Androcles. We should go."

"I do too," Andronicus said, meeting Lycus' glare with a scowl. "Which way, Droc?"

"That way," Androcles said, pointing north. "I

can feel it; it's like a fire. I can feel it pulling me."

Androcles started off in that direction, not giving anyone time to question this last odd remark. Andronicus gave Euthymius a troubled look, and Thymi answered with an equally troubled shrug. Theodotus started after Androcles without waiting, leaving the three of them standing in the rain.

"You can't be serious!" Lycus shouted. "He can feel a fire pulling him? Andronicus, he's not in his right mind. Most likely he's gotten sick from the cold. We'll all be sick soon enough."

"You're probably right," Andronicus replied, "but what else are we supposed to do? We can't just sit this storm out. If Androcles says there's a cave over there, we might as well see if there is. Hell, maybe Theo is right, and the gods have led us toward it." Lycus scoffed in response.

They all started off toward where Androcles had pointed. The little light that had remained of the day began to fade, leaving them in the dark abyss of water and thunder, occasionally lit up by a long, slender claw of lightning crashing down somewhere around them. Andronicus could only hope that the lightning would not find them. He remembered Philander telling them as boys that lightning liked to find metal, and all five of them were still dressed in their armor.

The mud began to lose any firmness it once held. Rocks and mud and water slid under Andronicus's feet with every step, and he knew that soon they would not be able to walk. He could see Euthymius not far to his right. He hadn't seen the others since the last flash of lightning.

At that moment, he remembered his dream from a fortnight earlier. The memory came crashing back to him, and he felt chills run through his already freezing body. The night before Niko died, he had dreamed of a mountain in a storm. The dream had been interrupted by the attack, and he had not thought of it since, but now it all came back to him. He had been on a mountain, eerily similar to this one in a nearly identical storm, and there had been a light, not a flash of light like the lightning but a constant shining brightness coming out of the mountain itself.

Andronicus looked around, half expecting to see a light in the distance, but all he saw was the pouring rain.

"Here!" someone shouted ahead of him. "Over here! I found it! Over here!"

Andronicus stumbled forward. A moment later Euthymius appeared at his side. They grabbed onto each other for balance and moved carefully forward until they found Androcles standing next to a large rock waiting for them. Andronicus looked around for Lycus and Theo but couldn't see them. As he came up to Androcles, he looked around the rock and was amazed to see a small slit next to it, and what looked like a small cavern behind.

"The others are already inside!" Androcles shouted. "Follow me." He stepped forward into the opening. A second later he was gone. Andronicus was amazed he had found the hole in the first place. It seemed impossible, and again the odd dream came back to him. He bent down and crept forward, Euthymius right behind him. He moved under the rock and felt it extending forward. For a moment he felt the air leave him, and felt as though the walls were closing in. Then the feeling passed.

Andronicus crept forward, feeling along the rocky walls with his hands. Then, without warning, the ground fell out beneath him, and he fell onto the hard, rocky floor. A second later Thymi fell beside him with a grunt.

"Sorry about that," Androcles said in the total blackness. "I guess I should have warned you about the step there."

"Aye, that would have been nice," Lycus said irritably from Andronicus's right.

"Ease up, Lycus," Theodotus said. "Androcles did find this cave."

"How did you know it was here?" Lycus asked, sounding a bit less aggressive.

"I told you," Androcles replied. Again Andronicus heard something odd in his brother's voice. "I felt it. A warmth, like a fire. Can you really not feel it?"

Andronicus took a second, and to his utter surprise, he could feel it—something pulling him in. It was down deeper in the cave, but Andronicus could feel it.

Suddenly, a bright flash lit up the cave, followed by a deep booming roar above them. The flash only lasted a second, but in that moment, Andronicus could see the entire cave. He and Euthymius were sitting on the ground in the middle of a small cavern, and Lycus and Theodotus were standing to their right. Next to them was a decrepit skeleton, sitting up against the wall, every fiber of hair and clothes long gone.

"It's this way," Androcles said when the flash was gone, and the cave was nothing but black again. "Come on."

"What is?" Lycus demanded. "What the hell are you talking about?"

"You can't feel it?" Euthymius asked.

"Feel what?" Lycus shouted, his voice echoing above the pouring rain. "Now you feel this fire too?"

"I feel it too," Theodotus said confidently. "Zeus has sent us a cave for shelter, and a fire for warmth. Do you really not feel it?"

"I feel it," Andronicus said, nodding pointlessly in the dark, "but it's not a fire. It's something else."

"What?" Euthymius asked, sounding a bit frightened.

"I don't know, but not a fire," Andronicus said, the chills creeping down his spine again. "I think I dreamed about this place."

"What do you mean?" Lycus asked in exasperation.

"The night before we were attacked, the night before Niko died," Andronicus added softly, hating the words as he said them. "I dreamed of this mountain and this storm."

"Was there a light coming out of the heart of the mountain?" Thymi asked. "In your dream?"

"Yes," Andronicus replied, surprised. "How did you know?"

"I had the same dream," Thymi said, sounding as frightened as Andronicus felt.

"What are you two talking about?" Lycus said, sounding much less confident than he had a moment earlier. "Are you saying you two had the same dream about this storm?"

"I think so," Andronicus said, not quite sure what it meant.

"Then why the hell did we come up here?" Lycus shouted. "If you all knew a storm was coming, why did you bring us this way?"

"The gods wanted us to be here," Theo said, startling all of them. "They brought us here for a reason, and they sent us the dream for a reason."

"You had the dream too?" Andronicus asked.

"Yes," Theo answered, sounding as if he were talking to the gods now instead of them. "I heard a voice coming out of the light in the mountain, and just before I could see who was speaking, I woke up, to Lycus's shouts."

"You mean the shouts that saved your lives," Lycus added stubbornly.

"That was what happened in my dream as well," Thymi said, ignoring Lycus. "Just before I could see the light, I woke up."

"Me too," Andronicus added.

"You're all joking, right?" Lycus said, sounding like he was at the end of his wits. "You all had the same dream, of this very night, and you can all feel some crazy fire in the mountain that is pulling you in, and Androcles can find hidden caves in the darkest of nights? This is madness!"

"You're right," Andronicus agreed, wondering what was going on. "But we *did* have that dream, and Androcles *did* find this cave, and I *can* feel something pulling me deeper."   "Come on!" Androcles shouted from deeper in the cave. "What are you waiting for?"

Andronicus got to his feet, and tried to shake off some of the water drenching his hair and clothes. They walked slowly down the dark cave, bumping into the rocky walls as they stumbled through the dark. Their soaking wet sandals made squishing sounds with every step, and their armor clanged against the rocks.

As they went farther into the cave, Andronicus could feel the ground sloping down under his squishing feet. He also felt whatever *it* was getting stronger. His whole body seemed to be buzzing with a soft energy. His eyes slowly adjusted to the pitch black, and he could just make out which way the passage was bending, which allowed him to walk a little faster.

They continued going down for more than twenty minutes into the heart of the mountain. Andronicus had no idea how far down they had gone, but he guessed they were probably all the way down the mountain they had climbed, buried beneath a million tons of rocks and dirt. The buzzing feeling had become positively electric. Andronicus felt as if his whole body was teeming with light, and the warmth was pulling him ever forward.

The passage became a little clearer as they walked, and Andronicus could see rocks here and there. It wasn't until a minute later that he realized there was actual light in the cave. He couldn't see the source of it yet, but there was definitely a light up ahead. Andronicus sped up, slipping between rocks, turn after turn. He could hear Lycus still bumping into rocks and grunting behind him.

Finally, they rounded a bend and saw that the next turn had to be the final one. The light was too bright now. Andronicus stepped around the final bend, with Lycus and Euthymius right behind him, and saw Androcles and Theodotus standing together in a well-lit opening.

The opening was bigger than a room, with a high ceiling of smooth rock above them. Andronicus looked around and immediately noticed several strange markings on the wall to his left. They were dark and old, probably carved into the rock with a knife. The marks formed an odd kind of symbol, some language probably long forgotten. Andronicus examined the mark as Lycus and Thymi joined Androcles by the source of the light.

Ignoring an immense urge to join the others, Andronicus took a moment to stare at the odd symbol.

Somehow Andronicus felt as though he had seen it before. It certainly was not Greek, and yet it still felt familiar. He reached out and ran his hand over the odd markings. His fingers tingled as they touched the surprisingly smooth rock.

"Can you see it?" Androcles said from behind him, making him turn around. Andronicus stumbled over to where the others stood in a kind of stupor, unable to feel a single step he took.

In the corner of the cave, where the others had all gathered, was a pool, which appeared to be the source of the light. Andronicus stared down into its depths alongside his companions. The pool wasn't very deep, maybe three feet at the most. The water was a clear filmy blue, and at the bottom was a cluster of rocks.

They weren't like any rocks Andronicus had ever seen, and he wasn't even sure they were rocks. They shone with a bright white light, illuminating the whole cave. Andronicus peered into one of them, and his eyes filled with its brightness. The light was so bright, it matched the lightning they had left behind a thousand times over, and yet it didn't hurt his eyes. It felt like cool water and warm sunlight all at once.

"Can you see it?" Androcles asked again, with a reverence to his voice.

"I see it," Lycus answered coldly, standing next to Andronicus.

Andronicus stared into the light, unable to tear his eyes away. He tried to see what the others were doing but was continually drawn back into the light. He felt the light fall around him, like hands clawing at his sides, drawing him closer.

When he felt his foot touch the water, he tried to stop himself but couldn't. He noticed the others stepping in beside him, as transfixed as he was. He opened his mouth to say something, but the words vanished at the edge of his lips. The light was pounding in his head, drawing him ever forward. The bright rocks seemed to be shining brighter than Apollo himself now, dimming out the rest of the world.

As Andronicus stared into the light, he began

to see shadows. He could see things in the shadows, strange things. At first there were only odd shapes dancing about in the light, like smoke. Then they started to grow and take shape. The smoke cleared, and Andronicus could see a city, as clear as day. At first he thought it was Sparta, but as he looked at it, he realized it wasn't any city he had ever seen. There was something strange in the heart of the city, but before he could see what it was, the city fell away. The shadows pulled and stretched, and a moment later there was a desert, bigger than any Andronicus had ever seen. Sand stretched out as far as the eye could see. Andronicus thought he saw someone walking through the sand, and then the wind kicked up, and the sand blew the desert back into the shadows.

When the shadows settled, Andronicus was looking at a vast jungle, huge and ominous. Before he could even look around, the shadows changed again. Now there was a mountain as high as the sky itself. In the blink of an eye, the mountain was gone, replaced by a forest and then by a placid sea. The calm sea changed into a stormy one, and then that was gone as well. The shadows began to change so rapidly that Andronicus could no longer take them in. He saw cities, large and small, new and old, strange and foreign. He saw forests and jungles, mountains and valleys, fields of grass and fields of dirt. He saw rivers and lakes and seas, the likes of which he had never seen before. He saw fire and ice, life and death. A thousand people in one, a million lives he had yet to touch. He saw everything, everywhere, all at once, all in a single instant, a solitary glimpse.

It was all foreign and strange beyond belief, and yet it all had a strange familiarity to it, as if Andronicus had seen all these things already, a thousand times and again.

When the last city fell away, Andronicus wasn't sure what came after it. The shadows showed him so many other things, all of them strange and terrible and completely foreign to him. As he watched one vision fall away into the next, and then the next, and the next, he felt his hand dip into the water. The last things he saw he did not understand at all. There was darkness and light. In one of the visions he appeared to be floating through the night sky, blackness and stars the only things around him.

Andronicus had a final moment of clear thought as he watched his hand reach down for the nearest rock. In that moment he saw the others reaching down beside him. Andronicus tried to scream, to pull his hand back, but it was as if he had lost control of his body. Just before he touched the rock, he thought he heard a voice speak, but he couldn't make out the words.

When Andronicus's fingers touched the shining rock, he felt a jolt go through his body. His eyes filled with the brightest light he could have imagined, blinding him, and his ears started ringing in deafening agony. The whole world filled with light and sound. Andronicus had wondered what being struck by lightning would feel like, and he thought it must not be as bad as this. The light got brighter and louder until the world fell away, and Andronicus was immersed into the bright water.

Act II
A Strange New Land

Chapter 12
A Strange New Land
1

Andronicus awoke on his back with a sharp pain piercing his head. His ears were filled with a high ringing sound, and his eyes were clenched shut against the immense brightness. He tried to remember what had happened, but all he could recall was the bright light, and he wondered if he really had been hit by lightning.

He tried to open his eyes but then closed them immediately. He sat up slowly, shielding his eyes with his left arm, and propped himself up with his right. He took several minutes to adjust to the bright light all around him. After his eyes finally became accustomed to the brightness, he opened them slightly and looked around. He was in a field he didn't recognize at all. He searched for the others but didn't see them anywhere.

"Androcles!" he shouted. The pain in his head shot up with the effort, and he winced and clutched his temple. No one answered, only a bird far off in the distance. He called out again but heard nothing.

He slowly got to his feet, his head pounding relentlessly. He looked around and realized instantly that he wasn't in Persia anymore. He had not been in Persia long, but the land he saw around him was like nothing he had ever seen before.

The dirt was an odd reddish color, like dirt stained by blood after a great battle. Rough patches of tall yellow grass reaching nearly up to Andronicus's neck were scattered around him. Trees unlike any he had ever seen before were mixed in amongst the tall grass, some tall and thin with thin leaves and some short and fat with lush canopies atop their odd thick branches.

Andronicus looked around in painful confusion, feeling more disorientated than he had ever felt. He had no idea where he was or how he had gotten there. He called out for the others again and was again greeted by a lone bird's call. He looked down at himself, and saw that he was still wearing his armor and cloak, which was still wet. Besides that all he had was his sword, his clothes, and his old comb tucked behind his belt.

His head felt like it had been split in two, but he tried to remember what had happened. He remembered a mountain, and he tried to think of where he had been, still not recognizing anything at all. They had been in Persia; he could remember that much at least. They had been moving through Persian lands, chasing pirates. He remembered seeing the ruins of Troy with the others.

Andronicus felt his stomach drop as he remembered being ambushed and Niko's grisly death. The pain in his head mixed with the knot in his stomach, and he turned and vomited into the dirt. The pain in his head rang out louder than ever as he emptied his guts, coughing and spitting.

As he wiped his mouth with his arm, he tried again to remember what had happened. After they buried Niko, they had begun heading back to Greece. Then he remembered the storm. They had climbed a mountain in search of shelter. The pain in his head made it hard to think clearly, but he concentrated as hard as he could.

He remembered Androcles finding a cave hidden beneath a boulder on the side of the mountain. They had entered the cave, and then there had been something in the cave. Some thing that had drawn them to it.

Andronicus's head started pounding harder and harder as the memory returned to him, but he pushed on, ignoring the urge to retch again. They had entered a cavern, and there had been a pool of water, but not normal water. And there had been something in the pool. They looked like rocks, but Andronicus knew they were not.

The rocks had begun to glow, and he had been totally transfixed. He remembered staring into the light and seeing shadows. They had shown him things—great things, strange things. But no matter how hard he tried he couldn't remember what he had seen. The last thing he could remember was a moment of panic as he saw himself reaching for the rocks. Then there was nothing, just a flash of bright light, and now this.

He tried to remember what had happened after he touched the rock but drew a blinding white blank. All he remembered was a warm feeling coursing through his body as he reached into the water, like a kind of buzzing, and then nothing but light.

All at once Andronicus came to the abrupt realization that he could be dead. Suddenly, he felt very afraid. An icy chill crept down his spine, turning the hairs on his neck as it went. He had not felt such fear since Thermopylae. The uncertainty crept through his mind like a disease. For a moment he began to panic, and he felt his heart pounding inside his armored chest. He closed his eyes and took a deep breath, then looked at the sky.

The sky was a perfect blue with a few thin clouds in the distance, and the sun standing high overhead. It was hard to tell for sure, but he thought the sun looked bigger than usual. Andronicus let out a long exhale, feeling his heartbeat ease. Wherever he was now, he didn't think it was the house of the dead. Apollo had no business in Hades' house. He felt reassured that he wasn't in the underworld, though he supposed that didn't necessarily mean he wasn't dead.

After a long deliberation, Andronicus started walking in a direction he hoped to be north, though he had no way of knowing.

He walked for hours through the strange new world he had woken up in, seeing bizarre plants and animals he had never seen or heard of before. Everything looked different than it should. He saw a pack of wild dog-like animals running in the distance, but their bodies were twisted and elongated, and their faces were snarling, sneering nightmares. He saw strange-looking orange deer with long, twisted horns that pranced through the tall yellow grass, jumping in graceful strides, higher than Andronicus had ever seen any animal jump.

When a small group of horses ran by to his left, he stopped dead in his tracks. He had seen both white horses and black horses in his life, but never a horse with black and white stripes. He watched in utter disbelief as an entire herd of striped horses ran in graceful unison along the edge of the tall grass, their striped bodies gliding easily across the plain. Andronicus stood there for a minute longer watching the herd, wondering what kind of strange land he was in, before continuing his journey.

2

Andronicus had no idea where he was. It had been at least four hours since he had woken up in this strange new land, and he had already seen more bizarre and alien-looking plants and animals than he would have ever believed existed. Besides the striped horses and the prancing orange deer, he had seen a huge grey beast with a great horn atop its face, which he had kept his distance from, and a small herd of what he thought might be elephants. He had never actually seen one, but they were huge and grey and had long tusks, just like in the stories he had heard as a boy.

Pools of water were spread out over the ground, as if it had just rained, and there were animals everywhere Andronicus looked, none of them familiar to him. One of the birds he saw looked a bit like the cranes back in Greece, but he had also seen at least a dozen terrifyingly strange birds, each one more peculiar looking than the last.

Andronicus kept walking, not sure where he was going or where he was coming from. He still had no idea what was happening to him, where he was, or how he had ended up here. Deep down he told himself that the bright light had brought him here, but he tried to ignore that. That didn't make any sense, but so far as he could tell, there was no logical explanation for how he could have come to this place without having any memory of the journey.

The last thing he could remember was reaching

down into the pool of water and touching one of the shining rocks beneath its surface. After that there was nothing but bright light, blindingly bright and yet not painful. He remembered feeling like he was floating through the light, as if it were water. Then there had been shadows, so many shadows, but he still couldn't remember their shapes.

The possibilities of what might have happened raced through his head, one after the other. As he walked alone through the plains, it felt more and more obvious to him, no matter how absurd it seemed, that whatever the light was, it was what had brought him here, wherever here was. He knew it was still entirely possible that he was dead and that when he touched the light, it had been as if he had been struck by lightning, and this was the underworld. He looked up at the sun for reassurance, hoping its presence meant he was not in Hades house. But if this isn't hell, then where the hell is it? He let out a hollow laugh at the thought.

He kept walking toward what he hoped was north, although he still had no real way of knowing yet. Even if he was walking north, he didn't know what lay ahead of him, or behind him, or all around him. He wondered if he was even in the same world. Was Greece out there somewhere, waiting for him? He honestly didn't know. Or was he in a totally new world, far away from Greece and Persia and everything he had ever known? Both seemed equally possible. Either way, he figured the best thing to do was keep moving and hopefully find the others, or at least find someone to speak to.

3

About an hour later as Andronicus walked through the open plains, he saw the first truly unbelievable animal. At first he thought it was just a tree and kept on walking. Then when he was about a mile away, he saw one of the "trees" move. Again he stopped dead in his tracks, peering ahead and wishing his vision was as good as Lycus's. He strained his eyes to see if the tree was really moving amongst its companions. Sure enough, it was.

Andronicus hurried forward, eager to get a closer look at this giant moving thing. As he got closer, he saw that it was not a tree at all but some kind of great colossal horse, both terrifying and beautiful at the same time. The creature stood taller than a house. Its legs alone stretched higher than Andronicus stood, and it had a neck even longer than that. It had two small horns where its ears should be, but otherwise seemed to have a head similar to a horse, only longer and thinner. Its body was covered in a pattern of brown circles against yellow skin. The horse walked from tree to tree on its long slender legs, eating the leaves at the top of the great flat canopies, which no other beast could reach.

Andronicus found a rock to sit on and watched the great horse eat for over an hour. He sat there in utter amazement, admiring the brown-and-yellow pattern on the creature's body and the way it moved about so gracefully despite its size. A herd of the strange orange deer were grazing in a field of tall grass to his left, and a few of the black-and-white striped horses were far off in the distance. Andronicus felt a moment of peaceful serenity as he watched the magnificent beasts all around him. In that moment he felt sure that he was still alive, and that he was still in the world, just far away from Greece. He had no idea where this was or where his companions were, but in that moment he felt confident that he would find them soon enough.

4

The great horse was still eating from one of the large flat trees, flicking its long pink tongue out and snapping off small branches of leaves, when out of nowhere it whipped its long thick neck around. The towering beast stared at something in the distance for a moment and then took off in a slow gallop. Andronicus looked to his left and saw the orange deer prancing away as well, the striped horses already well ahead of them.

Before Andronicus could join the beasts in their

flight, he saw a new beast emerge from the brush nearby. He had never seen one in person, but he had certainly heard of lions before. A lioness was creeping toward him, crouched low to the ground, her long, sharp teeth bared menacingly. The lion was much larger than he would have expected, and she looked immensely powerful. Andronicus knew he could not outrun her, which left him with only one other choice.

He drew his sword and got into a low stance. The lioness emitted a low, steady growl as it crept forward, sending his heart racing. The beast stopped about fifteen feet from him and crouched even lower on her hind legs, staring him right in the eye. Andronicus had never seen a lion before, but he had seen enough predators in his life to know what was coming next.

For a moment they just stared at each other. Andronicus stood bent over, sword in hand, waiting for the inevitable pounce, wishing more than anything that he had his shield. The beast was perched on her hind legs, her sharp white teeth bared, ready to rip him open like she probably did to all the poor beasts she came across. Andronicus took a second to size the cat up and guessed it to be bigger than a mule, much bigger than he would have guessed a lion to be from the stories he had heard as a child.

When the great cat finally leapt at him, Andronicus acted swiftly and confidently. He quickly lunged forward and ducked to the side. He flung his sword up at the flying beast while trying to duck under it. The lion saw him duck as she flew through the air and reached out with one paw to claw at him. As his sword plunged into the beast's belly, her paw slapped his shoulder. Andronicus felt the lion's long, sharp claws rip through his flesh like knives. Each claw cut to the bone, leaving four deep scarlet gashes running across his shoulder.

Andronicus fell to the ground as the cat fell on its side behind him. He scrambled to his feet, ignoring the blood pouring down his chest as the lioness slowly stood up. When she turned to face him, he saw his sword buried to the hilt in her chest. Andronicus started backing up, hoping the beast would fall before it could charge him again. The lioness gave one last hollow roar before lunging at him. She only made it about ten feet before falling forward onto her face.

Andronicus approached cautiously, ready for the beast to leap up and strike at him, then carefully pulled his sword from her chest. The lioness was still taking slow, short breaths, so he plunged his sword into the beast's upper neck, ending her pain and her life in one motion.

Andronicus was beginning to look at his shoulder when he heard the sharp, angry howl of another cat. He looked to his left and saw another smaller lioness creeping toward him, even lower to the ground than the first. As the lion slunk closer to him, he picked up a rock and prepared for another fight, ignoring the blood pouring from his shoulder. This lion didn't lunge at him but rather crept toward him. Once she was too close, Andronicus swung his blade in a long arc and caught the beast's nose. Blood sprayed across the dirt, and the cat jerked back in response.

The lion pounced back and forth in the dirt, bringing her paw up to her wounded face. Andronicus threw the rock, striking her again in the face, and she let out an angry howl. Andronicus let out his own mighty war cry, which rang out across the empty plains. The lion gave him one last angry look before slinking back into the brush from which she had come.

Andronicus stood up and looked around for any more of them. Seeing no more lions, or any other animals, he finally seemed to have this strange world all to himself. He looked down and saw that the entire right side of his body was covered in blood, then turned his head away from the deep red lines running across his shoulder. Blood was pouring out of each cut, and he knew he had to stop it quickly. He carefully unstrapped his armor with his left hand, keeping his right arm curled up tight. As he set the armor down, he noticed four long dents running across the chest, and imagined how much worse his wounds would have been without it.

He picked up a handful of red dirt and shoved

it into the wounds on his shoulder, stemming the flow of blood until he could patch it up properly. He clenched his eyes tight and let out a low groan as the pain in his shoulder seemed to explode. There was a waterhole not too far off, so he made his way over to it, dragging his armor behind him. When he reached the pool, he collapsed into the dirt and let his face hit the water.

He drank for a long time, not realizing how thirsty he had been. After drinking his fill, he started cleaning his wounds and washing the blood off himself. When he finally had the cuts cleaned to his satisfaction, the pool had turned a vile red. As he was finishing, he noticed something move in the water. He stood up abruptly, grabbing his sword and preparing to fight whatever new beast this might be. A long, scaly head poked up out of the water, and Andronicus quickly moved away from the pool. He didn't know what the creature was, but he didn't care to find out.

His wounds were clean but still bleeding a bit. He knew he would have to do a better job eventually but sufficed for the time with ripping a piece of cloth from his red cloak, and wrapping it around his shoulder. A dark stain quickly spread across the red cloth, but after a while Andronicus could feel that it had mostly clotted.

Once his shoulder was tended to, he walked a good distance from the pool with the creature in it and then went about gathering some sticks and branches from the trees and bunching them together. After adding some of the tall grass to the pile, he looked around for the right rocks. Once he found some that he thought he could work with, he sat down to attempt a fire. He was only able to use his left hand, trying not to move enough to open the cuts back up.

It took nearly an hour, but eventually he was able to make himself a small fire. He walked back to where the dead lioness lay and began to skin its hind leg. He knew he could not take it with him, so he simply cut off a few good pieces of meat and went back to his fire. He picked out a nice sturdy stick and skewered a piece of lion flesh on it.

He stuck the other end of the stick in the dirt, so the meat rested just over the fire, then sat back to rest and enjoy the warmth. He couldn't help thinking that Archelaus would be proud of him for faring so well in such a strange and hostile wilderness. He chuckled to himself as he turned the meat over, wondering where in the world he was. Perhaps even more puzzling, where was everyone else?

5

As Andronicus sat cooking the meat of the beast that had nearly killed him, he watched the sun set, presumably in the west, although he couldn't be sure just yet. The sky turned an incredible array of colors as the sun sank, pinks and oranges and yellows and reds, and everything in between. It reminded him of the sunsets back home in Sparta. This sunset was a truly magnificent spectacle, and yet it was just a sunset, the same as he had always seen. Again he felt a soft sort of reassurance that he had not left the world behind completely.

As the sky turned black, he turned his attention to the fire and let his thoughts wander. He wondered where he was, where his friends were, and where his brother was. He wondered what had happened to them, and to him. He wondered if he was indeed dead. He wondered if he was in another world. He wondered more than he had ever wondered before. Most of all he wondered what that bright light had been. Even as he thought of it, he could feel the warmth return to him. He wished he knew what it was and what it had shown him. He knew that whatever the shadows had shown him had been important, but he couldn't remember any of it, only cryptic flashes: a desert, a storm, a mountain, and other things he didn't understand.

He took the cooked meat off the stick and pulled a long strip off with his teeth. He chewed the meat for a moment and was pleased with the result. After a moments consideration he decided that cooked lion meat was quite good indeed, especially when it came off the back of a lion that you killed yourself.

After his supper, Andronicus put out the fire and began walking again. He had no intention of sleeping anywhere near a dead carcass out in this foreign wilderness. He wondered briefly what would become of the rest of his kill and guessed it would go to the wild dogs he had seen earlier, them or the carrion birds. He had to think for a moment what other kinds of beasts might live in this land. Lions and elephants he had at least heard of before, but the other animals were all strange to him, and they were likely not the only ones. There was no telling what kind of monsters he might come across in this strange foreign place.

Andronicus stopped walking, and looked up at the night sky for a long time. The sky was filled with stars, as many as there always were, if not more. Even though the sky was filled with stars, he didn't recognize any of them. Back in Greece he had gotten rather good at what Philander called astrology. Andronicus knew he should be able to see many of the old constellations, but he couldn't. He could tell the stars here formed constellations of their own, but they all looked foreign and unfamiliar to him.

He kept walking, with no real idea why. It seemed less likely with each step that he would actually find his friends. He had no reason to believe they were even out there. Any kind of conventional logic seemed pointless; only wondrous and fantastical ideas seemed possible. It felt like he was in the most bizarre dream ever. Soon he would wake up and find himself lying in the dry beige dirt of Persia with his friends beside him. Even Niko would be there, because none of that had really happened; it had all just been a dream. Or perhaps they had never even left Greece. When he finally woke up, he would find himself in his own bed with Gaia next to him and his mother snoring in the other room.

Andronicus came upon a fallen tree and sat on its trunk, wishing things could be that simple. Life had always been simple, even when it wasn't. He had always known what to do, or at least where to go. Now he was completely lost and alone. It didn't even seem to be the same world. He was as naked and exposed as he had ever been in his life, and he wished desperately that he could talk to his brother, or Thymi, or even Lycus.

It had been dark for a long time, and his shoulder was stinging like nothing he had felt before. Andronicus stood up and looked around for any large animals. It was dark, but the moon was full, and the sky was clear. He could see a few horses in the distance, but other than that it seemed to be safe. Andronicus picked a nice spot next to the fallen tree, then laid his red cloak on the ground, noticing the few new inches that were gone from it. It was too dark to check his wound, and it felt dry, so Andronicus lay down for the night, hoping he would be safe from any terrible monsters that might be lurking around.

It was hard to fall asleep. His mind was racing with questions and thoughts, and images of all the beautiful and terrifying things he had seen that day. Andronicus stared up at the stars for a long time, wishing he recognized them, but feeling comfort in their presence nonetheless. He slid seamlessly from the night sky above him to the night sky all around him. He sat up and looked around, seeing blackness everywhere and stars in every direction, even below him. He looked down at himself, and saw clothes he didn't recognize at all. Fear gripped him, but before he could scream, the dream changed.

Suddenly, he was on his feet. He looked down, afraid to see stars again, but saw only dirt, normal brown dirt. He looked up, hoping he would see his friends, but instead he saw a tall dark man standing next to him. The man was looking off in the distance, but before Andronicus could ask him who he was, he was gone.

For a moment it felt like he was floating, and then somehow he was in a chair. Andronicus looked around, utterly confused, and then he saw his brother sitting across from him. Androcles looked different. He had much longer hair and an odd-looking shirt. Androcles opened his mouth to speak, and a loud trumpet blast blared.

Andronicus snapped awake in a panic. His cuts tore open as he reached for his sword, but he didn't even notice. He jumped to his feet, clutching his sword and gasping for air, then fell backwards as he saw a giant grey beast in front of him. He banged his head on the tree as he fell and let out another yell. The mighty beast scuttled away. Andronicus looked around in confusion as his head rang with pain.

After a minute of disorientation, he got to his feet and looked around. He was still in whatever strange land he had woken up in the day before. The giant grey beast joined a few others, and once he saw one of their tusks, Andronicus realized they were elephants. The tusks of an elephant were worth a fortune back in Greece, and he thought about trying to take one, before remembering he didn't know where Greece was.

He put his sword down and slowly sat back down, trying to remember his odd dreams. He had never had dreams like that. They were so vivid and real. The dreams were leaving his brain faster than he could remember them. All he could remember were brief flashes: his brother, but with long hair, a tall dark man, and the night sky below him. As he remembered that frightening image, he decided to let the dreams go. He knew there were many more, but he wasn't sure he wanted to recall them.

After sitting there for a long time, he stood up and threw his cloak over his shoulder. The sun was barely up, but it was already too hot to wear a cloak. Andronicus began to walk again, not knowing where he was going. He no longer thought he would find his friends, but perhaps he could find some people who could tell him where he was. Once he found out where this bizarre land was, he could find his way back to Greece, and hopefully find his friends there. That seemed like the only way to see them again now.

The sun rose, and more animals began appearing across the land. Andronicus stopped occasionally to drink. He was beginning to get hungry, and he wished he had taken more of the dead cat with him. There were plants all around him, but he didn't know anything about them. For all he knew every one of them was poisonous.

When the sun was all the way above him, he finally found some berries that looked like some of the berries he knew from back home. He knew how hard it would be to kill an animal with his wounded arm, so he decided he would try the berries. He popped a few of them in his mouth and sighed at the pleasant taste.

After eating half a handful of them, he sat on a rock not far away to wait and see if anything would happen to him. Eventually, he decided the berries were okay and went back to the bush. He ate most of the berries and then resumed his march to nowhere.

After a while his stomach began to hurt, and for a moment he feared the berries had indeed been poisonous, but then he thought he had just eaten too many too fast.

The day went by without incident. There were no more lions, but he did see most of the other animals from the first day. The tall horses were still his favorite, and at some point he changed his direction to follow them. He still didn't know which way anything was, so he figured it didn't really matter.

When it began to get dark, Andronicus started looking for food again. He saw a tall slow-looking bird sitting by a pool of water, and he walked toward it, staying low to the ground.

He was about to throw his sword at it when he spotted a perfect-sized rock. He picked it up and took careful aim with his left arm. He knew he would only get one shot, and he had to hope he wouldn't open his wounds yet again. After a few deep breaths, Andronicus threw the rock at the bird. His cuts opened again, and he winced in pain. The rock struck the bird in the side, and it let out a loud squawk, then stumbled to its left. Andronicus leapt at the bird, raising his sword.

The bird began to fly, but Andronicus brought his sword down in a quick blow. The bird let out another squawk, then fell over. Andronicus quickly drove his sword through the bird, then looked down at his shoulder. A light trickle of blood was running down his chest, but he ignored it.

He picked up the dead bird by its neck and started toward the nearest waterhole. When he reached it, he sat down in the dirt, took a quick drink, and then began plucking the bird, while keeping an eye on the water for more of the scaly beasts.

By the time Andronicus had the bird plucked and butchered and a small fire going, it was well after dark. The bird didn't have as much meat as he had hoped, so he roasted little strips, one at a time. The bird didn't taste nearly as good as the lion had, but it quelled his hunger all the same.

Andronicus ate all the stringy meat the bird had to offer and then sat by the fire for a long time, enjoying the warmth of the flames. He wished he could just lie down and go to sleep next to his fire, but after his rude awakening that morning, he wanted to sleep somewhere with better cover. He reluctantly got up, wincing at the pain in his shoulder, and kicked dirt over his fire.

Andronicus walked for another hour before he found another big waterhole. He drank his fill again and then saw a large flat tree nearby. The way the tree curved made him believe he might be able to climb it. It looked like the best cover he was going to find, so he walked over to it, trying to decide how best to get up. After getting a small running start, he managed to lift himself up the side of the large tree without tearing the cuts on his shoulder again and then climbed up into the canopy.

He found a nice flat spot in the tree's thick branches, then laid his cloak down for the night. As he lay back in the tree, he looked at the stars again. They seemed to be the only familiar thing in the world, and he didn't even recognize them. The moon was still full, and it gave him comfort to see the old familiar ball.

An animal screeched in the distance, but Andronicus ignored it, knowing he was safe in the tree. He was truly out in the wilderness now, like Thymi used to talk about when they were kids. He recalled the night of their first test, when he lay looking up at the stars with Euthymius. He wondered again where his friends were now. Were they all out there somewhere in their own strange land? Were they all back in that cave wondering where he had gone? Were they all dead?

His mind raced through a field of questions, none with any answers. The fear that he might be dead had mostly subsided, but the fear that he was no longer in the same world was still strong. He fell asleep with his mind bouncing from one question to the next.

As he slipped away from the tree and the foreign stars above him, he fell into a world of shadows. At first he saw magnificent landscapes. A sea of trees spread out below a hill, greener than any trees he had ever seen. A snowy mountain, stretching high above the clouds. A desert of sand, bigger than the sea of trees had been, bigger perhaps than a real sea.

After the desert he found himself in a room with high shelves, each lined with neat rows of rectangular leather objects. Sitting across from him was a balding man in a yellow robe, reading a scroll with careful precision. As the man looked up, he changed and became a boy with one brown eye and one blue. The boy stood up and looked like he was going to say something, and then the whole world fell away from Andronicus.

Chapter 13
Chaka
1

Andronicus awoke suddenly to the sound of shouting voices. He rolled over out of his sleep in an instant, and saw five tall dark skinned men standing at the foot of the tree. They were shouting up at him in a language he couldn't understand at all. Each of them held a long wooden spear, all pointed up at him. The spears were crudely made, bent and curved from the branches they were made from, and the blades were just sharpened rocks, but Andronicus knew they could pierce his skin easily enough.

He couldn't understand a word of what the men were saying; it sounded like odd gurgling to him, completely unlike any language he had ever heard before. They all had darker skin than anyone he had ever seen. The Persians had dark men in their army, but these men's skin was truly dark, like the night itself. They wore small cloths around their waists and nothing else. Each of them had to be at least seven feet tall, and their crooked wooden spears each looked to be ten feet long.

As the men shouted up at him in gibberish, they appeared to be getting more and more agitated. Andronicus raised his hands, to try to show them he wasn't a threat, and two of the men jumped back, thrusting their spears up at him. Andronicus hesitated a moment, wondering if he should strap on his armor. He hoped he wouldn't need it, and began slowly sliding down the side of the tree. When he was down the men quickly surrounded him, and all pointed their spears at him.

Andronicus tried to tell them he didn't want to fight, but they didn't understand him anymore than he did them. He still had his sword strapped to his side, but he didn't want to fight these men. Each one of them looked as strong as an ox, and his shoulder was still a pained bloody mess. One of the men stepped forward and started talking to Andronicus in their odd language. The man spoke for a while in a deep calm voice, and then looked at him expectantly. Andronicus had no idea what the giant man wanted from him.

He raised his left hand slowly and pointed at himself, and then pointed north, hoping they might simply let him go. The man standing beside the first man started yelling angrily, and then one of the other men started shouting as well. The leader shouted at the second man, who shouted back, and then they were all shouting. The one who had begun the shouting fell silent, and gave Andronicus a look of utter loathing.

Andronicus didn't know what the men were saying, but he knew what that look meant. Just as the angry man stepped forward and lunged his spear, Andronicus stepped lithely to his left. He drew his sword with his left hand, and flipped it around in a quick motion. Before the man even knew Andronicus was armed, he brought the sword up above his head. The man tried to pull back his spear, but Andronicus struck down on it as hard as he could. He felt the wood of the man's spear splinter into pieces under his heavy blow.

Two of the other men shouted in outrage and flung themselves at Andronicus. He moved swiftly and confidently, striking first one spear, and then the next. They were fast, but clearly untrained, and his sword deflected the spears expertly as he stepped toward the man nearest him. Andronicus ducked again and hit the man's spear before lunging forward and punching the man hard in the gut with his right hand.

Pain seared through his shoulder as he felt the cuts reopen. He kicked the man's spear away, but before he could hit him again, a big black fist hit him hard in the face.

Andronicus took a step backward, feeling a bit dazed, and looked around. He was surprised to see that the other three men had all backed off. The man who had hit him stepped back as well, and the angry man who had started it all stepped forward. He dropped the broken end of his spear and glared at Andronicus with wild furious eyes. Andronicus did not need to be able to talk to him to recognize the challenge. The other four men stepped back, apparently ready to allow Andronicus to face the man alone. Andronicus flipped his sword around and placed it back in its sheath, and raised his hands to fight. Blood was again trickling down his chest from his wounds, but he ignored it.

The other men stood silently and watched as Andronicus and his single attacker slowly stalked each other. Andronicus had never seen a bigger man in his life. These men all seemed to be giants, but this one was definitely the biggest. His entire body was covered in large flexing muscles, and his big balled fists looked big enough to crush a man's skull. The gigantic angry man stood hunched over, and still towered over him.

Andronicus and his challenger waited a moment longer, glaring each other down, slowly circling each other. Andronicus had enough time to wish he had strapped on his armor. He took one last deep breath, and then the tall man lunged forward. He moved quicker than Andronicus had expected, and he wasn't able to get out of the way in time. The man struck Andronicus on the side of the head with a big powerful hand, and grabbed his right shoulder, trying to bring him down. Andronicus let out a howl of pain as the wounds on his shoulder tore wide open. He could feel warm blood spreading across his chest as he regained his balance.

Andronicus gathered himself quickly and punched the man hard in the gut twice, ignoring the pain. The man bent over and Andronicus punched him several times in the face before he flung himself on Andronicus. The man outweighed him, but Andronicus was trained for combat. He was able to turn the man mid fall, and he landed hard on his head. Andronicus quickly jumped on top of him, and started pummeling the man's face with both hands.

He beat the man relentlessly, pounding down as hard as he could, not giving him a chance to even defend himself. When Andronicus felt hands on his shoulders pulling him up, the man under him was covered in almost as much blood as he was. Two of the others pulled Andronicus off their comrade, and threw him into the dirt with frightening ease.

Andronicus reached for his sword, but felt only air. He looked down and saw that his sword was gone. One of the men was holding it, and all four of them were now standing over him. The man who had first spoken stepped forward again. He said something Andronicus couldn't understand, and then offered Andronicus his hand. Andronicus moved to defend himself at first, and then realized the man wasn't threatening him.

They all seemed to be eyeing him differently now, as if he were some kind of strange and intriguing thing they had never seen before. He hesitated a moment before taking the man's hand. The man pulled him up in one quick easy motion. Once Andronicus was on his feet, they looked each other in the eye for a long time, sizing each other up. Andronicus had never had to bend his neck more to look a man in the eye.

After a long time, the man finally lifted his hand and pointed at himself. "Chaka," he said in his strong, deep voice. Andronicus nodded, then pointed at himself, and offered his own name. As Andronicus said his name, the men looked at each other in amusement, as if not understanding it. Andronicus said his name again more clearly, and Chaka replied with "Jocus." Andronicus figured it was close enough for now and nodded. He pointed to himself and said "Jocus," then pointed at Chaka, and said "Chaka." Chaka broke into a wide grin and clapped Andronicus on his uninjured shoulder. He said something to the others, and they laughed.

The man whom Andronicus had beaten up had gotten to his feet and was walking toward them, his face still a bloody mess. He shouted something, and looked like he would fight Andronicus again, but Chaka stepped in front of him and spoke with the man for some time. Andronicus heard the word "Jocus" used more than once, and the man finally seemed to back down, though he still looked furious. They walked back to where Andronicus and the other three stood. Chaka pointed to himself again, saying "Chaka," then to Andronicus and said "Jocus." Then he pointed at the man Andronicus had fought and called him Kwesi. Chaka introduced the other three as Obi, Dayo, and Chiomi.

When the introductions were complete, Chaka pointed west and said something to the group. Then they started walking off in that direction. Andronicus wasn't sure if he was meant to follow them or not. He didn't know what these men wanted from him or whether he was now their captive, but the one called Dayo was still holding his sword, and he knew he could not survive this place without it.

Andronicus called out to them to wait. They stopped and turned around, though he knew they didn't know what he was saying. He ran back to the tree, climbed up and grabbed his cloak and armor, then climbed back down. As he strapped on his armor and threw the cloak over his shoulder, the men stared at his bronze armor with wide, curious eyes.

Chaka reached out and touched the metal,
then quickly withdrew his hand, completely fascinated
by it. Andronicus realized they had never seen metal
before. He laughed as they all bent down to admire his
armor. Chaka reached out again, and touched the dent
in the armor that the lion's claws had made. He drew
his finger along the line until it reached the connecting
line on Andronicus' bloody shoulder. Chaka looked up
at him in surprise, and Andronicus nodded.

Chaka took a step back, utterly bewildered.
The other men were all standing back as well, staring
at the armor in awe. Andronicus laughed again and
banged twice on the chest plate with his fist. It emitted
a dull clang, which he was more than used to, but the
men all jumped back at the sound. They looked from
Andronicus's armor to each other and then back to the
armor. They talked to each other in their odd language
and then looked back at him.

Andronicus wasn't sure what they wanted, so
he pointed west, where they had been walking. Chaka
nodded and said something to the others. They all
nodded and then began walking again, though they
continued to stare at his armor. Andronicus walked
with them, having no idea where they were headed.
He followed the strange men blindly across the plains,
again wondering where in the world he was.

2

The six of them marched through the hot, open
plains mostly in silence. Occasionally, someone would
say something to the others, and they would either
nod or laugh and then fall silent. Andronicus walked in
the middle of the group, between Obi and Chaka.
Kwesi walked off to the side, shooting glaring looks
Andronicus's way. He was reminded of how Lycus used
to glare at him when they were kids after Lycus had
been beaten.

The sun rose steadily as they walked. When it
reached its peak, Chaka stopped the group at a small
water hole to rest. Kwesi and Chiomi went off to the
east without a word. Andronicus assumed they were

going to get food. He sat in silence with his supposed captors as they all drank from the murky pool of water.

Kwesi and Chiomi returned not long after with a bundle of large fruit. Kwesi handed two to Chaka and Obi and then spit on a third and threw it down at Andronicus's feet. Andronicus glared at Kwesi's bruised and swollen face as the rest watched, and for a moment Andronicus thought he would have to fight the man again. Thankfully, Kwesi turned to eat his lunch, but not before spitting once more on Andronicus's fruit.

Andronicus picked up his fruit and cleaned it off, wishing he had his sword. He took a bite of the colorful fruit and was pleasantly surprised. It was quite good. While the others ate, Chiomi began crunching a bunch of leaves and berries with his hands. When he seemed satisfied with the result, he walked over to Andronicus and nodded at his bloody shoulder, holding his hands out. Chiomi said something Andronicus couldn't understand, but he knew what he was asking. Chaka said something as well, nodding in approval.

Andronicus looked at the grey-green slimy mess in Chiomi's hands. It smelled foul, but he reluctantly reached up and removed the bloody rag from his shoulder, wincing at the way it clung to the wound. The wound was a series of dark red lines crusted in dried blood. It had begun to smell, and Andronicus turned his head away as Chiomi rubbed the concoction into his shoulder.

Andronicus was surprised at how good it felt. He had expected the slimy mess to burn, but it soothed the pain right away. Chiomi spread it across the four cuts, covering them entirely. Once the wounds were no longer visible under the slime, Chiomi gave Andronicus a curt nod and went back to his place by Obi. Andronicus wasn't sure how long he was supposed to keep the stuff on, but he trusted that Chiomi would let him know.

3

When they were done eating, they resumed

their march. They walked the rest of the day, seeing many strange beasts along the way. Andronicus saw large herds of the striped horses and the orange deer. He even saw a herd of eight of the tall horses walking together. Obi spotted a pride of lions in the distance, and the group made sure to give them a wide berth. Chaka pointed toward the lions, then pointed at Andronicus' shoulder with a questioning look. Andronicus nodded, and they all looked impressed, even Kwesi.

As they passed a large waterhole, Andronicus saw a huge, fat grey animal like he had never seen before. It walked slowly and clumsily toward the water before opening its imposingly large mouth to drink. Andronicus was amazed at the size of the beast's mouth, and thought a child could fit inside it.

When the sun set, the group found a good patch of dirt away from the grass and lay down for the night. Dayo stood guard, and Andronicus assumed the others would take shifts. Again he lay awake for a long while, his mind whirling with questions. So far the only answer he felt sure of was that he was not dead. Other than that he had no idea where he was or how to get back home. He also wondered where the others were, and if they had woken to find themselves in a strange land as he did. Were they somewhere near, searching for him? Or were they right where he left them, and he was the only one who had been pulled away? Perhaps they were all dead, and only he had made the journey.

He fell asleep sometime later and had an awful dream of the fat grey beast eating him whole. As the huge mouth closed on him, he snapped awake with a start. He sat up slowly, making sure not to move his right arm. For an instant he hoped they might all be sleeping, and he could take his sword back, but Dayo was still wide awake. He was looking up at the stars, but Andronicus knew that he was aware of him. As if he had heard the thought, Dayo turned to look at Andronicus with a peaceful but attentive expression on his face.

Andronicus lay back down on his cloak, and

Dayo returned his gaze to the sky. The thought of the fat grey beast from his dream kept Andronicus awake for a while, but eventually he fell back to sleep.

In his dream, he found himself on the deck of a ship in a terrible storm. The wind howled all around, and rain whipped at his face. Andronicus turned to look around the ship and saw Dayo, sitting cross-legged on the deck, looking peacefully up at the sky. Rain poured over his face, but he stared unblinkingly up into the dark night. Andronicus started to walk toward him, but someone came up behind him and grabbed his arm.

4

In the midst of his dream, Andronicus felt a hand shaking his arm, and the storm fell away. He opened his eyes, and saw Chaka kneeling over him. The sun had not yet risen, but light had begun to spread across the plains. Andronicus rose, trying to forget his dreams, and saw that Obi was already roasting some meat over a small fire. The men ate their breakfast as they seemed to eat all their meals, in silence.

When they had all eaten their fill, Obi put out the fire, and they got underway. Andronicus had no idea where they were taking him, but he followed nonetheless. They walked the whole day again, seeing all the many beasts of these lands. At sunset they stopped and set up for the night.

They did this for six days before they reached their destination, the five men taking turns gathering food and setting up fires. Andronicus simply walked, ate the food that was given to him, slept, dreamed his wild dreams, and then began the whole process over again.

The burning in his shoulder had gone down a little more each day since Chiomi had put the ointment on it. Andronicus wasn't sure how long he was meant to keep the stuff on, but so far it had been four days. On the fifth day it simply crumbled off his arm, revealing a still ugly, but much better looking scar that had begun to form. Chiomi looked at the wound in an odd way when he inspected it, as if he had expected it to be even more healed than it was. Andronicus, however, was pleasantly surprised by the effect.

The next day, the sixth day since Chaka and his party had found Andronicus, a small mountain appeared on the horizon. It didn't take him long to realize they were walking toward it. It was the first mountain he had seen since he had woken up here. It wasn't a huge mountain, less than half the size of the mountain the cave had been under, but it ran well out of sight along the horizon.

When they finally reached the base of the mountain the next day, Andronicus thought they would take a rest and eat, but the others simply started up the mountain without stopping. Andronicus would have liked a breather before embarking on such a steep climb, but had no choice but to follow the others up the slope, trying not to use his right arm for support.

It took them several hours to reach the top. By then Andronicus was panting for breath and trying hard not to pass out, but the others all seemed fine. Andronicus looked down and saw a small village lying on the other side of the mountain. Obi climbed a high rock and retrieved a long, twisted horn that lay there. It looked like it had belonged to some magnificent beast. He gave the horn three loud blows. It sounded different than any horn Andronicus had heard, Greek or Persian. The three short blasts were high and long, a clear greeting call.

As soon as the last blast from the horn rang out, Andronicus saw people emerging from the huts in the village and gathering at the base of the mountain. They looked small from this height, but he could tell the village was most likely more than fifty people strong.

They descended the mountain much faster than they had climbed it. Andronicus had to step carefully so as not to lose his footing and tumble down. When they reached the bottom, a great commotion arose as the people saw Andronicus. Some people screamed and shouted, but most people just stared in fascination.

Obi and Dayo each embraced a woman, and

Chiomi greeted two young children. Chaka and Kwesi instantly began a heated conversation with an older man wearing a big frilly headdress. As Andronicus's new acquaintances joined their people, a circle formed around him. Men, women, and children all gathered to stare at him. There was much chatter and many big round eyes. Kwesi and Chaka's conversation grew louder and louder until the old man shouted something, and Kwesi stormed off.

Chaka led the man over to Andronicus and introduced Andronicus as Jocus. Then he introduced the tall, stoic-looking man as Challah. Challah said something to the crowd, and they all broke into chatter again. Challah spoke for a while, none of it discernible to Andronicus, until the crowd started to disperse, and people went back to their huts.

Chaka led Andronicus to a small clay hut in the middle of the village. Chaka rested his hand on the hut and said "Jocus." Andronicus understood and was flattered. He wasn't sure whether they had accepted him because of the lion wound, his armor, what he had done to Kwesi, or simply out of kindness, but they clearly had accepted him, at least temporarily.

He had to duck his head to enter the hut. In it he found a cot made up for him. Andronicus turned to Chaka and nodded. Chaka smiled and clapped him on the back before leaving him alone for the first time in days. Andronicus wondered what Dayo had done with his sword. He would have to wait until he could get it back before he could leave. In the meantime, these people seemed to be friendly enough. For the first time since waking up in this strange new land, Andronicus actually felt safe.

Chapter 14
Swihmehe
1

Andronicus stayed in the little mud hut for the rest of the day, not yet ready to go out and face all the people. They seemed nice enough, but he didn't like the way they all stared at him, like he was some kind of alien.

As the sun began to set, he heard people gathering on the far side of the village, accompanied by the sound of drums beating. He also saw the glow of what could only be a large bonfire.

Chaka arrived to fetch him, a pretty young woman in tow. She smiled brightly at Andronicus, and he lowered his guard slightly. She had the biggest, whitest teeth he had ever seen. She said something to him, pointing toward the fire, and he nodded and got up.

"Manyara," Chaka said in his deep, calm voice, pointing to her. Andronicus nodded and repeated the name. He assumed the girl was Chaka's wife, and he was surprised when he felt a pang of jealousy. At that moment he felt a pang of guilt as well, realizing he hadn't thought of his own wife even once since waking up in this strange land. He knew he should be thinking about getting back to Gaia, but he wasn't. He was thinking about getting back to his friends, his brother, his mother, and Sparta, but he hadn't thought of Gaia once until now. He admired Manyara's physical stature as they walked, and wondered why she made him think of Gaia.

Manyara was tall, like all the people there, though not nearly as tall as Chaka. She stood only a few inches shorter than Andronicus, and had a tight, muscular body, fitter than any woman he had ever seen. He could tell she was young, though not as young as Gaia had been when they married. She looked nothing like the girls he knew back in Sparta, including Gaia. Gaia was short and olive skinned and a bit pudgy from her life of leisure. Looking at Manyara, he had never been more impressed with a woman in his life.

When they arrived at the bonfire, everyone turned to stare at Andronicus. The drums ceased, and a hush fell over the crowd. For a moment the only noise was the crackling of the immense fire. Andronicus felt like they were waiting for him to say something, but he couldn't speak their language.

The tall, somber man named Challah stood up, and everyone turned to face him. He began speaking to the crowd, too fast for Andronicus to make out anything. He had been trying to learn what he could of their language, but had only managed to pick up a few words, none of which he was sure of. When Challah stopped speaking, he and everyone else turned back to Andronicus.

"Jocus," Challah said. Andronicus wasn't sure what to do. He stood up and lowered his head before the man, hoping it would be taken as a sign of respect. There was a soft murmur from the crowd, and Andronicus hoped it wasn't bad. Challah said something else, then put his hand on his chest. Andronicus had an inkling that Challah was telling him he was the chief. Andronicus nodded slowly, and Challah nodded back.

Challah walked over to where Chaka sat, and Chaka jumped to his feet. Challah touched Chaka's shoulder and said something that sounded like "gitembo." Andronicus wasn't sure, but he thought he was saying that Chaka was his son, which Andronicus already knew to be true. Chaka and Challah looked exactly alike, and their names made it all but certain.

Challah moved on to Kwesi, who also rose, repeating the word. Andronicus was not surprised; he had already guessed that Chaka and Kwesi were brothers. He guessed that since Chaka had part of Challah's name and was introduced first, he was the older son and likely the next in line to lead the village, if they did things that way here.

Then, to Andronicus's surprise, Challah stepped in front of Manyara, and she stood as well. Challah touched her shoulder and said a word that sounded like "gitembo," only slightly different. Andronicus wasn't sure whether Manyara was Chaka's wife or sister; either seemed plausible.

After Challah had introduced all five of his children to Andronicus, he walked around the fire, addressing all the people again.

"Swihmehe," Challah said, turning to Andronicus. Several women yipped in response, and nearly all the men began stamping their feet in the dirt. The drums started pounding again, and men and women got up and began dancing around the fire. Andronicus watched in awe. He had never seen anything like it. Their large, muscled bodies swayed the way the oracles did in old Spartan tales.

As the drumming and dancing continued, large slabs of meat were thrown over the fire. Various fruits were passed around, and the next thing Andronicus knew, the whole village was having a feast, all in his honor, as far as he could tell. He sat next to Chaka and Manyara and tried to learn what words he could.

At one point he was asking Manyara how to say "hut" when Chaka appeared carrying a clay bowl. He bent down and held it out for Andronicus. The bowl was full of brown, chunky liquid with some kind of meat in it. Andronicus took it from Chaka, not wanting to offend him, and lifted the bowl to his face. He took a deep whiff. It made his nostrils sting and his eyes water, but it smelled surprisingly good.

Andronicus looked at Manyara, and she gave him an approving nod. He turned back to Chaka, gave him a nod of thanks, then brought the bowl up to his lips and drank a big gulp, eating a piece of the meat as well. At first it tasted good, but in an instant his mouth went from enjoying the food to being completely on fire. Andronicus dropped the bowl and began coughing as the stew burned his throat. For a moment his ears rang, and then he heard laughter.

He looked up through his tears and saw Chaka roaring with laughter. Challah was also laughing, as was Dayo and most of the tribe, from what he could tell. Even Manyara was struggling to hold back a smile. Dayo handed Andronicus a bowl of water, still laughing, and Andronicus gulped it down. A moment later Manyara offered a small yellow fruit, and Andronicus ate it. It soothed the burning somewhat, although his mouth still stung.

Andronicus turned to Chaka with a furrowed brow, and Chaka burst into laughter again. There was no malice in it, and after a moment, Andronicus was able to join in the laughter as well. After that the dancing resumed, and Andronicus went back to trying to learn new words.

Manyara was quite good at teaching him. By the time the feast was over, and people were returning to their huts, Andronicus was confident he had learned the names of at least two of the fruits and was positive that "gyioto" meant fire, though he couldn't say it correctly no matter how many times he tried.

Andronicus found himself really laughing for the first time in weeks. Even before the storm and the mountain he had been sullen. Ever since Niko died, everything had been all wrong. But now Andronicus smiled and basked in the warmth of these kind, generous people, and Manyara's gentle smile.

When the night was over, and the fire had burned low, most of the villagers back in their huts, and Kwesi and Chaka were both snoring loudly in the dirt, Manyara walked Andronicus back to his hut. He wanted to take her inside, to lay her down, and take her then and there, but he knew that was a bad idea, even if she would have him. He had been lucky to find these people and have them take him in rather than kill him, and he was sure that sleeping with the chief's oldest daughter on the first night would not be well received.

Andronicus had to settle for a soft touch of her hand. It felt smooth against his calloused fingers, and he didn't want to let go. He stared into her big brown eyes for a long time, and she stared right back into his sharp green ones. Perhaps it was because they couldn't communicate with words, but Andronicus had never stared into anyone's eyes like that. They couldn't say a thing to each other, but in that moment they both felt each other, and knew.

Finally, she pulled her hand back from his and said something like "dyoto." Andronicus had no idea what it meant, so he just smiled and tried to repeat it. Manyara giggled as he failed to say whatever it was, and he smiled back. He felt warm for the first time in months.

She turned away and skipped off toward the fire. Andronicus watched her go, then went into his hut. He still had a thousand questions, but suddenly they all seemed less important. He thought about the people here, about Chaka and Chiomi and Chief Challah, and especially Manyara, and he thought that perhaps he could stay here for a while.

2

Andronicus learned quickly that the Swihmehe were an efficient people; everyone served a purpose. The hunters and gatherers always came back with food, and the builders kept the huts together. They were a simpler people than Andronicus had ever seen, and yet they lived well. They had no tools that weren't made of stone, and their huts were made of mud and sticks. Back home these people would be called barbarians or even savages for living as they did, but Andronicus didn't think of them that way at all.

Over time he began to learn their language. The days turned to weeks and the weeks to months as Andronicus gradually learned the ways of the Swihmehe. In the mornings he would go hunting with Chaka and his troupe, learning their ways of the hunt one day at a time, and teaching them a few things as well. In the evenings he would take language lessons from Manyara. Between Chaka and Manyara, Andronicus soon began to understand the Swihmehe language well enough to get by.

He found the people absolutely fascinating, especially the way they lived so peacefully with the land. They didn't take any more than they needed, and they didn't build anything more than their simple huts. They didn't have a house of worship or a barracks for soldiers. They didn't have a blacksmith or even a baker, but it didn't matter; they didn't need them. The only hut that didn't look exactly like the rest was Challah's, which stood on the far side of the village, next to the mountain.

They didn't have any of the pillars of civilization that the Greeks took pride in. They didn't have temples or libraries, and they didn't sow the land. They were, in essence, savages, at least to the average Greek. And yet they seemed happier than the Greeks, more at peace with the land. They ate what the land provided for them. They slept when the sun slept, and they rose with it in the morning. They had so much less, and yet they seemed to be so much more content.

It made Andronicus wonder if this wasn't a better way to live. Society seemed to be a wonderful idea, meant for civilized people. Those who lived without what the Greeks considered necessary were seen as savages. But Andronicus hadn't seen any savagery so far. In Sparta savagery had been a way of life. He had been raised for war and had gone to war at only sixteen. In his years in Swimha, he had only seen four men die. Three of them were killed in the hunt, and the fourth fell climbing the mountain.

For all the fear of savagery and lawlessness, their society seemed to be far less savage than so-called civilization. It came as a shock to Andronicus, and it made him curious. He had always taken it for granted that the Spartans lived the best life anyone could, but now he wasn't so sure. The Swihmehe lived in peace alongside other tribes in the area. Andronicus had seen them on hunts before, and Chaka always steered clear of them, but they didn't go to war. Apparently, there had been fights in the past, but not for many years.

Even though the Swihmehe lived like savages and had so little compared to the Greeks, they also had things the Greeks did not. The Swihmehe used herbs and medicines that Andronicus had never heard of before, like the stuff Chiomi had put on his shoulder, and many others. An old bald man named Grito was the village healer, and Chiomi was his apprentice. Every other day one of them would find Andronicus and apply a new layer of muck to his shoulder. He didn't know what they were putting on him, but it seemed to be working, though not nearly as fast as they seemed to expect. The cuts slowly began to heal over the growing years. Within the first year the cuts had sealed, and a few years after that they were nothing but four long rough white lines in his skin.

Once his shoulder was healed, Andronicus was able to truly learn the Swihmehe ways of the hunt. In Greece he had hunted deer and boar and once even a black bear. In the land of Swimha, the game was far more abundant.

The fields where the animals roamed were flat and open, with only the tall grass to conceal the hunters. The Swihmehe learned their hunting skills from the beasts themselves. Their favorite tactic was for some of the men to creep through the grass until they were near their prey, as the lions did. The rest of hunters would charge from the other side, just as the wild dogs did. The herd would flee directly into the waiting hunters' spears, giving them a few kills each time. Andronicus taught Chaka and the other hunters about tracking, but the game was plentiful enough that they didn't need it.

Andronicus was able to prove himself a worthy hunter over time. Two years after he arrived in Swimha, he was made an official member of the tribe. He still wasn't sure why they had accepted him so graciously. He had tried several times to tell them how he had gotten there, but they didn't seem to understand, not that he understood either. They didn't seem to care how he had come to their land, just that he was strong and useful.

There was a big bonfire the night he joined the tribe, much like the one on his first night. The people cheered and danced and feasted in his honor. By then Andronicus knew enough words to have conversations, and when he didn't know a word, he knew how to ask Manyara.

It hadn't taken Andronicus long to fall in love with the Swihmehe people and the land of Swimha, and it took even less time for him to fall in love with Manyara. He had first lain with Manyara a few months before the ceremony. By the time he was being indoctrinated, he hoped they would be able to stop hiding their affair. He still felt guilty about betraying Gaia's trust and his own sacred vows, but he could not deny the way he felt about Manyara, and he didn't want to.

Andronicus knew that Chaka was aware of them and that he approved, or rather, he didn't disapprove. Challah seemed to like him quite a bit as well, and Andronicus hoped Challah would be accepting. It was Kwesi that worried him the most. He had not warmed to Andronicus at all since their brutal fight that first day, and he would often find a reason to pull his sister away from Andronicus. He just hoped he wouldn't have to fight Kwesi again.

When the day finally came for his induction, Andronicus stood before Challah, the whole village looking on, and took his vows. Manyara had made sure he knew the words. When Challah finished his bit, Andronicus began speaking in the Swihmehe language as best he could.

"I, Jocus, promise to keep the ways of the Swihmehe," Andronicus recited, carefully enunciating every word in the foreign tongue. "I promise to protect my own and keep the peace of the land. I promise to follow the path of the great elephant." Andronicus had learned rather quickly how much the Swihmehe admired, and practically worshiped the elephants. "I vow to keep the elephant and the Swihmehe in my heart until the day I die."

Andronicus wasn't sure he had gotten it all right, and he wasn't even sure what half the words meant, but Challah and the rest of the village all seemed to be content with his response. Challah began speaking again, most of which Andronicus couldn't understand, and turned back to the tribe. When Challah was done, he turned to Andronicus and nodded, and everyone began cheering and whooping. Within seconds they were all on their feet, dancing and celebrating. Andronicus joined them as a fellow tribesman for the first time.

3

One day Andronicus was out hunting on the plains with Chaka, Kwesi, Obi, and Dayo, and a few others. They were two days away from the village, following a small herd of water buffalo. When they finally caught up to the herd, Andronicus made his way around them, being the stealthiest in the group. He took aim with his long spear and then threw it at the nearest buffalo. The spear hit it just above the neck, taking it down in one shot. The beast let out an awful moaning howl, then keeled over.

The hunters ran over to it and quickly went about building a sort of gurney to carry it home. It took nearly an hour, and when they lifted it Andronicus couldn't believe how heavy the buffalo was. Nevertheless, the seven of them carried it all the way back to the village.

It took them two and a half days. When they got back, Andronicus was dead tired and sore all over. He limped over to his hut, wincing at the pain in his back, and found Manyara there waiting for him. He lay down and eagerly started trying to tell her about the hunt, and his kill.

"Tell me about something other than the killing," Manyara said after a few minutes. "What other animals did you see?"

"The same we always see," Andronicus said slowly, still needing to reach for every word. "Zebras, giraffes, elephants. But we cannot kill them; it is against your father's rules."

"They are not my father's rules," Manyara said as she lay back against Andronicus's chest. "They have been the ways of our people forever."

"They are not bad rules," Andronicus said, running his hand through her coarse black hair. "Some animals are too good to kill."

"You think too much about killing, Jocus," Manyara said. "I know you say your people like killing, but you must let it go."

"It is not that my people like killing," Andronicus said, not quite sure that was true. "We are just the best at it. That is the way of my people. I cannot help it, really. I was taught how to fight my whole life."

"Your life is not over," Manyara said, sitting up and looking Andronicus in the eye. "Just because you have fought and killed does not mean your future will be full of fighting and killing. I once heard of a man who walked the land until he was old, and when he got home, he never left his hut again."

Andronicus let out a hearty laugh, then leaned

forward to kiss Manyara. He didn't believe he could ever let go of his Spartan ways, but he felt like he could try for her.

"What will I do if I cannot fight?" Andronicus asked with a smile when they broke away.

She smiled back at him. "You could be a husband . . . and a father. I know my father will give us his blessing."

"No more fighting then," Andronicus said, gazing into her eyes. They kissed again and then let things go where they would.

4

A few years after being accepted into the tribe, Andronicus finally married Manyara. Challah led the ceremony and seemed even more pleased than Andronicus could have hoped. Most of the Swihmehe people still viewed Andronicus as an outsider, but many also viewed him as a folk hero. Challah and Chaka were impressed not only with his skills with his blade but also with the blade itself, not to mention the red cloak he still had with him and his dented but still shiny bronze armor.

On the night of their wedding, Andronicus dressed in his full Spartan attire, donning his armor and strapping his scabbard to his side. He had only been wearing his breastplate in the cave, and it was all he had left of his once-magnificent armor. He wished he had brought his helmet; he knew the Swihmehe would have loved seeing the frilly red plume atop it.

As he threw his cloak over his shoulders, a momentary wave of guilt washed over him. The faces of his friends ran across his mind's eye, not his new friends in Swimha but his old friends: Thymi and Theo and Lycus, and especially his brother. He wondered for the thousandth time where Androcles was. He wondered if Androcles was searching for him or if he was settling down in some strange foreign land just as Andronicus was. He also wondered if Androcles had stayed behind in the cave and was now back home in Sparta, mourning Andronicus alongside their mother. As always the train of questions led to the looming possibility that Androcles was dead, followed immediately by the still prominent possibility that Andronicus himself was dead.

He shook his head and tried to rid himself of the dark thoughts. He was getting married—again—and he didn't need to think about death and loss. There were never any answers anyway. He had no mirror or glass to look at himself in, so he drew his sword. The blade maintained its polished shine, and Andronicus looked at himself in its reflection. He had not cut his hair since arriving in Swimha, yet it barely brushed his shoulders. He had used his old knife to shave that morning, and double-checked his handiwork in the sword's reflection.

When he was satisfied that he looked decent, he stepped out of his hut, where Chaka stood waiting for him. Chaka's youngest brother stood next to him, beaming excitedly at them. Chaka looked Andronicus over, staring for a long time at his cloak.

"Does everyone in your land wear such clothes?" Chaka asked in his deep voice.

"No," Andronicus answered in Swihmehe. He was able to manage conversations well enough now. "Only Spartan warriors wear them."

"Warriors or hunters?" Chaka asked, tilting his head to examine the cloak more closely.

"Warriors," Andronicus said firmly. "Everyone in Sparta is a hunter. These cloaks are only for soldiers. And this armor was made by the finest . . ." He hesitated, not sure how to say "blacksmith" in Swihmehe, or if they would even understand. He settled for saying the word in Greek. "The finest blacksmith in the world."

As expected, Chaka and the young boy gave him an odd look when he said the word "blacksmith." He spent the next ten minutes trying to explain what metal was.

When they arrived at the great fire pit on the edge of town, where all ceremonies took place, they found the whole village waiting. A good number of people eyed Andronicus with disdain as he stepped forward in his Spartan armor and red cloak. Most, however, looked happy and more than ready to celebrate. One thing he had learned about the Swihmehe was that they loved to celebrate and have feasts. They didn't even need a reason, but when they had one, the celebrations were even greater.

Andronicus walked over to where Manyara was waiting for him. She was wearing a simple brown dress and a purple flower in her hair. Andronicus looked a little silly next to her in his fine Spartan attire, but he didn't care; she looked perfect.

Challah came forward, and a hush fell over the crowd. They stood silently, waiting for their noble leader to speak.

When he did begin speaking, Andronicus concentrated as hard as possible on the words; he still had trouble understanding Challah sometimes. Then Andronicus and Manyara stood together before the chief and spoke the words of the Swihmehe people.

"I take this woman to be my wife," Andronicus said as she gazed at him adoringly. "I will watch over her all of my days." Flashbacks of the day he had married Gaia filled his head, but he quickly shoved them away. "I will meet her again in the great lands beyond," Andronicus continued. "I shall father her children and teach them the ways of the Swihmehe. I shall love this woman, and only this woman, until the day I die." He felt an odd sort of guilt as he spoke such similar words to those he had spoken in Greece in front of his friends and family.

Andronicus and Manyara knelt side by side before Challah, who chanted the old words of their people. When he finished, the crowd cheered, and Andronicus and Manyara rose as man and wife. He took the cloak from his back and wrapped it around her shoulders. It was not a Swihmehe custom, but everyone cheered nonetheless. Andronicus felt guilty about remarrying, but he was committed. He was in a strange, distant land, and had found a woman he loved. He knew his old life was truly gone now.

By the third course of the great feast, everyone in the village was smiling and having a good time from what Andronicus could tell; everyone except

Kwesi. As Andronicus had feared, the huge man had not taken kindly to him marrying his sister. Kwesi glared at him the whole night until finally Chaka sent him away. Andronicus had expected Kwesi to act as such and was actually surprised he hadn't done more. He had not, however, expected Obi to be glaring at him all night as well. At one point he asked Chaka what Obi's problem was, and Chaka told him Obi had always loved Manyara, ever since they had been children. Andronicus understood and didn't think any more of it as he went back to the celebration.

5

After marrying Manyara, everything seemed to fall into place for Andronicus. Not a day went by that he didn't think about his friends and about the many questions he still had, but he was able to settle down. He didn't know where Greece was, how to get back there, if his friends would be there, or if they were even alive. What he did know was that he had a good life here, as good as he ever had in Sparta.

In Sparta he had been a renowned warrior and an honored member of the community. He had great friends and got to live with his family. He had been married to a beautiful and powerful woman, and they had made love every night. But he realized now that was all they had done. His life in Sparta had been a sham, an empty shell, not what he wanted for himself but what he had been told to want by the culture in which he had grown up.

He had never truly loved Gaia. He had made love to her and told himself he cared, but the way he felt about Manyara, he hadn't even known such feelings were possible. She made him want to be something different than he had always been, something better. He remembered the way his mother always talked about his father and liked to think it was a bit like that.

Over the years Andronicus grew to truly be one of the Swihmehe. He hunted and walked the land with Chaka and Dayo and spent his nights with Manyara.

Once they had been married for years, they

began to wonder why Manyara had not taken with child. Grito did some strange tests, moving his hands along their bodies, inspecting their most private areas. When he was done, he pronounced them both physically fit for conception, though Andronicus had no idea how the old man had reached that conclusion.

The years passed, and Andronicus grew more and more comfortable in Swimha. The questions never left, but he learned to live with them. He still didn't know how he had come to find the Swihmehe people, but he had decided it was meant to be. He no longer felt the need to see Greece again. He was more than happy to stay with the Swihmehe until he died. It wasn't as if Andronicus let go of his past completely, but he gradually committed himself to his new life.

He spoke openly and often with Manyara and Chaka about his past. He told them about his old life, his friends, and his family. He told them about Greece and the war he had fought in as a boy. He even told them all that he could remember about the day that had brought him to Swimha. Chaka always listened, but Andronicus could tell he didn't believe or understand most of what he was saying. Manyara knew him well enough to know it was all true though. She was fascinated with his stories. Part of him wished he could bring her back home to Greece to see it all, but he knew that would never happen.

The thing that made it difficult to stay, however, were his dreams. They had become less frequent as he settled into his new life, but they never went away. He had always had dreams, but they had seemed meaningless to him before. Most nights he would still have normal dreams, but some nights he would have a different kind of dream, dreams that were far too real and bizarre beyond belief. It wasn't often that Andronicus could remember what he dreamed about, but he began to think that he was dreaming of the things he had seen in the shadows of the light, and wondered what they could mean.

6

Many years went by, though the Swihmehe

didn't keep track of things like that. As much as he enjoyed his new existence, living with the Swihmehe made Andronicus appreciate some of the little things that came with Greek life. He had always known what year it was, even what day, and had never considered how he knew. Men like Philander had seemed simple and useless when he was young, but now he realized just how much they actually did.

The Swihmehe didn't know what year it was or even what a year was. Andronicus tried to explain the concept of time to them, but it was like trying to teach them about the gods. Everyone seemed to like Andronicus's stories about gods and titans and beasts that were half man, but he could tell that no one believed them. To them the only gods were the elephants, and the rest was all just part of Swimha.

Andronicus tried to track the years by observing the stars, but at some point he lost count. He also tried to count the rainy seasons, but it rained too often to tell. Time moved forward at the same pace it always had, but now it went by untracked.

The best way for Andronicus to track time came from watching the children grow. When he had arrived at the village, Chaka's youngest brother, Choko, could not have been more than six or seven. By the time the boy grew into a man and had his own children, Andronicus knew many years had passed. There was something freeing in not knowing though. There were no numbers here, no rules, and it gave life a sort of easiness that he had never felt in Greece.

Andronicus knew he must be getting old, but he never felt it. His hair grew, though extremely slowly, and his beard gradually began to fill out as well. He often wondered why he didn't look his age, but merely chalked it up to good health. He had never gotten to see his parents grow old, so he didn't know what they might have looked like. He knew that eventually he would be old and grey, like Challah had become, but as more years passed, he still appeared to be the same strong young man he had been when he first woke up in Swimha.

Manyara stayed much the same as she had

been when they met as well. She seemed to maintain her youth in a way that the rest of the tribe did not. Challah grew old, and Chaka and Kwesi both grew older as well. Grito died of old age, and Chiomi took his place. It seemed that only Andronicus and Manyara were staying young. It confused Andronicus more than anything, and if he thought about it enough, it scared him as well.

7

Years after Andronicus had given up on ever being a parent, Manyara finally became pregnant. The entire village celebrated the news, Challah most of all. He had grown old and frail over the years and wanted desperately to have more grandchild before he moved on. Chaka and Kwesi had both taken wives over the years, and Kwesi was now a father of two, though Chaka was still childless as well.

When the village had a feast to celebrate the news, everyone was merry, congratulating Andronicus and Manyara. Even Kwesi was in good spirits. Kwesi still didn't like him, but he had accepted Andronicus's presence long ago. The feast was a grand time. Andronicus was filled with the same fatherly pride his father had felt some fifty odd years earlier and felt truly at peace with the world.

In the midst of the frivolity, Andronicus heard two loud, sharp horn blasts. There was a long pause in which the feast seemed to stop all at once, followed by two more sharp, quick blasts of the horn. Andronicus knew what it meant. Enemies were approaching.

The mood quickly shifted as everyone went from raucous celebration to the realization that they were about to be attacked. Most of the men ran to their huts and grabbed their spears. Andronicus fetched his sword, the only sword in Swimha. The women all scurried into hiding, and then the men formed a welcoming party for whoever was coming.

Ten minutes later a group of about twenty men stepped out of the darkness and into the light of the large fire. They were fierce and tall, just like the Swihmehe, but they were covered in white chalky war paint. Each one had a different configuration of white lines on his face, chest, and arms. Andronicus had seen these men before and knew they did not approve of his presence. They lived not far away, but the two tribes normally steered clear of each other.

A fierce-looking man with a white line going down his nose stepped forward. "You have disgraced the lands of Swimha," he said angrily. "You have let this outsider lay with one of your women. Now he has spawned a demon baby. This pale monster will be the death of us all. Kill him, atone for your mistakes, and we will go in peace."

"And what if we do not?" Chaka replied, glaring at the man with fire in his eyes. Andronicus saw the man falter the smallest bit at the rage on Chaka's face.

"If you allow this monster to continue living here, we will have to kill him ourselves," the man said. Andronicus gripped the hilt of his sword, hoping these men wouldn't make him kill them. He hadn't killed anyone in years, and he desperately wanted to keep that part of his life behind him.

"You will do nothing!" Chaka shouted. "You will leave our land and not return, or you will face me yourself. This is a joyous day, and you are not welcome here."

"You would choose this outsider over the people of your own land?" the man said, sneering.

"He is of my land!" Chaka shouted. "He is of the Swihmehe! And he will father my sister's son. He is my people, not you!"

"So be it," the man said. Andronicus had expected a fight, but he and his men simply walked away, leaving the threat hanging in the air.

That night the entire village seemed restless. People whom Andronicus had been friends with for years shot him bitter, angry looks. Manyara seemed more concerned with her people than her own safety. While Manyara sat with the other women, talking but mostly praying, Andronicus stood on the edge of the village with Chaka. They stayed up the entire night, watching out for the men who had threatened them.

The attack did not come that night or the next. For three months the Swihmehe had scouts posted all around the village every night. When the attack still didn't come, and no one had heard anything from the Swihmacha, the Swihmehe let their guard down. Andronicus also finally let himself stop worrying about the threat and focused on the child they were going to have.

He had asked Manyara long ago, and she had agreed to let him name the child after his brother. Despite his inability to measure time, he knew it had been many years since he had last seen Androcles and the others. The questions still burned in his mind every day, though he had learned to suppress them. He still thought of his friends often, about where they might be and what they might be doing. He wondered if any of them had gotten married or had children of their own.

It was a happy time for Andronicus, perhaps the happiest of his life. He had a family, a home, and purpose. He was finally going to be a father, which made him nervous and proud at the same time. He thought of his own father for the first time in years, and wondered if his son would look at him the way he had looked at Aristocles.

Chapter 15
The Massacre

1

Andronicus rose with the sun, as he did every morning. He rolled over with a yawn and gazed at Manyara as she slept. He ran his hand gently over her round stomach, trying to feel movement from his son; somehow he was sure it was a son. Manyara moved her head slightly, and Andronicus pulled his hand back, not wanting to wake her. He put on his brown loincloth and walked out to greet the day.

A thick mist was hanging over the land, making it hard to see. Andronicus looked up the mountain to make sure someone was standing guard. Ever since the threat they had received, they always kept at least two guards up on the mountain. He strained his eyes to see through the mist, looking for the lookout. He thought he could see someone standing up there, but couldn't be sure.

Suddenly, Andronicus felt an odd certainty creep over him. Goose bumps spread across his flesh, and the hairs on his neck stood up. Without knowing what he was doing, he ran to Chaka's hut. Chaka was already up preparing breakfast.

"Chaka," Andronicus said, "who is on watch right now?"

"On watch?" Chaka repeated, looking groggily at Andronicus as he let out a yawn. "On the hill?"

"Yes, on the hill," Andronicus replied impatiently. "Who is up there right now?"

"Dweiyo," Chaka said, rubbing his eyes, "and Obi."

Andronicus felt the chill wash through him again. He thought of the night they had celebrated his child, the night the Swihmacha had threatened his life along with Manyara and the baby. He tried to remember what Obi had been doing that night. He couldn't remember Obi being there at all. He remembered Chaka telling him that Obi had always loved Manyara though. He also recalled the look on Obi's face the night of their wedding.

The mist hid the plains from sight. Andronicus knew the Swihmacha could come at any time. He still wasn't sure Obi had betrayed them, or even that an attack was coming, but he knew they were vulnerable. He hesitated for a moment, not wanting to worry anyone needlessly, then decided to err on the side of caution.

"Chaka," he said quietly, not wanting to start a panic, "I think the Swihmacha are coming. I think they are going to attack us."

"If the Swihmacha were coming, we would hear the horns," Chaka replied confidently. "I told you, Dweiyo and Obi are up there. You can see them through the mist, see? We are fine."

"I think Obi is going to let them come," Andronicus said gravely. "without warning us."

"What are you talking about?" Chaka asked, glaring at Andronicus. "I have known Obi since I was born, he would never betray our people." Andronicus lowered his eyes from Chaka's stern gaze. He knew he had no way to prove that Obi had betrayed them, and more importantly, no way to convince Chaka the Swihmacha were coming.

Just as Andronicus was trying to figure out how to convince Chaka that an attack was imminent, a scream arose from the south side of the village. Their heads snapped around together, and Chaka looked over at Andronicus, his eyes full of fear and regret. He jumped to his feet, raced inside his hut, and returned a second later with his spear. Chaka started off toward the scream, but Andronicus hesitated.

"Come on!" Chaka shouted, just as another scream rang out. It was followed by a shout and then another. "They are here, move!" Chaka looked desperately at Andronicus.

"You go!" Andronicus said. "I will be there in a moment. I need my sword."

"No sword!" Chaka shouted frantically. "Just take a spear." Andronicus knew that without the sword he might not be able to defeat the Swihmacha.

"Go!" Andronicus shouted. "I will be right behind you. Go!" Chaka stared at Andronicus for a moment, then turned and ran toward the rising commotion.

Andronicus raced back to his hut. When he entered, he found Manyara sitting up with a frightened look on her face.

"Jocus, they are here for our baby," she said, her voice shaky.

"I will not let them hurt you or the baby," Andronicus reassured her, grabbing his armor from the corner. "Just stay in here, and stay down. I will come for you when the fighting is over."

"But what if they find me?" she said, grasping her belly in her arms.

"They will not find you," Andronicus said, giving her the most reassuring smile he could muster. "They are here for me."

"They are here for the baby too," she said, holding him back as he got up to leave. "They must know where our hut is. They knew about the baby as soon as we knew." Andronicus felt his stomach drop; he hadn't thought of that. If Obi had indeed betrayed them, he had likely told the Swihmacha exactly where to find Manyara.

"Go to your father's hut," Andronicus instructed. "Your nephews and sisters will be there. Watch over them and your father." Manyara nodded, and then they both left the tent.

All the shouting was still coming from the south side of the village. Challah's tent was to the north. Andronicus held Manyara's hand a moment longer, staring into her big, scared eyes, then turned to join the battle.

Andronicus ran past huts and screaming women and children until he found the fighting. Chaka and ten Swihmehe hunters were fighting nearly twice as many Swihmacha. Both sides had long hunting spears unsuited for close combat and no other weapons, save for rocks they picked up. Most of the fighting had reduced to simple fistfights, groups of large black men rolling in the dirt, bashing at each other's faces.

Andronicus gripped his sword firmly and knew what he had to do. He saw Dayo lying unconscious on the ground, getting pummeled by two large men with war paint, and stepped toward them. The nearest man lunged at Andronicus with a loud cry, but he easily ducked the blow. They were not prepared for the lethality of a well-made sword. Andronicus slashed at the first man, sending a thick spray of blood across the dirt.

The man collapsed with a howl, bringing his hands up to the long red gash across his torso. He looked down at his chest in shock and then back up at Andronicus, as if, in his last moments, he realized just who Andronicus really was. Andronicus swung the sword again, taking the man's head clean off.

Swihmacha and Swihmehe alike stared at Andronicus in fear and wonder. He could tell none of them had ever seen a man's head cut off before. The second man who had been kicking Dayo ran at Andronicus with a large rock held above his head. Andronicus dodged him easily and then plunged his sword through the man's chest. The man's eyes nearly bulged out of his head, either with fear or shock or pain, or perhaps all three.

Andronicus pulled his sword loose, and the man dropped to his knees, his face a comical mask of terror. Andronicus stepped toward the next man, who tried to run, but Andronicus was too fast. His sword swung through the air, cutting through flesh like butter.

It had been many years since Andronicus had killed a man, and he was a little disturbed to find how much he was enjoying it. Whether it was the knowledge that these men were here to kill his wife and child, a desire to protect the people who had saved him, or whether he simply enjoyed the sport of it, he genuinely didn't know.

It didn't take him long to cut through the entire Swihmacha war party single handed. Within a minute eight men lay on the ground, dead or dying, all covered in deep, bloody cuts from Andronicus's sword. The men he hadn't killed ran away as soon as they saw the carnage. The Swihmehe men who were still on their feet looked at Andronicus with fear and admiration. Chaka stared down at the sword in awe, watching the thick droplets of blood fall from the end of the blade.

Andronicus was about to speak, to try and tell them he wasn't a monster, when a scream rose from the other side of the village. It was followed by a second, which could only be the scream of a child.

"Manyara!" Chaka said urgently.

"She is with your father," Andronicus replied, "and the other children." Chaka didn't wait to respond; he bolted for his father's hut. Andronicus followed him, the others in tow.

The run through the village seemed to last a lifetime. Andronicus felt like he was in a nightmare, the kind where he was trying to run from a monster, but his feet didn't seem to work.

When they reached the hut, to Andronicus' horror, Chaka's youngest brother lay dead on the ground, blood pooling under his head. A tall Swihmacha man covered in war paint was standing over Kwesi's daughter with a spear raised over his head. Chaka lunged at the man and plunged his own spear through the man's back and out his chest. The young girl screamed again as blood rained down over her.

"Yeseh!" Chaka said to her, in a panic. "Where are Manyara and Father?" Yeseh continued to sob but pointed at the large hut. Andronicus ran toward it and just beat Chaka inside.

The second he entered the hut, he could smell the stench of death and blood. The fire had been scattered, the embers now emitting only a dull glow. Andronicus squinted, trying to see through the dark. Then he felt the air leave his body. He fell to his knees, and the sword dropped out of his hand and hit the dirt with a dull thud.

Two Swihmacha men were standing in the hut. One of them was standing over Challah, preparing to plunge a spear through his chest. The other man was standing over Manyara's body. Andronicus could see a dark gash in her belly where the spear had killed their child.

Tears rolled down his face as he looked at Manyara's big brown eyes. They were the same eyes he had stared into every day and every night for the past twenty years. They were the same eyes that could warm him with a single glance. And yet they were not the same eyes. Manyara's eyes had been full of life, and love, and beauty. The eyes Andronicus stared into now were empty dead orbs staring into nothing.

Andronicus heard the noise of anguish Chaka made as he saw his sister. He started toward the man standing over Challah, but Andronicus pulled him back. In a kind of haze, Andronicus rose to his feet, lifted his sword, and stepped toward the man.

The man barely had time to realize Andronicus was there before his head left his body. Then

Andronicus turned to the man who had killed Manyara. He looked down at her again, and saw that the man had also stabbed her in the neck. Blood covered her body and face, soaking into the dirt around her.

Andronicus looked up again just as the man came at him. He sidestepped the spear with ease and swung his sword deftly across the man's throat. The man's eyes grew wide and full of terror and surprise, just as all the others had. Andronicus stood over him as he fell to the ground, watching the blood squirt from the gash on his neck. He writhed in the dirt for a few seconds before dying with a mangled gurgling sound. Andronicus watched his eyes the whole time. When the life was gone from them, the fear still showed. Andronicus turned again to Manyara and fell to his knees.

"Manyara," Challah coughed from behind Andronicus, "Jocus, Manyara." The old man sounded short of breath. Out of the corner of his eye, Andronicus saw Chaka go to his father's side. Andronicus felt lightheaded as he stared down at his dead wife.

"Manyara," Challah coughed again. "Yeseh, Chako."

"Manyara and Chako are dead, Father," Chaka said, his voice breaking in a way Andronicus had never heard from him before. Challah broke into sobs, his frail, old body trembling with sorrow. Chaka began to weep as well.

Andronicus continued to stare down at Manyara as Chaka and his father wept behind him. Challah's gentle sobbing was soon joined by a chorus of wailing from outside. Andronicus felt as though he were in a dream. His head swam with the sounds of sobbing and wailing, and his nose was filled with the stench of death. Finally, he looked away from Manyara's haunting eyes and saw his sword lying next to her. There was blood all along the blade and splashed across his arms.

Andronicus picked up the sword and rose to his feet. He heard Chaka say something to him, but it sounded like it was coming from a mile away.

Andronicus walked out of the tent and found a dozen women wailing over the dead children, but he barely heard them.

Men and women alike shrank away from Andronicus as he walked through the village. Everyone was afraid of him now. The same people who had treated him as one of their own for years now looked at him like some sort of demon. The people who had never liked him at all now ran in terror at the very sight of him. Andronicus saw them run, but he didn't care. He walked through the village like a drunkard, ignoring the mayhem all around him.

When he reached the edge of the village, he kept on going, walking toward the Swihmacha village. The Swihmehe had never planned on attacking the Swihmacha, even though they knew they could. They had assumed that if the Swihmacha attacked, they would be able to fight them off, just as they had. They had underestimated, however, just how strongly the Swihmacha felt about Andronicus.

The Swihmacha thought he was a devil, a monster from a foreign land who had come to kill them all. He had thought they had been wrong, but as he trekked through the hot plain, he knew they were right. He would be the one to kill them all, men women, and children alike.

Andronicus had already lost his life once. He had lost everything and everyone he cared about. Manyara had been his new life, a life he could be proud of. Without her he didn't know what he was. It had been decades since he had killed, but a sleeping beast had been awoken, and now it was terribly hungry.

2

It was dark when Andronicus reached the Swihmacha village. He didn't know if he had walked for one day or two, stumbling along in a sort of fugue state the entire time. A great fire was burning in the center of the village, and drums and shouts filled the night air. The Swihmacha were not the great celebrators that the Swihmehe were, and Andronicus knew it took a special occasion for them to act in such a manner. It filled him with a dark rage to know that the joyous shouting he was hearing was in honor of the murder of his wife and child.

Andronicus walked openly up to the village. When he was a hundred yards away, someone shouted, followed by someone else. A minute later ten men were running toward him, spears in hand. Andronicus just kept walking, a stony expression of hate etched on his face.

When the men reached him, before they knew what was happening, three of them had tasted Andronicus's steel. They stabbed at him clumsily with their spears and tried to bring him down, but he deflected and ducked their blows with pristine skill, striking at them one by one, as if he had never stopped being a soldier at all.

By the time one of them thought to throw a rock at him, the others had all been slain. The man stood up, raising the rock over his head, but his expression turned to one of comic surprise as Andronicus's sword flashed out at him. The rock fell onto his head with a heavy thump, and he tumbled to the dirt, blood pouring from his neck and head alike.

Andronicus stepped from one man to the next, making sure they were all dead. Once they were all lying still, soaking the dirt in their blood, he heard more shouts, and more men came out to challenge him. He cut them down just as easily as he had cut down the first group, then kept moving forward. Andronicus slew the last two guards and then made his way toward the bonfire.

When he stepped into the light, the shouts of joy turned to cries of fear. The women and children tried to run, and some of the men tried to stop him, but Andronicus quickly killed them.

The air filled with screams and cries of pain and anguish. Andronicus moved swiftly, killing everyone in sight. He had never killed a woman before, but he killed them now. There was no thought or emotion as Andronicus carried out his massacre; no guilt, no pity, no mercy. They tried to run from him, but he slashed at them all, ending them one by one.

At one point a young boy charged him with a rock in hand, and he didn't hesitate to cut the boy down. As Andronicus slid into the old carnal routine of killing, he thought he saw a pair of red dots in the darkness, like eyes staring at him.

Andronicus didn't know how long it took or how many he killed, but when he was done, no one was left alive in the Swihmacha village. He was sure he had seen a group of children run away with at least one old woman with them. For a moment he thought about going after them but then decided against it.

As he stood among the dead, he felt the world slowly coming back to him. He saw the eyes of the dead women he had killed staring blankly up at him and felt his stomach turn. He turned around and retched so hard it brought him to his knees. His whole body began shaking, and he struggled for air. After a few minutes he regained control of himself and sat down amongst the dead.

Andronicus knew what was waiting for him back at his village, and he felt no rush to return. He spent the whole night with the people he had slain. He didn't sleep a wink, nor did he try. He thought about Manyara and the baby and the dozens of people lying around him that he had killed. But more than anything he thought about the shining stones in the pool. He thought about the shadows he had seen, and wondered if they had shown him this.

3

By the time the sun rose, Andronicus knew what he had to do. He was not meant to stay in Swimha. He had tried to make it work because he wanted Manyara, even though he knew he wasn't meant to have her. He wondered why it had taken until Manyara had gotten pregnant, and thought that maybe it was a sign. He knew he was already close to fifty years old, and would likely never live long enough to find Greece, but he couldn't stay any longer. His time in Swimha had come to an end, a far bloodier end than he could have ever imagined.

A few hours after the sun had risen,

Andronicus finally got to his feet. His neck and back felt stiff from sitting still all night, and he realized he had barely moved since he had sat down. He looked around at the dozens of bodies lying around him and felt sick. As he scanned the terrible mass of slain bodies, he did a double take. He approached one of the bodies and stared down at it, rage pumping through his body. Obi was covered in Swihmacha war paint, but Andronicus still recognized him.

He wished there was something more he could do to him. Obi had no wife or siblings, his parents were dead, and Andronicus had slaughtered his new people. There was nothing more Andronicus could take from him, and yet it still didn't feel balanced. Obi had taken away everything. Manyara had become Andronicus's whole world, and the baby hadn't even gotten to see the world yet.

After a long time of staring down at Obi, Andronicus turned away and began walking back to the Swihmehe village. Along the way, he found a pool of water where he could wash off all the blood, scrubbing at it with his fingernails. He didn't return to the Swihmehe village until just before nightfall.

Everyone stared at him like he was some kind of monster. People he had called friends for two decades shied away from him like he was toxic. Some women and children were still wailing as Andronicus made his way to his hut, not looking anyone in the eye.

When he got there, the first thing he saw was the bed in which he and Manyara had lain just the night before. Staring at it, he realized he could not stay there any longer. He took his few belongings—the hunting stick he had made years ago, a small clay pot for cooking, his old comb, and, of course, his red cloak.

Just before he left the tent, Andronicus saw a small piece of cloth. He had seen Manyara wear it on her arm more times than he could recall, and he decided to take it with him. He carefully wrapped it around the side of his armor, then left the hut for the last time.

As Andronicus walked through the village, people either glared at him or shrank away from him.

Suddenly, a large hand fell on his shoulder. Andronicus turned around and saw Chaka staring at him. For a moment Chaka didn't speak. He looked like he had been crying.

"I want to go with you," Chaka said finally, looking Andronicus in the eye.

"What?" Andronicus asked in surprise.

"I know you are leaving," Chaka said, "and I want to go with you."

"You cannot come with me, Chaka," Andronicus said softly. "This is your home, and these are your people. You have to stay and watch over them, you are going to be chief soon."

"I cannot," Chaka said, tears welling up in his eyes. "I have failed my people. I have failed my father and my sister."

"*I* failed your sister," Andronicus said through clenched teeth. "I was meant to protect her, and I failed. I cannot stay here any longer, but you have to."

"No," Chaka said, looking down. "I cannot stay here and face my father. I will go with you."

"Chaka, you do not even know where I am going."

"Of course I do," Chaka insisted. "You are going back to Greece to find your old friends. Yes?"

"Yes." Andronicus nodded slowly. "I am going to try and find Greece, but more likely I will end up dying in the dirt somewhere alone. You do not want to come with me, Chaka, trust me."

"I do not want to; I have to," Chaka said firmly. "I know what you did last night. Kwesi followed you. He saw you kill the Swihmacha. I know what you did for my people and my sister. I will not let you go alone."

"Your father is old, Chaka," Andronicus insisted. "You will be the chief soon. Your people need you. Your wife needs you."

"Kwesi will be chief," Chaka answered softly. "I have dishonored my family. I have already spoken to Nyarai; she knows I have to go."

"You have done nothing wrong," Andronicus said. "What happened here is my fault. You do not have to leave. Stay with your family, and let me go."

"I cannot," Chaka said simply. "I am going with you." Andronicus could tell that Chaka was not going to take no for an answer. He knew this journey was not going to end well, and he didn't want to drag Chaka into some awful death, but part of him did like the idea of not having to go it alone.

"Fine," Andronicus said reluctantly, not understanding why Chaka would want to leave. "If you really must come, then we will leave in the morning."

Chaka nodded, then went back to his hut to prepare his things and spend his last night with his wife. Andronicus knew he couldn't sleep in his own hut; it was too full of memories. He walked over to a tree just outside the village and laid his old cloak in the dirt. He sat against the tree for a long while, thinking.

He thought of Manyara, and their baby, but not as much as he should have. He felt guilty, and he knew how wrong it was, but he couldn't help but feel a twisted sort of hope. He realized he had resigned himself to living and dying with the Swihmehe, but now that he was leaving, a whole new world of possibilities seemed to have opened. Every time he tried focusing on what he knew he should be thinking about, his thoughts wandered off toward shining rocks and magical lands.

Chapter 16
Setting Out
1

Andronicus and Chaka said their goodbyes at the edge of the village. Each member of the tribe came up to Chaka and thanked him, then said farewell. He accepted each of their thanks with a simple nod and an embrace. Very few of them even looked at Andronicus. Word of what he had done had spread quickly, and he knew it was good that he was leaving.

Some of them did say goodbye to him though, and a few even embraced him as well. Chiomi gave him a warm hug and wished him good fortune.

Andronicus thanked him for all of his care and kindness over the years. Chaka's younger sisters both said goodbye to him as well; they knew how much Manyara had loved him. Dayo was badly bruised, but he gave Andronicus a tight hug and cried a little as he thanked him and said goodbye.

The last to say goodbye was Kwesi. People were saying that Kwesi was chief now because Challah still hadn't come out of his hut, and they said he wasn't eating. Andronicus felt terrible for the old man, but he knew he wouldn't want to see him. He just had to hope they would all be alright without Chaka, and again wanted to tell Chaka to stay.

Kwesi stepped forward and stood before Andronicus, gazing sternly at him. The two of them stood in silence, neither breaking their gaze, just as they had on the day they first met. They had fought that day, and Andronicus had won. Kwesi had seemed to hate him the entire time they had known each other, but now that their time had come to an end, Kwesi actually looked remorseful.

Andronicus had so much he wanted to say to him. He wanted to tell him how sorry he was for getting his sister and little brother killed, how sorry he was that he was taking Kwesi's older brother away, how much he now wished he had never met the Swihmehe, or that they had killed him that first day. But Andronicus didn't say any of that; he simply stared into Kwesi's eyes, wishing he could.

Kwesi didn't say anything either. He just stared back, then finally gave Andronicus a curt nod. The simple gesture said more to Andronicus than any words Kwesi had ever spoken to him. In that nod there was empathy, acceptance, encouragement, and forgiveness. Everything the two men had never said to each other said in the simplest fashion of all.

Andronicus tried to return the nod with the same weight, but it felt empty. He tried to say all the things he felt in silence. To convey all his remorse, regret, and guilt with his eyes. Kwesi's lip tightened the tiniest bit, and Andronicus thought he understood. In that moment Andronicus felt like he and Kwesi were finally brothers and that they finally understood each other. He felt a pang of regret that he had to leave but knew there was no other way.

When Andronicus turned to leave, Kwesi finally spoke.

"Go in peace, Jocus," he said in his deep, stoic voice. "Go with the pride of the Swihmehe." More than a few onlookers looked furious at that. Andronicus met his gaze once more. Kwesi held his head high, holding to the notion he had just passed. Andronicus felt tears wanting to build up in his eyes, but he fought them off. It would not do to cry in front of them now.

Andronicus stepped forward and held out his hand. The two men shook hands for the first time, twenty years after they had first met and tried to kill each other. Andronicus nodded once more, wishing they had made their peace years ago.

Kwesi turned to embrace his brother, whispering something into Chaka's ear. Chaka smiled and clapped Kwesi on the back. Andronicus felt guilt wash over him again at the thought that he was taking Chaka away from his home, his wife, his family, and his rightful place as leader.

Chaka had asked to join him, but Andronicus knew that Chaka had no idea what he was getting into. The journey would be long, and arduous, and most likely very dangerous. The chances that they would actually make it back to Greece were slim to none. He didn't even know which way Greece was, or if it was even out there.

Andronicus still felt strong and healthy, but he knew he would begin to show his age soon. He was already in his fifties, and he didn't know how long it would be before he would not be able to travel. The prospect of actually making it back home seemed almost impossible. They would likely travel for as long as they could and then end up having to live and die in some foreign place with foreign people. They would both die far away from Swimha and probably Greece as well.

Andronicus couldn't tell Chaka any of that. He wanted to. He wanted to tell Chaka not to come, that it was folly, that they would never find Greece, or the others. If they were lucky, they would be able to die together, with at least one friend by their side. But more likely they would die alone, and afraid. As Andronicus watched Chaka say his last goodbye to his wife, he wanted to tell him those things, but he didn't. Deep down he wanted Chaka to come with him for selfish reasons; he wasn't ready to go alone.

Andronicus took one final look at the Swihmehe tribe. He had lived with these people for twenty years, and he had grown to love them. He had even come to think of himself as one of them, but that was all gone now. Most of the people he had known for so long now looked at him like he was a monster, the very devil the Swihmacha had accused him of being. He supposed, in his own way, he had brought the legend to life. He and Chaka stood before the tribe and waved one last time. Everyone waved to Chaka, and a brave few souls even waved to Andronicus.

And then they left.

When they were halfway across the valley, they heard a loud whoop behind them. The Swihmehe hunters shouted in unison, once, twice, and a third and final time. Their final shout echoed across the mountain and over the plains, and then it was gone, nothing but a reverberating memory that would echo in Andronicus's ears for many years to come.

2

Andronicus and Chaka walked all day, stopping only once. Neither of them said very much. They were both still coming to grips with their extensive loss. Andronicus had lost his wife, his unborn child, and his hope for a peaceful life. Chaka had lost his wife as well, along with his sister and brother and his future role as chief. And they had both lost their home. They had not walked more than two hours when the realization began to truly sink in, that they might never have a place to call home again.

They had brought a few belongings with them, thrown together in a sloppily made bag that hung over Chaka's shoulder. Inside the bag were rocks for fire making, a rock bowl for cooking, two wooden bowls, two sharpened rock knives, a few raggedy clothes for each of them, and an old lion claw that Chaka claimed was good luck. They also each had a large hollowed-out gourd filled with water and a big brown rolled blanket strung over their backs. Besides that, Andronicus still had his sword, his terribly weathered scabbard, his breastplate, his old comb, and of course, his red cloak.

That was everything in the world that they could call their own. As far as they could tell, it would be all they would have for the foreseeable future. Andronicus supposed if they killed any animals they might be able to barter the pelts with someone, and he intended to do just that, but he had no idea when they might see other people again. For all he knew, they could be alone with the plains and the animals for months before they found people again. It was only one of a thousand new questions as they marched into the unknown.

When the sun set, and the light began to fade from the land, they set up camp for the night. Chaka went to find something to eat while Andronicus worked at starting a fire. They had brought enough food for a week, but Andronicus knew that there was almost always meat to be found in these lands, along with nuts and berries.

When it was almost completely dark, Chaka came walking into camp with a good-sized hare and a few small fruits. Andronicus skinned the hare, and soon they had a nice dinner, splitting everything evenly.

After eating mostly in silence, they put out the fire and laid out their blankets. Andronicus marveled at how peaceful it was out in the wild. It had been a long time since he had slept under the stars without the crying of someone's child or someone coughing not far away.

He stared up at the stars and thought about the life he had just left behind. He loved the Swihmehe, not just the friends he had made but the tribe itself. They were good people, strong and hard working. They lived in harmony with the tremendous wildlife around them, and yet they were not afraid to take what they needed. He had thought he would spend the rest of his life with them, and part of him wished he still could. Having Chaka with him made it easier, but he would still miss the Swihmehe very much.

They were heading south, and he had no idea when they would find another village. There were several other villages in Swimha, but Chaka knew where they were and how to avoid them. Andronicus thought it best not to see anyone else for a little while.

The memory of what he had done was still too fresh. He wondered what had become of his massacre. Had the bodies been consumed by lions? Dogs? Vultures? Would someone go back to bury them? He doubted that, and he felt guilty for leaving them the way he had. For all they had taken from him, they were still people, and they deserved to be buried, or at least burned, not eaten. He rolled over on his blanket and tried to shake off the awful images that his mind kept conjuring.

Andronicus tried to focus on his old friends and how he would see them again someday, but the memory of what he had done kept reappearing, and as he fell into sleep, he found himself back in that village. All around him were dead bodies. The bodies of the Swihmacha lay on the ground at his feet, but next to them were brown men.

Andronicus looked around and saw hundreds of dead bodies spread out across the bloody red dirt. Everyone he had ever killed lying on the ground around him. He looked around, wanting to get away from them, but they were packed too closely together. The entire ground around him was covered by the bodies of his dead. Andronicus opened his mouth to shout, but nothing came out. He tried to take a step forward, but his feet felt like they weighed a thousand pounds. He looked around in a growing panic, trying to find a way out of the field of corpses.

Then, to his horror, one of the bodies began to move. It slowly sat up and then rose to its feet, standing taller than even the tallest Swihmacha, taller than any person could possibly be. When it was fully upright, the figure towered over Andronicus. It took a long stride forward. Andronicus tried to run, but his feet wouldn't move. He stood paralyzed, frozen in fear, as the giant shadow stepped toward him.

He heard an awful hissing whisper, and then he saw its eyes. They were red and glowing, but Andronicus knew they were eyes. His bones turned to ice as the shadow hissed something he couldn't hear. Then the rest of the corpses started moving. They slowly began lifting themselves up, and he finally let out a scream as one of them grabbed his leg.

Andronicus snapped awake with a shout. He grabbed his sword and lifted it to kill the monster grabbing his ankle, but when he looked down, nothing was there. He sat back, panting heavily, and saw Chaka looking at him. Chaka didn't say anything; he just stared silently, which made Andronicus even more unsettled. A moment later Chaka rolled over, and Andronicus lay back down, trying to get his breathing back to normal.

It took a long time to fall back to sleep after that. Andronicus was terrified of finding himself back in that awful graveyard, but eventually he drifted off to sleep. This time he dreamed of a vast jungle, full of life and beauty. In the morning he barely remembered the awful nightmare, and by noon it was gone entirely.

3

They walked all day, barely speaking as they passed herds of animals and vast open fields. They were both naturally quiet people, and they made suitable traveling companions. Andronicus was left to his thoughts as they walked through the magnificent countryside. Even after so many years, this world still amazed him. He could only imagine what he would find between Swimha and Greece. He stared out at all the marvelous creatures roaming the magnificent plains and wondered what kinds of strange new things he might see in their travels.

At midday they found a large watering hole

and some more fruit. They rested there briefly before continuing on.

When the sun began to set, they set up camp again, repeating the ritual of the night before. They repeated this ritual for weeks and then for months. They rose with the sun each day and would begin walking not long after. They would walk all day, only stopping once or twice to eat or drink, then stop at sunset and find food and a place to sleep. They would chat often enough as they walked, but mostly they stayed quiet, admiring the plants and animals they passed.

4

Three months after they had set out, they saw the first village. It was smaller than the Swihmehe's, looking like it probably held less than fifty people. The small cluster of huts was not far from a body of water that was so large it could almost be called a lake. Staring at the glistening water, Andronicus wondered how often they had to fend off animal attacks. On the far side of the pool were several striped horses and two orange deer.

Andronicus and Chaka started toward the village with hopes of bartering for some food. When they were nearly within shouting distance, a small group of men came out brandishing spears. He and Chaka both held their hands out, offering peace, but Andronicus's sword hung at his side, ready if he needed it.

When the group was halfway to them, they came to an abrupt halt and began talking to each other, turning from one to the other in what looked to be a panic. After a moment four of the men turned and raced back to the village. The other two started walking toward the Andronicus and Chaka, much slower than before. Andronicus was thoroughly confused. He had never seen a welcoming party do that, anywhere.

Just as Andronicus was about to shout to them, one of the strangers beat him to it. "We do not want to fight!" the man shouted nervously in the language of the Swimha. "My friends have gone back to our village to get you food. You can fill your water jugs at the great water, and then you can go. Please leave us alone." Andronicus was at a loss for words. He had expected hostility, not instant submission and total compliance.

"You are very generous," Andronicus replied, bowing his head. "My friend and I thank you." The man flinched at the sound of Andronicus's voice and shied away with every word. Andronicus stepped toward the man, and he and his companion scurried backwards.

Andronicus was about to ask what was wrong when it dawned on him. They knew who he was, and what he had done. He knew that some of the women and children had escaped, and they must have gone to other villages. The story of the white-skinned man who had massacred a village must have travelled far by now. He wondered how long they would have to walk before people wouldn't be afraid of him.

When the other men returned with food in their arms, Andronicus and Chaka each took two fruit and a dead hare but left the rest. They also filled their gourds with water. Then they left, making sure to give the village a wide berth. Andronicus felt bad that they were so afraid of him. It made him feel even more like the monster he had been accused of being.

5

They continued traveling southeast through the land of Swimha, moving slowly and stopping only occasionally to meet with the people that would have them. Once they had gone far enough, Andronicus was sure they didn't know what he had done to the Swihmacha, but they still seemed wary of him. Occasionally, they met people who were interested enough to talk to him, but no one would let him into their village.

After a while they tried to avoid villages and people altogether. Many months after they had left the Swihmehe behind, people were still afraid of Andronicus. He wondered what it was about him that made people so afraid. He knew it could just be as simple as his skin color, but he felt like it was more than that. It was as if the people knew that Andronicus was a predator and should be feared. He supposed it didn't really matter in the end. All that mattered was that they were afraid of him. He felt like a leper, and he didn't know what he would do without Chaka's company.

They walked day after day, moving far slower than Andronicus had anticipated. They gradually made their way out of the land of Swimha and into unknown territories that they had only heard tell of. As they trekked farther south, the people they met started to change in subtle ways. Their huts were shaped differently, and their accents and even the language itself started to change. Andronicus and Chaka found themselves having to learn as many new words as possible when they met people, until one day they were speaking a language that the Swihmehe would barely understand.

Andronicus found it fascinating that the language itself could blend so easily across the land. Each change was small, but over time, and taken altogether, they became significant. From one village to the next the people could understand each other, but the villages far apart were speaking almost totally different languages. Without ever consciously learning a new language, Andronicus and Chaka found themselves speaking a language quite different from the one they spoke when they left.

They would only spend a day or two with most of the tribes, if they would even have them. One village found Andronicus fascinating, and he and Chaka spent several weeks with them, enjoying the break from their trek. Andronicus couldn't believe how good it felt to be with people again who didn't hate or fear him. Everyone still looked at him like he was some kind of alien, but he knew it was just his skin and not what he had done.

He wanted desperately to be able to forget it all and put it behind him the way he had the Persian war. He didn't like what he had done as a boy, but he had learned to live with it long ago. He had forgiven himself for leaving Leonidas and his men, and for all the Persian slaves he had killed. It was all behind him. But what he had done to the Swihmacha, and what they had done to Manyara, he couldn't get rid of that.

Every night Andronicus would lie awake for a long time, whether in a strange village or out in the wilderness, dreading the dreams he knew would come. While living with the Swihmehe, he had had the dreams less often over time, but since his departure they had returned in earnest. It was as if they were trying to make up for lost time. Only now the dreams weren't all fantastical and wondrous; many of them were downright terrifying.

Most often he would dream of that terrible night. Sometimes the people would look like the Swihmacha, and sometimes they would look Persian. No matter how hard he tried, he could never stop his arm from bringing its relentless tide of death to everyone around him. The dream always ended the same way. At some point during the fighting he would look into one of their eyes, and they would be a horrible glowing red. Everything would stop, and Andronicus would see the creature with the red eyes about to speak. Then he would wake up in a panic, sweating and panting.

On the nights he didn't have to suffer through the awful nightmare, he would dream of far more mysterious things. He liked those dreams, even though most of them meant nothing to him. He liked to see the things his dreams would show him; he knew they were things most people would never get to see. Sometimes he would dream of a massive jungle and sometimes a great desert. There were mountains and seas and cities like he had never seen before. There were people too. He would forget them all as soon as he woke, but he knew he was seeing the same people in many dreams, and he wondered if he would ever get to meet them.

Walking through the plains every day, with Chaka as his trusted but silent companion, Andronicus had nothing but time to ponder his wild and bizarre dreams. On the days he would awake from an exciting and mysterious dream, he would spend half the day trying to retain some piece of whatever he had seen. On the days he would awake from the nightmare, he would quickly find something around him to focus on or get Chaka to talk about something. It got to the point that Andronicus's whole day would depend on what kind of dream he had the night before.

6

One day the two wayward travelers were walking through a vast dirt field. A few trees were scattered to the left, and a bit of dry, dead grass was up ahead and to the right, but other than that the land was barren. They had not seen any animals for four days, and they were beginning to worry they were coming to the end of these lands. Andronicus knew all too well what happened to fools who tried to cross a desert, and he had no intention of being a fool.

After some debate, they decided to journey onward, rather than turning back. They continued south, moving a little faster now, in hopes of finding food. They had stayed with a tribe called the Hyagodi for seven days less than a fortnight before and even gone on a hunt with them. After Andronicus killed a water buffalo with his sword, the Hyagodi insisted that they take as much food as they could with them.

They only had rations left for one more day when they finally came across a village in the barren land. The huts appeared to be made of a different clay than all the others, and they were odd and lopsided.

Andronicus and Chaka approached the village in plain sight, as they always did. When they were about a hundred yards out, a group of hunters came out to meet them. Andronicus was surprised to see they were armed with slings rather than spears. The tallest and fiercest looking among them stepped forward and shouted at them in a deep voice. Andronicus could barely understand the man's words, but he thought he had asked who they were.

Andronicus had not had to try to converse with a man speaking a completely different language since the day he met Chaka, though at least this time they probably knew a few of the same words. Careful not to move too fast or alarm the men, Andronicus introduced himself and then Chaka.

By then Andronicus was used to being gawked at, but these men appeared terrified of Chaka as well. The leader of their group spoke again. Andronicus thought he heard the word "want," but he couldn't be sure. He pointed to himself, then to Chaka, made a walking gesture with his fingers, and pointed south. The skittish welcoming party glanced nervously at each other, not saying a word. Andronicus found them to be almost comical. They were large and lean and muscular, but they seemed as frightened as field mice.

Finally, the leader spoke again. Andronicus had no idea what the man said, but it didn't really matter. He knew these men were no threat to him. He and Chaka followed the men back to their village, where they found more frightened people. A man who looked to be about a hundred years old hobbled out to greet them.

"I am Gobu," he said in an accent they could actually understand. "I am sorry for my people's cowering," the old man said, pausing after every other word, "but we do not see outsiders very often. And when we do, it is usually not very pleasant."

Andronicus looked over the tribe, the children hiding behind their mothers, the mothers hiding behind their husbands, and the men looking like they were going to wet themselves.

"We are no threat to you, old man," Andronicus said, hoping some of the other people would understand him and relax a bit, but they all flinched away from his loud voice. "We are just passing through. If you have any meat, we have a deerskin pelt to trade."

The old man nodded and said something to the leader of the greeting party in their own language. The man turned and hurried off, presumably to get the meat.

"We do not hunt here," the old man said in his croaky voice. "The animals do not come this way. Most people do not come this way either." That explained the absence of spears and axes, but it made Andronicus wonder what the man had gone to fetch.

Just then the man returned with a large woven basket in his arms. He placed it at Andronicus's feet and stepped back. Andronicus stared down into the basket, and a large grin spread across his face.

"What is this?" Chaka asked with a disgusted look. "This is not meat."

"It is, brother," Andronicus said as he smiled broadly at the old man. Chaka stepped backward, covering his nose from the stench. Andronicus reached down and grasped one of the slimy grey masses from the basket, and brought it up to his nose. He took a deep breath, filling his nose with the rich, pungent odor. It had been more than twenty years since he had smelled it, but no boy who grew up in Sparta could ever forget the smell of fish. He turned the fish over in his hands, admiring its freshness; it had surely been caught that day.

"Where?" was all he could manage to say. The old man gave him a toothless smile and pointed south. "From the great water."

Andronicus wasted no time. He gave the old man the pelt he had promised and picked up the fish basket. He thanked the old man and then set off toward the south, Chaka giving him and the fish a wide berth.

Twenty minutes later Andronicus could smell it, the same smell he had grown up with. Even over the strong stench of the basket of fish in his arms, he could smell the sea. Once he could smell it he began to run, knowing it had to be up ahead. Chaka didn't believe Andronicus's stories about a great water, but he ran nonetheless, keeping away from Andronicus and the fish basket. Andronicus ran up a small hill covered in moss and sand. When he reached the top, he came to an abrupt halt and stared out at the vast blue sea. He turned to see Chaka staring as well in dumbfounded fascination.

Andronicus had never seen Chaka look at anything the way he looked at the sea that day. The largest body of water in Swimha was maybe a hundred feet across. The largest body of water they had seen since leaving the Swihmehe was about 250 feet across. The body of water that stood before them now, stretched farther than either of them would even believe. Chaka looked as though his entire view on the world was changing in that moment, and Andronicus had to smile.

The water was a sapphire blue that shimmered dazzlingly as it moved about with the wind. It moved in slow, rolling hills breaking over here and there, eventually sliding into heavy white waves that pushed onto the beach. The waves rolled onward, rising slowly, and rolling over, becoming a hollow tube for just a moment before crashing over themselves and ending in a chaotic white mass of foam and water that stretched up the sand. All that just to slide back and do it all again, and again and again until the end of time.

It had been many years since Andronicus had last seen the sea. Chaka had never seen it. They spent a full day just sitting and watching the waves. Seeing the sea again made Andronicus more hopeful than he had been since waking up in Swimha. Maybe he really could find Greece.

As the sun set, Andronicus went swimming, just as he had done as a boy in the Aegean. The water was much warmer than the Aegean, and after a while even Chaka was splashing about in the waves. After they swam Chaka built a fire, and Andronicus gutted two of the fish. Once the fire was going strong, Andronicus skewered the fish and cooked them. When the pinkish meat had turned white, he removed the fish from its skewer and took a big bite. He had not eaten fish in so long that it was hard to tell, but he thought this was the best fish he had ever eaten. Chaka watched apprehensively as Andronicus wolfed down his fish, then began gutting two more.

"Go on then," Andronicus said impatiently. Chaka only made a face and shook his head stubbornly, eyeing the fish like they were going to jump up and bite him.

"I ate the tree squirrels you killed," Andronicus

said as he ripped out the guts of a fish. "I did not want to either, but you made me. Now I am making you eat this fish. Eat it." Chaka gave him a mistrustful look but reluctantly took the skewer. He slowly removed the fish and took a small bite. His face instantly brightened, and he took another bigger bite, then broke into a big grin.

Andronicus let out a hearty laugh. "You had better like it. That is probably all we are going to be eating for a long while." Chaka's smile faltered for a moment, but he continued eating his fish, and he even asked for another when he was done.

7

In the morning they packed up their belongings and then made their way off the beach and up the coast, heading west now. They walked that whole day without seeing anything but ocean, sand, and seabirds flying overhead. Andronicus was surprised to see that the seabirds here looked exactly like the seabirds back in Sparta.

In all the years Andronicus had spent in strange lands, these seabirds were the only identical match to anything from his past life. He had seen many animals that resembled animals from home in one way or another, but never an actual match. As he watched the seabirds fly overhead, he became more and more convinced that these were indeed the same birds.

The idea that Greece could be across the sea came to him on the second day of walking up the beach. By the sixth day the idea had consumed him entirely. He was sure that Greece had to be somewhere across the sea, and he was determined to find his way there, no matter how long it took.

Andronicus shared these thoughts with Chaka, but he didn't seem to agree. Chaka had become quite certain that the great water was the end of the world. He now believed that the great water surrounded all the land, and that no matter which way they went, they would find it eventually. Andronicus knew better though; he had crossed a sea before. He knew that just because they couldn't see the other side didn't mean it wasn't there.

He didn't know if Greece was across this sea or another, but he believed it was out there. Andronicus began to realize just how big the world might actually be. The Greeks thought that they knew everything that mattered and everywhere that mattered, but they had never heard of the Swihmehe, and the Swihmehe had never heard of them. It seemed now that Greece might be just a small piece of a much bigger puzzle.

There was no way to know which way Greece lay, so Andronicus kept them moving west. He wasn't sure if he was trying to walk around the sea or find a way across it, but he thought they should stay by it. There were more than enough fish to eat and enough freshwater streams nearby to keep them going. Andronicus decided they should just follow the coast until he came up with a better plan.

8

They continued moving west, keeping close to the sea for a long time. They each had a long spear, and they learned to use them to catch fish. Luckily, the fish swam right up to the beach, and Andronicus got quite good at spearing them in one try. After a month Chaka was able to spear fish almost as well as Andronicus.

After months of eating nothing but fish and berries, the land finally became less barren. More plants began to appear amongst the trees. As soon as the grass started, the animals returned as well.

The first time they saw a deer, they spent the entire day tracking and hunting it. When it was nearly dark, they finally managed to spear the quick beast. They quickly made a fire, and enjoyed their first red meat in months.

After supper they found a small pool of water and filled their water jugs. As Chaka sat drinking, Andronicus looked down at the rippling water. The ripples slowly subsided, and his face emerged as the water calmed. Once again he was amazed at how little he had aged over the years. He didn't know exactly how long it had been, but he knew it had been at least twenty odd years since the storm and the cave, and he didn't seem to look a day older. His father had begun to show gray hair very young from what he could remember, but Andronicus's hair was still the same jet black it had always been. He didn't know how old he was, but he knew he was over fifty, and yet he still felt as strong and as youthful as ever.

They made camp a few hundred feet from the watering hole, making sure to stay upwind of it as well. They had learned long ago not to sleep too close to a watering hole, lest they wanted unexpected nighttime visitors.

After eating the last of the deer, they lay down in the dirt to sleep. Within a minute Andronicus heard Chaka snoring on the other side of the smoldering fire. He looked up at the countless stars above as he listened to the soft crackling of the embers. He still didn't know the stars' names, but he had come to know them as well as he had known the stars back home. He could make out shapes if he wanted, just as the old men did back in Greece. The stars were so abundant he could make them into anything he wanted, and yet they always seemed to form the same things—the things from his dreams.

He was slowly beginning to let go of the awful nightmares. Many nights he would have normal dreams, the kind he had as a young man, before he touched the rocks, the fantastical nonsensical kind that he didn't remember when he woke up. Most often, however, he would have the different kind of dreams. Those dreams were terribly vivid and uncomfortably familiar. As he kept seeing the same things in his dreams, he began to remember them better. Perhaps it was because he kept having the same dreams over and over again, but it felt like he had been there before, like they were memories rather than dreams. He felt an unsettling certainty that they were things yet to come. Things he had seen in the shadows of the light.

It was only the same few dreams that he could remember. A mountain, higher than anything he had ever seen, stretching up into the clouds and out of sight. A jungle, thicker than he could even believe, stretched out like a sea beneath him. A coliseum, back home in Greece, full of cheering people, with him standing beneath them, raising his sword. A ship at sea, a ship far bigger than any he had ever seen, with towering masts and massive billowing sails. And an endless desert, a sea of sand. This one always gave him the chills. Whenever he dreamed of the desert, he would wake up covered in cold sweat.

Andronicus didn't know what the dreams meant, if they were visions of the future or just dreams. Or perhaps they were memories, things that had happened to him when he touched the light. Seeing as he had been transported to a strange new world in the blink of an eye, this possibility didn't seem too far-fetched late at night. Whatever they were, Andronicus would dream of them often. Those dreams and others. Some of the dreams Andronicus didn't understand at all; they were too bizarre and alien for his mind to comprehend, and when he awoke from those dreams he was in a cold sweat as well. Each night as Andronicus drifted off to sleep, he wondered which strange world he would find himself in this time.

9

The next morning they packed up and headed west again. They still kept within a few miles of the sea, letting it guide their course. There were more villages the farther west they went, but they didn't bother with most of them. Between the fish and the game that had returned, they were able to feed themselves well enough on their own.

They kept walking beside the sea, day after day, until one day Andronicus realized they were no longer traveling west. Once he was paying attention to it, he discovered they were getting closer and closer to moving north. Finally, after more than a year of walking by the sea, they were heading directly north. Once he was sure of it, Andronicus felt newly invigorated. He didn't know how to explain it, but he had the feeling they were going in the right direction.

For the first time in years, he felt confident in his plan. When the sea began to turn west again, Andronicus continued north. They had been walking for years by then, but he finally felt like he knew where to go. Chaka didn't care which way they went. It was all the same to him, and he seemed to just be along for the journey. Andronicus had no idea what lay to the north, but he now felt sure that was the way they were meant to go.

Chapter 17
Gods and Demons
1

Months after leaving the sea behind, they entered a land even more abundant in life than Swimha. The grass grew tall and thick, and the animals came in droves. Great herds of gazelles and zebras roamed the fields, and there were more elephants than even Chaka had ever seen. Whenever they came across a good sized watering hole, it would already be occupied by several other species.

The animals kept their distance from the traveling pair, for the most part. Many of them would run as soon as they saw Andronicus and Chaka, which told them a village of experienced hunters was somewhere in the area. Occasionally, a lioness or hyena would get a little too bold and come looking for a quick meal. Those foolish beasts would leave with a gash from a spear if they were lucky, and dead if they weren't.

Chaka always made sure that they only killed an animal when they had to. And when they did he would make sure they took every last scrap that they could, which meant they often ate much smaller beasts than Andronicus would have preferred. He didn't mind indulging Chaka's beliefs; after all, it was still more his land than Andronicus's. They would strip the meat, salt it, and dry it in the sun, making it hard and chewy but able to last for weeks. It was a trick Andronicus had learned back in Sparta, and it allowed them to keep moving instead of having to hunt every day. Andronicus would remove the pelts carefully with his sword, and eventually they would find a village willing to barter for them.

2

One day, more than a year after they had left the sea behind, they came across the carcass of a massive bull elephant. It was being savagely devoured by a pride of lions, all of them soaked in its blood. It was by far the biggest elephant that either of them had ever seen. When alive, it must have stood at least fifteen feet high at the shoulder, maybe more. Its tusks were each twice the size of the lions that had killed it, two nine-foot curved spears, each thicker than a man's head. Down at the end of each tusk the fine white turned a dark bloody scarlet, drops of blood falling into the soaked red dirt.

Lying some twenty feet beyond the elephant were four dead lionesses and a dead lion, their bodies torn and mangled. The elephant had skewered more than half the pride before being taken down. Andronicus couldn't decide which he was more impressed with, the gargantuan elephant or the pride that took it down.

The three remaining females were digging through the mighty beast's stomach, stripping away pieces of meat to bring to their hungry cubs. Atop the back of the great elephant sat a huge male lion. The thick red hair of his mane blended seamlessly with the blood that soaked his muzzle, giving him a truly sinister look. A bloody strip of flesh hung from his jaws, as he lazily chewed the meat his wives had killed.

Chaka was mortified. Andronicus knew that elephants were like gods to the Swihmehe, and to see such a mighty god fallen was clearly a great tragedy to Chaka. His face went from horrified anguish to fiery rage. Andronicus saw a fury in Chaka's eyes that he had only seen once before, on the day his family had died. Chaka raised his spear to attack, but Andronicus reached out and stopped him.

"No," Andronicus said, his voice forceful but quiet enough not to catch the lions' attention. "They bested him. They deserve the spoils of battle." Chaka turned his fiery glare on Andronicus, and for a moment it looked like he might hit him.

"They disgrace him!" Chaka shouted. Tears of rage welled up at the corners of his eyes, and his lips trembled with anger. Andronicus understood Chaka's love for the gods, and he sympathized with him, but he also believed that a beast that had bested another beast in combat deserved the spoils of victory. He felt himself being torn between the ideals of gods and the virtues of battle. He wondered what Archelaus would think about the matter, followed quickly by Androcles and then Euthymius.

One of the lionesses had looked over when Chaka shouted, and was now giving them a long studying look. She crawled out of the elephant's stomach and started to stalk toward them, leaving bloody tracks behind her.

Andronicus snapped out of his trance and picked up a rock. He stepped forward, meaning to just send the beast off. The cat emitted a low, grumbling growl as it slinked forward. He shouted and hurled the rock at her. The rock struck the cat in the head, and she let out a sharp roar. Instead of running away though, she got low to the ground and began growling.

Andronicus was amazed at the lions' brazenness, and he wished he could have seen the fight they had with the elephant, though he would never tell Chaka that. The other two lionesses had begun to creep over as well, and Andronicus began to fear they might have to really fight these bold cats.

Just as he reached for his sword, preparing for a fight, he felt a brush of wind go by his face. Out of the corner of his eye, he saw the spear fly past his head. It flew straight and true, sinking into the lioness's shoulder. She let out a terrible howl and staggered as she tried to remain on her feet. Chaka was past Andronicus and on her in an instant. He pulled his spear out as she tried to claw at him with her now useless paw, and he plunged it through her heart with a cry of anger. The other two lionesses issued identical roars and then charged. Chaka ran toward them, but Andronicus knew he couldn't take them both alone.

Andronicus raised his sword and took a split second to aim. The lions were coming at Chaka from two sides. Chaka was in a rage as he charged the nearest one and seemed blind to the lion at his back. Andronicus took a deep breath and then threw his sword with both hands as the lion leaped. The sword flew by Chaka's head just as he plunged his spear into the other lion. Both cats fell down to the ground at the same time. Andronicus ran forward and finished off one cat while Chaka killed the other.

Chaka turned to find Andronicus's furious expression.

Before either man could speak, the big male lion let out a loud rumbling roar that rang out across the land. He casually lumbered down from the elephant's back and took a few steps toward them. Andronicus pulled his sword free, preparing to take the big beast down. But after roaring a few more times, the lion slumped off in the other direction, the cubs at his heel. Andronicus wondered how long the little pride would last without their hunting mothers, and guessed they would all be dead soon enough. When they had gone, Andronicus turned back to Chaka.

"They were not yours to kill," Andronicus said in a low tone that showed his displeasure.

Chaka's lip curled up in anger. "They were defiling him!" His voice cracked slightly as he said it.

"He was theirs to defile," Andronicus replied, his voice picking up as well. "Those lions killed the biggest elephant I have ever seen, and they lost four of their own doing it. They deserved to eat their fill."

Chaka looked down for a moment, as if deep down he agreed with Andronicus, then he glared back up at him. "They killed him," he said stubbornly. "They deserved to die."

"And their children as well?" Andronicus said angrily. Chaka looked down again, a hint of shame in his eyes now.

"Did you think of the children when you killed the Swihmacha?" Chaka asked, giving Andronicus a loathsome look. There was nothing he could say to that. Chaka was right; he had killed an entire village for what a few of them had done. He remembered the little group of children who had run away with an old woman, and chills crept down his spine. He could still see the lion with its few cubs at its heel walking away in the distance, and he felt sick at the eerie similarity.

"Fine," Andronicus said, not meeting Chaka's eyes. "You got your revenge, just like me. They are all dead, and now this mighty elephant will go to the scavengers who have no right to him at all."

"No!" Chaka barked. "He will not go to the dogs."

"Well, we are not going to bury the damn thing," Andronicus said. "It would take weeks to bury this thing."

"We will burn him," Chaka said. Andronicus waited a long time, not breaking his stoic frown, before reluctantly nodding in agreement.

He started clearing the brush as Chaka went for wood to start the fire. As Andronicus looked over the mammoth-sized elephant, he couldn't help thinking what a shame it was to let so much fine ivory go to waste. Most villages would barter for good ivory. He looked around for Chaka, and when he didn't see him, he brought out his sword again. The blade was still sharp, and he thought he could take the end of the tusk off in one blow. He raised the sword over his head, but just before he swung it down, Chaka came running out of the brush.

"Stop!" he shouted. "What are you doing?"

"This ivory is worth more than everything we have combined," Andronicus said, lowering the sword. "We should take it with us."

"You defile him just as the beasts do!" Chaka shouted. "You are no Swihmehe!"

"No!" Andronicus shouted back, getting angry. "I am not. I am Spartan, and in Sparta when you come across a fortune lying dead on the ground, you take it."

"Even if the fortune is that of a god?" Chaka said in a quieter but still stern voice. Andronicus stopped to ponder this for a moment. He wondered what he might do if he ever came across the dead body of Apollo, his golden harp in his arms. If he saw the winged shoes of Hermes just lying in the road, would he take them? He remembered the stories of the gods and their punishments as a child, and he remembered Chief Challah and the other village elders telling similar stories of elephant gods around the fire back in Swimha.

"There are no gods, Chaka," Andronicus finally said in a low dark tone. He turned back to the elephant. "There are only men and beasts and death. This beast is dead, and we are not." With that Andronicus raised his sword again, and brought it down hard. He heard Chaka's anguished cry as the old blade cut through the thick tusk in one clean swing. The bloody end of the great tusk fell to the dirt with a heavy thud.

Andronicus turned back to see tears running down Chaka's cheeks, leaving dark lines down his dirty face. Neither of them said anything for a while. Finally, Chaka went back to making a pyre for the elephant, his face still wet with tears. Andronicus bent down and lifted the heavy tusk with a grunt. It weighed much more than he had expected. He only had about two and a half feet of it, but it weighed as much as a large rock.

Andronicus let Chaka give the elephant its funeral while he washed the blood off the tusk. He felt like an outsider now, a thief.

After cleaning the tusk, he wrapped it in his cloak, trying not to listen to Chaka's words as he prayed over the mighty beast. He knew Chaka would not help him carry the ivory, so he made a sling for it out of his cloak. It would slow them down, but he couldn't bear to leave such fine ivory behind.

Chaka built a pyre around the great dead carcass. Once the wood was set, the brush cleared, and Chaka's prayers were complete, he set fire to the mighty fallen beast. Chaka cried and prayed and clearly had a deep religious experience as he knelt and watched the huge fiery blaze. Andronicus sat on a log a short distance away, staring into the massive flames. It was definitely the biggest fire he had seen since waking in Swimha, and he feared what might happen if Chaka lost control of it.

Andronicus lay down to sleep in the dirt, as his cloak now held the tusk. His eyes stung from the smoke, and his nose was filled with the strong scent of the tons of burning flesh. He slid slowly from the smoky plains into smoky woods. Andronicus looked around, and saw a forest of thin trees. He had never seen the forest before, or even the trees, but they felt familiar all the same. The smoke was thick and black and coming in the from the east. It didn't smell at all like the fire of the elephant had, but it had a pleasant scent nonetheless. Screams came from the direction of the fire, and Andronicus began to walk that way despite the thick smoke.

He was trudging uphill through the thin, smoky forest when he heard a sharp howl. He looked over to see a dark shape moving toward him. Andronicus drew his sword just as the wolf leaped at him, and then he jerked awake, sword in hand.

He looked around and saw Chaka carefully adding more brush to one side of the great burning beast. The sun was already up, but its light had turned orange due to the smoke from Chaka's fire. Andronicus got up and sat back down on his log, not wanting to intrude on Chaka's ritual. He knew how upset Chaka must be with him, and he wondered if he shouldn't have let the ivory go. Seeing what was becoming of the great fallen beast as its body continued to burn, Andronicus thought he should have taken all the ivory. The beast's skin and flesh was burnt to a black crisp, and the bones and ivory were beginning to blacken and burn as well.

In the end it took Chaka the better part of two days to burn the great elephant. A few animals came to inspect the scent it was sending across the land, but they all fled from the great billowing flames. Andronicus stayed off to the side the whole time, feeling shame and anger. Shame for what he had done and anger that he felt ashamed.

When the funeral was finally finished, they made camp for the night. They didn't say so much as a word to each other all night. Andronicus skinned and cooked one of the lionesses they had killed, and they ate silently over a fire, never meeting each other's eyes. The next morning they packed up. Chaka said a final prayer over the elephant's ashes, and then they set off again, heading northeast.

3

They walked through unknown lands for weeks without speaking. Chaka seemed determined to show his anger with Andronicus, even though Andronicus knew he wasn't going to leave him. They had come too far to go back to Swimha; it would probably take years just to find it, if they even could find it again. Chaka had come to help find the lands Andronicus had told him about, and Andronicus knew he wouldn't turn back now. Every time Chaka meant to say something to Andronicus though, he would see the polished white ivory hanging from his shoulders, and the rage would fill him again.

One cold, cloudy day they were walking through a large open plain, preparing to stop and set up camp, when they heard and then saw a group of hunters in the distance. Andronicus wasn't sure if they had been seen yet, and he quickly crouched down, Chaka doing the same. There looked to be at least a dozen hunters, and they were heading their way. Andronicus knew they wouldn't be able to get by unseen; there wasn't enough cover.

Staying low to the ground, he ran over to a dead tree about twenty yards away and put the tusk and the rest of their things under the tree's decaying trunk. After a moment's thought, he unstrapped his armor and laid it down on top of the rest, then pulled some brush over it. He stepped away, looking down at everything that he owned covered by a bit of dead branches and decided it would have to be good enough. He ran back to Chaka, staying low to the ground, and hoped he hadn't been seen yet.

When the hunting party was close, they stood

up slowly to greet them. They lowered their spears and showed their hands but prepared themselves for a fight nonetheless. As the men approached, Andronicus counted an even twelve hunters. They looked tall and fierce, much like the Swihmehe. When they were close enough, Andronicus saw that the men were almost as tall as Chaka. Each man had white markings across his face and body, all unique, similar to the Swihmacha's war paint yet somehow more ominous.

The hunters encircled them, and then one of them stepped forward. More than seven feet tall, he stared down at Andronicus with cold dark eyes. Thick white lines ran under his eyes and across his face, giving him an intimidating look. The man grunted something in a language Andronicus had never heard before. Andronicus slowly raised his hands and made the gesture he always made to strangers—he pointed to himself and then made a walking gesture and pointed north. Even as he did it, he knew that these men were not going to let them pass.

The man glared and shouted something angrily. Several of the other men shouted as well, and none of them sounded close to welcoming. Andronicus's hand crept down to the hilt of his sword, not breaking his gaze from the tall man before him. The leader shouted something to his men, and they all shouted back in unison.

Neither Andronicus nor Chaka needed to understand the language to know what would happen next. Chaka raised his spear and turned to the man nearest him, and Andronicus drew his sword and stepped toward the leader. Before he was able to reach the man, a huge musclebound giant lunged forward and swung a spear at him. Andronicus ducked, feeling the wind of the man's spear on his neck. He stood up and prepared to strike at the man as he swung again, like he usually did to clumsy fools with spears. This man however, was not clumsy. Andronicus stepped to the side as the man pulled back his spear and then he swung it sideways at Andronicus.

Andronicus had not expected the man to be so

quick, and the spear struck him on the side of the head with a loud whack. Andronicus fell to the ground, and before he could get up, a foot came barreling into his gut. Retching and gasping for air, Andronicus turned over to see Chaka being beaten and kicked by three men. Another foot connected solidly with Andronicus' face, and he fell back, sprawled out in the dirt. His head rang loudly, and he saw the leader step over him just before someone hit him again. Then everything went black.

4

When Andronicus came to, he was sitting against a sturdy wooden post planted in the ground. He tried to sit forward and bring his hand up to his face, only to discover his hands were bound behind his back. Another rope bound his feet. He looked up and saw Chaka tied to a post across from him. Chaka's face was a swollen, bloody mess, and he was still unconscious. It was night, but a bright light was coming from somewhere off to Andronicus's right, where he heard many people shouting and whooping. Andronicus could tell they were somewhere within the hunters' village, and he guessed they were having a bonfire, most likely in celebration of capturing them. He only hoped the ceremonies wouldn't involve killing or eating them.

He looked around hurriedly, trying to see anything he could use to get free, and saw his sword stuck in the dirt to his right. They were in the center of a large circular arena with four huge wooden posts in the ground. All around him was nothing but flat red dirt, and his sword was too far to reach. He tried wriggling his hands free, but he could barely budge. The ropes were too tight.

The shouting coming from beyond the nearest huts became a loud chant. It sounded as if more than a hundred people were chanting in unison. As the dull, heavy thumping of drums joined the chorus of voices, Andronicus's heart began to race. The festivities sounded as though they were coming to a head, and he knew they had to escape now.

Andronicus struggled against the ropes and finally managed to loosen the rope around his wrist a tiny bit, but his right arm was still locked in place. He worked as fast as he could, but it wouldn't budge. He felt the strain it was putting on his shoulder as he struggled, but he kept going. He glanced over at Chaka, who was still unconscious, his head flopped to one side, blood dripping from his mouth and the gash on his forehead. The drums picked up their pace, and Andronicus's heart quickened with them.

By the time the drums reached a thundering pitch, Andronicus was sure that a procession of warriors was going to come around the corner at any second. He continued to struggle against the ropes, but he could barely move. His arm had locked into place, with the rope pulled tight against his wrist. He knew the rope would loosen if he could just get his shoulder free, but it had become stuck. The veins on his neck stuck out as he pulled on his shoulder. The booming crash of the drums seemed to get louder by the second, and he could tell they had begun to move toward him. A loud whoop went up from just over the nearest hut. The thundering noise pounded relentlessly into Andronicus's head.

Andronicus closed his eyes and clenched his teeth. He took a deep breath before wrenching his shoulder forward and out of its socket, tearing his flesh and breaking his bones. The pain was immediate and excruciating. Andronicus let out his breath in a painful whimper, and his eyes filled with tears as soon as he opened them.

His shoulder felt like it had been stabbed by a burning blade, but his arm was loose. He wriggled a bit and felt lightning shoot through his whole right side, but the rope around his hand shifted as well. He wriggled again and had to bite on his lower lip to keep from crying out. The coppery taste of blood filled his mouth, and more tears rolled down his face. The rope shifted again, and he felt his right hand begin to free itself.

Andronicus took another deep breath and then used what little strength he had in his broken arm to pull his hand up. It came free of the ropes. He had felt like he was being stabbed a moment before, but that was nothing compared to what he felt now. As he wriggled the ropes off his left hand, his right shoulder felt as if a blade dipped in molten steel was resting between his arm and his torso.

Once his arms were freed, he leaned forward and used his left hand to undo the rope around his ankles, his right arm hanging limp and useless at his side. The pain in his shoulder had drowned out the noise around him for a moment, but now it came flooding back. In an instant the thundering bellow of the drums and chanting came crashing down upon him. Andronicus had to stop untying the ropes and brace himself with his left arm as he struggled not to faint. The loud voices chanting in their foreign tongue sounded closer than ever. He shook his head and began working at the rope around his ankles, his fingers flying as he untied his legs. Then he remembered his sword.

He rolled onto his left side and crawled toward the blade. He pulled it out of the dirt and then easily cut the rope around his legs. Trying not to move his right arm, he stood up and limped over to Chaka. Still using only his left arm, he began cutting Chaka free from the post. The procession was getting louder, and he knew they would be upon him at any moment.

"Chaka," Andronicus whispered so loudly it was nearly a shout, "Chaka, wake up." Chaka's head still hung against his chest, and he showed no signs of waking. Andronicus cut the rope around Chaka's hands, and he fell forward.

"Chaka, I need you to wake up," Andronicus said, his voice filling with panic. He had no idea how the oncoming procession had not managed to reach them yet, but he knew it would be only seconds. Andronicus pulled the rope free from Chaka's hands, and he slumped down into the dirt.

As Andronicus pulled the final rope away from Chaka's legs, Chaka still lay unconscious in the dirt. The shouting was clearly coming from just around the corner now, and he knew he had only seconds to act.

Chaka was too big to carry, especially with a broken arm. He knew he couldn't fight the hunters with his left hand, and he was out of time.

"Chaka!" Andronicus shouted, shaking Chaka's unconscious body. "Chaka, wake up!"

Chaka was not waking up, and the hunters would be there any second. Andronicus stood up, ready to flee. He started running away from the booming noises coming toward him but then stopped and turned back.

He shoved his sword into his belt, then bent down and picked Chaka up with his left arm. He let out a cry of pain as his right shoulder shifted with the weight of Chaka's body. Chaka was even heavier than he had expected, but somehow he managed to get beneath him. Andronicus stood up, Chaka on his shoulder, and let out another cry of pain. As Andronicus ran around the corner with Chaka on his back, he heard a shout and knew someone had heard his cry.

5

Andronicus ran past huts with no one in them, Chaka's limp body slung over his left shoulder like a dead animal. His right arm hung at his side, flopping about as he ran, sending shooting bursts of pain through his shoulder. Andronicus couldn't feel a thing though; he couldn't hear a thing either. His body was filled with more adrenaline than it had been in decades, perhaps more than ever before. The angry shouts and war drums were a thin buzz in his ears as he ran awkwardly through the village. Finally, he reached the end of the huts and ran into a field of grass.

He saw a tall tree far off in the distance but knew he wouldn't make it that far. There was a muddy water hole not far to his left, and he stumbled toward it. Andronicus fell into the mud with a splash, bringing Chaka crashing down with him. Chaka let out a low grunt as his body hit the ground with a squelch and rolled over. Andronicus quickly rolled around in the mud, covering his body in dark slime.

Andronicus pulled Chaka behind some grass and laid him down. Seconds later the first of the hunters came running out of the village, and Andronicus ducked down. From his vantage point, he watched as the hunters came flooding out, holding torches and spears. They were still covered in the white war paint they had been wearing earlier. The hunters shouted and whooped as they ran into the field, their spears high above their heads. They ran past him at full speed, none of them taking the time to check the muddy pit.

Once nearly thirty men had run past them, the drums ceased their listless banging, and the whoops of the hunters died away in the distance. Andronicus heard worried chatter coming from the village, but it sounded like mostly women and children. He crawled painfully back over to Chaka and checked on him. Chaka was breathing normally, but the gash on his head was still bleeding, and a mixture of blood and mud caked his face.

Andronicus shifted to try and move Chaka's head, and a bolt of pain shot through his shoulder. He finally looked down at it and felt his stomach turn. His arm had completely detached from his shoulder, and it looked truly awful. His arm ended in a big ugly ball resting in front of where it should go into his shoulder, and it looked a dark reddish purple color in the moonlight. The old scars stood out eerily on his shoulder, four deep white lines running from the top of his shoulder to what was now the top of his arm, though it should have been his bicep.

Andronicus turned his head away in disgust, not wanting to look at his mangled arm. He knew he had to reset it, but he didn't know how to do it without help. Chaka still lay unconscious in the mud, and he knew the hunters would return eventually, most likely not running this time. All he could do now was wait and hope that he could fix his arm once they were safe.

6

Andronicus waited until the hunters were all

gone before moving again. He knew that some of the hunting party that had gone in search of him would be back soon enough, so he had to act fast. Chaka was still unconscious, though he had mumbled a few times. At the edge of the village stood two guards, each of them holding a torch. The pit Andronicus and Chaka were in was only thirty yards from them, and the light from their torches barely reached them. Andronicus knew that if the hunting party returned, one of the men would surely see them lying there, and that would be the end.

Working slowly, so as not to be seen or heard, Andronicus lifted Chaka over his left shoulder again. The adrenaline that had surged through his veins earlier was gone, and Chaka felt as heavy as a horse. After nearly ten minutes of struggling, Andronicus managed to get on his feet, with Chaka slung over his back. He was behind a bit of brush but would have to leave that cover to escape. The light of the guards' torches dwindled a few yards away from them, but Andronicus still thought the guards might be able to see him.

As he stood there, struggling to think, barely able to stay on his feet, his mind filling with panic, a pack of wild dogs began howling in the distance. Andronicus didn't waste a second. He couldn't see the guards, but he knew his only chance was to run now, with the guards hopefully looking toward the sound of the dogs.

Andronicus leapt out of the muddy pit and started running. He never looked back toward the guards; he just hoped they wouldn't see him. Normally, he was good at hiding his footfalls, but with Chaka's extra weight it was hard to run softly. The dogs continued to howl, and he didn't hear any voices as he ran.

When he reached a tree, he hid behind it and laid Chaka down again. Chaka mumbled something under his breath as his head hit the dirt, but Andronicus didn't have time to check on him. He peered around the tree and saw both of the guards still staring off toward the dogs. He let out his breath in a shuddered sigh of relief.

A yelp shot across the land, and a second later the dogs stopped howling. Andronicus guessed the hunting party must have found them. He watched the guards say something to each other and then return to their post. He couldn't help but laugh to himself; they had been saved by a muddy pit and a pack of wild dogs.

As he lay against the tree, Chaka let out a deep moan and rolled over. He began to say something when Andronicus threw himself on top of him, holding his left hand firmly over Chaka's mouth.

"Quiet," Andronicus whispered into Chaka's ear. "They are still nearby." Chaka let out another moan, his eyes still caked shut with dried blood. Andronicus turned his head toward the guards. They were still staring in the direction of the dogs. He waited for about ten minutes, resting against the tree, struggling to cope with the horrendous pain going through the whole right side of his body.

Eventually, he managed to get Chaka over his shoulder again and started walking. He made it as far as he could and then stopped, carefully lowering Chaka to the ground. When Chaka hit the dirt, his eyes fluttered open, and he looked around in confusion.

"What happened?" he asked, coughing as he sat up.

"We got taken captive," Andronicus said, wondering how to tell Chaka what had happened. "But I got us out."

"How?" Chaka asked, looking around in the darkness.

"It does not matter," Andronicus said as he helped Chaka onto his feet. "Can you walk?"

Chaka nodded. "I think so," he said, taking a tentative step.

"Good," Andronicus replied, starting to walk. "We are still too close to their village. We have to keep moving."

"Where?"

"Somewhere we can hide. This way for now."

Andronicus started walking, trying not to focus

on the burning pain in his chest and arm. He had seen
people dislocate their arms before, and he knew what
he had done was far worse than that. Looking down at
his mangled shoulder made his stomach turn, so he
ignored it and just focused on staying on his feet.
Chaka walked next to him, swaying a bit with every
step. They walked for nearly an hour, until they found
a big rock sticking out of the ground with a place
underneath for cover and a few trees nearby. They
crawled under the rock, and within seconds Chaka was
out cold again. Andronicus slowly sat back against the
rock, wincing in pain. He tried for a while to go to sleep
but wound up spending the whole night in the worst
pain he had ever felt.

Chapter 18
Hard Truths
1

Andronicus decided to wait another day before
trying to find the old dead tree where he had hidden
their belongings. Chaka had awoken several times
during the night, groggy and confused, before
dropping back into restless sleep, and he had mumbled
constantly throughout the night. Andronicus spent the
night keeping watch but mostly just cradling his
crippled arm. When the sun came up, he crawled out
from their spot under the rock and walked over to a
watering hole not far away, wincing with every step.
His shoulder still felt like there was a fire burning
within it, and he knew he had to reset it somehow.

Chaka awoke not long after and limped over to
join him. He dropped to his knees heavily, cupped
water in his hands, and began drinking from the pool
in big gulps. After drinking for a full minute, Chaka sat
back and began cleaning the bloody mess covering his
face. Even after being washed a bit, the gash on his
head still looked bad, and he was moving much slower
than usual.

"I need you to help me with my shoulder,"
Andronicus said.

"There is nothing I can do," Chaka replied
apologetically, his voice weak. "I do not know

medicine."

"I do not need medicine," Andronicus said as he crawled over to a nearby tree. "I need you to push my shoulder back in place."

Chaka shook his head apprehensively, looking at the mangled mess that was Andronicus's arm. "That is a bad idea. It will just make it worse."

"Not if we do it right," Andronicus grunted as he leaned against the tree. He sat up straight, his shoulder resting firmly against the trunk. He took a sturdy-looking stick from the ground and bit down hard on it, then pointed to the exact spot Chaka was to push. Chaka shook his head again, looking scared. Andronicus gave him a look that said there was no other way, and Chaka nodded reluctantly.

Andronicus closed his eyes. His shoulder already hurt worse than anything he had ever felt before, but he knew it was about to get much worse. He knew they could make the problem much worse than it already was, perhaps even so bad that he could die. If he didn't do this now though, his arm would never be the same again. He took three deep breaths and then nodded. Chaka shoved his full weight against Andronicus's arm in one motion. The pain was unfathomable and immediate. The fire seemed to explode out of his arm like lightning. White spots appeared against Andronicus's closed lids, and then he felt himself slip away into darkness.

2

When he came to, he was still slouched against the tree. His shoulder was throbbing softly. When he looked down, he saw that his arm looked like an arm again and was resting in a crudely made sling hung around his neck. He looked up hazily, squinting against the light, and saw that the sun was going down to his left, meaning he had spent the entire day unconscious.

He looked around and saw Chaka sitting by a small fire over by the watering hole, skinning a rabbit. He was using the old knife they had brought from Swimha. He looked around again and saw the rest of their belongings lying in the dirt next to him.

Andronicus's sword was resting beside his armor, along with the rest of his things. He looked to his right and saw the ivory lying on the ground, separate from their other possessions.

"You brought the tusk," Andronicus said with a harsh, raspy cough. "Why?"

Chaka glanced up at the sound of his voice but then looked back down quickly. He didn't say anything for a long time. He finished skinning the rabbit and skewered it over the fire, not looking at Andronicus. Andronicus just sat there staring at him, waiting for an answer. Chaka watched the meat slowly char, his face lined in conflict.

"You saved my life," Chaka said finally, still not looking up from the fire.

"That is not why you got it," Andronicus said, wincing as he sat up. "You could have left it there or let me go for it later."

Chaka finally looked up at him, his face a mixture of emotions. He looked angry, tired, and hurt, but there was something else there too, and Andronicus couldn't quite place it.

"You were right," Chaka said softly, looking back into the fire.

"Right about what?"

"The dead do not need," Chaka said eerily, the orange flames dancing in his eyes. "Not even the gods." His eyes welled up, and his bottom lip began to tremble. "I am alive because of you, Jocus," Chaka said. "If you say we need the tusk, then we need it. If you say we need to cross the great water, then we will." Chaka turned back and stared into the fire.

"I still do not know who you are, Jocus," he said after a long pause, his eyes reflecting the crackling orange flames. Andronicus raised his eyebrows and started to speak, but Chaka waved him off. "I know who you are, but at the same time I do not. You came to us many years ago. When I first saw you, I did not even know *what* you were. I had never seen a man like you before." Chaka let out a dry chuckle. "A short, fierce-looking man with light skin, a yellow shirt made of stone, and a big red blanket hung on your back." They both laughed. Andronicus still remembered the looks on their faces when he had put his armor on.

"I thought we would kill you and bring you back to our village. But we did not kill you. When you beat my brother in that fight, I could not believe it. No one had ever beaten Kwesi before, not even me, and you did it after being attacked by a lion."

Andronicus just sat against the tree, silent, listening to Chaka talk. It was more than he had said in weeks, if not months.

Chaka removed the charred rabbit from the spit and started to cut off pieces of meat. "When we took you in, it was only supposed to be for a little while. I do not know if Manyara ever told you that."

"No," Andronicus said softly, taking a piece of meat when Chaka offered it.

"My father only agreed to let you in because of what you had done to Kwesi." Chaka laughed. "It seems strange now that we let you in for beating one of us, but it was so impressive." Andronicus bit into the charred rabbit and winced at the taste. "We are not a warrior people, Jocus; you know that." Chaka bit into his own piece, and they sat in silence for a moment chewing the tough meat. "I wanted you to teach us how to fight."

"You never asked me to teach you to fight," Andronicus said. "I would have taught you."

"I know." Chaka nodded, and his eyes watered up again. "Manyara asked me not to. She said you spent too much time thinking about fighting and killing, and she was going to change you."

"She couldn't change me." Andronicus sighed and put down the meat. "No one can. I was born to be a fighter. It is all I have ever been."

"It is not all you have ever been," Chaka said. "You were good to my sister. You were good to my people."

"And look how it ended," Andronicus said. "How long did your people have peace with the Swihmacha before I came?"

"What they did was not your fault."

"Then who's fault was it?" Andronicus shouted, wincing again as his shoulder flared up. He shifted against the tree and glared at Chaka. "Because of me, Manyara is dead, and Chako, and all the rest who died that day. Because of me you will never see your home again."

"I made the choice to leave," Chaka said. "You told me not to come, but I did anyway. Do you know why?" Andronicus shook his head slowly. He had never gotten a real answer as to why Chaka had come, and he realized he wasn't sure he wanted to know. "It was not because of the land you spoke of," Chaka said, "where the huts are made of rock, big enough to fit a hundred people inside, and there are great gods who rule over everything. It was not because of the story you told where you touched a magical shining rock that brought you to us." Chaka stared intently at Andronicus. "I came with you because there is something inside you."

"What are you talking about?" Andronicus asked, feeling a harsh dryness in his throat.

"I have known you for many years, Jocus, and you look exactly the same as the day I first met you. You have more scars, but not one hair on your head has gone white. I was young when we met, and now I am old. But you are not. Your face has not changed at all, and you are as strong as you ever were." Chaka stopped and sighed. "I used to think you were a liar, or crazy. I did not know where you came from, nor did I care, but I never really believed your story."

"And now?" Andronicus asked. Chaka looked at him with a seriousness he had never seen on his face before.

"Now I suppose I really do believe," Chaka said. "We should have died by now, Jocus. We should have died last night, but we did not. You saved us. You saved me." Chaka stopped and looked down, but Andronicus knew there was something more he wanted to say.

"Go on Chaka," Andronicus urged. "Say it all."

"Whatever happened to you that day, it changed you," Chaka said. "You say in your homeland people die all the time. You said your own father died when you were only a child. You should be dead by now, or an old man."

"I know," Andronicus said. He had never said it aloud, but he had been thinking about it for some time. He still didn't know why he looked so young, but he had begun to suspect it wasn't just his looks. Chaka was right. He was too young. It had been too long. He should have grown old and frail by now, and his hair should have gone white. Chaka's hair was already speckled with grey, and his face had many lines that hadn't been there when they met.

"Like I said, whatever happened to you that day, it changed you. I can feel it. You are not like other people, Jocus. It is not just your skin or your skills. There is something about you, and I think it came from those rocks."

"I know," Andronicus nodded. He hadn't spoken this open about it since Manyara had died. "Whatever happened in that cave, it did change me. I still feel the same, but I suppose that is the problem. I should feel old by now, but I do not. I feel as strong as I ever did. Well, maybe not at the moment." He looked down at his swollen and bruised shoulder.

"You are not getting older, Jocus," Chaka said. As soon as the words were out of his mouth, Andronicus knew they were true. He hadn't ever put the thought together, but now that it was said, it was more obvious than he could believe. "Perhaps you never will," Chaka added, eyeing him oddly.

"You think I cannot die?" Andronicus asked, knowing it wasn't true.

"No." Chaka shook his head. "I know you can still die; everyone dies, but you may have to wait for a long time."

"Most people would kill to be able to live forever," Andronicus said.

"That is because they know it cannot happen," Chaka replied. "But it is happening to you. Someday I will be too old and weak to travel. What will you do then? And what about when I die? You will still be the same man you have been all this time."

Andronicus stayed silent. He hadn't considered that. He knew Chaka was getting older; he had known for some time, but he hadn't thought much about it. But Chaka was right; eventually, he would be too old to keep going. Then Andronicus would have to go it alone. The thought of walking day after day through the plains all alone terrified him.

"You do not know that," he said, trying not to agree with Chaka, and failing. "We could find Greece before then. Or somewhere else maybe."

"You are not looking for somewhere else, Jocus. You are looking for Greece. We do not even know if we can find it, or how long it will take."

"We can find it," Andronicus insisted. "I know it; I can feel it. And when we get there, we can get some answers. Someone must know what happened to me. We will find Greece and the answers. We just have to keep going."

Chaka nodded solemnly. ""I will keep going, but I fear I will never see Greece. You may, but I will have died long before you find your home again."

"You never know, Chaka," Andronicus said with a sad smile. "You may see Greece yet. It seems as though nothing is certain anymore." Chaka nodded slowly, then tossed away the bone he had been chewing.

3

After supper they discussed their route out of the hostile lands of the Kahli. It seemed safest to travel at night until they were far enough away, so they waited until just after sundown. When the light was gone from the land, they gathered their belongings and set out again. The ivory was in a bag slung over Chaka's shoulder, along with most of their goods. Andronicus was able to carry a small bag on his left shoulder, but his right arm lay in the sling, totally useless. He tried to move the fingers on his right hand and winced at the pain it sent through his arm. He didn't manage to move his fingers, but he thought it was a good sign that he could still feel pain in them.

They crept across the land for the next two

nights. They were moving much slower than they had been before their run-in with their captors. Andronicus was only able to carry the small bag, and Chaka was still weak from his own wounds. And as they traveled farther north, Andronicus began to worry more about the wound on Chaka's head.

The gash was at least five inches long, starting at his forehead and moving up through his hair, and it had started to take on a nasty color. Green had joined the shades of red and brown, and the skin around the cut was turning a nasty dark shade of red. Andronicus knew the wound was infected and needed treating, but he had no medicine to give him.

One night, more than a week after they had escaped, Andronicus held his sword over a fire until it was red hot. Chaka bit down on a stick, just as Andronicus had done with his shoulder. Chaka closed his eyes and clenched his fists. Andronicus counted to three and then pressed the knife into the cut. The hot blade seared through the gash as Andronicus tried to cut and burn away the infection. Chaka let out a pained cry, but he didn't move. Andronicus wanted to turn away from the awful smell of burning hair and flesh, but he had to work as fast as he could.

When he was finished, Chaka let out a long, deep sigh and tumbled down into the dirt. Tears covered his face, and he wiped them away, wincing as he touched the burnt cut.

Andronicus thought he had been able to get rid of most of the infected skin around the cut, but he feared it might be too late. Chaka had been walking slower and slower and needed to take more frequent rests every day. Andronicus knew that if they did not get Chaka help from a proper healer, he would probably die.

Andronicus began carrying the heavy bag over his left shoulder, which slowed them down even further. Chaka's skin had taken on a terrible ashy color, sweat shown out across his entire body, and he walked slumped over, like a man struggling with every step. Andronicus had to get Chaka help soon, if it wasn't already too late.

4

Their movement had become painfully slow, as Chaka had to lean on his spear just to walk. His wound looked awful, and he seemed to be slipping in and out of consciousness as he stumbled along. Andronicus was carrying most of the weight, which wasn't easy with his mangled shoulder, and he felt like they were barely moving. They kept walking north through dry open plains, hoping to find a healer before Chaka got any worse.

Three weeks after they had escaped from the Kahli, they were trudging through the plain when Andronicus saw a big black mass in the distance. At first he had no idea what it was and was a bit nervous. He could tell it was many miles away, but it was so big that it looked much closer. As they drew nearer, the black shape getting bigger all the while, Andronicus realized it was a massive herd, bigger than any he had ever seen.

He had seen water buffalo often since waking in Swimha, but never in a group of more than a hundred or so. This was a group of thousands, though just how many, Andronicus had no idea. It looked as big as the army he had marched with against the Persians.

As it got closer, and he saw more of the thousands of buffalo running together, he thought it looked bigger than the Persian army as well. It seemed impossible that so many beasts should be able to move together without trampling each other to death.

"They are going south to find the great water lands," Chaka said in a raspy voice, snapping Andronicus out of his trance. "When I was a boy, a man visited my village and told us a story about the great migration. Did we ever tell it to you?"

"No," Andronicus said, certain he would remember such a story.

"The great herd only comes as far south as our village once in a lifetime, or so my father used to tell me," Chaka continued, staring out at the massive herd. "But there was a man who came to Swimha who used to walk many lands, and he said the great herd moves south every year in search of the water lands. It is not just the buffalo but the elephants too."

"How do they all run together like that?" Andronicus mused. "They should be leaving a pile of trampled bodies in their wake, but there are none."

"The buffalo have been running together long before we walked these lands, Jocus," Chaka said. "They were here before us, and they will be here after us. This is more their land than ours. We are only a small part of Swimha."

"Do you think we are still in Swimha?" Andronicus asked.

"I do not know," Chaka said sadly. "Before, Swimha was the whole world to me, but we left my homeland long ago. The same animals may roam here, but this is not Swimha." They sat in silence for a long while, watching the herd move past them.

"What was the legend?" Andronicus asked.

"The what?" Chaka said, sounding confused.

"The legend your father used to tell you about the great migration. You said there was a story about it."

"Yes," Chaka nodded slowly as he gazed out at the multitude of roaming buffalo. "They say the great herd are our ancestors. As the Swihmehe die, they return to the land as the wildebeest and the buffalo. Once in a lifetime, the great herd moves south and collects the new souls. If the legend is true, my father and my father's fathers are out there, and so is my sister."

Andronicus looked over at Chaka at the mention of Manyara. Chaka was still gazing out at the herd, but there were tears in his eyes. Andronicus remained silent and turned back to look at the buffalo.

"I will be part of the great herd soon," Chaka added.

"No," Andronicus replied. "We will find a healer. You are not going to die."

"I am, and you know it." Chaka coughed. "It should not have taken this long."

"And they should not be able to run together

like that without killing each other," Andronicus said, pointing at the herd. "But they are. And you are not dead. You just have to keep moving, and we will find a village."

"I will keep walking until I cannot get up," Chaka said with a sigh, "but you know I do not have long."

Andronicus hated it, but he knew Chaka was right. The cut on his head looked worse than any wound Andronicus had ever seen, and it wouldn't take much longer to finish him off. He refused to give up on finding another village though; he just hoped the next village they encountered wouldn't be like the last one. As long as they kept moving, there was still hope, but Andronicus didn't know how much longer Chaka would be able to keep moving. Despite his assurances to the contrary, it seemed all too certain that he would be burying his friend in this strange and foreign wilderness.

Chapter 19
Healing
1

As the sun rose in the east, Andronicus looked over at Chaka and was sure it would be his last day. Chaka's skin had become an ugly grey color, except for the dark blackish-red lines running from the horrible greenish-brown cut on his head down into his tired face. His eyes were a vile red, as if they were filled with blood. Chaka ate slowly, not saying a word, struggling just to chew. When he had gotten a bit of food down, Andronicus gathered their things, all of which he was now carrying, and they set off.

Each step Chaka took looked like it would be his last, and his breath came out in terrible rattling coughs. His eyes stared off into nothing as he stumbled along like a drunkard. Andronicus didn't know what to say to him or if Chaka could even understand anything. He looked like he was barely conscious.

Andronicus was starting to think about where he should take Chaka to die when he saw a village from afar. It was across a shallow valley, at the top of a small hill. Andronicus let out a long sigh of relief and told Chaka to rest. Chaka immediately collapsed into the dirt and began struggling for his water pouch. Andronicus knelt down to help him with it, gently bringing the gourd to Chaka's lips.

"There is a village over there," Andronicus said. "I am going to get you help. Wait here." Chaka nodded weakly. Andronicus strapped his sword to his side and left the rest of their things with Chaka. He started off, then went back and grabbed the bag with the block of ivory in it as an afterthought.

2

The village looked small as he ran up the hill beneath it. He could only hope the people would be kinder than the last people he met.

As he reached the top of the hill he heard shouts rising from the village. A moment later five men ran out with long spears in their hands. Andronicus put his left hand up in peace, but not before making sure his sword was ready for a quick left-handed draw if he needed it. His right arm still hung useless in his makeshift sling.

When the men reached him, they spread out quickly, encircling him. A tall, fierce-looking man with a long dark scar running across his face stepped forward and spoke loudly. Andronicus didn't know what language he was speaking, but he was able to understand a few words. It wasn't the same language as the hunters who had taken them captive, which was a good sign.

Andronicus slowly brought his hand down to the bag slung over his shoulder, never breaking eye contact with the scarred leader. He reached inside, moving at a snail's pace, and took out the block of ivory. All five men lowered their spears when they saw the shiny white object. The leader began speaking quickly, and Andronicus couldn't make out anything he was saying.

Andronicus still wasn't sure if they were hostile or not, but he knew Chaka didn't have time to waste.

Andronicus handed the ivory to the leader, and the man stopped speaking in mid-sentence and stared at Andronicus as if he couldn't believe his eyes. All five men exchanged comical looks of surprise.

"Healer," Andronicus said in the tongue he thought the leader had spoken to him. The man looked even more surprised, but Andronicus couldn't tell if he had understood him or not. He repeated himself, and then said the word in every language he had heard since leaving the Swihmehe, hoping one would work. The leader looked at a short stocky man to his right and said something in a language Andronicus had never heard before. The short man nodded, and then the leader turned and nodded to Andronicus.

Before Andronicus could say anything else, the leader started marching back toward the village. Andronicus looked around and saw the other men waiting for him. He started after the leader, and the others followed. He wanted to tell them that he didn't have time for this, but he didn't know how.

As usual, all the villagers gathered to stare at Andronicus as he was marched into the village. He was used to being regarded as an alien, being the only white man anyone in these lands had ever seen. As they reached the center of the village, an old bald man came out of a big hut. He was wearing a loincloth and a large odd-looking headdress.

"Do you speak Twahli?" Andronicus asked without any real hope.

"I do," the old man replied in a croaky voice. Andronicus let out a deep sigh of relief.

"Thank the gods," he said to himself. "Do you have a healer in your village?"

"I am a healer," the old man said, carefully enunciating every word.

"My friend," Andronicus said, pointing across the valley. "He needs help. He is sick."

The old man stayed silent for a while, staring at Andronicus. The entire village, including the men who had fetched him, were all gathered around, waiting for the old man to speak. Andronicus wanted to tell the old man to hurry up, but knew he had to wait.

"You come bearing gifts?" the old man asked, then turned to the scarred man who was still holding the block of ivory. He stepped forward and handed it to the old man without a word. The old man held the ivory up and admired it for a moment before handing it back.

"I have more," Andronicus said, feeling the awful slowness of it all. "I will give you all of it. Just help my friend, please." The old man took another painfully long silence before finally giving Andronicus a curt nod.

"Bring him to me," the old man said, then turned away before Andronicus could reply. The scarred man stepped forward, giving Andronicus an expectant look. Andronicus didn't waste any time. He ran off in Chaka's direction, the same five men from before now following him. Ignoring the pain shooting through his shoulder, he ran as fast as he could, hoping he was not too late.

3

When they finally reached Chaka, he was unconscious. The short, stocky man said something in the language Andronicus couldn't understand, and the others nodded. Andronicus knelt beside Chaka as the others watched. He placed his hand on Chaka's forehead and felt the heat rising off him.

"Help me with him," Andronicus said to the leader. The man shook his head. "Sick," he said in a low voice, staring unmercifully down at Chaka.

"No help, no ivory," Andronicus said, glaring fiercely at the man.

"We take," the man said, pointing at Andronicus's limp right arm. Andronicus slowly reached for his sword with his left hand, ready to kill the man, when one of the others stepped forward. He was much younger than the rest, barely as old as Andronicus had been when he first went to war. The boy knelt across from Andronicus, and placed his hands under Chaka's back. He looked at Andronicus with a wary smile. Andronicus nodded, and they lifted Chaka up. It was nearly impossible to do with just the two of them, but a moment later one of the other men joined in, and then another, and finally even the leader and his stocky friend.

It took the six of them nearly an hour to get Chaka's unconscious body back to the village. Sweat was pouring off Chaka like rain, and their hands kept slipping as they struggled to carry him. They walked past all the murmuring watchers and went to the large hut in the middle of the village. They bent down and carried Chaka into the hut.

Inside, a fire was smoking in the corner. The old man was sitting beside it mixing something in a bowl. They laid Chaka down in the dirt away from the fire. Everyone but the scarred man and Andronicus got up and left. The scarred man walked over to the entrance of the hut and knelt there silently, standing guard.

Andronicus turned to the old man. "Can you save him?"

"I can give him medicine," the old man said, standing up. "But beyond that, it is not for me to decide." He knelt beside Andronicus, reached into the bowl, and scooped out the brown paste he had been mixing with his fingers. Andronicus couldn't tell what was in it, but he had to trust the man.

The old man spread the paste over the nasty cut on Chaka's head, completely covering it. It didn't look at all like the green muck Chiomi had put on Andronicus's shoulder back in Swimha, and it smelled much worse. When the old man was done, he stood up and walked back to the corner. He returned a moment later with another bowl, this one filled with a steaming dark brown liquid.

"He must drink," the old man said sternly.

"He is asleep," Andronicus replied.

"He must wake," the old man said, then laid the bowl in the dirt before walking back to the fire, not offering any solution. Andronicus took a deep breath and tried to calm his mind. Then an idea came to him.

"My things," he said softly in Twahli. "I need to get my bag." Andronicus stood up and started toward the door, but the scarred man blocked his path. The old man said something to the scarred man in their language, and he replied angrily. The old man repeated his order, and after a lingering glare, the scarred man left. Andronicus turned to the old man, about to ask what he had said, when the scarred man returned with Andronicus's bag in his hands.

Andronicus couldn't remember seeing any of the men pick up the bag; he must have been too focused on Chaka to notice. The scarred man threw the bag down in front of him, glaring angrily. Ignoring him, Andronicus reached inside and fumbled around. After a moment of searching, he found the bag of salt they had gotten from a village by the sea. He took out a pinch and held it under Chaka's nose. It was an old soldier's trick he had learned from Archelaus.

After a few seconds, Chaka's eyes fluttered open. He looked around in confusion, utterly bewildered.

"You have to drink this, Chaka," Andronicus said, lifting his head up. The old man appeared at his side and brought the bowl up to Chaka's lips. Chaka looked as though he was struggling just to stay awake, but he slowly drank the liquid. It took nearly ten minutes for him to drink it all, and when he was done, he immediately fell back into a deep sleep. The old man walked back to the fire.

"That is all?" Andronicus asked.

"That is all," the old man replied as he sat down beside the fire. "Now he will either live or die. There is nothing more we can do."

"You said you are a healer," Andronicus said angrily, "there must be something more you can do."

"I have done all I can," the old man replied. "Everything that can be done for him has been done. Now it is time for him to win this fight on his own."

4

Andronicus waited anxiously for four days before Chaka finally woke up. The old man, whom Andronicus now knew as Nnamdi, had given him a small hut to sleep in while he waited for Chaka to heal, in exchange for the block of ivory. Nnamdi seemed to be an honorable man. He was the leader of the village, and Andronicus could tell that if not for Nnamdi, he would have been turned away already.

In talking to Nnamdi, Andronicus learned several important things. First, the village was just a week's walk from what Nnamdi called the Great Jungle. From what he told Andronicus, it sounded like the jungle was truly massive. Andronicus would need time to heal, and so would Chaka, if he made it, before they could even try to cross this Great Jungle. Andronicus would have been happy to stay with Nnamdi and his tribe, the Bahitu, until they were both fit to travel, but the second piece of information made him truly scared.

Nnamdi told Andronicus that he knew of the hunters who had captured them. They were called the Kahli, and they ruled over all the lands south of the jungle. Nnamdi said it would likely take months before they were out of the Kahli's hunting territory. The Kahli sounded more like a Persian warlord than any of the tribes Andronicus had come across. They took a monthly tax from every other village, killing two male children any time a village couldn't pay up.

They didn't take food, as they didn't need to. They were the best hunters in the area, and they could feed themselves with ease. It was skilled labor they wanted from the other tribes. In the case of the Bahitu, they wanted their cloth. Nnamdi showed Andronicus their skill in sewing, as well as the pile of tools and trophies they had already set aside for the Kahli.

Nnamdi told Andronicus that the Kahli had already come looking for him two days earlier and would almost surely be back. He also told Andronicus that the Kahli would find out about him eventually. Andronicus knew it was true and that he had a serious problem. Chaka still had not woken, and Andronicus's right arm was still useless. He couldn't run, and when the Kahli came for him, these people would give him up, so he couldn't hide either.

He had no desire to try and fight them again,

at least not yet. He had been fully armed, both in weaponry and body, and been defeated. He felt a bit helpless as he pondered the situation. For the first time in his life he had an enemy that he didn't know how to defeat, and it scared him.

5

Andronicus spent four days waiting with Nnamdi in his large hut. Chaka lay in the corner, breathing a bit better than before but not much. As they waited, Nnamdi told Andronicus all about the Kahli and his own tribe, the Bahitu. He also told him about the Great Jungle, or at least what he knew of it.

Andronicus had seen all different kinds of wilderness since waking in Swimha, and he wasn't afraid of a jungle, but Nnamdi made him afraid. Nnamdi made it sound like this jungle was not only massive but actually impenetrable. His people had lived by the jungle for generations, and no one had ever crossed it and returned. Andronicus still firmly believed that north was the way to go, but now he wasn't sure what to do.

The day he had arrived, Nnamdi had agreed to take a look at his shoulder. After inspecting it from all angles, Nnamdi made several small corrections with his hands, shifting the arm ever so slightly. Each small adjustment sent bolts of pain shooting down Andronicus's side, and he had to close his eyes so as not to tear up. Nnamdi told him he had done an expert job at realigning it himself, but it would still take a very long time to heal.

Andronicus was outside sitting on a rock just outside the village, watching a herd of buffalo when Kofi, the scarred man whom Andronicus had met on the first day, came walking up to him. He was one of the only people in the village who could speak Twahli.

"Your friend is awake," Kofi said. Andronicus let out a deep sigh of relief. He gave Kofi a nod of thanks, then hurried back to the village. He wasn't sure what he should tell Chaka. He had been trying to think of a way out of their situation, but so far he hadn't come up with anything.

When he got back to Nnamdi's hut, Chaka was sitting up and drinking from a bowl of water. Nnamdi was sitting by the small fire, as he seemed to be most of the time. Andronicus knelt beside Chaka and studied his face. He looked much better than he had in weeks. His skin was a healthier color, and the lines running from the cut had started to fade.

"Where are we?" Chaka asked in a weak voice.

"In a small village near a jungle," Andronicus told him, speaking slowly in Chaka's mother tongue. "The people here have agreed to let us stay until you are ready to continue on." Chaka put the bowl down and sighed. He looked gaunt, and his eyes had a faraway gaze.

"I thought I was going to die," he said softly, looking at Andronicus.

"Not yet, brother." Andronicus smiled, and clapped him lightly on the back. "We still have a jungle to cross." Chaka's mouth bent into a slight smile, but his eyes stayed dark. He grabbed the bowl and drank more water. Andronicus looked over at Nnamdi, who was sitting cross-legged with his eyes closed and his hands resting on his knees.

"You said they agreed to let us stay here," Chaka said. "Why?"

"The ivory," Andronicus said, smiling faintly. "I gave it to them in exchange for a small hut on the far side of the village." Chaka closed his eyes, and his brow furrowed as Andronicus continued speaking. "Nnamdi," Andronicus gestured to the old man, "he convinced the others to let us stay. He says we can stay longer if we like." Andronicus hesitated, wondering if he should tell Chaka about their problem. Chaka gazed off in silence for a moment, and then a pained smile stretched across his face.

"The ivory," he said. "I called you a monster for taking that tusk. And what did you say?" Chaka looked at Andronicus for a response.

"I do not remember," Andronicus replied, still thinking about the Kahli.

"You said, 'The dead do not need, and we are not dead,'" Chaka said, staring off into space. "You were right, Jocus." Andronicus nodded slowly, not sure what to say.

"How long do you think they will let us stay here?" Chaka asked, glancing at the old man.

"I do not know," Andronicus replied, finally deciding to tell Chaka the truth. "If it were up to them, I think we would be welcome for some time. But they are not the only people here. The hunters, the ones who took us, they come through these parts, and take whatever they want, and they will be back."

"What will you do when they come?" Chaka asked, setting the bowl aside. "I am too weak to fight, and even if I was not, those men are better fighters than me. And you." Chaka looked at Andronicus's swollen shoulder, "you will not be able to swing that sword of yours for a long time."

"I know." Andronicus sighed. "We cannot fight them, at least not now. Perhaps we can offer them some of the ivory."

"Those men do not need your ivory, Jocus," Chaka said, lying back in the dirt. "If they want an elephant's tusk, I am sure they can kill one and take it."

"Well, then I guess we just have to hope that Nnamdi can help protect us for now." Andronicus saw the old man's head move and thought it must have been at the sound of his name.

"How long have I been out?" Chaka asked, taking another drink.

"Four and a half days," Andronicus said, looking him in the eye. Chaka's eyes were still bloodshot, but looked far better than before. Chaka looked as if he didn't believe it could have been that long, but Andronicus held his gaze firmly, and Chaka nodded in understanding.

"So," Chaka said, setting the bowl aside again and taking a piece of meat from Andronicus, "what have you learned about these people while I have slept?"

"They are good people," Andronicus said after a moment's thought, "at least from what I can tell. They are not as good at hunting as the Swihmehe, but they are much better weavers." Andronicus nodded at the new sling around his arm. It was a fine weave of light strings that was soft and easy on his swollen dead arm. Chaka admired it for a moment and then nodded.

"We should learn that trick before we go into this jungle."

"Agreed," Andronicus said with a nod.

"Your arm," Chaka said, pointing at it. "Can you feel it?"

"Yes," Andronicus replied, looking down at it. "I am sure someday I will be able to use it again, but not now."

"And what about me?" Chaka asked. "I thought that cut was the end of me."

"The infection seems to be healing," Andronicus said. "I have no idea how Nnamdi did it, but whatever he gave you, he saved your life."

"His life was not mine to save," Nnamdi said from the corner. Andronicus and Chaka both spun toward him in shock. The old man had spoken in Swihmehe. They hadn't heard anyone else but themselves speak Swihmehe in years.

"You speak Swihmehe?" Andronicus said, gazing at the old man in wonder.

"I speak many tongues," Nnamdi replied, still sitting in his cross-legged position.

"How do you know our language?" Chaka asked, struggling to raise his voice.

"I visited the land of the Swimha in my youth," Nnamdi replied. "I stayed there for three years."

"You must have known my father then," Chaka said, sitting up straighter.

"Who is your father?" the old man asked.

"Challah," Chaka said proudly, "son of Choko, chief of the Swihmehe." The old man gazed at Chaka for a moment, his head slightly cocked, as if he was gauging whether or not it was a lie.

"You are Challah's son?" Nnamdi asked without giving away any sign of his thoughts toward Challah. Andronicus knew that telling Nnamdi this was a risk; they didn't know what he thought of Challah. But Challah was a good man and an honorable leader, and

Andronicus thought Nnamdi was as well, so he had to hope they had been friends.

"I was his eldest son," Chaka said, his voice cracking slightly. "I forfeited my birthright as chief to follow this man on his journey to his homeland."

"Challah is dead then?" Nnamdi asked, looking Chaka in the eyes.

"I do not know," Chaka said, sounding both sad and ashamed. "When we left, he was weak but still alive. We had been attacked by the Swihmacha."

"And you left your people?" Nnamdi asked, looking surprised for the first time.

"Not before he killed the Swihmacha," Chaka said, gesturing toward Andronicus, his gaze never faltering. "Jocus went to their village alone and killed them all."

Nnamdi looked at Andronicus in wonder. "You killed the Swihmacha?"

"I did," Andronicus replied, not knowing how Nnamdi might feel about that either.

"Why?" Nnamdi asked, raising his brows slightly. "You are not Swihmehe. Why avenge their chief?"

"The Swihmehe took me in," Andronicus said. "I took a wife, built a home. I respected Chief Challah, and his people."

"So, why did you leave?" Nnamdi asked. Andronicus hesitated, not sure how much to tell Nnamdi. They all sat in silence for a long moment as Nnamdi waited for Andronicus's answer. Finally, he looked Nnamdi in the eyes and told him the truth.

"I left in search of the thing that brought me to the land of the Swimha." Nnamdi squinted, giving Andronicus a curious look.

"I am not sure, I understand you," Nnamdi finally said.

"I am from a place called Sparta in a land called Greece," Andronicus explained. "Many years ago my kin and I came across a great white light in a dark cave. We touched it, and I woke up in the land of the Swimha without any sign of my kin. Chaka and I left the land of the Swimha in search of this light." Nnamdi gave Andronicus an odd look. No one spoke for some time, and Andronicus was sure that Nnamdi didn't believe him.

"How old are you, Jocus?" Nnamdi asked, staring at him fiercely.

Andronicus shrugged. "I do not know." He knew he had to be in his late fifties at least, but he had lost track of the years long ago. "But I am older than I look."

"I believe we have much to learn from one another, Jocus," Nnamdi said, looking him firmly in the eye. Andronicus nodded, wondering what the old man meant. Nnamdi knowing Swihmehe was something he hadn't expected, and now he wanted to know more. This village seemed like the perfect place to rest and heal before taking on the jungle. The only thing Andronicus had to do now was find a way to avoid getting killed by the Kahli.

Chapter 20
Better to Burn Out
1

The Kahli hunters arrived just after dusk on the fifth day. Six of them came walking up the hill, casually holding their long spears at their sides. Andronicus walked out with Nnamdi to meet them. He knew he couldn't run or hide, so he just had to take his chances.

As they approached the tall, intimidating men, Andronicus recognized the man who had led the party that attacked him and Chaka. He was tall and fierce like his companions but much older than the rest, and Andronicus knew he was their leader. He hadn't noticed before, but the man had to be in his forties at least, but he still looked as strong as a bull elephant.

His cold, dark eyes moved from Nnamdi to Andronicus, resting for a while on the latter's swollen mess of a shoulder. He was eying Andronicus more like stolen property than a human, and it made him feel weak. When the man finally turned back to Nnamdi, he began giving orders in their native language. When he was done, he turned back to Andronicus with a look of contentious triumph. Nnamdi replied, but the tall man's face didn't change in response to his words.

One of the Bahitu ran up with Andronicus's ivory in his arms and dumped it at the hunters' feet. The tall man looked down at the tusk, then back at Nnamdi and said something short and stern.

"He says it is not enough," Nnamdi said, lowering his eyes. "He wants you and Chaka. I am sorry, Jocus. There is nothing more I can do."

"Tell him I can give him something else," Andronicus said, hoping the plan he had been forming might work.

"What more do you have to offer?" Nnamdi asked.

"My armor," Andronicus said, knowing it was the only thing left. It was either that or his sword, and he would never give that up.

"What is that?" Nnamdi asked, giving Andronicus a puzzled look.

"The golden shirt," Andronicus replied, "the one I brought with me." Nnamdi nodded slowly, but he didn't look convinced. Nevertheless, he sent his man off to get it. When the man returned, he dropped Andronicus's armor at the hunters' feet beside the ivory. It made a dull clunk as it hit the dirt. The tall man frowned as he looked at the armor. It had lost its shine long ago and was covered in dozens of dents and divots. The steel straps on the side had even begun to rust. It looked nothing like it once had. The leader turned to Nnamdi and shouted angrily.

"They do not want it," Nnamdi said. "They want you."

"Tell him I can give him something else," Andronicus pleaded, looking the hunter in the eyes.

"What?" Nnamdi asked before relaying the message.

"I can make things," Andronicus said, unsure if he could actually accomplish what he was thinking of. "Tell him I will make him a golden cup. To drink from," Andronicus added when he realized Nnamdi didn't know what a cup was. "Tell him he will want to see it before he kills me."

"How will you make this, cup?" Nnamdi asked, intrigued.

"Just tell him I will make it," Andronicus said, still staring at the fierce hunter. "It will take me a few moons, but I will make it."

Nnamdi shook his head but reluctantly relayed Andronicus's message to the hunters. The leader listened to Nnamdi, but never took his eyes off Andronicus. He stepped forward and stared down into Andronicus's eyes like a hungry wolf. Andronicus stood his ground, but he knew the man could kill him whenever he wanted, which was an entirely new feeling for him. He wished more than anything that his right arm was healed, but there was nothing he could do about it.

The tall man stared down at Andronicus with a mixture of contempt and curiosity now. Finally, the man turned to Nnamdi, said something brief in their language, and then started walking away. Two of the Bahitu ran up with finely woven baskets full of blankets and handed them to the other Kahli hunters. The hunters took the baskets and the ivory, then marched off after their leader. Andronicus turned back to Nnamdi, wondering what the man had said.

"He said you have until the great rains fall," Nnamdi said, answering his unspoken question. "Then he will kill you."

"How long until the great rains?" Andronicus asked, picking up his armor and dusting it off.

"Two moons, maybe three. They do not want your iron shirt," Nnamdi added, shaking his head. "It is ugly."

"I told you, it will not be a shirt," Andronicus said with a wry smile. "It will be a cup."

2

The Bahitu allowed Andronicus and Chaka to stay with them, even though the Kahli had taken the ivory. They were a kind people, and they treated them well from the start. The Bahitu were the best weavers Andronicus had ever seen, better even than the Greeks. Within weeks he had them weaving new things they had never heard of before. They were fascinated by his old red cloak, and he wished he could tell them how it was dyed, but he didn't know. All of their cloth was brown, but it was a sturdier weave than Andronicus had ever seen.

Ever since he had awoken in Swimha, Andronicus had been drinking from bowls or gourds, but now he had water bags again. The Bahitu were able to sew him fabulous new bags out of a water buffalo hide. Andronicus' had thrown his old sandals out years ago and had been on bare feet ever since, but now he had the Bahitu make him sandals. It felt a bit odd after so many years without them. He had them make Chaka a pair as well, but Chaka wouldn't wear them. He had been walking on bare feet since he was born, and he didn't like the idea of shoes.

While the Bahitu sewed, and Nnamdi prayed, and Chaka healed, Andronicus worked on his new project. He was no blacksmith, but he had spent enough time as a young man in Niko's father's workshop that he thought he might be able to get it done. His own mother had been a blacksmith's assistant when he was young. He knew that the hardest part would be building a proper fire that could melt the bronze. Shaping the metal would just be a matter of fitting the right stones together, but his fire needed to be special.

He created several practice fires, seeing if he could get them big enough without losing control. The first two he tried weren't hot enough, and the third nearly burned the village down. After apologizing profusely to Nnamdi and promising he wouldn't start another huge fire, he knew he would have to do something different. He had hoped he could do it with a normal campfire, but it was clear he needed to build a blacksmith's station.

Andronicus walked the land for a week, alone at first and then with Chaka once he was able. He walked all throughout the lands of the Kahli, looking for the right stones. The Kahli must have been told to leave him alone because one day as he was walking, two hunters saw him from a distance but never came near him. It was hard to find good stones because most of the rocks were either too big or too fragile.

Eventually, Andronicus found the stones he was looking for near the base of a small mountain about a day's walk from the village. They were black and rough, like they had already been burnt, and Andronicus knew they would work. Normally, he wouldn't have had a problem getting the rocks where he needed them, but his right arm was just barely beginning to have movement again, and he knew it would still be a long time until he could carry boulders. After a great deal of convincing, Andronicus got a few of the Bahitu to help him, and a week later he had his stones ready.

The needles the Bahitu sewed with were fine-tuned and perfect, but their crafting tools were crude and flat. Andronicus spent weeks hammering away at the big rocks he had brought back. Everyone looked at him like he was crazy, which he knew he may be, but he began to see the shapes he wanted in the rocks. First he moved the larger stones into place, or rather Chaka moved them while Andronicus instructed. Over time, a small rock oven was formed.

It took a full month just to build the oven. When he was satisfied with it, Andronicus stuffed it with dry grass and lit a fire. The oven wasn't perfect, but it worked. The fire burned much hotter than the open fires had, consuming the grass in seconds. The fire blazed brightly but went out far sooner than he had hoped. He remembered the way Niko's father had stoked his fire using a big baglike object and tried to remember how it worked.

Andronicus took his plans to Nnamdi first, who seemed interested, if not confident. He lent Andronicus five of the best weavers, and they began to sew the bags according to Andronicus's instruction. He had them set up two wooden stocks and weave the bag into them. They argued at first when he told them it needed a hole at both ends, but they did it. When they were done, Andronicus tried them out and let out a laugh. The women looked insulted, and he had to explain he wasn't insulting them; he was just amazed that he had gotten working bellows made in a little village in the wild.

When Andronicus built another practice fire, it was a great success. He had more grass and plenty of wood and got two children to work the bellows. The fire burned hotter than the last, sending embers flying as the bellows stoked it. The Bahitu were alarmed at the ferocity of the fire, but Andronicus was ecstatic. He finally felt like he would be able to accomplish his goal.

Once he was satisfied with his rock oven, he began working on the rocks that would shape the metal. First, he made a deep bowl, small enough to fit atop the oven but sturdy enough to hold the metal. Once his bowl was finished, he fashioned the stones that would shape the metal itself, carefully hammering away day after day.

There was something peaceful about the blacksmith work, and it made Andronicus think of Niko more than he had in many years. He wished Niko had stayed behind with his sons and his wife. He could have been a blacksmith like his father, and no one would have thought any less of him. He could have had the kind of life they all dreamed of, but he had chosen the path that Andronicus laid out for him. There was no way for Andronicus to deny it; he had been the reason they all went. He had been the one they all followed, either to death or into the unknown.

The Bahitu went on with their lives around him, and Chaka slowly began to hunt more as Andronicus needed less help. Chaka showed the Bahitu the ways of the Swihmehe hunt, and they were very grateful. Everyone seemed to think that Andronicus had lost his mind, but he knew what he was doing.

Nnamdi came to him one day, with a worried look on his face, and told him that the rains would come before the next full moon. Andronicus simply nodded, then went back to his work. He knew that to Nnamdi it looked like he had just hammered large black rocks into odd, useless shapes, but it all had a purpose.

3

When the time finally arrived to make the cup, Chaka and Nnamdi both sat by watching curiously, as did a few other Bahitu. No one spoke much; they just sat watching Andronicus build his fire. He had gathered a pile of sticks, grass, and wood, enough to last for many hours, and had all his tools in place. Beside the rocks he had shaped for casting, he had a number of long, sturdy sticks as well as a pair of new mitts. The Bahitu had looked at him like a loon when he asked for them, but they had sewn them better than Andronicus could have wished for.

Andronicus stoked his fire, waiting anxiously until it was hot enough. The same two boys were helping him with the bellows again. Embers began to fly as the fire grew hotter, and a red light shone out, illuminating the spectators' faces.

When Andronicus was satisfied with the fire, he had Chaka take the big bowl-shaped rock with gloved hands and place it over the fire between two other rocks. His arm was still too weak to lift it himself, and Chaka was glad to help. There were a few murmurs as Chaka set the bowl on top of the rock oven, and then everyone fell silent.

After about fifteen minutes, Andronicus saw little tendrils of smoke rising from the bowl, and he knew it was time. He picked up his old armor and held it up to the light for a moment. Now that the moment had come, he found he didn't want to give it up so easily.

His armor had been with him through most of his life, and had saved his life on numerous occasions. As he examined the dented metal, he thought of his old friends. Niko had been buried in his armor, but Lycus still had his, or at least he had in the cave. Andronicus wondered where Lycus was now, and if he still had his armor. The light from the fire danced off the bronze metal, and for a moment the fire flickered off two dents like a pair of red eyes staring at him. It gave Andronicus the chills. He stepped forward and dropped his armor onto the rock bowl.

At first nothing happened, and the people

watching began to murmur again. Andronicus just waited, hoping it would work. After a few minutes, the metal began to shine in a way it hadn't before. It lightened gradually until it almost looked new again. Then the metal started to bend inward, the sides of the breastplate drooping down. Slowly, the shape of the armor was lost.

Andronicus watched as the four deep lines on the shoulder faded and then disappeared. The entire chest plate caved in, and the whole thing began to fold in on itself. There was one flickering moment where the rusted steel straps on the side of the armor stood out in stark contrast to the golden metal. As the red steel slowly melted, it looked like blood running down the sides. Then the metal collapsed, and the rust disappeared.

As the metal melted, the crowd murmured with excitement and awe. Some people gasped, and others screamed. One man got up and ran away, as if he thought Andronicus was doing some kind of black magic. Chaka and Nnamdi both got up and approached the oven, gazing at the growing pool of metal in wonder. Andronicus chuckled, then picked up one of his sticks. He poked the pool with it, and the stick sunk in easily, then almost instantly caught fire. Andronicus threw the stick aside, happy with the result.

"This next part is the hard part," he said to his audience. "Will you help me, Chaka?" Chaka looked up in surprise and then nodded, his eyes quickly returning to the shining golden pool.

Andronicus wasn't sure what everyone was thinking, but he knew none of them had ever seen anything like this. He put on his mitt and had Chaka do the same. Working in unison, they lifted the bowl. Andronicus couldn't put any weight on his right arm yet, so Chaka had to do almost all of the lifting, but he was up to the task. Andronicus led Chaka over to the other rocks he had set up a few feet away and then halted. He knew they only had one shot at this.

As carefully as they could, Andronicus had Chaka slowly tip the bowl over and let the golden metal pour down into the other rocks. First, they poured the metal into a small bowl-shaped rock until it was half full. Then Andronicus had Chaka stop. Next he had Chaka pour the metal into a tight gap that Andronicus had created between two small rocks. Chaka poured carefully, and then stopped when Andronicus instructed. There was still a little more than half of the metal remaining in the big bowl, so they put it back on the fire.

As Chaka brought the bowl back to the fire, Andronicus began his work. He had taken painstaking care to turn one of his rocks into as perfect a sphere as he could. He placed it into the small bowl full of liquefied bronze, making the golden liquid rise up to the edge of the small black bowl. Andronicus let it rest, then turned to the smaller rocks. A small amount of metal was slowly running out of place. Andronicus took another stick and quickly tried to move the metal back into place. The stick caught fire like the last one, but he kept poking and prodding until the metal was mostly where he wanted it.

Then they waited. Everyone seemed fascinated by the slow-moving golden liquid, and some of them even wanted to touch it. Andronicus told Nnamdi to tell them not to and then lit another stick on fire to emphasize his point. Nnamdi seemed especially fascinated by the metal, and was watching every part of the process with wide, curious eyes.

An hour after the metal was poured, Andronicus knew it was time. First, he tried to remove the circular rock from the bowl, but it wouldn't budge. He had feared this might happen, and he wasn't sure whether to try and remove it now, or let it cool more. He remembered Niko's father once telling them never to leave part of a smelting job for later. He took one of the rocks he used for hammering and began methodically hammering away at the sides of the circular rock, slowly loosening it from the metal's hold.

Suddenly, the rock came loose. Andronicus lifted it up and looked at the underside. The metal had dried to the bottom of it, and the rock looked rather impressive with its perfect shape and half-golden shine. Andronicus had no more use for it, and he offered it to Nnamdi, hoping it wouldn't be taken as an offense. On the contrary, Nnamdi seemed genuinely honored to be given the rock, and all of the onlookers watched with wide eyes as Nnamdi held it up to them. They all cheered and crowded around him, and Andronicus chuckled again, happy he was able to impress them so much with his novice blacksmith skills.

He looked back down at the small bowl and was pleased to see that the metal had indeed taken the shape of a cup, and was even smoother than he would have guessed. The metal was still fused to the rock beneath it, and Andronicus went about breaking it free. It took a long time, and at one point he feared he had broken the metal, but it came out fine. The end result was indeed a cup shape, about as big as a large hand, with a good shape to it. Andronicus was quite pleased with himself, not having any real experience or tools.

The handle was much harder to do, as it had not quite taken the shape he had hoped for. It was close enough that he could tell it was meant to be a handle, but that was not how it had turned out. Instead it was a sort of twisted stick shape with tendrils of weeping metal going down the side. Andronicus figured it could have come out worse, and thought he might still be able to shape it to his liking. Once he had his two shapes, he turned to his audience and told them he was finished. Several of the Bahitu cheered, and many of them bowed their heads to him before leaving. Nnamdi went with them, excitedly showing off the half-bronzed rock.

Andronicus walked over to where Chaka was still standing by the fire, staring down at the bubbling pool of metal. The look on Chaka's face was somewhere between reverence and fear. It was a bit like the look he had when he saw the sea for the first time. Andronicus sat beside him and stared down at the pool as well. The gold bubbled and swirled, and the orange licks of flame whipped up around the sides of the rock.

Andronicus was entranced by the sight of it,

unable to turn his head away. The orange flames kicked up again, and then there they were, two little red dots, like eyes, floating in the middle of the golden pool. They stared up at Andronicus with fiery fury, and for a moment he saw his hand moving toward the pool. He had a moment of the most haunting déjà vu as he remembered reaching down helplessly into a pool of shining water. Fingers wrapped around his wrist and pulled his hand away. Andronicus shook his head and saw Chaka holding his arm, looking at him like he was mad. Andronicus turned back to the pool, and the red dots were gone. It was just a pool of molten bronze once again.

"You said it would burn you," Chaka said, eyeing him warily.

"It would have," Andronicus said in a breathy voice. "Thank you. I do not know what came over me."

"You scare me sometimes, Jocus," Chaka said, releasing his arm.

"I know," Andronicus said softly. "I scare myself sometimes too."

"What will you do with the rest of it?" Chaka asked, pointing at the half-full bowl, clearly wanting to change topics.

"I will let it cool," Andronicus said, trying not to think about the fiery eyes. "I do not need any more of it right now, but I can still use it again later." Chaka nodded, and they returned to staring at the fire and the bronze. The two of them spent half the night watching the fire die and the bronze harden. Andronicus didn't know what Chaka was thinking as he stared into the flames, but he thought about his old life and felt like he had burned part of it away. As much as he wanted to live, he hated that he had to melt down his own armor to appease a man he wanted to kill.

4

Andronicus spent a fortnight hammering away at his newly shaped metals. Once he had the cup ready, he worked at getting the handle attached for a full week. When the two pieces were finally connected, it wasn't pretty, but it was indeed a cup. He continued shaping it and polishing it until it actually resembled something like a chalice. He hoped it would do, being the only bronze cup anyone around here had ever seen.

The Khali arrived the day after the first rains fell. It was still pouring when they arrived, and almost everyone was sheltered in their huts. The Kahli hunters walked up the hill the same as they had before, slow and confident. Their war paint had either been forgotten or more likely was washed away by the rain. The leader stepped forward, ignoring Nnamdi this time, and walked right up to Andronicus.

"Gift," he said in his calm, intimidating voice. This was the first time Andronicus was able to understand him, and somehow it made him even more frightening. Andronicus took out the cup and held it before the man, knowing it might not be enough. The man stared at the cup for a long moment. Andronicus had no idea what he was thinking. This man made him feel like a child, and he hated it. His arm still hung in its sling, but he clenched his fist, making sure not to wince at the pain.

After a painfully long silence, the man finally gave Andronicus a curt nod then held the cup up, letting it fill with rain. Then he drank from it. He lowered the cup and looked at Andronicus. "More," he said flatly.

"I can make another," Andronicus said meekly, hating the sound of his own voice. He wasn't even sure he had enough bronze for another cup, and he had not intended to give it all away. The man glared at him, then turned and headed back down the hill. Two of his men accepted baskets of goods from the Bahitu, then they all marched off down the hill again.

Andronicus was shaking with rage as he watched the Khali hunters trudge down the muddy hill. He had never felt like less of a man in his entire life. At that moment he didn't care about making it back to Greece, or finding his friends, or getting his answers. The only thing he knew was that he was going to kill that man. He would have to wait until his arm was healed, but once he felt up to it, he would end it, either with that man's death, or his own.

5

Andronicus went about rebuilding his rock oven while the rest of the Bahitu returned to their lives. Chaka helped Andronicus when he needed it, but more often he went on the hunt. Chaka had always been a hunter, and Andronicus could tell how much he enjoyed it. While Chaka hunted, and Nnamdi prayed, and the rest of the village sewed, Andronicus worked. Taking the stones he had used the first time, he began shaping them for his new plan. It was slow and painfully monotonous, but Andronicus continued pounding away at the rocks with his left arm.

His left arm had never been so strong in his life. After his fight with the lion when he first arrived in Swimha, he hadn't been able to use his right arm for months, but this time was much worse. He watched as his right arm slowly lost its definition, and his left arm gained it, until his arms looked comically lopsided. It didn't matter. In his mind all he had to do was wait. Once his arm had healed, he could get it back up to strength in no time.

6

When the time came to forge again, far fewer people showed up. Andronicus didn't mind. He didn't really want people to see what he was going to make this time. Nnamdi and Chaka both sat by the fire, and a few other people sat a little ways away. Andronicus made sure all his tools were in place before starting, and then he lit the fire. It took a long time to get a good fire going beneath all the rocks, but once it took, it quickly began to grow. The same two children had volunteered to work the bellows again, rhythmically pushing them up and down.

When hot embers began flying out, Andronicus knew it was time. He nodded to Chaka, who got up and lifted the heavy rock bowl. Andronicus had left the rest of the bronze in the bowl, and it looked the same as he had left it. Chaka placed the bowl on top of the hole in the rocks and then returned to his place beside

Nnamdi.

They waited patiently, none of them speaking. The only sounds were the loud crackling of the fire and the pulsing whooshes of air from the bellows. After a while, the metal began to shine brighter, and everyone perked up.

Nnamdi walked over to watch it happen. Chaka and Andronicus joined him as the metal began to move. It had looked much more impressive the last time when they had watched the armor collapse into itself, but it was still beautiful to watch the bronze turn molten. When he thought it was ready, Andronicus poked a long stick into the metal, and it sank all the way in, catching fire as it did. He threw the stick into the dirt, and Chaka stomped it out.

"Just like last time," Andronicus said to Chaka, who nodded as he slipped on the mitts. With a grunt, he lifted the heavy stone bowl. Andronicus led him over to where he had his rocks waiting and guided him as he poured the bronze down. The golden metal slid out in chunks and waves until the stone bowl was empty. It still had a golden sheen, but Andronicus was satisfied. He nodded to Chaka again, and Chaka placed the bowl in the dirt.

"You boys can stop that now," Andronicus said to the boys working the bellows. "As for the rest of you, the fun is over. This will take me many days to finish." There was a soft chatter from the small crowd, and then they began to disperse. When the onlookers had all left, Chaka sat down next to Andronicus.

"You are not making another cup, are you?" Chaka asked with concern.

"No, I am not."

"You are making something that you do not want these people to see," Chaka said, suddenly realizing what was going on.

Andronicus nodded. "Yes."

"You are making a weapon, aren't you?"

Andronicus nodded again.

"So, you plan to fight them?" Chaka looked both angry and concerned.

"Not all of them," Andronicus whispered,

staring into the fire, "just him." Amongst the dancing orange flames, he saw the two red dots floating steady amidst the chaos. As Andronicus stared back at them, he imagined cutting the tall man's throat.

"You do not have to, Jocus," Chaka said seriously. "We are lucky they did not kill us. Why would you want to fight them again?"

"They only beat me because I was not prepared," Andronicus said, needing to defend his skill as a warrior. "I underestimated them. That will not happen again."

"And what if you do kill him?" Chaka asked, standing up. "What will happen then? Are we going to stay here with the Bahitu? As soon as we leave, the Kahli will kill them. Is that what you want, for this village to die, just so you can kill one man?" Andronicus hadn't thought of that, and for a moment guilt began to sway him.

If you kill enough of them, they'll never bother the Bahitu again. Andronicus felt a chill wash over his body, and for a moment he felt like he would vomit. He shook his head, and when he looked up, there were the eyes, staring out of the fire at him like the eyes of a demon.

"If I kill enough of them, they will leave the Bahitu alone," Andronicus said, feeling dizziness wash over him as he spoke someone else's words.

"For what, so you can have revenge?" Chaka asked.

"Not just for me," Andronicus said, standing up. "For the Bahitu, and for you. They tried to kill you, or have you forgotten?"

"I have not forgotten," Chaka said seriously. "I will never forget. Not because the Kahli nearly killed me, but because you saved me."

"I did not," Andronicus said, turning away. "Nnamdi saved you. He gave you the medicine."

"And how did I get to Nnamdi?" Chaka asked. "How did I get away from the Kahli when I was asleep? They would have killed me or eaten me or done whatever they wanted with me, but you got us out of there. You saved me, Jocus, and then again with

Nnamdi and again with your cup. You even saved me back in Swimha when the Swihmacha came."

"They came for me, Chaka," Andronicus reminded him. "They never would have killed anyone if I had not been there. You would not have had to escape anything if you had never met me. You would still have a father and a sister . . ." Andronicus's voice broke as he said it. "I did not save your life, Chaka, I ruined it."

"My life is not ruined," Chaka protested. "I have had pain, as all men must, but I have also had joy. If we never found you, I would never have left my home. I would never have seen the sea or the jungle. My life is not ruined, Jocus, and neither is yours. You do not have to kill anyone. We can just leave."

"No," Andronicus said, staring into the dying fire, feeling a rage that didn't even feel like his own. "That man must die."

7

Andronicus spent a fortnight working on his new project. At first he had meant the blade to be for Chaka, but Chaka didn't seem to want it. After a week it was clear that Andronicus was making a knife, but Chaka showed no interest in it. He spent his days out with the hunters, catching greater game than the Bahitu had ever caught before. One day they returned with a full-grown male buffalo that Chaka had speared, and the village threw him a great celebration.

Andronicus didn't join them. Part of him wanted to, but he had other things on his mind. As the rest of the village sang and ate and laughed, Andronicus sat on the edge of the hill sharpening his new bronze blade and staring out over the plains for the Kahli. He wanted to join the fun, to dance and laugh like he had back in Swimha, but he couldn't. His mind was too full of hate. All he could think about was the man who had beaten him and emasculated him and how he would kill that man. His thoughts were dark and cloudy, as if he couldn't quite think right. Andronicus heard a laugh close by and turned around to see Chaka walking toward him with a young girl behind him.

"Jocus," Chaka said cheerfully, "come join us. I am going to show them the buffalo dance, but I need your help."

"Someone has to keep watch for the Kahli," Andronicus said, turning away from Chaka's smiling face.

"They are not coming tonight," Chaka said, sitting down beside Andronicus. "Their chief accepted your cup, he will leave us alone for now."

"If the Kahli saw that you killed a buffalo, they will come for their share," Andronicus responded bitterly. "I am just trying to keep everyone safe."

Chaka laughed. "They are safe, Jocus. You do not have to sit here all alone. Come dance with us."

"You thought we were safe from the Swihmacha too, remember?" Andronicus said angrily. The smile fell from Chaka's face like a rock, and Andronicus instantly felt guilty. For a moment Chaka looked like he might actually hit him, and he prepared to accept the blow. Instead, Chaka slowly got to his feet.

"Fine then," Chaka said, staring down at Andronicus with contempt. "Sit here and be hateful all night."

Chaka turned and walked away, and Andronicus went back to sharpening his blade. He knew he shouldn't have said that. He wanted Chaka to leave him alone, but he shouldn't have said that. It was no more Chaka's fault that the Swihmacha had come than it was Manyara's. Andronicus felt the anger subside a bit as he thought of her face. He didn't think of her as much as he used to, which made him sad. He still loved her, but he had begun to let her go. He wondered what she would think of his plan to kill the Kahli, and knew.

Chaka was right. He knew it, but he couldn't get the dark thoughts out of his head. It was as if they were from the outside, trying to take hold of him. His head felt heavy and dull, and it hurt worse than it had in years. He stared down at the tiny sparks his hand made as he slid the rock across the blade and tried to clear his mind of the darkness. It felt foreign, and yet far too familiar.

In his heart he knew Chaka was right, but his desire to kill was greater than it had ever been. It scared him a little. The last time he had felt this kind of rage, he had done the worst thing in his life. He forced himself to remember that night, even though it always gave him nightmares. He could still see the field of corpses he had created, the men, the women, and the children. There had only been a few children, but he had killed them all the same. As he pictured their faces and what he had done to them, an old dream returned to him. He had been standing amongst the dead, and one of them had risen. There had been red eyes, much like the ones he kept seeing in his fires, and he wondered if they were the same. It felt as if his rage was coming from the eyes, or with the eyes, or perhaps the other way around. The dark rage made him a better killer, but it also made him more carnal, like a beast.

Andronicus regretted that day more than any other day of his life, and he had many days to regret. If he went ahead with his new plan, he knew he would only have another day to regret. A kind of calm washed over him, and he felt the dark thoughts slowly recede. For a moment it felt like warm water cascading down his body. It was a bizarre sensation, and then it was gone. A moment later, Andronicus couldn't quite remember what it had felt like. He looked down at the golden blade in his hands and nodded slowly. A calm resolution set in, and the dark thoughts dissipated.

Andronicus stood up, feeling as light as a feather, and walked back to his hut. He placed the blade beside his sword and then headed off toward the celebration.

When he got there, he found Chaka leading a dozen laughing men and women in a dance around the fire. Chaka saw him and stopped dancing for a moment. Andronicus tried to say what he felt in a look, and Chaka nodded, then gestured for Andronicus to join him. Andronicus smiled and joined the awkward procession around the fire, laughing for the first time in months.

8

Andronicus no longer planned to kill the Kahli. He didn't quite know what had happened to him on the hill, but the darkness that had been hanging over him for months was finally gone. He felt free again, but they still couldn't leave yet. His arm had healed enough so that he no longer needed the sling, but he wasn't ready for the jungle yet.

A few days after he had abandoned his revenge plot, Andronicus asked Nnamdi to show him the jungle. He had heard about it ever since they arrived, but he still hadn't seen it. Nnamdi said he was too old for the jungle, but he sent two of the village's strongest men to lead Andronicus. Chaka came along as well, and the four of them set out at dawn the next day.

The jungle was much farther away than Andronicus had thought, and it took them four days to walk there. When they arrived at the edge of it, Andronicus couldn't believe it. He had been hearing stories about the Great Jungle ever since he arrived in the land of the Kahli, but nothing could have prepared him for the sheer size of it. It was the biggest thing he had ever seen, greater than any mountain or city, perhaps even the sea. It stood as tall as a small mountain and stretched off in both directions, just like the sea. They camped outside it for one night, and Andronicus heard all kinds of strange noises coming from the massive dark abyss.

The next day they trekked through the jungle for a few hours. The two Bahitu men refused to sleep in the jungle, but they spent enough time inside for Andronicus to know that the jungle would be a very different kind of traveling than he and Chaka had ever done before. There were vines and bushes everywhere, and Chaka had to use Andronicus's sword to cut their way through.

When they left the jungle at sunset, Andronicus knew his arm would need to be fully healed before they could attempt the journey. They slept outside the jungle again that night and then began the long walk back to the village the next day.

9

Andronicus finished his work on the bronze blade, which was now meant for Chaka to use in the jungle. Andronicus told this to Chaka, and he seemed pleased, if not excited. The blade was much shorter than Andronicus's sword, but it was bigger than a knife, and far sharper. It was a little more than a foot long, and he had shaped it into a nice curved blade, sharp on both sides. He couldn't make a real steel handle, so instead he dulled the other end of the knife and then wrapped it tight in deer hide, giving it a nice firm grip.

When the blade was finally done, he gave it to Chaka, along with a sheath made of deer hide. Chaka pulled the bronze blade out and admired it. Andronicus had sharpened it to a fine point and polished it with the sap of a nearby tree. Chaka held it up to the light and flinched back as the glint from the sun flashed across his eyes. He looked over at Andronicus, who laughed.

"I do not know how to use a weapon like this," Chaka said, holding it apprehensively.

"I will show you," Andronicus said, smiling as he clapped Chaka on the back.

10

When the Kahli returned, Nnamdi offered them five baskets of food instead of two, along with several things Andronicus had shown the weavers. They had made cloaks and sandals for the Kahli. After looking it all over carefully, the Kahli leader nodded and then left in peace without bothering with Andronicus. Andronicus had explained to Nnamdi what he had made and that he had no intention of giving it to the Kahli, but he also told him he could continue to show him new things to sew. Nnamdi agreed to give the Kahli the extra baskets in exchange for Chaka killing extra buffalo for the Bahitu. Andronicus knew that eventually the Kahli would want him again, but for now they seemed happy enough with their new trophies.

After that Andronicus worked every day at strengthening his arm. Chaka's wounds had healed, and he spent his days hunting and roaming the land, as his people had always done. Andronicus did what his people had always done as well; he trained. At first he spent day after day just lifting different rocks and logs with his arm, slowly building the muscles that had been torn apart.

Some days it hurt even worse than the original injury. Andronicus pushed his body well past its limits, forcing his arm to heal faster. Every day it hurt, but the progress was obvious. By the time the great rains returned for a third time, Andronicus could lift a heavy rock over his head, though it still hurt terribly. Once his arm was strong enough, he began really training again, and Chaka often joined him.

Andronicus practiced the old swings and movements that he had learned as a youth. Chaka was clumsy with his blade at first but slowly began to figure it out.

Over time Chaka learned how to swing a blade, and Andronicus got his arm ready for the next stage of their journey. His body felt strong enough, but he wasn't quite ready to go into the jungle. He dreamed about the jungle often, being stuck in that dark world for days, weeks, or even months. It grew more frightening as the prospect of actually living in the jungle grew closer.

11

Andronicus was finally ready to move on, feeling strong and rested. Chaka was ready as well, but before they could leave, the Kahli came for him one final time. This time Andronicus had helped Chaka kill a buffalo, and they had six baskets of meat ready to give them, along with more sandals, cloaks, and sleeping bags. Andronicus stood in the background as Nnamdi spoke with the chief. He couldn't quite bring himself to meet the Kahli leader's eye. He still felt ashamed, and he didn't want the blind rage to return. Andronicus watched as the Kahli man shook his head and then pointed right at him. Andronicus had thought the man was done with him, but he could see in his eyes that he was not.

Nnamdi shot Andronicus a frightened look, then gestured for him to come over. Andronicus approached them, still not meeting the man's eye. Andronicus's sword was hanging at his side, wrapped in a new sheath the Bahitu had sewn him. The Kahli man stepped forward and shoved Nnamdi to the ground. He pointed at Andronicus's sword with a silent, menacing scowl. Andronicus finally met the man's eye and felt the rage come rushing back. In an instant, the hatred returned, along with the urge to kill the man. Andronicus took a deep breath and tried to calm himself.

"You cannot have this," he said in a clear calm voice, even though his heart was racing. "I am sorry," he added. "We can give you another buffalo, or more—"

"We can kill our own buffalo," the tall man said, cutting him off angrily. "I want your special rock." He pointed at the sword again, and this time Andronicus knew the man wasn't going to just leave. He no longer wanted to kill this man, and he was afraid of what might happen if he did. He slowly placed his hand on the hilt of his blade.

"Please," Andronicus said, staring up at the man's dark eyes. "Take the meat. We will give you two more buffalo and cloaks for everyone in your village, but I cannot give you what you ask for."

"Then I will take it," the man grunted, stepping forward. Andronicus drew his blade, and the man stopped. His scowl got even darker, and his eyes filled with their own rage. "We should have killed you long ago," the man snarled.

"Yes," Andronicus agreed calmly, "you should have."

The man was still quick and skilled, but Andronicus was ready this time. As the man lunged, Andronicus swung his blade. It cut across the man's chest, leaving a dark red line. The Kahli leader looked down at his chest, then back at Andronicus, his eyes blazing with hate. Andronicus felt a momentary hesitation at the terrifying look, but stood his ground.

The man lunged again, faster than before. Andronicus slashed out again, but this time the man fell on top of him. He hit the ground hard and felt all the wind leave his body. As Andronicus gasped for air, strong hands wrapped around his throat and began to squeeze. Realizing he still had his sword in his hand, he brought his hand up, and encountered resistance. He thrust the sword again, and again. Finally, the hands loosened their grip on his neck until they released him completely.

The fierce, menacing Kahli leader swayed and then fell back onto his side. Andronicus pushed him off and scrambled to his feet. He looked down at the man and was surprised at all the damage he had done. The man's entire left side was ripped apart from the blade, his blood leaking into the dirt in torrents. The man was still glaring up at him, but Andronicus could see that he was dying fast. He heard a grunt close by, and Andronicus turned to see Chaka pulling his own blade from the belly of one of the other Kahli hunters. The third man lay dead at Chaka's feet.

When the last man fell, Andronicus's stomach dropped as he looked around at the dead bodies. He had not meant for this to happen.

Nnamdi was sitting in the dirt a few feet from Chaka, a horrified look on his face. He looked up at Andronicus and began to cry. "You have killed us," Nnamdi wept. "They are going to kill us all now."

"I am sorry," Andronicus replied, knowing the old man was right. He didn't know what else to say as Nnamdi continued to weep. "I could not let him take my sword. I did not want to kill him," Andronicus insisted, feeling a mix of emotions. He had wanted to kill the man before, but he had decided not to. The boiling rage he had felt had only returned for an instant. It was gone before the man had attacked, and now all he felt was guilt and shame.

He knew that Nnamdi was right, but there was nothing he could do. The only way he could protect the Bahitu now would be to kill all of the Kahli, like he had done to the Swihmacha, and he had no desire to do that. He knew he should have found another way to appease the man, but what was done was done.

"We have to go, Nnamdi," Andronicus said, hating himself for what he had done to these people, who had helped him and Chaka so much.

"Go?" Nnamdi said, looking up at him with big wet eyes. "You cannot go now. You must help us fight the Kahli. They are going to come for you."

"I know, and I am sorry," Andronicus said sadly. He looked over at Chaka, who was staring at the dirt in shame. "If we stay, they will fight, but if we leave, they might let the rest of you live." Andronicus wasn't sure if he believed his own words or not.

"We helped you," Nnamdi pleaded, staring at Andronicus in horrified disbelief. "We took you in, and we did everything we could to keep you alive. How can you leave us now after you killed the Kahlimah?" Andronicus didn't know what to say. He knew that leaving the Bahitu now might well be a death sentence for them, but the alternative seemed too dangerous for him and Chaka.

"I . . . I am sorry, Nnamdi," Andronicus said with a pained voice, placing his hand on Nnamdi's shoulder. Nnamdi dropped his head back in his hands and resumed his weeping. Andronicus looked at Chaka, who nodded sadly. They left Nnamdi there next to the dead men and hurried back to the village.

When they got to the huts, the people began asking them what had happened.

"Nnamdi will tell you everything," Andronicus told them as Chaka quickly packed their things. "He will take care of you."

"You are leaving!" someone shouted, and the little mob began getting restless.

"I saw you kill the Kahlimah!" someone else yelled, then a dozen people were shouting at him.

"I am sorry," Andronicus said, holding out his hands and hoping they wouldn't attack him. "I had to. He attacked me first."

"The Kahli are going to come for us!" a woman shouted. "This is all your fault. You cannot just leave now." Andronicus looked back and saw Chaka stepping out of the hut with their bags tucked under his arm. They were new bags that the Bahitu had sewn for them, which made it even harder. They began walking toward the other end of the village, and the little mob chased after them, still shouting angrily. Andronicus wanted to get away from them as fast as possible. He knew they weren't any threat to him, but he didn't want to hear them; their words were too painfully true.

He knew he was likely leaving these people to be killed. Even if the Kahli didn't kill them, there would be punishment. Andronicus knew the Kahli all too well, and he hated that he was leaving behind a people he had truly grown to care for. He wished he could at least save some of them, or even just Nnamdi. If the jungle wasn't so ominous, he could at least try to take them with him, at least for a while. But in the jungle, they would be slowed to a crawl. Andronicus knew his only options now were to run or fight.

It felt more shameful than anything to know he was choosing to run rather than to fight. It wasn't the first time he had ever run from a fight, but that didn't make it any easier. He had been raised never to run from a fight, to stand his ground. His own father had chosen to die rather than run from a fight.

As they left the Bahitu behind, the people still wailing and shouting, Andronicus had to wonder if he could take on the Kahli by himself. There were at least fifty hunters, if not more, and they were all big and strong. He and Chaka still had the only blades, but the Kahli knew how to fight. It was too great a risk. Even if he could defeat them all, in the end he would have to slaughter another village.

He knew there was nothing to be done, so he ran, alongside Chaka, feeling the same kind of shame he had felt as a boy, running from Thermopylae, knowing those he left behind would die a death that was meant for him as well.

Chapter 21
Into the Great Jungle
1

When they finally reached the edge of the Great Jungle, it was well after dark. They had been running for three straight days, hoping no one would follow them. Andronicus knew that whatever the Bahitu's fate, they had already likely met it. He wondered if Nnamdi was still alive, or if any of them were. He had half expected the Kahli to catch up to them, but either they had outrun them, or the Kahli weren't chasing them.

Andronicus knew he would never know what happened after they left. All he knew was that he had abandoned the Bahitu. They had been good to him, better than anyone except the Swihmehe. They had taught him more about the art of sewing than he could have imagined. They had also clothed him, fed him, nursed him and Chaka both back to health, and given them a place to stay for what Andronicus knew was at least several years. Now they had abandoned the Bahitu to an unknown terrible fate. Chaka seemed to be just as disturbed by it as Andronicus, but they hadn't said more than a few words about it since they left.

They set their things beside an old fallen tree a few hundred yards away from where the jungle really started. Andronicus looked up at the looming mass of dense foliage and felt chills go down his spine. They were not even in the jungle yet, and he could already hear shrieks, howls, cries, and the singing of a thousand birds. They ate in relative silence, and Andronicus spent that night dreaming about monsters and beasts from the jungle's deep, dark depths. He dreamed of everything from the giant snakes Nnamdi had told him about, to the Minotaur he had heard stories about as a child.

When the sun rose the following morning, Andronicus and Chaka rose with it, ready to start the next phase of their journey. Chaka looked like he had gotten a good night's sleep, as he usually did.

Andronicus felt uneasy as he stared up at the

vibrant green wall of trees. They rose higher than some mountains he had seen, and were covered in green leaves and vines all the way up. At the base of the trees were tangled messes of bushes and even more vines. Andronicus didn't like the idea of going through the unknown depths of the thick jungle, but he knew there was no way around. Nnamdi had told him that the jungle stretched all the way to the sea, both to the east and the west. He knew all too well what was waiting for them back south. That left only north, through the great and terrifying jungle.

The two travelers ate a quick breakfast, both staring up at the menacing sight before them. There was still no sign of anyone following them. Andronicus knew they wouldn't be followed into the jungle, but he still felt anxious. He wanted to get a feel for how far they would be able to travel each day once they were inside. He still didn't know how big the jungle actually was, but he hoped they could get through it in a year, two at the most.

They ate quietly, staring up at the giant trees that stretched out of sight in either direction. After gathering up their things and covering their tracks, they finally entered the Great Jungle. There was no place to simply walk in because the shrubbery was too thick from the start, so Andronicus drew his sword and cut his way in. Once they had breached the border, Andronicus saw a sort of path they could follow. He stepped into the vast green world, and Chaka followed.

As soon as the large trees were behind them, and in front of them, and all around them, everything changed. The light became patchy and spread out, just a few thin beams falling here and there. The ground squished and slid under their weight, and Andronicus felt bugs crawl over his sandaled feet as he walked. Even the air seemed to change, becoming thick and heavy, and Andronicus felt it filling his lungs with every breath.

It was hard to see the sun and, therefore, hard to judge the time of day, but when Andronicus caught a glimpse of it right above them, he made them stop for lunch. It was only midday and they were both drenched in sweat. They had trekked through unbearable heat in the plains and never sweated so much. It was definitely hot in the jungle, but it wasn't just the heat; it was the air. It felt thick and sticky, and it slowed them to a crawl.

Andronicus had no idea when the sun set, but when the light began to fade, they stopped and set up camp. He looked down at the ground on which they were to sleep and shuddered. A hundred bugs of every size and shape slithered and crawled and wormed their way about.

He tried to remember how many snakes they had seen since entering the jungle, probably nine or ten. As he stood there, a screeching howl rang out, followed by the shriek of a large cat attacking its prey, followed by an even more terrible screech, and then silence for a few moments before the birds resumed their singing.

Andronicus looked at Chaka, who appeared as uncomfortable as Andronicus felt. Andronicus decided to wrap himself in his old Spartan cloak, and Chaka wrapped himself in the big brown cloak the Bahitu had sewn him. They were both sweating like pigs and very uncomfortable, but they felt relatively safe from unwanted night guests.

It felt like it took all night for Andronicus to fall asleep in the hot, noisy jungle, but when he awoke in the morning, he felt like he had slept for a week.

He gazed over at Chaka and saw him snoring loudly, his cloak rolled up beneath him. Andronicus looked up to see where the sun was and was surprised to see that it was high enough to have been up for hours. They must have slept in later than they had in years. He woke Chaka, and they ate some nearby fruit in a hurry, then started moving again.

Andronicus didn't know what lay to the north, but he still felt that was the way they were meant to go. He was determined to keep them moving north, but it wasn't easy in the jungle. On the plains, he had used the sun and the stars for direction. Now, under the many layers of thick vines and branches, a hundred feet below the tree canopy, it was nearly impossible to tell which way was north and which was south. For all he knew they could be walking in a big circle.

Time and space both ceased to be manageable as soon as they entered the world of the jungle. Andronicus remembered the stories Nnamdi had told him about how big the jungle was, and he began to fear they would never make it through.

After a full day of walking, it felt like they had barely moved at all, and he wasn't even sure if they were going the right way. Everything looked the same everywhere they went, and the jungle only seemed to get thicker. Andronicus wondered again how long it might take to reach the end, shuddering at the thought.

2

On the second day they moved even slower than the first. When the sun set, they had to quickly make camp before the light was completely gone. There was no way to travel through the thick jungle at night. The light from the moon and stars fell away a hundred feet above them, and the jungle floor where they slept was as black as could be, and damp as well. Again they wrapped themselves up for the night despite the heat. Andronicus had been able to observe a bit of the jungle life already, and he didn't really fear the animals bothering them at night, but he did fear the bugs.

This time they went to sleep just after the light faded and were able to wake with the sun. Moving through the heavy tangles of vines, branches, and leaves didn't get any easier on the third day, or the fourth. Andronicus blessed his sword every morning and every night and silently thanked Karpos for making him such a fine blade. If not for the sword, he was sure they would not have been able to make it even this far, never mind through the entire jungle. He wished he could have made Chaka a sword of his own instead of just a dagger. It was still immensely helpful to have a second blade, but it couldn't cut through the vines like the sword.

Taking turns using the sword to cut through the vines and brush, they were able to keep moving forward at the very least. Andronicus had no idea how far they were travelling each day, but they kept moving. In truth he didn't even know if they really were moving forward; they could just as easily be walking right back to where they had started.

They moved through the jungle day after day, becoming increasingly accustomed to jungle life. They learned how to avoid the deadlier predators, of which there were many, and how to seek out which animals to kill, of which there were even more. It didn't take them long to realize their best food options were high above them. The ground was covered in bugs and snakes, with the occasional animal they could eat, but the trees were full of animals ripe for the taking.

They began climbing trees with spears to hunt, which slowed their progress even more, but it kept them busy and full. Andronicus was good at climbing, but Chaka was amazing at it. He used his long arms and tall body to reach branches Andronicus never could. Sometimes Andronicus thought Chaka moved through the trees better than the animals. Chaka became excellent at tree hunting, but he refused to kill more than half of the animals they came across.

Andronicus knew that many animals in Swimha were forbidden to hunt, and he respected that, but he had not expected Chaka to begin adding new animals to the list as they marched farther into the jungle. There had only been a few kinds of monkeys in Swimha, most of them small and quick, but in the jungle there were hundreds. There were quick little monkeys in the trees and big, strong monkeys on the ground, and Chaka refused to kill them all. He usually caught different kinds of squirrels and other rodents instead of the bigger game.

One day Andronicus was doing the hunting, and he managed to kill a fairly big monkey with bright beautiful fur, and a somewhat humanlike face. Chaka cursed him up and down, but in the end, he ate the poor beast as well. It was the best meat Andronicus had tasted since entering the jungle, and he tried convincing Chaka to allow it, to no avail. If anything Chaka just became more stubborn about what they were allowed to eat, and Andronicus didn't push the matter.

They trekked through the jungle for months before they finally broke down and ate their first snake. Andronicus hated the slimy creatures, and even Chaka seemed to dislike them. In the plains, snakes had been much smaller and yet much easier to spot. In the jungle they saw snakes that looked like they could eat a man whole, and they blended into the jungle far too well. They finally killed and ate a snake one day because they hadn't found anything else to eat. They were surprised to find that it was much better than they had imagined, so snake joined the menu.

3

Andronicus counted each day as they moved through the vast jungle, struggling to keep it accurate. Chaka tried to help, but he had never really learned numbers. Every day Andronicus told himself the new number over and over, but each day was so similar to the last that it got harder to keep track.

Somewhere between 160 and 180, Andronicus lost the exact count. A hundred days after that, he had lost it entirely. They pressed on, walking day after day, cutting through the jungle with no way of knowing how long they had been there. Once he stopped counting the days, Andronicus truly had no idea how long they had been inside. He couldn't even track the seasons, as it seemed to always be a rainy season.

When it wasn't raining, the heat was dreadful, and the air was thick and heavy. What the jungle had in abundance was plant life. Andronicus supposed it made sense; he knew that rain gave plants life, and it seemed to rain almost every day. In the plains fruit had been scarce, and the animals had room to run. In the jungle, fruit hung all around them, many that Andronicus had never seen before. They came in every color imaginable and varied in size from the smallest grapes to large, misshapen gourds. Nnamdi had warned Andronicus about all the poisonous plants he knew of, but as they kept seeing strange new plants, Andronicus decided to just stay away from all berries and only eat fruit that looked familiar.

Game was also abundant, from small rodents to large, lazy animals that walked the jungle floor. The trees above them were always filled with the songs of a thousand birds and the howling of monkeys. The predators stayed away from them for the most part, and they stayed away from the predators. The cats kept their distance, and the snakes barely moved when they saw them. Their eyes slowly grew accustomed to the nights' darkness, and they became experts at seeing and hearing danger before it found them. When a big cat would come near them, they would crouch down and wait for it to pass, and it usually worked. Only once had they been detected, and that most vigilant and unfortunate cat had tasted Andronicus's steel before it could eat them. Andronicus realized quickly that the jungle was not used to having men come through it, and everything seemed wary of them.

4

They trekked through the jungle day after agonizingly hot sticky day. Andronicus had lost the count of days long ago, but they kept moving forward, he hoped. He guessed they had been in the jungle for two or three years, but he knew it could just as well be five or six. The days all mashed together, each one no different from the last. They woke, they ate, they walked, they hunted, and then they walked, they ate, and they slept. They repeated the routine through jungle that all looked the same, day after day, after day after day until it all became a mindless blur.

Andronicus had finally begun to grow a beard again some time along the way. He hadn't shaved since leaving the Bahitu, and his stubble slowly grew into a beard. It became the best way for him to judge the time. His hair still wouldn't grow the way it had before he touched the stones, but he thought he had gained an idea of how fast it grew now. When he had lived in Sparta, he would cut his hair twice a year, letting it fall down his neck. When he lived with the Swihmehe, Manyara had only cut his hair twice, and it had never grown past his shoulders.

He hadn't cut his hair since then, and it fell in tangled matts down his neck, past his shoulders and onto his back. The beard that now covered his face was slowly becoming thicker and blacker and filled his whole hand when he ran it through. He was well aware of how wild he looked, and he was glad Chaka was the only one around to see it.

Water was not hard to come by in the jungle either. It pooled all around them in plants and hollows and occasionally on the ground itself. Large pools of water like the plains had were rare in the heart of the jungle, but whenever they came across one, Andronicus would spend a long time staring at his reflection in the water.

Still no change. Beneath the matted hair, the dirt, and the grime, he still looked exactly the same, not a day older. And it wasn't just his face; his body still felt young and healthy and strong, and he had never experienced any of the plights of the elderly, despite his injuries. It made no sense that his hair would still grow, and yet not the way it always had but far slower. It made no sense that he was not getting any older. It made no sense that he had woken up in Swimha. None of it made any more sense than it had that first day. But as they walked deeper into the depths of the jungle, it almost did seem to make some kind of twisted sense.

There was a ritualistic kind of chaos about the jungle. There was more life in the jungle than Andronicus would have believed existed in the whole world. Seeing so much life, so many different plants, animals, bugs, and birds, Andronicus could almost make sense of it all. There were answers in the jungle; he could feel it, but he knew he didn't dare search for them. Just trying to keep moving straight ahead was hard enough.

The days all blended together too well, and Andronicus feared for his own sanity. Chaka seemed to be adjusting just fine; he loved all the animals, and he didn't even seem to mind the constant rain. For Chaka it was much easier to just let time pass. Andronicus spent far too much time thinking about his mysterious predicament. In the plains it had been much easier to lose himself in the scenery, but the jungle all looked the same, just more plants and trees. It gave Andronicus nothing to think about but himself.

It was impossible to be sure, but he thought he was in his sixties at least by now. It seemed absurd because he still felt just as young and vibrant as he always had, but he knew he had spent at least twenty years with the Swihmehe. He had counted at least ten rainy seasons before they reached the Bahitu, and they had spent several years there as well. Andronicus had been thirty-one when he touched the rocks, and with the unknown amount of time in the jungle constantly increasing, he knew he had become an old man.

Chaka had to be getting old as well. He had been much younger than Andronicus when they met. Now he looked at least ten years older than Andronicus, but not nearly as old as he should. Chaka had a fair amount of grey in his hair and a few wrinkles in his face, but he was still as strong as ever. Andronicus didn't know how old Challah had been, but his hair was as white as snow, and he had looked like an old man from the start. Chaka was likely that old now, but he didn't look like it at all.

They had both seemingly stopped in time. And in the endless jungle, it seemed like the world had stopped with them. There was no way to judge time, or distance. They didn't know which direction they were going, or where they were going. They didn't know what lay ahead or behind. They were completely lost in the biggest most intense wilderness imaginable.

Chapter 22
The Perpauca
1

Andronicus and Chaka trekked aimlessly through the vast jungle, well after they had lost all sense of time. They continued moving forward as best as they could, never certain they were going the right way. The jungle seemed to be truly endless, and they both had to wonder how big it really was. Each day seemed identical to the last, and their entire world became nothing but green trees. They climbed the trees and cut them, they went through them and around them, but always there was just another tree and then another, on and on and on.

One day Andronicus was cutting through the thick vines with Chaka not far behind, when suddenly the vines stopped, and he found himself looking out over a cliff. He walked to the edge and looked down. The trees below the cliff were at least a few hundred feet down, and Andronicus knew the ground would be a few hundred feet below that.

Chaka walked to the edge next to him, and they both looked out over the vast jungle spread beneath them. Andronicus could not believe the sight of it, thick green jungle stretched as far as he could see in every direction. There were hills and valleys, but it was all covered in thick jungle.

As Andronicus stood beside Chaka, admiring the magnificent spectacle of the Great Jungle, an odd feeling crept over him. One second he was looking down at the trees, thinking how the jungle was like nothing he had ever seen before, and the next second he realized he had seen it before. He had seen this exact place before in his dreams, or visions. Memories came rushing back of massive ornate landscapes, a mountain, a desert, a stormy sea, and a jungle. Once the thought came to him, he was certain he had dreamed not only of this jungle before but of this very cliff overlooking the jungle. It should have made him happy to know that one of his dreams had come to be, but it just filled him with more uncertainty. It made him wonder if he would reach those other places as well and, if so, how long it would take.

They spent the whole day staring out at the jungle from above, seeing the world they had been living in from a completely different view. Andronicus couldn't believe the magnificence of it all. He had seen oceans and mountains and plains and some of the greatest cities in the world, but none of that came close to the splendor of the Great Jungle.

When night came, they set up camp by the cliff and went to sleep under the open stars for the first time in years. Andronicus stayed up most of the night trying to remember every last bit of astronomy he had learned over the years, including what Philander had taught him back in Greece. As far as he could tell, the stars above the jungle were the same as the stars he had been looking at ever since he awoke in Swimha. Andronicus wondered if he would ever get to see the old stars from his childhood again.

He was also able to make out that they were unbelievably still heading north, so far as he could tell. He didn't know if they had stayed true to north the whole time, but he knew they had been going north for at least the last few weeks. There was still no telling how far the jungle went, but he was confident that if they continued going north, they would find the end of it someday.

As he lay there staring up at the stars and thinking about his life, he slipped into a dream. At first he didn't realize he was dreaming. It was night, and he was in the jungle, and it felt like every other night. Then he saw something through the trees, a light in the distance. It grew nearer, followed by another light and then another. Andronicus reached for his sword as the fierce painted warriors of the Kahli stepped out the bushes. The firelight danced across their eyes, and Andronicus saw they didn't have any pupils; their eyes were completely white, and the light from the fire turned them red. A shiver ran down his back, and then he heard the voices start to whisper. They weren't speaking any language Andronicus had ever heard. They didn't even sound human.

Andronicus closed his eyes and shook his head,

trying to turn away the awful voices. When he opened his eyes, he wasn't in the jungle anymore. He was in an open field, and it was daytime. The land didn't look like anywhere he had ever been. There was a yelp of some wounded animal nearby, and Andronicus turned around and saw Lycus kneeling in the dirt, cutting open the belly of a wild dog. Andronicus called out to him, but Lycus didn't look up. He ran over to him, and called out again, and again Lycus ignored him. Andronicus saw red cloth wrapped around one of Lycus' hands and wondered what had happened. He called out one last time, as loud as he could, and Lycus finally looked up. He had a strange expression on his face, somewhere between fury and terror.

Andronicus started to call out again, but he felt himself slipping away. Lycus became fuzzy, and then the world around them turned to smoke. Andronicus closed his eyes and felt water spray against his face. He opened his eyes and saw himself on the deck of a huge ship. A storm was raging, and before he could speak to one of the many men running around him, the ship crested a massive wave. Andronicus grabbed hold of the nearest railing as the ship hurdled down the side of the wave. As the ship pounded into the ocean below, Andronicus lurched forward.

He sat up abruptly, and looked around at the jungle. He was sitting next to Chaka, between where the brush ended and the cliff began. There were a few chitters from the birds in the trees, but other than that the jungle was silent. Andronicus lay back down on his cloak, his heart still racing. He hadn't had such vivid dreams since entering the jungle, and he found that he actually missed it. Now he wasn't so sure though. The look on Lycus's face in the dream gave Andronicus the chills. It took a long time to fall back asleep, and when he did, he dreamed of war.

2

It took them two full weeks to find a safe way down the cliff. They searched for a place where they could walk safely down to the ground below but had no luck. As far as they could tell, the cliff went on for miles in both directions. Eventually, they decided to climb down.

They walked the cliff for another three days before Andronicus found a place he felt was right. Trees were growing out of the side of the mountain, and they climbed carefully down the vines and branches, praying the whole way down that the trees wouldn't give way and drop them to their deaths.

It took an entire day and most of the night to climb down, but they made it safely. The moon was full, giving them enough light to see their hands and feet and where to step. Once they dropped below the tree line, the moonlight faded, but there were also many more vines to grab hold of, and it didn't take them long to reach the jungle floor.

Once they had their feet back on the ground, they set up camp at the foot of the cliff and went about building a small fire.

The pair sat in silence, eating a snake they had killed on their way down. Andronicus was staring at the fire as he chewed the charred rubbery meat, thinking about Greece, when he heard something move behind him. He leapt up and grabbed his sword. Chaka took out his knife and held it up, ready for a predator to appear. They looked around but couldn't see anything through the thick trees and blackness.

They heard a rustling noise to their left and then another to their right and two more right in front of them. By the time Andronicus recognized the sound as human feet, they were surrounded. The fire they had built was still burning between them, and Andronicus knew that whoever was out there could see them clearly.

Andronicus clutched his sword in his hand, ready to cut down whoever was hiding in the shadows. It had been so long since they had come across another human that he had begun to think there weren't any people in the jungle at all. When they had first entered the jungle, they had seen the marks and tracks of other people occasionally, but as they trekked farther into the heart of the jungle, signs of other people had ceased to exist entirely.

The bushes in front of them began to tremble and then to shake. Andronicus didn't know if they were close to the end of the jungle or who these people might be, but he knew they were likely hostile. The leaves in front of them rustled some more, and he saw them moving. Andronicus clutched his sword and prepared for the attack.

The leaves moved again, and a short figure stepped out into the open, holding a short spear in one hand and staring up at them both. At first Andronicus thought it was a child; he only came up to Andronicus' midriff and was below Chaka's waist. Andronicus lowered his sword and let out a relieved sigh as the figure came toward them.

The person stepped forward into the light, and Andronicus realized it wasn't a boy at all. The man had even darker skin than Chaka, but he had grey hair and a chalky beard. Andronicus raised his sword again, and the man jumped back with a high-pitched yelp. He stared up at them both with big bright eyes that stood out in stark contrast to his dark face. He didn't say anything, just stared up at them in fear and wonder, like they were the first normal-sized people he had ever seen.

Andronicus took a small step forward, and the little man leapt back, throwing his hands up above his face. He tripped over a rock and went sprawling in the dirt. Several of his companions hiding in the bushes let out shrieks and squeals as their comrade fell. Andronicus quickly lowered his sword. After a moment the small man stood up, staring at Andronicus as if he were some kind of beast. Slowly, the others came out of the bushes as well, all staring at Andronicus and Chaka in stupefied awe. They were all just as short as the first man, most even shorter.

Andronicus looked around at all the tiny people and then looked over at Chaka. He couldn't help but let out a snort of laughter in response to the expression on Chaka's face. Chaka was looking down at them the way an elephant looks down at a mouse, as if he were afraid they would crawl up his leg like bugs. He looked just as frightened of them as they were of him.

Andronicus could tell the tiny terrified little men would not be any threat to him, and he put his sword away. He turned back to the little man who had first stepped out and held out his hands in peace. Again, they all flinched at his movement. Andronicus looked at Chaka, who shrugged, the comical look of disgust still on his face. Chaka stepped forward, and all the little people flinched back in fear, many of them actually falling to the ground in terror.

Andronicus didn't know who the tiny people were or where they came from, but he was quite sure they had not seen anyone but their own for a long time, probably not for generations. After a long time of Andronicus trying to start communication and the little men flinching back in fear, he finally managed to get them to take him to their village.

3

The little people fascinated Andronicus from the very beginning. Their village started on the jungle floor in an open patch of dirt between four huge trees that stretched high above the rest. The little people had made ladders and ropes to climb up the trees, and the rest of their village stretched up through the branches and vines. It was like no village Andronicus had ever seen, and it seemed to rise out of sight above him.

From the moment they saw Andronicus and Chaka, the little people treated them like gods. The women looked almost exactly like the men, except that they had small bared breasts, and the children were as small as spider monkeys. Everyone in the village stared at them in fear and wonder.

That night the people held a feast for Andronicus and Chaka. They had meat, and fish, probably from a river somewhere nearby, and all manner of fruit.

They ate like kings for the first time since entering the jungle. Andronicus loved every minute of it. Chaka, on the other hand, spent the night looking down at the little people as if they might bite him. At one point during the festivities, a group of tiny children ran up to him, and for a moment Andronicus thought Chaka was going to swat them away like flies. Instead he let one of them climb up his back like a tree. Then he shook the small child off, and the rest of them scurried away.

Andronicus spent all night trying to communicate with the first man who had emerged from the bushes, who seemed to be the chief, or at least some kind of leader. Andronicus had learned many languages over their travels. He wasn't fluent in all of them, but he could at least communicate with the people of the plains from the Great Jungle all the way back to Swimha and down to the Great Sea. The language of the little people, however, wasn't like any other language he had heard. It didn't even sound like they were saying words; it was more like odd clicking sounds with their tongues.

Andronicus tried to learn the man's name, and by the end of the night, he thought he knew what the man called himself, though Andronicus wouldn't dream of pronouncing it. He had tried to tell them their names as well. He introduced himself as Jocus, as he had since the day he had met Chaka. None of them were able to say Jocus or Chaka, though they came as close as their clicking tongues would allow.

When the feast was over, and the rest of the little people were climbing up the trees like monkeys, the man Andronicus had been speaking to led him and Chaka over to a small hut on the ground. He showed them in, and they found several cots that looked like they were for small children. Andronicus pushed two of them together, and Chaka took the rest, and after a few minutes they each had a cot that would fit them.

The tiny man said something to them and then left. Chaka lay down and fell asleep almost right away, clearly glad to have a bed to sleep in. Andronicus stayed up for a long time, thinking. He was still shocked that they had found people so deep in the jungle, and even more shocked at the people themselves. He thought about how remarkable it was that there were so many different kinds of people in the world. It made him wonder who else might be out there. As always his thoughts eventually found their way to his old friends, and he wondered if any of them had met such strange people in their travels.

4

The next morning Andronicus awoke to find three small men staring down at him in fascination. They all jumped up and fled as soon as he opened his eyes. He sat up and saw Chaka snoring loudly next to him and decided to let him sleep; he knew they would stay at least a few days. It would be a perfect place to rest a while before returning to the endless dank jungle.

Andronicus walked out into the center of the tiny people's village and looked at all the small faces staring up at him with wide eyes. They seemed a bit absurd to Andronicus. They all had dark black skin, the darkest he had ever seen, and huge white eyes, and they all cowered in fear as Andronicus neared them, the men and the women. Before he could say anything, two little men ran out with breakfast for him. He picked out a few fruit from the bunch they had brought him, then sat down to eat as the two men scurried off.

The chief came out and walked over to Andronicus, still gazing at him as though he were Apollo himself. Andronicus smiled at him and held out a fruit, gesturing for the man to sit down. The small man took the fruit with a trembling hand and then sat down. He bit into the fruit as if it were magical. Andronicus couldn't help but laugh.

Chaka stepped out a moment later, and many of the little people who had been watching Andronicus ran away at the sight of him. Chaka frowned at the villagers, then walked over to Andronicus as they scurried off.

"I do not like these little people," Chaka said as he sat down, his brow furrowed.

"And why is that?" Andronicus asked, taking a bite of the fruit. "They have been perfectly kind to us. They fed us and gave us shelter. And to be honest, I think they think we are gods." Andronicus thought

Chaka would find the idea as amusing as he did, but clearly Chaka did not.

"We are not gods, Jocus." Chaka said seriously.

"And how do you know that?" Andronicus asked with a sly smile. "How else do you explain what has happened to me?"

"You are not an ordinary man Jocus," Chaka said. "I know that." The chief of the small people was still sitting next to him, gazing at them in awe, not understanding a word. "But that does not make you a god. You once told me there are no gods, and yet now you wish to act as one."

"I am not acting like a god," Andronicus protested. "They think I am a god, and I have no way to tell them otherwise." Andronicus tried to look innocent, but Chaka gave him a troubled look. Andronicus could tell Chaka didn't like any of it. "It is not as if we are going to stay with them like we did with the Bahitu," Andronicus insisted. "It is just a nice place to stop and rest for a while before we resume our journey."

"And just how long do you expect we will stay here?" Chaka asked gravely.

"A week," Andronicus replied. "Two at the most."

5

It turned out that leaving was much harder than Andronicus had anticipated. Living with the tiny people was much nicer than the ceaseless trekking through the jungle. They fed Andronicus and Chaka more food than they could ask for and treated them like kings. Andronicus loved living amongst the tiny people, whom he had named the Perpauca, which meant "tiny people" in Greek. They lived much the way the people of the plains lived, hunting when necessary and never taking more than they needed.

The thing that fascinated Andronicus most about the Perpauca was their mastery of the jungle's poisons and toxins. Andronicus had learned early on which plants were poisonous, and they had been lucky enough not to get bitten by the poisonous spiders and snakes. The Perpauca had spent generations studying the poisons, and Andronicus wanted to learn it all.

He still couldn't understand a word they said, but they taught him about all kinds of plants and insects and other ways to get poisons. Andronicus had never realized how many there were or how many different things they could do. Some of the toxins made people fall asleep right away, and some caused paralysis. Some caused people to break out in hives, and some caused them to shriek in pain. Most of the poisons were lethal, but they all seemed to kill in a different way. Some didn't even leave a trace.

The Perpauca used blow darts to expel their poisons, and they were masters at it. Andronicus had seen other tribes use blow darts before, but the Perpauca had perfected the art. They made slim tubes out of the branches of certain trees, about two feet long, and thin sharp darts, dipped in their choice of poison. They had a special way of firing the darts, so they could hit a target more than fifty feet away.

After a month with the Perpauca, Chaka was ready to leave. Andronicus, however, was determined to master the art of the blow dart and learn all the poisons he could. He told himself, and Chaka, that he wanted to stay to finish learning about the different plants and toxins, but in truth he was just glad to have a place to stay for a while. He was afraid of what would happen to his mind if he walked through the jungle for much longer. And while he would never admit it to Chaka, or even to himself, part of him enjoyed being looked at as a god.

6

Andronicus lost track of how long they stayed with the Perpauca, but eventually he thought it had to be years rather than months. He still couldn't speak their language, but he had learned to communicate with the chief. He still couldn't say the chief's name properly and had resorted to calling him "Glick" a long time ago. It was the closest thing he could say to part of the man's name, and Glick certainly didn't seem to mind the nickname.

Eventually, Glick finished showing Andronicus the last of their poisons. As soon as Chaka heard it, he began pestering Andronicus to leave. Andronicus knew they shouldn't stay any longer, but he didn't want to go. He didn't know how long it had been since they had met the Perpauca, but it had certainly passed the two weeks he had promised Chaka it would be. It was amazing how easily he had become comfortable, but he knew it was time to move on. There was only one thing left he had to do before leaving the Perpauca behind.

Glick had shown him a concoction they made, which was taken once by every male in the tribe, and on that day they would become a man. Andronicus had seen four boys eat the mixture since he had arrived, and all four had exhibited incredibly odd behavior. It was as if they were seeing things he was not. He tried to ask Glick what it was for. Glick motioned to his head, expanded his hands, then pointed to his eyes, and expanded his hands again.

Andronicus nodded, thinking he knew what Glick was trying to say. He didn't know what other people saw when they took it, but he had an idea what he might see. His dreams were all too scrambled and hectic to remember, and he yearned for a chance to see them more clearly. Andronicus wasn't sure if it would work or not, but he desperately wanted to try the concoction before moving on. He just wasn't sure if he was allowed.

Andronicus went to Glick's hut and motioned to the thick green mucky liquid that sat in a bowl in the corner. Glick looked at him in surprise, as though he had never even considered the idea of Andronicus taking their sacred remedy. Andronicus could see that Glick was struggling with the idea. On one hand this was their sacred potion, the thing that made them men. On the other hand, Glick still viewed Andronicus as a sort of god. In the end it seemed Glick decided that sharing the sacred potion with a god would be OK, because he slowly got up and retrieved the stuff.

He handed the bowl to Andronicus with a

hesitant look on his tiny face. Andronicus gave him a nod to indicate he was aware of what he was asking, and Glick nodded back. Andronicus took the bowl and walked back to his own hut. Chaka's hut was right next to his, and he was sitting in front of it sharpening his bronze knife. He looked up when Andronicus came around the corner and put down the knife.

"It is time, Jocus," he said, looking anxiously at Andronicus. "You have learned your poisons, so let us leave this place, as we should have long ago." Andronicus looked down at his feet as Chaka reminded him of the promise he had made.

"We will," he said. "I just have one last thing to do before we go."

"What now?" Chaka asked in exasperation.

"I have to take this," Andronicus said, holding the bowl out for Chaka to see. "And when I am done, we can go."

Chaka looked at the green muck in alarm. He had also watched the boys eat the stuff and then act wildly. One of the boys had never been right afterward, and Chaka fully mistrusted the concoction.

"Jocus, you cannot," he said, getting to his feet. "You should know enough about poisons by now to know this is one of them. It is a poison of the mind."

"Glick says it will expand my mind and make me see more," Andronicus argued.

"Glick is a foolish little man," Chaka said bitterly. He had never liked the Perpauca and had only tolerated them for so long because they brought him fresh fruit and meat three times a day. "He knows about poison and medicine, yes, but he is not the wise man you think him to be. He is not Nnamdi, Jocus. You should not take this poison."

"I will be alright, Chaka," Andronicus assured him. "I will be done by tomorrow, the day after at the very latest, and then we will leave."

"You once told me we would stay here for one week, two at the most," Chaka reminded him, "do you know how long ago that was?"

"No, I do not," Andronicus said, looking back down at his feet.

"Neither do I," Chaka said sternly. "Take your poison, Jocus. In three days' time I leave with or without you."

"You are going to leave without me?" Andronicus said in a mocking tone. "And where will you go?"

"Farther than you," Chaka grunted, then stormed off. Andronicus looked down at the green muck again and thought about just packing up their things and leaving that night, but he couldn't do it. His curiosity was too strong. He wanted to know what the stuff would show him. More than anything he wanted to get a clearer glimpse of the visions he had seen so long ago when he had touched the glowing stones. The scattered dreams weren't enough; he needed a closer look.

Andronicus knew the custom was to walk deep into the jungle and take the stuff there, then find one's way back to the village, so that's what he did. He took only his sword and cloak and began walking deep into the jungle.

After he had walked for a few hours, he found a small stream and sat to drink and eat. He knew not to take the stuff on an empty stomach, so he ate plenty of fruit before forcing the green muck down.

It tasted disgusting. It was sour, and it smelled rotten. Andronicus had to gag down every bite. It took him nearly ten minutes, but he finally managed to get it all down. He waited by the water, drinking often to wash away the foul taste as he waited for the drug to take hold.

7

Andronicus waited for almost an hour, sitting by the stream and tossing rocks into the trickling water. He was beginning to wonder if Glick had given him a defective batch when he started to feel funny. The sun had nearly set, and only a few slim beams of light made their way to the jungle floor, but everything started to get brighter. Suddenly, the plants all around him looked greener than any he had ever seen, a kind of vibrant green so bright, he had never seen anything like it. The water, which had been clear a moment earlier, now shown with all the colors of the rainbow.

The entire world around Andronicus seemed to come alive with a sort of effervescent glow. The calls and songs of the birds high above him began ringing with a harmony he had never noticed before. As he listened to the noises above and all around him, he thought he could actually see the sounds moving through the air, like a wavy mirage on a hot day. The world became a spinning whirling vortex of sound, and smell, and more color than he knew existed. Everything felt as if it were one. One heartbeat beating in a thousand chests. One life made up of a million souls. The jungle itself was truly alive and awake in a way Andronicus could never have expected.

He could feel everything around him, everything he had never felt before. Every little thing, from the plants to the bugs to the birds, they all seemed to be calling out to him, calling for him to join them, to come home. As the sun slowly fell away, and the light began to fade, the glow began to fade as well.

In a matter of minutes, the jungle went from a glowing, vibrating world full of life to a dark, dank blackness pounding down on him like an angry drum. It was as if the jungle that had been alive and singing a moment earlier had suddenly noticed him, an outsider in its presence, and closed in on him. The birds ceased their singing, and the only remaining noises were the howls of monkeys up in the trees and the scurrying of an animal somewhere nearby.

As the blackness enveloped him, Andronicus's lungs began to tighten. His breath came in short bursts, and he realized he was starting to panic. He closed his eyes and focused on the good noises that were still there, the humming of the wind through the trees, the occasional whistle of a bird, and the endless chirping of the crickets. When he opened his eyes an unknown time later, he was breathing normally again.

To his surprise, his eyes quickly adjusted to the darkness. It was as if his eyes cast light upon everything they saw. Now that he could see again, the feeling of claustrophobia started going away. He stood up and looked around. He was still in the same jungle he had been in for years, but everything looked different now.

He started to walk through the black jungle with no idea which way he was going. The noises blurred together into a ringing sensation in his ears. He kept walking through the jungle, stepping over moss and logs and ducking under vines as if it were as light as day.

As he stepped over a small stream, he heard a rustling noise above him. He looked up and saw two yellow eyes staring at him out of the blackness. At first he couldn't see what they belonged to; he only saw a thick branch covered in leaves and vines. Then one of the vines moved, flicking back and forth. Andronicus realized it was a tail just as the cat leapt down from the tree.

It landed a few feet away and looked up at him. It was hard to make out the cat's body because it was as dark as the night itself, but its yellow eyes were unmistakable. Andronicus stared into the two yellow orbs staring back at him, and they began to glow like the trees had before. At first it was just the cat's eyes, then it was as if he could feel the beast, like they were one and the same.

Andronicus stared in wonder at the black shape standing in front of him. He wondered why the cat had not attacked him yet. He still had his sword in his hand, but if the beast was smart and quick, it could kill him easily. He stood his ground, staring into the cat's eyes, waiting for it to attack. He couldn't tell if it was because of the drug or not, but he felt an intense connection to this beast. It was as if the cat's eyes were trying to tell him something. For some reason it reminded him of the red eyes he saw sometimes in his dreams, but these eyes didn't make him feel cold and sick; they made him feel warm, and safe.

Andronicus didn't know how long he stood there with the jet-black cat, neither of them moving. It could have been five minutes or five hours. When the cat finally turned its head away, the light from its eyes left, and Andronicus could just barely make out the dark shape as it gracefully leapt back into the trees and disappeared into the darkness.

Andronicus stood there for a long time after the cat left, trying to think what it could mean. His mind was racing in a way it never had before, leaping from one thought to the next. He tried to calm his mind and focus his thoughts, but it was difficult. He was sure that when the young boys took the potion it was a bit of a nightmare for them, but Andronicus was an old man with the fit body of a young man, and he was able to deal with the effects well enough.

It was well past dark, but he didn't feel the least bit tired. His body was filled with a humming feeling. It felt warm and familiar in an odd sort of way. Then Andronicus realized where he had felt it before: in the cave. He remembered the way the glow of the rocks had seemed to fill him up, and he felt that same sort of warmth now. Thinking about the cave and the rocks quickly led to thinking about his visions.

Andronicus closed his eyes and concentrated as hard as he could. His mind was difficult to control; the drug was making his brain work in an unusual way. At first all he could see were colors and movements, and then it began to clear. His eyes were still closed, but he could see shapes forming in his mind. He realized he was beginning to remember the visions, something he had waited years for.

The first thing he saw was a massive army, all with long spears, chanting in unison. The army quickly fell away and was replaced by a city. Andronicus didn't recognize the city, and before he could try to focus on it, it morphed into a huge mountain, bigger than any Andronicus had ever seen. The top of the mountain was covered in snow and stretched high above the clouds. Then the mountain fell away too and was replaced by a desert as big as a sea. Men were fighting each other. Andronicus couldn't see who they were, but one of them was cutting the others down in quick succession.

The fighting men were replaced by new men, who were holding things Andronicus didn't recognize at all, and bright flashes of light were coming from their hands. Then there was only one man, standing over a field of corpses. The man had an odd-looking hat on his head, sort of square shaped with a long, flat brim, and he was wearing a long dark coat that fell past his knees. Andronicus had never seen anyone like him.

The vision became clearer, and Andronicus could just make out the man's face. He had dark eyes and a scar running across his mouth. At first Andronicus thought the man might be him, but as he saw him clearer he realized it wasn't. He concentrated as hard as he could, trying to see the mysterious man's face. Then the man moved, as fast as anyone he had ever seen, faster even than Andronicus. The man's hand dropped to his side, and then there was a flash of light.

Andronicus opened his eyes with a start and saw two red dots floating in the darkness. He blinked, and the red dots turned yellow. A large, dark shape began creeping toward him. It took him a second to recognize it was a cat, though not the same one as before. This one looked to be a spotted shade of yellow. Andronicus scrambled to his feet and reached for his sword. The cat let out a sharp howl and then ran at him. Andronicus's sword slipped out of his hand, and he put his hands up as a simple reflex. As the cat ran at him, he felt his heart leap into his throat.

At the last second, as the spotted cat leapt, with Andronicus kneeling there like a wounded deer, a big black shape jumped in front of him, sending the leaping cat tumbling backwards. The cat jumped to its feet and let out an awful shriek before charging the dark newcomer. The black shape was a blur. It disappeared and then came crashing down onto the oncoming beast with all its weight.

For a brief moment there was an awful screeching racket as the two large cats fought each other. All Andronicus could see was a tangled mass. Finally, they split. The spotted cat let out a low, grumbling growl, stalking the black cat, and the black cat stood as still as a rock. The spotted cat looked like it was going to pounce again when the dark one let out a roar. It was louder than any beast Andronicus had ever heard, and the defeated predator fled in fear through the trees.

The black shape turned and looked at Andronicus lying on the ground. When he looked into the shining yellow eyes, he knew it was the same beast as before. He wasn't sure what the cat was going to do, but he knew it could easily kill him if it wanted to. But this time he wasn't afraid. He just sat there, staring into its glowing eyes, feeling the beast's energy in a way that still seemed foreign to him. Finally, the cat turned around, and slunk away into the darkness, just as it had done before.

Andronicus picked his sword up and followed it. His mind was still full of whatever the concoction was, but its effect was beginning to weaken. He was just wondering how long it had been when the light began to show again. At first he couldn't believe it was already morning, but the light quickly spread. The plants and the light had the same sort of vibrancy they had the day before, only not as strong.

Andronicus realized he had no idea which way the village was or how to get back there. Every direction looked exactly the same, and he didn't know where to go.

As he was trying to get his bearings, he saw the black cat jump down from a tree. Andronicus was amazed at the beast. It was as if it were protecting him; he had never seen anything like it.

The shining black beast stared at him for a long time, then turned and walked away. Andronicus decided to follow it, hurrying to catch up. The cat never turned around to look at him, but he could tell it was going slow enough for him to follow.

When they reached a small clearing, the cat turned around and stared at him again. Andronicus didn't know what the beast was trying to say, but he was certain it was trying to tell him something. Then it turned and left. This time instead of following, he stood and watched as the beautiful, agile beast glided up a tree and out of sight.

Andronicus was wondering what to do next when he heard voices in the distance. He walked toward them and soon found his way to the village. Everyone looked at him like they had never seen him before. Glick ran out to meet him and started shouting in his language. Andronicus didn't know what he was saying, but he thought that he had probably come back too fast.

He wished he could tell Glick about the black cat, how it had showed him the way home, but he thought it better not to.

Chaka approached and gave Andronicus a questioning look. Andronicus nodded slowly, and Chaka let out a deep sigh. It was still early in the day, and Andronicus knew Chaka would want to leave right away. The drug had mostly worn off, so he went and joined Chaka as he gathered their things.

"What happened to you out there?" Chaka asked, looking concerned.

"I saw . . . things," Andronicus said, thinking about everything that had happened over the night.

"And what about that? What happened there?" Chaka asked, pointing at Andronicus's sword.

He looked down and noticed the hilt had blood on it. He drew the sword and winced at the scratchy feel of the dirty blade as it came out. The entire blade was covered in dried blood, from tip to hilt. He couldn't remember using his sword at any point, and he felt a chill run down his spine. For a moment he told himself it could just be mud from when he had dropped it, but it only took a moment's inspection to see that it was indeed blood.

Andronicus tried to think of where the blood could have come from, and he could only think of one thing. He tried to tell himself that he was wrong, that the black cat had been real. He couldn't decide which was more likely, that the drug had made him see a cat that wasn't there or that it had made him forget killing something at some point in the night. The cat had been real; he felt it, it had been more real than anything he had ever seen.

He felt even more confused than he had been before taking the drug. He had been expecting, or at least hoping, that the drug would help give him some answers or help him remember the visions. That at least, the drug had succeeded in. As Andronicus packed his things, he thought about what he had seen when he closed his eyes. Some of it had been the same things he kept dreaming of, like the mountain and the desert, but some of it had been new.

The memory of the man he had seen just before snapping out of it returned to him, and he felt the hairs on his arms and neck stand up. Whoever the man was, he had looked terrifying. Andronicus remembered the way his hand moved like lightning, and then the flash, and he wondered what it all might mean. The experience had merely generated more questions. Andronicus finished his packing, then met Chaka outside to say their goodbyes to the tiny people and return to their seemingly unending jungle quest.

Chapter 23
Through the Great Jungle
1

Once the Perpauca village was behind them, and they were back to trekking through the dense jungle, the travelers quickly fell back into their previous rhythm. They would trek all day, either hiking or climbing, with one of them breaking trail with the sword. If they happened to find an easy meal they would take it. If not, they had both become excellent jungle hunters. Whenever they came across a stream or a pool of water, they would rest for a while, fill their water bags, then continue on, always hoping to find some sign of the end of the jungle, but never finding it.

When they lay down to rest at night, they would usually wrap themselves in their blankets. They also stuck bits of moss in their ears, not because of noise but to deter unwanted visitors. The jungle was full of deadly creatures, and Andronicus didn't know how they had not died already. The large predators usually stayed away from them, but the small ones were always around.

Glick had given Andronicus a small, ornate-looking wooden box before they left. It was one of the most finely carved boxes Andronicus had ever seen, and he couldn't quite fathom how the little jungle people had managed to create something so beautiful. The craftsmanship would have made any Greek man proud, and in all his time with the little people Andronicus had never seen anything else like it. Inside the box were twelve little squares, separated by thin, perfectly flat pieces of wood. The box was rectangular and small enough to fit in one hand.

On the top of the box was a symbol that Andronicus had never seen before, carved so perfectly into the wood that there was no indentation whatsoever. The symbol sent chills down Andronicus's spine every time he looked at it. He had tried to ask Glick what the symbol meant, but Glick had just stared up at him with his big brown eyes and slowly shook his head. Andronicus wasn't sure what that was supposed to mean, but he accepted the gift nonetheless.

Chaka didn't like the box at all. He knew what was inside it, and he wanted no part of it. Andronicus had only opened the box once, and he didn't plan on opening it again any time soon. He was glad the box was made so well and would be able to stay shut. Inside the dozen small spaces were twelve different powders. Andronicus knew every one of them and what they could do, and he always kept the box wrapped tightly in a cloth.

They had accumulated quite a bit of junk to lug around with them over the years. Andronicus had his sword with its hide sheath, which the Bahitu had made for him. He still had his Spartan cloak as well, which had been patched many times over the years, but still held together. They each had the two large water bags and a few halved gourds that they used as bowls. They also had a collection of rock tools as well as the bronze knife. Besides that they each had a bag slung over their shoulders with some spare clothes and rags as well as two blankets each.

The jungle was so hot and the air so thick that they could only move so fast. They both sweated profusely, and they had to drink water constantly. Luckily for them, there was enough water in the jungle for them to drink as much as they wanted. Their days were filled with the constant struggle of pushing through the jungle. Their nights were spent silently pondering the depths of the endless world through which they were moving.

Andronicus had never meant to be in the jungle for so long. If he had known the place was this big, he would have tried to find a way around it. Now that they were as deep as they were though, there was no turning back. Andronicus had no idea how long they had actually been in the jungle. He was sure it had been a few years before they found the Perpauca, and at least two years with them, maybe three. Andronicus tried to guess how long it had been since leaving the Perpauca, and thought it was already probably a few years as well, but it was just so hard to tell.

Time in the jungle seemed endless. There were no stars, no moon, no sun. Only a few beams of sunlight managed to penetrate the trees and reach the jungle floor. Andronicus made sure to check his reflection every time he came across a large pool of water. He didn't know why he still did it; he always saw the same thing. His hair was long, wild, and matted, and his beard was thick and black, but under all the tangled hair he could still see his face, and it still hadn't changed a bit. Only his eyes had changed. They were still the same piercing green they had always been, but now they had a look that Andronicus hadn't seen there before. His skin had grown much paler than it had been in the plains, perhaps more than it had ever been.

As they spent more and more time inside the jungle, Andronicus's thoughts began to darken. When they had first entered the jungle, he had been confident and determined. But as they spent year after hopeless year trekking through the seemingly endless jungle with no other humans in sight, it was harder to keep his thoughts together. He began to wonder if he was dead, and if the jungle was hell. Chaka was not much for small talk, so Andronicus was left alone to his dark thoughts day after day, month after month, and year after painfully slow year.

He didn't know when it started, but sometimes he heard voices speaking in his head. Sometimes they spoke Greek, sometimes Swihmehe, and sometimes languages he didn't understand. Whenever he was talking to Chaka, they would go away, but if the silence lasted long enough, the voices would return. Andronicus didn't like it at all; it felt foreign and bad, and he tried to make them stop. He knew he was losing his own sanity and could do nothing but pray for the jungle to end.

One thing that always made the voices go away was thinking about his dreams. He didn't have them like he used to. In the plains he would have vision-like dreams almost every night, but in the jungle they were as rare as the sun itself. He still remembered the same flashes of the dreams though, mostly magnificent landscapes and cities that he had yet to see in real life. He had become certain that the dreams were indeed visions and that he knew where they came from.

He had no idea how any of it worked, but he was beginning to put things together. He knew that the glowing rocks had brought him to Swimha. He knew that they had given him visions of the future and that they were making him stay young. Whatever had happened in that cave had changed him forever; that much he was sure of. It made him wonder if his old friends could still be alive as well, also the same age they had been that day. Whatever it was, it seemed to have rubbed off on Chaka too.

When they had left the Swihmehe Chaka had been in his forties. They spent at least fifteen years before entering the jungle, and countless years inside. Andronicus knew Chaka had to be at least sixty years old by now, and yet he still looked young as well. It wasn't like he hadn't aged a single day like Andronicus, but he still looked in his forties. His hair was sprinkled with grey, but it had been for years. It was as if somewhere along the way, Chaka had stopped aging too.

It was more than Andronicus could hope to understand. He wondered if Manyara would have grown old with him if she hadn't died, if they would have lived for centuries together in peace, raising a little boy who would never grow old.

Andronicus tried to talk to Chaka about his thoughts, or his questions as he called them, but Chaka was never very interested. Andronicus wasn't sure just how many questions he had, but he asked them every single day. Where exactly did I wake up? Are Swimha and Greece even in the same world? Where are my friends? Did they wake up in strange lands as well? Are they not getting older? Do they have friends who have stopped getting older like Chaka? Will I ever find them? Will I ever find Greece? Is it even possible to find Greece? How big is this damned jungle? Is there an end to it all? Is there an end to me? Will I ever die? Am I already dead?

The questions went on and on, constantly, without any answers. Chaka and Andronicus had never been a chatty pair of travelers, but on the plains Andronicus had at least been able to walk under the open sky, and breathe normally. In the dank, dark jungle, it was much harder to stay positive. Andronicus spent most of his time being torn apart by all the things he didn't know. He contemplated his very existence daily, never really sure of anything.

Andronicus didn't know what was going on in Chaka's head while they walked, but his was filled with dark questions and even darker memories. Too often he saw the faces of the innocent people he had slain back in Swimha. He knew he would likely never be rid of them, nor should he be. Perhaps he was cursed to walk aimlessly through the endless jungle, never reaching the end and never able to die.

Occasionally Andronicus would try to force Chaka into a conversation about his questions, but Chaka would just shrug them off. He said they were questions for a white man. The Swihmehe had no worry about such things. Chaka would talk about the plants or animals or even listen to Andronicus tell stories about Greece, but he would not talk about the things Andronicus really wanted to talk about.

Andronicus wanted someone to talk to about

what the hell was going on. Chaka had only talked to Andronicus one time about not getting older and how he had thought he was going to die. Now that he was alive, Chaka didn't want to talk about death at all. Andronicus wished he could put his obsessions aside and just enjoy the jungle like Chaka seemed to, but he couldn't get rid of all the dark thoughts. The occasional whispering voices didn't help at all.

2

The jungle never really seemed to change. The land went up and down, and sometimes there were breaks in the trees above them, but the jungle all looked the same. They saw new trees, birds, and animals all the time, but the jungle itself was always the same. As the days stretched on, seemingly without end, they saw more animals than they knew could possibly exist, and yet there were never any people. The utter lack of humanity would likely have been unbearable if either of them were on their own, so they were glad for each other's company.

Andronicus and Chaka didn't actually talk most of the time, but just having each other there was enough. They were both quiet men, and they had been travelling partners for so long they had said most everything they had to say, except of course to really discuss the greater situation. In addition to companionship, they worked perfectly as a team. They had been on the move for so long that they had become masters at it.

While one hunted, the other prepared camp and a fire. While one broke trail with the sword, the other lugged the bags on his back. They knew how much water to drink and when to eat. They knew when to sleep and when to wake if danger appeared. The routine of their days became automatic and hypnotic. It was easy to turn off their minds and simply walk, especially with such magnificent surroundings.

No matter how far they walked or how much everything blended together, they still saw new and incredible things all the time. Andronicus was sure the jungle was unlike anywhere else in the world, and part of him felt lucky to see sights that no human eyes had seen before. It was something special to be the first people to walk through a land, but it was also dangerous.

They came across beasts Andronicus had never seen before, and he knew the creatures had likely never seen humans either. They saw more of the sleek yellow cats with brown patterns on rare occasions, usually just catching a glimpse of them as they crept by. The spotted cats looked like lions, and yet there were definite differences. Andronicus made sure they kept their distance from the bigger beasts, but they still came across them every now and again. Only one of the cats was bold or foolish enough to try and kill them. Chaka was the one holding the spear that day, and he acted swiftly and surely, even though he hated to kill such a beautiful creature.

When he had killed the beast, he insisted they take every last bit of it. Normally when they killed an animal in the jungle they would eat what they could but leave the rest for another creature to find. They didn't have enough salt to spare, and meat was easy to find in the jungle. But Chaka insisted they take every scrap of what he called the *hakahitu*, which in Greek more or less translated to the marvelous cat.

They spent the rest of the day with the dead beast. First, Chaka cut off large slabs of meat for them to roast. Then he got to work on removing the pelt. Andronicus knew Chaka would want no help, so he focused on maintaining the fire and also keeping an eye out for any of the marvelous cat's friends. The cat tasted even better than the lions from the plains. Chaka made sure they both ate as much as they could, but they still had to leave a good bit behind.

Chaka took the magnificent pelt with them when they moved on. He had cut it perfectly, and Andronicus was sure they could sell it for a fortune if they ever made it out of the jungle. Until then it would serve as a fine blanket. Chaka also took all eight of the beast's claws. For weeks after that he carefully cut holes in them, and eventually strung them together into a fine necklace. Andronicus never would have guessed Chaka to be one for ornaments, but he had to admit the necklace gave him a powerful look. It made Andronicus wish he had taken the claws of the lioness that had cut his shoulder.

The cats weren't the only amazing beasts in the great jungle. Other than the snakes, cats, and other predators, there were hundreds of different kinds of monkeys. Andronicus found most of them annoying, but Chaka loved them all, and they all seemed to love him. Sometimes little monkeys would come down and ride on Chaka's shoulder as he walked, and he always loved it.

None of the monkeys ever threatened them, not even the big ones. And some of them were huge, much bigger than Chaka even. They were big and fat with dark black fur, except for their backs, which were greyish silver. Their massive arms looked like they could rip a man in half. They also had long, sharp white teeth. To Andronicus they looked like massive killing monsters, but to Chaka they were something else.

Chaka would walk up to them and put out his hand, and they would either turn away and run or approach him and touch his hand lightly, but they never harmed him. He did it again and again, and it always amazed Andronicus. It didn't make sense why some beasts seemed to leave some people alone. The lion in Swimha had attacked him, and yet the black cat in the jungle had helped him—if, indeed, it had been real. It was like some of the beasts could see into a person's soul.

3

One day, years after they had left the Perpauca behind, they came across the most amazing monkey Andronicus had ever seen. It was massive, the biggest one they had ever come across. It was fat and had bright orange fur. Its face was dark and round, like a giant circle, and it had long, powerful arms that it used to swing from the trees. It was perched not far from them, and, of course, Chaka approached it.

Andronicus couldn't help but approach the

beast as well; he had never seen anything like it. Chaka walked right up to it and held out his hand. Right away the giant orange beast held out its own hand and touched Chaka's. It made a heavy grunting sound, and Chaka laughed as if he could understand the thing.

"You are a special one," Chaka said to the beast as he stroked its orange fur. "Look at him, Jocus. Have you ever seen anything like it?"

"No, I have not," Andronicus said, in awe of the creature. The giant black monkeys looked fearsome, but even though this creature was much bigger, it wasn't imposing at all. Andronicus stared into the beast's big black eyes, and for a moment it was like he could see into the animal's soul. He knew the creature was looking back at him, having its own thoughts, and it was remarkable.

They spent the rest of that day sitting with the giant orange monkey and slept that night knowing it was still nearby. The next day it was gone.

Andronicus thought they would never see another beast like it, but a few weeks later they came across a small family of them. The females were much smaller and looked more like the other monkeys, only orange, but there was another giant male with a big round face.

A long time after that, they came across a large herd of elephants deep in the jungle. Chaka was beside himself with joy. Neither of them would have guessed they would ever find elephants so deep in the jungle, let alone more than twenty of them. They walked in a line, and the one in front would break trail for the others. The elephants looked almost identical to the elephants of the plains that the Swihmehe worshiped, certainly more than the jungle cats looked like lions.

The jungle elephants had darker skin than the elephants from the plains. Andronicus guessed that was because the plains elephants had much drier skin. The jungle elephants were huge, but none of them were as big as the mammoth elephant whose tusk they had once carried.

Once they found the elephants, Chaka insisted that they follow the herd. They both knew they were going well off track, but there were enough gaps in the trees this far north that they could see the stars well enough to regain their bearings, if needed. It was also nice to have a break from breaking trail all day.

After following the elephants for weeks, and praying more than Andronicus had ever seen him pray, Chaka finally said they could continue on their own. He also said he had been told by the elephant spirits that the end of the jungle was coming soon. Andronicus wanted to know more, like when it would come or how Chaka had heard these spirits, but all Chaka would say was that the spirits had told him the end would come soon enough.

4

Not all the beasts in the jungle were spectacular. They thought that they had seen the worst the jungle had to offer, until one day they came across the most gigantic snake either of them had ever seen. It was coiled into a massive pile that was as big as an elephant and as thick as a large tree trunk. When they stumbled upon it, the beast lifted its colossal head to stare at them. It flicked out its long pink tongue and let out a terrible hiss that kept Andronicus awake for many nights afterward.

They both ran, thinking they heard the snake moving behind them. They ran and ran and ran, all day, and when they finally stopped, they saw no sign of the snake. That night they decided to take turns sleeping, with one of them keeping an eye out for the monstrous beast. They didn't see it again that night or any other, but they both lived in fear of the beast long after.

Not all the deadly beasts in the jungle were huge, intimidating monsters. Some of the worst killers were as small as a pebble. There were more spiders than Andronicus could ever dream of keeping track of, but Glick had given him antidotes to the worst of them. Andronicus was sure that as they moved farther away from the Perpauca, there were likely more new spiders, but he felt confident that he had enough in his potion box to keep them both alive.

He only had to use the stuff once, when Chaka was bit by a small black spider with nasty red dots on its back. Andronicus had seen the spider before and had a powder that he gave to Chaka with some water. He was ill for three days, but he lived through it, which he thanked Andronicus for profusely. After that Chaka was much less wary of the box and its contents, and he even agreed to carry it in his bag from time to time.

When Andronicus was a boy, he had thought the tales about centaurs, and Minotaur, and other fantastical beasts were just silly stories that couldn't possibly be true. However, the more amazing and wondrous beasts they saw as they moved through the jungle, the more he wondered if those old legends really could be true. He half expected to come across one of the mythical creatures someday. He or Chaka would be cutting down vines, slowly making their way forward, and then all of a sudden they would see what looked like a horse, only it would have the torso of a man. Andronicus would ask the centaur how to escape the jungle, and of course the centaur would understand, as it would surely speak Greek. The legendary creature would tell Andronicus the way out, and he would lead them to freedom at last.

But no centaur ever appeared. There was nothing from Greece in the jungle, and nothing from the jungle in Greece. It seemed ridiculous to think that the two worlds were one and the same. Andronicus thought that by now they must have traveled farther than the whole known world, and yet they still hadn't found an end to the jungle. No matter how crazy or unlikely as it seemed, Andronicus still believed that one day he would find Greece again.

5

Slowly, over a number of weeks, the jungle began to grow less dense. There was more space between the plants and fewer animals than before. They still saw large monkeys from time to time, but they hadn't seen a cat in months. It was hard to tell because the jungle canopy was so high above them, but it looked like the trees were growing shorter as well. It also rained less.

When they had first entered the jungle, it rained once or twice a week. Once they got deeper into the jungle, it rained nearly every day. A few times while in the heart of the jungle, it had rained for weeks on end. Now as the jungle seemed to slowly lessen, so did the rain. Andronicus became increasingly certain they were getting close to the end of the Great Jungle, and it made him move faster.

He had no idea how long it had been since they entered the colossal green world, but he knew it had to be many years. He told Chaka that he thought they were getting close one day, and Chaka simply nodded in agreement. Andronicus felt like he would go mad if they didn't leave the jungle soon, but Chaka still seemed to enjoy the jungle life.

6

Even though Andronicus had noticed the jungle shrinking, and expected to find the end, when they finally reached it, it still came as a complete surprise. Andronicus and Chaka exited the jungle the same way they had entered it. One second they were stomping their way through the trees, stepping over the thick vines that covered the jungle floor and hacking at leaves and branches, and the next moment, Andronicus swung his sword and was immediately blinded by light.

Andronicus stumbled backward into Chaka, covering his eyes. When he finally opened them again, he saw Chaka kneeling in a massive field of grass, a plain.

Andronicus stumbled out of the trees and felt the cold air hit his lungs. He took in the thin air too fast, and began coughing profusely. Tears of joy ran down his filthy cheeks and into his bushy beard, and his coughing quickly turned to laughter. Andronicus made his way over to Chaka and fell to his knees beside him. Chaka's face was also wet from crying.

The two men embraced, crying like children,

and thanked the gods that they had finally made it. Andronicus realized in that moment that part of him had expected never to leave the jungle; it had been so long, so endless, so hopeless. But now they were looking out at a plain of grass and dirt that looked eerily similar to the one they had left when they entered the jungle.

Andronicus felt his stomach drop and his blood run cold. The possibility that they had made a massive ten-year circle suddenly occurred to him. This plain could very well be the same exact plain or a similar plain but on the wrong side of the jungle. He knew he had kept them moving north as best he could, but he might have failed. For all he knew north wasn't even north in the jungle.

He decided not to share that thought with Chaka. He felt confident they had come out on the other side, but the idea of the terrible circle remained with him.

The sun was slowly approaching the horizon, and Andronicus realized he had not seen a real sunset since the day they had sat on the edge of the cliff. They quickly made a fire, relishing how much easier it was in the dry dirt.

When they had a small fire going, they sat down to watch the sun, placing a large snake they had killed over the fire to roast. They jokingly made a pact that they would never eat another snake again after that. The sun moved faster as it dropped below the horizon. The sky was a beautiful mix of colors, blending so smoothly with each other that Andronicus couldn't tell where one ended and the next began.

As he watched the sun sink, he thought of Apollo. He always used to think about Apollo when he watched a sunset, though he hadn't thought of the god in many years. The only god he had thought about in the jungle was Hades, wondering if the jungle was his house or not. Watching the sun again and thinking of Apollo made him think of Greece.

If they had come out on the right side of the jungle, which Andronicus believed they had, Greece lay somewhere ahead, or so he hoped. Andronicus didn't know what lay between them and Greece, but after making it through the jungle alive, he knew they would surely be able to handle anything.

Long after the sun had dipped out of sight, the sky remained bright and colorful. Andronicus and Chaka sat silently under the array of colors. When the colors finally faded, they were replaced by stars. They hadn't seen the open night sky so clearly in years, and both men lay on their backs and stared up at the sky.

"You told me once that they have names," Chaka said, bringing Andronicus out of a trance he had been in as he stared up.

"Who?" Andronicus asked. "The stars?"

"Yes."

"They do," Andronicus said, nodding. "At least in Greece they do. I am sure they have other names in other lands. But I thought you were not interested in that sort of thing. I used to tell Manyara about the stars, but you thought it was foolish."

"That was long ago, Jocus," Chaka said, "and far away. Now I wish to know their names."

"Why?" Andronicus asked, genuinely curious.

"So I will know what to call them when we get to Greece," Chaka said with a smile.

Chapter 24
The Blood Moon
1

Andronicus and Chaka slept under a sea of stars, still in the shadow of the Great Jungle. They meant to leave the next day, but they wound up spending a week sleeping next to the jungle, entering it every day for food and water. For years they had feared it and hated it and wished to be rid of it, but now that it was behind them, neither of them could seem to let it go. The Great Jungle had become a part of them. It had taken a part of them as well.

When they finally did move on, they packed up their camp, said a solemn goodbye to their dreadful home, and began walking north again. It took three whole weeks before they could no longer see any jungle behind them. It felt odd being back on the plains, but it also felt good. They had gotten so used to the thick green trees and having to walk slowly and carefully that being able to walk freely through the open dirt felt amazing. They ran for the first time in years, sprinting as fast as they could, the wind in their faces. It felt more freeing than anything Andronicus had ever experienced in his life. As they traveled they saw most of the same animals they had seen in Swimha: zebras, giraffes, gazelles, even elephants.

For the first few weeks out of the jungle, the whole world seemed eerily quiet. There was an occasional bird call or an animal noise somewhere in the distance, but other than that the only noise was the wind. It was so quiet that Andronicus thought he could hear voices on the wind, whispering in languages he couldn't understand, but he just chalked it up to having lived in the loudest place imaginable for so long. He had grown used to falling asleep to the sound of hundreds of birds and monkeys, all competing to be the loudest. The newfound silence was nice during the day, but it kept him up at night. He found himself longing for the horrible squawking call of some bird to help him get to sleep.

Not long after they left the jungle, Andronicus had the old nightmare again. It had been years since he went back to that night in his sleep. It wasn't the same as before though. He was walking through a village in the dead of night with bodies spread out around him. When he looked up at the night sky, he saw the moon was a bloody red. As he stared at it, the moon split apart and became two big bloody red moons, like haunting eyes. Andronicus thought he heard a voice hiss something, and then he awoke with a start.

He sat up, dripping with cold sweat, and looked over at Chaka, who was snoring peacefully. Andronicus thought about the old dream and realized then that he hadn't had the nightmare in years. He couldn't even remember having it once in the jungle. Chills crept down his damp spine as he thought about the two red moons. It was strange how they had looked like eyes, but they had been moons, two of them, each a bloody red. Having the nightmare again troubled Andronicus greatly. He couldn't fall asleep again that night, and he lived in fear of the dream for weeks after.

2

They didn't come across any people after leaving the jungle for nearly three months. When they finally came across a village, it was similar to the ones they had encountered many times before. At first the people were alarmed at the sight of them, Andronicus a white man and Chaka standing over seven feet tall, but Andronicus made sure they showed no sign of a threat, and the villagers slowly lowered their guard.

The people there didn't speak any language Andronicus knew, but it sounded a lot easier to learn than the Perpauca tongue. Andronicus went through his old song and dance with his hands, trying to tell the people they meant no harm and that they were just passing through. It was a bit surreal to be talking to normal humans again after only seeing the little people and no one else during their long trek through the jungle.

Eventually, Andronicus managed to convince the leader of the village that they weren't a threat, and the villagers offered the wayward travelers food and a place to sleep that night. Andronicus and Chaka thanked them as best as they could without words. After dinner the leader showed them to a small hut on the far side of the village.

It was crowded with the two of them and their gear, but it was certainly better than many places they had slept over the years, like jungle trees and mossy jungle floors, and muddy pits under a tide of rain. Having a roof over their heads was all the comfort they needed. Andronicus fell asleep with the utmost ease and slept right through the night.

3

Andronicus awoke suddenly with a dull ringing in his head. As soon as he opened his eyes, the ringing became a clamor, and he quickly shut them again. He lifted a hand to his pounding head and felt the cool sticky texture of what could only be blood covering the side of his head and face. He opened his eyes again and looked down at his hand. It was more red than white.

He sat up slowly, holding onto his head, and looked around. He was no longer in the hut, but he thought he wasn't very far away. For a sickening moment, he felt a terrible sense of déjà vu as he awoke in a strange place with his head pounding. The memory of the day he had awoken in Swimha washed over him, making his hairs stand on end. For a moment he thought he would vomit, like he had on that day, and then it was gone.

Chaka was lying in the dirt a few feet away. Andronicus crawled over to him. Chaka also had a deep cut on his head, in almost the exact same place where the Kahli had hit him years earlier. Andronicus shook his shoulder gently, and Chaka rolled over, letting out a groan. He opened his eyes and then closed them again.

"What happened?" Chaka asked, coughing as he tried to sit up. He made it halfway and then let out a harsh cough, spraying blood across his chest, and fell back into the dirt.

"I do not know," Andronicus said in a raspy voice. "I think they hit us in the head while we were asleep." He looked around and didn't see anything. All of their possessions were gone; everything they had managed to keep all the way across the jungle had been robbed in the night.

Andronicus tried to think of everything they had lost. His sword and sheath, his Spartan cloak, all the things the Bahitu had sewn them, the blankets, the water bags, the blade he had made for Chaka, Chaka's spotted pelt, the box Glick had given him, and all the trinkets they had brought all the way from Swimha. It was too much. Andronicus knew there was no way he could just let them go. He had been willing to let the Kahli live, but he could not forgive this.

Andronicus slowly stood up and looked around. The village was nowhere in sight. He helped Chaka to his feet, and they started walking. Andronicus wasn't sure which way they had been taken from the village, so he chose south. They walked for over an hour until they found water. They drank their fill and washed the blood off themselves.

"What are we going to do when we find them?" Chaka asked as he splashed water over the back of his neck.

"I am going to ask nicely for our things," Andronicus said sarcastically. "What do you think we are going to do? We are going to kill them and then take back what is ours."

"How are we going to kill them without weapons?" Chaka asked. "They took our blades and our spears."

Andronicus took a moment to think. He had not really considered how he would attack them; he had never really been without his sword. There had been at least twenty men in the village, and without any weapons, Chaka was right; they wouldn't be able to fight them all. Andronicus sat in silence for a long while, thinking. Chaka eyed him curiously, waiting for an answer to his question.

"We could make weapons," Andronicus suggested.

"What kind of weapons could we make that would kill a whole village?" Chaka asked. "I know of only one weapon that can do that, and they stole it from you."

"I will think of something," Andronicus said, more to himself than to Chaka, already thinking about how he would go about it.

"There must have been twenty men in that village," Chaka pointed out. "Are you going to kill them all?"

"If I have to," Andronicus said.

"How?" Chaka asked, looking exhausted.

"The same way they took it from us," Andronicus said menacingly. "I will sneak up on them in the middle of the night."

"We could just leave," Chaka suggested. "We do not have to go after them."

"They took everything!" Andronicus shouted.

"We do not need any of it," Chaka said. "We are out of the jungle, so we do not need blades anymore. And we can make new water bags. We do not need to go after them, Jocus."

"You may not, but I do," Andronicus said stoically.

"You thought you had to kill the Kahli too," Chaka reminded him. "Why did you let them live?"

Andronicus let out a long sigh. He was still furious, but he knew Chaka was right. "Fine," he said. "If I do not have to kill them, I will not."

"Thank you," Chaka said, sounding relieved.

"But I am still going to get back what is mine," Andronicus said.

4

They decided to split up and search in different directions for the village. Andronicus had no luck, but when he returned to the place they had camped, he saw Chaka approaching with fruit in his hands.

"They left," Chaka said as he handed Andronicus a fruit.

"What do you mean?" Andronicus asked.

"I found their village," Chaka said, "but no one was there. They took everything with them."

"Are you sure?" Andronicus asked, worried for a second that Chaka might be lying to save him from killing them.

"I will take you there in the morning," Chaka said, biting into his fruit. "You can see for yourself."

5

When they arrived at the village around noon the next day, Andronicus saw that Chaka had been telling the truth. The village was deserted. After circling the village looking for tracks, he deduced they had headed west.

They set out after the villagers at a fast pace, hoping to catch them en route to wherever they were going. As they walked through the quiet plains, Andronicus thought he could hear voices on the wind, and he wondered if he was finally going mad.

Normally, there was just one voice in his head, his own, but now it was as if a group of people were having a chat just out of sight. If they weren't in an open plain, with nowhere to hide, Andronicus would have thought people were hiding nearby. At one point he asked Chaka if he could hear any voices. Chaka just shook his head, giving Andronicus a curious look.

When night fell, and there was still no sign of the thieving villagers, they stopped to rest. Without their belongings there was no camp to set up, so they simply picked a nice patch of ground, lay down, and went to sleep.

Andronicus had the same awful nightmare again, a sick combination of the night he massacred the Swihmacha and the massacre that hadn't happened yet, where he would kill the thieves, all under twin bloody red moons.

6

In the morning they had nothing to pack up, so they simply set out again. It was easy to follow the villagers' tracks. They had taken everything of value with them, so they were a slow-moving caravan, and it was only a matter of time before Chaka and Andronicus caught up with them.

Andronicus was filled with rage when they finally spotted the villagers in the distance. He had never been robbed before, and he meant to make them pay for it.

He and Chaka crept around to the group's left, keeping low to the ground. They stalked the caravan from afar until the villagers stopped for the night. A large group of men made a big fire while the rest of the villagers set up camp.

As the people settled for the night, and the light faded, the moon began to change. To Andronicus's utter horror, the big full moon slowly began to get darker, not the way it usually did, but an awful bloody red. It should have been totally foreign to Andronicus, but it wasn't. It was just like the red moons in his dream, and it made him feel cold and scared. He could feel the dark thoughts trying to come out, and he struggled to suppress them.

They waited until well after everyone had lain down for the night before making their move. The villagers had no huts or tents, merely sleeping under the stars with their possessions piled all around them. As Andronicus had hoped, there were only four men standing watch, one facing each direction. He noticed the one facing west seemed especially sleepy. His head kept bobbing, and he continually rubbed his eyes.

Andronicus let Chaka take the sleepy one, and he took the one facing south. That guard looked like one of the bigger men among the tribe. He was tall with wide shoulders and strong arms. He had a long spear resting next to him as he sat and stared up at the strange red moon. Andronicus noticed the moon was even darker than before, and far too close to the color it had been in his nightmare. The hairs on his neck stood on end, but he tried to ignore it.

Andronicus could tell he would not be able to sneak up on the man, as Chaka would likely be able to with his. He crouched behind a bush about twenty feet away from the man. He had spent countless nights listening to the birds sing in the jungle and had gotten quite good at mimicking their calls. He let out a call he had often heard in the jungle, though one probably not often heard in these parts.

Andronicus peered around the bush at the guard. He was on his feet, searching the darkness for the source of the noise. Andronicus made the call again, softer but more clearly. When the man started toward him, Andronicus picked up a good-sized rock in his right hand.

He could hear the man approaching slowly, and stayed down. When the man was nearly upon him, Andronicus leapt out. The guard looked utterly stunned to see Andronicus pop out from behind the bush. He had clearly believed the noise to be a bird of some kind, and was now stunned silent to see a white man holding a rock over his head.

Realization donned in the man's eyes, and he opened his mouth to call for help. Before the man could make a sound, Andronicus smashed the rock into the side of his head. The man fell to the ground, blood already gushing from the wound. He looked up at Andronicus in surprise and tried to call out, but Andronicus brought the rock down again, feeling the sickening crunch of the man's skull as the rock broke through it.

Andronicus pulled the rock from the dead man's skull, wincing at the squelching noise it made. The rock was dripping thick red droplets of blood into the dirt, and Andronicus let it fall from his hand.

The dead man collapsed into the dirt, making a dull thud. A voice called out from the other side of the camp, and Andronicus knelt down quickly.

He had a moment to run over to the camp before the other guard came around the corner. The second guard noticed his friend lying on the ground, and started walking towards him. Andronicus didn't give him time to find out if his friend was alright. He rushed over, crept up behind the man, then snapped his neck in a single fluid motion, just as Archelaus had taught him a lifetime ago. He caught the dead man as he fell, and lowered him silently to the dirt.

Andronicus looked around to see if anyone else had heard and saw nothing but the terrible blood-red moon staring down at him.

He crept into the camp, staying low. As he passed the sleeping people, he heard voices speaking in the distance. There was no mistaking it now; there were voices somewhere nearby. Andronicus didn't know how the people weren't being woken by it. It sounded like an entire crowd.

From what he could tell, everyone else was still asleep. Men, women, and children were scattered about, many snoring loudly. Andronicus's eyes had gotten very good at seeing in the dark while they were in the jungle, and now he tried to locate their belongings without having to actually search through everything. Everywhere he looked he saw bundles of goods, baskets of food, blankets, and cloths piled amidst the sleeping people. He tried to concentrate, but the strange whispering made it difficult.

He heard a noise on the other side of the

camp, and then he saw Chaka slinking out of the darkness. He was holding a spear, and the tip of it was dark black in the reddish moonlight. They nodded silently to each other amidst the sleeping villagers.

Andronicus motioned for Chaka to look through the people's things on his side of the camp. Then he went from one pile to the next, hoping to find their belongings. Most of the piles contained the same sort of junk: hairbrushes, makeshift knives, and other useless trinkets. One of the piles had a knife that didn't look half bad, and Andronicus took it.

After searching through seven bags, Andronicus began to worry they wouldn't find their things before someone woke up. Then, as he was searching through his eighth pile, he noticed the man who had welcomed them lying on the ground. Andronicus crept past several other sleeping bodies to get to him. Next to the man was a large blanket, covering his pile of goods. Andronicus lifted the blanket, and there it all was: his old bag, the water bags, his red cloak, Chaka's spotted pelt, and lying beside the man, Andronicus's sword.

Andronicus picked up his sword and stood over the sleeping thief, looking down at him. The voices had become a clamor now. He couldn't tell what most of them were saying, but he thought he heard one voice telling him to kill them, in Greek. He tried to ignore the voices and focus on the people around him instead.

Standing over the sleeping thieves with his sword clutched in his fist, the memory of what he had done in Swimha came rushing back. The cold dark memory of a field of dead bodies flashed before his eyes. When he opened them, he saw a field of bodies around him now. They weren't dead, but he knew he could make them dead. Andronicus clenched his teeth and his fists, glaring down at the thieves with pure hatred. He wanted to kill them, but he didn't like the way it made him feel.

When he had first killed a man in battle, when he was young, he had told himself he hated it. When he saw the faces of the Persian slaves as he ended their lives, he had felt nothing but guilt and remorse.

But when he had fought the Persian elites, he had enjoyed killing them. He had told himself at the time that he was just doing his duty, that he didn't like it any more than Euthymius did, but he knew that wasn't true.

Andronicus was no longer a boy, he was an old man, and he could no longer deny the way killing made him feel. He didn't enjoy killing just for sport, but killing a man who had wronged him, killed his people, or robbed him in the night, that was different.

He stared down at the sleeping face of the man who had treated them kindly, welcomed them into his home, and then beat them and robbed them in the night. He felt the strongest urge to just reach out and end the man. He knew he could do it without waking anyone else. Now he was quite sure the voices were urging him to do it.

Andronicus tore his eyes away from the sleeping thief and looked up at the moon. All the hairs on his body stood on end at once, and he felt his heart lurch. The moon was no longer shaded red, it was entirely red. The moon looked like it had been dipped in blood, and Andronicus knew right away that it was an evil thing.

He looked back down at the thief and felt things starting to slip away. For a moment he felt like he was watching himself. He lifted his arm, his sword in hand. He felt pure, total, inexplicable rage like he had never felt before. It felt foreign, like it wasn't his own, and yet it was enveloping him. Just as he was about to drive his sword down, he heard a cracking noise as a twig snapped behind him.

Snapping out of his trance, Andronicus turned and saw Chaka glaring down at the man as well.

"We should go," Chaka whispered as softly as the wind, but somehow louder than the whispering voices. Andronicus shook his head as he glared down at the thief. His thoughts had become a cloudy blur of rage and anger. Thieving was something he had despised since he was a boy. He had despised it in Sparta, he had despised it in Swimha, and he despised it still. Staring down at the thief who had hit him in the night and robbed him blind, the old fire burned hotter than ever. He blocked out the whispers as he felt the rage boiling over.

"Do not do this, Jocus," Chaka said, his hand resting on Andronicus's shoulder. "You have told me many times how much you regret killing the Swihmacha, and they murdered your wife. How do you think you will feel if you kill all of these people merely for stealing your sword?"

Andronicus glared at Chaka, feeling the same kind of rage he had felt as a young man, the same kind of rage he had felt the night he had murdered all those people, and so much more. Andronicus looked back down at the sleeping man, his bare chest exposed and ready to accept Andronicus's blade. He gripped the hilt of his sword so tight it began to shake.

"I will not help you kill these people," Chaka whispered, pulling his hand away. "We have what is ours. I am leaving."

Andronicus watched him go. Then he looked down at the man again, the rage still burning within. He looked back up at the moon. It was still the awful bloody red. Andronicus stared up at it, trying to understand what it meant.

He felt like it was all connected: the strange voices, the awful nightmares, the thieves, and now this blood moon. Andronicus wondered if the moon had turned red just for him, as a sign of some kind. He couldn't tell if he was supposed to kill the villagers or not. The voices certainly seemed to want him to do it, and he had done it in his dreams, but that didn't mean he had to make it real. He looked back and forth between the sleeping thief and the moon for several minutes.

Finally, after a long and terrible inner debate, Andronicus turned and walked away, leaving the thieves where he found them, unharmed—apart from the guards.

He found Chaka waiting for him just outside the camp. Chaka looked immensely pleased and relieved that Andronicus had not slaughtered the thieves. He gave Andronicus a curt nod, indicating his gratitude. Andronicus knew that if not for Chaka, he would have done something terrible again. He didn't think about it nearly enough, but it was just one of a thousand times Chaka had saved him over their many years together.

With their belongings in hand, they started walking north again, wanting to get far away from the thieves before they woke up. The voices had gone away as if they hadn't ever been there in the first place. After a few hours of walking, Andronicus wondered if they ever really had been there. The moon only stayed red for an hour or so longer and then slowly reverted to its regular color. After a few hours, it was still a shade of red, but nothing like it had been before.

As they walked, Andronicus tried to understand the rage that had filled him. He was no longer a young man, no matter what he looked like, and he wanted to know just why he felt the way he did. It was not just anger; it was a dark sort of fury. He knew it wasn't just about the strange moon, as much as he wanted it to be. It was something within him; it always had been. He remembered that Lycus used to experience the same thing during battles, which made him wonder where Lycus was now and if he still felt the rage as well. For a moment he felt the strangest feeling that Lycus was somewhere close by, but he knew that was impossible.

Chapter 25
Diamonds
1

Armed, clothed, and in full possession of all their worldly belongings once again, Andronicus and Chaka returned to their seemingly never-ending journey north. Andronicus didn't know where they were headed, but after the jungle, he believed they could handle anything. There was no telling how long they had been traveling together. To Andronicus it felt like it had to be at least fifty years, though he knew it was probably far less. He still looked the same as he always had. His hair and beard had become truly wild, but underneath it he was still the same.

He wished he knew how long it had been, and how old he now was. No answer would really surprise him. He could be ten years older, or twenty, or fifty. He could even be dead. He didn't like to think about it much, and he certainly thought of it a lot less than he used to, but he knew he could be dead. Even if he was dead, he thought it would be alright. Whatever this world was, there were people and animals and beauty, and most importantly, he had Chaka.

Andronicus tried to think of how he might tell the people back home what had happened to him, if he ever got home. He couldn't think of a single scenario where everyone wouldn't think he was crazy. Although he didn't like to think about it, he knew that most of the people he knew back in Sparta were most likely dead by now. Archelaus could still be alive, but he would never believe Andronicus's story. The only person in Sparta who might actually listen to him was his mother, if she was still alive.

Andronicus felt guilt and shame wash over him as he realized he hadn't thought of his mother in far too long. From the moment it had all happened, for years now, Andronicus had thought of the others. He wondered where he was, and where they were, but he always knew where his mother was. She was right where he had left her. His goal had always been to get back to Greece, to get back to them, but in his heart he knew it was to get back to her.

He still felt guilty about Gaia, but when he thought of his mother, he felt only shame. Not only had he left and never come home, he had taken his brother as well. Athenia had lost her husband in battle, and then her sons had gone away and never returned. Andronicus knew she might be dead by now, and he felt anger and shame at the thought. If it were true, then all he could hope was that Androcles had made it home and that she had gotten to see at least one of her boys before she died.

Andronicus still believed he would make it back to Greece one day, and he prayed it would be before everyone was gone. If anyone was still alive when he arrived, he would have to explain why he was still so young, and that was where things would get tricky.

Whenever he got the chance, Andronicus would look at his reflection. It was the same every time. His hair still grew, albeit far slower than it once had, but his face remained the same. It had a hardness that hadn't been there before, a dark, cold look in his green eyes, but his face itself was the same as it had been since the day he awoke in Swimha.

The scars of his past were still visible on his skin. He ran his fingers over them often to make sure they were still there. The four white lines still stood out on his shoulder from where the lioness had clawed at him. The mark where he had been stabbed in the arm during his massacre of the Swihmacha people was also a constant reminder of what he had done. More than a dozen small cuts he had gotten in the jungle still showed. The scar he looked at most often, however, was the small white dot on his left side. It was his first scar, the one he had gotten in the battle of Plataea, when Niko had pulled the arrow out of his side. It was the only real scar that he had gotten in his previous life. That was how he had come to think of his life in Sparta, as a previous life.

Whether the life he had been living since then was real, he still didn't truly know. There were many signs that it was indeed the same world he had come from. The sky, the sun, the moon, some of the trees and birds; much of the world was as it was in Greece. The old stars had even returned. When he first noticed it in the jungle, he had been hopeful but still unsure. Now there could be no mistake; the stars from Greece were back. Some of the nameless constellations from Swimha were still there, and some were gone, but now he could see the old Andromeda and the mighty Aries he had known as a boy.

It made it seem possible that they actually would make it back to Greece. Everything about the world around him seemed as real as it ever had. The grass, the dirt, the birds, the trees, all of it was as it should be. He was the only oddity. The world had gone on normally, and he was the one who had stopped.

The strangest part was that Chaka had stopped getting older as well. Andronicus knew he had stopped, because he had been aging when they were back in Swimha. It was somewhere along the way that he had stopped.

The sun rose and fell, and rose and fell. It moved south as the days grew shorter and then north as the days grew longer again. It had become the only way for Andronicus to mark the passing of time. Sometimes he would wonder if time had ceased to exist and if he would simply go on living forever, walking strange new lands for eternity, with Chaka at his side.

But then he would look at his scars. They were his windows to the past. He remembered how he got every one of them, and to him they were proof that the past had happened. Every time he received a new scar, he would smile to himself, knowing in his heart that he was still alive.

If the past is real, and the present is real, then the future will surely come. If time was indeed real and still moving forward as it should, then it must be Andronicus who had ceased to move forward. It was as if his own time had stopped, but the world all around him kept moving. And somehow Chaka had stopped as well.

Andronicus had no real sense of how it all worked, but he knew it was because of the glowing rocks. Now more than ever as he and Chaka walked through plains and into drier lands, he thought about what those rocks could have been. When they had set out from Swimha, many years ago, Andronicus's intention had been to find Greece and his home. Now he simply wanted answers.

Before, his questions had been wild and confusing, and yet they had been much simpler; questions like, where am I? How did I get here? Am I still alive? Where are my friends? Are they still alive? Am I still in the same world? What were the rocks?

Now his questions were far more profound, and far more alarming. Now he had questions like, why do I still look young after all these years? Why does

Chaka still look young? Are the others still alive? Are they still young as well? What happened in that cave? What were those glowing rocks? What did they do to me? And what was it they showed me in the water?

As time kept moving forward, and Andronicus stayed the same, the questions just grew louder. Before it had been a deep curiosity, but Andronicus began to become obsessed, the way he had once obsessed over questions about his father. He had gotten his answers to those questions, and he would get his answers to these questions as well.

He tried to talk to Chaka about it from time to time, but Chaka didn't like talking about it. He clearly knew they were both much older than they looked, but he never seemed to want to discuss how or why. Andronicus guessed Chaka was scared of such thoughts, so Andronicus left him alone for the most part.

Over time Andronicus' mind became consumed with the questions. They rolled around in his head from the moment he woke to the moment he slid into haunted dreams full of things he couldn't understand. Sometimes he dreamed about the jungle and sometimes about Swimha. His favorite dreams were about Manyara. Most often though he dreamed of things he didn't understand at all, things he had seen in visions long ago but could never quite remember when he woke.

Sometimes he would dream about cities he had never seen, about massive armies clad in gold and silver, men wearing armor like he had never seen before, and buildings that looked like they were made from steel. The dream that came the most was the one where he was in a great desert of nothing but sand as far as the eye could see. He would dream that he and Chaka were walking through the desert under the stars. Somehow he knew in his heart that he and Chaka would have to cross it before they could reach Greece.

Whenever Andronicus would awake from a dream in which he saw something truly strange, he would try to remember it, but he rarely could. He was becoming more convinced every day that his dreams were showing him the future. He grew more sure every time that the dreams were memories from the glowing water, some of the many things he had seen but couldn't remember.

2

Time moved on, seasons passed. Andronicus and Chaka walked ever onward, slowly making their way north but also moving west now. Andronicus believed the land getting drier meant they were headed toward Persia, and he began guiding them northwest, in hopes of finding the old empire.

Andronicus spent his days deep in thought. Chaka had always been content in silence, and he seemed none too perturbed by Andronicus's newfound quiet. When they did talk it was usually Andronicus telling Chaka stories about Greece. He told Chaka all about his time in the war when he was young, and about the terrible journey that had ended in the heart of a mountain. Before, Chaka had never seemed interested in Greece, but the farther they walked, the likelier it felt that they would actually find it someday. And while Chaka didn't seem to care to discuss the matter of their outward appearance, and their seeming lack of aging, he did seem to be acting now as if he believed he would someday come to Greece with Andronicus.

Chaka had learned several languages since leaving the Swimha, most of them similar to Swihmehe, and he asked Andronicus to teach him Greek. The first thing Andronicus tried to teach Chaka was his real name. Since the day they met, Chaka had always known and referred to him as Jocus.

Even though Chaka was eventually able to pronounce it, he absolutely refused to call him anything but Jocus. It was extremely slow going teaching Chaka Greek, and they usually spent most of their days in long silences, but Chaka gradually began to learn more of Andronicus's mother tongue.

3

After having been robbed in the night, they tried to stay away from villages. There was nothing they really needed from them anymore. When they came across other people, Andronicus would try to barter with them if he could, but they no longer stayed in any villages. They had learned that lesson the hard way.

The land slowly changed as they moved north and west. The hills and valleys gradually flattened out into plains again. The animals were still much the same, but there were new buffalo that Andronicus had never seen before, and as always, there were new birds to be found. It always amazed Andronicus how many kinds of birds existed.

One day they came across the body of a dead elephant. It had no wounds that they could see, and certainly no lions eating it. From what Andronicus could tell, the beast had simply died, and the scavengers had not found it yet. It was nowhere near the size of the mighty elephant they had seen long ago, but it was big, and its tusks were long and sturdy. This time Chaka had no objections as Andronicus hacked off both tusks.

They were big and heavy. Andronicus fastened ropes around them, so they could each carry one on their back. Chaka built a pyre and burned the elephant's body before the scavengers could get to it. The tusks were heavier than Andronicus had expected, each probably around sixty pounds. Chaka wrapped his tusk in his jaguar pelt, and Andronicus wrapped his in his cloak, making them easier to carry on their backs, but they were still hard to walk with. It slowed them down far more than he had anticipated, but they kept them anyway, knowing they would find a use for them eventually.

4

Soon after taking the tusks from the dead elephant, they found the perfect place to dispense with them: a village unlike any other they had come across before.

Andronicus and Chaka were trudging along

with the big tusks strapped to their backs when a group of men appeared on the horizon. The men were coming from the west, walking straight toward them.

Andronicus expected to see the same kind of people he had seen everywhere else since leaving the jungle. These men looked similar to everyone else, a few of them holding spears, but there was one major difference: all six of them were decorated with huge shining diamonds. Some of them had large sparkling diamonds inside their ears and lips, others had them adorned on their heads, and all of them had them strung around their necks with string.

Andronicus had not seen a diamond since he had been in Sparta, and even then only in the high temple, and he had never seen a diamond as big as some of the ones he saw now. To see such large diamonds hanging on an ugly string around these men's necks looked absurd. Andronicus realized they had hit the jackpot. All six men were staring at the ivory tusks with wide eyes, and Andronicus knew they would be able to work out a nice trade.

The men took them back to their village and brought them before the village elders. The three elders were covered in diamonds from head to foot. Andronicus had to wonder how in the world these people had come across so many perfect diamonds. The elders spoke in a language he didn't understand, but this was not his first time experiencing that. Andronicus used his hands to tell the elders where they were going. It took a long time, but he was able to convince them to take the ivory and give them some diamonds in return.

The elders offered to let them stay in the village, but Andronicus and Chaka were both hesitant. Their last such encounter still made them wary. These people seemed nice enough though, so Andronicus convinced a reluctant Chaka to spend the night. They took turns sleeping and standing guard throughout the night.

In the morning, the villagers offered them breakfast. They stayed there all day, and the villagers seemed more than happy to have them. Andronicus had no intention of staying for a long time, but it was nice to spend time with people for a while.

5

Andronicus and Chaka wound up staying with the diamond-clad villagers for several months. It was the first village they had slept in since being robbed of their goods, and they were both comfortable there. The villagers were simple people. It didn't take Andronicus long to find out where all the diamonds came from either. They picked them out of the river, right out of the mud. They came out looking murky and ugly, but after being cleaned and polished, they were beautiful shining stones.

Their language was complicated, and Andronicus didn't try very hard to learn all of it, just what he needed to get by. One thing he was able to understand, one very important thing, was that he was not the first white man these people had ever seen. Ever since he had touched the rocks and woken up in Swimha, everyone he had come across had dark skin and looked at him like an alien. These were the first people he had met since then who had seen a white man before, and he took it as a sign that they were indeed headed in the right direction.

Andronicus and Chaka would join the village hunters whenever they went out. They were glad to be part of a hunt again, and wound up teaching the hunters quite a lot. Once they taught them how to hunt the bigger game, the villagers began having feasts almost every night. The hunters and the village elders alike thanked Andronicus and Chaka profusely and presented them with two bags of diamonds, each bag bigger than an apple.

After several months of resting, hunting, and graciously accepting the thanks of the people of the village, Andronicus was eager to get back on the road. Chaka seemed more content to stay, certainly more than he had been in the jungle with the little people, but he didn't argue when Andronicus said it was time to leave. They packed up their things and then said their goodbyes.

6

The first night after they had left the village, Andronicus carefully dumped out all of the diamonds they had been given, counting and inspecting each stone in the light of the fire. There were 146 small diamonds, 68 medium-sized ones, and 6 big ones.

Andronicus knew that the six large diamonds alone were enough to buy an army. With the others included, he thought they would have enough to buy a small city if they wanted. The thought of him reigning over a small Greek city made him laugh. Chaka thought the diamonds were beautiful, but he didn't believe they could be worth so much. He thought it was an outrage that Andronicus had traded fine ivory for such tiny stones, no matter how sparkly they were. Andronicus tried to explain the worth of diamonds to Chaka, but he still didn't believe it. He told Andronicus that he had grown too fascinated by shiny rocks and forgotten that they are just rocks, they don't all make you live forever.

7

They headed north again after the village of diamonds. Andronicus knew that the sea lay not too far to the west; that much he had been able to get out of the village elders. He knew what lay south, the Great Jungle, and below that more plains, Swimha, and the sea again. North and east were the only options. They had been moving north for so long now that it seemed foolish to turn east, even though he had the strangest feeling that was where they were meant to go.

After trading for the diamonds, they didn't stop to meet with many people. They were able to feed themselves more than well enough, both being expert hunters and gatherers. They didn't have a strong desire for shelter, enjoying the feeling of sleeping in a field under the stars after so much time in the dank, dark jungle.

The only reason to stop and meet with people was to see if they were speaking the same language as the last people they had met and to inquire what lay north. The people in the lands they were passing through spoke languages that Andronicus couldn't understand. They changed from one village to the next far more than the languages south of the jungle had, which made him wonder how close they were getting to the world he had left behind.

Chapter 26
Getting Close
1

Time moved ever onward as they continued travelling north. How much time, Andronicus was never really sure. He and Chaka both looked the same as they had for as long as he could remember. Their hair and beards gradually began to grow out again, though not nearly as matted as it had been in the jungle. Andronicus watched the sun make its long rotations across the sky at least twelve times after they left the jungle. He didn't know if that meant it had been twelve years, or six, or twenty-four for all he knew. He often wished he had paid more attention to Philander's lessons when he was a child.

Andronicus was beginning to wonder how far the plains stretched when things finally began to change. The plains grew dryer and the animals scarcer. They no longer saw herds of striped horses and prancing deer or the great long-necked horses of the south. Eventually, there weren't any elephants anymore either. The buffalo remained, and there were far more scavenger dogs around. Andronicus took it as an encouraging sign. The land was beginning to look much more like Persia.

As the landscape changed, so did the people. Small villages made of mud huts became small towns made of clay and then finally small cities made of stone. After so many years walking through the plains finding many villages that all looked the same, it was bizarre to see square structures again. Chaka was amazed. Andronicus had told him about such places, but this was his first time seeing them. They were still wary of trusting others, but they couldn't resist sleeping in one of the stone buildings for a night.

After leaving the first town with stone houses, Andronicus half expected it was a fluke, but sure enough, two weeks later they found another village, also made of stone buildings. They began stopping at more villages than they had in years, trying to learn the new languages as best they could. They never stayed in any one place for very long, but they moved slowly enough that Andronicus gained a basic understanding of whatever language the people were speaking.

The people's skin had begun to change as well. Ever since Andronicus had awoken in Swimha the only people he had encountered had dark black skin, or darker black skin. Now, after so many years, he finally saw people with brown skin again. They looked more and more like Persians, and Andronicus became more convinced that soon they would find Persia somewhere to the north.

As Andronicus gradually learned the language, and came across steadily bigger towns, he finally gained his first real pieces of information. After so many years of searching blindly, without knowing where he was going or what he was looking for, he finally had some answers.

First, he found out where they were.

He had been right all along. He wasn't dead or in another world. He had always believed that one day he would find the land he had left behind, and it seemed he finally had. He found out that Persia was not to the north but far to the east. North of them was the sea, but to the east was the westernmost part of a nation called Carthage. As soon as Andronicus heard the name, he knew he had heard it before, and felt exhilarated. He racked his brain, trying to remember lessons he had barely listened to a lifetime ago.

From what he could recall, Carthage had been a budding nation across the Mediterranean, to the west of Egypt. This meant that Andronicus finally had some answers, at least a few. If Carthage lay to the east, and Egypt lay beyond that, then Greece *was* to the north. He wasn't crazy, and he wasn't dead. He had trusted blindly that he would find his way home, and after so many hopeless years, it finally seemed possible.

If he could reach Egypt, he knew exactly how to get back to Greece, and he could do so in short order. Considering everything they had been through, the journey from Egypt to Greece would be easy.

The idea that they had set out from Swimha to find Greece so many years ago, and now they might actually get there, was dizzying. Even though Andronicus had always trusted, he still could not believe that he might have actually found his way back. He couldn't wait for Chaka to see his home and perhaps even meet Andronicus's old friends. It no longer seemed likely that he would find his mother or Archelaus waiting for him. He had been hopeful that they might still be alive, but that was before he received his second big answer.

The towns west of Carthage were still primitive compared to Greece, but they were far more advanced than the villages of the plains had been. Not long after he learned where they were, Andronicus learned when they were. It took a while to verify, as these people weren't using the same calendar as the Greeks. After a long conversation with a well-educated elderly man who had been to Egypt, Andronicus was able to learn what year it was back in Sparta.

He had left Sparta in 465 BC. If the man he spoke to was to be believed, it was now 406 BC. It had been sixty years. At first Andronicus refused to believe it. He knew they had been traveling for a long time, but it couldn't have been sixty years. He interrogated the poor man until he was clearly scared out of his wits, but eventually Andronicus had to accept it. It didn't seem possible, which of course it wasn't. If it was indeed true, that meant he was ninety years old.

As he left the old man's hut, he felt like he might pass out. He had thought thirty, maybe forty at the most, but sixty years. He was older than almost every person he had ever met. He tried to think how it could be possible. He knew he had spent at least twenty years in Swimha, perhaps more. They had walked for years before reaching the land of the Kahli and more years after the jungle. It still didn't seem possible. When Andronicus began to realize how long they might have actually been in the jungle, he shuddered at the thought.

He looked down at himself and flexed his muscles, feeling the youthful strength in them, and shook his head in disbelief. He had his first answers, but they only made his other questions all the more serious.

Now that he knew where he was, he could work out in his mind where Swimha might fall on a map. He laughed at the mental image. Swimha was so far south that it would cover a dozen maps to show the way to Greece. Swimha was indeed in the same world, only farther than Andronicus could have ever believed possible. He had been moved in a second, across the entire world. He felt chills move down his back as he thought about what that actually meant.

Knowing the year made the other questions more important as well. When he had thought he was fifty, it had seemed interesting that he still looked so young. Now that he had confirmed that he was actually ninety-two years old, it was more than just interesting. The gravity of what had happened in that cave sixty years ago came crashing down on Andronicus. Whatever those stones were had been more profound than he had ever imagined.

It made him wonder if he even should return to Greece. There could no longer be any question that his mother was dead. He felt ashamed knowing she had died alone, without any of her family present. Everyone he knew would be dead. He supposed it was possible Gaia could still be alive. He thought about going to his old home and finding his young wife, now turned old and grey. He wondered what he could possibly say to her, but there wasn't any scenario in his head that didn't end with her thinking he was cursed somehow or that she was crazy and seeing an illusion.

He supposed the only people who might actually be around were Niko's boys, although there was almost no chance they would remember their father's old friend from when they were small children. Realizing no one would be waiting for him back home, he began to wonder if there wasn't a better use of his endless time. Egypt was said to be the oldest nation in the world, and Andronicus had heard tales as a boy of their magnificent library.

But he immediately felt himself torn. The idea of going to Egypt in search of answers made sense, but he couldn't deny his longing for Greece. He didn't know what would happen when he got there, but he and Chaka had been searching for it for so long that he couldn't stop until he got there. He wondered what kind of life Chaka could find in Sparta, and guessed they would find out soon enough.

2

They kept walking north until they reached the sea. It was a welcome sight after so many years, and they spent a week camping by the water, just like they had back in Swimha.

There was no way to cross the sea though, which would have shortened their journey. The villages they encountered were inhabited by farmers and herders, not seafaring people, and they had no boat that Andronicus would trust with such a voyage. Sailing to Greece from there would take weeks, and require a large, sturdy ship with a competent crew, and none of these could be found.

After resting by the sea, they headed east for Carthage. Andronicus knew there would be ships big enough to travel to Greece there, and they had more than enough diamonds to book passage. They kept close to the water as they walked, eating fish almost every day, just like they had long ago.

As they moved closer to real civilization, Andronicus's vision-like dreams became more frequent again. Occasionally, he would dream of the sky-high mountain, covered in snow and clouds. Sometimes he dreamed about massive armies at war. Once or twice he even dreamed about being amongst the stars with no sun or moon and no land or sea, just countless stars and the endless black night all around him. Most often though he would dream about the desert or the storm.

In the desert dreams it was always night, the land lit by thousands of stars. He would see two figures trudging through the endless sand, and he knew it was him and Chaka. It was a peaceful dream, but a frightening one nonetheless. Andronicus had been taught as a boy how foolish it was to try and cross a desert, but he believed it was going to happen. He had dreamed of the jungle long before he ever saw it, and it had been plenty real. Andronicus still remembered the intense feeling of certainty he had experienced when he took the Perpauca's drug in the jungle. He had been certain that the dreams were not just dreams, but visions of the future, meaning he would walk through that desert someday.

The certainty that what he dreamed would be real only made the dreams about the storm all the more terrifying. In those dreams he could never tell if it was night or day, but it didn't matter, they were the same thing when the clouds are that dark, and the rain is falling that heavily. There was always a flash of lightning in the dream, which would light up the world for a split second. In that flash Andronicus could see the sea. The waves were as big as mountains, rolling onward one after the other without end. The boat he was on would crest the top of a gigantic wave and then plummet down the other side. The boat would crash into the water and splinter apart, and Andronicus would feel himself launched into the water. Then he would snap awake, panting and covered in cold sweat.

Andronicus believed they were both visions, and he dreamed of them both more often, until every night he dreamed of one or the other. He became certain over time that he would have to make a choice. Soon he would have to decide whether they were going to test the sea and pray that the storm wouldn't come or take their chances with the desert. Andronicus didn't know which one was more foolish, or frightening. He told Chaka about both dreams in great detail, and asked him which way he thought they should go, but Chaka would just shake his head in response.

"It is your choice, Jocus," he would say. "They are your dreams, and it is your home. I follow you."

Sometimes Andronicus wondered what Chaka really thought of him. He knew they were the best friends either of them had ever had, but Chaka seemed to treat him like he was some kind of legend, not in the way the Greek people spoke of Zeus and Poseidon but in the way they spoke of Jason and Heracles. It was like Chaka had decided Andronicus was more than human, and that's why he still followed him. Andronicus had to wonder if Chaka was following him, or the light. He knew that whatever that light had been, part of it was in him now, and keeping him young. Whatever it was, however it worked, it was clearly keeping Chaka young as well, and Andronicus wondered what would happen to Chaka if they were ever separated, and if Chaka ever thought about that.

3

As it turned out, Carthage was much farther than Andronicus thought it would be. It took them longer than he ever would have guessed to finally reach the western most edge of the Carthaginian's Empire. As they continued east, passing many villages and towns, it seemed that most of the people spoke the same language, which made it easier for Andronicus to learn. Even Chaka was able to learn enough to speak with people without Andronicus's help. The more Andronicus was able to speak with the people outside Carthage, the more he realized Carthage would be a dangerous place for him to go.

Evidently, during his time away from Greece, his countrymen had not been idle. The Greek cities were still at war with each other, but they were also at war with both Carthage, and a growing nation called Macedonia, to the north of Greece. The Carthaginians hated the Greeks. Andronicus was glad his skin had grown so dark during his travels. His complexion had grown very dark in Swimha, and then in the jungle he had become pale, but years back in the plains had turned his skin back to dark, not as dark as the Carthaginians, but darker than most Greeks.

There were many black people in most of the towns they passed through, so no one ever gave Chaka a second look, except to gape at how tall he was. Andronicus, on the other hand, had to come up with an elaborate backstory of how he had defected from the Sicilian army after their wars with Athens and fled to Carthage to aid in the fight against Greece. It wasn't hard for him to feign hatred for the Athenians, for he had once hated them. It was funny how quickly his old Spartan loyalties returned, even after so many decades away from it all.

The story worked for most people they encountered, but not everyone. Andronicus got into more fights than he had since his drunken days with Lycus in his youth. For the first time since he had left Swimha, Andronicus's skin color became a danger to himself and Chaka. As they got closer to Carthage, it became clear that they would almost surely not be able to book passage across the sea. Even if they could, Andronicus would not have done it. He was too afraid of the storm from his dreams.

When he heard about what was beyond Carthage, between them and Egypt, Andronicus knew it was the way. It was said that there was a massive desert, The Great Desert, the people called it. The stories of the desert were all bleak and depressing. Everyone told them that no one had ever crossed the desert and lived. Andronicus had seen the desert a thousand times in his dreams. He knew it would be the desert from his dreams, how could it not be? It became clearer to him by the day that the desert was the way to go, no matter how absurd it seemed. They had crossed the Great Jungle, and it only seemed fitting that they should cross the Great Desert as well.

Carthage itself seemed an unnecessary risk, so he simply steered them around it to the south and then back east. Close to the sea were small villages and some larger towns, so they strayed even farther inland.

They realized quickly that the dry lands were

not like the plains at all. The plains had always been hot and dry, but there had always been water. As they moved into drier lands, Andronicus and Chaka had to learn to conserve their water for weeks at a time.

They had always been able to manage with only two water bags each, but now they needed more. They had both learned to sew quite well during their time with Nnamdi and the Bahitu, so they set out to find a good animal hide to turn into bags. They were walking through a dry mountainous desert by then, and the only large animals were the big-horned goats that climbed the sides of the mountains. It took them a few weeks to finally kill one, and they immediately went about turning its pelt into their new bags. Even with four bags for water, they still had to conserve more than ever before. Watering holes grew scarcer the farther they went, and it hardly ever rained.

The animals became scarce as well. Where in the plains life had been abundant, the dry lands held less and less life. They stopped seeing buffalo, and even the scavenger dogs disappeared after a while. The only animals they saw were the occasional fox or rabbit, but mostly they saw goats, and the beasts were far better mountaineers than Andronicus or Chaka could ever hope to be.

Whenever they managed to make a kill, they had to make the meat last for days, which was difficult due to the heat. On several occasions they found themselves eating rotten meat, and spending a day and night in awful retching pain sending it all back up.

Some days they didn't eat at all. Both of their bodies began thinning as their diets became more strict. Andronicus couldn't be sure, but he thought Chaka was finally starting to look a bit older again for the first time in years. He still looked as strong as an ox and healthy, but his salt-and-pepper hair had finally begun to turn white. There were also new lines around his eyes and mouth that Andronicus was sure hadn't been there before.

Once Andronicus noticed this, he made sure to stare at himself long and hard whenever they found a pool of water, which was less frequent all the time. At first Andronicus thought he might finally start to age again as well; that whatever the curse had been it had ended when they left the jungle. But deep down he knew it wasn't true. By that time it had been many years since they had left the jungle, and he still looked exactly the same as he always had. His hair and beard were still growing, but his face had not changed.

The mystery of Chaka finally showing signs of change was more interesting to Andronicus than anything. He desperately wanted to know how it all worked. He believed he could get some answers in Egypt, but that would take time. He knew Egypt was not far away, considering how far they had come, but it was on the other side of the Great Desert.

They had entered the desert long ago—no lands as dry as the ones they walked through could be called anything else—and yet the Great Desert still lay ahead. The farther they walked into the hot dry lands, the fewer people there were. They were consistently told that the final village before the Great Desert was called Kaminan. Every person they asked told them not to cross the Great Desert, warning that no one could survive the crossing, but they kept on moving toward it anyway.

No matter how many people tried to discourage them, Andronicus was certain they had to cross the desert. He had seen it in his visions, and he had dreamed about it a thousand times. The more barren the land got, the more it looked like Andronicus's dream, and the more convinced he became that it was the right way. Chaka seemed less sure about crossing the Great Desert, but he knew Andronicus would not be deterred. Andronicus was sure that they would make it; he had dreamed about it too many times not to. The light wouldn't have shown him the desert if he wasn't going to cross it. Besides, the light had shown him so many other things that he was sure would happen someday. He told himself these things over and over, but beneath it all was a dreadful fear of the sea and the storm.

4

It was slow going even with Andronicus pushing them forward, traveling south around Carthage and then east to Kaminan. They reached the village several years after first reaching Carthage. The people in Kaminan used the same calendar as the people west of Carthage. Andronicus knew he was fast approaching one hundred years old, and he was inwardly waiting to just drop dead of old age one day, but he remained as youthful as ever.

The Great Desert began just a few miles east of Kaminan and stretched farther than anyone really knew. Andronicus and Chaka stayed in the village for a few days preparing for the final stage of their long journey. They had crossed the plains. They had escaped the Kahli. They had lived in the Great Jungle for countless years. They had walked all the way from the jungle to the sea. The only thing left between them and true civilization was the Great Desert. Andronicus was sure that he and Chaka were the only humans who had ever crossed the entirety of the Great Jungle, so it was only fitting that their journey home should end with them being the first men to cross the Great Desert as well.

They heard a hundred different stories about people who had claimed to have made the journey, but Andronicus knew they weren't true. He tried to find someone who could tell him with certainty how big the desert really was, but he could tell no one knew for sure. Some said the desert would take a hundred days to cross. Some said it would take a year. Others said it would take ten years. Most, however, said that it could not be done.

Andronicus didn't know how far the desert stretched, but he knew they would make it across. He was positive that his dreams were showing him the future, and they showed him the desert as often as anything. As optimistic as he was, the fear of running out of water in the desert was very real, and it wasn't hard to convince Chaka that they needed another two bags each.

They lingered in Kaminan for a few weeks while they sewed additional water bags. The people of

Kaminan were fascinated by the skill of their sewing and fed them graciously in exchange for teaching them. It was a comfortable few weeks on the surface, but both men were restless. Deep down they both feared the desert. The jungle had been deadly in a thousand different ways, but it had always been full of life. The desert was completely devoid of life. It was a true wasteland in every sense of the word. Even the buzzards stayed away. The only things they would find once they entered it would be what they brought with them. That and sand. Lots of sand.

They had been told about the endless rolling dunes, but Andronicus remained determined to cross them anyway. He felt like it was the last stage of their quest, the final hill they had to crest before they were done.

They had started down in Swimha, more than thirty years ago. They had probably crossed more land than any men before them. They were the first men to ever cross the Great Jungle, and now Andronicus would see them be the first men to cross the Great Desert as well.

Before they set out, Andronicus either purchased or prepared as much food as he could. By the time they were ready to enter the desert, they both had large bags slung over their shoulders, some carrying nuts and berries, the rest carrying water.

Once their gear and provisions were ready, they set out from Kaminan. They walked for five days before they found a small watering hole, which was only an inch deep. Less than a hundred yards beyond the lone pool of water, they could see the sand. They had been in the desert for years by then, but they had never seen so much sand in one place. Once the sand started, they couldn't see the end of it, and they knew it would stretch for hundreds of miles.

Andronicus was quite sure that the pool would be the last water they would see for a long time.

They stayed beside it that night. Chaka went to sleep quickly, like he always did, but Andronicus stayed up for a long time, staring up at the stars, thinking about his many old questions. He felt like he was closer than ever to finding his answers. All he had to do was cross this last massive obstacle, and he could finally return home.

Chapter 27
The Great Desert
1

The next day they set out just before dawn and walked as far as they could before the sun rose to its highest point. When it got too hot to continue, they stopped to rest and eat. In every direction all they saw were great rolling hills of sand. The sand rose and fell. It trickled down itself and then lifted up and flew with the wind from time to time in a dusty haze. It crept into their sandals as they walked and ground under their feet with each step. It seemed like the entire world had turned to dust.

Andronicus couldn't help feeling that this was the end of the world, that neither Egypt nor Greece lay ahead of them, only death. Dry, barren, slow death. He was almost tempted to turn back, but he didn't. He knew that Egypt lay ahead, and he knew the only other way was to face the sea and the storm.

Andronicus and Chaka learned quickly that it took much longer to walk in the sand than it did in the dirt or mud. Every time they brought their feet down, the sand would move under them. They began to lift their legs higher as they stepped. Once they got into a rhythm, they began to make better pace, though they looked rather absurd doing it, especially Chaka.

By the end of the first day, Andronicus had drunk almost a quarter of one of the six bags of water they carried, which were meant to last him an indefinite amount of time, across an unknowably large and infamously deadly desert. Chaka had drunk even more. They didn't drink with dinner that night, and they went to bed with dry mouths that felt like they were full of the sand on which they slept.

The next morning, Andronicus awoke before dawn. His lips felt like burnt meat, crispy and dry. They ate a small bit of their food and took a sip of water each. They got up, and realized that their tracks from the previous day had been blown over by the sand. They looked in every direction and saw only dunes. The sky had already started turning blue, and the stars were fading away. They set off toward where the sun was beginning to glow beneath the horizon, hoping it was an indicator that they were heading east.

They had to stop when the sun made it halfway to its peak, as the heat became unbearable. The heat in the desert didn't come in waves but rather as a constant, overbearing presence. It encompassed them completely, crashing down on them and then rising back up from the endless sand. Everywhere Andronicus looked he saw waves of heat rising off the sand. When he stared in one direction for too long, the heatwaves played tricks on his eyes and showed him things he knew weren't there.

They sat and rested, both trying to regain their waning strength. Andronicus rubbed his lips together and felt them cut at each other. He brought a finger to his lower lip, and saw he had drawn a small drop of blood. He looked at Chaka and saw a man in desperate need of water. Chaka's skin had begun to crust and break. His hands were covered in small cuts where his dry skin had broken, and the sand dug into each of them. Andronicus looked down at his own hands and saw that they too had begun to crack.

After they had rested for a while, they each took a small sip of water and then continued on. They walked another two hours before they had to stop again. They were both quiet, sullen men to begin with, but now they walked in utter silence. The only sound was the rustling of sand in the wind. Neither man dared waste any energy on speech. After another long rest, they resumed their journey once again. The sun had now risen high above them, and their only guide was the tracks they left behind. As far as Andronicus could tell, their tracks remained straight, but he knew they could be going south or north just as easily as they could be going east. With the sun high above them and the dunes rolling from one to the next, they could even be going west, back where they came from.

2

When the sun finally set, and the stars emerged, Andronicus could see they had not strayed too far off course. They had been going approximately northeast for the last few hours, which suited their cause well enough. They sat and ate in silence, at first enjoying the cool night air on their burnt bodies, then later cursing the cold wind chill that cut across their broken skin and into every crack.

They had only walked the desert for two days, and they already looked like they had spent a month out there. Andronicus decided that from then on they would have to travel at night; the desert sun was just too strong. He didn't know why he had not thought of it from the start. Whenever he had the dreams it was at night. He should have known that would be how they would have to cross. He had not dreamed of the desert or the storm for weeks, and wondered what it might mean. He feared he might have made the wrong choice but remained determined to best the immense desert.

That night they remained awake. For most of the night they sat in silence, each contemplating the vast endeavor on which they had embarked. After Andronicus caught himself drifting off to sleep for the third time, he sat up and looked over at Chaka, who was also nodding off.

"Chaka," Andronicus said in a rough, croaky voice, wincing at the harsh dryness in his throat. "We need to stay awake."

"I am trying," Chaka said, rubbing his eyes and letting out a long yawn. "The sun here is greater than any I have known."

"I know," Andronicus said. "I always thought Swimha was the hottest place in the world, but this place is truly unbelievable."

"What do you think happened here, Jocus?" Chaka asked, staring out at the rolling hills of sand lit by the moon and stars. "Do you think this place was always this way?"

"I do not know," Andronicus said. "I suppose so." He let out a long yawn. "They say Persia has always been dry."

"I do not believe that," Chaka said. "I think the lands here once had life. Why would the gods put a wasteland like this in the world?"

"The gods?" Andronicus laughed. "I thought you did not believe in gods. Only elephants."

"The elephants are the gods of Swimha," Chaka said. "My people have worshipped them for generations, and they watch over us. But there are no elephants here, and you say that there are no elephants in Greece either."

"That is correct," Andronicus agreed. "I had only heard tell of them before I came to Swimha."

"Then there must be other gods here," Chaka said matter-of-factly. "Your people give them names, titles, and stories, but if they truly exist, why would they make a place like this?"

"I do not think the gods of my home are real, Chaka," Andronicus said, wondering what his brother and Theo would say if they heard him. "They are just stories to tell to children. The Persians have their own gods as well. When we get to Egypt, you will learn about their gods. Either they all exist, or none of them do. Either way, they are all the same thing."

"And what is that?" Chaka asked.

"Just stories people made up to answer all the questions," Andronicus sighed.

"If there are no gods, then who put the rocks in the pool that brought you to us?" Chaka asked.

Andronicus looked at him in surprise, his mind already racing down this new track. He had never really wondered how the rocks had gotten there. He had always been more concerned with what they were and how they worked, but it was an interesting question to add to his list. Whatever the rocks were, how had they ended up in that cave, and how was there a path leading through a mountain to reach them?

"I have no idea," he admitted.

"Only gods should have the power to do what they did," Chaka said. "Perhaps it was the gods who put the rocks in the cave."

"Perhaps," Andronicus mumbled, considering the possibility of gods for the first time in a long time.

"Look," Chaka said, pointing toward the hill behind them. Andronicus saw the faintest hint of light beginning along the horizon. They sat in silence and watched the light slowly spread across the land. When the sun finally appeared fifteen minutes later, Chaka was already snoring loudly. They had broken one of their spears in half and made a little makeshift tent in the sand to protect them from the sun while they slept.

Andronicus stayed up a while longer, thinking about what Chaka had said. It just added to the great mystery of the rocks. Andronicus looked out over the vast desert, knowing that Egypt was on the other side. He couldn't help but feel that he was closer to his answers then he had ever been. All that stood before him and the world he had come from was one massive, blazing desert. He didn't know how far the desert stretched, but somehow he knew they would make it. Andronicus fell asleep as the sun rose, feeling more hopeful than he had in fifty years.

3

They slept in the shade until the sun had nearly set again before rising. They ate a small meal as the sun disappeared behind the sand. They both refrained from drinking any water, and tried to eat only what they needed. They packed up their things and set out as the light faded from the land.

They made much better time walking at night. The sand still moved beneath their feet, but the sun didn't beat down on them, and they had the stars to guide them east. Andronicus counted some thirty-eight dunes they crossed that night and wondered how many more they would have to cross before they reached Egypt. As the sun rose again, they set up their tents and took a sip of water.

The small sip of water didn't come close to quenching Andronicus's thirst, but he knew it was all he could have. His mouth felt dry and burnt, like his skin. It felt as though the sand had managed to get everywhere. There was sand in his ears, eyes, mouth, and all the other places you might imagine. The entire world had turned to nothing but sand. No animals, no plants, no water, not even dirt, just endless waves of sand as far as the eye could see.

Andronicus was pleased with the progress they had made during the night. They had drunk far less water and crossed many more dunes, and it made him feel optimistic for the first time since entering the desert. Chaka looked more drained than usual, but Andronicus knew he would adjust; he always did.

He guessed that if they walked at night and slept during the day, taking just three to five sips of water per day, they would have enough water for roughly 150 days. Andronicus did not know how far the Great Desert stretched, but he knew that at the end of it lay Egypt, the mighty land he had heard of as a boy. He only hoped they would have enough water and food to get them there.

4

Andronicus and Chaka walked through the devastating desert night after night. Every day they would set up their tents and lie in the shade, feeling the heat vibrating all around them. The sand that slid down and touched their arms or legs was scorching hot. Their little makeshift tents barely lent them enough shade, and often Andronicus would wake with a terribly burnt leg or arm that would pain him for days after.

Andronicus thought he had known heat before. The plains had seemed so hot when he was in them. When they were in the jungle, he thought that was what true heat was. Now, Andronicus knew that true heat resided in the Great Desert and in the Great Desert alone.

A month in, he realized just how foolish the endeavor was. All the stories had told them not to go and so had all the people, but Andronicus had trusted his visions. He no longer had the desert dream while he was sleeping; he was living it. Every night while they walked through the endless sand, he would remember the shadowy vision of two men walking through a great desert. There was no longer any doubt at all that he and Chaka were the two men, and they were fulfilling the vision.

Andronicus wondered constantly if he had made the right choice. Sometimes he wondered if he had made a choice at all. He told himself it was his idea to travel through the desert, but perhaps fate had drawn them there. It had seemed like there were only two options, the desert or the storm at sea, but perhaps that was just in his head. Maybe they could have taken the sea and not seen so much as a single dark cloud. Maybe they would have found that storm and died in it. But none of that mattered anymore. Whether Andronicus had chosen it or it had been fate, the only thing now was to cross the desert, or die trying. He told himself every day and night that they would make it, but as the weeks turned to months, it became harder to believe.

5

The fruit they brought didn't last much beyond the first week. The salted meats they had prepared for the journey lasted much longer. Andronicus had worried the sun would harm the meat, but Chaka insisted it would just get rougher, and Chaka was right.

The meat lasted an incredible sixty-eight days. It tasted sour and chewy as their supplies began to run out, but it was still nourishing. Once the meat was gone, all they had left were nuts and dried berries. The berries lasted another twenty-three days after the meat, and the nuts another thirteen days after that, and then they were out of food. Andronicus silently cursed his stupidity. He could not believe how arrogant he had been. He had led them both into a death trap, even though he had been warned a hundred times.

They were completely out of food, and they each had only one water bag left. They continued walking every night, though it got harder and harder to keep walking through the sand without any food. Day and night the only sound was the wind swirling the sand about, and the angry growling of their stomachs. They had been losing weight ever since they entered the desert, but they both grew dangerously thin once they ran out of food.

Chaka looked worse than Andronicus had ever seen him. Even when Chaka had been nearly dying due to the nasty cut on his head, he had looked better. Now he was rail thin, and his bones were visible all over his body. The powerful muscles that had always covered his body had grown frail and weak. His skin was cracked and crusty, and his face seemed to hang in an awful way. It made Andronicus sad to see his once-mighty friend looking so ill and misshapen. He knew he must look just as bad, and was thankful he couldn't see himself.

6

One morning as they set up their tents to hide from the sun, Andronicus felt an odd sort of restlessness. The sun was barely up, and his body was covered in cold sweat. He turned to Chaka to say something, but he was already snoring loudly. Andronicus lay back and let out a deep sigh, wondering what could be wrong now. As he drifted off to sleep, the feeling only got worse.

Suddenly, Andronicus was standing on wood rather than sand. He looked down and saw long brown planks under his feet. A gust of wind splashed a spout of water into his face. He looked up as he wiped seawater out of his eyes. What Andronicus saw sent chills down his spine. He was standing on the deck of a ship, a huge ship, but a ship that he had seen before, only never in the light of day. Every time he had ever seen this ship, it had been riding the waves of a terrible storm in the blackness of Poseidon's wrath.

Andronicus took a tentative step toward the bow. A cluster of men were standing at the side of the ship, staring out at the open sea. They were wearing clothes that Andronicus had never seen before, and they all wore big brown boots rather than sandals. As he approached, none of them seemed to notice him. He looked out at what they were all staring at and felt his stomach drop.

In the distance, a huge mass of angry black clouds was forming. Andronicus recognized it at once. It was the storm. He had only ever seen it from within, but there could only be one storm so terrible.

A strange horn sounded somewhere high above his head, and he looked up to see where it had come from. To his amazement, there was a little platform high up at the top of the towering mast, and a man was standing atop it.

Andronicus felt someone bump into him and saw men running all over the ship. Clearly, preparations were being made for the storm, but he knew they would not be of any use. He knew how this would end; he had seen it a thousand times. They would enter that terrible storm, and they would fight off the inevitable as long as they could, but eventually they would plummet down one of the mountainous waves, and then they would crash and die. The dream always ended with dying. Andronicus looked around at all the men hustling about the ship and wondered how the dream would end this time. Would he stay in the dream until that wave came?

One of the men ran past him, and Andronicus did a double take. He stared as the young man yanked on a rope attached to something high on the mast. Andronicus didn't know who he was, and yet he looked so familiar. It was as if Andronicus had seen him before, many times, and yet he knew he hadn't. He wondered if he had seen this boy in his visions before, in the ones he couldn't remember.

Suddenly, the boy stared right at Andronicus. Feeling like he should say something, he opened his mouth to speak, only to feel a hand shaking him from behind. Andronicus turned to see who it was and saw Chaka looking down at him.

Andronicus was completely disoriented for a few seconds as he stared up at Chaka's dry, crusted face. He rolled over and felt sand moving under him. As the world slowly came back to him, he sat up. Chaka packed his things, but Andronicus just sat there thinking about the dream, knowing full well that it was not just a dream.

He had thought that he had made a choice, that he had chosen the test of the desert over the test of the storm, but now the dream was back. What made him angry was that this time he had dreamed of the beginning of the storm. He had seen enough to know that wherever and whenever that was, it was not here or now. They could have taken the sea to Egypt, and the storm would not have come, but now he would have to face the storm anyway, if they even made it out of the desert. He did take it as a good sign that he was once again dreaming of the future though, and he hoped it meant they would survive.

7

One hundred and twenty-four days after entering the Great Desert, twelve days after running out of food altogether, they finally reached the end of the dunes. It was the middle of the night, and the moon was just a sliver off to their right. Andronicus and Chaka hobbled along, their bodies moving awkwardly in their weak, emaciated states. They reached the top of an especially tall dune and stumbled their way down.

It took a few minutes before Andronicus's feet registered that they were walking on dirt instead of sand. As soon as he noticed it, he fell to his knees. Chaka stopped to help him up, clearly unaware of what Andronicus had realized.

"Chaka," Andronicus rasped, wincing at the way his throat scratched. "Chaka, the ground. The sand."

Chaka looked down and then released Andronicus. He fell back into the dirt, but he didn't care. Chaka fell to his knees beside him and put his hands down on the ground.

"We made it," Chaka gasped, his voice barely audible. "We made it."

"Come on," Andronicus said, coughing as he stood up. "We should try to find some water." Andronicus had to take an inhale of breath between his words. His body had never felt so weak in his entire life. He knew that if they did not find food and water soon, they would both die. Some part of him had tried to convince himself that he couldn't die, that he had become immortal, but now he thought differently. He could feel his body slowly shutting down, and he knew he would die if he didn't eat.

Chaka looked even worse, his once hugely muscled body was now just skin and bones. The hint of the muscles were still somewhere beneath his awful leathery looking skin, but they were nearly gone. His seven-foot tall figure looked inhuman without the muscles. He looked like some kind of stretched out monster.

The two starving men ambled back to their feet, and continued walking east. Now that they knew their feet were back on solid ground, they began moving faster than they had in months. Less than two hours after reaching the dirt, they found a cactus. It had long prickly thorns, but they took their time, carefully removing them from the bottom.

They were both desperate to drink from the cactus and even more eager to eat it. Andronicus knew that some desert cacti could be poisonous, but he decided he would rather die of poison than starve. They carefully pulled the thorns out before cutting a hole in the trunk of the plant, using the kind of patience only old men could show in such starvation.

When they finished removing the thorns, they took turns drinking from the base of the tree. It was the first time in weeks that they were able to drink more than a sip at a time, and it felt more refreshing than Andronicus could have imagined. He hacked off the branches with his sword, and they each ate far too much. They threw up into the dirt and then ate some more. The cactus was bitter and rough, but Andronicus savored every bite. It was amazing to be eating anything at all. After eating their fill once again, they decided to stop for the night. The sun hadn't risen yet, but a faint light was already forming in the east.

That day they slept on dirt for the first time in months. Andronicus thanked the gods for letting them find the end of the sand. He slept that day with a full belly, and woke feeling better than he had in weeks. Even Chaka looked refreshed. They both drank more from the cactus and ate another branch. The sun was still providing some light, so Andronicus cut what remained of the cactus into pieces small enough to carry. They didn't know when they would find another cactus or anything else, so they made sure not to eat too much.

The end of the sand and the appearance of a living plant meant they really were coming to the end of the desert. They had walked so long among the dunes that Andronicus had truly begun to think they would both die there. Now they had food again, at least for a time, and water too. All they had to do now was walk through the dry wastelands until they found a village, and then they would be saved. They could rest and nourish themselves back to health. From there all they had to do was walk north through Persian lands, which might prove difficult, though it would be nothing compared to the jungle or the desert.

Once they made it past Persia, it would be a short journey to Greece, considering how far they had come. Andronicus wasn't sure what they were going to do once they got there, but it didn't matter; they would do it together. He didn't know if there was a single person that he had known left in Greece. He did know it would be an odd adjustment, much more so for Chaka than for him. Andronicus thought about his home, and when he went to sleep, he dreamed of walking through the streets of Sparta again with Chaka looking around in amazement at his side.

Chapter 28
The End of a Long Journey
1

Eight days after they had left the sand dunes behind, it felt like they no longer had any bones in their legs. Each step through the deep sand had been a great effort, and now that they were back on solid ground, their legs felt like feathers. Their water jugs had almost dried up in the dunes, and they had begun to seriously fear death, but they filled up a bag and a half each at the cactus, and had food for three days.

There was no other water in the wasted lands they walked through, and no creatures. Then Andronicus saw a bird flying overhead for the first time since entering the dunes, and took it as a good omen. It wasn't long after leaving the dunes that they realized they had not left the desert after all. All the horizon held was dirt shimmering in the glare of the sun, along with the occasional dead tree. It made Andronicus wonder if Chaka hadn't been right. There had been life here once, but now the desert was slowly growing, like a sickness.

The sun was as hot as it was in the dunes, so they continued walking at night. The relief of leaving the dunes behind was quickly replaced by the realization that they might not even be halfway across the desert.

2

They had been walking all night, and the sun was just rising when Andronicus thought he saw movement on the horizon. He stopped and squinted to see what it was. He couldn't make it out, but after a few seconds he was quite sure there was actually something moving. He had seen many things in the heat that hadn't been real, but this was different. They started walking toward the movement. About fifteen minutes later Andronicus saw a group of dots moving toward them.

At first he saw only six dots crossing the brow of a low hill in the distance. As the dots came down and turned toward them, he saw another five behind them. They were approaching too quickly to be on foot. As they grew nearer, Andronicus counted eleven riders heading straight toward them. The sight of other humans was a welcome relief, followed by sudden fear.

Andronicus knew the riders would not want to help them. No one came this far into the desert to do strangers good deeds. The only kind of men Andronicus had ever known to venture so far into the middle of nowhere were bandits, either men on the run or men on the hunt. Either way Andronicus knew if they found the diamonds he had in his pouch, they would surely kill him and Chaka for them.

As the riders galloped toward them, Andronicus tried to think of a peaceful way out of the situation, but he couldn't come up with any way to avoid fighting the men. He didn't even know what language they might speak. Andronicus felt his confidence falter as he saw Chaka's weak look of desperation.

"Chaka," Andronicus coughed, his voice still raspy, "we have to fight."

Chaka nodded slowly, but he didn't look strong enough to fight off one man, let alone half a dozen. Andronicus pulled out his water bag and took a large gulp. He knew that the riders would have more water, and that he would either die or be able to take their water when he was done. He nodded to Chaka, and Chaka took a big gulp from his bag as well.

The riders were coming at them at full speed now and would be on them soon. As he set his things down and drew his sword, Andronicus saw the wooden box fall out of his cloak. The odd symbol on the front stared up at him, and he was hit with a sudden idea. He picked up the box and carefully cracked the top open. He made sure to keep his head away from the box, so as not to inhale any fumes.

A white powder was in one of the compartments. It had been an opaque colored paste when he got it back in the jungle, but it had turned to white dust long ago. Glick had told Andronicus about it, but he had never used it himself. The stuff was supposed to give a burst of energy. He knew it was their best chance at being able to defend themselves against the oncoming riders. Andronicus gave half of it to Chaka, who took it without question, despite his previous aversion to the box. They put the powder in their mouths and took another gulp of water.

At first Andronicus didn't feel anything. Then his face started to tingle. By the time the riders were almost upon them, Andronicus felt like his whole body was buzzing with electricity. It was similar to what he had taken in the jungle, but completely different at the same time. This stuff was like a burst of pure energy; Andronicus felt ready to take on all eleven riders himself.

"Finish off that bag," Andronicus said, nodding to Chaka's water bag. They both downed the last of their water as the men rode up to them. As the water ran down Andronicus's throat and into his stomach, it tasted like the sweetest nectar. Water had never been as good and refreshing in his long life. For a moment he felt a rush go through his head, and his knees grew weak. Then his strength returned in earnest. He felt better than he had since they had started through the desert.

Andronicus gave Chaka a look of caution and encouragement as the riders encircled them. Each rider wore brown robes that covered their heads and faces. They rode tall, strong horses, and they each had a long curved sword pointing at the weary travelers.

A big man with a black sash across his chest reined in his horse, and it took two steps forward. "Glish ah bah!" he shouted in a language Andronicus knew he had heard before. He wasn't sure, but he thought the man had asked who they were. He tried to remember how to say "merchant" in the man's language, but the only thing he could remember how to say was "I have pelts and meats to trade." Seeing as he had neither pelts nor meat, he was at a loss.

"Glish ah bah!" the man shouted as he towered over them. Andronicus stayed completely still. He knew that the moment he or Chaka moved, the riders would attack. His sword rested on his hip, free for his right hand to draw, but he withheld.

"Gahneh seya hun," Andronicus said, trying to sound calm. He hoped it meant "I wish to trade," but he wasn't sure. Several of the riders looked at each other before the lead rider burst out into harsh, dry laughter. The other riders joined in, sharing a raucous laugh at whatever Andronicus had said.

"Djohuneh kayame nuh domahtah sehn," the lead rider said in his rough voice, and the other riders laughed again. The only word Andronicus understood was *domahtah*, which meant, "kill you." He turned his head slowly until his eyes met Chaka's. Their eyes locked for a moment, and Andronicus knew that Chaka understood what they had to do.

The white stuff was making Andronicus's mind race. He quickly took measure of the riders. It was like his perception had been turned up, and he could see clearer than normal. His heart was beating like a drum, and he had to keep from shaking. He raised his hands slowly, making a final attempt at peace. The lead rider shouted something Andronicus couldn't understand and then reared his horse.

As the beast reared, Andronicus drew his sword, stepped forward, and drove it deep into the horse's bare chest before its feet returned to the ground. The beast let out a terrible screech as it fell with the rider still on its back. Andronicus turned just in time to see the two nearest riders swing their swords on him. He ducked one sword and deflected the other, rising as another rider came at him.

Andronicus weaved past the man's sword and plunged his own into the man's gut. He pulled the dying man down off the horse and took his sword before leaping onto the horse. Once on horseback Andronicus saw Chaka fighting off four riders with difficulty. One rider lay dead at Chaka's feet, but the others were bearing down on him. Andronicus pressed the horse forward, clashing his sword and the stolen blade against two rider's curved swords. Andronicus slew the riders one by one as he made his way to Chaka.

Andronicus fought harder than he had in decades. He hadn't had a real sword fight since leaving Greece, and the old thrill of battle came rushing back to him. As Andronicus cut down one rider after another, he felt alive for the first time in years. Each time his sword ended another man's life, Andronicus let out a loud war cry. The riders who had been so confident and imposing a minute earlier now looked at Andronicus with nothing but fear.

When only two riders were left, they turned to flee. Andronicus rode after them and cut them down before they could get away. His mind was still racing, but he was completely focused on killing. He drove his sword into the final rider's back with a cry to the heavens. He felt better than he had ever felt. It was as if in battle his body remembered its true purpose.

As Andronicus pulled his blade from his last rider's back, he heard a terrible cry, a cry that would haunt him for many years after. At that moment he remembered Chaka, who was surrounded. His heart lurched as he turned around and saw Chaka down on one knee with a sword sticking out of his back. The tall brown man pulled the blade from Chaka's back, sending blood spewing across the dirt, and then charged Andronicus alongside his last remaining companion.

They rode toward each other at full speed. Just before the horses passed each other, Andronicus threw his extra sword at the lead man. It spun through the air twice before plunging into his face. As the dead rider fell from his horse, blood spraying down his face and chest and on to his horse, Andronicus saw a look of terror on the last rider's face before he swung his sword at him. The rider did not even have time to swing as Andronicus removed his head with one clean blow.

When the last rider was slain, Andronicus jumped down and ran to Chaka's side. Chaka was on his knees, bent over, blood running down his back and dripping from his cracked lips. Andronicus looked at the wound and felt his whole body weaken. The sword had pierced Chaka's lung and possibly even his heart. Andronicus knew Chaka did not have long, but he didn't want to believe it.

He helped Chaka onto his back, then brought his water bag to Chaka's trembling lips. Chaka leaned forward and took a small sip, and then his head fell back into the dirt. His breathing had become short and quick. Blood curdled at the corners of Chaka's mouth as he struggled for his last small breaths.

Andronicus didn't know what to do. He had always been able to save Chaka. They had always been able to save each other, but now he was at a loss. Nothing in the wooden box could help Chaka. Andronicus tried to lift Chaka up, to put pressure on the wound, but as he lifted him up, Chaka began coughing terribly, blood shooting across his chest. Andronicus lay Chaka back in the growing red pool. He felt more helpless than he ever had in his life. Tears fell from his eyes and onto his dying friend's chest.

It looked like Chaka was trying to say something. His lips were moving, and he had a look of determination in his eyes. Andronicus leaned in close and put his ear next to Chaka's trembling lips. At first all he heard was Chaka's rough breathing. Andronicus looked at Chaka and saw the determination still there. In a way, Chaka looked at peace, with one last thing to do. He coughed out a spurt of blood and then tried to speak again. Andronicus dropped his head back down to listen.

"What?" Andronicus asked his old friend. "I cannot understand." Chaka looked him dead in the eye and spoke clearly.

"Find them, Jocus," Chaka whispered, gasping for air between each word. "Find . . . your . . ." Chaka let out another cough of blood, and then his head fell back into the sand. Andronicus clutched Chaka's hand in his own, staring into his friend's dark-brown eyes. Chaka's hand felt rough, cracked, and lifeless. Chaka's whole body looked thin and weak, and Andronicus knew it was all his fault. He had forced them into the desert, and in the end, he killed his best friend.

"Go in peace, brother," Andronicus whispered, trying to lend the moment some gravity. "Perhaps one day we will meet again."

Chaka's eyes slowly turned and met Andronicus's. They remained silent for a time, Chaka lying there with a dark pool of blood spreading around him and Andronicus kneeling over him, clutching his hand. It felt like it lasted hours, though Andronicus knew it was only seconds.

Chaka's lips curled into one last grin before his hand slipped from Andronicus's, and he took his last sharp intake of air. His stern brown eyes lifted and took one final look at the sky. When the air left his body, Andronicus felt Chaka's body shrink beneath him. He slumped and slid into the blood pooling around him. Andronicus stared into Chaka's lifeless eyes and felt more sorrow than he had ever felt in his life.

A hint of a smile lingered on Chaka's face for a moment before his lips slumped like the rest of him. Chaka's body was dusty and looked like it was decaying already. His hair was white, and his face was old and wrinkled. Andronicus thought that Chaka finally looked his true age for the first time since they had left Swimha.

3

Andronicus spent the rest of the day in a stupor. First, he searched the dead riders scattered about the dirt and found a small spade on one of their horses. It took him hours to dig the hole, though it seemed to go by in seconds. When he had dug a grave, Andronicus stood over it for a while, staring down into the dark pit that would be his friend's final resting place. He had never dreamed of Chaka actually dying, even when he almost had. Now that he was gone, Andronicus felt empty, without any purpose at all.

He thought for a moment about finding a nicer place to bury Chaka, then decided against it. Everywhere Andronicus turned there was nothing but empty desert. It seemed right to bury Chaka right where he had been slain, covered by the very dirt that was soaked in his blood.

Andronicus looked at Chaka's limp body and began to cry. He had never felt a greater loss in his long life. He had lost his brother and his friends. He had lost his wife and his unborn child. He had lost him home, twice, and everything else in the world. He had lost everyone and everything he had ever loved. But Chaka was different. Chaka had always been there, always. When Manyara died, and Andronicus was ready to give up, Chaka was there. When the jungle began to drive Andronicus mad, Chaka was there. Chaka had been there every day since the day they met.

The thought of going on without him made Andronicus feel empty. He knew his friends could still be out there somewhere, that they could be looking for him just as he was looking for them, but he didn't know where they were. He knew it could take another fifty years to find answers to his many questions, and the thought of going through that without Chaka made Andronicus feel ill.

As he knelt beside his friend, he considered killing himself and joining Chaka, just taking his old sword and slitting his wrists. He knew how to do it, so he would die quickly. Then he realized he didn't even have to use a blade; he had a whole box of poisons. There were at least three he knew of that would be painless. For a moment Andronicus actually considered letting their journey end together.

Then Chaka's last words returned to him. He hadn't really heard them when Chaka said them; he had been too focused on trying to save him. Now as he knelt beside Chaka's body, he thought of the words. "Find them," he had said. Andronicus wasn't sure exactly which them Chaka had meant—his friends? His answers? His home? The shining rocks? Maybe Chaka meant all of it. Find them, all of them, everything he was searching for. Find it all.

The thought of going on alone scared Andronicus more than anything, but he knew he had no choice. He had to continue for Chaka now.

Andronicus lifted Chaka's frail body. He was as light as he had ever been, but it was still difficult for Andronicus to make his way over to the grave he had dug. The white powder had worn off, and Andronicus's weak muscles felt like rubber. He fell to his knees beside the grave and then lowered Chaka into it, his tears falling all the while.

Andronicus made sure Chaka was laid out straight and then laid the spotted jaguar pelt across his chest and arms. He thought about putting Chaka's necklace on him as well, the one he had made in the jungle from the claws of the same cat. Andronicus took it out of Chaka's bag and turned it over in his hands, feeling the smoothness of the claws. It was too beautiful a thing to leave in the dirt, and Andronicus felt he had to take something of Chaka's with him.

He lifted the necklace over his head and let it fall onto his chest. Then he picked up the spade and stared down at his old friend's withered face one last time, the tears falling like rain. After a long time, Andronicus shoveled the first load of dirt onto Chaka. Covering his friend in dirt and leaving his body in the ground in such an awful, desolate place was the hardest thing Andronicus had ever done. More than anything he wished he could bring Chaka back to the land of the Swimha, so he could rest with his brothers, sisters, and his father.

4

When Andronicus was finished, the dirt above Chaka looked a bit fresh but otherwise indistinguishable from the rest of the desert. Andronicus found a large rock with a flat face and then used the bronze knife he had given Chaka to carve "Chaka Swihmehe" in the old Greek letters. The Swihmehe had never made letters of their own.

He laid the rock at the head of Chaka's grave. Then he put the old lion's claw Chaka had given him so long ago next to the stone. He took a step back and gazed upon his closest friend's final resting place, and wept.

5

Andronicus stayed next to Chaka's grave all night. He felt more alone than he ever had. As he sat there beside the soft mound of dirt, he realized he had never really been alone before. When he was young, he had his brother and mother. When he went to school, he had Thymi. When he went to war, he had Lycus and Niko. Even in his youth, when he was drinking and fighting every night, Lycus had been there with him. When Andronicus had gone into the cave that had changed his life, he had not been alone; he had been with his friends.

The only time in Andronicus's extraordinarily long life that he had actually been alone was the two days between waking up in Swimha and meeting Chaka and the others. They had taken him to their home, and he had been with the Swihmehe for many years. And then when Manyara died, and he had to leave again, Chaka had come with him. He thought about what it would have been like if Chaka had not come with him. What it would have been like to walk all of those years by himself, through the Great Jungle and the Great Desert and all of the lands in between?

He knew he never would have made it this far without Chaka. No man could cross the Great Jungle alone; he would have lost his mind. Chaka had been more than just a travel companion. Whatever it was that had touched Andronicus, whatever was keeping him young, had touched Chaka as well. Andronicus still didn't know exactly how old Chaka was, but he knew he was much older than he looked. However it all worked, Chaka had become a part of it, and now he was dead.

Andronicus thought again about going on without Chaka, and he felt truly hopeless. He still knew where he had to go and how to get there. Egypt lay at the end of the desert, and now Andronicus had enough food and water to get there, not to mention his pick of the horses. It just didn't feel right without Chaka. Reaching Egypt was all he had dreamed of since he had heard about it, but it didn't feel the same without Chaka to experience it with him.

Andronicus had been as excited to show Chaka the world as Chaka had been to see it. Chaka had spent countless hours learning the languages of Egypt and Greece, hearing the stories Andronicus would tell, and learning how to live in such places. He had wanted so badly to see the great buildings Andronicus spoke of, but now he never would. Chaka had only gotten to see dirt and sand.

When the sun finally began to rise, Andronicus realized he had been sitting next to the grave all night. He got to his feet, wincing at the stiffness in his joints, and made his way over to where the riders still lay. As expected, each of them had a water pouch. He went from one to the next, searching through their belongings and taking any valuables.

When he was finished, he chose the finest horse among the lot, a large black stallion that looked strong enough to pull a cart with no wheels. Andronicus unsaddled the remaining horses and let them roam free. Once upon his new steed, he rode over to take one final look at Chaka's grave. It looked bleak and empty, not at all worthy of the man who lay beneath it. Andronicus wished he could have given Chaka a proper Swihmehe burial like he deserved, but there was no great fire, no dancers.

6

Andronicus rode east for the rest of the day, following the tracks of the bandits he had killed. Not long after midday, he reached the small mountain range the riders had come from. The tracks turned north, up the nearest hill and out of sight. Andronicus knew Egypt lay to the east, and he sat on his new horse, and thought about just letting it go. He didn't even know if there were any more of them in the hills.

Andronicus sat there for a long time, thinking. Then he turned his horse north and rode up the hill, following the bandit tracks. He decided Egypt could wait a little longer. He had no doubt that the bandits had a camp somewhere, and he intended to find it.

The tracks were easy to follow, even as it grew dark. Andronicus rode slowly up the hill, enjoying not having to walk. When he reached the top, he looked down into a long valley, and in the distance saw a large fire burning. Andronicus walked his horse down the hill as quietly as he could. When he came to a dead tree, he dismounted and wrapped the horse's reins around a sturdy branch.

The horse was surprisingly docile for his size, and seemed content to stand by the tree until Andronicus returned for him. Andronicus took his sword and walked down the hill as the last tendrils of daylight wavered on the horizon. The fire was still a ways off, but he could hear voices shouting.

As Andronicus got closer to the camp, he saw at least a dozen men either sitting around the fire or walking around the camp. There were five large tents, and he knew there were likely more men inside. For a moment he thought about leaving. He had killed the riders earlier, but Chaka had helped, and so had the white powder. It had been years since he had fought so many men, and he was still in such terrible shape after crossing the desert.

As Andronicus stood in the darkness debating what to do, he remembered Chaka's mangled cry as the sword pierced his back. Chaka had told him to find them, and found them he had. He knew that wasn't what Chaka meant, but he didn't care. Andronicus drew his sword and crept over to the camp. He wanted to walk straight in and kill them all, but he waited.

Most of the men were shouting, and Andronicus realized many of them were drunk. The seven men sitting around the fire were all drinking, and none of them were armed. Two men were packing something into a crate, both of them also unarmed. Four other men were standing around on the far side of the camp, each one with a sword at his hip.

Andronicus crept around the camp. He had gotten good at being stealthy over the years, and none of the men noticed him as he came up behind them. The four men were talking in what sounded like some kind of Egyptian slang. Andronicus had been studying the language for the past two years, and recognized a few of their words. He wasn't sure, but he thought they were talking about their missing party.

They were standing in front of one of the tents, not far from the fire. Andronicus knew there was no way he could sneak up to them without being seen. For a moment he thought about just charging in, slashing the first four men, and then charging the rest of them. It was more or less what he had done when he had massacred the Swihmacha, but they had not been armed with swords.

In the end he decided to take a more practical approach. He hid behind the large tent and kicked a rock. A second later, Andronicus heard the voices stop. Someone said something that he couldn't make out, and then footsteps were coming toward him.

Andronicus clutched his sword and prepared for a fight.

He let the first man pass as he stood flat against the tent, hidden in the shadows. The first man was looking around in front of him, searching for the source of the noise. When the second man emerged, Andronicus struck. Before any of them knew he was there Andronicus drove his sword through the second man's neck and then wrenched it forward, sending blood spurting down over the man's chest. Then he drove his sword through the first man's back. He pulled the blade free and turned to see the other two men drawing their swords in alarm.

Andronicus leapt at them. One of them shouted, alerting the rest of the camp to his presence. Andronicus clashed his sword against the two bandits' curved swords. He hadn't fought anyone with a sword since he had woken in Swimha, but his skills returned to him quickly. He ducked one man's blow, deflected the other, stepped to his left, and then brought his sword down onto one of the men's arms. Andronicus's sword cut through flesh as well as it ever had, and the arm dropped to the dirt, still clutching the sword.

As the now one-armed man fell to his knees with a howl of pain, Andronicus stepped toward his companion. The man swung his sword twice, Andronicus deflected both blows and then drove his own sword up into the man's throat. As the man dropped his sword and reached up to his gushing neck, Andronicus turned to see the rest of the camp charging at him.

At least eight drunk men were running his way, and several others were emerging from the tents. Andronicus thought he might be able to take on all of them. After all, they were mostly drunk, but he decided to fight smart. Andronicus ran away from the men, feeling a bit like a coward, until he was far enough from the fire that all he could see was shadows.

Andronicus turned around to see the men still chasing him much further back than he had expected. Either they were drunker than he thought, or he had truly become an expert at seeing in the dark.

When the drunken bandits finally stumbled over to him, many of them falling along the way, Andronicus almost pitied them. Had he stayed in the light, they might have been able to at least fight him, but they stood no chance in the dark. Andronicus moved quickly from one man to the next.

A few of them tried to strike out at him, but none of them came close. Andronicus was still faster than any of them, and they could barely see. It wasn't hard to cut down all eight of the drunken bandits, even as weak as he was. When they were all down, Andronicus went around making sure each of them was dead. He heard voices shouting from the camp, so he started back in that direction.

When he reached the camp, he found six men strapping on armor. One of them turned around as Andronicus entered the camp, and he shouted to the others. Andronicus drove his sword through the man's chest as the rest turned to see why he had shouted. Andronicus pulled his sword free and slashed at the nearest man before he could react.

The final four bandits huddled together, facing Andronicus down. They each had a sword in hand, three of them had breastplates, and two of them had wicker shields. Andronicus got in the old fighter's stance that he hadn't been in for decades. He knew they would try to surround him, so before they could, he ran at the men, and kicked one of the wicker shields. The man went flying backward, taking one of his companions with him. Andronicus landed on his feet but nearly lost his balance. While he was trying to steady himself, one of the other men swung his sword. Andronicus tried to duck the blow, but he felt a terrible sting as the sword cut through his lower back. He fell to one knee with a cry of pain.

Before he could even think, the other sword was coming down at him. Andronicus flung his own sword upward, and the two blades clanged together. Andronicus jumped to his feet, barely able to feel the cut in his back, and faced the two men as the other two got to their feet. He swung at the one on the left, and their swords clashed. He deflected one blow and then another, and then saw a hole. He slashed at one man's left arm, cutting it deeply. The man didn't fall, but he turned away, clutching his arm.

Andronicus fought with the second man as the other two charged back in. He managed to drive his sword through the man's chest just before the other two reached him. He pulled his sword free just in time to deflect another blow. The last two men both had breastplates and wicker shields. Andronicus deflected their blows, but every time he took a good shot, they deflected it with their shields.

The longer the fight went on, the more he could feel the cut in his back and the blood running down his leg. His arms began to feel weak, and he knew he wasn't swinging his sword with the same power as before. He caught a break when one of the men tripped, and Andronicus brought his sword down on the man's head, lodging it in his skull. Andronicus tried to pull it free, but it wouldn't budge. The final bandit swung at Andronicus, and he had to leap to the side to avoid his flashing blade.

The man turned and charged at Andronicus again. Andronicus had no sword, and none were close by. Without thinking, Andronicus grabbed a nearby rock and flung it at the man. It struck him just above the eye, taking a flap of skin with it. The man stopped for a second and reached up to his face, and Andronicus was on the man before he could react.

He brought the man down, falling on top of him. He had no sword, so he grabbed the man by the throat and squeezed. The bandit tried to stab Andronicus with his sword, but Andronicus brought his knee down on the man's hand. He squirmed as Andronicus choked the life out of him. At the very end, he looked like a wild horse, his bulging eyes staring madly up at Andronicus.

Once Andronicus was sure the man was dead, he fell off him. Two men were still alive, the one-armed man and the nearly one-armed man. Andronicus took care of them both before tending to his own wound. There was an alarming amount of blood on his back. He couldn't see the whole cut, but what he could see looked deep. He tore a blanket into pieces, and wrapped it around his bleeding back.

He searched the camp thoroughly before leaving. He found a bag full of different looking coins and was sure they would be useful in Egypt.

He left the bandits' fire burning, illuminating all the dead bodies as he limped back to his horse. He was pleased to find it waiting peacefully for him. He mounted the horse and set off back down the hill.

7

At dawn Andronicus found a nice flat spot in the shade of a small mountain. He tied his horse to a dead tree. Then he took a small bowl from his new supplies, filled it with water, and held it to the horse's mouth until it drank its fill.

Andronicus took a drink as well. The water was as refreshing as any he had ever tasted. He had only taken a few sips a day while crossing the great dunes for fear of running out. Now he had eight water bags filled to the brim and no companion to share them with, save his new horse. The fact that he was seeing dead trees meant he was entering lands that got at least some water.

Andronicus sat in silence as he ate the food he had scavenged from his victims. He missed Chaka more than he could have been prepared for. He had lost people before—in fact, he had lost everyone he ever cared about—but he had not been prepared to lose Chaka. He had been friends with Chaka for over sixty years. It was hard to believe, but if the Carthaginian calendars were correct, it had really been that long. They had crossed all of Africa together. They had fought together and laughed together. Chaka had saved his life countless times, as he had Chaka's. They had crossed the Great Jungle together and had bested the Great Desert, but in the end he had fallen to bandits and thirst.

Andronicus cursed the riders who had killed Chaka. To think that such a skilled fighter and honorable man should be bested by a band of thieves. Andronicus had always suspected he was still mortal—

he could certainly be wounded—but Chaka's death seemed to confirm it. Whatever light had touched Chaka to make him live so long had not been enough to keep him from death. Andronicus feared it would not keep him from death either.

8

The rest of the journey to Egypt was much easier for Andronicus. He now had a strong horse, new supplies, and plenty of water. It took another two weeks to go from the eastern edge of the Sahara to the great pyramids of Egypt, and it went by quickly.

He had heard tales as a boy of Egypt's mighty pyramids. It was said that they were great stone structures higher than the clouds themselves. In his days of war with the Persians, he had again heard tales of these great achievements of the Egyptian builders.

When he finally encountered a road cutting through the vast desert, Andronicus knew he was getting close. He now wore the brown robes of one of the riders he had slain, and when he came upon other riders, he was able to pass as a merchant. The bandits had, in fact, had several valuable pieces, including three bright rubies. Andronicus knew that when the time came he would be able to trade them.

As the road became wider, and he passed more riders and peasants, Andronicus knew he must be truly close. The road twisted around a large mountain, and when he finally turned its corner, there it was, a stone lion with the head of a man, at least sixty feet high. In the distance behind it was the first pyramid. It was still some miles away, but Andronicus could see it clear as day. It was larger than any stone structure he had ever seen. He stopped for a moment to admire it before pushing his horse onward. The entire ride down he stared at the great pyramids.

They seemed impossible. Andronicus could not imagine how men could have ever built something so huge. And yet he had done things that no man should be able to do. His entire life had become something that no one should be able to do, and yet he did it. It made him wonder if it had been regular men who had built these impossible stone structures, or something else. The pyramids were impressive and by far the biggest manmade things Andronicus had ever seen, but it was the statue that kept drawing his attention.

He stared up at the great stone cat, and stared at its human face. It looked older than anything he had ever seen. He knew that the pyramids were around two thousand years old, but no one knew how old the statue was. Chunks of stone were missing from it in several places, and the sides of the structure had wavy lines that could only be made over a very long time. Andronicus wondered just how old this great stone beast was, and if such a creature had ever roamed the earth. There were similar stories of half-human creatures back in Greece, but no one had ever seen them. This stone beast looked so old that it actually made him wonder.

The other people on the road were walking right past it as if it were not the most amazing thing they had ever seen. Andronicus guessed that if you see anything every day it no longer seems great, but it was hard to think that he could ever walk by such an incredible sight without staring at it. He had walked through beautiful lands for years, seeing the same things every day, but he still took time to admire them. He decided that the people walking by without looking up at the beast were either scared of it or too foolish to appreciate how magnificent it was. Perhaps they knew something he didn't, some old legend about the great stone cat with a man's head.

Andronicus turned away from the stone cat as he rode past it and stared up at the towering pyramid before him. It seemed like such a strange thing to build—an odd shape, an odd color, an odd building. What had been its purpose? As Andronicus rode solemnly into Egypt, he realized what a spectacular place it might be, and he let his mind wander about the old, storied country.

Act III
A Life Lost and A Life Found

Chapter 29
The New Old World

1

The road leading into the ancient city of Memphis filled with people until it became a bustling marketplace. Merchants and trading carts lined both sides of the big dirt road, and the road itself was filled with people from all over the Egyptian empire. Andronicus saw gypsy traders from Persia and African hunters with lion skins and elephant tusks. He saw bald men in priest's robes, and men who looked very much like the bandits he had killed. There were children playing with sticks, and people selling goods. Every so often he caught the scent of some foreign dish that made his mouth water.

He saw at least six different types of soldiers within a half mile, some wearing black leather, and some wearing gold-plated Egyptian helms. Men-at-arms stood watch over the merchants, and others marched in groups through the crowd. Andronicus felt overwhelmed by it all as he rode amongst them. He felt like an outsider, a stranger, as if he really were coming from a different world, back to one he barely remembered.

As Andronicus rode his horse through the dense crowd, he didn't make eye contact with anyone. He received a few odd looks from passersby, but most people didn't seem to notice him at all. He had cut his hair not long after he found the main road and given himself a nice close shave, hoping he would blend in.

When he had finished cutting off his long black locks and what remained of the beard he had been growing ever since leaving the jungle, he hadn't known what to do with it. It didn't seem right to just let it go in the wind. It wasn't hair that he had grown over a summer, or a year, he had been growing that hair all the way from the Great Jungle. He didn't know exactly how long it had been, but he had learned enough to know it had been at least ten years since the jungle. In the end he burned the hair. It made an awful smell, but it gave him a small bit of relief, as if he were letting go of a piece of his past.

It seemed like the past was all he had now, although he knew he likely had plenty of future yet to come. It depressed him greatly to know that no one he knew would be in that future. He knew his friends and his brother could still be out there somewhere, but he no longer believed he would ever find them. He had been able to keep the hope alive when Chaka had been alive, but ever since his death Andronicus had been forced to face some hard facts.

He didn't know what he was supposed to do next, or where he was supposed to go. He knew that Greece wasn't far away now. He could book passage by the end of the week, and be in Greece by year's end. He knew how achievable his goal was, and yet he no longer felt any urge to go home. Everyone he had known would be dead by now. The only ones who could possibly still be alive would be Niko's boys, and they would have to be in their eighties at the least. The thought of going home actually scared him now.

Looking around at all the strange and interesting faces, Andronicus wanted to stay. He had heard of the great library of Memphis when he was a boy, and he was sure he could get into such a place now. He wondered what he might be able to find if he spent time in that library.

As he rode through the busy crowd, he thought about all that he might be able to learn in a place like this. It might be the best way for him to get his answers. There was no reason to go back to Sparta; he knew what he would find there. Egypt was a much older country than Greece, and Andronicus knew it would be the best place to search for clues. It seemed like the best thing for him to do now was go to the library and at least see it for himself.

Andronicus soaked in the busy atmosphere as he rode. He had not seen a larger marketplace since he had left Sparta, perhaps not ever. A group of young boys swinging sticks ran past and around Andronicus.

One boy even ran right under his horse. A soft smile appeared on Andronicus's lips for the first time in months. He turned away from the playing children, still smiling, and found a tall, barrel-chested man with a thick beard blocking his path. The large man grabbed the reins of Andronicus's horse, and brought him to a quick halt. Andronicus's hand instinctively dropped to his sword, but he withheld from drawing.

"Who are you?" the man barked in a rough, scratchy voice. He spoke the common Egyptian tongue with a thick accent, but Andronicus had spent enough time learning the language when he was in Carthage to understand him.

"I'm a merchant trader from the lands west of here," Andronicus answered, trying to look non-threatening.

"What have you to trade?" the man demanded. "I see naught but a horse."

"I have precious stones," Andronicus said, smiling blandly. "I mean to take them to the high temple."

The man glared up at Andronicus. "You're loyal to the pharaoh then?" The man's tone sounded hateful, and Andronicus tightened his fingers around the hilt of his sword. He had heard about the turmoil that had been brooding here, and guessed this man was part of whatever revolution was going on.

"I'm loyal to no man in this country," Andronicus said with a cold flatness to his voice. The man flinched at the look Andronicus gave him. "I want no part in your affairs with the pharaoh." There was a tense moment of silence between them. The crowd bustled by completely unaware while they glared at each other, Andronicus on his horse, and the tall man blocking his path. If the man attacked, Andronicus would have to kill him, and he didn't know what might happen then.

Finally the man broke his gaze and looked to the hilt of Andronicus's sword. "I see you have a fine sword there, of western making. If you truly have no claim in the pharaoh's affairs, then perhaps your sword may be bought. Arkos the brave will offer you one hundred gold pieces to fight for him in the battles to come."

Andronicus laughed humorlessly. "This is not my country, and this is not my fight. My sword is not for hire." Andronicus moved his hand away from the hilt while giving the man a fierce look, and the man suddenly looked uncomfortable under his stern gaze. "Now, I suggest you move aside before your fight does become mine," Andronicus added.

The man gave one last look of anger before releasing the reins and storming off. Andronicus watched him go, looking for others. He noticed several men standing in the crowd, some of them looking around, others looking toward him. He realized how out of place he must look, even with his new haircut. He was dressed in the ragged clothes of a dead bandit that he had been wearing for weeks, and he still had Chaka's claw necklace around his neck, not to mention the tattered red cloak slung over his horse's back. He tugged on his horse's reins and picked up his pace through the crowd.

2

Andronicus marched his horse through the rest of the marketplace without anyone else stopping him. When he was near the city walls, he asked a merchant where he could find the high temple. The man gave him directions, and Andronicus offered him a bronze piece in return. The man looked up in surprise, but Andronicus rode off before the man could thank him.

The ride up to the temple took him past a great stone structure in the shape of a pharaoh that was under construction. Andronicus watched as hundreds of slaves worked slowly through the glaring heat. Soldiers with whips stood by, striking at those who lagged behind. Most of the slaves' faces were dark, and Andronicus knew they came from places he had probably been to, and stayed in. These were the people he had known for years, brought to the modern world for this, to be worked to death.

Andronicus had seen slaves in the Persian army; he had killed more of them than he liked to remember. He had even known some of the Helot slaves back in Sparta. It was hard to call the Helots slaves compared to the poor souls he saw now, killing themselves so a great stone man could be made, and yet a slight chill went up his back as he thought of them. It had been a long time since he had thought of the old burnt woman who had cursed him so long ago. That was before everything, before the cave, and the rocks, and Niko's death. As he remembered that woman, and the other Helots, and the Persian slaves, he pitied them all.

But never in his long life had Andronicus seen people treated so terribly as he did now. As he rode by them, an old dark-skinned man as frail as a leaf fell to the ground, a stone brick twice his size strapped to his back. A split second after his knees hit the dirt, a whip cracked. Blood spurted from the man's arm where the whip struck, and he cried out as he struggled to stand. The soldier shouted at him before striking again. The old man took the lash with a cry and a whimper.

Andronicus jumped down from his horse and grabbed the soldier's hand just before he struck again. The soldier turned around furiously, ready to strike whomever had grabbed him, but stopped when he saw the look on Andronicus's face.

"The old man is doing the best he can," Andronicus said in a stern, commanding voice. "If you continue to strike him, he will die. Then you will have to find another man to take his place, and two jobs will take the time of three." The soldier looked confused, but he lowered his whip. He looked at Andronicus in confusion for a moment before turning back to the old man. He pulled the old man to his feet and pushed him forward. The old man stumbled but stayed upright, wincing with each step. The soldier looked back at Andronicus as if to get his approval, apparently taking him for an authority.

Andronicus waited until the old man was past the soldier's watch before returning to his horse. He hated seeing people in such a state, but knew there was nothing he could do. He had probably done too much already. He needed to stay out of sight and trouble, not go looking for it. Andronicus felt a pang of guilt as he rode away from the slaves, wishing there was more he could do for them.

3

As Andronicus rode up to the city stables, the stable master asked him his business. Andronicus jumped down and told the man he was there to see the great temple and that he might be staying for some time. The stable master told him the price to keep his horse there was one gold piece per week for as long as he wished to stay. Andronicus thanked the man and paid for three weeks in advance. The man brightened right up at the sight of Andronicus's gold and hurriedly helped him with his horse.

Andronicus left the stables and walked the rest of the way to the temple. As he approached the great temple, he had to stop and admire the magnificent architecture. He had heard the Egyptians had built some of the greatest structures and buildings in the world, and now he knew it to be true. He had to wonder how many slaves had been whipped to death building this great temple though, how many had died of thirst, and how many had simply fallen dead from the heat itself. Andronicus climbed the steps two at a time until he reached the entrance. A short, bald man in a pale silk robe came forward with his hands outstretched and a troubled look on his face.

"How may I help you, my lord?" he asked in a high voice, bowing slightly. It was hard to mistake the sardonic tone of the man's voice as he called Andronicus a lord, or the look he gave Andronicus's ragged clothes.

"I'm no lord," Andronicus answered politely. "I'm simply a weary traveler, who seeks an audience with your high priest."

"What, may I ask, is your business with the high priest?" the man asked in a condescending tone. "We do not usually allow 'weary travelers' in to see our high priest."

"My name is Andronicus of Sparta," Andronicus said in his most commanding voice. It felt odd to use his real name after so many years of being Jocus, but that part of him had died with Chaka, and he would have to be Andronicus once again. His voice echoed off the tall stone pillars and reverberated through the hall. "I have traveled across many lands to be here. Now I seek the vast knowledge of your people. I would study at your great library, if you would permit me. Now, if you would please take me to your high priest."

The bald man looked taken aback. He hesitated for a moment, seemingly debating what to do, then nodded and told Andronicus to follow him. He led the way through the temple, passing magnificent statues of stone and gold. There were statues of sphinxes and lions alike. Most of the statues were of men, though not all of them were human. Some of the statued men had the heads of beasts—wolves and eagles. Andronicus supposed it was not so different from the stories his people told of the Minotaur and centaurs, and he wondered again if any such creatures had ever existed or if they were all just stories.

After climbing a tall flight of stairs, the bald man led Andronicus into a large room with a great open balcony and bright billowing curtains. Another man in the same kind of orange silk robes sat at a large stone desk in the middle of the room, leaning over a piece of parchment. The man was older than the first man, probably in his fifties. He was wearing a silk turban, and he had a stern brow over his thoughtful eyes.

The man who had led Andronicus there went to his older counterpart and whispered into his ear. Then he stepped back from the older man and bowed his head.

"So," the old man said in a stern voice without looking up from his parchments, "Herman tells me you wish to learn from us?"

Andronicus bowed his head slightly. "Yes, high priest, I have come far to be here. I would learn your ways, if you would have me."

"There is no need for pretense here. My name is Horus. What is it you seek, my friend?" he asked as he finally looked up from his work. He had a hard face, the kind that would make most men cower in fear, but Andronicus also saw intelligence behind the man's eyes.

"I wish to know your history, your religion," Andronicus said, not lying but not telling the whole truth either.

The old man did not break his piercing gaze. "Yes, but why?" Clearly, the man was not going to take Andronicus in without knowing who he was.

"Your country is as old as mine, older perhaps," Andronicus said. "I have seen the lands west of here, and now I wish to stay here for a time. Your history is as rich as any, and I would like to learn it."

"You're a warrior," Horus said bluntly. It was a statement, not a question. "Not a scholar. Now answer my question. Why are you here? You say you came from the lands west of here, and yet you come by horse, not by sea."

Andronicus had not expected such a fierce inquiry. He had thought he would be able to simply say he wanted to learn, pay them in diamonds, and be left alone. He realized he had probably not chosen the best story to tell.

"I seek answers, high priest," Andronicus said, looking the man in the eye. "Answers you may have in your library. I do come from the lands west of here, I assure you. I crossed the Great Desert."

"You crossed the Great Desert?" the high priest repeated, eying Andronicus carefully. "By yourself?"

"No. I set out with a companion, but we were attacked by raiders, and he was killed."

"And how did you escape these raiders?" Horus asked. "I have never heard of desert raiders leaving anyone alive."

"I killed them," Andronicus said, unconsciously moving his hand toward the hilt of his sword.

"You killed them," Horus repeated, still eyeing Andronicus intently. "How many were there?"

"Eleven," Andronicus answered. "My friend killed four of them." He decided not to tell the priest about the second group of bandits that he had sought out and killed. There was no need, and the man would likely not believe it anyway.

"You killed seven raiders with that sword?"

Andronicus still couldn't tell if the man believed him or not. "Seven clumsy, untrained raiders would never stand a chance against any true Spartan warrior," Andronicus said, holding the man's gaze. The old man stayed silent for a moment as he sized Andronicus up, as if for the first time.

"What are the questions for which you seek answers, lord Spartan?"

"My questions are my own," Andronicus replied, his tone more forceful than he had intended. "Welcome me or turn me away," he continued, lowering his voice, "but leave my motives be. You have my word that I mean no harm to you, your temple, or any man in Egypt."

The priest sat back and thought about this for a time. "And why should we allow a stranger to stay with us and learn our ways?" he asked finally.

"I will pay you," Andronicus replied, reaching into his pouch. "I have diamonds, enough to last a very long time."

"Diamonds, you say?" Horus suddenly looked much more interested. "May I see one?" Andronicus reached into his pouch and brought out one of the smaller stones. Light from the sun was coming through the large window, and it bounced off the stone, making it sparkle and shine. The high priest reached out for the diamond, a thin smile spreading across his face, but Andronicus closed his fist, then put the stone away.

"Very well," the high priest said as he sat back down with a sneer. "You can stay here. Study our teachings, read our books, search for your answers, whatever they may be. The price to stay is one of those diamonds every three months." The priest looked at him as if he expected a protest, but Andronicus was more than happy with the arrangement. If necessary, he had enough to stay there for a hundred years.

Andronicus nodded in agreement, and the priest waved his hand and returned to his work.

Herman quickly emerged from the shadows and ushered him out of the room.

Andronicus followed the bald man through seemingly countless hallways, until he showed Andronicus into a small room in the middle of a dark corridor. The room had a bed on one side and a wooden table and chair on the other with a chamber pot in the corner.

Andronicus thanked Herman, who quickly disappeared down the hallway, leaving Andronicus alone in his new room. He closed the door behind him, marveling at the feeling of privacy. He had not had his own bed to sleep in for a long time, and he went immediately to test it. It was hard and unyielding, but it felt as soft and comfortable as anything he had slept on in years, and within minutes he was asleep in his new home.

That night Andronicus dreamed of a great coliseum, bigger even than the temple. He knew it had to be of Greek making, but he had never heard of such a massive coliseum anywhere in Greece. The many rows of steps going up the sides of the coliseum were covered with thousands of cheering people. He looked around and saw a tall, muscular black man standing not far away with a Greek sword in his hand.

Andronicus ran to him. He didn't care if it was a dream; he just wanted to see Chaka again. He reached out and spun the man around, expecting to see the face of his friend. To his surprise the tall black man was not Chaka but a complete stranger, though he seemed to recognize Andronicus. The tall man pointed and shouted, and Andronicus looked over to see two dozen men charging at them. The rest of the dream was a cloud of blood and death, and Andronicus reveled in it.

4

The next morning Andronicus slept in late; it had been so long since he had a real roof to sleep under. When he finally did wake, he dressed slowly and then went in search of the library. The vast temple's halls twisted and turned, and they all looked alike. The building seemed even bigger from the inside than it looked from without, and again Andronicus was struck by how impressive the Egyptian architecture was.

After walking aimlessly through the halls, Andronicus ran into a priest. Like the others, he was completely bald and wore the same orange-and-brown robes as the rest, but somehow he looked out of place. His face was round and pudgy, and he had small, beady eyes. Andronicus had to stifle a chuckle as he watched the man teeter down the hall. He had a stack of scrolls in his arms, and he appeared to be struggling greatly with keeping them in place.

The priest looked up when he heard Andronicus, gave a start at the sight of him, and the scrolls all came tumbling out of his hands onto the stone floor. The man's face turned bright red, and he quickly started gathering the papers. Andronicus bent down to help him.

"Oh, uh, thank you," the man said in a nervous voice. "Very kind."

"No trouble," Andronicus said casually in his best Egyptian accent. "Do you by chance know where the library is?" Andronicus nodded to the scrolls as he handed the man one of them. "Something tells me you do."

"Oh, well, um, yes, actually I do," the man said in his mousy voice. "It's, um, back that way. Go down this hall, then uh, take the third left, then the second right, then go down that hall until you come to the fifth passage on the left, then, um, go down there."

"Could you just show me," Andronicus suggested. "I don't think I'll be able to find it on my own. I am going to need some time to learn these halls."

"You must be the soldier—I mean the merchant," the priest corrected quickly, staring at Andronicus in fear.

Andronicus let out a chuckle at the frightened look on the man's face. "Relax," he said calmly. "You do not need to fear me, and yes, I am the soldier *and* the merchant. My name is Andronicus. What's yours?"

"I'm Imhotep," the man said, looking down at his feet.

"You haven't been here very long, have you, Imhotep?" Andronicus asked bemusedly.

"Just a month," Imhotep said with a sheepish look on his face.

"Good," Andronicus said as he helped the lad to his feet. "Now how about that library?"

Imhotep showed him the way to the library, though Andronicus guessed he would need to be shown many times before he would remember it all. When they finally arrived, Andronicus was amazed. He had seen the libraries in Sparta, Athens, and Corinth, but they were nothing compared to this. There were more scrolls and papers piled in the tall circular room than Andronicus would have believed existed. He realized as he gazed upon the stacks and stacks of paper that he might be in Egypt for much longer than he had initially thought.

5

Andronicus's first year in the temple of Memphis passed much without incident. He spent most of his days in the library, with Imhotep translating for him at first. Andronicus grew fond of the young man. He was clumsy and probably couldn't fight off a child if he had to, but he was an outcast in the temple, and Andronicus could tell he was a loyal sort.

In his heart Andronicus knew he was using this man. He had found someone who was easy to befriend and who wouldn't leave, because deep down Andronicus was afraid of being alone. The weeks after Chaka's death had been the hardest, loneliest days of his life. He needed someone to keep him from his own thoughts. Imhotep was nervous, mousy, and fat, but he was also helpful. Andronicus didn't know how to read the scrolls, and he needed someone to teach him.

Most of the other priests stayed away from him. Horus would come by every so often, wanting to see what Andronicus was reading and trying to find out what he was searching for. Andronicus would tell him that he was just looking through some old documents, and then the high priest would leave him alone for a time.

Imhotep never asked Andronicus what he was searching for, but he always helped nonetheless. Andronicus could tell the boy had never had a real friend before and was glad for the company. Andronicus didn't necessarily want his only friend in the world to be a fat, scared little man, but he much preferred Imhotep's company to the dark spiral of his own lonesome thoughts. Having Imhotep around to chatter on about nothing distracted him from Chaka's absence, and drowned out his own inner monologue. Inside the temple, Andronicus found a sort of home, amongst the papers and scrolls with his clumsy new friend.

Outside the temple, however, things were far less placid. Tensions were growing between the people of Memphis and their new pharaoh. Andronicus wondered when this Arkos he had heard of would attack. He knew that when the day came, his place would be here, watching over the books and the priests. The priests had been good to him, or had at least been accommodating, and he would do his part to help them if needed.

Andronicus cared not at all for the pharaoh of Egypt. The Persians had lost control of Egypt some fifteen years earlier. Whether Psammuthes or Hakor ruled didn't matter to him; they were just names. He only cared that the temple and the library remained unharmed and that his agreement with the high priest continued. When the fighting ended, the slaves would still be slaves, and the lords would still be lords. Neither ruler was offering any plans to conquer foreign lands or advance the empire. It was a simple game of who got to be number one, and Andronicus wanted no part in it. Neither man was a true ruler in his eyes.

6

In the eleventh month after Andronicus had moved into the temple, the revolution finally came. At first he watched from a high window along with Imhotep and some of the other priests as Arkos's men stormed the streets and then the palace. Fires raged in the distance, and screams rang throughout the city. Andronicus heard a shout from below and looked down to see a group of armed men climbing the temple steps. He knew the soldiers would leave neither the priests nor the library untouched.

Andronicus ran to his room and grabbed his sword, then ran to the temple entrance, hoping he was not too late. When he reached the large entrance hall, he found the pharaoh's guards already slain, along with Herman.

When the rebel soldiers saw Andronicus, they rushed forward, forming a circle around him, their swords outstretched. Andronicus held his own sword firmly as he waited for them to attack.

"This temple is a sacred place!" Andronicus shouted. Many of the priests cowered in the corner, helpless. "The priests here will take no part in this war. Leave now!" Andronicus glared at the men with fire in his eyes, daring them to challenge him. It had been more than a year since the desert, and he had gotten himself back in shape in that time, and was once again his usual imposing force.

"Who are you?" a tall man with a large chest asked, stepping forward. "You're no Egyptian. What are you doing here?"

"I'm a guest of the high priest," Andronicus said. "He has allowed me to stay here and study."

"Well I'm revoking your rights to our lands," the man said with a sneer. "You should have hidden with the rest of the cowards here. Now we have to kill you."

"No," Andronicus said, glaring at the man. "Now I have to kill you."

Andronicus raised his sword, and the eight men surrounding him did the same. There was a tense moment of silence as Andronicus faced down the men he was about to kill. He held his sword at just the right angle to see the reflection of the men behind him. He hadn't fought since the night Chaka died, but he felt ready. He could feel his heart racing and the old fire pumping through his veins. He took a deep, steady breath as he stared into the eyes of the men before him.

Finally, a man standing behind Andronicus stepped forward and raised his sword to attack. Andronicus spun around, and his blade slashed across the man's chest before he knew what had happened, spraying blood across the white marble floor. The man cried out as two more of his comrades lunged. Andronicus deflected their blows with ease, then plunged his sword through one of their chests. Two more men stepped forward as Andronicus wrenched his sword free, and then his sword was clashing against five others.

The great hall was filled with the echoes of clanging metal and the grunts and cries of the men as Andronicus cut them down one by one. It had been longer than he cared to think about since his training in battle, but it came back to him like it was yesterday. The rebel soldiers outnumbered him eight to one, and yet they were overmatched from the very start. Andronicus pressed forward, slashing through them with carnal delight. They fell one by one as Andronicus slashed and stabbed them with his sword, feeling the warm spray of blood on his arms and face.

When only three men were left, they dropped their swords and ran for the door. Andronicus grabbed a sword and threw it at the nearest man. Before he hit the ground, Andronicus threw another sword, hitting another man square in the back and sending him sliding across the blood-covered marble.

The final man reached the door and bolted down the steps, taking them four at a time. Andronicus ran after him, picked up a spear from one of the dead door guards, and let it fly. It flew straight and true, whistling through the air until it pierced the man's back, sending him tumbling down the final few steps.

When Andronicus returned to the great hall, some of the priests rushed forward and thanked him profusely. The rest shied away from him like he was a monster, unable even to look at him. Andronicus nodded curtly to the men around him and then brushed them away. They were looking at him like he was some sort of prophet. The others regarded him as if he were one of their hound-headed demons come to life. It reminded him of the way the Swihmehe had looked at him after he had killed the Swihmacha, and he hated it.

"You killed them all by yourself," Horus said, in awe as he approached Andronicus. "How?"

"I told you," Andronicus said, trying not to look like the monster he felt like, "ten clumsy, untrained men are no match for a true Spartan warrior."

"You are too humble, sir," Horus replied. "Those were not clumsy, untrained men. They killed our guards, all six of them. Those men were trained mercenaries."

"Still no match for a true Spartan warrior," Andronicus insisted.

"No match for you maybe," Horus said. "I don't believe that any man trained to fight in Sparta could have done that. I don't believe there are many men alive who could have come out of that unscathed, as you have."

"I've been fighting for a long time," Andronicus sighed, accepting a cloth from one of the priests and wiping the blood from his face. "But I suppose I have always excelled at killing."

"You become more intriguing by the day, Andronicus," Horus said, bowing his head. "You're welcome here for as long as you wish, free of charge. We will not forget what you have done for us this day."

Horus turned to the other priests and began shouting commands. They quickly went about removing the bodies. Andronicus stayed by the entrance, ready to fight whoever else came looking for trouble, but no one did. When the fighting was all ended, they kept waiting for someone to come looking for the men Andronicus had killed. Well after dark, Andronicus decided he could go and rest and leave someone else on watch for a while.

The next day, when the revolt was over, and all the fires were put out, a troupe of one hundred soldiers came marching up to the temple. Andronicus knew he couldn't fight that many, and he had to hope that Horus could take care of it this time. Horus spoke with the commander for some time before the host turned around and left. Andronicus later discovered that Horus paid the man with bricks of gold and the diamonds Andronicus had given him over the last year. When the soldiers left, Andronicus and the priests went back inside. For weeks afterwards everyone in the temple was ready for another attack, but it never came.

7

After saving the priests from an unknown fate at the hands of the revolutionaries, Andronicus became something of a hero around the temple. Where before most of the priests wouldn't look at him or acknowledge him, now they all greeted him right away, and more importantly, they were most willing to help him find his way through the massive ancient library.

He had spent most of his first year in the library just trying to learn how to read Egyptian. He had never learned to read before, not even in Greece, and hadn't realized how difficult it was. When he had lived in Sparta, reading had not seemed important. Euthymius had learned to read when he was still a boy, but Andronicus had never tried. Now he struggled greatly trying to learn how to read a foreign language. He had learned to speak more than a dozen languages in his travels, including Egyptian, but reading was a very different sort of thing.

Andronicus could remember nearly everything about fighting and the animals of the plains and jungles. He could remember the faces of people he knew decades ago. He could remember the stories he heard as a boy about gods, heroes, and monsters. He had always had a good memory, but none of that helped him remember the sounds all the little shapes and symbols meant. There seemed to be a thousand different shapes on the pages, and he had to learn them all.

Most of the time he had Imhotep read for him while he followed along, trying to learn as they went.

Imhotep still had no idea what Andronicus was looking for, but he always read whatever he was asked without question. Mostly they read old histories of Egypt. It was a fascinating place, and they both enjoyed the old stories, but they gave Andronicus none of the answers he was searching for.

8

A year after Psammuthes overthrew Hakor and named himself pharaoh of Egypt, Hakor retook the throne. The second revolution was far shorter and less bloody than the first. Psammuthes had not been kind to the people in his single year in power, and they quickly rose to help Hakor regain his title.

When the scant fighting ended, a small group of soldiers came to the temple and met with Horus. They asked for nothing, simply checking to make sure everyone was unharmed. As quick as that, the second revolution was over for Andronicus and the priests.

9

With the Egyptians leadership struggles over, things went back to normal, and Andronicus got back to work. The temple bustled with people every day, but he ignored them. He spent nearly all of his time in the library, slowly learning to read, first Egyptian and then Greek. It took him years, but eventually, he was able to read every word of the old texts on his own. Imhotep still sat and read with him most of the time, even though he still didn't know what he was supposed to be looking for.

In truth Andronicus didn't know what he was looking for either. He told himself he would know it when he saw it, but he knew that probably wasn't true. The answers he wanted wouldn't be written down on some ancient scroll. They were out in the world somewhere. In his heart he knew he should not be shut away in a stone building. He should be out in the world, roaming the lands as he had done for so many years. Instead he stayed inside, reading and talking and telling himself he was searching for answers.

The one thing he hoped for was to read of

someone else who had been through what he had. Of course, no one would write the full truth. It would be madness to write that they had touched a glowing rock and awoken in a strange land and then ceased to age altogether, but he still hoped to find some part of the truth somewhere in all the old scrolls.

He searched for years, finding no sign of the rocks, or ageless men. What he did find were histories mostly, though there were hundreds of other works as well. Works about medicine, military strategies, religion, and history. There were even dozens of scrolls about astronomy and mathematics, things Andronicus had thought only the Greeks knew about.

The years of peace and stasis were not terribly unkind to him. He enjoyed reading, and he found it comfortable after traveling for so long. It gave him a sense of peace and a feeling of connection to the past. After so many years of knowing nothing, to have the world's largest source of knowledge at his disposal was a bit overwhelming. But Andronicus found a deep comfort in the knowledge of others and remained confident that he would find some scrap of information somewhere in the seemingly endless library.

When he wasn't reading, he ran through the streets to keep himself in shape, and practiced with and sharpened his sword. Aside from that he walked through the city quite often, observing the people. He always made sure to stay away from where the slaves were working, knowing he would only get himself into trouble. It was nice to be in a city rather than a village or a town. Memphis was one of the oldest and largest cities in the known world, and Andronicus walked every street, taking it all in over the years.

Chapter 30
The Marks of Time
1

Andronicus awoke on November tenth, 380 bc, and went about his usual routine. He had grown very comfortable in his life in Egypt, though he could see trouble on the horizon. After washing and dressing, he left his room and headed to the library. When he arrived he found Imhotep already reading a dusty old piece of paper.

Imhotep looked up as Andronicus entered the room and broke into a big grin. Imhotep had grown fatter and balder over the years. He actually was bald, unlike most of the priests who shaved their heads every day. He stood up with a grunt as Andronicus approached.

"Hello Im," Andronicus said casually. "What have we got today?"

"This is a scroll from 2982," Imhotep said excitedly, pointing to a frail, old scroll. "I believe it's the chronicles of a man who travelled through Persia."

"Very good," Andronicus said, taking the scroll delicately. "And what are you reading?"

"An old manual on farming," Imhotep answered, sitting across from Andronicus. Andronicus nodded, trying to feign interest. There was nothing more boring than manuals, especially about farming. Imhotep returned his smile eagerly, and Andronicus turned to the scroll before Imhotep could start telling him about farming.

He read the scroll without much interest at first. The man who had written it had not been a poet by any stretch of the imagination. The chronicles were simple and precise, more like a ledger than a journal. The man had gone from one village to the next, much as Andronicus had done for many years. Andronicus was barely paying attention as he read when he suddenly stopped short. As he reread the passage, he felt his heart quicken.

"Imhotep," he said, trying to keep his voice steady, "take a look at this." He turned the scroll around and showed it to Imhotep. "Have you ever seen a symbol like that before? Like he describes here?"

"I don't think so," Imhotep said, scrutinizing the text. "It's certainly not Egyptian. And it's not Persian either. What is it?" Imhotep looked up at Andronicus, his curiosity quickly turning to concern. "Andronicus, are you alright?"

Andronicus had to grab hold of the table to

steady himself. The whole world had begun to spin, and his ears filled with a ringing sound. For a moment he thought he might faint, and then it began to pass. Imhotep ran for some water, and by the time he returned, Andronicus was feeling fine again.

He returned his attention to the scroll, staring at the symbol. He had thought for years that when he found what he was looking for he would know it when he saw it, but he had not expected it to hit him like that. Looking down at the symbol, he felt chills go through his whole body, making the hairs on his neck and arms rise.

"What is it?" Imhotep asked anxiously. "What does it mean?"

"I don't know what it means," Andronicus said, "but I think this is what I've been looking for all this time."

2

"Andronicus, what's going on?" Imhotep asked in a worried voice as Andronicus ushered him into his room. "What was on that page?"

"Sit down, Im," Andronicus said as he shut the door. "I need to tell you a story that I should have told you a long time ago."

"What story?" Imhotep asked, sounding more curious than frightened now.

"My story," Andronicus said, and then he began. He started at the beginning, when he was a boy. He told Imhotep about his friends and the battles they had fought in. He also told him about the mission he had been sent on, about the curse the burnt woman had put on them, and how things had started going wrong. He paused for a moment when he got to the point in the story where Niko died, and then he carried on.

When he got to the storm, he told Imhotep the whole story in great detail, including the way Androcles had seemed to know about the cave and the way it had pulled them in. When he got to the part about the cave itself, he had to stop again, his heart racing.

He told Imhotep about the glowing rocks and

the visions, which he could barely remember. Then he told him what had happened next. He watched Imhotep's face go from interest to confusion as he told him about waking up in Swimha. It took a while, but eventually he was able to get Imhotep to understand the story, though Andronicus didn't think he believed it.

Imhotep sat silently through the entire tale, through the plains, and the jungle, and the plains once again. Andronicus tried not to leave anything out. He realized how hard it was to properly tell a story that lasted a hundred years without taking forever.

When he got to the desert, he had to stop again. He waited a long time, fighting back tears. Imhotep never said a word; he just sat there waiting for Andronicus to continue. Finally, Andronicus told him about being ambushed by raiders in the desert and about Chaka's death. After that it was a quick jump to the present.

When he was done telling his life's story for the first time in fifty years, he looked at Imhotep, awaiting a response.

"So, how old are you?" Imhotep asked after a long moment of silence.

Andronicus smiled. "I'm one hundred and sixteen years old." He couldn't help but wince as he said the words. He waited for Imhotep to laugh or call him a liar, but he just sat there, deep in thought.

"I've known you for fourteen years," Imhotep said after a long silence, not looking at Andronicus. "If you had seen me all those years ago and not a day since, you probably would not recognize me. But you still look exactly the same as you did the day I met you." Imhotep looked up at him. "You say you're one hundred and sixteen years old. Well, I think I believe you."

Andronicus couldn't believe it; it had taken him years to convince Chaka it was all true, but Imhotep had accepted it on the first telling.

"You believe me?" Andronicus asked, sounding both shocked and relieved.

Imhotep nodded, a grave look on his face. "But

you still have not told me what happened this morning. What was in that scroll?"

"Oh, right." Andronicus suddenly remembered why he was telling his story in the first place. "The symbol. You remember the cave I told you about? The one with the rocks in it?"

"You mean the cave where there are magical rocks that make you live forever and can send you from Persia to Africa in a split second?" Imhotep said sarcastically. "I think I remember you saying something about it, yes."

"Right," Andronicus said, frowning at him, "well, that symbol was carved into the wall in that cave. It was the only thing there besides the pool with the rocks. Someone had carved it into the wall, probably with a knife. It was deep, and it must have taken some time. I don't think my friends or my brother even noticed it, just me."

"So someone was there before you," Imhotep said thoughtfully, "which means they must have touched the stones as well."

"I suppose they must have," Andronicus agreed. He had pondered that thought more than he could say.

"I wonder how old they are," Imhotep mused with a longing look in his eye. Andronicus had spent countless nights asking the same question, and a thousand others.

"I don't know," Andronicus said, "I suppose they could be thousands of years old. I have no idea how any of it works."

"Well, what does that scroll mean?" Imhotep asked excitedly. "The page with the symbol from the cave, what else did it say?"

Andronicus shrugged. "I don't know. I stopped reading as soon as I saw the mark."

"Well what on earth are we waiting for?" Imhotep asked, getting to his feet.

They walked back to the library in silence, finding the scroll right where they had left it. Andronicus picked it up even more gingerly than before, and held it up to the light. The symbol stared up at him like an eye watching its prey. He felt chills go down his back again and wondered for the millionth time what the symbol meant.

3

Crasseth, 2982, Euphrates River.

The river continues flowing north to south. I believe it will take me at least another two years to reach the end of it. The villages here are primitive. The people would make fine slaves for the pharaoh.

The river has gotten wider. The people living along the shores here are fishermen as well as hunters. They would make fine slaves for the pharaoh.

I met an old man. He had light skin, like the Greeks. He had strange black marks upon his skin, written in ink as black as a crow upon each of his forearms. He had many goods to trade. He had silk and skins as well as gold and gems. The man asked me what year it was. He also asked me which way to the city of Troy. I told him I have never heard of Troy. He thanked me and left. He was a very strange man.

The river turns east now. The villages are still small, and the people primitive. The people here would make fine slaves for the pharaoh.

4

Andronicus put the scroll down with delicate hands. An old man with light skin and marks on his arms. Andronicus wondered if the old man could still be alive 2,602 years later. If he could find that old man, he would surely have the answers Andronicus was after, at least some of them.

He looked up at Imhotep, who was sitting silently across from him, waiting for Andronicus to tell him what it meant. Andronicus handed the scroll over carefully and let Imhotep read it for himself. When he was done, he gave Andronicus a curious look.

"This old man," Imhotep said thoughtfully, "you think he's the one who carved the mark on the wall?"

"He has to be," Andronicus said, trying to will it to be true. "We've read more scrolls in this place than the rest of the priests combined, and we've never seen this mark before. Now it shows up in a simple chronicle of a slaver, on the arms of an old man. It can't be a coincidence."

"Perhaps it's the mark of a people," Imhotep suggested, "and the old man and the man from the cave were simply from the same place."

"Why would a man have taken the time to carve the symbol of his people on the wall?" Andronicus asked. "It can't be that simple. The mark means something." He looked at Imhotep earnestly, waiting for him to argue. Imhotep sighed and set the scroll down. Andronicus could tell he wasn't convinced.

"It says the man was going to Troy," Andronicus said, still trying to convince Imhotep. "The old man asked for the city of Troy."

"What of it?" Imhotep asked. "Troy fell to Agamemnon in 1184, did it not?"

"Actually, it fell to Odysseus," Andronicus said, "but that doesn't matter. The cave wasn't far from the ruins of Troy."

"What are you getting at?" Imhotep asked.

"The old man had the mark on his arms, he was searching for Troy, which, by the way, was barely even a city in 2982, and the only other place the mark has ever shown up is on the wall of the cave a few weeks' walk from Troy. He must have been the one to carve the mark."

Imhotep sat thoughtfully for a while, rubbing his hand over his chin. "I suppose you have a point," he said finally, "for the mark to show up like that, so close to Troy, and the old man asking for Troy. You make a fine case, Andronicus. I'm convinced. The old man must have been in the cave. But that still doesn't tell us what it means or where he might be, if he's even still alive, which, of course, should be impossible.

"It doesn't matter," Andronicus said with a wan smile. "At least now I know what to look for. I had forgotten all about the mark on the wall; I've not thought of it in years. Now at least I have something to look for in all these old scrolls."

5

When Andronicus got back to his room, his mind was racing. He hadn't thought of that symbol in a very long time, and yet there was still something oddly familiar about it. He sat there thinking hard about where he had seen it before, and then a strange idea occurred to him. Andronicus went to the corner of his room, took out his cloak, and brought out the wooden box. He stared at the odd symbol carved into the box and felt chills again.

The symbol was not the same, but there were definite similarities. It looked as though the two marks could be from the same language. Andronicus could only shake his head in disbelief, wondering how the Perpauca had gotten the box. He had always suspected they had not made it themselves, seeing as they had nothing else that resembled its craftsmanship. Now it seemed all but certain that they had been given the box, and whoever had given it to them was the person that Andronicus needed to find.

He thought again about the description of the mysterious old man and wondered if he had traveled through the Great Jungle as well. Now that Andronicus had been studying for years, he knew that the Great Jungle was named the Congo, and it was believed to be the biggest jungle in the world. If this mysterious stranger was hundreds or even thousands of years old, then it was likely he would have crossed the jungle as well. Andronicus had more questions than ever. He couldn't fall asleep at all that night, his mind so full of new possibilities.

6

Andronicus continued searching through the library for any other record of the symbol, to no avail. He and Imhotep spent years sifting through the shelves looking for old histories of Troy and the neighboring towns and cities. They read every day, always hoping to see the symbol again but never finding it.

Eight years after Andronicus had found the symbol on the scroll, he knew it was well past time to leave. The questions about him had begun years before, whispers of the man who didn't age. The old priests, the ones who had been there as long as Andronicus, remembered what he had done for them during the revolt. They also remembered what he had looked like back then. It wasn't hard to forget, as he looked exactly the same, twenty-four years later.

The younger priests had begun calling him a sorcerer, and he feared they would soon confront him about it. Every day when he went to the library he saw one or two priests who seemed out of place, the sort who normally wouldn't be there. Andronicus didn't know how long they had been watching him, but once he caught on, he knew he had to leave.

If not for Imhotep, he would probably have gone long ago. Imhotep had become a true friend. He wasn't like Chaka, strong and sturdy, a great warrior, and ever dependable. Imhotep was fat and clumsy, and scared as a mouse, but he was dependable in his own way, always present and always ready to help.

Andronicus thought about taking Imhotep with him, but he knew it wouldn't work. Chaka had been well suited to life on the move, walking all day, sleeping under the stars, and having to fight from time to time. Andronicus didn't think Imhotep would be able to handle any of that, but he wasn't ready to say goodbye to his friend, and he didn't want to be alone.

Eventually, the time came when he knew it had to be done. Everywhere he went, eyes followed him. When he walked the halls, he heard hurried footsteps behind him. Horus had died four years earlier, and ever since, the new high priest had grown increasingly suspicious of Andronicus. Now he had people following him and watching him.

7

On the day Andronicus meant to leave, he went about his daily routine as if nothing were different. When he arrived in the library, he noticed two priests sitting nearby, clearly waiting to spy on him, but he ignored them. Imhotep was seated at his normal place, a pile of old scrolls next to him. He looked up as Andronicus came over and handed him a scroll.

"This is from a merchant sailor who traveled to Troy around 1468," Imhotep said. Andronicus nodded silently and took the scroll. He began reading, though he didn't take in a single word, his mind fixed on his departure. He knew it would be hard to leave with the priests watching him, but he felt his many years of experience would get him out safely. After a few hours, the spies both looked like they were going to fall asleep, neither one paying attention to them.

"Imhotep," Andronicus whispered, his eyes on one of the spies, who was nodding off.

"Hmm . . .?" Imhotep said without looking up from his scroll.

"I'm leaving tonight," Andronicus said. Imhotep's head snapped up, and his eyes went wide. Andronicus could see the fear on his face.

"What are you talking about?" he whispered, clearly trying not to panic.

"They're on to me Im," Andronicus said, looking at the spy again. "They have been for a while. I've been a fool to stay this long. They've begun to call me a sorcerer."

"They're just scared is all," Imhotep said. "They think you're some kind of immortal or something, that's all."

"They're right," Andronicus whispered. "I am immortal, Im. I'm one hundred and twenty-four years old. I would rather not answer the questions they clearly mean to ask me."

"Then let me come with you," Imhotep whispered, looking truly fearful.

"You know I can't," Andronicus said sadly. "Where I'm going I will have to fight and kill. And besides that, I'll be walking from dawn to dusk every day. You wouldn't be able to keep up. You'll be fine here. The priests respect you now. I only hope your friendship with me will not affect anything."

"So that's it, then," Imhotep said in disbelief. "Just like that, you're leaving."

"I have to, Im, I've already stayed here far too long. I've not aged a day in nearly one hundred years. Someday you're going to die of old age, as will every priest here, and I'll still be thirty. For a long time I wasn't convinced, but once I turned one hundred and still felt as strong as ever, I knew. I'm not going to die, at least not by old age. So, I have to search. I've searched for answers here for as long as I could, but there are other libraries. You've been a good friend, Imhotep, a loyal friend. I wish you good health and fortune."

Andronicus stood, and Imhotep looked up at him with tears welling in his eyes. Andronicus gave the bald man a curt nod and then turned away, walking out of the library without looking back. He couldn't bear to see Imhotep's crestfallen face.

8

Andronicus waited until the middle of the night to leave. He had packed his things in a rucksack he had purchased in the city. He hid the bag of diamonds and the box of poisons inside his old Spartan cloak and rested Chaka's old necklace on top. He also took the scroll with the mark on it; he didn't know what he meant to do with it, but he thought he should take it with him. The last thing he did was strap his sword to his side. It had been a long time since he had used the blade, but he had kept it sharp.

He slipped out of his room, making sure not to let the door creak, and peered into the hallway. As he had feared, a man was sitting on a wooden stool at the far end of the darkened hall. He knew the man was stationed there to watch him. He also knew the man probably wasn't a priest.

Andronicus waited until he was sure the man wasn't looking before he moved. The guard wasn't asleep, but he was nodding off, bobbing his head up and down every few seconds. Andronicus had packed his sandals in his bag, and he crept down the hall on bare feet, his sword already drawn.

Just as he came up to the guard, the man looked up in surprise. He opened his mouth, but before the man could shout, Andronicus brought the butt end of his sword down hard on the man's head, knocking him unconscious.

Andronicus hurried to the front entrance. At first he had hated these halls, with their seemingly endless turns and passages. It had taken him years to stop getting lost in them, but years he had spent, two dozen of them, and now he knew the way like the back of his hand.

Within minutes he was crouched behind an old statue looking out at the temple's front gate. Four men were standing guard, each with a spear in his hand, and none of them looked very sleepy. Andronicus knew there was no other way out, and that the guards had almost surely been told not to let him leave.

He stayed behind the statue trying to think of a way to escape without having to kill the guards. His time in Egypt was done, but the priests had always been good to him, and he had no desire to kill men needlessly. He thought about paying them off, but that wouldn't work either. As soon as the priests discovered he was missing, the guards would be killed anyway. In the end he knew there was no other way; he would have to kill them.

He sheathed his sword and opened his pack, taking out the old bronze knife he had made in Africa. It had lost its shine over the years, but the blade was still sharp to the touch. He slid out from behind the statue and tiptoed toward the gate.

As quick and as quiet as a jungle cat, Andronicus grabbed the guard's head and slit his throat. Before the guard fell, Andronicus was already onto the next one. His knife flashed in the moonlight as it flicked across the man's neck.

The other two guards turned around as the first guard hit the ground with a clash of metal. Andronicus drew his sword, and charged the one on his left. The guard looked stunned as he watched his comrades fall to the ground, blood gushing from their necks. He only managed to get his hand to the hilt of his sword before Andronicus's sword plunged through his chest.

The final guard started shouting for help. He was more than twenty feet away, so rather than charge the man, Andronicus simply threw his knife. The knife flung through the air like a shining star, whirring as it went, until it sank itself deep into the man's chest, bringing his shouting to an abrupt halt.

Andronicus heard alarm bells ringing in the distance and voices shouting from within the temple, and he knew he had only seconds. He pulled the knife free from the dying guard, who let out a sickening cough, spraying blood across Andronicus's face. Andronicus plunged the knife into the man's heart, ending his suffering, and then he ran.

Once the temple was behind him, he slowed to a fast walk, trying to avoid any soldiers. He had been planning his escape for weeks, and he knew the best way out of the city. Bells continued to ring. The streets were empty, but he heard people running somewhere close by as he made his way to his chosen gate on the east side of the city.

When he arrived, he found a half dozen armed men standing guard. Andronicus knelt behind a barrel in an alley across from the gate and watched. Two more guards walked by, and Andronicus waited restlessly for them to return. More bells were ringing throughout the city, and he knew he didn't have long.

A minute later the two guards went walking by in the other direction. Andronicus snuck out from behind the barrel and crept through the alleys, moving around the two patrolmen.

He crept to the end of another alley just next to where the two guards would be walking. When he heard them approaching, Andronicus drew his sword. He waited until their footsteps were nearly upon him, and then he leapt out and swung his sword before either of them could react. His swing caught one of the guards just above the neck and sank deep into the man's face. Andronicus tried to pull his sword free, but the blade was embedded in the guard's skull.

The second guard let out a frightened shout as he registered what had just happened. He drew his sword and stepped toward Andronicus with a scared but determined look on his face. Andronicus released his sword and pulled out his knife. The man took a wide arching swing at Andronicus, but he ducked the blow, stepped toward the man, and sank the knife deep into his neck. The guard's eyes went wide as he fell to his knees, choking on his own blood.

Andronicus pulled out the blade and shoved it into his belt, then bent down to get his sword. He had to use his foot and both hands to wrench it free. Then he sheathed it and made his way back to his first hiding spot, across from the gate. When he got there, all six of the guards were still standing their post. For a moment Andronicus thought his plan wouldn't work, that he would just bring more soldiers down on top of him and get himself trapped.

One of the guards turned to the others, and they began speaking. A moment later that guard shouted to the others, and then he and two others left in the direction of their dead comrades. Andronicus waited until the three men were out of earshot and then rushed out to fight the remaining three. They saw him before he got to them and drew their swords.

"Halt!" one of the men shouted. "This gate is guarded on the orders of—"

Before he could finish, Andronicus swung his sword at the man. He blocked Andronicus's blow, but Andronicus threw another, faster this time. It caught the man under the arm, and he took a wobbling step backward as one of his companions charged. While Andronicus engaged the second man, the third man shouted for help. Andronicus dueled with the guard until the man took a wrong step, and Andronicus shoved his sword through the man's heart.

Andronicus pulled his sword free and turned to the last guard. He dropped his sword, held his trembling hands up, and began to sob.

"Please," the man begged, his legs shaking

with fear. "Please, you don't have to kill me."

"Get out of here!" Andronicus shouted. "You never saw me."

The man turned and fled. Andronicus heard shouts not far away, and he knew the rest of the guards would be on him soon. He ran out the gate and into the open land. When he was far enough from the city walls, he turned back and took one final look at the ancient city of Memphis, which he had called home for so long now. It looked huge and sturdy, like something that had stood the test of time. Somehow Andronicus knew he would see it again someday.

Chapter 31
On the Road Again
1

Andronicus walked for hours, until the city was well out of sight. He found a shadowy spot hidden beneath a cluster of rocks and crawled under it to sleep for the night. It felt odd sleeping in the dirt again after having a bed and a roof over his head for the past two and a half decades, but it also felt familiar. He had spent more than half his life sleeping in dirt and mud and sand, but that didn't make the rock any softer. He spread his old cloak beneath him. It had been a long time since he had slept on it, and it felt like home.

As Andronicus lay there and looked up at the stars, he reflected on his many years in Egypt. He had learned more than he could have ever hoped when he arrived at the city. He had always known how to fight and how to survive, but he had never given any thought to learning about anything that didn't involve survival. In the library of Memphis, he had learned so much more than he could have ever imagined. Had he known just how much a man could learn from reading, he would have mastered the skill back in Greece.

By reading books and discussing with the priests, Andronicus had learned about all manner of things. He had known fighting since he was a boy, but now he knew about tactics, and strategy, not just how to kill a man. He learned how to achieve victory in war, not just battle. In Greece he had not been privy to politics, and in Africa politics were overly simple, but Andronicus had learned much about politics in the library, the politics of the Egyptians, the Greeks, and the Persians. He found that he didn't care much for politics though.

What he liked best were the histories. The old stories of the pharaohs of Egypt, of the great Greek legends he had heard of growing up, of the Hebrew prophet Moses, who led his people out of Egypt and slavery and brought them back to their homeland. Andronicus found all the histories enthralling. He supposed that was because he himself was now part of history. He had fought in a great Greek war that had happened more than a hundred years ago. He had been considered a hero of that war, and now it was taught to children as something that happened long ago.

He wondered if he would ever see the city of Memphis and the great temple again, and figured he probably would. When he arrived in Egypt, he had been a ninety-eight-year-old man, still fit as an ox, wondering when he would drop dead of old age despite his appearance. Now he was 124. He had been the oldest man he had ever heard of for the past twenty years and had no reason to think he would not continue to stay young.

It gave him a sort of peace to know he had all the time in the world, literally. It was why he had stayed in Egypt for so long. He had thought often about where to go next and had decided to make his way around the Mediterranean, then walk across what was now called Macedonia, and make his way back into Greece from the north. It was well past time that he returned to his homeland.

He wondered what Greece would be like. It had been nearly a full century since he had last seen it. He knew there would be almost no chance of anyone he had known still being alive. The only way would be if one of the others had found their way home as well and was waiting for him there, but that didn't seem very likely. It was much more likely that one or all of them had already died.

Andronicus had come close to dying many times since awakening in Swimha. If not for Chaka, he surely would have died long ago. He wondered if the others had found someone to help them as he had, someone to keep them safe and sane. He had no doubt he would not have been able to cross the Great Jungle alone. If not for Chaka, he likely would have lost his mind there. He knew Chaka had stopped growing old at some point during their travels, and he wondered if any of the others had seen the same thing with someone, wherever they were. It was frustrating still not having any real answers.

Being back in the wilderness, away from people and buildings and without a roof over his head, Andronicus found himself right where he had been before he came to Egypt. He had spent more than twenty years in that temple, and while he had learned a great many things, the only thing he had really found in regards to his situation was the mention of a symbol he thought he recognized, that was over two thousand years old. It all felt like a giant waste of time, but he just reminded himself that he had all the time in the world to waste.

That first night he went to sleep wondering about the future, and he dreamed the old dreams for the first time in many years. He dreamed of sky-high mountains and stormy seas, of armies he had never seen before, and of battles big and small. He dreamed of cities he had never been to but which he knew he would see one day. He dreamed of strange and foreign things, buildings and people and animals the likes of which he had never come across in his travels or his studies. He reveled in the dreams, even though they still frightened him, but he had not seen the sights for so long, and even though they were all things he hadn't even seen yet, they felt like being back in touch with a part of himself that he had lost for a time.

2

Making his way out of Egypt took longer than Andronicus anticipated. His violent departure from

Memphis had not gone unnoticed. Several times a day, he needed to quickly leave the road and hide from groups of soldiers as they galloped by, presumably looking for him. He could only imagine what they were saying about him back in the city. Everyone would be talking about the ageless man who had fled the great temple and killed a dozen guards to escape. He was lucky the road was straight and flat; otherwise one of the raiding parties would surely have caught him unawares.

Other than the soldiers and the occasional merchant, the road was empty, more of a path carved through the desert than a road. He would have left it and traveled by sun and stars, as he had done for so many years, except for the merchants. They sat atop wagons with oxen or mules pulling them along, and their wagons were always filled with salted meats, fresh grain and bread, and fine wines from the east.

Andronicus bought wine from every merchant he met. Whenever he saw a cart approach, he would take out a gold piece and hold it up before they could try and run. In the end they would barter with him, even though many of them knew he was the one the soldiers were searching for. They would always accept his gold in exchange for their finest wines and meats.

In Sparta Andronicus had never noticed the difference between different wines; they had all been the same to him. The Egyptians, however, had given him a taste for the decadent, although he would still drink whatever he could get. His small pouch of diamonds was still full. He also had two heavy sacks full of gold, so paying the merchants was never a problem.

In Memphis he only drank occasionally at night, always staying clear headed to read during the day. Now back on the road, with copious amounts of wine and no one to talk to, Andronicus began drinking earlier and earlier in the day, until he would awake to a drink. He told himself he was doing it to stave off boredom, but he knew that wasn't true. The wine was the only way to escape the drowning loneliness of traveling alone without Chaka beside him.

3

Eventually, Andronicus reached the land of the Israelites. He had heard about these people and read nearly all of their histories in Egypt, but he had never actually met any of them. The road continued east into the Persian Empire, but Andronicus turned north, into the hills.

He had purchased a horse a few weeks before from an old man who had been driving a small cart with four horses. Andronicus had given him a small diamond, and the old man had dropped to his knees to thank him, then offered him the largest of the lot.

The horse was tall, lean, and strong. He had a shiny brown pelt except for a white line that ran from his eyes down his snout.

His first day with the horse had been difficult and frustrating. The horse was restless and hard to manage, the polar opposite of his last horse in Egypt. When that horse died Andronicus had not mourned him. He had not ridden the beast in years, and it meant he could stop paying the stable master. Now he missed that calm old horse very much.

Day by day, however, Andronicus and his new steed grew more accustomed to each other. It was only a beast, but Andronicus was glad for the company. It was also much easier to drink the day away atop a horse than it was on foot. Riding into the land of Israel Andronicus drank more and more. The horse didn't seem to mind, and it always managed to go the right way, even when Andronicus was passed out on its back.

4

Andronicus finally found the Hebrews, or at least some of them. He was riding his horse over the crest of a tall, rocky hill. When he reached the top and looked down into the valley, he saw a village in the shadow of a mountain. He made his way down the mountain, and when he reached the bottom, three men came out to greet him.

None of them were armed, but they were all

large and fearsome looking, with bushy black beards and dirty brown robes. The one in the middle held out his hands to Andronicus.

"I am Yaakov. What brings you to our village?" the man asked in Hebrew. Andronicus had learned most of the language with Imhotep and was able to understand the man well. He could read Hebrew, and he could understand it, but he had only ever tried to speak it to Imhotep, so he knew his accent would be terrible.

"My name is Jocus," Andronicus said, not sure why he had given the man his Swihmehe name. "I am making my way north, to my homeland." He knew he had a terrible accent, but the men looked like they understood him. "If you have any food you can spare, I have gold."

"How do you know our language?" the man on the left asked curiously.

"I spent many years in Egypt, and I read much about your people," Andronicus explained.

"You are Egyptian!" the man on the right shouted. "You are not welcome here!"

"I am not Egyptian," Andronicus said quickly. "I am Greek. I am going back to Greece. I was exiled from Egypt."

"What were you exiled for?" Yaakov asked, eyeing Andronicus curiously.

"For killing a guard," Andronicus lied. He didn't know what the Hebrews would make of his real story, but he decided not to find out.

"If you want to go to Greece, why don't you take a ship?" Yaakov asked. "It would be much faster." For a moment Andronicus felt a chill go through his bones, and an image of a giant hundred-foot wave came at him. Then it was gone again, and there were just three bearded men standing before him, no waves or water at all.

"I do not like the sea," Andronicus confessed. "I would rather take my time on land."

"Very well, you may stay with us tonight and join in our supper," Yaakov said, seemingly as much to the other two men as to Andronicus. Andronicus thanked him, and they led him back to their village.

The village was small, likely less than fifty people altogether. The first thing he noted about the Hebrews was that the men all had beards—every one of them. The second was that the women were seemingly all beautiful.

Andronicus took an immediate liking to the Hebrews. They were simple folk, much like the Swihmehe and many of the other tribes he had met in Africa. They didn't hunt like the Africans though. They planted where they could, but mostly they were herders. They lived in a barren wasteland, devoid of most animal life, with soil too rough to grow crops, but they had found a way to prosper.

Andronicus couldn't help but admire them. He knew how they had been treated in Egypt, and he had heard the story of Moses, the man their god chose to lead them out of captivity. Andronicus liked the story, and believed part of it was even true. They were the first people he had ever heard of who believed there was only one god; one single, all-powerful god ruling over everyone.

Andronicus couldn't help but find the idea a bit amusing. He had grown up believing in the gods of his father. He had met people in Africa who believed in all manner of gods. Some worshiped the sun and some the stars. The Swihmehe had believed the elephants were the gods, and the Perpauca had believed Andronicus was a god. In Egypt he had found gods similar to the ones he had known as a boy, only with different names and different stories. But the Hebrews believed in just one god and that they were his chosen people.

Andronicus had never been overly interested in gods. In Greece he had always accepted that the gods were real without a second thought. He hadn't believed in them the way Theo had, or even the way his brother had, but he had not disbelieved. When he arrived in Swimha, the way he thought about the gods had been forced to change.

Even now Andronicus felt that he couldn't think about gods, or a god, the same way as everyone else.

People believed in the gods their parents told them about. Andronicus probably would have had an easier time believing in gods if not for one simple fact. All the gods he had ever heard tell of and all the religions and all the stories left out the most important thing of all. Religions can tell you what happens when you die, they can explain the sun and the stars and the land and the sea. Religions can answer the questions a normal person would ask, but Andronicus was no longer normal. The one thing that every single religion seemed to be missing was the magical glowing rocks that bring you across the world and make you cease to age. As soon as Andronicus could find a religion that could account for that, he would devote himself to it fully, but so far no religion had. The way Andronicus looked at it, he had a piece of the puzzle that everyone else was missing. When he heard stories of gods and the way the world worked, he knew they must be false because they were all missing his special piece.

5

It took Andronicus a long time before he finally grew weary of the taste of mutton. The Israelites were a fine people whom Andronicus knew he could live with for years in peace and harmony, but he felt he had nothing more he needed to learn from them. He had spent years in the library learning about them, and after almost a year of moving slowly through their land, passing from one village to the next, Andronicus decided it was time to move on. He took his time, staying with people whenever he could, but he had begun to grow restless living with the Hebrews. All their talk of their god and their faith made him think more about his questions.

In one small village in the depths of a mountain pass, Andronicus spoke with the village elder about some of his questions. He told the man his story and at the end asked him what his god would make of it all. The old man had shouted at Andronicus and called him a blasphemer and a liar. Andronicus left the village that night and walked for hours before resting. After that he knew he couldn't tell just anyone the truth and expect them to accept it.

He moved slowly north from Israel, stopping less as he entered the Persian Empire. Andronicus couldn't help but feel unwelcome in Persia. As he passed by the heart of the empire he didn't dare stop and talk to anyone, lest they discover he was a Greek. He couldn't help but think of all the Persians he had killed as a young man and of his friends who had been killed by Persians, especially Niko.

He moved much slower through Persia than he would have liked. He thought that not stopping to trade with villages or merchants would let him travel faster, but having to keep to the mountains and the hills slowed him down tremendously. He didn't mind though; he had gotten used to the slow passage of time. It was hard, however, to live day to day without anyone to talk with.

Andronicus had scarcely been alone in his long life. There had been times that he was alone, but they had all been brief. As a young man he had always had his friends. When he was sent to Swimha, he was only alone for five days before Chaka found him. The longest he had been alone had been after Chaka died, until he got to Memphis. In Egypt he had at least had Imhotep to keep him company, but now he was truly alone, living in the mountains and the rocks, far away from any people.

His hair slowly began to grow out again. He had not cut his hair since first arriving in Egypt, nearly thirty years earlier, and his hair once again reached his shoulders. He had stopped shaving once he left Egypt, and it took nearly four years to grow the beginnings of a beard. His hair was the only outward part of him that ever changed. The rest still looked the same as it always had.

Two years after leaving Memphis, Andronicus entered Asia Minor, the place where he had touched the stones. The fastest way back to Greece was to stay by the sea and book passage with a ship, but instead he headed northwest, toward the ruins of Troy. His curiosity was just too great. He didn't know if the cave and the rocks would still be there or if he could even find them again if they were, but he had to try.

6

The barren hills looked the same as the day he had last seen them, just like him. It wasn't hard to find the ancient ruins; everyone still knew where they were. The second he saw the old, dead city, he was hit by a wave of nostalgia. The last time he had looked upon those crumbling ruins, he had stood next to Euthymius, Lycus, Androcles, Theodotus, and Niko. He had been a captain of Sparta, leading an important expedition. He wondered for the millionth time if he was the only member of that expedition left alive.

He didn't stay by the ruined city long. It made him feel oddly cold to look at something that had been so grand but which now lay decaying in the sun, nothing but a simple sight for wayward travelers. He walked south from Troy, trying to follow the same path as they had before. He was able to move faster than they had the first time because he had a horse, but it still took a while to find the place where they had been ambushed.

Eventually, he found what he was looking for: a large round stone with Greek markings carved into its face. The markings were old and faded and nearly indiscernible, but Andronicus knew what they said. The rock said Nikopheros, Sparta, 31. Andronicus remembered Lycus carving into the stone with his knife. Then he remembered burying Niko, and he felt tears roll down his dirty face.

Andronicus knew the rock had left the exact place it was meant to be, and there was no one left to remember Niko but him. He took the stone and placed it in one of the bags slung across his horse's back. He thought he could find a better resting place for it than this barren wasteland. He knew Niko's bones were buried somewhere close by, and he said an old prayer to Zeus on Niko's behalf before he left.

It took a while for Andronicus to remember where they had gone after Niko died. It had all been a bit of a blur. He thought he remembered heading north and decided to go that way. He couldn't remember exactly how many days after Niko died they had found the mountain, but he was riding a horse this time, so it would be hard to tell anyway.

Once he reached the mountain range, Andronicus found they all looked the same. It had also been pouring rain the last time he was there. He rode slowly, taking his time studying each peak and valley. Then finally, everything felt familiar.

Memories of that fateful day crashed over him in waves. The moments leading up to the cave had always been a bit fuzzy, but now they came back as clear as day. Andronicus shivered as he remembered how the storm had come out of nowhere. They had gone up the mountain in search of shelter, stumbling through the rain.

He looked up at the steep, rocky slope and felt a chill creep down his back. He knew it was the right mountain; he could feel it. He dismounted and tied his horse to a tree. The horse was even more restless and fidgety than it usually was, which seemed like further proof that they were in the right place. As he started up the mountain, it was uncanny how similar everything looked, as if no one had been there since his last visit.

He knew he was in the right spot when he felt the pull of it, just as it had been before, but he couldn't find the cave. He searched until the sun went down and then finally stopped and found a place to rest.

That night he had stranger and more vivid dreams than he had had in decades, maybe ever. He dreamed of the mountain, the sea, and the coliseum. He dreamed all the old, familiar dreams he had seen so many times. But he also dreamed new dreams: a desert made of ice, a beach with black sand, a great fire in the woods.

He awoke from the last dream with a start, sweating and panting, then lay back down slowly. He looked up at the thousands of stars above and tried to remember what he had just seen, but could only see flashes.

When the sun finally rose hours later, he had a

quick breakfast and then resumed his search, but he still couldn't find the cave. He wondered if there had been a rockslide or a cave in. Even if the entrance to the cave had been covered, he did not believe the inner cavern could have collapsed. It still had to be down there, buried by a literal mountain of dirt and rocks. Or maybe it had moved as well. The thought had never occurred to him until then, but the rocks had sent him across the world to the middle of Africa, and gods only knew where they had sent the others. So, it was perfectly reasonable that the rocks could have moved themselves as well.

7

Eventually, Andronicus decided to move on from the mountain, though he promised himself he would return there someday. He could still feel the presence of whatever it had been. The buzzing feeling he had felt occasionally throughout the years was stronger there than ever. Each night he dreamed of the shadowy visions he had seen in the water, and each night they showed him something different. Sometimes he would remember bits of it when he awoke, but usually it would return to a blur as soon as he opened his eyes. Some of it involved things he had dreamed of many times, but most of it was new, strange and confusing.

He would have stayed longer and continued his search, but the place began to give him the creeps. Some nights he woke up in a cold sweat, and all he could remember were the haunting red eyes he had seen back in Africa. He didn't know what it meant, but just thinking about it made his heart race.

He had run out of wine months ago, and his head yearned for a drink. Sleeping in the shadow of the mountain, being so near to where it had happened, made him want a drink more than ever. He knew there would be wine for him as soon as he left Persia, so he finally left the mountains and headed north again. It was a long way from the mountains of Troy to the edge of Macedonian rule, but Andronicus had time to spare. As far as he could tell, he had all the time in the world.

8

Moving through Persia was much more difficult than traveling through Egypt or Israel. He could no longer trade with any of the merchants. Even if he wanted to, none of them would take gold from a Greek. Without the wine he moved faster though. He drove his horse harder than the beast was meant for, but it didn't falter.

Once he crossed the Granicus River, it was not far to the sea. Andronicus knew he would have to take a short sea voyage into Macedonia or spend at least ten years walking all the way around, probably more. He still feared the sea and dreamed of the storm quite often, but he decided to take a ship anyway.

It was not hard to find a vessel that would take him. He found a small Thracian vessel readying for departure. Andronicus offered the captain a small fortune in gold for safe passage—and for the captain's silence. The captain agreed heartily, and they left that day.

It took a week and a half in the small Thracian ship, and Andronicus spent most of the voyage retching over the side of the deck. As a boy he had been used to life at sea, but that had been a hundred years ago, and he had lost his sea legs in that time. He also spent the entire trip fearing the storm from his dreams, but there was never so much as a cloud. When they reached the other side, Andronicus thanked the captain and gave him another two gold coins.

Andronicus felt a range of emotions as he set foot in what had been Greek land when he left. Now it belonged to the Macedonians, as did many of the nearby regions, from what he had heard. It still felt like being back home though.

Not a minute after getting off the ship he heard two men shouting at each other in Greek, and he almost cried. It had been a hundred years since he had heard his mother tongue used so freely. Hearing it now, being used to curse and shout, made Andronicus feel more at home than anything else could have. In his mind's eye, he could see Sophos yelling at his crew of Spartans, and he smiled to himself.

The captain had allowed Andronicus to take his horse across the sea, for another small fortune in gold, and now Andronicus mounted his horse and set out for Sparta. Along the way, he returned to buying wine as often as possible. He had never noticed it as a young man, but now as an old man, he thought that Greek wine was better than all the others.

Moving through Macedonia was pleasant and easy. Everyone spoke his language, and no one looked twice at him. Everyone on the road was a Greek. A few times he came across groups of riders who were looking for trouble, but Andronicus had no desire to fight his countrymen, and he managed to defuse such situations without having to resort to violence.

Chapter 32
Home Is Not Home
1

Andronicus finally returned to Greece on April 5, 363 bc, one hundred and four years after he left. He was immediately struck with how everything had changed, and yet nothing was really different. When he left, Greece had been split into more than a dozen city-states, all united against the Persian invasion and yet still enemies in their own right. Now, from what he had heard, Greece had largely unified itself. Most of the cities had become members of a pact called the League of Corinth. The Thebans, the Magaerans, the Messenians, and even the Athenians had all joined with the Corinthians in this new alliance.

Now only Sparta remained by itself. Andronicus felt an odd sort of pride in his people's stubbornness. Even when all of Greece had unified, and the Macedonians were growing stronger in the north, the Spartans remained independent. It reassured him to know that Sparta had not grown weak in his absence.

Andronicus rode from Thessaly, purposefully making his way toward Thermopylae. It was out his way, but he wanted to revisit the place where he had become a man so many years ago. It had all happened so long ago, and yet he still remembered it well. He wondered if there would be any marks of the old battle, any sign of the momentous event that had taken place there.

When he arrived at the pass, he barely recognized the place. He walked over to the heart of the pass, where the fighting had taken place, and looked out on the open field where the Persians had been encamped. He tried to imagine a million men spread out across the green field. The hills were the same, but everything else looked different. The huge valley that the Persians had been encamped in was now covered in grass and weeds. The place where he stood, where hundreds of men had died, was rocky and uneven, with weeds and grass growing here and there.

The wall they had built before the battle was gone. All that was left were a few bricks in a thin line. The rest were gone, either stolen or broken.

Andronicus walked over to the old goat path and stared up at it, trying to keep his anger at bay. That old path had been the downfall of King Leonidas and his brave men. It had also led to an entire war that could have ended there. The path was still hidden well, brush having grown all around it, but it was still there, ready for another ambush should another war ever come to the pass of Thermopylae.

Other than the few stones that were left, nothing remained to tell people what had happened there. It made Andronicus angry to think that his old friends had been forgotten so easily. He realized he had not thought of Gaios and Diokles in decades, and it made him feel ashamed. He knew there would be no record of them back in Sparta. Leonidas would still be remembered, but not the others. All that was left of their legacy now was his memory of them.

Andronicus walked over to the stones, took out his knife, and carved their names into the stones. He carved one for Gaios, one for Diokles, and one for Perikles. He didn't know how old they had been when they died, so he just carved their names and the mark of Sparta. When he was done he set them next to each other in a patch of dirt beside the ruins of the wall. He stood over the rocks for a long time, remembering the men he had known and fought alongside so many years ago.

2

Andronicus spent the night at the pass where the Spartans had been camped, and he dreamed of that first battle. He dreamed he was a boy again fighting beside Lycus and Niko. They fought the Persians as they had so long ago, and won.

As the fighting ended, the dream changed. It turned from day to night in an instant, and then they were all sitting by the fire. Niko and Lycus were laughing cheerfully, Diokles was tearing apart the leg of a chicken like a wild animal, and Gaios was staring into the flames. Andronicus felt warm as he sat amongst his brothers in arms, like he was home.

Then the king appeared. All the laughter and noise fell away. Andronicus looked around, but there was no one there, only the old king. Leonidas looked him dead in the eye,
and the flickering firelight danced off his weathered beard. Andronicus felt like a child again, his hairs rising on end as the mighty king stood over him.

"Find him," Leonidas said in his rough kingly voice. "Find him and train him. It has to be you."

"Find who?" Andronicus asked in a whiny child's voice he barely recognized as his own.

"I told you, Andronicus, son of Aristocles, you are not meant to follow, you are meant to lead," Leonidas said with the same reverence Andronicus remembered.

"We should never have left you," Andronicus said, tears welling up in his eyes as he stared up at his dead king. "We should have died with you that day. Everything since then has been all wrong."

"You were not meant to die here, Andronicus," Leonidas said, his face as hard as stone. "You have a far greater purpose to serve."

"How do I find the answers?" Andronicus asked desperately, hoping the king would tell him. "Where do

I go?"

"Keep searching, Andronicus, son of Aristocles," Leonidas said, and then everything began to fade away. "Find your answers, and find the boy." Andronicus tried to ask who he was talking about, but Leonidas was already gone.

Andronicus found himself in a forest. He was walking up a slope, surrounded by tall trees. It didn't look like any forest he had ever seen before.

As he looked around at the trees, he realized people were behind him, following him up the hill. He didn't recognize them, but they all looked like soldiers. Just then there was a shout from somewhere up ahead. A man came running toward them, and the next thing Andronicus knew, they were all running up the hill together.

Just as he began to get his bearings, he heard screams up ahead. Andronicus and his little band of fighters ran out into a clearing, and he saw a huge wooden wall. Behind the wall was a fire. The night sky glowed an ugly orange color as smoke rose from the forest structure. The screaming was coming from inside the walls.

Andronicus and his men charged through the gate. Fire was raging everywhere, huge billowing flames engulfing whole houses. Andronicus heard someone shout above him, and he looked up just in time to see a barrelful of water coming at him.

Andronicus jerked awake as the water hit him in the dream. For a moment he felt panic as he awoke to find himself soaking wet, but he quickly realized it was just sweat. He didn't know where that forest was or who lived there, but the thought of that fire made him shiver in the cold night air. He knew it was a vision of the future, not just a meaningless dream. He had dreamed of the desert all the time, and then he had lived the dream, and he had never dreamed it since. He knew for certain that the stones had shown him things from the future, but he had never had such a vivid dream of the past before.

Andronicus felt chills go down his sweat-drenched body as he thought of how King Leonidas had stared at him. He had thought that he had forgotten the old king's face, but in the dream it had been as vivid as it was in real life. Andronicus thought about what the king had said to him in the dream, and he didn't know what to make of it. He wasn't sure if Leonidas had been telling him to keep searching through the libraries or stay on the road. He had no idea who the boy the king had spoken of was, and had no idea where to look for him.

The dream left him with even more questions than he had before. He couldn't fall back asleep after the frightening end to the dream, so he sat up the rest of the night, looking out at the vast sea of stars above. He wondered the same thing he always did as he gazed at the stars: where were his friends? It seemed less likely all the time that they were all still alive, but he still hoped he would see them again, or at least one of them.

3

From Thermopylae, Andronicus rode down through the lands around Athens and then Corinth. He knew he was stopping far too often for wine, and yet his purse never seemed any emptier. Every time the big bag of gold emptied, he would find a wealthy merchant on the road, give him one or two small diamonds, and the bag would be filled to the brim with gold once again. First the bag had been full of Egyptian coins with the faces of ancient pharaohs, then it had been Persian coins, with their odd markings and smooth surfaces. Now the bag was full of Greek coins, the same coins he had once coveted as a young man.

The bag of coins was the only reason he was not turned away by most people. His outward appearance had become haggard and alarming once again, and he had begun to stink of wine and sweat. Most of the people he passed on the road shot him dirty looks and hurried by. Occasionally, soldiers passing by saw his tattered old cloak and recognized it for what it was. They would nod in greeting but shy away as soon as they got close enough to catch Andronicus's scent.

One day he was riding down the same road he had been on for weeks, finishing off the last of a bag of wine, when he looked up at the mountain to his right. A jolt of recognition hit Andronicus so hard he dropped the bag and nearly fell off his horse. He shook his head and then looked back up at the mountain. His head was heavy from the wine, but he could not mistake that mountain. It was a mountain he had not seen for a century, but one he had once known quite well. It was the mountain he had passed every time he had ever entered or left Sparta. In a sense it was the marker of Sparta's border.

Andronicus was on Spartan soil. He was finally home.

4

Andronicus wept when he caught his first glimpse of Sparta. The old city lay right where he had left it. The high white walls stood firm, and the temple stood out on the tall hill behind them. He could see the helots plowing the fields outside the city walls, but he felt no pity for them now. He was glad to see the old people again. He hadn't realized how much he had missed them. Andronicus sat atop his horse for a long while just staring at the old city, his true home.

Before he entered the city, he buried half of his belongings beside a tree he knew he could remember, including the bag of diamonds, the box of poisons, and Chaka's old necklace. He also took out his old cloak and flung it over his shoulders. He had washed it, along with himself, a few days earlier, and he looked more Spartan than he had in many years. He had even shaved the small beard he had been growing since Egypt and combed his tangled hair.

Just like in the old days, a troupe of six men came riding out to meet him before he even got close to the gate.

"You there!" the lead man shouted in the old Spartan accent Andronicus had not heard in nearly a hundred years. "Who are you, and what business have you in Sparta?"

"I am Andronicus of Sparta, son of Aristocles,"

Andronicus said in a loud, commanding voice. "I have been away since the war. Now I have come home."

"You fought in the war?" the commander asked suspiciously as he and his men rode up to Andronicus. The men behind the leader looked green and weak, but their leader had the look of a war veteran. Andronicus took a moment to size up the troupe and felt confident he could take them. He couldn't help but feel disappointed in his people. In his day the welcoming guard was not one soldier with a cluster of fresh recruits behind him, but a troupe of six of the fiercest men imaginable.

"Aye." Andronicus stared at the lead man with his iron gaze and thought he saw the man falter slightly.

"Which war?" the man demanded. "Athens or Persia?"

"Persia," Andronicus said truthfully, knowing the man was speaking of a different war than the one he had been in.

"Where have you been since then?" the man asked, lowering his spear. "The rest of us returned years ago."

"I went to Egypt," Andronicus explained. "I studied at the great temple in Memphis. Now I intend to study at the Spartan temple."

"Whom did you fight under during the war?" the man asked skeptically. Andronicus could already tell he should have said he had fought in the Athenian wars.

"Perikles," Andronicus said, deciding to tell as much of the truth as he could and hope it got him through.

"I have never heard of Perikles," the man said, raising his spear again.

"Perikles was my captain," Andronicus said. "He died in Lycia. A man called Sophos took command after him. And who are you to claim to know every man who fought for Sparta in the war?" Andronicus was pleased to see the man blush and shift in his saddle, then slowly lower his spear again.

"I'm Herodotus," the man said, much less

aggressively than he had been a second before. "I don't claim to know every man who fought in the war. I know most of the men who fought in the war who came back, but I suppose if this Perikles died in Lycia, and you left to go to Egypt, I would not know you."

"No," Andronicus agreed, "you would not."

"How old are you?" Herodotus asked. "You still look strong enough to fight."

"I assure you I'm still strong enough to fight," Andronicus said with a faint smile. "But I'm also past the age of a soldier, and I reserve my right to retire."

"We shall see," the man said, turning his horse around. "I'm taking you to the temple to meet with the council."

"Very good." Andronicus nodded politely and extended his arm. "After you then, Captain Herodotus."

Andronicus rode up to the gates behind Herodotus, the other guards spread out around him. As they rode he noticed that the archway of Hermes was gone, replaced by two ugly stone pillars.

"The archway," Andronicus said to the man next to him, "what happened to it?"

"Archway?" the boy repeated, looking confused. "What archway?"

"The archway of Hermes," Andronicus said, not knowing how anyone in Sparta could not know the archway of Hermes. "The golden entrance to the city of Sparta."

"The archway of Hermes was destroyed in the earthquake," another man said, eyeing Andronicus oddly.

"When was this earthquake?" Andronicus asked, glaring up at the awful new entranceway to the city.

"The earthquake?" the first man said, laughing. "It was a hundred years ago. I guess you must have missed it while you were studying in Egypt." The men all laughed, but Herodotus didn't turn around. Andronicus knew the captain had heard him, and he wondered if he had just blown his cover. Andronicus realized then just how careful he had to be with what he said to these men.

They rode through the old cobblestone streets, passing few people as they went. So much had changed since he had left. Andronicus wondered if it was the earthquake or simply the mark of one hundred years passing.

They turned onto a wide stone road that stretched up a hill and out of sight, and Andronicus recognized it at once. It was the main road, the same one that had been there when he was a boy. He remembered the day he had marched down this road with Lycus, Euthymius, and Niko as boys, through a crowd of people, off to face their first test as young Spartans. He found it amazing that he could remember it so clearly so many years later.

Once on the main road Andronicus knew where they were going. The old road had led to the great temple, and unless that had been destroyed in the quake as well, it likely still did. When he came around the final bend and saw the immense stone building, he knew it was the same temple from his youth. As they approached, Herodotus called out. A minute later a balding man with a great white beard and a long white toga came out to greet them.

Two Helot slaves hustled behind him, one holding a pitcher of water and the other a stack of scrolls. Some things never changed, Andronicus thought with a pang of guilt and regret. The old woman's burnt face floated before his eyes, her terrible howling words and her cackling laughter ringing in his ears, and then it was gone.

"Herodotus," the old man said with a lazy smile as he sauntered over to them. "What have you got here?"

"A deserter," Herodotus announced in a commanding tone. "This man claims he fought in the wars against the Persian revolts. He says that after the war he traveled to Egypt and has been there ever since."

"A deserter," the old man tittered, shaking his head disdainfully, but the passive smile remained. "What a pity. You there, deserter," he called out to

Andronicus. "Why have you come back to Sparta? Do you wish to atone for your crimes?"

"I would seek a private audience with you and any other high priests of this temple," Andronicus said, looking at the man with a mixture of feigned respect and actual contempt. "Then I'll answer your questions."

"Show some respect!" the young soldier sitting next to Andronicus shouted. Andronicus saw the slap coming from a mile away, and his own hand flashed out instinctively, striking the man across his nose and sending him toppling backward into the dirt. The man to Andronicus's left reached for his sword, but Andronicus grabbed him by the collar of his breastplate and threw him down into the dirt as well.

"Seize this traitor!" the old man shouted in a high voice, the pretentious smile finally gone from his face. Herodotus and the other four men all drew their swords, and Andronicus reluctantly drew his own. He had no intention of killing Spartan soldiers if he could help it, so he knew he would have to fight carefully. Herodotus raised his sword and called out, and the other men charged at Andronicus.

Andronicus reined his horse and charged the man to the far left. He clashed his sword against the rider's, and then swung it around and smacked the man hard on the back with the flat of his blade. The man tumbled off his horse as the other three turned and charged Andronicus again.

This time they circled him, and Andronicus found himself fighting all three men at once. Herodotus and the old man, along with his two slaves, stood on the sidelines watching as Andronicus parried and dodged the three blades expertly. He had been correct in his assessment of the guards' skill and again felt disappointed in his countrymen. As soon as he saw his chance, Andronicus punched one of the men off his horse.

Down to two opponents, Andronicus kicked one off his horse and was about to knock the final rider on the head when the man flung his sword into the dirt and leapt off his horse, yielding. Andronicus spun his horse around, ready to fight, and saw the other five men getting to their feet, some nursing bloody noses, all of them looking up at him in fear and admiration.

"Who are you?" Herodotus asked, staring in amazement at Andronicus.

"I told you who I am," Andronicus said, his sword still clutched in his hand, "and what I seek."

"Quickly," the old man said to the two slaves standing behind him, "go and fetch the other high priests. Tell them to convene in the hall of Apollo and wait for me there." He reached out and whipped the slaves, who ran back up the steps.

"My lord," the old man said, turning back to Andronicus and bowing, "my deepest apologies. I confess, I thought you to be a liar. But only a true Spartan warrior could fight with such skill."

"Aye," Andronicus agreed with a nod, "but I'm no lord. I was a captain once, but no longer."

"Then what are you, my gallant friend?" the old man asked, the lazy smile returning to his face. Andronicus could tell he was not going to like this man.

"I'm simply a wayward traveler who has found his way back home."

"Very well," the old man said, bowing again. "Shall we head into the temple then?" Andronicus nodded curtly and climbed down off his horse. Herodotus did the same, and he and two of the men Andronicus had fought followed him into the temple, keeping their distance from him now.

Once inside they walked through winding passageways, much like the temple in Memphis, until they entered a large room with a high stone ceiling. Andronicus recognized the room at once. He had been there as a boy, just back from Thermopylae, and spoken with the high priests of that time. The old stone table sat exactly where it had on that day, and just as on that day, the table was surrounded by old men in white robes. They all turned around when Andronicus and his cohort entered. For a moment he half expected to see Archelaus turn to greet him, but, of course, it was an entirely new group of men.

"What is the meaning of this?" a gaunt man

with greying whiskers and small dark eyes demanded of the balding priest. "Why have you gathered us here in such fashion?"

"My friends," the balding man said to his peers, "we have an honored guest. This is, um, what was your name again, son?"

Andronicus frowned at the old man. He didn't care for being called "son" by this pompous fellow, who was probably seventy years his junior.

"My name is Andronicus, son of Aristocles," he said, his eyes traveling around the table. "I have been away for many years, traveling at first and then studying in Egypt. I have returned to Sparta to study in your library."

"And why should we permit you to use our library?" the gaunt man asked, sneering at him.

"I have gold to rent a room, and gems as well."

The gaunt man looked even angrier than he had a second before, but several of the other men around the table looked quite interested.

"This is not a brothel, boy," the gaunt man said with his doglike sneer. Once again, Andronicus had to fight the urge to slap the man for calling him "boy." "We are not common innkeepers to be bought so easily. We—"

"Now hold on, Myron," a kind-looking man with bushy white hair said, resting his hand on Myron's shoulder. "Let's hear the man out. What kind of gems are you speaking of, Andronicus, son of Aristocles?"

"Diamonds," Andronicus replied. There was an excited murmur from the table as the priests whispered to each other.

"May I see one?" the curly-headed man asked.

Andronicus reached into his pack that still hung around his shoulder. He rummaged around until he found the small sack of diamonds; most of them were hidden outside the city, but he had brought enough to barter with. He felt around until he located a good-sized stone, and pulled it out. The reveal was met by a chorus of gasps from the priests and soldiers alike as the stone sparkled in the firelight.

"Myron here can be a bit hasty," the bushy-haired man said with a broad smile. "I believe we can accommodate you here."

"You would permit this . . . this intruder into our midst?" Myron asked.

"He is no intruder," the man replied. "He's a Spartan. He fought in the war, and now he wishes to stay in the temple. He's also willing to pay generously for the accommodation. Is that right, Andronicus?"

"Aye," Andronicus answered, giving Myron a look that dared him to challenge his story. Myron looked like he was going to say something else, but one of the other priests came up and whispered in his ear. Myron shot the man a furious look and then stormed out of the hall.

"Don't mind Myron," the balding man who had led Andronicus in said, offering a placid smile. "He can be rather wary of outsiders. Though, of course, you're not an outsider."

"Andronicus," the curly-headed man said as he approached him, "I am Sophokles, and I believe you've already met Nikanor," he said, nodding to the bald man. "May I show you to your room?"

Andronicus nodded, then followed him down a hallway. The temple was big but not nearly as big as the temple in Memphis.

By the time Andronicus was shown to his new lodgings, he was quite hungry. He pulled out three gold coins with a dead pharaoh's face on them and flipped them to Sophokles.

"Where do I go to eat?" Andronicus asked.

"We have a dining hall," Nikanor said from the doorway. "I can show you there if you like."
Andronicus nodded with a grunt and then followed the man through a few passageways until they reached a large hall with four long wooden tables. At each table sat a number of priests, eating their supper.

As soon as they entered, Andronicus was hit by the scent of roasting meat and fish. He smelled all the old foods he had forgotten about: onions and olives and fish of every kind. He noticed a table off to the side with food on it. He headed straight for it, leaving

Nikanor standing alone, talking to no one.

That first meal back in Sparta was the best he had had in years. He sat alone, many of the priests giving him furtive glances, and relished the Spartan food. After wolfing down a third plate of fish, Andronicus rose to leave and found Nikanor waiting for him.

"Is there anything else I can get for you?" Nikanor asked, his condescending tone unmistakable.

"Wine," Andronicus replied, then walked past the man without waiting for a response. He was able to find his way back to his room easily enough.

Not long after, he heard a knock at his door. When he opened it, one of Nikanor's slaves was standing there holding a large flagon of wine. The boy was hunched over, holding the flagon up to Andronicus, not daring to look at him.

"What's your name, boy?" Andronicus demanded, though not unkindly.

"Aesop," the boy said, still not daring to look up at him.

"Have a drink with me, Aesop," Andronicus said as he took the flagon from the boy.

"I cannot, sir," the boy said quickly.

"Why not?" Andronicus asked as he poured himself a cupful.

"We are not allowed to drink the priests' wine," Aesop said nervously, still looking at his feet.

"Well, this is not the priests' wine," Andronicus said after a big gulp. "This is my wine. I purchased it, and I say you're allowed to have some, so drink." The boy looked nervously down the hall, as if he expected Nikanor to appear at any second and begin whipping him.

"I . . . I cannot," the boy stammered, then hurried away down the hall. Andronicus watched him go, pitying the lad, and then returned to his room.

After finishing off most of the flagon, Andronicus finally stumbled into bed, drunk as a mule. *I'm in Sparta*, Andronicus thought just before he dozed off. *I'm really back in Sparta.*

4

The next morning Andronicus made his way down to the dining hall for breakfast. After a hearty meal that reminded him of the old days, he made his way to the library. The library was a bit disappointing. After spending years and years only to read less than half the works in the library in Memphis, he had expected to find a similar library in his home city. He supposed he should have known better. The Spartans had never been a people to write much; they were the ones others wrote about. The library was a simple stone room with three walls covered in shelves of scrolls. The room was only half the size of the dining hall and merely a fraction of what the library in Memphis was.

Andronicus was the only person there, and he wandered around the room, looking at what sort of scrolls there were. At first glance, few of them looked like they would be of any use to him. It had taken him twenty-four years to read just a portion of what was in Egypt, but he thought he would be able to read everything of worth in the Spartan library within a few years. He still didn't know exactly what to look for, or if he would ever find anything useful, but he felt he had to at least try.

5

Being back in Sparta, back in his home, the place he had spent so long searching for, was nothing like Andronicus had expected. He didn't know what he had been hoping to find. All that he had in Sparta had died long ago. Now all the city held for him were memories of people and things long forgotten by everyone else. Being home was not at all the great relief he had thought it would be. He had foolishly hoped that returning home would be the end of his journey, that when he finally made it back, he would be finished. Instead he found that Sparta had all but forgotten him. Everyone and everything he had ever loved was dead, or lost.

The city was still the bustling, energetic place he remembered from his youth, only it was no longer meant for him. His Sparta had died long ago, and the new Sparta had no place for him. He was like a final reminder of a forgotten story. Eventually, he realized that it wasn't the city that had changed or even the people; it was him. He had changed too much since his Spartan days, and he knew this was no longer where he belonged.

He tried going back to his first home, back in Gytheion. He made it all the way to his parents' house. He stood in front of the door, his mind filled with images of his mother and father, and brother. It was too much, and Andronicus left without speaking to the people there or looking inside. He made his way down to the old cliffs that his father used to take him to as a boy, and stared out at the majestic sea for a long time. It was still his home, and yet it wasn't. He could feel some of what had been, but it wasn't the same. It wasn't for him.

Andronicus went back to the temple in the city. He only stayed to go through the library, searching for clues about magical rocks or ageless men, and even that wasn't easy. The histories and stories he had read in Egypt had at least been interesting; the histories in Sparta were dull and poorly written. It took him a little more time to finish each scroll while he slowly made the local wine merchants rich.

From the very beginning, being back in Sparta was painful. Everywhere Andronicus went he was reminded of someone he had loved and lost or some promise he had failed to keep. He tried to track down the descendants of Gaios's son and of Niko's boys. He couldn't find any record of Daios, but he did manage to track down the great-granddaughter of one of Niko's sons, though she was old and widowed. Andronicus tried talking to her one day, but it was too painful. The knowledge that this frail old woman was the descendant of the man he had loved as a brother was just too bizarre and painful.

After several months of drinking, he finally got the courage to visit the old cemetery where his father's grave was. He half expected to find a grave of his own and one for Androcles and Euthymius and all the others. When he got there he found none of that. His father's grave was still there, right where it had been for a hundred and thirty years, next to the men he had died with. Andronicus stared down at his father's grave and burst into tears. No one else was around, so he let himself fall to his knees and weep.

He didn't know what he had expected, but certainly not to cry. He was only a little boy when his father died, but he had spent most of his young life trying to live up to the man. His father had always told him he would be a great Spartan warrior someday and fight to defend Sparta. Fulfilling that dream had been the proudest time of Andronicus's life, but he had never reached that height again. The next time he had fought for Sparta, he had failed completely, getting nearly all of his men killed. He knew he was far from the man his father had wanted him to be, but he wasn't sure what to do differently. He wished there was a new war he could fight in, but it was peacetime. There was nothing but the cold, dark library, and the dusty old scrolls.

Andronicus wiped the tears from his face and stood up with a heavy sigh. He looked around at the other graves and noticed Lycurgus's grave just three over from his father's. He still remembered the story Archelaus had told him about how Lycus's father had gotten his father killed. He didn't feel the same anger he once had. Perhaps it was because they would have all died years ago anyway, but Andronicus no longer cared what had happened when he was a boy. He had become an old man, the oldest he had ever heard of, though it was still impossible to tell by looking at him.

Before leaving the cemetery, Andronicus took out the stone that had marked Niko's grave. He couldn't find an empty space that looked right, so he laid it down by his father's grave. Niko's father had not been a soldier and would not have been buried, but Niko had died in battle, and he deserved to be honored with the other Spartan warriors. Andronicus said a prayer to Ares that he had read in a book for both Niko and his father, and then he left.

Andronicus spent the next seven years drinking, whoring, and wasting away his time in Sparta, waiting with faithless hope that his brother or his friends would show up, and eventually, he had to move on. Sparta felt too eerie, and it made him anxious all the time. It was memories, all the people he had known, all the people he had lost. He hadn't made a friend like Imhotep to help him through the books and the boredom, and he felt completely alone. Sparta felt like a ghost town, and he knew he had to go. Every night he would drown away the voices in a sea of wine. Too often he would stumble into the library with the front of his clothes stained red, and the priests would shoot him disdainful looks.

At some point he realized he wasn't having the visions anymore. He didn't know if it was because he was back home, because he had stopped moving, or because he was just too drunk to dream, but he decided it was the latter. Sometimes he missed them, the dream about the mountain or the coliseum. Mostly he was glad to be rid of them. No more storms at sea, no more things he didn't understand, no more haunting red eyes.

The wine didn't only stave off the dreams; he had begun to grow fat as well. His stomach, which had remained hard as a rock for over one hundred years, grew soft and plump, and his arms were noticeably smaller and weaker than they had always been. It had been years since he had last used his sword, but he still sharpened it every week.

Once he decided to leave, he packed up his things and went and found Sophokles praying in the great hall. Andronicus walked slowly over to the man, trying to hide his daytime drunkenness. Sophokles looked up when he heard Andronicus coming and rose to his feet.

"Andronicus," Sophokles said, beaming at his drunken benefactor, "how are you this morning?"

"I'm leaving," Andronicus said, cutting to the chase. "Thank you for all that you've done for me." Andronicus reached into his bag and pulled out a good-sized gem and handed it to Sophokles.

"You're leaving?" Sophokles said, looking alarmed. "To go where?"

"Athens to start," Andronicus said. "I'm told they have a much bigger library there. Perhaps it will have what I seek."

"And what is it you seek, Andronicus," Sophokles asked, eyeing him intently. "You never did tell me."

"Answers," Andronicus grunted, then turned around.

"Answers to what?" Sophokles called after him as he walked away.

"To everything," Andronicus called back over his shoulder, then turned the corner.

Outside the temple, he walked down the old stone road. He was wearing his old Spartan cloak, which was noticeably faded compared to the other soldiers he passed, and a new bag he had sewn slung over his shoulder. While sewing the bag, he had pricked his fingers more than he ever had before, probably due to his drinking, but he still remembered the technique the Bahitu had taught him, and it came out light and sturdy.

As he walked down the road, he was acutely aware that he might never see Sparta again, but it didn't bother him at all. The streets and buildings were too full of memories, memories of people long dead, and it gave him the chills. He knew he would probably live long enough to get the opportunity to return, but something inside him told him he shouldn't.

When he got to the stables, he gave the stable master a gold coin and then mounted his old brown steed. The horse had grown fat and lazy over the years, just like its master, but that suited Andronicus just fine. He was not in any rush.

After leaving the stables, he rode down the main road to the ugly new gateway, frowning as he looked at it. The new gateway felt like a perfect analogy for the entire city, and he hated it. He reached into his saddlebag as he rode, took out a pouch of wine, and took a long swig.

When he got to the main gate, he tipped his head back, finishing off the wine, then let out a long belch, a last goodbye to the city he had once loved. Herodotus was standing guard, just as he had been the day Andronicus had arrived. He saw that Andronicus was dressed for travel and came down to say goodbye. Andronicus stuck out his hand, and Herodotus shook it with a look that Andronicus couldn't quite place. He had known Herodotus for years now, and never seen that look. Then it donned on him, it was pity. Andronicus had been a great many things in his extraordinarily long life, but pitiful had never been one of them.

Andronicus turned away, trying to hide his shame, and rode out of the city and down the old road. He only made it a few miles before he left the road and found a shady spot to sleep for a while. Nothing was waiting for him in Athens that would not be there if he took his time, and he certainly had no shortage of time to spare. It seemed a perfectly reasonable thing to take an afternoon nap during his travels, or so he tried to convince himself. Part of him tried to suggest that he had travelled for forty years through the worst conditions imaginable, and never needed a nap, but he ignored that. If he had wine when he was in the jungle, he surely would have slept during the day. Chaka would have too, he told himself as he drifted off.

Chapter 33
The Academy
1

Andronicus raised his hand to block the sun from his eyes as he woke. He sat up slowly, squinting, and looked around in confusion. For a moment he had no idea where he was. Then he remembered going into the woods to get his buried belongings. He felt like he had slept for a long time, but the sun was still high above him. Then he realized that the sun was actually higher than it had been when he had fallen asleep. He had slept for nearly a full day.

He walked over to his horse, rubbing his

aching head, and fumbled around in his saddlebag, pulling out a sack of wine. He brought it up to his lips and then stopped. He stared down at it for a moment, debating with himself. He knew it had become a problem, and he should stop, but it was an awful struggle. Finally, he put the wine away and took out a water bag instead. He drank half the bag in one gulp, enjoying its refreshing coolness.

He lifted himself onto his horse with a grunt and dusted himself off. Once back on the road, he started riding north. The sun was already beginning to go down to his left, and he had to squint from the brightness. His head was pounding like a drum, and the motion of the old horse's languid movements made his stomach turn.

Andronicus retched over the side of his horse a few times before the sun went down, but he didn't take a drink. He passed a few other travelers on the road, and they all gave him a wide berth. Only a day on the road, and already he looked like a drunken vagabond again, which in a way he supposed he was. When the last light was gone from the land, and the road was empty and barren, Andronicus kept riding. Riding through the night under a sea of stars reminded him of Chaka, which just made him want to drink even more.

He knew he probably wouldn't hold to it, but he told himself he was not going to drink until he reached Athens. He wasn't afraid of dying from the drink, like some old drunks do. He wasn't even afraid of being killed in a fight while he was drunk, feeling confident he could still handle a blade while intoxicated. What really scared him was that the drink would immobilize him, make him weak and stupid, which it already had. He knew he couldn't truly find what he was looking for while he drank the days away. Andronicus finished off four bags of water that night and felt confident he could kick the drink entirely.

2

He stuck to his pledge for two and a half days. On the third day his body started fighting him. He broke out in a cold sweat and was barely able to stay on his horse. He lasted a few hours like that before giving in and drinking a whole bag of wine. He felt a wave of guilt, followed by numbness, and then he felt better. He started riding again, and when his horse tripped over a rock and fell forward in a heap, Andronicus fell flat on his face in the dirt and was snoring within seconds.

3

The sound of his horse's loud braying brought Andronicus out of his stupor. Disorientated, he looked at the dark world around him. It was night, and the horse's horrible screeching rang through the woods. Andronicus brought a hand up to his face and felt dried blood caked to his cheek. He got up, and walked over to where the horse was lying on its side, writhing and braying in agony. The poor beast had snapped its front leg at the knee, and Andronicus knew he had to end its suffering.

He drew his sword and knelt beside the old horse. He tried resting his hand on the beast's neck for a moment, but it was writhing around too much. Its screeching was awful. Andronicus impaled its heart with his sword in a clean, fluid motion. It gave out one last horrible scream and then fell silent.

Andronicus didn't know what to do with the dead horse. It was too big to bury, and it was too windy to burn it without burning half the woods down with it. In the end Andronicus just left him there. It didn't feel right to abandon the beast after it had served him well for so many years, but a little wine made that seem less awful. Andronicus pulled his saddle bag off the dead horse and threw it over his shoulder, then started down the road on foot.

After that he had to drink much slower because he was walking instead of riding, but he didn't mind. It felt good to walk again after seven years of lying around, even if he was walking slowly. It took him over a month to walk from Sparta to Athens. He had once made the trip in a week, but he just reminded himself that he had all the time in the world.

By the time he reached Athens he thought he might have even lost a little weight.

4

Athens looked nothing like it had the last time he had seen it. In 471, when he had last seen Athens, it had been a city in ruins. The Persians had razed the city twice during the war, and it had done little to heal itself in the ten years after. Now, more than one hundred and twenty years after that, the city had more than healed itself.

Even from a distance the city was a spectacle. The stone pillars looked as white as snow and made the stonework in Sparta look old and decrepit. Even as he walked past fields well outside the city, people were all about, most of them tilling the fields or picking either cotton or crops.

As he approached the city, five soldiers rode out to meet him. He made sure to keep his hand away from his sword. When they reached him, they circled him, and a large fierce-looking man with a thick black beard trotted forward on his horse.

"Welcome to Athens," the man said in a deep, gruff voice. "What is your business here?"

"I am Andronicus of Sparta," Andronicus said, taking care not to let his voice slur. "I come seeking a place in your temple to study and learn."

"A Spartan, come to learn," the man said with a laugh, his companions joining in. "Can you even read, Spartan?"

"Yes, I can," Andronicus replied. "I can read several languages, in fact." They all burst into a fresh bout of laughter, their leader the loudest among them.

"What do you want, Spartan, really?" the man said as the laughter died down.

"I already told you," Andronicus said, trying to keep his voice even. "I wish to study at your temple. I would like an audience with the priests. I'm sure they will be willing to take me in."

"And why would the priests take in a fat, drunk Spartan to study at our temple?" the man asked.

"Because I can pay them," Andronicus said

with a smile, "and I can pay you as well."

"What have you got to pay me with?" the man demanded. "Your Spartan coins are no good here."

"What about my diamonds?" Andronicus asked, taking one out of his pocket. "Are they good here?" The soldiers all fell silent, and the leader stared at the stone with a hungry look in his eyes.

"How many of those have you got?" he asked eagerly.

"Enough," Andronicus answered, not liking the look in the man's eyes.

"Suppose we take those gems from you," the man said, reining his horse closer to Andronicus. "Suppose we take everything you have and leave you here for the carrion birds." The other five men also moved in, trapping Andronicus.

"If you can take them from me, you are welcome to them," Andronicus said with a lazy smile, his hand creeping back toward the hilt of his sword.

"You think because you were born in Sparta you can fight us?" the leader said with a smirk. "You're no Spartan warrior. You're a fat drunkard."

"Then you should be able to best me quite easily," Andronicus said. The men laughed again, but their leader glared down at Andronicus.

"I would kill you in seconds," he said. "Hesiod, put this drunken fool in the dirt where he belongs." The man to the leader's right jumped down from his horse and drew his sword. Andronicus drew his own sword, knowing he couldn't kill any of them if he wished to enter the city.

The man stepped forward and swung, but Andronicus easily parried the attack. The man swung again, and again Andronicus easily blocked him. He toyed with the man for a few seconds, enjoying the feeling of clashing swords again. Once he grew tired of the fight, he parried a blow while swiping the man's leg, knocking him onto his back. Andronicus kicked the sword out of his hand and held his own sword to the man's throat. Andronicus looked up at the leader with a smile. The man glared at Andronicus and shouted for two more of his men to take him.

They both dismounted and approached Andronicus, one on either side, swords drawn. When they swung, Andronicus stepped backward, blocking one blow and sidestepping the other. He clashed his sword against the man on his right and then punched the man in the face. The guard stumbled backward, and his comrade took his place, swinging his sword wildly at Andronicus. It only took a single punch to drop him as well. Whatever achievements Athens may have made over the past century, they certainly hadn't been practicing their fighting.

The first man came charging back, blood running down his face, and swung his sword at Andronicus. Again Andronicus struck him in the face, this time with the hilt of his sword, sending blood shooting out of the man's nose.

"Enough!" the leader shouted.

Andronicus turned just in time to see the leader running at him with his sword raised. Andronicus blocked the blow while tripping the man. He fell into the dirt next to his men, and Andronicus kicked him in the gut. He keeled over, and Andronicus put his sword to the man's throat.

"I may have grown fat and drunk," Andronicus said, his voice carrying over the fields, "but I am still Andronicus of Sparta, and it will take more than the likes of you to kill me. Now if you would please, escort me to the temple." Andronicus removed his sword from the man's throat and stepped back. The leader was on his feet in a second, glowering at him. For a moment Andronicus thought he was going to charge him again, but then he turned to his men and said something that Andronicus couldn't hear. Then he turned back to him.

"Very well," the leader said angrily. "I'll take you to the temple. Let the priests decide what to do with you."

5

The brutish leader led Andronicus inside the temple, leaving his men waiting outside. One of them had already run ahead to tell the priests they were coming.

Right away it was apparent that the temple was much greater than the one in Sparta. They walked through a maze of halls before entering a room where several old men were waiting for them. When they entered, one of the men got up, and nodded to the lead soldier, who nodded back and then left, but not before shooting Andronicus a last angry glare.

"We were told you come from Sparta," the old man said. Andronicus answered with a nod.

"And you have come to see our temple?"

"No," Andronicus said. "I have come to see your library and to study."

"You have come to Athens to study?" the man looked taken aback.

"Yes," Andronicus replied.

"And we are told you have diamonds to pay us with?" another man said from the corner of the room.

Andronicus nodded.

"Perhaps you should go to the Academy," the first man suggested.

"What is the Academy?" Andronicus asked, wondering what kind of place this old fool was trying to send him.

"It is a school," the old man said with a smile. "A place for men to study and learn about science, mathematics, and philosophy, especially philosophy."

"A school for grown men," Andronicus mused. He had never heard of such a thing.

"We thought it was an absurd idea as well," the third man said, "but it has been working quite well."

"It all comes down to the teacher," the first man added. "If Plato were not there to guide it, the Academy would have failed long ago."

"Plato," Andronicus said with a raised brow. "This is the man that runs a school for grown men?"

"He has help," the priest answered. "He still travels quite often, but he is there enough to teach and to guide the others. Some of his students are rather remarkable. If you truly wish to study and to learn, the Academy is where you ought to go."

6

The soldier whom Andronicus had humiliated led him from the temple to the Academy. Neither man said so much as a word the whole way there. When they arrived, the soldier warned him not to cause any trouble and then left in a hurry.

Andronicus was a bit disappointed with the looks of the place. He didn't know what he had expected, but it was not the decrepit old building in front of him. It looked more like a home for the poor.

Andronicus approached the front door and knocked, not knowing what to expect. He heard some bustling inside. A moment later the door opened, and a short bald man poked his head out.

"Can I help you?" he asked in a high voice.

"My name is Andronicus of Sparta," Andronicus said. "I have come a long way to study in the library of Athens. I was told there is a man named Plato whom I should seek out."

"Who told you to seek out Plato?" the man asked, seeming a bit alarmed.

"I went to the temple of Zeus," Andronicus explained, eyeing the man coldly. "I told the priests there my purpose, and they told me to come here, to this . . . Academy, to find a man named Plato."

"Very well," the bald man said reluctantly, "come in then." He opened the door wider, and Andronicus entered.

Once inside, he saw three men with greying or white hair sitting around a table in the corner, apparently in the middle of a stimulating conversation. Bent over a quill and parchment at another table was a younger man, furiously scribbling something.

"Where is this Plato?" Andronicus asked the bald man, who was standing behind him.

"He is busy," the man said reproachfully, "with his students."

"I would speak with him now," Andronicus said. "We have terms to settle."

"I'm afraid Plato is very busy," the bald man said. "He cannot help you this very moment."

"Go and get him, boy," Andronicus demanded. "Now!"

The bald man flinched and fell back onto his butt. The three men sitting at the table looked up and laughed when they saw him on his backside. The man writing at the other table looked up in alarm when Andronicus shouted but then quickly returned to his work.

"I . . . I . . . I cannot," the bald man stammered as he got back to his feet. "He is a v-very busy man. H-he cannot be dis-disturbed by every man who w-wishes to speak with him." Andronicus could tell he had rattled the man badly, but he still needed to speak with Plato.

"Look, fool," Andronicus said in a cold, flat voice, only loud enough for the bald man to hear, "either you take me to Plato, or I'm going to cut off your head and find him myself." The bald man stared at Andronicus in fear for a moment, as white as a sheet, then nodded and hurried toward a side door.

Andronicus followed the man silently. When he passed the table where the three men were discussing what sounded like mathematical theory, they all fell silent and looked up at him. Andronicus gave them a simple nod, and they returned to their discussion.

The bald man led him into another room, also filled with mostly old men, all of them sitting at tables and talking with others, reading, or writing. Andronicus couldn't help but smile to himself. Perhaps this was the place he was looking for. The bald man kept walking through into a third room, which was larger and nicer.

This room only had one table, with three men sitting around it. One of the men was short and fat with long, curly hair and a thick black beard. The second man was tall and thin and balding a bit on top. He had a thick black beard with spots of grey. He had a look on his face Andronicus had never seen before, a sort of keen intelligence behind his pale eyes.

The third man looked to be much older than the other two, most likely in his seventies or eighties. He had a full head of curly snow-white hair and a long white beard that stretched well below his collar. He had a kind, friendly face, wrinkled and weathered yet still full of curiosity. The old man reminded Andronicus of his old teacher, Philander. He was sure the old man was Plato.

Plato looked up as the bald man led Andronicus into the room. The younger intelligent-looking man fell silent as Andronicus entered, and they all looked over at him.

"I'm terribly sorry to disturb you, Plato," the bald man said, staring at his feet, "but this man requested an audience with you right away."

"And any man who requests an audience should be granted one at once?" the intelligent-looking man asked.

"Well, uh, no," the bald man stammered. "He, uh . . ."

"I have come a long way to be here," Andronicus said to Plato, cutting the fool off mercifully. "I came to Athens to read what your library has to offer."

"Thank you, Phiokles," Plato said to the bald man, "that will be all." Phiokles bowed low and then hurried out of the room.

"You can read?" the thin man asked Andronicus as the door shut.

"I can," Andronicus said, turning to face him. "I can read Greek, Egyptian, Hebrew, and some Carthaginian."

"Impossible," the man said, his mouth curling into a thin smile. "It would take a man twenty years to learn to read all of those languages."

"And yet I can read them," Andronicus said, shrugging. "I can show you if you like."

"That will not be necessary at this time," Plato said, getting to his feet. "You must forgive Aristotle. He can be quite curious and skeptical. Now then, why have you really come to Athens? Surely you are not here simply to admire our library. You must be seeking something."

"I am," Andronicus answered, thinking carefully about what to say next. "But what I seek is my own business. Know that it does not bode ill for any man in Athens. I wish no harm upon you."

"You are from Sparta," the fat man said, speaking for the first time. "Athens has been at war with Sparta for over one hundred years."

"I had no part in those wars," Andronicus said. "The only wars I have ever fought were against the Persians. I hold no ill will toward Athens."

"So you have come seeking unknown answers in our library, you know how to read four different languages, you claim to have fought against the Persians, and you have gold to pay us with," Aristotle said. "You sound like quite the man, Andronicus of Sparta. Exactly how old are you?" Andronicus could tell this man was too smart to fool; he needed a way around him.

"I'm forty-two years old," Andronicus lied, not knowing how long he might want to stay in Athens. "I fought when I was young and traveled after that. I spent many years in the library in Memphis, where I learned to read and write."

"So you can write as well," Aristotle said with a hint of a laugh. Andronicus could tell he didn't believe a word of it.

"Yes, I can," Andronicus said, keeping his voice even. He looked back at Plato, hoping he would tell Aristotle to back off, but he simply stood there, watching intently.

"You must be a truly remarkable man," Aristotle mocked, "to have done so much in your time."

"Well, Aristotle, how many languages can you read?" Andronicus asked.

"Six," Aristotle said, a hint of a blush creeping up his neck.

"And you know mathematics as well?"

Aristotle nodded reluctantly.

"And physics? And philosophy?" Aristotle answered each question with a reluctant nod.

"And how old are you?" Andronicus asked.

"I'm thirty-four years old," Aristotle said, no longer meeting Andronicus's eye.

"And yet you have had time to learn all of

these things." Andronicus saw Plato smiling out of the corner of his eye. "I wonder, Aristotle, do you think I'm lying because I'm a Spartan or because I'm a soldier?"

"I meant no offense," Aristotle said, meeting his eye once again. "It simply seems impossible for a man to have done all those things in just forty-two years."

"Come now, Aristotle," Plato said, finally speaking up. "You have learned more in your thirty-four years than most men could learn in a thousand years. The work you are doing will change the way we look at the world forever, and yet you are still a young man. Why should this man not be able to have done all those things he has claimed?"

"Apologies, friend," Aristotle said to Andronicus with a slight bow. "I meant no offense." Andronicus responded with a nod, but he knew he would have to be careful around this one.

"So," Plato said, walking around the table, "you have come seeking answers, and yet you cannot tell us the questions. How can we help you find what you seek?"

Andronicus hesitated, not sure how much he should tell these men. Then he reached into his pouch and took out the old scroll from Egypt. Aristotle and the fat man both perked up at the sight of the old papyrus.

"Is that from the library in Memphis?" Aristotle asked excitedly.

"It is," Andronicus replied, nodding. "But it will not be missed. It is a simple ledger made by a slaver traveling up the Euphrates River nearly two thousand years ago." Andronicus laid the scroll out on the table, and all three men huddled around to admire it.

"This symbol," Andronicus said, pointing at the mark on the page, "have you ever seen it before, anywhere?" The three men were silent for a long while as they leaned over the parchment. Andronicus could tell both Plato and Aristotle were reading it, even though it was written in old Egyptian.

"Very interesting," Plato said finally. "I don't believe I have ever seen the mark before. What does it mean?"

"That is one of the many answers I seek," Andronicus replied. "I saw this mark myself once, in a cave not far from the ruins of Troy."

"The man from the ledger was headed to Troy," Aristotle said, looking up from the scroll. "Perhaps he was the same man who put the mark in the cave."

"I'm quite sure he is," Andronicus agreed, "sure that he was, that is." Aristotle gave Andronicus an odd look, then returned to the paper.

"So you saw this mark in a cave," Plato said, "and then you found it in a scroll in Egypt and nowhere else."

"Right." Andronicus chose not to show them the mark on his box of poisons just yet.

"Most interesting," Plato said thoughtfully. "I'm sure Aristotle would be willing to help you in your studies. If you mean to stay with us, that is."

"I do," Andronicus said. "I have gold and gems to pay you with."

"No payment is necessary," Plato said, holding his hands up. "Learning is free here at the Academy. It was my old friend, Acedemius, who thought of the idea, a school for men to learn, a place where mathematics and philosophy can be pushed to their limits and beyond. I like to think we have achieved his dream in some small way."

7

Andronicus settled into the Academy quite nicely. For the first time in a very long time he felt like he was a part of something bigger than himself. The Academy was like nothing he had ever experienced before. It was more than just a school for adults; it was a commune of the greatest minds in the world, not necessarily teaching each other but simply discussing and debating and learning with each other.

Plato was often abroad; he traveled to Sicily quite often to give lectures to the priests there, as well as the other Greek cities. When Plato was gone, Aristotle led most of the discussions. Over time

Andronicus grew to like Aristotle. He was without a doubt the smartest man Andronicus had ever met. Aristotle knew math, physics and military strategy, as well as several languages, and he knew more about philosophy than anyone besides Plato.

At first Andronicus tried to simply search through the library for clues, as he had in Egypt and Sparta, but the urge to join the academic discussions was too great. When he asked Plato if he could join the Academy full time, he was accepted with open arms. All he had to do was avoid getting drunk and making a fool of himself. Right away his aimless reading became the studying of science and math.

Whenever Aristotle was in charge, the conversations would focus on the sciences, military strategies, or some other technical thing. When Plato was there, the conversations would always be centered in philosophy. Plato would often speak of his own teacher, a man named Socrates, who had been just a few years younger than Andronicus. He also liked to talk about his idea for a perfect society, a city run entirely by its people. He had an idea for a form of government where no one man was in charge but rather a counsel, selected by the people. He called it a republic and insisted it would be the foundation of all society one day. Andronicus didn't believe it would ever work, but he guessed he might be around to find out either way.

When Plato was not debating governance and philosophy with his students, he would spend countless hours locked away in his study, writing down his ideas. He said he wanted his ideas to remain his own, and that if he did not write them down, they would be mangled and twisted by a thousand other minds, and his words would be used to destroy everything he loved. Andronicus could tell that Plato was close to the end of his life, and he knew that he simply wanted his legacy to be untarnished.

Aristotle, on the other hand, seemed far less concerned with what could be done with his ideas. He was more interested in creating the thoughts than protecting them. Aristotle's intellect floored

Andronicus. His mind was able to grasp concepts in a matter of days that took others years to understand.

Quite often Aristotle would try to trick Andronicus into giving him some answers. Andronicus knew that Aristotle still didn't believe his story, and he made sure to keep his guard up when talking to him. Sometimes Aristotle would slip in a question about the Persian wars, as if he were trying to trip Andronicus up. Luckily, Andronicus never did slip up, though he grew worried that Aristotle would eventually discover the truth about him anyway.

Plato simply wanted to talk to Andronicus. It was as if he knew that Andronicus was even older than him. Plato would ask him about the African plains, and Andronicus would spend hours telling him about his younger days. He told Plato much of his story without ever really telling the truth. Before the end, Andronicus was sure that Plato knew some piece of the truth. Andronicus had told him too much for Plato not to know he was much older than forty.

One day Plato asked Andronicus into his study. Plato was alone in his room, wrapped in blankets beside a fire, and Andronicus could see that he didn't have long to live. Plato beckoned him over, and Andronicus sat on the floor beside him. Neither of them said anything for a while; they just sat in silence, staring into the fire. It reminded Andronicus of the way he and Nnamdi used to sit by the fire.

"You know things," Plato said abruptly, bringing Andronicus out of his trance. He wasn't sure how to respond.

"Sorry," Andronicus said, pretending he hadn't heard the old man.

"You know things, Andronicus," Plato said, turning to look at him. As Andronicus regarded the old man, he saw a look on his face that he hadn't seen before. "Great and terrible things," Plato continued. "Things that most men will never get to know, or have to know."

"How do you know that?"

"I am very old," Plato said with a sigh. "I am very old, and very intelligent, and very wise. They are not the same thing, you know."

"I know," Andronicus said softly, meeting the old man's kind eyes. "I'm very old too," he added.

"I know," Plato said, smiling. "How old, I could not say, but I guess you are older than I am. Am I right?"

"Yes," Andronicus said, his voice barely above a whisper. He had no idea how the old man would react.

"Are there others?" Plato asked, the faint smile still on his lips.

"There were," Andronicus replied, nodding. "There were five of us. I don't know how many are left though, if any."

"One of the many answers you seek?" Plato asked, still smiling.

Andronicus could only nod, still unable to believe Plato had guessed so much on his own.

"What will you do if you find them?" Plato asked, his face growing serious.

"I don't know," Andronicus replied, his voice cracking slightly.

"Does Aristotle know?"

"Does he know what?" Andronicus asked.

"Any of it."

"I don't know. I don't think so."

"You should tell him," Plato said, turning back toward the fire. "He's the smartest man I have ever known. If anyone can help you find your answers, it's him."

"He won't believe me," Andronicus said, "and telling people the truth can be very dangerous for me. I found that out the hard way."

"Aristotle is not like other people," Plato said. "If you tell him the truth, he'll believe you. I won't be here much longer, Andronicus; I think you know that. This is the only way I can help you."

Andronicus sighed. "Alright. I'll tell him, though it may mean I'll have to leave Athens."

"It may," Plato said with a snort, and then he began to laugh. Andronicus joined in, and the two old men laughed heartily beside the fire.

Chapter 34
Wise Men and Wise Words
1

Plato died three weeks later, at the age of eighty. Andronicus had turned one hundred and forty-nine just a few days before. All of Athens had a celebration to honor their greatest teacher. Hundreds of Plato's students from all over Greece came to pay their respects. Aristotle did not say a word the entire day after Plato's passing, and everyone left him alone; they all knew he was Plato's closest pupil.

Already there was much debate as to what would become of Plato's school, the Platonic Academy, as it had been named. Many of Plato's students came forward, claiming they were the right man to lead. Most thought that Aristotle would take over, but Andronicus knew he wouldn't. Aristotle was likely the only man who could keep the Academy as Plato intended, but Andronicus knew he would want no part in that.

After the festivities ended, and the debate about succession had died down a bit, Andronicus went to speak with Aristotle. He found him sitting alone in Plato's study, crying. Aristotle wiped his face with his sleeve when Andronicus entered, but Andronicus could see his eyes were puffy and red.

"You loved him," Andronicus said, sitting across from Aristotle. "As he loved you." Aristotle burst into a fresh bout of tears and hid his face in his hands. Andronicus sat by and waited; he had never been the kind to offer comfort. He waited until Aristotle stopped crying before addressing him again.

"They have already begun to fight over the Academy," Andronicus said. "Without you to guide them, I fear Plato's dream will be lost.

"Plato's dream will never be lost," Aristotle insisted, wiping away tears. "One day the world will be as he imagined it, living in peace and prosperity. The rich will be poor, and the poor rich, enemies will become friends. Nations that have hated each other since the beginning of time will rejoice in harmony."

Aristotle poured himself a glass of wine, and Andronicus noted that the jug was more than half empty. "All men will be equal and live in tranquility and kinship. But I'll not be the one to lead us there."

Andronicus remained silent, not knowing how to respond. He did not believe what Aristotle was saying to be true, but he let him go on anyway.

"Or perhaps Plato's dream is already dead," Aristotle said sadly, looking over at Andronicus. "Plato dreamt of a world where all men could be educated. A world where people could live in harmony and be the masters of their own lives. He wished to see his republic come to life."

"It may not be too late," Andronicus said, not believing it himself but trying to comfort his friend.

"Where?" Aristotle asked angrily. "Here in Athens? That's a laugh. And certainly not in Sparta. The Macedonian king grows strong in the north, and soon he will come for Greece. On that day Plato's dream will truly die."

"It will not happen in Greece or Macedonia," Andronicus said, choosing each word carefully, "and certainly not in Persia or Egypt. But I believe one day Plato's dream will come true." He knew it was possible, that someday, somewhere it could be done. "It may happen a long time from now in a place far away, but there will be a republic one day, and on that day the thinking men of the world will rejoice and remember wise old Plato of Athens and his many teachings."

Aristotle smiled, nodding sadly. "This academy is no longer the place for me," he said, wiping away the last of his tears. "I have to move on."

"Where will you go?" Andronicus asked, pouring himself a glass of wine.

"To Macedonia," Aristotle answered, sounding quite sure of it. "A year ago I received a message from King Philip. He asked me to go north and tutor his son and the other boys who are to be officers one day."

"You would rather teach those boys than the men here at the Academy?" Andronicus asked.

"Oh, yes. Men are vain, and loathe to accept anything new. Children are full of curiosity and wonder. With them I may actually be able to truly teach. With the men here I would simply be telling them what I know and waiting to see what stuck. Besides, this young boy will be a king someday. I can do more by teaching him than I could possibly do here in Athens with these bickering old men."

"And what of the Academy?" Andronicus asked. "Plato loved this place."

Aristotle let out a long sigh and stared into the fire burning in the corner. "Perhaps you should be the one, Andronicus," Aristotle suggested. Andronicus laughed. He knew he could not, but he didn't know how to tell Aristotle why.

"No," Andronicus said softly, gazing into the fire. "I cannot."

"Why not?"

"Because I can't," Andronicus said, then finished off his wine.

"I believe I have learned everything there is to know in the city of Athens," Aristotle said, standing up. "Everything, except for one last thing."

"And what is that?" Andronicus asked, fearing he already knew the answer. He poured himself another glass, preparing for what was about to come.

"The mystery," Aristotle said, meeting Andronicus's eyes.

"What mystery?" Andronicus asked slowly. He knew he was cornered; it had been years in the making.

"Your mystery, Andronicus. Too much of your story is impossible, and yet it holds truth as well; I know it. At first I did not believe you could read four languages, but now I have seen you do it. I did not believe you could be a warrior and a scholar, and yet I have seen you fight, and I have seen you read more than most men could in a lifetime." Aristotle stopped and looked down at his feet, his face turning red. "I have seen your sword, Andronicus, the one you keep wrapped in the red cloak under your bed."

"You searched through my belongings?" Andronicus asked in surprise. Aristotle looked uncomfortable, but stayed his ground.

"I did," Aristotle said, meeting Andronicus's gaze. "I'm sorry, but I wanted answers. I wanted to know if your story was true.

"And what did you find?" Andronicus asked gravely.

"I found the sword," Aristotle repeated, looking like he was ready to flee if Andronicus became hostile.

"What of it?" Andronicus asked, not knowing where he was going with this.

"I saw the mark on the blade," Aristotle said. Andronicus continued to stare at him, waiting for him to explain his meaning.

"I said I saw the mark on the blade," Aristotle said again, expecting recognition from Andronicus but receiving none. "The mark on that blade is the mark of Karpos of Sparta." Andronicus felt his stomach drop. He had no idea Aristotle knew who Karpos was; he didn't know anyone alive knew who Karpos was. He knew his skin must be as pale as snow.

"Karpos of Sparta?" Andronicus repeated, trying to imply he did not know of him.

"You know who he was, Andronicus," Aristotle said, not unkindly. "Any Spartan man carrying a sword made by Karpos of Sparta knows who he was."

"Who was he?" Andronicus asked, struggling to keep his voice even.

"He was the personal blacksmith of King Leonidas. He died at Thermopylae, and all of his swords were thought to be lost to the Persians. How did you come by this sword?"

Andronicus remained silent, debating whether or not to tell Aristotle the truth. He considered Aristotle to be a friend, and he was certainly the smartest man he knew, but it still seemed an incredibly foolish risk to tell anyone the truth. He wanted to tell him, but it seemed too dangerous. What made up his mind was what Plato had said to him. The old man had known the truth, at least part of it, and he had told Andronicus to trust Aristotle.

"It was given to me," Andronicus said finally.

"Given to you by whom?" Aristotle asked.

"It was given to me by Karpos of Sparta,"

Andronicus replied, staring into Aristotle's eyes. "It was one of the final three swords that he ever crafted."

Aristotle didn't say anything for a long time. He just sat there, staring into Andronicus's eyes, weighing the truth of his words. Andronicus kept waiting for him to laugh or shout or just say something.

"Go on," Aristotle said finally, breaking the long, tense silence. "Tell me your story, Andronicus of Sparta. It will not leave this room; you have my word. Tell me the truth, and I will believe you." Andronicus was surprised by Aristotle's reaction. He had thought he would laugh and call him a liar, but instead he appeared to believe Andronicus and genuinely wanted to know how it could be possible. Andronicus had another inner debate, much shorter this time, and then decided to tell him everything.

"Well, I'm not sure where I should start," Andronicus said, pouring more wine.

"From the beginning," Aristotle replied as he sat back down and accepted a cup from Andronicus.

"I am not quite sure where the beginning of this story is. I suppose I should start with my beginning. I was born in Sparta, in the year 496," Aristotle's eyes got wide, and his face grew a bit pale, but he did not interrupt. "My brother, Androcles, was born two years after me. We started training at the age of six, as all Spartans do. When I was sixteen, me and two of the other boys from my class, Lycus, and Nikopheros, were chosen to join King Leonidas' guard amassing outside of Thermopylae."

2

Andronicus told Aristotle his entire life's story, sparing no detail. At first Aristotle just listened, but when the story came to the cave and the rocks, he couldn't hold his silence any longer. Aristotle began asking questions, most of them regarding the rocks and the visions. He seemed especially fascinated with what Andronicus could remember about the rocks themselves, and the glowing water, and the shadowy visions. Andronicus answered his questions the best he could, but he still didn't have most of the answers himself.

When the story reached Swimha, Aristotle began asking a myriad of questions about Africa, from the type of plants there were to the different animals to how the Swihmehe and other tribes had governed themselves. It took Andronicus the entire night to tell Aristotle all of it, and they went through three jugs of wine, most of it consumed by Andronicus. By the end they were both dead tired, but Andronicus knew that Aristotle believed him.

"You're not meant to be in a place like this, Andronicus," Aristotle said after a long yawn. "You have a greater purpose. You have lost sight of it, I think. Too much wine and too many books have dulled your senses. You should be searching for your friends and your brother. If you have lived this long from touching the rocks, it stands to reason that they should still be alive as well."

"Keeping yourself alive for one hundred and fifty years is harder than you might think," Andronicus said, finishing off the last of the wine. "Especially while traveling. That's why I stay in libraries now, much safer."

"You stay in libraries because you still haven't gotten over the death of your friend, Chaka," Aristotle said. "When Chaka was alive, you had a purpose; you were still in search of the answers. But ever since he died, you have been stuck. You think that looking through old books is your way of searching, but it isn't. It's your way of hiding. You found the mark from the cave in an old scroll from Egypt, and that has validated your wasted time for the past thirty years. The answers you seek are not in some book in Athens or Sparta or any other place. The answers you seek are out there," Aristotle waved his hand in a big circle, "and they're searching for you as well. I don't believe you're the only one to have survived. I think the others are out there. They are the answers, each one of them. Should you ever meet again, the possibilities could be endless. Just imagine what kind of impact you could have on society."

"I don't want to have an impact on society,"

Andronicus said angrily, getting to his feet. "I never asked for any of this. I never wanted to live for one hundred and fifty years. I was meant to die a soldier, in battle, like my father and his father before him. I'm not a teacher or a leader or any other damned thing. I'm just one of the unlucky fools who was cursed by those infernal rocks."

Andronicus stormed out of the room without waiting for Aristotle to respond. He hated that a man one hundred years his junior could cut to the core of him so easily. He went to his room and then straight to the jug of wine at his desk. He upended the jug, emptied its contents into his belly, and then stumbled over to his bed.

He wished that old age would have cured him of his temper, and his insecurities, but it hadn't. Aristotle had sent him into a fury, simply by telling him the truth he had been denying for years. For a moment he thought about what Aristotle had said, about the others, about getting back to the hunt. He thought about traveling again, but that reminded him of Chaka, and thinking about Chaka hurt too much. His thoughts slowly turned to less important matters, and a few minutes later he was snoring loudly.

3

Aristotle left Athens less than a month after Plato's death. Andronicus was sad to see him go, but he believed he would see him again. Leadership of the Academy was given to several of the other students, who would run it as a sort of council, but Andronicus knew it would not be the same. Without Plato and Aristotle there to guide them, the discussions in the Academy quickly turned from philosophy and science to politics, a matter Andronicus wanted no part of.

Not long after Aristotle departed, Andronicus left the Academy as well. Rather than moving on from Athens, however, as Aristotle had suggested, he simply moved into the temple of Zeus. The priests were more than happy to welcome Andronicus and his gold. Once back in a library, it was easy to slip back into his old ways.

The scrolls were easy to consume, as was the wine. Andronicus spent day after aimless day drinking, and searching fruitlessly for things he knew were not there. In his heart he knew he was wasting a gift. He had been given eternal life, or so it seemed, and he was using it to drink away his days in a dusty old temple surrounded by people he despised.

What made it even worse was Aristotle's frequent letters from Macedonia. He had begun teaching the young prince and a number of other boys and was taking steps to open his own academy. Aristotle praised the young prince in his letters, going on and on about Alexander's intelligence and level head. He would end each letter by saying what a fine king Alexander would make someday and that Andronicus should be there to fight beside him when the time came.

Andronicus thought about leaving Athens almost every day. It sounded good, there was certainly nothing for him there, and the idea of getting back to his old life was appealing. The thought of joining an army again, however, was quite unsettling. He knew he could do it without being discovered. The only man in Macedonia who knew the truth about him was Aristotle. He could go to Macedonia under some false name, or perhaps even as Andronicus of Sparta if he wished. He could join King Philip's army and help teach the young prince how to fight. But he was scared. He had grown fat and slow, and he didn't know if he could be the man he once was. More than anything he feared he couldn't give up the drink, and he knew he couldn't go to war as a fat, drunken slob.

As his inner struggle worsened, Andronicus slid deeper and deeper into the bottle. By the time he finally did decide to leave Athens, he looked worse than he had since leaving the jungle. His hair was long and disheveled, tangled and matted. His beard was thick, coarse and wild, and stank of wine. Rather than buying a horse, Andronicus chose to walk to Macedonia, as he had done in his youth.

He quickly found that it was much harder to walk all day while constantly drunk. He would walk for a few hours, stumbling down the road, before finding a place to sleep. Other travelers gave him a wide berth, whether because of his alarming appearance or simply because of his smell, Andronicus didn't know or care.

Occasionally, ruffians would approach him, most likely to rob him. Sometimes it was soldiers and sometimes it was just fools with blades, looking for easy money. Whoever they were, as soon as they drew on him, Andronicus would throw down his things and draw his sword. His appearance was unseemly and haggard, but apparently he still looked opposing enough, because usually when he drew his sword on someone, they would leave. He ended up treating the people on the road the way he had once treated the lions of the plains.

It was lonely traveling alone, lonely and hopeless. It had been fifty years since Chaka had died. It seemed an absurd thought to Andronicus, but it was true. It still felt like it had happened just yesterday. He could still remember the way Chaka had looked before he died, the way he had grown frail and weak, and he knew it was his fault. He wondered if Chaka would still be alive if they hadn't crossed the desert. He had begun to stop aging, just like Andronicus, and he certainly hadn't looked the eighty-four years he had been at the end. Andronicus wondered for the millionth time how it all worked, and if he would ever know.

Chaka's last words came back to him often. "Find them," he had said. Andronicus still didn't know exactly who or what Chaka was referring to, but he knew what he meant. He had told Andronicus to keep searching, to not give up, but instead Andronicus had slithered into a sack of wine. Andronicus knew what he was supposed to do, but it was just too much easier to drink away his troubles. His purse never seemed to grow any lighter, and he never looked a day older, but he knew he was wasting away.

Chapter 35
Through Hell and Out the Other Side
1

By the time Andronicus reached Macedonia, he was a complete mess. His hair and tattered clothes were covered in dirt and vomit, and he smelled horrid. It had been over a year since he had not been drunk. He drank when he woke, which was usually sometime in the afternoon, until he dropped into a restless sleep. No matter how much he drank though, he could no longer escape the dreams, though it did make them harder to remember. Every night he would dream of things he didn't understand. He tried to remember them in the mornings, but his morning drink would blur it all together.

Macedonia was different than it had been twenty years earlier. There was more of a military feel to the place. Andronicus began having to avoid the roads much more as soldiers marched to and fro through the budding kingdom. He didn't have to listen very long to hear the people praising King Philip. Everywhere he went in Macedonia, they all spoke of the coming invasion. The closer he got to the capital city of Pella, the more he heard.

King Philip had conquered the Thracians, and he was in the process of conquering the Greeks as well. In Athens the scholars had spoken of the Macedonians and Philip like allies, but in Macedonia the people spoke of Greece like she was theirs for the taking. It made Andronicus mad to hear common folk speak of Greece in such fashion, but he knew they might well be right. He supposed in the end it didn't matter who led the attack. All that mattered was that Greek men were going to invade Persia, and Andronicus wanted to be a part of it despite himself.

It had been more than a hundred years since Andronicus had gone to war with the Persians, but he still felt that old fire. He knew it wouldn't be the same people he had fought with his friends, but he would be battling their descendants. They had killed too many of his friends, and he had killed too many of them. He knew he had to be with the army when they fought

Persia again, but he didn't know how he was going to prepare in time.

2

The first thing Andronicus did once he reached Pella was find Aristotle, who had told him where to go in his letters. He stumbled his way there while enjoying a fine wine from Larissa. When Andronicus arrived at the large white stone building that Aristotle had told him to find, he sat down to rest before going inside. As he sat in the building's shadow, Aristotle happened to come out.

"My old friend," Aristotle said merrily as he walked up to Andronicus. "You made it. How are you?"

"Mphm," Andronicus grunted in response, getting to his feet. Aristotle took a step backwards as Andronicus's stench hit him. "How did you get such a fine building as this?" Andronicus asked, gesturing up at it.

"Well," Aristotle said, smiling modestly, "the king wishes his son to get the finest education. He has awarded me every kindness and spared no expense in making the Lyceum the finest school of any kind in the world."

"The Lyceum," Andronicus repeated with a frown. "That's what you call this place?"

"It is," Aristotle nodded, looking Andronicus over. "My own attempt at Plato's dream. Not much different than the Academy, really."

"Then why did you leave?" Andronicus said accusingly, slurring his words. "When you left, the Academy went to hell. And what did you leave for? So that you could start a new one, with the Macedonian king's money."

Aristotle frowned, not responding to Andronicus's drunken accusation. In truth Andronicus didn't even care; he was just too drunk to stop himself.

"I see you lost some weight," Aristotle said after an awkward pause.

"Aye." Andronicus nodded drunkenly. "I walked here from Athens."

"When did you leave?" Aristotle asked curiously.

"341," Andronicus answered, followed by a belch.

"That is almost a year ago, Andronicus," Aristotle said slowly.

"A year?" Andronicus grunted, looking confused, "what year is it now?"

"It is 340," Aristotle said sadly, "it is may of 340."

"Well I'll be damned," Andronicus said with a bemused chuckle, "no wonder I lost so much weight."

"Andronicus . . ."

"What?" Andronicus barked.

"You have to stop this. You may not be able to die of old age, but that doesn't mean you need to try to find out if you can die by wine."

"I can still fight," Andronicus slurred. "I could be as drunk as a mule and still beat ten men in a fight." He let out another large belch as if to confirm the fact.

"You are as drunk as a mule," Aristotle insisted.

"Good, then go get me ten men to fight." Andronicus let out a hearty laugh, followed by another belch.

"Do you have a place to stay?" Aristotle asked, trying to change the subject.

Andronicus shook his head. "No. I thought you would tell me where to go."

Aristotle sighed. "Very well. I know of a place. I can take you there."

Aristotle went inside to get a couple of walking sticks, and some water. As they walked through the city, Aristotle told Andronicus all about Macedonia and the young prince. Many of the people they passed gave them curious and frightened looks, as if they couldn't believe a man like Aristotle would be seen walking with such a disgusting vagrant. Several times as they walked Andronicus went to take a drink, but each time Aristotle stopped him.

By the time they reached the small house

Aristotle had arranged for him, Andronicus was feeling quite ill. When they entered, Aristotle made a fire while Andronicus sat in the corner, holding his pounding head. He tried to drink some water as Aristotle began roasting some vegetables and a nice chunk of meat over the fire, but his stomach wanted wine. When the food was ready, Aristotle called him over.

"What will you do now that you're in Macedonia?" Aristotle asked as they sat down to supper.

"I haven't thought about it much," Andronicus admitted, his head resting in his hands. It was the longest he had gone without a drink in months, and his head was pounding like a drum. The smell of the roasting meat made his stomach churn, and he had to keep from vomiting.

"Well, think about it now then," Aristotle said.

"I suppose I'll find the biggest library and start searching," Andronicus said, his hands covering his eyes to shield them from the dim light of the fire.

"Searching, is that still what you call it?" Aristotle asked, giving Andronicus a disapproving look. "I call it something else."

"Oh, and what's that?" Andronicus asked angrily.

"Hiding."

"Are you calling me a coward?" Andronicus asked, finally taking his hands off his eyes.

"Not at all. I have no doubt that you're the bravest man I have ever met. But you have grown scared. Not of any man," Aristotle added quickly in response to the look Andronicus gave him. "I think you're scared of yourself. Of what you could do. Of what you could become."

Andronicus wished there was a jug of wine nearby. He hated hearing Aristotle's words because he knew they were true.

"I'm not saying you should go and save the world," Aristotle added. "I think you should be a soldier again. Even if just for a little while."

"Be a soldier again?" Andronicus said in mock surprise, as if he hadn't been thinking of it himself. "I haven't been a soldier since before your grandfather was born."

Aristotle nodded. "I know, but you're still a soldier, Andronicus, or at least you can be. You always were a soldier, even when you didn't want to be. I remember every bit of the story you told me, and I still believe it. You tried to live in Africa with your wife, but when she was taken from you, what did you do?"

Andronicus turned away from Aristotle, wanting a drink now more than ever. He could still see the faces of all the people he had killed that day so long ago. He wondered how many generations he had ended, one hundred years later.

"I don't mean to guilt you Andronicus," Aristotle said gently. "I'm simply trying to remind you who you are. I have known other men whose wives were killed, but you're the only one I know who massacred the people who did it. In your travels throughout Africa, how many times did you have to fight your way out of trouble? Even when you were in Egypt, trying to live in peace, when the war came to your door, you fought, and won, as you always have. Even after nearly dying of thirst and starvation in the Sahara Desert."

"Enough!" Andronicus shouted, slamming his hand on the table and standing up despite his pounding head. "I hear your words, but I can't do it."

"Yes you can, Andronicus," Aristotle insisted. "You don't have to be a king, just a foot soldier. I know many of the king's officers. Cleitus the Black is King Philip's chief of guard. I can introduce you to him, and he will give you a place amongst his ranks. King Philip is planning to march on Persia within the next two years, and you can be there when he does."

The thought of fighting the Persians again was more appealing than anything Andronicus had thought about for a long time. In his heart he knew he wanted to do it, to fight again, as he was meant to. Much louder than that, however, was the insistent pounding in his head, demanding he find a drink and fast. The thought of fighting the Persians again was nice, but it quickly was eclipsed by the pounding.

"I can't," Andronicus said with a sigh, sounding defeated. "Now point me toward the nearest wine merchant before I get sick."

"You're already sick, my friend," Aristotle said sadly. "You must stop this madness."

"I can't," Andronicus said, sounding more sad than angry. "It hurts too much."

"You have to accept what happened, and move on," Aristotle insisted. "You don't know how long you're going to be alive."

"I don't mean it hurts like that," Andronicus said, looking Aristotle in the eye. "I mean it hurts my body. It hurts almost as badly as having my shoulder torn apart did."

It was true. Andronicus had tried to stop drinking after leaving Sparta and again after leaving Athens, and a dozen times in between, but it had never worked. Every time he tried he reached a point of such physical pain that he had to give in and drink again. He didn't know how he had let himself reach such a place, but he had no idea how to get back out.

"I have heard of this," Aristotle said, sounding interested, "when men drink so much wine that their body literally can't be without it."

"Exactly," Andronicus said, nodding.

"I have seen men recover from such an illness," Aristotle added with a smile.

"Impossible," Andronicus replied. "I've tried. It's too much."

"Then you didn't try for long enough," Aristotle said matter-of-factly. "Maybe it takes longer for you because of, you know."

"Perhaps," Andronicus said, nodding curiously. He hadn't thought of that. Most things took a terribly long time for him now. His hair grew painfully slow, and his wounds healed slower than most, so it made sense that it would take a longer time to kick such a terribly strong habit.

"It will take time, and it may hurt worse than you know," Aristotle said, "but it is in our darkest hours that we must focus to see the light. If you make it through to the other side, you can start to live again, and perhaps someday you will find your light once more."

"Alright," Andronicus said, sounding tired but feeling a touch of hope for the first time in years. "I'll try."

3

Aristotle was right; it did hurt worse than he knew. At first it was just Andronicus's head that hurt. Then his stomach began to spin around inside him, and it became impossible to keep any food down. The first few nights were the worst. He barely got any sleep, and when he did it was racked by nightmares, all of the worst things he ever dreamed of: the terrible storm, the fire in the woods, the haunting red eyes, all the dreams he couldn't understand.

He would awake from the dreams covered in sweat and then go back to sleep feeling ill. His body shook violently day and night. Aristotle told him constantly to drink more water, but Andronicus just vomited it all back up anyway. He had to force the water down, just so he had something he could send back up. One moment he would have a fever and be sweating like he was back in the jungle, and the next he would feel like he was out in the snow, shivering like a babe.

Not long after the fevers started, he began to hallucinate. He would see all manner of things in the dark room with him. Sometimes it would be beasts, the kinds he had seen and the kinds he hadn't. In the middle of one terrible feverish dream, Andronicus saw a man with a wolf's head walk into the room, just like the old statues in Egypt. Other times he saw his old friends. Andronicus knew that some of the people he saw were dead. Archelaus came by and laughed at him for being so weak and pathetic. Manyara came by and cried as she saw him tossing and turning, soaked in sweat. When Chaka came, it was almost too much. Chaka didn't say a word or show any sign of emotion; he just stood in the corner and watched Andronicus's struggle in silence.

As the hallucinations persisted, Andronicus

wondered if he was going mad. Aristotle continued to care for him as much as he could, sending in a nurse whenever he had to go teach the boys. Andronicus lost himself in the fever and the dreams, the days began to mix, and he was never sure if it was day or night. His body felt like it was dying, and his mind was trapped in a black hole.

After a month of the terrible fevers and dreams, Andronicus finally started to feel himself again. His temperature dropped, and his body shook less and less. The dreams never stopped, but he started dreaming more of the pleasant ones and less about the fires and storms and endless black pits. He still stayed in bed most of the day, but little by little, he began doing more until he was finally ready to begin training so he could join the Macedonian ranks, even if only for a while.

4

It took three full months before Andronicus felt strong enough to start training. His head had felt clear for weeks, but it took a long time for his body to adjust to sobriety again.

King Philip was already laying siege to the city of Perinthus, the last city before Persian territory. Within a year's time the Macedonians would meet the Persians in battle, and Andronicus needed to be there when they did. While King Philip and his army lay siege, and Aristotle spent his time tutoring the prince, Andronicus trained his body, harder than he had in a hundred years, perhaps harder than ever.

From dawn to dusk Andronicus pushed his body past its limits. At first he just ran for miles and miles, flushing every last drop of alcohol from his system. It felt better than he would have believed to be free of it. It felt like being young again, which in a way he still was.

Andronicus trained his body for six months, striving to regain the physique he had lost. His stomach had grown pudgy and round, so he ran every day. He ran a little more each day, until he was running from dawn, until well after noon. Once he felt lean and healthy again, he began to work on his muscles. He still remembered the old drills that Archelaus used to make them do to get strong. Once he found the right boulders, it was just a matter of lifting them properly. Archelaus had taught him dozens of exercises, and he still remembered them all. He spent months strengthening every muscle in his body, from front to back and top to bottom.

It took the better part of a year before Andronicus truly felt like he was himself again, truly himself for the first time in decades. Once his body was back to being the muscular, intimidating force it had been in his youth, Andronicus went to the quartermaster. Aristotle had already made all the necessary introductions, so the man was expecting him. Andronicus asked to train with the other soldiers. The balding quartermaster looked him up and down and grunted his assent, clearly not expecting much from Andronicus. They all knew what a drunk he had been, and he was excited to show them who he really was.

Andronicus stepped to the middle of a dirt ring, and a tall, fierce-looking soldier stepped in across from him. The man was holding a wooden practice sword, and the quartermaster tossed one to Andronicus as well. The tall soldier assumed a battle stance, but Andronicus stood perfectly still, not taking his eyes off his opponent. A few onlooking soldiers chuckled and whispered amongst themselves. Andronicus could tell they thought he was a joke, and he felt invigorated by what he knew was about to happen.

The big soldier stepped forward and raised his sword above his head. Andronicus couldn't believe the man's poor form, and didn't feel at all guilty for what he was about to do. As the man stepped toward him and swung, Andronicus acted as he always had, with fierce precision. He took a quick step to the side and swung his sword into the big man's gut. The man bent down as he let out a loud guffaw. Andronicus brought his sword down hard on the man's back—so hard the wooden sword cracked in half and even left a bloody line across the man's back.

The soldier fell onto his face with a pained grunt. Andronicus put his foot on the man's back and pressed him into the dirt. He looked over at the men who had been laughing at him a moment earlier and was pleased to see fear in their eyes. He released his beaten opponent and looked over at the stunned quartermaster.

"Aristotle told me you were a mighty warrior who had lost his way," the balding man said, eyeing Andronicus much differently now, "but I did not expect that."

"Have you ever known Aristotle to tell a lie?" Andronicus asked.

"No I haven't," the man admitted. "You're welcome to train here with me and my men, sir, but I think you may be above our skill level. You should be with Cleitus the Black and the king's guard."

"Where can I find this Cleitus?" Andronicus asked, recalling Aristotle mentioning him.

The quartermaster laughed. "You don't find him, friend. He finds you. But perhaps your friend Aristotle can help you in that regard."

Andronicus thanked the quartermaster and gave a final look at the group of soldiers staring at him. The big man he had fought was just getting to his feet, a nasty red bruise already forming on his back.

Andronicus went straight to Aristotle's. Swinging a sword again had made him eager to get back to fighting for real.

5

Andronicus was finally ready to begin real training and join the Macedonian army full time. Aristotle arranged a meeting between him and Cleitus the Black, the captain of King Philip's guard. If all went well, Andronicus would join the king's guard. The thought of being a member of a king's guard once again gave him chills. He still remembered the look in Leonidas's eyes as he had told them to go, the faint light from his torch bouncing off his rough, weathered face. Andronicus had been charged with protecting that king as well, and Leonidas had been killed by

Persians.

Now he would be charged with the protection of King Philip II of Macedonia on the cusp of his invasion of Persia. Andronicus cared not at all for Philip or for Macedonia; he knew the war would not reach Sparta. All he cared about was getting a second chance at the Persians. They could have killed the Persians when he was a boy. They could have ended them. They had chased them all the way back to Asia. But then the Spartans had chosen to go home.

The day he had left the battlefield of Plataea, with his brother and his friends beside him, and an arrow wound in his hip, was still one of the most shameful days of Andronicus's life. When they left Thermopylae, at least they had been able to say the king had ordered them to leave. When they left Plataea, there was no honorable reason. Every man among them had known they could defeat the Persian empire if they kept going, but they didn't.

Now Andronicus had a second chance at killing the people who had killed his father, his friends, and even his king. It didn't matter that he would be with Macedonians instead of Spartans or that he would be taking orders from men just a fraction of his age. All that mattered was that he would get to kill Persians again, to do what he was born to do. His destiny may have changed drastically over his long lifetime, but at the start, he had been destined to kill Persians, just like his father.

Andronicus felt excited for the first time in decades. Getting himself back in shape felt amazing, and he could only imagine how good it would feel to be back in the heart of a battle again.

Andronicus knocked on Aristotle's door. A moment later, Aristotle opened it and welcomed him in. It was much darker inside than out, and it took Andronicus's eyes a moment to register the man sitting in the corner.

As soon as he saw him, Andronicus knew why they called the man Cleitus the Black. He had long, shiny black hair that hung over his face in wet mats. His beard was trimmed on his cheeks but grew thick and black around his mouth and chin. Andronicus had never seen a beard manicured like that before, but thought it was an impressive look. Around Cleitus's shoulders hung a heavy black wolf-skin cloak linked around his neck by a black chain. His leather soldier's garments were all dyed black as well.

Besides Cleitus's clear fondness for black, Andronicus thought the word could also be used to describe the man's demeanor. He had a dark gloominess in his eyes, and his face was etched with despondency. His thick brow only added more cloudiness to his eyes, and his nose was long and bent to one side. He reminded Andronicus of Archelaus, his old teacher from another lifetime.

"You're Andronicus of Sparta?" Cleitus said in a rough, stern voice, much like Archelaus's.

"I am," Andronicus said, meeting Cleitus's dark eyes.

"Aristotle tells me you're a fine warrior."

"Aristotle tells it true," Andronicus replied, trying to gauge the man, and failing.

"Why do you not fight for Sparta?" Cleitus asked, leaning forward.

"Sparta is no longer my home," Andronicus said, feeling a pang of regret as he spoke the words, knowing them to be true. He still thought of Sparta as his true home, and he thought of himself as a Spartan, he always would, but he knew there was no longer any place for him there.

"Why do you wish to fight for Macedonia?" Cleitus asked, staring intently at Andronicus.

"I'm told that King Philip means to fight the Persians," Andronicus replied, meeting the man's iron gaze with his own. "I have unfinished business with them."

"So you wish to kill Persians. Is that all?" Cleitus asked, sounding disappointed.

"Yes, I wish to kill Persians, but that is not why I wish to join King Philip's ranks."

"Then why do you want to join the king's ranks?" Cleitus gave Andronicus a cold, black look. Andronicus thought the man was the best interrogator he had ever met, and still had no idea what he was thinking.

"Because I owe it to Aristotle," Andronicus said. "He saved my life, and he asked me to be by the prince's side when the fighting comes."

"Aristotle saved your life?" Cleitus asked, his eyes twinkling with amusement, the first sign of emotion he had shown.

"He did," Andronicus said, nodding. "Not from any man or beast, but from myself."

"And now he wishes for you to fight alongside the prince," Cleitus repeated, sitting back in his chair and returning to his cold, emotionless demeanor.

"I do," Aristotle said from the corner. It was the first time he had spoken since Andronicus had arrived. Cleitus turned his cold gaze toward Aristotle, who shifted uncomfortably in his seat. "This man is the finest warrior I have ever known, and I believe he would serve the prince well as his guard."

"What do you know of protecting princes?" Cleitus asked, turning back to Andronicus.

"Nothing," Andronicus replied, "but I know more about fighting and killing than any man in your army."

"Are you prepared to defend that statement?" Cleitus asked, rising to his feet.

"I am," Andronicus said, standing as well and not taking his eyes off Cleitus.

"Good." Cleitus stepped toward the door, and Andronicus followed. Aristotle tagged along behind, a nervous look on his face.

Once outside, Andronicus and Cleitus drew their swords and sized each other up.

"That's a fine sword you have there," Cleitus said with a cold smile. "We shall see if you know how to use it." He swung his sword in a hard, clean blow, but Andronicus parried it easily. Cleitus swung again, and Andronicus stepped back to dodge it.

Andronicus swung his sword, and it clashed against Cleitus's. They did a sort of dance for a while, stepping and sidestepping each other, their swords ringing out in the quiet morning air. Andronicus looked for an opening but failed to find one. Cleitus was giving him a better fight than he had had in a very long time. Finally, Andronicus found his opening; Cleitus was an expert swordsman to be sure, but Andronicus had been fighting much longer. He noticed that every time Cleitus swung down from the left side, he left his right leg momentarily open.

Andronicus waited patiently for the right time to strike. As soon as Cleitus raised his sword over his left shoulder, Andronicus kicked his right leg out from under him. Cleitus went sprawling in the dirt, and before he could regain himself, Andronicus had his sword resting above Cleitus's throat. Cleitus looked up at Andronicus in surprise and then slowly nodded. Andronicus pulled his sword away and sheathed it, then helped Cleitus to his feet.

"As always, you speak true Aristotle," Cleitus said as he dusted the dirt off his black cloak. "This man truly is a skilled warrior."

"And knowledgeable in strategy as well," Aristotle added with a smile.

"Very well," Cleitus said, meeting Andronicus's eye. "You will join Prince Alexander's personal guard. When can you leave?"

"Today," Andronicus replied happily.

Chapter 36
Eyes of Land and Sea
1

"I've already told Alexander a bit about you," Aristotle said as he led Andronicus up a long, winding stairway that went up a tall hill to where Alexander and the other boys were waiting. Cleitus had agreed to let Aristotle take Andronicus to the prince alone. Andronicus knew he reported to Cleitus now, but he was glad to be alone with Aristotle for this first meeting.

"Oh, and what did you tell him?" Andronicus asked, waiting for Aristotle to catch up.

"That you're a true Spartan warrior," Aristotle said, beginning to pant as they continued climbing. "And that he can learn much in the ways of battle from you."

"So you told the boy that I can teach him what you cannot," Andronicus said, a little annoyed.

"Yes, I suppose I did," Aristotle answered thoughtfully. "You told me that when you were a boy you had two teachers, one for battle and one for philosophy, did you not?"

"That's right," Andronicus had to stop again to wait for Aristotle.

"OK, are you ready then?" Aristotle said once he caught his breath. Andronicus grunted and then followed Aristotle into the training yard, where they found a small group of boys cheering on two boys who were fighting wildly in the dirt. They were not using swords, but both boys had blood smeared across their noses and mouths.

"That's enough!" Aristotle yelled when he saw them. The boys who had been cheering all stopped as soon as they heard Aristotle, but the two fighters kept going.

"Alexander! Hephaestion!" Aristotle yelled at them, "stop this at once!"

"No," Andronicus whispered to Aristotle, "let them finish. I would see what this prince is made of." Aristotle gave Andronicus a disapproving look, but he let the boys continue. The other three boys who had been cheering looked at Andronicus fearfully, and then turned back to the fight.

Andronicus watched with the others as the two boys rolled around in the dirt, punching each other. He was a bit disappointed in what he saw; he had hoped the boy already knew how to fight. He still didn't know which one was the prince, but neither boy could fight especially well. They were only sixteen, but Andronicus was quite sure that he, Lycus, or Niko at age sixteen could have easily beaten both of these boys single-handed.

Andronicus let the boys fight for a minute longer before stepping in and wrenching one off the other. The boy went sprawling in the dirt and jumped to his feet, ready to attack whoever had thrown him. He had a strong look, short curly brown hair, and a lean fighter's face. The boy was tall and looked to be stronger than the other boys and had certainly beaten the boy lying in the dirt.

"Andronicus," Aristotle said from behind him, "this is Hephaestion." Andronicus looked around and was surprised to see Aristotle pointing at the boy who was standing.

"And this," Aristotle said, helping the loser to his feet, "is Prince Alexander of Macedonia."

Alexander looked like no one Andronicus had ever seen. His hair was a golden blonde that Andronicus had only seen a few times before. His neck was tilted slightly to the left as if he were deep in contemplation, but Andronicus could tell that he always looked that way. He was short for his age, much shorter than the boy he had been fighting, but he had a strong look about him as well. His most remarkable characteristic, however, was his eyes. His left eye was dark brown, like dirt after a short rain, and his right was bluer than any eye that Andronicus had ever seen, like the sky on a cloudless day.

Alexander eyed him curiously. "You're the Spartan?" he asked with all the authority that comes with royalty.

"I am," Andronicus answered in a stern voice, meeting the boys mismatched eyes. "I'm here to teach you boys how to fight."

"We know how to fight," Hephaestion said.

"Do you now?" Andronicus asked, raising one eyebrow. "And I suppose you're the best fighter amongst this lot, yes?"

"I am," Hephaestion said, nodding confidently.

"You there, boy," Andronicus pointed at one of the three boys who had been watching. "What's your name?"

"Cassander," the boy answered nervously, but he stepped forward nonetheless.

"Do you know how to fight, Cassander?" Andronicus asked. The frightened boy was taller than the others but much thinner. He had long, greasy black hair and eyes almost as blue as Alexander's right eye.

"Yes, sir," Cassander said, nodding, "but not as well as Hephaestion."

"Good, come here." Andronicus gestured for the boy to approach him.

"What's this?" Hephaestion asked angrily.

"I'm going to teach Cassander how to knock you on your ass," Andronicus said. Alexander and the other boys laughed at that. Even Aristotle let out a chuckle.

"I'd like to see you try," Hephaestion said menacingly.

"Good. Now, shall we use swords or continue on as you were?" Andronicus asked.

"It doesn't matter," Hephaestion said. "He won't beat me either way."

"Very well," Andronicus said with a knowing smile. "No swords it is then. Take your places, boys."

Hephaestion and Cassander got in the middle of the yard and faced each other. The other two boys who had been watching began cheering for Cassander, but Alexander remained silent, watching his friends intently.

"Begin!" Andronicus bellowed. Hephaestion lunged at Cassander and knocked him back into the dirt. Before Cassander could react, Hephaestion began pummeling him with his fists.

"Stop!" Andronicus shouted. The cheering boys all fell silent at the sound of Andronicus's voice, but Hephaestion continued pounding Cassander into the dirt. Andronicus grabbed Hephaestion by the back of his shirt and sent him flying across the yard.

"I said stop, boy!" Andronicus shouted. "If you wish to train with me, you'll do as I say."

"Who said I wish to train with you?" the boy asked as he jumped to his feet.

"Cassander, on your feet," Andronicus said without taking his eyes off Hephaestion. Cassander slowly stood up, wiping away the blood that Hephaestion had drawn from his nose and bottom lip. Cassander ambled over to where Andronicus was waiting for him. He looked like he had no desire to continue. Andronicus leaned down to whisper in his ear.

"He charges like a bull," Andronicus said, "with all his weight on top. When he charges you, take a step backward and to the left. Then, as fast as you can, bring your right knee up into his gut. When he bends over, kick his left leg out from under him. Then when he falls into the dirt, jump on top of him, but instead of punching him blindly, bend his left arm behind his head. Then wait for my instruction. Have you got all that?"

Cassander gave Andronicus a semi-confident nod, and then the two boys faced each other again, waiting for Andronicus's signal. Alexander was watching with a fierce look of concentration on his face.

"Begin!" Andronicus shouted. Hephaestion charged, just as he had before, but this time just as Hephaestion reached him, Cassander stepped back and brought his right leg up. It caught Hephaestion unprepared and knocked the wind out of him with an audible thump. He bent over in pain, and Cassander quickly kicked his left leg out from under him. Hephaestion went down hard, and Cassander jumped on top of him.

Before Hephaestion could so much as take a breath, Cassander had his arm locked behind his head. Hephaestion writhed in the dirt, trying to get free and still struggling for air.

"Cassander!" Andronicus said, cutting through the sound of the cheering boys, "bring your left leg around his head." Cassander did as Andronicus instructed. "Now fall backward, and take his arm with you." Cassander tipped backward, holding onto Hephaestion's arm, and Hephaestion came up into the air, his arm bent awkwardly behind him.

"I yield, I yield!" Hephaestion shouted.

"Release him," Andronicus said. Cassander let him go, and Hephaestion went tumbling into the dirt, clutching his arm. Cassander beamed up at Andronicus in amazement, clearly shocked he had beaten his much stronger friend.

"It worked!" Cassander exclaimed, getting to

his feet. He ran over to the other boys, who all congratulated him, none more than Alexander. Andronicus glanced at Aristotle as the boys cheered, and Aristotle smiled and gave him an approving nod.

"As I said before," Andronicus stated, turning back to the boys. "I'm here to teach you how to fight."

"We will be most eager to learn from you, master Spartan," Alexander replied, speaking for all of them, "even Hephaestion." Everyone turned to look at Hephaestion. He was still on the ground holding his arm.

"I'm sorry," he said, meeting Andronicus's eye. "I was wrong. I would be happy to have you teach us."

"Good," Andronicus said, helping him up. He was already impressed with the boys, not with their skills in fighting but with their sense of honor. Aristotle had taught them well, and with the addition of tactical knowledge, these boys would be ready to conquer the world.

2

"That was a nice trick you showed Cassander," Aristotle said as they walked back down the steps. The boys had all gone down to the water, and Andronicus and Aristotle were headed back to Andronicus's house, which was not far from where the prince stayed. "Where did you learn it?"

"From my first teacher, when I was much younger than them. Who has been teaching them?"

"King Philip has a master at arms who has been teaching them, or so he says," Aristotle said, a trace of annoyance in his voice. "Now you see why I've been asking you to do it. Those boys will lead armies someday, so they ought to know how to do it properly."

"Aye," Andronicus agreed. "They have much to learn. And I suppose I'll have to be the one to teach them."

"Yes, you will," Aristotle said, "and quickly. Philip is already planning to lay siege to Byzantium. He will be upon the Persians in less than a year's time, and I fear he will want his son by his side when he does."

"And I suspect those boys will follow Alexander wherever he goes," Andronicus said, reminded of his own childhood friends.

"Oh, yes," Aristotle agreed, "those boys would follow Alexander if he walked into a pit of lions."

"He's a strong boy," Andronicus said thoughtfully, "curious though."

Aristotle smiled. "He's the most curious boy I've ever met. He's fascinated by the old stories, especially the Trojan war. I can't tell you how many times I've thought about telling him your story."

Andronicus gave Aristotle a grave look.

"I never have," Aristotle said quickly, "and I never will, though I suspect you may tell him yourself someday."

"Fine," Andronicus said, "just so long as you don't."

As they continued down the path, Andronicus saw a woman come out of a small stone house and start toward them. At first he thought she was a slave, but as she approached, he realized she had the sort of regal quality that only came with royalty. Her natural beauty was made even more striking by her royal apparel.

"Queen Olympias," Aristotle said, bowing slightly. "How are you this fine day?"

"Is this the Spartan you've brought to teach my son?" she asked, her voice cutting through the air like a knife.

"Yes." Aristotle nodded and turned to Andronicus. "This is Andronicus of Sparta, an old friend of mine and a student of Plato's."

"Have you ever fought in a real war, Andronicus?" Olympias asked, eyeing him coldly.

"Aye," Andronicus said, nodding. "When I was young."

"And have you ever protected a king?"

Andronicus already disliked this woman. She had the air of pompous wealth that Andronicus had always mistrusted.

"Aye," Andronicus said. "I was a guard to the

king of Sparta."

"And you left your king?" Olympias asked boldly. Andronicus said nothing, letting the words hang in the air. Thus far he hadn't lied, and he wanted to avoid it if possible. King Cleomenes had been king of Sparta for decades, and Andronicus knew this woman could trace his lie if she wanted to. Andronicus swallowed and was about to answer, when Aristotle spoke up.

"Andronicus served Cleomenes loyally," he assured her. "But after the war, he wished to study. He left his king to come to Athens and find Plato. Now he has come to Macedonia at my request because those boys need to know how to fight."

"I thought *you* were teaching my son how to fight," Olympias said, glaring at Aristotle.

"I'm teaching the boys strategy," he said, "but I can't teach them how to handle a sword. I'm merely an academic. This man can teach your son how to defend himself in battle."

"Is that what you're going to do?" Olympias asked, turning her fiery gaze back to Andronicus. He nodded slowly, taken aback by the woman's ferocity. "Can you assure me that my son will live through the war that is coming?"

"I can assure you that I'll do what I can to teach him how—"

"No, I want you to promise that you'll keep my son alive." She glared at Andronicus, and he shifted his gaze uncomfortably. She frightened him in a way he couldn't explain.

"Fine," Andronicus grunted, meeting her eye again. "I'll keep your son alive, but I can't make any promises for the others."

"I don't care about the others," Olympias said, waving her hand in disdain. "My son is going to be king, not them. Keep him alive, Andronicus of Sparta, or you'll answer to me." She turned around and began marching down the hill. Andronicus glanced at Aristotle, who gave him a wary shrug, and then they continued walking, neither saying a word about Olympias's threat.

Andronicus trained the boys from dusk till dawn every day, pushing them harder than they had ever been pushed. By the end of the first month they all hated him, except for Alexander. He seemed more eager to learn by the day as Andronicus taught them new ways to disarm a man and fight off opponents. Mostly he taught them the sword, how to beat one man or three, and how to fight as a unit.

Twice a week Aristotle joined Andronicus, and together they taught the boys tactics and strategy. Aristotle had only studied warfare a bit, but his immense intelligence was always of use. Andronicus had not only studied warfare extensively in his youth in Sparta, he had also read dozens, if not hundreds, of texts on warfare and strategy in his many years spent in libraries and temples. Between the two of them, the boys could not have asked for a better environment in which to learn how to lead armies and wage war.

When Alexander turned sixteen, his father ordered his tutoring to end and his training to begin full time. Once he saw what Andronicus had done for his son and the other boys in such a short time, Philip demanded that they study from him until it was time for them to join the army. Before he returned to the front, the king asked Andronicus personally to prepare his son for the war that was coming.

Andronicus liked the king at first; he even reminded him a bit of Leonidas. Philip was a warrior-king. He led his men into every battle, and he had the scars to prove it. He had a bad limp on his left side, and he walked laboriously because of it. His stocky arms were covered in small white lines where blades had cut him over the years. His voice was rough and deep and not very kingly to Andronicus's ears, but powerful nonetheless.

One thing Andronicus did not wholly approve of was that the king had already taken seven wives, and it was rumored that he meant to take another. Andronicus had seen the king's other wives, and they were all as regal and as beautiful as Olympias. Each of them were royalty in their own right, and several of them had given Philip daughters. Alexander was Philip's only son though, and therefore, his heir, but Alexander had eight sisters by four different mothers. Every time the king was with one of his other wives, Andronicus noticed the prince scowling at them, and he could tell that Alexander wished that his father loved only his mother.

When the king left with his army to take the ancient city of Byzantium, he left Alexander as regent and heir apparent to the Macedonian kingdom. Alexander was only sixteen, but he was smart, and he had Aristotle with him to counsel him. Part of Andronicus wished he was going with Philip, where the fighting would be. He knew he would be of more use to Alexander, but he was eager to get to the fight.

Alexander was more than eager to take command, something he had been anticipating for his entire life. After Philip left with the army, Alexander expected to begin kingly duties full time, but instead his training with Andronicus continued. While word of his father's campaign kept coming back, it became increasingly difficult to train Alexander and his friends. Not only were they constantly interrupted, Alexander no longer seemed to want a teacher. Now that he thought he was in charge, he was done with his childlike lessons.

Rumors of Philip's conquest came back every day, and the city grew restless. Andronicus did his best to try and keep the prince and the other boys focused on their training, but more and more Alexander spoke of marching off to join his father.

4

One day Andronicus was woken by a loud bang at his door. A moment later, Alexander barged in, with Hephaestion and Cassander right behind him. All of them looked eager and excited. Alexander marched in with a scroll in his hand, holding it out to Andronicus. Andronicus shook the sleep off himself in an instant, the way only a soldier can.

"What's this?" Andronicus asked, taking the

scroll. He quickly read the message. "Thracian Maedi have taken up arms against the crown. They are amassing a force in the north and mean to march on Macedonia while King Philip is away. Please respond at once."

Andronicus looked at the young boy's eager face and shook his head. "You can't," he said, already knowing what Alexander wanted to do.

"I have to," Alexander said. "My father left me the regent, and heir apparent. If Thrace means to move on us, and my father is away, I'm the one to defend Macedonia. It's my duty."

"You're not ready to go to battle," Andronicus said as kindly as he could. "None of you are. Maybe in six months but not now."

"You've been a fine teacher, Andronicus," Alexander said. "I appreciate everything you've taught me. But I'm the prince, and the king regent while my father is away. The choice is mine, not yours." Andronicus frowned at the boy prince, but knew better than to try and deny him. "I'll take what men I can north and repel these rebels. I expect you'll be there to fight alongside me."

Andronicus eyed the prince carefully. On one hand he saw a young foolish boy seeking fame and glory. But beneath that he saw something else, something kingly. There was a spark in the boy's mismatched eyes, a look of triumph. Andronicus knew there was nothing more that he could say. After all, the prince had given a command.

"Very well, my prince," Andronicus said reluctantly, bowing his head. "I'll accompany you into battle. I don't guarantee victory. All I can promise is that I'll keep you alive. But I can only promise to keep *you* alive."

"I believe you already have kept us alive, Andronicus," Alexander said with a smile. "We will not fall in battle to these Thracian rebels. Come now. I have a war council to convene, and I very much wish for you to be there."

5

Andronicus had reported to war councils in his youth, but he had never been a member of one. Besides him, the council consisted of Alexander and his closest friends: Hephaestion, Cassander, and Ptolemy. Philotas, son of Parmenion, Philip's lead general, sat at the head of one of the tables. Calas, another of Philip's leading generals, who had ridden in haste from Byzantium for this very council, sat at the head of another. Cleitus the Black stood in the corner with shadows covering his face. Aristotle was there as well; he seemed a bit out of place amongst all the soldiers and generals but was welcomed by all. When everyone was seated, Alexander stood up at the head of the great table and faced his council.

"I, Alexander, son of Philip, acting king regent of Macedonia and heir apparent to my father's crown, call this meeting to order." He looked around at the other men. "I trust you have all seen the letter I received." There was a murmur of agreement and a nodding of heads. "Good," Alexander said. "Now I wish to amass a host of cavalry to ride north and put an end to this rebellion before any other states get the same idea as these Thracian fools."

"Alexander is right," Calas added, rising to his feet, "and the king would agree as well. This treason must be dealt with at once. And it is past time for the prince to get his feet wet on the battlefield."

"That is not your place to say," Andronicus said from his place in the corner. "I'm the one teaching these boys the ways of war, I'll say when they're ready to fight."

Alexander gave Andronicus a crestfallen look, then turned back to Calas. "I am ready to fight," he said firmly, overruling Andronicus. "I may not be the best fighter I can be yet, but I can still defend my country, and it is my duty to do so."

"Hear, hear!" Hephaestion said, banging his fist on the table.

"I agree with the prince," Philotas said. He was a few years older than Alexander and looked as though he thought this council was beneath him. "The rebels must be dealt with," he continued, "and the prince is already sixteen years old. Tell me, Andronicus, is it? How old were you when you saw your first battle?"

"Sixteen," Andronicus replied, glaring at the young captain.

"Well, there you have it," Philotas said in a pompous tone.

"Aristotle, what do you think?" Alexander asked, looking hopefully to the older man. Aristotle gave Andronicus an apologetic glance and then returned his gaze to the prince.

"I think you're both right," he said with a heavy sigh. "I think the rebels must be dealt with, and I agree that you're the best one to do it. But I also agree that you may not be ready for battle. But I trust that Andronicus and your friends will keep you alive."

"Then it's settled," Alexander said, getting to his feet, not giving Andronicus a chance to argue. "Send word to amass the cavalry. We leave at dawn."

Alexander turned to leave, his friends right behind him. Cleitus got up and quietly followed the boys. Calas, the only real general among them, stood to leave, but Andronicus stopped him.

"Hold on," Andronicus said. "You have fought with Philip?"

"Since we were boys," Calas said proudly, "not much older than the prince."

"And you really think those boys are ready for battle?"

"Look, Andronicus," Calas said kindly, putting a hand on Andronicus' shoulder, "Cleitus told me about you. He said you are a true Spartan warrior, just like out of the old stories. He also said that you have been training those boys for months now."

Calas clapped his hands, and a slave boy came running with a jug of wine. Calas took it and shooed the boy away. He took a long swig from the jug, and offered it to Andronicus. For a brief moment Andronicus felt his guts tighten up, and he almost reached for the jug instinctively. But he shook his head, not taking his eyes away from the jug, and Calas took another swig.

"Now I know you think they're not ready

because when you were their age you were probably a much better fighter, but we're not exactly going to be fighting the Persian elites here. A horde of Thracian Maedi will be a perfect first test for the boy. And besides, he has you to make sure he doesn't get himself killed."

Calas let out a hearty laugh and then walked away. Andronicus looked over to see Aristotle saying goodbye to Philotas. The two soldiers walked out together, leaving Andronicus and Aristotle alone in the room.

"You really think they're ready for battle?" Andronicus asked. "They can barely fight each other, let alone an army."

"They're stronger than you think," Aristotle reassured him. "But I'm glad to see that you care so much for their safety."

"I've been ordered by the king to teach those boys how to fight," Andronicus said, "and now apparently I'm responsible for keeping them alive in a battle I know they're not ready for."

"You don't think you're up to the task?" Aristotle asked with a smug smile.

"You know damned well I can keep that boy safe against the Thracians," Andronicus said, "but that wasn't what I had in mind when I joined this army. I signed up to fight the Persians, not defend a boy playing at being king."

"You'll get your chance to fight the Persians. You just have to be patient. I'm sure you of all people know how to be patient," Aristotle added with a chuckle. Andronicus frowned at his wise friend. "I have no doubt that you would be of great use to the king if you were fighting with him," Aristotle said more seriously, "but I'm also sure that you're of far greater use by Alexander's side. He may be a foolish young boy full of hopes and dreams of grand adventures, but soon enough that boy will be king, and it will be him leading the fight against the Persians. And you can make sure he's ready when that day comes. That's how you can make a difference Andronicus. Not simply by being a great soldier and killing as many Persians as possible, but by teaching that boy how to be a great king. Then you can truly change the world, which is what you're meant to do."

"I'm not meant to do anything," Andronicus insisted, his temper flaring. "I have no great destiny or worldly purpose."

"You are almost one hundred and sixty years old Andronicus," Aristotle said flatly, "how can you not think you have a worldly purpose? You think it was an accident that you and your friends found that cave and touched those rocks?"

"You think it was destiny that brought us to the cave then?" Andronicus snarled. "Or perhaps you think it was the gods that led us there, like Theodotus did."

"I think there's a reason why you were chosen," Aristotle said, trying not to upset Andronicus.

"We weren't chosen!" Andronicus shouted. "It wasn't the gods or destiny or any other damned thing. It was a stupid accident."

"You said your brother found that cave in the middle of a storm," Aristotle said softly, eyeing Andronicus like he was a wild beast, "that he was drawn to it. You really think he found that cave by accident?"

Andronicus didn't answer. His fists were clenched as he glared down at Aristotle. He knew his friend was speaking the truth. Andronicus himself had spent countless nights thinking about how Androcles had inexplicably found the cave. There was no rational explanation for how it had happened. But the idea that it had been meant to be, that it had been preordained, made Andronicus angrier than anything. He could accept that they had been the unluckily fools to fall into the trap, but the idea that he had been chosen, along with the others, he simply was not ready to stomach.

On the heels of that came a new thought that he had never considered before. If it had been destiny, some kind of twisted fate that led them into that cave, what if he was the only one who was chosen? Perhaps the others had all died more than eighty years ago, and only he still walked the earth. On the other hand, what if it wasn't him who had been chosen? What if one of the others was meant to be there, and he and the others had simply followed? What if he was one of five people living through time, but he was not the one who it was all meant for? He wondered who it might be if not him. It couldn't be Lycus; he was far too angry and jealous to be the chosen one. He doubted it would be Theodotus either. He was smart, and devout beyond belief, but not the heroic type. He supposed it could be Thymi. That would make Andronicus happy. Thymi was kind and smart and loyal, and Andronicus knew he would be a wonderful leader. Then there was Androcles. His brother was the one who had found the cave, the one who the light had called to first. Perhaps he was the one it was all meant for.

Andronicus looked up and saw Aristotle smiling at him. He realized he had checked out for a time as he thought of his old friends. He sat down in one of the chairs, still frowning at Aristotle.

"You're too smart to think it was all an accident," Aristotle said gently. "I'm not saying you have to have a great destiny, or that it's your duty to change the world. I'm simply saying that there must have been some reason it was you five who found those rocks."

"And so now I must follow a child into battle," Andronicus said with a dry laugh, "and make sure he doesn't get himself killed."

"That child is the prince of the most powerful nation in the world," Aristotle reminded him. "By teaching him, and keeping him alive, you really are changing the world."

"You think I want to change the world?" Andronicus asked, his eyes blazing. "You think I care what happens to Macedonia?"

"No, I certainly do not," Aristotle said with a frustrated sigh. "I don't think you care about anything, and that's what makes *me* so angry."

"I make you angry?" Andronicus said, incredulous.

"That's right. You've been given the greatest gift I've ever heard of. Do you know how much I wish I could live for one hundred and sixty years? Do you know how much I could accomplish in that much time? How much I could change the world? In fifty years I'm going to be dead, and so will King Philip and maybe even Alexander. But not you, Andronicus, not unless you get yourself killed. You're going to be here long after we're all dead, and you're still going to be doing nothing, wasting a gift from the gods."

"Trust me, wise man, if I could give you this 'gift,' I would," Andronicus said, glaring at Aristotle. "I would gladly end my life today and let you live for eternity. It's not a gift to live forever, it's a curse. I've lost everyone I've ever known. I watched my wife die, my unborn child, my best friend. I wish I had died long ago with my people."

"I pity you, Andronicus," Aristotle said. "I hope someday you realize just what it is you've been given."

He got up, and left without another word. Andronicus sat there alone for a long time, staring into the fire.

Chapter 37
Out of Dust and Ashes
1

The young prince, and now king regent and protector of Macedonia in his father's stead, led a host of one thousand mounted soldiers north to meet the Thracian Maedi rebels, and Andronicus rode with them. Alexander rode at the head of a long column of riders, surrounded by his close friends. Hephaestion, Cassander, and Ptolemy were all chatting joyfully as they rode, but Alexander was silent and dour, a look of fierce determination on his young face. Andronicus rode a ways behind the boys, beside Cleitus the Black. While the boys chatted eagerly of the battles they hoped to see, the two veterans rode quietly, taking in the scenery.

Alexander left Calas behind to defend the city while he was away, but he took most of the city's soldiers with him, as well as nearly all the horses. The Thracians had already reached the northern border of Macedonia and were said to be burning villages as they made their way south. When Alexander got word of this, he pushed his host twice as fast, eager to prove himself to his father and his country.

Andronicus couldn't help but remember the last time he had fought in Greece. He had been leading his own mounted host to kill a band of rebels, eerily similar to what they were doing now. Only this time Andronicus wasn't in charge; a boy prince was, and this time it wasn't a hundred men but a thousand. Andronicus thought that he and his old band of Spartans could have given this lot a good fight though. Against a band of Thracian Maedi, however, this cavalry would be insurmountable.

This wasn't the first time Andronicus had been to Thrace. He had seen the people who lived there, and they were only slightly more civilized than most of the tribes he had known in Africa. The rebels they were going after were likely armed with little more than spears and axes. They wouldn't have armor or shields, and they wouldn't have horses. In a way Andronicus supposed it would be good for the boys to have such a sure victory in their first battle, although he did fear it might go to their heads.

The cavalry host marched tirelessly, and reached the rebels less than a fortnight after setting out. The horses were all dead tired, and the riders were deprived of sleep. Andronicus still didn't expect much from the rebels, but if they were even the slightest bit organized, they might be able to give the exhausted Macedonians a good fight. Alexander, in his eagerness to prove himself, might have actually hurt his chances of doing just that.

2

They saw smoke and heard screams long before they saw the Thracians themselves. The road wound up a tall, grassy hill. Beyond it was a village aflame. Alexander halted the cavalry and rode forward. He turned to face his men, a look of triumph and hate in his wild two-toned eyes. His blue eye seemed almost to glow while his brown eye looked like a deep black pit.

"Men!" Alexander shouted while the echoes of the Thracians pillaging behind him continued. "These beasts have betrayed us! They have brought fire and death to the innocent, and the defenseless. It is our duty, as soldiers of my father's army, to drive this sickness from our land. Now, ride with me, for Macedonia!" Alexander raised his sword high above his head. His great black steed, Bucephalas, lifted its front feet high in the air, raising Alexander above everyone. In that moment he looked every bit the hero he wanted to be. The young prince let out a battle cry and then charged up the hill.

As soon as Alexander spurred Bucephalas forward, Andronicus charged. He tried to keep up with Alexander, but Bucephalas was faster than all the other horses, and soon Alexander was ahead of everyone else. He crested the hill first, and for a moment was out of sight. Andronicus crested the hill behind him, and his momentary worry about the prince's safety disappeared the moment he saw the village below him.

The rebels were scattered about in bunches of threes and fours. They were either chasing down screaming, unarmed villagers or setting fire to their homes. The Thracians didn't notice the Macedonian army charging at them at first, and by the time they heard them, it was too late.

Andronicus watched nervously as the prince rode at a group of rebels, well ahead of the rest of the cavalry, and swung his sword in a long, sweeping ark. His blade slashed through a Thracian's collar, spraying blood across the dirt as he kept on riding. The men behind Andronicus cheered, but Andronicus kept riding toward the prince. Bucephalas ran into another rebel at full gallop, and Andronicus watched the man's neck break under the weight of the powerful horse.

A second later, Andronicus and the rest of the cavalry were upon the Thracians as well. If the Thracians had been dug in, positioned in a proper phalanx, the cavalry still would have beaten them, but scattered about as they were, the battle lasted only minutes. The Macedonians rode down every one of the rebels, cutting them down instantly. When the brief battle was over, Philotas, who was Alexander's second in command on the expedition, brought forward thirty Thracian prisoners and presented them to Alexander.

"You should kill these men, Alexander," Hephaestion said, jumping down from his horse and striding toward the prisoners. "You saw what they were doing."

"They are beaten, Alexander," Ptolemy said. "Take them as slaves. There is no honor in killing a man on his knees."

"There is no honor in burning villages to the ground either!" Hephaestion shouted. "They were slaughtering those people!"

"And now you wish to slaughter them as well?" Ptolemy yelled back.

Alexander looked at Cassander, who shook his head uncertainly. Alexander turned to where Andronicus and Cleitus were sitting by quietly on their horses, but neither man said a word, nor gave any inclination of what they felt the prince should do. Andronicus didn't want to tell the boy what he thought; he wanted to see what the future king would do on his own. Philotas didn't say anything either, but he also looked interested as he waited for the prince's order.

"Enough," Alexander said, cutting off his friends' bickering. "Thrace is part of our empire. I will not murder men from my own kingdom, no matter what they have done. Keep them as captives. We will sell them as slaves."

No one argued with the prince's command, not even Hephaestion, though his eyes blazed with fury. The prisoners were taken away, and the majority of the cavalry dismounted and set up a camp for the night, upwind from the burnt village. Alexander and his friends and generals, including Andronicus, stayed on their horses and watched the procession.

"What will you do with the people from these villages?" Philotas asked the prince. "Their homes are destroyed."

"Bring them back to Macedonia with us,"

Ptolemy suggested. "Allow them to join us."

"Ptolemy is right," Cassander said, nodding. "They will be more than willing to join us now that we have saved them."

"No," Alexander said, a twinkle in his oddball eyes. "They must stay here."

"Stay where?" Hephaestion asked. "Their homes have been burnt down. There are no villages left for them."

"Then we will build them a new one," Alexander said with a smile, sticking his chest out. Andronicus had not expected that, nor, apparently, had the others.

"Build them a village?" Hephaestion asked, clearly trying to hold in his exasperation. "Do you know how long that will take?"

"Not long at all if we help," Alexander replied merrily, gazing out at the open fields before him. "Out of dust and ashes a new city shall rise, and I shall call it Alexandropolis."

3

Alexander delivered on his promise. He and his men stayed on for five months, building the new town of Alexandropolis. Andronicus became more frustrated than he had been in a long time. He had succeeded in keeping the boy safe, but now he had to help build a damned village for some poor fools he couldn't care less about. No one in the small Macedonian army seemed especially happy to be stuck in the middle of nowhere building a village from scratch while a war was going on in the east.

Alexandropolis did not turn out to be the shining city that Alexander had imagined, but it was far bigger and better than the villages the people had lived in before. Most of the houses were made of wood, though a few were made of stone. A road led in and out of town, and several smaller ones intersected it. Defenses were set around the town, and Alexander ordered one hundred of his men to stay behind to live in, defend, and govern the newly founded town of Alexandropolis. The former villagers, now the town's new residents, praised Alexander and his men when they finally left to return home. Andronicus was as glad to leave the town behind as the rest of the men were.

Rumors of the war in the east were growing darker, and Andronicus was more eager than ever to ride to Persia. King Philip had failed to take the ancient city of Byzantium, but he still meant to lead his army into Persia. There were also rumors about the new Persian king, Arses, who had taken the name of his father and grandfather and now ruled as Artaxerxes IV. Under his father's rule, the Persians had expanded their empire farther than it had gone in decades, even going as far as reclaiming Egypt. It seemed inevitable that the two kings would meet in battle.

4

Alexander and his host returned to Macedonia in May of 338 to find Philip and his army already returned from Byzantium. The siege had failed, and the king had returned home in relative disgrace. Philip had won more battles than any king in the last hundred years, but the Greeks did not have a particularly forgiving memory when it came to kings losing battles to Persians. It seemed obvious to Andronicus that Philip would have to launch his invasion soon or have the Greeks rise up against him.

Within a month of Alexander and Philip being reunited in Pella, Andronicus was proven right. Word arrived from the south that some of the Greek states were planning to revolt against Macedonian rule. The Athenians and the Thebans were amassing near Athens, and the Corinthians were said to be raising an army themselves. When Philip heard reports of the Athenians pillaging sacred lands that belonged to Apollo, he finally decided to step in.

The king ordered his son to raise a host and ride south to meet the Greek rebels while he took the bulk of his army north to dispel the last of the Thracian revolts once and for all.

Andronicus went wherever the young prince went, and did as he was told, but inside he was getting fed up with it all. He had joined the army to fight the Persians, but instead he was babysitting a group of rich kids playing at war. Now it seemed he might have to fight the Greeks before he could fight the Persians, and Andronicus didn't know how he felt about that.

Alexander began recruiting soldiers from across the country, with the help of his generals. Alexander and his close confidants were the only ones who knew the host was being gathered to fight the Athenian rebels. The rest of the army was told they were going to attack Illyria. Alexander thought that if the Greeks got wind of the attack, they would be able to prepare, so he set up his elaborate ploy to fool the men.

Andronicus would have told Alexander not to do this if he had been asked, but the boy had gained far too much confidence after his victory in Thrace. Alexander spoke about the fight as if it had been an actual battle, and his friends only encouraged the idea. In reality it had been little more than a slaughter. One thousand mounted soldiers against a few hundred scattered bandits, lightly armed and with no real leadership.

Andronicus didn't like the new confidence the boys seemed to have. They walked around like they were real soldiers now, and didn't listen to anyone, least of all him. Alexander seemed to be holding a grudge from Andronicus's lack of trust in him. As soon as they returned to the city, Andronicus tried to make them resume their training, but they all refused, except for Cassander. He was the only one who apparently still thought he had more to learn from Andronicus. So, Andronicus spent the days training Cassander, and occasionally Ptolemy as well, while Alexander and Hephaestion played at being generals.

In reality Alexander was simply a name and face in this particular endeavor. Calas was really in charge of amassing the army and the attack itself. He and the other generals allowed Alexander and his friends to listen in on all of their war councils, and somehow they even managed to make the boy think he was in charge. The only real decision Alexander made regarding the attack though, was to spread the lie that they were meaning to attack the Illyrians.

5

Shortly before Alexander was to march south, the Illyrians attacked. As it turned out, the lies and rumors had worked far better than anyone had expected, though not in Alexander's favor. The Greeks had no idea the Macedonians were coming for them, but word had reached the Illyrians of the attack headed their way, and they decided to bring the fight to Alexander instead. It was the honorable thing to do, and Andronicus could have warned the boy this might happen, if he had asked.

The Macedonians outnumbered the Illyrians ten to one however, and pushed back the attack easily. The Illyrians didn't fight for very long before fleeing. The attack was unsuccessful, but it also crippled Alexander's plan. With the Illyrians defeated, there was no more reason to stay in Macedonia and continue raising an army without the truth getting out. If Alexander stayed where he was, the Athenians would know he was coming for them before the week was over.

Alexander went to all his trusted advisors, from Hephaestion to Aristotle, and even to Andronicus. Andronicus gave the boy the same advice he hoped everyone else had: attack the Athenians now. Alexander waited another day, listening to everyone's counsel on the matter, and then gave orders for the army to march south at dawn.

That night, the king returned. The Thracians had been easily beaten, and Philip had driven his men home in great haste, hoping to join his son against the Greeks. The two armies merged, and in the morning more than thirty thousand men marched south, now led by the king, with the prince at his right side.

Chapter 38
Civil War

1

Three days after the Macedonian army passed

into the lands of Boeotia, they met the Greek army. It was August second, 338 bc, and it would be the first time the Greeks and Macedonians truly fought. The Greeks had chosen to march out and meet the Macedonians head on rather than waiting to be attacked. Andronicus didn't like marching on Greece; he had signed up to fight the Persians, not the Athenians. He thought of all the time he had spent in Athens studying and drinking. It wasn't just the Athenians either; the army was made up of men from all over Greece. The Thebans, the Corinthians, and the Megarans, Andronicus had fought alongside them all in his youth, and now he marched against them behind a foreign king.

The Macedonian command received word that the entire Greek force was blocking the road near Chaeronea. They were said to be over thirty thousand strong and held a firm wall of phalanxes that stretched nearly a mile. The Macedonians had not expected to find quite so many Greeks, and Andronicus felt the mood quickly shift throughout the ranks. A nervous energy hung over the Macedonian soldiers as they marched down the road to meet their Greek counterparts.

Philip and his generals were all on horseback, leading nearly two thousand cavalry. Behind them, stretching far down the road, marched thirty thousand infantry, some Greek and Thracian, but most of them true Macedonians. Andronicus had seen many battles in his life, but he had never seen two massive western armies meet in battle before, and he had no idea what to expect. He knew it wouldn't be like fighting the Thracians or even the Persians. These were the same men he had fought against at Plataea and Salamis so long ago, or their descendants anyway.

The Macedonian army slowly spread out and formed their own phalanxes as they got closer, and continued marching toward Chaeronea in battle formation. When the Greek line came into sight, Philip ordered his army to halt. The Macedonians marched in unison, pounding their feet in the dirt, and stopped altogether, making an impressive sound.

Philip turned to face his men, riding down the line of infantry phalanxes and shouting encouragement, but Andronicus couldn't hear what he was saying. Alexander and the other boys were nervously eyeing the huge Greek force before them. Andronicus could tell they were now realizing what he had told them for months, that they weren't ready for a real battle. He knew he would have to protect them once the fighting began.

Philip came riding back up the lines, shouting battle cries to his men. A loud whoop went up from each phalanx as the king rode past. When he returned to his captains, he began shouting orders, laying out the plans for the battle. He took command of the right phalanx, accompanied by his cavalry. Alexander was given command of the left phalanx and was accompanied by most of the other generals and a much smaller cavalry.

Just before riding back to his command post, Philip turned to Cleitus. Andronicus was standing behind Cleitus and heard the king's words as he commanded Cleitus to keep his son alive no matter what. When Philip rode off, Cleitus turned to Andronicus with a look of pure conviction. Andronicus gave a curt nod and then moved over behind where Alexander and his friends sat atop their horses.

There was a moment of awkward hesitation after the king left. Philip was giving his men a rousing speech of some kind far down the line, but he was too far away for Andronicus to make out what he was saying. The soft echo of the king's voice swept over the quiet left flank as they waited for the prince's orders. Alexander must have felt the silence as well because he rode forward and turned to face his army.

"Men!" Alexander shouted. "You have followed my father into battle many times. You have bled with him, and you have lost brothers and fathers. Now I ask that you follow me! Those may be Greek men you see before you, but they are still our enemy. These rebels have betrayed my father's peace. They have defiled Apollo's sacred lands! Follow me now into battle! In the name of my father, Macedonia, and Apollo himself, ride!" Alexander's command was met by a thundering cheer from the men.

Andronicus was mildly impressed; the boy was certainly not as good as Leonidas, but for a seventeen-year-old kid he had done well, and he had done much better than his first attempt in Thrace. Andronicus doubted he could have given such a rousing speech at that age. Alexander's friends roared along with the rest of the army. The generals all stood by quietly, but they looked impressed as well.

At that moment a cry came from the far right, and Andronicus turned to see Philip's cavalry charge. A second later Alexander shouted, and then he charged as well. Andronicus rode with the rest of the men, staying as close to Alexander as possible. The light cavalry led by Alexander broke ahead of the massive infantry, riding at full speed toward the Greek line. Alexander was at the head of the pack, and Andronicus pushed his horse harder to keep up.

As they galloped toward a wall of Greek shields and spears, Andronicus felt a moment of fear—not for himself, but for the boy. He watched as Bucephalas ran past the spears and crashed his muscular black body against the Greek shields. The horse sent three men flying backward, breaking the Greek line. A second later the rest of the cavalry hit. Andronicus felt his own horse crash against a shield, followed by something digging into his foot.

Without looking down Andronicus started slashing with his sword, taking down every Greek man within striking distance. It felt amazing to be back in the fight, although it was hard to see the faces of the Greek men as he killed them. Somehow killing Persians, Egyptians, or Swihmacha, didn't have the same feeling as killing Greek men. Perhaps it was because Andronicus had fought beside the Greek cities in his youth, or maybe because he had spent so many years living in Athens. Or perhaps it was simply because they looked like him. He hoped it wasn't that simple, but he knew that it may well be.

As the Macedonian infantry charged into the battle, Andronicus tried to find Alexander. He spotted him pushing his way well into the Greek lines, and he was at least twelve rows into the phalanx. Hephaestion and Cassander were right behind him, slashing at the men around them. Cleitus was not far behind, trying to push his way toward the prince. Andronicus reared his horse and charged forward.

He grabbed the sword out of a dying man's hand and began slashing down with both hands, killing Greek men as he went. The Macedonian foot soldiers finally arrived, clashing against the Greek phalanx, and then everything became a chaotic mess. Andronicus continued making his way toward where the boys were fighting, but the Greek lines were pushing forward now. The more men Andronicus killed, the more the rest of the men slunk out of his way.

Just as he cut the final distance between himself and Alexander, he saw Cassander go down with his horse. A moment later two men grabbed Bucephalas's reigns and pulled. The large black horse went down with a terrible screech, sending Alexander tumbling into the dirt.

Andronicus leapt down from his horse and reached the prince just as an Athenian was preparing to skewer him with a long spear.

Andronicus drove his sword through the man's breastplate and out his back. He wrenched his sword free just as two other men lunged at Alexander. Andronicus managed to slash one, but the other was out of reach. Alexander was still on the ground trying to regain his bearings as the man moved to kill him. Then Hephaestion came riding out of nowhere and leapt off his horse and onto the man, driving him into the dirt. A second later Cleitus appeared, covered in blood and with a crazed look of bloodlust in his dark eyes.

Andronicus moved forward, and with Cleitus by his side they stood over the prince. The two seasoned fighters worked together, keeping the Greeks away from the boy. Hephaestion and Cassander were both fighting not far away, but Andronicus could do nothing to help them. His sole job was to keep the prince alive. Alexander tried to stand up, but Cleitus pushed him back down, making sure he was beyond the reach of the Greek swords.

Andronicus didn't know how long the battle lasted. For him it mainly consisted of standing over Alexander and making sure he couldn't fight. When horns began to blow, and the Greeks finally started to retreat, Andronicus was able to look around. Cassander and Hephaestion were standing together, both covered in blood and looking like they were going to be sick, but otherwise unharmed.

Calas rode over to meet with Alexander once the Greeks had gone. Andronicus was surprised he had managed to stay on his horse throughout the battle and noted that there was almost no blood on him or his horse. Andronicus wondered where Calas had been during the fighting; he certainly hadn't seen him. Even Alexander had blood splashed across his face and body, and he had barely been allowed to fight.

"Alexander!" Calas called out as he rode over. "Your father wishes to speak with you."

Alexander was back on his feet with his friends around him, but he had not heard Calas. He was looking around frantically, a look of panic in his eyes. Andronicus realized the boy was looking for his horse and began looking around as well. A moment later Andronicus saw the great black horse on a hill in the distance; there could be no mistaking such a magnificent beast.

"He's over there," Andronicus said, pointing. Alexander didn't hear him, continuing to look around in panic.

"Boy!" Andronicus said, and Alexander finally looked at him. "Your horse is over there on that hill." Alexander finally spotted it, and Andronicus saw the fear leave his eyes.

"You men!" Alexander shouted to a group of men still on their horses, "go get my horse."

"My prince," Calas said impatiently, "the king wishes to speak with you at once. He is waiting on the far side of the battlefield."

"Very well," Alexander said, then turned to his friends, who looked like they were all still trying to cope with the battle. "You stay here. I must speak with my father alone." Alexander started walking away, and Andronicus and Cleitus fell in behind him.

"You two stay here as well," Alexander ordered them. "The battle is over. You no longer need to hover over me." Cleitus shook his head slowly, not making a move.

"I gave you an order," Alexander said, clenching his teeth in anger. "Wait here until I return."

"Your father gave us orders too, my prince," Cleitus said, his face a mask of stone. "We are not to leave you until he says."

"Fine then," Alexander said bitterly, "but stay out of my way, and stay quiet."

2

When Alexander found his father, he was being congratulated by his generals. Most of them were old men who had not done any fighting at all, but Andronicus did notice Philotas not far from the king, and he was covered in as much blood as anyone. The king was also well doused in the blood of his enemies. Andronicus had expected Philip to look the part, but not actually get his hands dirty, but his hands were certainly dirty now.

"Father!" Alexander called as he approached the king. "You wish to see me?"

"Aye!" Philip bellowed once he saw his son. Philip looked his son over, beaming with pride. "This was your first real battle, son," Philip said as he embraced him. "That mess in Thrace was nothing, but this was a true battle, and a great victory. I'm glad we get to share it together."

"As am I, Father," Alexander said, his chest puffing out with pride. "May it be the first of many."

"Hear, hear!" Philip cried, and his generals roared their agreement. "Your friends," Philip said, "did they all live?"

"Yes, Father," Alexander said, nodding quickly.

"And that great black horse of yours," Philip added, "I'm surprised to see you off him. Did he fall?"

"He did," Alexander replied, "but he lived. I

sent a group of riders after him."

"Good." Philip beckoned a servant to bring him some wine. "That is a special horse you have there. I still remember the way you tamed that beast. Remarkable." Alexander didn't say anything, but he glowed in the face of his father's praise.

"The battle is over!" Philip shouted to his men as he took a swig of wine. "We have had a great victory this day." The generals and soldiers around the king all cheered.

"The battle is over, but we still have much to do," Philip continued when their voices died down. "The Greeks will run back to their cities, fortify their defenses, and wait for us to lay siege to them, one by one."

"But, Father," Alexander said, only loud enough for the king and a few generals to hear, "it will take years to lay siege to each Greek city, perhaps many years. The Persians will strike first if we wait that long."

Philip's ugly scarred face stretched into a crooked grin as he stared at his son. "My son speaks true," he said proudly. "We cannot lay siege to all of Greece. We do not have the time to conquer them, so we will make our peace."

"My king," Calas said, "forgive me, but you already did make peace with the Greeks, and the moment you left the country, they began to rebel."

"Aye," Philip agreed, "and that is why they are coming with us. We will need them when we meet the Persians, and with the majority of their forces with us, they won't dare attack us at home."

"It is a good plan, Father," Alexander said, "but how will you get the Greeks to join us? As you said, they are running back to their cities to man their defenses."

"Leave that to me, son," Philip said with a wicked smile. "Send word to every city in Greece, tell them I am holding a great council and that any who do not attend, will be known as enemies of both Macedonia and Greece."

Chapter 39
A Father's Love

1

In the aftermath of the battle, Philip called together a great gathering of Greeks and Macedonians. Representatives from every Greek state came to treat with Philip—governors and ambassadors and even some generals from all over the Macedonian empire, from Thrace down to Corinth. The only city that had not answered the king's summons was Sparta.

Andronicus felt an absurd sort of pride in his countrymen's stubbornness. Philip had sent an emissary to Sparta before the battle saying that if he succeeded in defeating the Athenians and the Thebans, Sparta would be next to fall. The emissary had returned from Sparta with a single word in response: *if*.

Philip had sent a second message immediately after the victory, telling the Spartans that if they did not attend his gathering, he would march on Sparta and kill them all. The second emissary returned with a much longer message, this one was four words: *We shall be waiting*. Andronicus had to stifle a grin when he heard it. The Spartans would never change. He only hoped a war with Sparta would never come. Then he truly wouldn't know what to do.

While the gathering of dignitaries and generals was forming, Andronicus scanned the room from his position behind the king, watching as the men filed in and took their places. The thin-lipped, angry-looking ambassador from Thebes sat next to the governor of Corinth, a heavyset bald man with a thick, furrowed brow and long white whiskers. A group of men from the Peloponnese were clustered together, eyeing the king fearfully. Andronicus recognized the marks of Achaea, Arcadia, Laconia, and Messenia as the men all took their places. There were a few others that he did not recognize. The balding Thespian general sat alone with his arms crossed, watching the king intently.

Then there were the defeated captains of the recent battle. The Megaran and Achaean generals sat together while the Chalcisian and Epidaurian men stood behind them. Sitting in front, directly across from Philip and Alexander, were the two defeated Athenian generals. Chares of Athens was old for a general; he had a bald spot atop his head, surrounded by thin white hair. Andronicus remembered seeing the man years ago in Athens when Chares was much younger. Chares had been at the Academy studying with Plato for a time. Andronicus shifted to his left so the man could not see him. Chares's face was lined and weathered, but he still had a stern demeanor. To Andronicus he looked exactly how a general should look.

Next to Chares sat Lysicles. The Athenian second-in-command looked to be at least thirty years younger than Chares. Lysicles had a thick bandage wrapped around his left arm and a deep, fresh cut stood out across his chest. He was glaring at the king with a fierce hate, and Andronicus was ready to act the second the man should move.

When everyone was seated, a tall thin man in a white toga stood up and walked to the middle of the room. He held up his hands and waited for the room to fall quiet.

"Gentlemen, lords, and generals," he said in a businesslike tone, "my name is Lycurgus." Andronicus felt his stomach drop like a rock. He had not heard that name in nearly one hundred and fifty years, and yet it still haunted him sometimes. He remembered the story Archelaus had told him well, on a stormy night so many years ago. He had told Andronicus the story of his father's death and how it had been Lycus's father, Lycurgus, who was to blame.

Andronicus had never met Lycus's father, and he hadn't seen Lycus in so long he could barely remember his face, but staring at this thin, squint-eyed man, Andronicus couldn't help but see a resemblance. He knew it was silly; this man must have been born a hundred years after all that happened, but he still couldn't stop his reaction to the name. He stared at the man along with everyone else, and felt a cold sweat forming on his back.

"I am here to orate these proceedings on the

behest of Philip the Second, King of Macedonia,"
Lycurgus continued, "we have gathered you all here
today to settle these matters once and for all."

"The matter of you taking our lands?" Lysicles
spat, quickly bringing Andronicus's attention back to
the business at hand.

"It is our right to take your lands," Parmenion
said from Philip's left. He was Philip's lead general, and
he had ridden at great haste to arrive before the
meeting, to show solidarity along the Macedonian
front. He was older than Philip, but it was clear that
the two were close friends. He barely had any hair on
his head, but he had a thick black beard. His face was
lined and weathered, and he had a certain fierceness
about him, a sort of stoic authority. "We defeated you
in battle," he continued. "We owe you nothing."

"That is not why we're here," Philip said in his
rough, scratchy voice. "We are here to make peace
between Greece and Macedonia, so we can move
forward together."

"What shall become of our armies?" the fat
Corinthian governor asked. "Are our men to follow you
into battle?"

"You may lead your own men into battle,"
Philip replied impatiently. "But you will march behind
me when I meet Artaxerxes in the field."

"So, it's true then," the Theban ambassador
said. "You do intend to march upon the Persians."

"I do," Philip grunted, glaring at the man.

"And who will defend Greece while all of our
armies are in Persia?" the Corinthian demanded.

"Defend Greece from whom?" Alexander
asked, and all the men turned to stare at the boy
prince.

"From our enemies, boy," the fat man
answered sternly.

"Which enemies are you referring to?"
Alexander asked, a wan smile on his face. "The
Persians certainly will not be able to attack Greece
while we lay siege to their lands, and by the end of this
meeting, none of you will have cause to attack each
other ever again. So, who exactly are you afraid of,

Governor?" The governor's heavy cheeks turned a bright red.

"What of the Spartans?" the fat man said defensively. "You think it's coincidence they're not here? They'll take all of our cities while you march to Persia."

"Sparta will not attack any of you," Alexander said, shaking his head.

"And why is that?" the fat man demanded.

"Because Sparta does not care about taking your cities. If they did they would have done so a thousand years ago, or any time since. Sparta is not here because they do not fear us, or you, or anyone. They will not attack you unless you give them reason to, which I do not recommend." There was a chattering of laughter from the men as Alexander sat back down.

"Yes, well," Lycurgus said, trying to get the meeting back on track, "as I was saying, we have gathered you all here to make a lasting peace amongst our cities. You will each be asked to make a pledge today to King Philip. If you refuse, you will be branded an enemy of the state, your cities will be ransacked, and your people enslaved."

"You wish us to give a pledge to you?" Lysicles exclaimed. He rose to his feet in anger, and Andronicus and Cleitus quickly moved in. Lysicles stepped forward, and the next second Andronicus was upon him. In a matter of seconds, he had the man on his knees, his arm bent behind his head. Lycurgus stepped forward, staring down at Lysicles, ignoring Andronicus completely.

"So, you do not wish to make this pledge to the king?" he asked in a chilling voice.

"Damn your pledge," Lysicles spat through clenched teeth, struggling against Andronicus's hold. "I kneel to no man."

"You are kneeling," Lycurgus said with a cold scowl. "Now I will give you one final chance. Do you refuse to pledge yourself to King Philip of Macedonia?" Lysicles glared up at the thin orator with hate in his eyes. Andronicus knew what was going to happen.

"I do," Lysicles said angrily, turning his scowl

toward the king.

"Very well," Lycurgus said. "Take this man outside. The king will decide how he should be executed once we are done here." Andronicus released Lysicles' arms and lifted him to his feet, pushing him out the door before he could protest.

Outside, Andronicus marched him over to three soldiers who were standing by and ordered them to take the prisoner to the cells. Once Lysicles was taken care of, Andronicus quickly returned to the meeting, not wanting to miss anything. As he walked in, Lycurgus was just getting ready to recite the oath the men were to give.

"Oath. I swear by Zeus, Gaia, Helios, Poseidon, and all the gods and goddesses," Lycurgus said, his high voice ringing out in the large room. Everyone else was dead silent, listening intently to the pledge they all had to recite. "I will abide by the common peace, and I will neither break the agreement with Philip nor take up arms on land or sea, harming any of those abiding by the oath. Nor shall I take any city, fortress, or harbor by craft or contrivance, with intent of war against the participants of the war." Andronicus thought it sounded a bit contrite, and he wondered who had come up with these awful words. "Nor shall I depose the kingship of Philip or his descendants or the constitutions existing in each state that swears the oaths of the peace." Andronicus looked around at the men as they listened to the oath, most of them appearing more than a little displeased. "Nor shall I do anything contrary to these agreements, nor shall I allow anyone else to do so, as far as is possible. If anyone does commit any breach of the treaty, I shall go in support as called by those who need, and I shall fight the transgressors of the common peace, as decided and called on by the Hegemon, King Philip the Second, of Macedonia."

A heavy silence fell on the room when Lycurgus finished. Most of the men looked pale and sick, as if they were about to turn over their people to their enemy forever. Chares was the first to rise. When he stepped forward, Cleitus stepped between him and the king and placed his hand on his sword. Chares ignored him and stared right at the king.

Before Philip spoke, Chares began to recite the oath, word for word, not taking his gaze off Philip. When he was finished, he got down on one knee and bowed his head. As soon as he stood up, the Theban ambassador was in his place, reciting the words.

One by one the others all gave the oath and then kneeled before the king, swearing their allegiance to Philip and Macedonia. When all the oaths had been taken, Lycurgus pronounced Philip the new Hegemon, the commander of the entire Greek army. Philip was the first official Hegemon since Leonidas had fallen at Thermopylae, which sent another wave of chilling nostalgia over Andronicus.

2

When the meeting was finished, and every state in Greece save for Sparta was sworn to Philip, the king took his men back to Macedonia. Andronicus travelled with Alexander and the other boys. Finally, there was a feeling of hope and eagerness in the air, because they all knew the real war was coming.

When they returned to Macedonia, Alexander and the other generals were all eager to begin the planning of the invasion of Persia. The day after they returned home, Alexander went to speak with his father, but instead found him in bed with a girl barely older than himself. Alexander went back to the generals alone and told them his father was not able to join them. The prince led the war councils himself, in his father's stead, but it had the feeling of a farce.

That night Andronicus went to find the boy and heard him crying by himself. Andronicus thought of going in and consoling the boy, but he didn't. He left the prince alone to deal with his troubles as he would.

For two weeks after that Alexander tried to speak to his father every day, and every day Philip would send him away. The king didn't seem terribly interested in beginning the invasion. He was far more interested in his many beautiful wives and mistresses. Eventually, Alexander sought out Andronicus for comfort, but Andronicus had never been the comforting type.

"I think he means to marry this girl," Alexander said bitterly, sitting at Andronicus's table with a sigh.

"I have no doubt that he does," Andronicus replied. "He already has seven wives. What should stop him from taking an eighth?"

"He does not love them," Alexander said, balling his hands into fists. He looked more like an angry little boy than a future king.

"Of course not," Andronicus agreed. "That's not why he marries them."

Alexander turned away in anger and stayed quiet for a long time, staring at nothing. Andronicus didn't say anything; he just waited for the boy to speak up.

"Were you ever married, Andronicus?" Alexander asked, looking up at him. The question took Andronicus by surprise, and for a moment he didn't know what to say.

"Yes, I was," Andronicus said, turning away from Alexander's eyes, "to the most beautiful woman I have ever known."

"Was she Spartan as well?"

"No." Andronicus shook his head slowly, staring into the fire. "She was African."

"You married an African woman?" Alexander asked, stunned. "Was she black?"

"Oh, yes," Andronicus said with a chuckle. "As black as anyone you have ever seen."

"And you took her to Sparta with you?"

Andronicus shook his head sadly. "No. We stayed in the land of the Swimha. I only left those lands after she died."

"Swimha?" Alexander repeated.

"A land I knew in Africa."

"How did she die," Alexander asked softly.

"She was killed," Andronicus replied, still staring into the fire.

"Who killed her?" Alexander asked, clearly unaware of how painful what he was asking might be.

"A neighboring tribe called the Swihmacha."

"What happened to them?"

"I killed them," Andronicus said. For a moment he could hear the screaming of women and children and the smell of burning flesh. When it passed, Andronicus looked over at the prince, who was staring at his feet.

"Why did they kill her?" Alexander inquired with all the ignorant curiosity of a royal child.

"For carrying my child," Andronicus answered sullenly. He sighed again. "It does not matter where you are, Alexander. People do not like when men and women of different colors marry."

"Then why did you marry her?"

"Because I loved her," Andronicus said as he fought off a tear trying to well up in his eye.

"I wish my father loved my mother," Alexander said sadly.

That snapped Andronicus out of his trance. He had been lost in memories long past for a moment, but the prince's whining brought him back. Andronicus had lost his father when he was six and lost his wife before she had given him a child. Hearing the heir of the Macedonian empire whining about his mother and father infuriated him.

"What are you so afraid of, boy?" Andronicus asked, glaring at Alexander.

"If my father marries this girl, this Cleopatra, and she has a son . . ." Alexander looked up at Andronicus in fear.

"You fear an unborn child," Andronicus said with disdain. "Your own brother, no less. Why should you fear such a thing?"

"Cleopatra is the niece of Attalus, one of my father's closest advisors. My mother is Greek. If this girl has a son, he will be the true Macedonian heir, not me."

"And what of it?" Andronicus asked.

"If Cleopatra has a son, I will not become king," Alexander said, his voice frantic.

"Why is it so important that you be king?" Andronicus asked. He paid close attention to the prince's every move. Alexander said nothing at first, just stared down at the floor, thinking. Finally, he lifted his head and met Andronicus's green eyes with his own blue and brown ones. When Andronicus saw the look in the boy's eyes, he felt the hairs on the back on his neck rise. It was a look he had only seen once before: on the face of King Leonidas.

"I need to be king," Alexander said softly. "I am going to conquer the Persians."

"I thought your father was going to conquer the Persians," Andronicus said. A heavy weight seemed to be hanging over the room.

"Perhaps he was meant to," Alexander said, "but it will be me, not him."

"How do you know this?" Andronicus asked, staring into the boy's mismatched eyes.

"I'm not sure," Alexander said. "I just do, as if something told me."

Something. The boy had not said *someone* but something. It sounded eerily familiar. Andronicus had been shown things as well. In his mind's eye, he saw a pool of murky, glowing water and shadows dancing in the rippling light. He still did not know what all the things he had seen were, but he knew some of them had already come to pass.

"What's going to happen to your father?" Andronicus asked, his eyes still fixed on the boy.

"I don't know," Alexander said, shaking his head. The look fell from his face, and his eyes appeared to take in his surroundings as if he were just waking up. Andronicus could tell Alexander had no idea what they were talking about. Andronicus told the prince to go and find his friends. He sat there for a long time after Alexander left, thinking about what the boy had said.

3

Less than a month later Philip married Cleopatra. There was a great ceremony and an even greater feast. Every Macedonian nobleman and officer in Philip's army was in attendance. Alexander was seated with his friends, far from the king's table, and he didn't look happy about it. Andronicus was stationed by the east door, on guard duty, and from his position he had a good view of the boys.

All night Alexander stared at Philip and his new bride with nothing but loathing. Andronicus knew the boy just wanted his father to love him, but his jealousy was dangerous. As the night went on, and more and more wine was poured, people began making prayers for a new prince. Andronicus watched as Alexander became further enraged.

Finally, Attalus, Cleopatra's uncle, rose to his feet, raising a large golden chalice above his head. "We pray to you, oh mighty Zeus," the drunken general slurred, "give our great King Philip a son, so we may have a true Macedonian heir to the throne."

Alexander rose to his feet with fire in his eyes and started toward Attalus. Hephaestion tried to pull him back, but he wasn't fast enough. Andronicus stepped forward, but Alexander was already moving toward Attalus.

"Let my niece give the king a son, so the king may have a true heir!" Attalus shouted again, staggering.

"You monster," Alexander shouted as he came at him. "What am I then, a bastard?"

Andronicus pushed past drunken noblemen and slaves carrying wine and food and reached the prince just as he went to throw himself at Attalus. Andronicus caught the boy and held him back while trying not to embarrass him in front of his father.

King Philip rose to his feet and drew his sword. He let out a drunken roar and ran at Alexander. Andronicus prepared to stop the king should he reach the boy, but instead the king's drunken feet slipped, and he stumbled to the floor, his sword clanging loudly against the marble. Everyone was silent as the sword echoed throughout the great hall.

"See there!" Alexander spat at his father, with the whole of the Macedonian government listening. "The man who prepares to lead us into Asia, fallen before he can even reach his foe." There was a murmur of laughter from those bold enough to dare it.

Two men rushed over and helped the king to his feet. Philip glared at his son with real hatred.

"Get out!" Philip growled. "Get out, you bastard. You will never be king. I will have a thousand more sons, and they will all be greater than you."

Alexander stared at his father with a mixture of contempt and pity. He shook his head one last time and then turned his back on the king. Hephaestion and Cassander followed Alexander out of the hall, leaving Philip with his new wife and his many guests. As soon as Alexander was out the door, Parmenion ordered the harpies to start their song again, and within minutes the king had a new glass of wine and had seemingly forgotten his only son's outburst.

Andronicus stayed at his post, wanting to go after the boys but knowing he could not. The party lasted several more hours, and the king had a grand old time, never mentioning Alexander the rest of the night. The party finally ended when the king passed out in his chair. Most everyone was drunk by then, so Parmenion began ushering people out. Not long after that, the king was taken to his quarters.

When Cleitus finally dismissed Andronicus, he went in search of the boys. He found Cassander and Hephaestion talking quietly in their villa while the prince slept on a featherbed in the corner. Andronicus walked over to the boys, and sat down.

"He should not have done that," Andronicus said.

"We know that," Hephaestion replied irritably. "I tried to stop him. It's good that you reached him before he got to Attalus. I think he actually meant to kill him."

"He did," Andronicus agreed, nodding. "I saw it in his eyes."

"But you did reach him in time," Cassander said, a sick look on his face. "Alexander didn't kill anyone."

"He may as well have," Hephaestion said. "To talk like that to the king in front of everyone . . ." Hephaestion shook his head sadly as if he couldn't believe what his best friend had done.

"It won't matter," Andronicus said. "At least not to the king. He forgot the whole thing within five minutes."

"People are going to tell him what happened," Hephaestion said, "people like Attalus. When the king hears what happened, he's going to come after Alexander."

"You think the king is going to kill his only son and heir?" Andronicus asked, giving Hephaestion a disapproving look. "Use your head, boy. The king may be mad, but he won't do anything to Alexander."

"You don't know that," Hephaestion said. "If he does come after Alexander, he'll kill us all, even you."

"He could try," Andronicus said smugly, "but he won't; I can assure you."

"But how do you know?" Cassander asked.

"I just do," Andronicus said, trying to reassure the boys. "Trust me; the king will not harm Alexander."

"You don't know my father as well as you think," Alexander said, surprising all three of them. His eyes were puffy and red from crying, and he had a defeated look to him.

"He may be angry," Andronicus said, turning to the prince, "but he won't harm you. I promise."

"And what happens if he does come after me?" Alexander asked, looking like he was going to start crying again. "Are you going to save me, Andronicus? Like you did in the battle."

"It will not come to that," Andronicus assured him, "but yes, if I have to, I will."

"We all will," Cassander added, getting to his feet. Hephaestion rose with him. Alexander smiled sadly and then turned and walked away. Hephaestion started to go after him, but Andronicus pulled him back, shaking his head slowly. There was nothing more to say to him that night. The best thing to do was to wait until morning and talk to the king before he could get drunk again.

Chapter 40
Run and Hide

1

After the public bout with his drunken father, Alexander began to fear for his life. Andronicus tried again to convince the boy that the king had just been drunk and that he would likely not even remember. The other boys pretended to agree with Andronicus, and together they tried to talk sense into the prince. Alexander likely would have listened and let the matter go, except for his mother. Olympias filled her son's ear with dark whispers far too often for Andronicus's liking, but there was nothing he could do about it.

Andronicus didn't like the woman at all, nor did he trust her. She had a cunning demeanor about her, and a sly, subtle way of talking to her son. The other boys could all hear the poison in her words, but Alexander was blind to it. He loved his mother, as any boy should, and listened to her every word. She would tell him that his father hated him, and no matter what anyone else said to the contrary, Alexander believed her.

Less than a week after Philip's marriage to Cleopatra, known since their marriage as Cleopatra Eurydice, Alexander fled the country in the middle of the night. His mother's whispers had convinced him that the king would make an attempt on his life, and he meant to flee before it happened. His friends tried to stop him; they took turns pleading with him to stay. In the end, Andronicus was the last line of defense.

"You're running away like a coward," Andronicus scolded as Alexander packed the last of his things, "from a drunken old man and an unborn babe."

"I'm running from the assassins my father has hired against me," Alexander said, sounding too much like his mother.

"Your father has not hired any assassins, boy!" Andronicus shouted, trying to control his temper. "Nor will he. He has spent nineteen years and a small fortune, grooming you into the finest battle commander a boy your age could be. Do you think he hired Aristotle to teach you just so he could kill you one day?"

"That was before he married the harpy,"

Alexander spat, echoing his mother's poisonous words. "The high priest says that she's with child and that it will be a boy. When my father has a true Macedonian heir, he will no longer have any need for me."

"That's your mother's foolishness," Andronicus said, trying to make the boy see the truth. "I know you love your mother, but her words are madness."

Alexander shot him a furious look, then stormed off. Andronicus tried to get word to Aristotle, but by the time he heard back it was too late. Alexander fled Macedonia with his mother and left Andronicus and his friends behind. Hephaestion wanted to chase after him, and Cassander seemed willing to go as well, but Andronicus stopped them.

Deep down Andronicus wanted to go after Alexander too. He had spent two years teaching the boy how to fight, and he wanted Alexander to be there when they went to face the Persians. He knew he had to stay, however. He had not come to Macedonia to teach Alexander and his friends; he had come to Macedonia to fight the Persians again. Teaching the boys had simply been his way in.

A voice in the back of his head told him that wasn't true though. He hadn't found Alexander by accident. He had been meant to find him. Told to find him. It had been more than twenty years since Leonidas had come to Andronicus in the dream, but he could still remember it vividly. Leonidas had told him to find the boy, and Andronicus was sure that Alexander was that boy; he had to be. Andronicus had found him and trained him, and now the boy was running away with his mother instead of fighting in the greatest war the world would ever see.

Andronicus thought about it often, going after Alexander. He knew the boys would all come with him. Aristotle could come, and maybe even Cleitus. Together they could find him, and bring him back. Alexander hadn't left any clue as to where he might be going, but Andronicus had found his way home from across the world, so he was sure he could find a missing prince if he really tried. Perhaps that was what Leonidas had meant, to find him when he fled and bring him back.

When Aristotle finally arrived, Andronicus told him what had happened. He also shared his thoughts about going after Alexander. To his surprise Aristotle disagreed. He told Andronicus to stay and wait, and the prince would return on his own. Andronicus didn't believe it, but he decided to trust in his wise friend and stay put.

2

With Alexander gone, his friends had no real place in the army, so Andronicus brought them to Cleitus. Cleitus knew the boys well and had seen them fight at Chaeronea, so he accepted them into the guard without question. Andronicus kept an eye on the boys as they all waited for the inevitable day when they would begin the march to Persia.

The boys were still new recruits, no matter how noble their blood was, so they were given low posts. Andronicus was moved from the prince's detail over to the king's. He began following Philip as he had followed Alexander, staying out of sight and yet always ready to step in when needed. Andronicus found it much different following the king than it had been with the prince.

Where Alexander and his friends would often talk to Andronicus throughout the day, either asking questions or simply chatting, Philip never spoke to him at all. Andronicus didn't mind though; the more time he spent in Philip's shadow, the less he liked the man. Philip was the king and ruler of the greatest empire in the world and had promised to overthrow the Persians. Every day Philip's generals would come to him with battle plans and military requests, and every day Philip would ignore them.

Rather than attending the planning of his own invasion, Philip spent his days with his many wives. It seemed the king had not even noticed the absence of his third wife and only son. Philip would go from one wife to the next, often spending the day with one and the night with another. He was also a sloppy drunk, not quite to the extent that Andronicus had once been, but still far too much for a king.

On the few occasions the king actually attended to his kingly duties, other than trying to procure more heirs, he would be terribly drunk and almost totally useless. At one memorable meeting, the king vomited on his own feet while Parmenion laid out the first steps of the invasion. The king proceeded to fall over into his own sick and was snoring loudly a second later. Andronicus and Cleitus had picked the king up and dragged him back to his chambers, where they threw him onto his bed, still covered in his own filth.

Andronicus wanted to resent the king for his drinking, but every time he tried, his own plights with the bottle returned to him. He tried to tell himself that Philip was a king, and should therefore be above such carnal instincts, and yet he was over a hundred years old, and should therefore be above such things as well. Meanwhile, he had lived at the bottom of a bottle for years, decades even. The king still held the people's respect, and he was a proven battle commander, but Andronicus could see that Alexander had been right; this king was not the one to lead the invasion of Persia. Having a trustworthy and reliable prince like Alexander seemed more important than ever.

3

Six months after Alexander fled the country, Hephaestion came to Andronicus and told him the prince was returning. He said that Philip and Alexander had spoken through a third party and had come to terms. Andronicus's first instinct was to go to Alexander at once and welcome him home with open arms. Another part of him wanted to go and shout at the boy for running like a scared dog and hiding with his mother. Hephaestion said that he and the other boys would be rejoining Alexander's company, and told Andronicus that he would be welcome to rejoin Alexander's guard.

Andronicus thought about it for a moment and then refused. The look of excitement fell from Hephaestion's face, replaced by a look of hurt and confusion.

"But he's back," Hephaestion said. "How could you not rejoin him?"

"You have trained with him since you were children," Andronicus said. "Your place is beside him. Mine is not."

"But it is," Hephaestion pleaded. "You taught us how to fight. You have to be with us when we go to Persia."

"I will be," Andronicus said. "Beside the king."

Andronicus left without letting the boy say anything else. He knew he should go back to Alexander's guard, but he still felt the betrayal of Alexander's leaving. For the time being, he decided to stay with Philip. It wasn't as if he couldn't still protect Alexander if he had to; he just wouldn't be following the boy any longer.

4

With Alexander back at his father's side, plans for the invasion accelerated. The king still seemed more concerned with drinking and festivities at home, but Alexander was able to get things moving again. While Alexander and his mother had been away, Philip had decided to marry their daughter, Alexander's only full sibling, to her uncle, Alexander of Epirus. The king was much more interested in the business of this new wedding than the invasion, so the war was left for Alexander and Parmenion to plan.

While Philip prepared for the festivities, Alexander met with the generals every day. Andronicus couldn't do it any longer; he knew his place was with the prince, not a drunken old king. One day while Philip was busy with his fifth and seventh wives, Andronicus went to Cleitus and requested that he be put back on Alexander's detail. Cleitus regarded Andronicus silently for a moment and then nodded. Andronicus returned the nod, not quite sure what Cleitus was thinking, and then left.

When Andronicus found Alexander and his friends, they were sitting with Aristotle, deep in a conversation about mathematics. When they saw

Andronicus, Cassander and Ptolemy jumped up to greet him. Hephaestion and Alexander remained seated, staring bitterly at him.

"What are you doing here?" Alexander asked. "You should be watching over my father, should you not?"

"Your father is a drunken fool," Andronicus replied. He sat down, and Cassander and Ptolemy took their seats as well.

"That's the king you are talking about," Hephaestion said, sneering. "You could be killed for saying such things."

"Perhaps," Andronicus replied casually, "but I'm not so concerned about the king. I'm far more interested in the affairs of the future king, the man who will lead the armies into battle."

"You said we weren't ready for battle," Alexander said, sounding like an angry child.

"I was right; you weren't ready," Andronicus replied, "but you proved yourselves anyway. Your place is here, at the head of your army. Just as long as you never run away from your duties again."

"I did not run from my duties," Alexander protested. "I ran from my father's assassins."

"It doesn't matter why you ran," Andronicus said, "just that you never do it again. If you ever think that assassins are after you, just remember that my job is to keep you alive, and I'm a better fighter than they are."

"So you wish to be my guard again?" Alexander asked, his blue eye giving away his hopefulness.

"I do," Andronicus replied, nodding slowly. "If you'll have me back, that is." Andronicus looked over and saw Aristotle giving him an approving smile.

"What about my father?" Alexander asked. "He'll want you protecting him."

"I have been living in your father's shadow for the past six months, and I don't think he even knows who I am," Andronicus said. "He won't even notice I'm gone. And I cleared it with Cleitus already."

"Well, in that case, welcome back, old friend,"

Alexander said cheerfully. Cassander clapped Andronicus on the back with a big grin. Andronicus noticed Aristotle stifle a laugh when Alexander called him "old friend."

The conversation returned to mathematics, and Andronicus sat back and listened. It was as if a terrible weight had been lifted off his shoulders. As soon as Alexander welcomed him back, Andronicus knew he was where he belonged, at least for the moment. He didn't know what was going to happen, but he knew he was meant to follow Alexander into battle, not Philip.

5

"He thought you had abandoned him," Aristotle told Andronicus once the boys left for the marketplace. Aristotle had grown balder over the years and had begun to grow a gut as well. He looked older than the last time Andronicus had seen him, but he still had the same curious look in his eyes.

"He was the one who abandoned us," Andronicus replied.

"He thought his own father was trying to kill him," Aristotle said, defending the prince's actions. "Can you blame him?"

"I told him Philip meant him no harm," Andronicus insisted. "But he chose to listen to his mother and run from his problems."

"Olympias is a dangerous woman," Aristotle said, surprising Andronicus. "I have known it since I first met her ten years ago. She will do whatever she thinks is necessary to make sure her son is king."

"What do you mean?" Andronicus asked.

"I have heard that the king has a new baby on the way," Aristotle replied, "carried by a wife who is of noble Macedonian descent. Should the baby turn out to be a boy, some in the empire would say the baby, rather than Alexander, should be the heir to Macedonia."

"It's not as if he's from Thrace or Persia," Andronicus pointed out. "His mother is from Greece. Athenian blood is just as noble and pure as

Macedonian blood."

"You don't have to tell me that," Aristotle said with a chuckle. "I'm as Greek as you are. More so, in fact. You have lived in other lands while I have only ever lived in Greece and Macedonia."

"Do you really think that this baby will pose a threat to Alexander?" Andronicus asked. "Alexander is smart and strong and has been training for years now. Would anyone truly follow a boy if Alexander has already become a man?"

"I'm quite sure that Philip means to keep Alexander as his heir," Aristotle said. "You say it true; he has spent too much time and money on the boy to turn to another. But it doesn't matter what you or I think. It's the boy's mother I'm worried about."

"You think she would move to kill this child or the mother?" Andronicus asked.

"I do," Aristotle replied, nodding gravely. "You should stay out of that woman's way, old friend. She's more dangerous than she seems."

"Is there anything we can do?" Andronicus asked.

"Like what? Have Alexander's mother killed?"

"No, not killed. Just stopped from killing that poor girl and her baby."

"You have killed hundreds of men, and if that girl and her baby die, Alexander's position will be secure," Aristotle said. "Why do you care so much?"

"Perhaps I have a soft spot when it comes to pregnant women being murdered for the crime of the child they carry," Andronicus replied, his teeth clenched.

"I'm sorry," Aristotle said, looking at his feet. "I didn't think—"

"Forget it," Andronicus said, turning away. "There must be some way we can stop her. She's just a woman."

"An extremely powerful and dangerous woman," Aristotle said. "I would stay out of her way. But if you really feel you must do something, tell Cleitus, make sure the girl is well guarded."

"Aye, I will," Andronicus said, sighing. "But I

doubt that will be enough to stop Olympias if she really wants the girl dead."

Chapter 41
Long Live the King
1

In the fall of 336 BC, the invasion was nearly ready to get underway. Rumblings of the initial destination were spreading through the ranks of the Macedonian army. It was said that Philip intended to march on Persia before year's end, and every man had to prepare himself. Tensions throughout the city and the army were higher than ever as the day grew nearer. A sense of being on the edge of a cliff seemed to envelope every man, woman, and child. It was the same sort of restlessness that enveloped any nation on the brink of war.

A wedding festival seemed like an excellent way to lighten the mood.

Andronicus learned that while Alexander and his mother were in hiding, they had gone to Epirus, where Olympias's brother was still king. Alexander, King of Epirus, was the young Alexander's own uncle and namesake. They had been welcomed into Epirus in secret and spent most of their time in exile there. Alexander told Andronicus all about it once he returned, and about what his mother had tried to do.

Olympias had tried to convince her brother to lead Epirus into war against Philip. She knew that if Epirus attacked Macedonia, the Persian invasion would have to be put off for years, and the blame would fall on Philip. She didn't seem to care that both nations would bleed needlessly. Olympias wanted nothing more than the downfall of King Philip, and she didn't seem to care how many people had to die for it to happen, just so long as her son became king.

Luckily for Macedonia and Epirus, Alexander was not as coldhearted as his mother. He knew that to wage war against Persia, Macedonia needed an alliance with Epirus.

After Alexander returned home, he spoke with his father about the situation with Epirus. Philip suggested that Cleopatra, Alexander's true sister and his own daughter by Olympias, should marry Alexander, King of Epirus. Alexander was against the idea at first; he didn't like the idea of his sister having to marry their uncle, but he knew it was common enough among royalty. In the end Alexander agreed to his father's proposal, recognizing that the alliance was vital to the war effort.

As soon as the wedding was announced, it became the talk of the city. Everyone wanted to attend. The anxiety of the coming war was still everywhere though, and Philip hurried the wedding forward in order to please the people. It took place just a month after Alexander returned from exile. People came from all over the Macedonian empire. Noblemen and their wives from across the country came to Pella to fill the coliseum.

Andronicus was chosen to be part of the guard in the coliseum rather than being stationed by the prince. He stood atop the high steps, watching as the people filed in. He and the rest of the guard were scattered across the wide arena, watching for any signs of violence or treachery. The noble people of Macedonia laughed and cheered as they filled the large coliseum, glad to be rid of thoughts of the coming war for a day. Children weaved in and out of the crowd, play fighting with sticks. When Cleopatra and Alexander of Epirus emerged from the small tunnel, the crowd erupted into applause.

Andronicus watched the couple greet the nobles as they made their way to their place at the foot of the tall steps. When the betrothed and their guests had all taken their seats, a trumpet call rang out. Everyone rose as King Philip entered the coliseum. The king walked slowly, as usual, limping on his bad leg. Andronicus could tell immediately that he was drunk, and he hoped he wouldn't make a fool of himself.

The king's hair had grown long and grizzled of late, and his face was an angry mask of wrinkles and scars. He struggled to walk a straight line as he stumbled toward his daughter and his brother/son-in-law. Andronicus had never seen a king who looked less like a king, and yet he did still have a sort of power to him, the same way Andronicus had still been a threat no matter how drunk he was.

Philip lumbered toward the center of the arena and raised his hands. The crowd cheered, and Philip laughed and smiled at his daughter. As Philip began to speak, Andronicus saw the guard nearest to him step forward, and wondered what he was doing. The guard walked slowly but confidently, giving no one reason to doubt his cause. Then the guard reached under his golden breastplate and drew a dagger.

Andronicus shouted to Cleitus, who was standing close to the king, but his voice was drowned out by a scream as the guard drove the dagger into Philip's back. A dozen more women screamed. Then everything seemed to happen at once.

The king's smile turned to a grimace as he fell to his knees. The guard pulled the dagger from the king's back and then ran for the nearest tunnel. The rest of the king's guard charged after him while Cleitus ran to the king. The assassin cut down a guard before running down the tunnel with two dozen shouting men close behind him.

The crowd broke into utter chaos. The entire coliseum filled with screams and shouts as panic took over. People ran in every direction, and nothing could be heard over the hectic clamor.

Andronicus ran down the steps, shoving people out of the way. When he reached the bottom, he saw Alexander emerge from the tunnel, his face etched with horror as he saw his father.

The prince stumbled over and fell to his knees beside the king, who lay dying in Cleitus's arms. Alexander reached out and placed his hand on his father's chest. Tears fell like rain from Alexander's eyes onto Philip's blood-soaked robes. The king's mouth twitched, and Alexander lowered his ear to hear his father's last words. Andronicus couldn't hear what the king said, but he saw the look on Alexander's face. It was the kingly sort of look he had seen on Alexander before, only much stronger now.

The king let out a final strangled grunt, coughing a bit of blood onto his son's face, and then he died. Cleitus began to weep as he lowered the king's head and gently closed his eyes. Alexander got to his feet, the same expression on his face, accompanied by tears running down his cheeks. Andronicus looked around, taking in his surroundings. Most of the people who had been scattering in panic had stopped and were now staring down at their dead king.

Andronicus saw the bride and groom huddled together in the front row, the bride a sobbing, horrified mess. Beside them was Parmenion, looking as though he would be sick. Behind him, standing in the third row, was Olympias. Andronicus wasn't sure, but he thought he saw her mouth stretched into a wicked grin. Her eyes were dry, a cold darkness behind them. Andronicus felt a chill as he watched her staring down at her dead husband.

Andronicus turned back to see Calas standing next to Alexander, who was still staring down at his father, his face somewhere between horror and wonder. His white robes stained red from his father's blood, Calas took his hand, and raised it high in the air. Alexander finally looked up from his father's corpse and saw all the people looking at him. In Alexander's blue eye Andronicus saw a boy who had lost his father, scared and alone. But in the brown eye, there was a different sort of look, a kingly look.

"Here stands Alexander the Third, first son of Philip the Second!" Calas shouted. The crowd fell silent as they watched in fascination. "King of Macedonia!" Calas bellowed. "Hegemon of Greece, and leader of the Persian conquest!"

The crowd broke into raucous cheers. Just seconds before they had been running like a herd of crazed cattle, and now they were applauding their new king like it was the reason they had all gathered in the first place.

Alexander looked from his dead father's body to the crowd of cheering people, and stepped forward, as king. Tears still covered his face, and his clothes were soaked with his father's blood. On the surface he looked like a boy who had just witnessed his father's murder, but under that Andronicus saw something else, something so much more powerful. Alexander's face changed as his mind caught up to the situation. He did not look pleased or excited to be king, but in that moment he looked ready.

What Andronicus saw on Alexander's face was a fierce determination. In a single terrible instant he had gone from a boy to a man, from a prince to a king. Andronicus fought to keep the tears out of his own eyes. It wasn't that this boy whom he had taught was now king or that he would be the one to lead the invasion. Andronicus felt a sense of purpose that he had not experienced in ages, a feeling he had almost forgotten.

As Alexander raised his hand to his people and waved to them as their king, Andronicus felt warmth wash over him. For a moment he didn't know what it was, and then it hit him like a rock. Andronicus fell to his knees and braced himself with one hand in the dirt. His body was alive with a force of energy he had not felt for decades. Short of breath, he had to gulp down air. No one noticed him kneeling as the crowd continued cheering.

He slowly rose to his feet, his entire body tingling with energy. He looked at the new king and saw nothing but power. In that moment Andronicus knew that Alexander of Macedonia was going to be a truly great king.

Chapter 42
The Orders of the King
1

After the king was assassinated, things happened very quickly. A kind of frenzied panic had taken hold of the entire city of Pella, and likely the rest of Macedonia as well. People began to question the young king's competency the moment he was crowned. The generals, however, were loyal to Alexander for the most part. They knew he had no part in his father's death and that he was the rightful ruler by law. It was the noblemen Andronicus worried about, as well as the common people.

The night of the assassination, Andronicus walked through the city streets on the orders of the king, listening to everything as he went. Everywhere he walked he heard whispers of who people thought might be a better fit for the crown and who might be plotting against Alexander. Some people even thought that Alexander himself was behind the murder. Nothing Andronicus heard as he walked the streets of Pella gave him any comfort.

Early the next morning, Alexander called a meeting of his closest advisors and generals. Andronicus had only gotten an hour of sleep before being summoned, but he was ready.

When he entered the stone palace where Alexander and his council were waiting, he noticed there were far fewer generals than there had been before Philip's death. He wondered if Alexander had dismissed them, moved them, or had them killed; every option seemed possible.

Cassander approached Andronicus with a serious look on his face. "Andronicus," he said, bowing slightly, "the king wishes to speak with you." Andronicus nodded, and Cassander led him to the front of the room. Nearly every eye watched them as they approached the king. Andronicus quickly took measure of the men standing around him and did not recognize an alarming number of them. He did see Parmenion on one side though, whispering with his son and two other men.

Alexander was sitting in a large, ornate throne with Hephaestion standing over his right shoulder and Cleitus not far behind them. He looked up as Andronicus came over and rose to greet him. Alexander had a strained look on his face, like he had not slept for days.

"You were down amongst the people last night, were you not?" Alexander asked in a croaky voice. He had heavy rings under his eyes, and the lines around his mouth were deep.

"I was, my king," Andronicus said with a slight bow of his head, offering Alexander the courtesies he now commanded.

"Tell me what you heard," the king said as he took his seat.

Everyone in the room fell silent in anticipation of Andronicus's report.

"The people are scared, my king," Andronicus said. "They fear you're too young to lead them against the Persians. More than that they fear there will be a revolt, that someone will make an attempt on your throne and send the country into civil war."

Silence hung in the room for a moment as Alexander and his advisors processed this information.

"And did they say who might make an attempt on my throne?" Alexander asked through clenched teeth. Andronicus could tell that this news was more troubling to Alexander than anything.

"There were merely whispers, my king," Andronicus said. "I heard no names mentioned."

"Your cousin," Hephaestion said. "Amyntas, it must be him."

"Amyntas is a good soldier," Parmenion said, stepping forward to stand before the king. "He has always been loyal to your father."

"It's for those very reasons that he's the most likely pick to replace Alexander," Hephaestion shot back. "He's a decorated soldier, he's twenty-nine years old, a more suitable age to be king, and he's of Macedonian royalty, with pure Macedonian blood."

"Enough," Alexander said, cutting Hephaestion off. "If Amyntas is my truest competition for the throne, he must be killed."

"Alexander, you must reconsider," Parmenion urged, looking appalled. "Amyntas is a true Macedonian and your cousin by blood. You don't even know if he's plotting against you."

"If he isn't plotting against me now, he will be soon enough," Alexander said, looking the older general in the eye. "He is too great a risk for me to leave alive."

"Very well, my king," Cleitus said from his place beside the fire. "It will be done." Cleitus turned to Andronicus and gave him a small nod. Andronicus returned the nod, knowing he would have to kill the prince himself.

"And Attalus as well," Alexander added bitterly.

"My king, you can't," Parmenion said, aghast. "Attalus is of noble descent. He—"

"Do not tell me what I can't do, Parmenion," Alexander warned, rising to his feet. "I am king, and he dishonored my name. He called me a motherless bastard, and I'll see him dead for it." Silence fell over the room again. No one dared question the king now.

"Very well, my king," Cleitus said. "It will be done."

"And who else?" Hephaestion asked the room at large.

"Yes, who else shall we murder?" Parmenion said boldly, glaring at the boys. Andronicus admired the old man's grit, but knew he was a fool to challenge the new king.

"Stay your tongue, old man," Alexander seethed, glaring at his leading general. "My father is dead. I'm king now."

"I'll have no part in this madness," Parmenion shot back. "I'll return to the Persian front where I belong and await you and your army there. Let me know when you're ready to face your true enemies." With that Parmenion turned and stormed out of the room, leaving everyone in stunned silence, their eyes turning back to Alexander.

"We could have him killed as well," Hephaestion suggested, glancing at Philotas. Philotas didn't say a word; he just stared at the king, who would determine whether he and his father would be killed.

"That would be unwise, my king," Calas said, stepping forward. "Parmenion is the most experienced commander we have, and he's no threat to you. Killing him would only harm our Persian campaign."

Andronicus looked at Philotas, and saw that he was as white as a sheet, but he looked like he was ready to fight to the death if he had to. Andronicus pitied his situation; the boy must know that if Alexander killed his father, he would be killed as well.

"Calas is right," Cassander added quickly. "Parmenion is too useful to kill. If he's truly leaving for the Persian front, then perhaps that is for the best."

"What of your cousins from Lyncestis?" Ptolemy asked. "They are of royal blood, are they not?"

"They are," Cassander nodded, "and I have heard whispers that they may have had a hand in your father's murder."

"Have them killed as well," Alexander said offhandedly. No one challenged him this time. Andronicus looked around at the dozen or so generals standing about the room. Most of them were in their forties at least. They had fought in many battles over the years and had been completely loyal to Philip, but they could all sense the shift in power now as the new boy king and his friends planned the murders of their foes.

"Is that all then?" Alexander asked hopefully. "There isn't anyone else, is there?"

"What about your father's bride?" Hephaestion asked. "Cleopatra. Cleopatra Eurydice, that is," he added in a mocking tone.

"What about her?" Alexander demanded.

"Her son, Caranus," Hephaestion said. "He's the greatest threat to you now. He is of true Macedonian blood. He could become a threat if you let—"

"I will not hear of this," Alexander said. "You dare talk of murdering my only brother?" Alexander lunged at Hephaestion, who took a step back in surprise. Andronicus caught the king before he could reach his friend.

"You have not slept in two days, my king," Andronicus whispered, so only Alexander and Cassander could hear. "You need rest. We can finish this later." Alexander pushed himself away from Andronicus and glared at him.

"Very well," he said. "We will continue this evening." With that the king turned and left, Cleitus close behind him. There was an awkward moment after Alexander left. Andronicus could tell that the generals wanted to discuss the new king, but they didn't dare with his friends still in the room. After a minute Calas left, and then the other generals followed. The boys left after, as did Andronicus.

He walked back to his home in deep thought. He had seen hints of greatness in Alexander, but he wanted to see it in action. The murdering of the boy's enemies made perfect sense to Andronicus; it was exactly what he would do in Alexander's place. However, the fact that Alexander would not harm the girl or her baby, even though he was Alexander's greatest threat, showed that he could be merciless and yet compassionate at the same time, or so Andronicus hoped.

He had to wonder what would become of Parmenion. He was leaving for the time, but he had challenged the king in front of the other generals. Parmenion was smart and loyal, and Andronicus wanted him to be there when the fighting started. It was a good thing Parmenion was leaving because it would give Alexander time to cool, but eventually they would have to settle their differences.

2

Later that night Andronicus went to find Alexander. Andronicus had slept most of the day, and hoped that Alexander had as well. When he found the king, he was eating supper, surrounded by his close friends. Right away Andronicus could see that Alexander looked much better than he had that morning. He still had rings under his eyes, but they weren't nearly as dark.

"I see you got some sleep," Andronicus said as he approached the table.

"Yes, thank you," Alexander said, looking up. "You were right." Alexander returned to his food, and Andronicus waited for him to address the orders he had been given that morning. When he didn't, Andronicus finally spoke up.

"The orders you gave this morning," Andronicus said, "do they still stand?" Alexander looked up from his food and stared at Andronicus. He didn't say anything for a moment, as if he were waiting to see fear from Andronicus, but he saw none.

"Why would my orders not stand?" Alexander asked.

"I thought that perhaps after getting some sleep you might have reconsidered," Andronicus replied, meeting the young king's forceful stare with his own, calculated, menacing scowl that he had developed over nearly two centuries. "I'm glad you did not."

"And why is that?" Alexander asked, a little taken aback at Andronicus's overbearing demeanor. Cassander and Ptolemy looked positively terrified of Andronicus. Even Hephaestion turned away from Andronicus's murderous gaze.

"Because it means you're ready to be king," Andronicus said. "Now then, about your cousin, Amyntas, how would you like it done?"

"What do you mean?" Alexander asked, looking much less confident than he had a moment earlier.

"Would you like it to look like an accident, or shall I kill him in the name of the king?"

"How could you?" Cassander asked before he could stop himself. He looked at Andronicus fearfully for a moment and then realized he had to continue. "I mean, you would have to fight him and all of his guards if you told them what you were doing."

"You're right," Andronicus replied, "I would." Cassander turned bright red and sat back down, trying to look anywhere but at Andronicus's death stare.

"Do it in the name of the king then," Alexander said, meeting Andronicus's gaze. "I'm neither a liar nor a coward. I'm killing them because it's necessary to keep my empire. Tell him why he must die. And if you can, tell him I'm sorry."

3

Andronicus went back to his home and took out his old bronze blade. He tucked it behind his back, knowing he would likely need it before the end of the night. He donned the fine new armor the king had given him and then set out to murder the prince of

Macedonia on the orders of a nineteen-year-old boy.

As he walked down a dirt road, toward Amyntas's palace, it occurred to him that this may well be the first man he had ever killed who meant him no harm at all. He had killed hundreds of men in his long lifetime, but nearly all of them had been in battle or at least combat, usually started by his enemy.

He supposed there was the one time, the time he tried not to think about. As he walked toward committing a murder, he couldn't help but remember what he had done so long ago. In a sense it helped him to think of it now, to remember what he was capable of. He had once butchered women and children alike. A whole village laid bare by him alone. This Amyntas meant him no harm, but he was a childless man, a soldier who likely wished for a glorious death in battle. It may not be glorious, but Andronicus could at least give the man a death in battle.

He realized as he walked that it had been a rather long time since he had been in a real fight to the death. He had been fighting more of late than he had in years, but not to kill. And the one battle he had been involved with had certainly not been one on one. He tried to recall the last time he had fought and killed in close quarters and realized it was before he had even returned to Greece, nearly thirty years ago.

As he reached the palace and started up the steps, he felt a touch of trepidation. He didn't know how many men would be awaiting him, but he felt ready. Under the nerves, was a feeling even more palpable, a feeling of excitement and even relief.

He climbed to the top of the stairs and found two guards standing there with spears in hand.

"What do you want?" the guard on the left demanded.

"I'm here on behalf of the king," Andronicus replied. "I have a message for Amyntas, the king's cousin."

"Amyntas is not taking any visitors right now," the other guard barked. "Now leave."

"Stand aside, or I'll have to cut you both down," Andronicus warned, giving the guards the same cold look he had given the boys earlier. They both faltered for a second but then regained themselves.

"Look, whoever you are," the first guard said, pointing his spear at Andronicus. "Amyntas is not going to hear any message from the king. Now, there are two of us and only one of you, so leave before we have to hurt you."

Andronicus smiled at the man, a cold, dark smile, and was glad to see the man falter again. He drew his sword, and both men pointed their spears at him, though neither of them seemed prepared for a fight.

"You'd better leave," the second guard said, trying to sound fierce but sounding more like a scared child.

"I'll give you one last chance to stand down," Andronicus said. "Get out of my way."

"That's it," the first guard said, thrusting his spear at Andronicus. Andronicus easily moved to the side, caught the spear with one hand, and slashed the man's throat with his sword. He felt his sword rip through the guard's flesh and watched the blood shoot out from his severed neck.

The second guard recoiled in horror and instinctively dropped his spear. Andronicus didn't give him time to regret the mistake. As the guard threw his arms up in terror, Andronicus plunged his sword through the man's chest. He pulled his sword out with a nasty squelch, and the second guard fell to the ground next to his dying companion. Andronicus stepped over them and walked into the palace.

He found Amyntas sitting at a table with several other men. Andronicus recognized two of the men who had been at Alexander's meeting that morning and knew immediately that he had walked into a trap. There were only two guards in the room, but Andronicus knew that more would be nearby, likely waiting for Amyntas's order.

"You must be the famous Spartan, Andronicus," Amyntas said, rising to his feet. "I have heard so much about you. I'm told my young cousin has sent you here to kill me."

"You hear it true," Andronicus said, glaring at the two traitors.

"I see you have already started your work," Amyntas said, gesturing toward Andronicus's blood-soaked sword. "Is that from my guards outside?"

Andronicus nodded slowly, glaring at Amyntas. The prince looked a bit unsettled, but Andronicus didn't see the fear he had wanted in the man's eye.

"I hear you're a fierce warrior, all the way from Sparta," Amyntas continued. "That's why I made sure to have enough men to kill you." As Amyntas said the words, he knocked on the table. The doors to either side of Andronicus opened, and soldiers poured into the large room. Within seconds Andronicus was surrounded by a dozen men with swords pointing at him. Andronicus stood his ground, still staring at the prince but keeping the guards in his line of sight.

"I'm here on behalf of Alexander the Third, son of Philip the Second, King of Macedonia, Hegemon of Greece, and leader of the Persian conquest. In his name you have been sentenced to death," Andronicus proclaimed, his voice reverberating off the stone walls.

"On what charges?" Amyntas asked from behind the cover of his soldiers.

"Treason," Andronicus replied. "Conspiracy to kill the king and take his crown for your own."

"And what proof do you have of this?" Amyntas demanded.

"None at all," Andronicus answered with a cold smile.

"Enough!" Amyntas shouted. "Kill him!"

Andronicus stood his ground as several soldiers stepped forward. He waited patiently as they crept in, their swords pointed at him. He took a second to size up the approaching men. The one to his left was short and thick with big, hairy arms and a determined look on his face. The one on the right was taller, younger, and more athletic looking, but he looked much more eager. The one in the middle was a step behind, and didn't look at all like he would make the first move.

Andronicus guessed correctly. The younger man flung himself ahead of the others. Andronicus stepped to the side, clashed his sword against the young man's blade, and then spun around and drove his sword through the back of his neck. He wrenched his sword out of the man's neck, nearly decapitating him, and sent blood flying across the room. Just as Andronicus's sword pulled free, the short man lunged at him.

Again his sword clanged loudly against the oncoming sword. Then he spun his sword around, bringing it down on the man's arm and cutting through flesh and bone alike. The man's arm fell to the ground, still holding its sword. As the second man hit the floor screaming, the third man charged, the rest of the men right behind him. The poor fool looked terrified, and Andronicus barely had to move to cut the man down.

Andronicus stepped back as two swords swung at him at once. He deflected the other blows coming his way and then slashed at one of the men. His sword caught the man under the arm but didn't pierce very deep. Before Andronicus could strike again, he was back on his heels, defending the barrage of blows raining down on him from three sides. He had his back to the wall and was fighting off four men, with another five waiting behind them.

Andronicus deflected, struck, and deflected, doing the old dance he had done a thousand times before. Eventually, he saw his moment and slashed out at one man's throat when he lunged too far. Before the man fell to the floor, Andronicus drove his sword through a second man's chest. He withdrew it, but before he could strike the third man, two more had taken the others' places. He looked behind them, saw three more men ready to jump in, and readied himself for a lengthy fight.

The guards all looked scared of him now. There was a moment's pause in the fighting as the new front men slowly circled him. Somehow during the fighting one of them had managed to get behind him, and now he was surrounded. The man who was missing an arm was still screaming on the floor, and none of the men seemed to want to resume the battle. Even though they had him where they wanted him, none of them made a move.

Finally, Andronicus reached behind his back and drew the bronze dagger he had hidden there. With a flick of his wrist, he sent the knife flying through the air. It sank into the closest soldier's neck, and he fell to the floor with a mangled cry. Andronicus turned to the man to his left and raised his sword. The man took a scared step backward, tripping over a body. He fell to the floor and lost his sword, and Andronicus turned to the next man.

The soldier stepped forward, looking determined, and raised his sword above his head, only to have Andronicus's sword come flying up through his gut. The man stepped back, with a comical look of surprise on his face, and then fell to the floor. Andronicus spun around to see only three men left standing, with Amyntas looking terrified behind them.

One of the soldiers looked like he was going to say something, but before he could, Andronicus sliced his throat. He cut down the remaining men with ease. It was as if they had already resigned themselves to being killed after seeing the carnage Andronicus had unleashed.

When all of the men were either dead or dying on the floor, Andronicus turned to face Amyntas. Andronicus was covered in blood and looked more terrifying than ever. He went from one wounded soldier to the next, driving his blade through their chests and ending their dying cries. Amyntas and his remaining followers cowered in the corner like children. Andronicus walked toward them, his blood-red sword in hand, and the two traitors began to whimper.

"Please, my lord," one of the traitors from Alexander's meeting pleaded. "I only came here to make sure the traitor, Amyntas, would be here for you when you arrived. I'm loyal to the king; I swear it." Andronicus ended his babbling with a sickening thud as he cleaved the man's skull in two. The other traitor didn't wait to be executed. He got to his feet and made for the door, but he only got three steps before Andronicus's sword went whirling through the air and into his back. The man fell to the floor, throwing his arms up in anguish. Andronicus walked over to him, pulled his sword out, and then plunged it back in, ending the man's whimpering.

Andronicus turned back to Amyntas, the only man left alive in the room. He slowly stood up and drew his own sword.

"I may not be able to beat you," Amyntas said, his head held high, "but I can at least die on my feet with my sword in my hand." Andronicus nodded slowly, meeting his eye as he did. They had a moment of peaceful understanding, both fully aware of what was going to happen next.

"Alexander asked me to tell you he's sorry," Andronicus said. "He hopes you understand."

"I do, actually," Amyntas replied, a tear rolling down one cheek. Then he stepped forward and swung his sword. Andronicus deflected several of his blows as Amyntas moved forward. Andronicus was more impressed with Amyntas's skill than any of his men, but Andronicus was more than warmed up. He let the man fight him for a minute before ending him with a swift blow to the chest. Andronicus made sure to pierce the prince's heart, so he wouldn't suffer.

When it was done, and Andronicus was alone in the carnage he had created, he grabbed a clean napkin off the table and wiped his face. After cleaning his face and his sword, he walked back home, still covered in blood. The whole walk back, people ran from him in terror.

4

After going home and cleaning up, Andronicus returned to the king's palace. He found Alexander sitting behind a large table, his friends around him, as always, along with Calas and two other generals whom Andronicus didn't recognize. They were deep in discussion, but they all fell silent as Andronicus approached.

"I hear you were successful," Alexander said as Andronicus bowed before him. "It seems you gave the people quite a scare, walking through the streets covered in blood."

"My apologies," Andronicus grunted.

Alexander smiled. "Not at all. It appears the people are now terrified of us all and would not dare so much as a whisper against me."

"What of Attalus?" Andronicus asked, wondering if he would have to kill him as well.

"He is dead," Alexander said. "Cleitus killed him, though he heard some disturbing news after."

"Attalus was receiving letters from Demosthenes of Athens," Hephaestion said, not waiting for the king. "The Athenians were asking Attalus to help the Greeks revolt against Alexander."

"It's not just the Athenians," Alexander added, sounding troubled. "The Thebans and the Thessalians have joined them as well. Not to mention the Thracian tribes that have begun gathering to our north again."

"They must have already forgotten the last time they tried to revolt against us," Cassander mused, shaking his head.

"They have not forgotten," Alexander said, his voice bitter. "They think they were defeated because of my father. This time we'll have to make sure they never rise against us again."

"Where will we go first?" Cassander asked the king, "the Thracians are closer, and they may even have more men, but the Athenians are surely the greater threat."

"We will ride south, to Thessaly," Alexander replied. "Calas," he said, turning to his ranking general, "muster as many cavalry as you can. We ride for Thessaly by week's end.

5

The night before the army was to ride south, Alexander and his advisors were busy planning the attack. Alexander was seated at a great table with Hephaestion and Cassander to his left. Calas and Philotas were both bent over a large map, deep in discussion. Andronicus and Cleitus were stationed by the door, and a half dozen other men were gathered about the room.

There was a knock at the door, and Andronicus

turned to answer it. He opened the door, his sword hand ready, and saw Ptolemy standing there, as white as a sheet. Andronicus stepped aside, and the boy stumbled in. The boys all rose when they saw the expression on his face.

"What is it?" Alexander asked, rising to his feet. "What happened?"

"It . . . I . . . your . . ." Ptolemy paused, fumbling for words. "It was."

"Out with it, boy!" Calas bellowed. "What's happened? Is it the Greeks? Have they attacked?" Ptolemy shook his head, but still couldn't find the words to say what he needed to.

"Ptolemy, what is it?" Alexander asked, staring his friend in the eye. "What's wrong?"

"It's . . . it's your mother," Ptolemy said, not meeting Alexander's eye.

"What about my mother?" Alexander asked, his face turning pale.

"She . . . she . . ."

"Quit your sniveling, and tell the king what happened!" Andronicus bellowed, finally snapping Ptolemy out of his daze.

"Alexander," Ptolemy said, a tear rolling down his cheek, "your mother, she had Cleopatra Eurydice killed. Cleopatra and her children."

Alexander's face turned to stone as he stared at Ptolemy. "My brother?" he asked. "She had my brother killed?" Ptolemy nodded, then burst into a fresh bout of tears.

"What about the girl?" Alexander asked, sitting back down with a defeated look. "Europa, my baby sister?"

"She's dead," Ptolemy sobbed, wiping his face with his sleeve, "your mother had them all killed."

"Why would she kill the girl?" Cassander asked, echoing everyone else's thoughts. "She was no threat to anyone. She was barely a year old. Why have her killed?"

"My mother is a spiteful woman," Alexander said, his face a mask of pain. "I should have known she would do this."

Everyone fell silent. Alexander wept quietly, his head in his hands, while Cassander patted him on the back. Ptolemy was a mess, crying like a baby in the corner. Hephaestion and Philotas sat at the table, each of them considering what to do about the queen mother. Calas stood off to the side, next to Cleitus, a troubled look on his wrinkled face.

"How did it happen?" Alexander asked, looking over at Ptolemy. "How did they die?"

Ptolemy's face grew pale again, and he looked like he might be sick.

"I need to know," Alexander said. "How did my brother and sister die?"

Ptolemy's lips moved, but no one could hear what he was saying.

"Speak up, boy," Calas ordered. "Answer your king."

"They were burned," Ptolemy blurted, bursting into tears again. "She . . . she had them burned alive."

Everyone fell silent again, except for Ptolemy, who was sobbing loudly. Andronicus looked around at the faces of everyone there, and they all showed the same horror. None of them could believe that a mother would burn babies alive. Cleitus was the one exception. His expression was cold and dark and full of hate, but there was no shock there, not like the others. Andronicus had never trusted the woman, but he had certainly not expected this of her. Alexander was right; he should have seen it coming. They both should have.

"I think I'm going to be sick," Ptolemy said through his tears.

"Outside!" Cleitus barked. He grabbed Ptolemy by the collar and dragged him to the door, then tossed him outside.

"Go easy on him, Cleitus," Cassander said. "He just had to deliver terrible news to a good friend."

"He should have waited," Cleitus said, glaring at him. "We're marching to battle tomorrow, and the king doesn't need this on his mind."

"I would ask you not to treat me like a child, Cleitus," Alexander said, raising his head. His eyes were puffy and red, but his face was dry of tears.

"Apologies, my king," Cleitus replied, bowing his head. "I only meant—"

"I know what you meant," Alexander said, "and I would ask that you treat me as your king, not as a child in need of protection."

Cleitus bowed low, then stepped back and resumed his place by the door.

"Alexander," Hephaestion said, his face wet with tears, "what will you do about our march?"

"We will delay one day only," Alexander said. Andronicus could tell he was barely holding it together. "So I may bury my brother and sister. Calas, inform the cavalry we will be leaving the day after tomorrow. Philotas, send word to your father. Reassure him that we will not be delayed in joining him. Hephaestion," he turned to his closest friend with a look of total sorrow, "make the arrangements for my siblings' funeral."

They all stood and bowed to the king before turning to leave. Everyone who had been given orders left at once, and Cassander went out to check on Ptolemy. Alexander turned to Cleitus with a dark look on his face.

"Cleitus," he said, "I want you to take my mother into custody. Any harm done to her will be done tenfold to you. Take her to her chambers, and keep her there until I arrive. I want guards stationed outside her door at all hours."

Cleitus nodded and then left without a word, leaving Andronicus alone with the king. Alexander walked over to the great table where he had been making war plans just minutes earlier and slumped down into his chair. He leaned over the table and held his head in his hands. Then he began to weep. Andronicus watched him carefully, curious what he would do.

"You said your wife was murdered, didn't you?" Alexander asked without looking up. Andronicus was taken aback by the question.

"That's right," he said, eyeing the king.

"For carrying your child, wasn't it?" Alexander asked, his head still in his hands.

"Right again," Andronicus practically

whispered.

"How was it done?" the king asked, finally looking up at Andronicus.

"They drove a spear through her belly," Andronicus said, meeting the king's gaze. "They killed our child first. Then they drove a spear through her throat."

"What did you do to them?" Alexander asked, nearly inaudibly.

"First I killed the man who did it," Andronicus said, turning to stare into the fire. "I cut his throat, and watched as he died, choking on his own blood. And then I killed the ones they had come with. Then I walked to their village and killed every man, woman, and child. I ended their people completely."

Andronicus turned back to the king, who was staring at the wall now. Alexander looked terribly conflicted, like he was balancing life and death in his mind.

"And then what did you do?" he asked softly. For a moment Andronicus wanted to tell him, to tell him all of it. It would surely help ease the boy's pain, and Andronicus would likely become his closest advisor if Alexander believed him. Andronicus thought the boy probably would believe him if he told, he liked stories too much not to. For a moment he was about to tell Alexander everything, but then he decided to hold back.

"I left," Andronicus said, breaking his gaze and looking away, "and I came to Macedonia."

"How did you get to Africa in the first place?" Alexander asked, "and how did you manage to get back before you were an old man?"

Andronicus knew he shouldn't have told the boy about Manyara. Whenever he gave someone a part of his story, they always came back with new questions.

"I did a lot of walking," Andronicus said, getting to his feet. "Perhaps I'll tell you my full story one day, but tonight you need to rest. And tomorrow you need to bury your siblings. Do not see your mother tonight, Alexander. Save that for tomorrow as well."

Chapter 43
Power and Might

1

The day after Alexander buried his brother and sister and their mother, he set out with his army. Calas had mustered just over three thousand mounted soldiers, as commanded, and they rode out of Pella in a long, winding line. Alexander rode Bucephalas at the head of a column of riders that stretched backward out of sight. Andronicus and Cleitus, along with the other generals, rode behind him. They rode the entire day, stopping only once to rest. Alexander barely to spoke to anyone except to order the army to move faster.

Alexander pushed his army across more than a hundred miles in less than a week. The army was approaching Thessaly, expecting to march into the city, but their scout riders informed Alexander that the Thessalian army was camped in the pass between Mount Olympus and Mount Ossa. Andronicus knew the pass well; he had gone through it many times in his life, it being the only way into Thessaly for two hundred miles in either direction.

Alexander halted his cavalry and called together a council of his generals. They had no camp, so Alexander knelt in the dirt, with his generals huddled around him.

"We should wait until they're asleep and then attack in full," Hephaestion said, kicking things off.

"Do not be so hasty, my young friend," Calas said. "I have been through that pass many times. If they're camped where they ought to be, and I'm sure they are, then they're in a perfect position to repel a cavalry charge."

"We should wait them out," Philotas suggested. "Surround them and force them out."

"You forget that they're not cut off from the other side," Calas said. "They can still retreat into Thessaly."

"What if they couldn't retreat?" Alexander mused, more to himself than his generals.

"What do you mean?" Hephaestion asked.

"What if we could get behind them and truly surround them?" Alexander said. Andronicus saw the twinkle in Alexander's blue eye and knew the boy was on to something.

"How?" Cassander asked, bending down to look at the map. "It's two hundred miles to get around Mount Ossa, and you can't get around Mount Olympus at all."

"The king is right," Andronicus said, causing all eyes to look at him. "There's another way through. A small goat path that climbs the side of Ossa. I used it once to get by a batch of soldiers I didn't care to speak with."

"You're full of surprises, Andronicus of Sparta," Alexander said with a smile. "Can we get across this path without the Thessalians noticing us?"

"If we're careful and quiet, yes, I think we can. We won't be able to bring any horses with us though."

"No matter," Alexander said with a wave of his hand. "Most of the army will stay here. Philotas, you are in command until we return. I'll take two hundred men across the path, and in the morning the Thessalians will be surrounded. If they have any sense at all, they will surrender. If they don't, you will attack from the north."

"The Thessalians are not a people to fight a battle they can't win," Calas assured him. "They think they have the position to beat us, but once they know we're behind them, they will surely surrender."

"I hope you're right," Cassander said, still looking at the map with a worried expression on his face.

"If they don't surrender, we'll kill them," Hephaestion added in a matter-of-fact tone.

"Right," Alexander said, getting to his feet. "It's a good plan. At nightfall we move. Cleitus, pick out two hundred of our finest men, and have them ready to move on my command."

2

At dusk, Alexander and two hundred men

headed for the goat path. Andronicus had of course been chosen, being the only one who had ever seen the path. When they got closer to the mountains, they left the road and crept through the fields. There were fires in the distance where the Thessalian army was camped, but Andronicus was confident they would be able to slip past them unseen.

When they reached the side of the hill, Andronicus searched for about ten minutes until he found the old path. He went first, with Hephaestion right behind him. As he crept up the side of the hill, trying not to knock any rocks loose, he realized the terrible irony in what he was doing. A Greek army was occupying a narrow pass to repel an invading army, and he, Andronicus of Sparta, who had fought in the battle of Thermopylae, was now leading that foreign army across a goat path, so they could surround the Greeks.

He stopped for a moment, faces long dead coming to his mind's eye: Diokles, Perikles, Gaios, and Leonidas, his king. Andronicus told himself that he *was* serving his king, his new king, Alexander, and pushed onward. He forced the guilt and shame down deep and led the Macedonians across Mount Ossa.

3

At dawn the Thessalian army was woken by the sounds of Macedonian horns behind them. Alexander's plan had worked perfectly, and the two hundred men were stationed at the mouth of the pass, blocking the path to Thessaly. Alexander stood at the front of the column, the red plume atop his golden helmet dancing in the wind. Across the pass they saw Philotas sitting on his horse at the head of the cavalry. Andronicus watched from his place not a hundred feet away as the Thessalian army scrambled to their feet and then slowly realized their predicament.

Fifteen minutes after the horns had blown, a man came forward to speak with Alexander. Andronicus glanced at Cleitus, who gave him a look that told him to stay vigilant but not move. They couldn't follow the king out to meet with the man; it would make him look weak and craven, but they both stood ready to charge if need be.

Alexander spoke with the man for several minutes before turning back to his men, a big grin on his face.

"They have surrendered unconditionally!" Alexander shouted. "They will be following us down to Larissa where they will gather their own horses and join our cavalry."

Calas and Philotas organized the actual surrender, making sure none of the Thessalians did anything stupid. It took most of the day to get the entire Macedonian army through the pass, and that night they all camped underneath Mount Olympus on the Greek side. Tents were set up for the officers, but Andronicus chose to sleep in the dirt with the men. As he lay beneath the stars he knew so well, listening to the bickering and laughing of the Macedonian soldiers, he drifted off to sleep.

In his dream Andronicus rode a grey spotted horse he didn't recognize. A roar went up from behind him, and he turned back to see an army dressed for battle. He looked around and saw Alexander not far away. He was riding Bucephalas, his great red plume dancing on top of his golden helm. Alexander raised his sword and shouted orders to his army, but Andronicus couldn't hear them.

He looked over to where Alexander was pointing and saw their foes. Across a small river was the Persian army. The Persians' brown faces began to change as Andronicus stared at them. He rode forward to get a better look. As he watched in amazement, the Persians changed to Greeks. The Persian general's pointed face began to change as well. It retracted into itself, and lines appeared on his cheeks. Finally, a big, bushy black beard sprouted out of the man's face. When the change was complete, King Leonidas sat on the horse. His face had the same look of determination as it had the day he died.

Andronicus tried to ride forward, to speak with the old king, but his horse wouldn't move. As he called out to Leonidas, he noticed the men beside him. Gaios and Diokles sat behind the king, and behind them was Niko. Andronicus opened his mouth, but nothing came out. He turned back to Alexander, to tell him not to attack. When Andronicus saw Alexander's face, a chill swept through his body.

Alexander had ridden forward as well and was only feet from Andronicus. Alexander was staring at him with his mismatched eyes, only the boy's eyes had switched; the blue and brown had swapped places, giving Alexander a sinister look.

Andronicus turned back to where his old friends had been but saw only the Persians. When he turned back to Alexander, his eyes were where they were meant to be, and he had a smile on his face. Then his face began to change as well. In an instant his eyes turned green, his golden hair turned black, and a scar appeared on his left cheek. Andronicus watched in stunned fascination as the boy morphed into his brother.

"You have to find them, Dron," Androcles said. The rest of the army had already started to fade, and then the dirt began to fade as well. Andronicus reached out to his brother, but he was too far away, and Andronicus couldn't move.

"I found him," Andronicus managed to say. "I found the boy. I trained him."

"No." Androcles shook his head. "You have to find him, Dron. You have to find them all. They need you. We all do."

Andronicus tried to ask what it all meant and who he had to find, but Androcles was already gone. The desert and the armies also vanished, and Andronicus found himself in the woods. He didn't recognize the woods, but they felt familiar all the same. Somehow it felt like these were his woods. Screams sounded in the distance, and a great orange glow filled the dark night sky. Andronicus started up the hill toward the fire, shouting, and then felt himself being shaken.

Andronicus snapped out of the dream with a shout and reached out with both hands. For a moment he didn't know where he was or whose neck he was wringing, and then reality came crashing home. Andronicus fell back, releasing Cassander's throat. Cassander looked at him like Andronicus was a rabid dog. Andronicus gave him the warmest smile he could manage.

"Sorry," he said through panting breaths. "Bad dream."

"About the war?" Cassander asked, massaging his bruised neck.

"Yes," Andronicus replied, nodding. "Among other things. Nothing that needs speaking of. Are we moving out yet?"

"Yes," Cassander replied, seemingly glad to change the subject. "We move out in less than an hour, Cleitus asked me to wake you."

Andronicus nodded, still thinking about the dream, then got to his feet. As Cassander walked away to wake the rest of the generals, Andronicus sat there, thinking. Androcles had told him to find the boy. For the first time, Andronicus wondered if Alexander might not be the boy he was meant to train. It gave him more to think about than he would have cared for, and he had that old sense of helplessness he hadn't felt in a long time as he packed his things.

4

After the Thessalian rebels surrendered the pass to Alexander, there was no more resistance in Thessaly. Alexander stopped his army in the city of Larissa, where the rest of the Thessalians joined the cavalry without incident. From Larissa the growing army rode south into the Peloponnese. They stopped again not far from Thermopylae. Representatives from several cities came to meet with Alexander and surrender to him. For three days they stayed by Thermopylae while Alexander met with dignitaries from all over Greece. By the end of the third day, only Athens and Corinth remained against him. The Spartans had still not shown any interest in Alexander's campaign.

With only Athens and Corinth left opposing him, Alexander pushed south again, into Athenian territory. Before they even got close to Athens, Alexander received word that the Athenian leader was waiting for him in Corinth and wished to parlay. Alexander agreed.

As soon as they entered the city, he demanded to be led to Diogenes, the man who was leading Athens and Corinth against him.

Two Athenian soldiers led Alexander and his entourage, which included Andronicus, through the city. They walked through the streets without speaking a word, passing women and children who stared at them in fear.

Eventually, they reached a large grove of trees in the heart of the city, said to be full of every kind of tree one could find in Greece. Andronicus had never actually seen the grove, though he had heard of it since he was a boy. He knew that the Corinthians believed they had every kind of tree in the world in that grove, and he had to smile to himself, knowing better than anyone how far from the truth that was.

Scattered about the grove, either sitting in the grass reading or walking amongst the trees were dozens of old men. The two soldiers were about to lead Alexander and his men into the grove, but he stopped and told most of his entourage to stay behind. Only Cleitus, Hephaestion, Cassander, Ptolemy, Calas, Philotas, and Andronicus followed the king into the grove.

Seconds later, a short balding man with a big white beard came bustling toward them.

"My lord Alexander," the old man panted as he reached them. "I am Theophanes, the keeper of these gardens."

"I wish to speak with Diogenes of Sinope," Alexander said in his most kingly voice. "I'm told he's in command of the Athenian army."

"You're correct, my lord," Theophanes said, nodding quickly.

"This is Alexander, son of Philip," Hephaestion said, glaring at the old man. "He is king, not a lord."

"My apologies, my king," Theophanes said, bowing low.

"Do you know where he is or not?" Alexander demanded.

"Yes, of course, my king," Theophanes said, bowing again. "Right this way."

He led them through the grove, describing everything as they went. Many of the old men shot them nervous glances and then hurried away. Even the birds and squirrels took flight as Alexander's procession marched through the quiet grove.

"As you will see, your grace, we have every tree found in Greece here," Theophanes bragged as they walked. "I dare say we have every kind of tree in the world."

The image of the Great Jungle came to mind, and Andronicus couldn't hold back his snort of laughter. The old man glared at him for a moment and then continued on, though his pace was painfully slow as he named each tree.

"Enough of this, old man!" Hephaestion barked. "No more of your trees. Do you know where Diogenes is or not?"

"Yes, of course," Theophanes said, picking up his pace. A minute later he came to a halt and pointed at a man lying in the sun.

As Alexander and his men approached Diogenes, the man did not even look up until Alexander stepped in front of him, blocking the sun.

Diogenes looked old and weathered. He had a thick white beard, and the little hair left on his head was as white as snow. He looked thin for a man of wealth, his ribs standing out on his chest. Next to Diogenes was a small pile of bones. Andronicus didn't see any weapons on the old man, and he didn't look like a fighter, but Andronicus kept his hand on his sword anyway.

"I am Alexander, son of Philip," Alexander announced, staring down at the man. Diogenes looked up when Alexander spoke but merely grunted and went back to his lounging.

"I am King of Macedonia and Hegemon of all of Greece," Alexander said, clearly disturbed by the old man's lack of interest.

"All of Greece?" Diogenes asked with a shrill chuckle. He had a high, scratchy voice that didn't match his face at all. "Have you gotten the Spartans to bend the knee then?"

"Sparta remains independent," Alexander replied, looking a bit sheepish as he glowered down at the old man, who was still ignoring him.

"So then," Diogenes said, "you are not Hegemon of *all* of Greece, are you?"

"I'm King of Macedonia, Ruler of Greece, Hegemon of the Persian invasion, and Emperor of the West," Alexander said angrily, adding on to his titles a bit.

"Oh, yes," Diogenes said with a laugh, "most impressive. Most impressive indeed."

"Most of the governors of Greece came to offer me their allegiances," Alexander said.

"Very thoughtful of them," Diogenes replied, closing his eyes again.

"Your rebellion has failed. Why did you not come to offer your respects as well?" Alexander asked. He was trying to sound intimidating, but Andronicus could tell he was on the verge of losing his cool.

"I have never offered my respects to any king," Diogenes said. "Should I ever come across a king worthy of them, perhaps I will." Andronicus felt a pang of guilt at Diogenes's words. He tried to tell himself that Alexander was a worthy king, but all he could see in his mind was the face of King Leonidas staring at him from across a strange river.

"You think I'm unworthy of your praise?" Alexander asked in a cold, calculating tone, bringing Andronicus back to reality.

"I think all kings are unworthy of praise," Diogenes replied casually.

"Is there anything I can do to change your mind?" Alexander asked.

"Yes," Diogenes said, meeting Alexander's eyes for the first time. "You can move aside."

"Come again?" Alexander asked.

"You're blocking my sun," Diogenes said, dropping his head back in the grass. "Step aside, great king, so Apollo may shine his light upon me once more."

Alexander stared openmouthed at Diogenes for a moment, incredulous. It was as if he thought no one would talk to him like that once he was king. For a moment as Alexander stood over Diogenes, Andronicus thought Alexander might try to kill the old man. Alexander's hands were balled into fists, and the old man was lying down with his eyes closed. Andronicus knew that killing Diogenes would likely send all of Greece into revolt, and he wondered if he should stop it.

The moment passed. Alexander's hands opened, and he let out a hearty laugh, then stepped aside. The sun fell upon Diogenes once again, and the old man's face stretched into a broad smile. Alexander stood there for a moment longer, noticing the bones beside him.

"What are those for?" Alexander asked, nodding toward the pile. Diogenes opened his eyes and reluctantly sat up. He took two bones from the pile and held them up to the light, side by side. He stayed like that for a moment, not saying anything, as Alexander and his entourage looked on.

"These bones were taken from two different men," Diogenes said, "and yet you can't tell them apart, can you?"

"Why should you be able to tell them apart if they're the same bone?" Alexander asked, like he was back in Aristotle's lessons.

"You shouldn't," Diogenes said with a chuckle, "and that's the point."

Alexander shook his head. "I don't understand."

"One of these bones comes from a slave and the other comes from a king," Diogenes said with a wan smile. "Which is which, great king?"

Alexander's expression hardened as he inspected the bones. Andronicus couldn't see any difference, and he quite liked the point Diogenes was trying to make.

"This is that of the king," Alexander said

confidently, pointing to the one on the left.

"Perhaps," Diogenes said as he lay back down. "I have lost track myself. You see, once a man is dead, he's no longer a king or a slave. He is simply a dead man."

Alexander stood over Diogenes a moment longer, looking conflicted. Finally, he turned and walked away, his men following close behind. As they walked out of the grove, Hephaestion began belittling Diogenes.

"That old fool should be grateful we left him alive," Hephaestion said through clenched teeth. "To speak to the king that way!"

"Calm yourself, Hephaestion," Alexander said with a smile. "That old man was right. In a way I admire him, and his views on life."

"You agree with that old fool?" Hephaestion asked in astonishment.

Alexander nodded. "I do. In fact, if I were not Alexander of Macedonia, I would like very much to have been Diogenes of Sinope, the great cynic." His remark was met by a murmur of uncomfortable laughter. Then they fell silent as they left the grove.

5

With Athens and Corinth back among the Greek states under Macedonian control, Alexander took his army north to Amphipolis. Alexander let the army rest in the city for two days, and then set out to the east to break the final Thracian revolts once and for all. A week after setting out from Amphipolis, the army met the Thracians at Mount Haemus.

Just like the last time Alexander led his men into Thrace, the Thracians were not a well-manned army. When it was done, Alexander called it the battle of Mount Haemus, and named it his first victory as king. Andronicus didn't think it ought to be called a battle at all; it was just another slaughter. The Thracians put up the best fight they could, and they died for it. Those who didn't die were made slaves and sent south to be put to work.

From Thrace Alexander moved his men east

again, into Triballi territory, wanting to end all threats before moving on to Persia. The Triballi were an ancient and strong tribe that had given the Macedonians trouble before. It had taken Philip over a year of fighting to get them to bend the knee, and it was there that he had received the wound that gave him a limp for the rest of his life. Like almost all of Macedonia's provinces, the Triballi had gone into open rebellion at the news of Philip's death.

Alexander pushed his men forward with a harshness he had not shown in Greece or Thrace. Andronicus knew he was eager to fight the men who had maimed his father. Alexander got his wish not long after his victory against the Thracians. The Triballi attacked near the base of the Lyginis River. The battle that ensued was more of a fight than the Thracian mess had been, but Andronicus still wouldn't call it a battle. The Triballi threw themselves against the Macedonian lines and broke like waves against a cliff.

The battle ended with a few score Macedonians dead, and more than a thousand dead Triballi, twice as many captives, and the rest of their army scattered. Alexander let his army rest for a day and bury the dead. The next day they set out after the final Triballi and Thracians who still remained. Three days later they reached the Danube. The Triballi, the Thracians, and the Getae had all come together to make one final stand against Alexander. They were only a few hundred by then, unorganized and poorly armed. The Macedonians crossed the river at night and attacked at dawn.

Alexander sat with his other generals as Philotas ran the cavalry through the rebels. The screams and shouts carried across the river as the Macedonians slaughtered what was left of the rebel tribes. When the fighting was finished, Alexander had all the prisoners executed. He said they had been given too many opportunities to surrender, and he had to make an example of them.

6

It took the better part of a year to secure all of

the northern tribes. Alexander was impatient to get his real war started, but he listened to his older generals' council. Everyone agreed that the best way was to secure all of Europe before taking the army east into Asia. When the last of the rebel tribesmen were taken care of, the army marched back to Pella for a final rest before the real war began.

The Macedonians all went to their families to rest and say goodbye. The massive Greek forces remained camped outside the city, waiting for the Macedonians. Andronicus stayed close to the king, but he liked to walk amongst the men and hear what they were saying. Everyone he spoke to was eager to get to the war, and he felt confident in the men's resolve.

Chapter 44
More than a Hundred Years in the Making
1

After several weeks of waiting for the invasion, the army finally set out from Pella in April 334 BC. The army consisted of five thousand cavalry and thirty-two thousand infantry. They came from all over Greece and Macedonia, men young and old. There were fourteen thousand Macedonians, most of whom had fought beside Philip for years, eighteen thousand men from the Greek cities, and five thousand mercenaries from abroad. Not all of the army truly believed in Alexander or his cause, and Andronicus knew that the first battle with Persia would be the most important.

Andronicus rode amongst the royal guard at the head of the long cavalry column. The army stretched far out of sight, first on horseback, some men holding banners. Then came the men on foot, each one carrying a ten-foot spear. The going was painfully slow with such a large force, but they trudged through the barren countryside nonetheless. It took over an hour to set camp every night and twice as long to pack up in the morning. Andronicus tried to remember if the armies he had marched with as a boy had moved as slowly, but he couldn't remember.

It took several weeks to move the massive army out of Macedonia and into Asia Minor. Getting the army over the small strait of water was the hardest part, but once they were all across and into Asia, they picked up speed. The roads were less well kept, but there was more space to spread the army out. They followed the mountain range south, toward where they knew the Persians were waiting.

As the army neared the Hellespont, Andronicus couldn't stop thinking about where he was. They were less than two days' ride from the ruins of Troy, and he knew he must be close to where *it* had happened. He wondered if the cave was still there after all these years, as he was. He considered going to search for it again but decided not to waste his time. He had spent months searching the side of the mountain and never found so much as a trace of the cave.

When they reached the old ruins of the ancient city, Alexander had the army stop and camp in the shadow of the massive and once-triumphant wall. Most of the men seemed to fear the dead city; many of them wouldn't even look at it. Alexander gathered his priests, and made grand offerings to the gods before the once mighty city. Andronicus stayed up half the night just staring at the old, decaying walls. The stories of Agamemnon and Odysseus and Hector and Achilles had been his favorites as a boy. He had spent his childhood dreaming of being a great warrior like Achilles someday, playing out those old legends with Lycus and Niko when they were children a thousand times.

He never could have imagined what kind of life he would actually have. Being so close to where it all began, he couldn't help but fall into memories. Andronicus spent the whole night reflecting on his long life and where it had led him. It was as if he had come full circle and found himself back at the beginning. Here he was, in the shadow of Troy, preparing to fight the Persians. The circumstances were certainly different, but the purpose was the same.

Andronicus didn't know whether it should make him happy or sad. For so many years all he had wanted was to find Greece again. If he had taken the time to do things right, Chaka might still be alive;

though for all Andronicus knew, Chaka would have
died of old age long ago. Then he had actually done it;
he had found Greece and made his way home, only to
find everything had gone away.

It was hard to remember those days, not
because of the pain or loneliness he had felt at that
time but because he had been too drunk to remember
much of anything. Andronicus wondered if it would be
different now that he was sober, if home might feel
like home again. But deep down he knew it wouldn't.
The Sparta he knew had died long ago, because the
Sparta he knew had been the people, not the city
itself. There was no home for him there, or anywhere,
really. It seemed his only home now was on the move,
where he had spent most of his life.

2

While Andronicus's mind was consumed with
his past and how close he was to it, Alexander and his
generals were planning their first attack. Scouts had
reported that the Persian army was near and were
preparing to make a stand at the Hellespont.
Alexander remained calm and confident as he issued
orders to his men, but they were buzzing with
anticipation. They went to sleep knowing that the next
day, they would go into battle.

In the morning the army went about their
normal routine, though with a noticeable quietness.
Every man in the army knew what would happen that
day, and they were all preparing themselves in their
own ways.

Andronicus dressed quickly and then walked
amongst the men, trying to gauge whether or not they
were ready. He concluded that they were. They were a
strong bunch, and most of them seemed to believe in
the cause. There were a few whom Andronicus knew
would not live through the battle, but that was always
the case.

When he reached Alexander's large tent, he
found the king already dressed in his magnificent
battle attire, looking at a map with Parmenion. They
glanced up when Andronicus entered and then went

back to their work. Andronicus approached Cleitus, who looked truly hungry for battle. The generals finalized their plan, and then the horns sounded.

The army marched east, towards their first great battle, and reached the Persian army much sooner than expected. They quickly spread out in battle formations. Then a scout came galloping up to the king.

"King Alexander!" the scout shouted as he climbed down off his horse. "The Persians have marched out to meet us. They are set up on the far side of the Granicus River."

"Memnon must think that the river will neutralize our infantry," Cassander guessed. Memnon was a Greek man, but he was the one leading the Persian army. He was a mercenary who had been fighting for Persia for years, and seemed to have a real hatred for his countrymen. The new Persian King, Darius, was back home in Persia, apparently trusting that his men could defeat the Macedonians without him.

"Memnon is right," Calas said. "To fight on the river with infantry would be a grave mistake."

"Calas speaks true," Parmenion agreed. "We should wait until dark and then have our infantry march around the river."

"It could take a week to march our entire infantry around the river," Hephaestion said, his eyebrows knitted together in anger.

"It won't matter," Ptolemy added. "If we keep the men far back, out of sight of the river, they can march around it without the Persians knowing. It won't matter how long it takes."

"They will know we must be doing something," Hephaestion said, urging Alexander to listen to him. "It's too risky. If we march our infantry around, and the Persians are ready for them, we could lose our entire army."

"We will begin the siege from our side of the river," Parmenion explained, clearly trying to remain calm while being questioned by a boy. "We'll keep half the army here, where the Persians can see them, and have the rest of the infantry sneak around. Then we'll be able to attack them on two fronts and disrupt their forward line on the river. That's what your father would have done."

"That is a fine plan, Parmenion," Alexander said, smiling faintly. "I have no doubt that my father would have agreed with you, but that is not what I am going to do."

"What then, my king?" Parmenion asked, already looking like he knew the answer.

"We're going to attack in full force. Right here, right now." Alexander had a wild look in his blue eye that Andronicus had seen before, and no one dared argue with him.

"We're not going to wait until dark either," Alexander said. "We're not going to wait at all. Sound the horns. We will march to Granicus at once."

"My king, I urge you to reconsider," Parmenion pleaded, but Alexander was already riding Bucephalas down the Macedonian line, shouting praises and orders alike at the men.

Parmenion shot Hephaestion a furious look. "You must know this is madness!" he yelled. "You're his closest friend. Beg him to reconsider."

"Yes, he is my closest friend," Hephaestion said, "and he is also my king, as he is yours. You seem to forget that fact far too often, General. Your king has given a clear command. You may not agree with the battle tactics your king has chosen, but he has chosen them. You will be placed in command of our largest infantry battalions, and you will lead them well. Is that understood, General?"

Parmenion glared at his much-younger peer, his teeth clenched in anger. As much as they hated each other, Parmenion had heard the harsh wisdom in the boy's words. Parmenion turned to his son, Philotas, who gave him a weary look and then reluctantly nodded to Hephaestion.

"Good," Hephaestion said, taking a more commanding role as Alexander rode down the line shouting to his men. "Now for our placements. Parmenion and Nikanor will take command of the left hypaspists infantries. Calas, you and Hegelochus will command the right. Ptolemy, you'll be in command of the greater cavalry assault on the left. Philotas will lead the companion cavalry on the right. Cassander, you and I will accompany the king among the royal companion cavalry."

The generals all nodded and then left to take up their posts. Andronicus turned to Cleitus, who gave him the usual nod. They didn't need to be told their job. They knew their only job was to ensure that the king did not die in battle.

They both rode after Alexander. When they caught up with him, he was in the middle of bolstering the infantry with a valiant speech about country and honor.

3

Once the generals spread out the line, things moved quickly. Less than two hours after Alexander gave the order to attack, Andronicus found himself sitting on his horse on the bank of the Granicus river, staring at the Persian army across the water. The river was only about twenty feet wide and not very deep at all by the looks of it. The two armies stood face to face less than one hundred feet from each other with only the small body of water between them. It was too much like his dream for Andronicus's comfort, and he knew this was it.

He let the weight of the moment wash over him. They had the opportunity to end something that had begun before he was born. His father had died fighting the Persians, Gaios had died fighting the Persians, Leonidas had died fighting the Persians, even Niko had died fighting them. The Greeks and the Persians had been fighting on and off for over two hundred years, and now they stood face to face with nowhere left to run. There was no pass to even the odds, no supply lines to cut off. There was only a small shallow river.

Alexander rode back and forth, looking more like a king than ever. Bucephalas's magnificent black coat shone in the sun, making him look even more fierce than usual. Alexander was dressed in his finest armor: a ruby-encrusted gold breastplate, gold-plated armbands, and his huge golden helmet with its great red plume on top. Under all the armor he wore white silk robes.

Alexander turned to his men one last time before calling for the charge. The Persians clearly felt they had the better position, and were going to let the Macedonians make the first move, so Alexander took the moment to address his men before the battle. Andronicus remembered the rousing words Leonidas had spoken before Thermopylae, how powerful it had been and how much it had affected the men, and he hoped Alexander could do the same.

"I look out upon your faces!" Alexander shouted, his voice carrying well down the ranks, "and I see men from all over Greece. Macedonians, Athenians, Corinthians, Thracians, Illyrians. We have been fighting each other all of our lives, but we have always shared one common enemy. There has always been one nation that is the true rival of Greece. The Persians tried to break us at Marathon, but they failed. They tried to break us at Thermopylae, and even though they cheated the great King Leonidas into death, they failed. The Persians have tried again and again to break us and take our lands for their own. Now it is our turn. Now we have come to break them! We will crush Darius's horde and take their lands for our own. We will enslave the Persian people, and for a thousand years the world will remember the great Macedonian army that broke the Persian Empire once and for all. Now, men of Greece, Macedonians, Athenians, Thracians, together we will triumph!"

Bucephalas reared up, kicking the air with his front legs, and Alexander was lifted high above everyone else. He thrust his sword into the air and let out a mighty war cry. The entire army met his cry with their own. A thundering boom went up from the Macedonian line as the soldiers roared and pounded their shields. Andronicus was impressed. Not only had Alexander touched on many of the same points as Leonidas, he had also gotten nearly the same result.

Andronicus let out a cry of his own, much louder than the others, and saw many faces turn to see who had such a fierce battle cry. Alexander took his place at the head of his royal cavalry, and Andronicus got behind him, next to Cleitus. Hephaestion and Cassander were next to the king, roaring wildly and waving their spears over their heads.

The Persians seemed to be a little caught off guard. They had clearly expected Alexander to hold off on the attack, as Parmenion had suggested, and were now frantically trying to get into position before the Macedonian charge. The Macedonian army was spread far down the river in both directions. In the center, facing the bulk of the Persian force, were the Greek infantries. Parmenion and his younger son led the left flank, and Calas led the right. Together they made up the center of the Macedonian line. On the far left, beyond Parmenion's position, was Ptolemy and the Greek cavalry. Ptolemy was at the head of more than four thousand horsemen, mainly Greeks.

On the far right, beside Calas's infantry, was Alexander and his royal guard, with Philotas in command. They were less than two thousand, the smallest force among the army, but the Persians quickly shifted their forces over to that side. The Persians' center shifted left, and their entire cavalry moved over to face the royal guard. Andronicus wondered why they were moving their stronger force out of the middle, to where Alexander was. Once in position, the Persians waited for the Macedonians to charge.

Alexander rode forward, nearly to the edge of the river. Andronicus thought it was foolish to ride within range of the Persians' archers but knew not to interrupt the king now. Alexander looked to his left and signaled to Philotas. Philotas hailed his men into lines, and then charged toward the river, leading the half the cavalry. The other half remained behind with Alexander. As they charged down the mud bank and into the river, spears and arrows began raining down on them. Andronicus watched as men and horses alike fell into the river.

Once Philotas had crossed the river, the Persian cavalry charged him. Most of the Persians elite satraps charged down into battle. Andronicus watched as the battle grew ugly, and looked over at Alexander, wondering what he was waiting for. Philotas and his men held strong, and soon more of the Persians cavalry were leaving their flanks to join in the battle. As soon as he saw this, Alexander loud out a cry, and charged forward with the rest of the cavalry. Andronicus charged forward with them.

As they charged toward the battle, Andronicus looked down the river and saw Parmenion shouting orders, and his infantry battalion started marching forward.

Andronicus heard the old sounds of war as he charged forward on his spotted grey horse. Alexander charged his men to the right, and around the battle Philotas was beginning to lose. Alexander and his company charged around, and then turned hard into the battle. They hit the Persians from the side, unprepared for a second charge.

Alexander let out a battle cry, and Bucephalas shot across the river. Andronicus pushed his own horse forward, but Alexander had gotten a good jump, and Bucephalas was the fastest horse he had ever seen. Alexander hit the Persian line hard, swinging his sword at them and killing a man with his first blow. He only had to fight alone for a few seconds before the royal guard joined him.

They pressed forward, and in a matter of seconds they had broken through the first line. Alexander pointed toward the Persian generals, who were all charging their way toward him, and let out a loud cry. This time the entire cavalry charged as the king did, but they only made it about twenty feet before the rest of the Persian cavalry arrived. The two cavalry lines hit each other with a violent crash, and then everything erupted into chaos.

Within seconds the battle became a hectic bloodbath. Andronicus lost all bearing and dove headlong into the filth of battle. For a moment he stopped caring where the others were or where the king was and let the old beast take over. The other Macedonians quickly got out of Andronicus's way as he cut down one Persian rider after another. At some point he must have grabbed another sword, because when he came to he had a sword in each hand, both of them dripping with blood.

He came out of the haze of battle for a moment and looked down the river. The two infantries were in a stark, messy battle, many of the soldiers fighting in the river itself. The water of the Granicus had turned a dark, murky red as it quickly filled with dead men. Andronicus could not see Ptolemy and the other cavalry, but he knew the cavalry he was in was beginning to press forward. Alexander's feign tactic appeared to have worked. He turned back to look for the king and instead saw Cassander trying to fight off two Persian riders.

Andronicus rode toward him and took one of their heads off with a swing of his sword. The other man turned to watch his companion's head go flying into the dirt, and Cassander took the opportunity to drive his sword through the man's chest.

"Where is the king?" Andronicus shouted over the clamor.

"I don't know!" Cassander replied. "Cleitus and Hephaestion were still with him when I last saw him!"

"This way!" Andronicus shouted, pointing to where the Persian command was, knowing Alexander would try to push in that direction. "Stay with me!"

Andronicus pressed forward again, cutting through Persian soldiers as easily as he had once cut through jungle vines. Cassander stayed behind him, taking care of anyone left and trying to keep up.

When they found the king, Alexander was still riding Bucephalas, a mad look in his eyes. It was not the kingly look Andronicus had seen, but rather the same old look he used to see in Lycus's eyes during battle—the same look he guessed was in his own eyes during battle. It was the crazed look of a killer, a man so deep in the thrall of combat that he would cut down anyone who opposed him, be it friend or foe.

Andronicus looked toward the center again and saw that Parmenion's infantry had broken a hole through the Persian line. The Greeks had surrounded the Persians' front and were cutting through their weaker rear forces. In the distance Andronicus saw the Persian generals galloping away. The entire rear of the Persian army was retreating, and he knew they had won. Alexander let out another battle cry, trying to push his men further.

Andronicus rode after him and saw Cleitus emerge through the crowd. His black robes were stained red, from his feet to his collar. Blood was also splashed across his dark face, giving him a truly sinister look. Andronicus watched him cut down three Persians with ease as he made his way over to where Andronicus was fighting beside the king.

"Forward!" Alexander shouted, pointing toward the fleeing generals. "Keep pressing forward!"

"Alexander!" Cassander shouted. "We have to hold back! If we keep going, we're going to lose half the army!"

"The battle is won, Alexander!" Hephaestion added. "Turn to their infantry, and we'll cripple them!"

For a moment it looked as though Alexander was going to press forward anyway, and then his eyes slowly came back to reality, first the blue and then the brown. The king looked around at his men, all of them covered in blood, and then looked at where the battle was still raging. Andronicus looked as well. He could not see Parmenion, and he hoped the general was still standing, but either way, his infantry had pushed the Persians back.

Alexander shouted orders again, and a moment later his companion cavalry was charging back to aid the Macedonian infantries that were deep in battle. The cavalry rode in and cut down the remaining Persians.

Minutes later the battle was over. The vast bulk of the Persian army was fleeing across the horizon while Alexander's army cut down the remainder. Andronicus looked out over the Macedonian army and felt invigorated. They had done it; they had beaten the

Persians. He knew the war was far from over, but looking at the battle-hardened men around him, he believed they were going to win.

Act IV
The Boy King and The Forgotten Soldier

Chapter 45
Doubts

1

After the battle, Alexander was praised as a true war hero, just like his father had been. Parmenion was recognized as having led the main charge, and most knew that he was responsible for breaking through the Persian lines, but Alexander was given the bulk of the credit for the victory. The story of how Alexander had been told to wait but refused, quickly spread through the vast army. The morning after the battle, every man in the army knew that Alexander had given the order to attack at once.

Andronicus didn't like the way that victory sat with the young king. Alexander had a new air about him, as if he thought he were some sort of legend now. Hephaestion, Cassander, and Ptolemy didn't help any. They all followed him around like dogs, filling his ears with praises for his battle genius.

Andronicus followed the king from a distance as he walked amongst his wounded men. Cleitus walked beside him, never taking his eyes off the king. Cleitus still wore his thick black tunic, even though it was covered in blood, and it was far too hot for such heavy attire. Andronicus noticed that Cleitus looked even more dour than usual, practically glaring at the king.

"What's bothering you?" Andronicus asked him as they passed a whimpering man with a bandaged stump where his leg used to be.

"He acts as though he fought like some kind of hero," Cleitus growled under his breath.

"I wasn't with him during the worst of the fighting," Andronicus said as he stepped around a dead man, "though I should have been. But from what I did see he fought bravely. Did he not?"

"I saved his life," Cleitus said in a low voice, so only Andronicus could hear.

"What do you mean?" Andronicus asked. They stopped walking for a moment, and Cleitus leaned in close. "During the battle, there was a rider, some nobleman from the looks of him. He and Alexander fought for half a minute, and the Persian won."

"If he won why is the king not wounded?" Andronicus asked.

"Because as he swung his blade at Alexander, I stepped in and cut his arm off," Cleitus said. "As soon as I did it, Alexander drove his sword through the man's chest."

"What of it?" Andronicus asked. "You did your job; you protected the king. Why blame the boy for that?"

"I don't blame him for needing my help. I blame him for telling his little friends that he killed that man in single combat."

"You heard him say that?" Andronicus asked, surprised that Alexander would lie about such a thing.

Cleitus nodded sullenly. "I heard it. He's been boasting about the different captains he killed himself, and I know for a fact that at least two of them were killed by Hephaestion."

"Why would they lie?" Andronicus asked. "He already has the victory. And the credit that should rest with Parmenion is his simply because he made a rash decision, and it happened to work."

"He is not satisfied with taking false credit for the victory," Cleitus said, his face darker than Andronicus had ever seen it. "Now he has to take false credit for individual glories as well."

"He's just a boy," Andronicus said, defending the young king but feeling unsure, "and this was his first real taste of battle."

"How old were you when you fought your first battle?" Cleitus asked.

"Sixteen."

"And have you ever taken credit for a thing you did not do?"

"No," Andronicus replied after a moment's

thought, "I haven't."

The two men began walking again, following the king and his friends at a reasonable distance. They fell into silence once more, and Andronicus began thinking about what Cleitus had told him. He wondered, and not for the first time, if Alexander was really the great king he wanted him to be. He owed the boy nothing. Alexander was the king of a nation Andronicus had no true ties to. His own people, the Spartans, were the only Greeks not currently fighting for Alexander.

When he saw Alexander at his kingly duties, he saw sparks of greatness, of potential. When it came to politics, he saw the teachings of Aristotle in the young king, and when it came to battle, he saw the flashes of Leonidas. Andronicus wanted desperately for Alexander to be the great king that he knew he could be. Alexander was set up to conquer the world and bring it together, if he so desired.

Andronicus wondered for the thousandth time if he should be following a twenty-year-old boy into war. Aristotle had brought him to Alexander and told him to be a soldier again, but he had said to do it only for a time, just to get back into the world again. Training himself and the boys had been the perfect way for Andronicus to leave the drink behind and get back to life. But now the drink was behind him, and he was still following the boy he had trained. He wondered for the first time in a long while what he might do if he left Alexander, and where he might go, and he hadn't the slightest idea.

2

After the victory at Granicus, Alexander marched his army south. The lands they marched through were dry and desolate, but Parmenion had made sure the army was well stocked, knowing they would have no ties to the sea. Even though the army was massive and moved at a snail's pace, Alexander drove them tirelessly. Less than two months after crossing the Granicus River, the army reached the great city of Sardis.

Sardis had been conquered several times over the centuries, but never without great bloodshed. When Andronicus was a boy, the city had been under Persian occupation, but before that it had belonged to the Cimmerians. Sometime after Andronicus left Greece, the city had been taken by the Athenians. Not long after the Athenians took it, Cyrus the Great retook the city for Persia, and the Persians had held it ever since. It was the first major city in their empire.

Alexander seemed overly eager to prove himself in his first siege as king. He gave hurried orders to his generals, but before the siege could begin, the Persians surrendered the city, knowing all too well what would become of a long siege. Alexander marched his entire army into Sardis and had a massive feast in honor of the victory.

The people of Sardis were removed that night and taken to ships to be brought back to Macedonia as slaves. Andronicus watched them go with a bitter taste in his mouth as the king and his cohorts celebrated drunkenly in the governor's palace. The people being shipped off were not soldiers; most of them weren't even men. Far too many of the new slaves were children, and Andronicus hated his part in it all.

He wondered again if this was the right place for him. To have lived so long and seen so much, just to follow a boy-king into war. Seeing the decimated faces of the children, cold and scared and without their mothers, Andronicus couldn't help but feel ashamed. He still hated the Persians, and he wanted his revenge, but it wasn't these people he wanted to harm. The Persian army needed to be destroyed, not their homes and families.

Andronicus knew that if they did not kill or enslave the children, in fifteen years there would be a new war, but that didn't make it any easier to watch. Part of him wanted to turn away, to go join the king and have a drink. It had still only been a few years since he had left the bottle behind, and his thirst was still great. Looking at the crying faces of the newly enslaved children didn't help, but Andronicus stayed anyway and watched the slaves getting hurried along like cattle, to be marched off to the ships dozens of miles away. Long after the festivities had died down, Andronicus remained outside the city, watching the poor people being driven down the road and into the dark night.

3

The army continued moving south from Sardis, going from one city or town to the next. In each city Alexander would hold ceremonies, officially declaring that place a free democracy under the protection of Macedonia, sworn to serve and fight for him, their new king. Whatever soldiers the cities could muster would join the main army, and a few Macedonian soldiers would stay behind to ensure the city remained under Macedonian rule.

The first city that required a real siege was Miletus, by the sea. It was an ancient and wealthy city, and it predated even some of the great cities of Greece. For many centuries Miletus had been a part of Greece, but the city had been ruled by many different cultures. It had been both Greek and Persian over the years. When Agamemnon sailed to Troy, Miletus stood beside their sister city of Troy. It was the last city on what had once been the Trojan coast, and was now the westernmost tip of the Persian Empire.

The Macedonian army marched in and surrounded the city on three sides. The Macedonian navy sailed in not long after, closing off the seaside face of Miletus. With the city surrounded, Alexander gave his orders for a siege. This time the Persians did not surrender at the sight of Alexander's army.

Alexander and Hephaestion stood in command of the land forces while Nikanor, Parmenion's younger son, led the naval forces. The Persians had a much larger navy at port, outnumbering the Macedonians three to one, but they were cut off from the open sea. If Nikanor held the line with his ships, the Persian fleet would be useless. The two navies floated less than a hundred feet from each other, waiting for the first strike. Alexander was still eager to prove himself, but he decided to use more caution than he had at

Granicus.

After a weeklong siege, there was a brief naval battle. Andronicus stood beside Cleitus and watched as the king observed the battle from afar. Nikanor led his men to victory, and when the fighting was done, the Persians opened the city gates. Alexander marched his army in and proclaimed himself the conqueror of the city. Alexander took full credit for the victory, though any man who had seen the fighting knew Nikanor to be the true hero.

4

After Miletus, none of the other cities put up a fight. The huge Macedonian army marched east, taking town after town, never stopping for more than a night. There was no sign of the Persian's army or defenses until they reached the massive city of Halicarnassus. It was not as old as many of the other cities, but it was much bigger. It had been under Persian rule for decades but was, in truth, a Greek city. The last time Andronicus moved through these lands, after his time in Egypt, Halicarnassus had been merely a budding town, not even worth stopping at for the night.

Now the city had become immense. It had never been part of any Greek alliance, but its citizens had worshiped the old gods before the Persians took over. Since taking the city, the Persians had done quite a bit of building. There were high stone walls, well built for a siege, and the buildings inside looked to be quite ornate. For a time Darius himself had called the city home.

Now the city was occupied by the Persian navy, along with the remainder of the Greek mercenaries who had pledged themselves to Darius. Memnon still led the false Greek forces. He had been beaten at Granicus, but he was still in command of a few thousand men. Andronicus heard that Memnon had been denied entry back into Persia, and King Darius had ordered him to stop the invasion or die trying.

Memnon was the last real Greek threat to Alexander's throne. He had been leading the Persian navy to victory after small victory against the weak

Macedonian navy. There were rumors that Demosthenes of Athens was preparing an army to march on Macedonia should Alexander lose a battle to Memnon. Andronicus had even heard it said that Sparta might be preparing for war as well, should Alexander be defeated. Andronicus knew that if they lost a single battle to Memnon, Alexander could very well lose his whole empire.

Alexander was well aware of the importance of the battle to come, and he made sure that only he and Hephaestion were in command. Everyone else was stationed as captains. Alexander set his army around the city, surrounding it entirely. Memnon knew Greek siege tactics well and had archers and catapults stationed on all sides of the city, ready to repel the attacks.

On the second night of the siege, Andronicus went to speak with Alexander. He found him in council with his generals. Andronicus stepped quietly to the side, where Cleitus stood in the shadows, and listened in on the war council.

"Why should the spies not tell us the truth?" Cassander asked Parmenion.

"They're not spies," Parmenion said, clearly trying to get through to the boys. "They're mercenaries. With one breath they tell you they're loyal to Alexander and wish to see him victorious. And with the very next breath they tell you they can only help you if you pay."

"And pay them we have," Hephaestion said, glaring at Parmenion.

"It doesn't matter!" Parmenion shouted. "Those men have no honor. They will take your money and still fight for Memnon, who is their captain, in case you've forgotten!"

"We paid them. They will have the gates open," Hephaestion insisted. "You're just being a paranoid old man."

"And you're being an arrogant young fool!" Parmenion shot back.

Hephaestion looked at Parmenion with pure hatred. He drew his sword and stepped toward him, but Cleitus and Andronicus rushed between them. A second later Philotas had his sword drawn as well, shouting at Hephaestion for threatening his father.

"Enough!" Alexander shouted. "Get out, all of you." The din died down, and everyone began leaving the tent.

"Not you, Calas," Alexander said as Calas made for the door, "nor you Cassander." The two men stayed behind as the others all left. Once the instigators were gone, Andronicus and Cleitus returned to their position in the corner, and Alexander made no objection.

"Tell me true, Calas," Alexander said. "Do you think these spies will betray me?"

Calas lowered his eyes. "I do."

"Thank you," Alexander said, waving his hand. Calas nodded and hurried out.

"They pledged themselves to me?" Alexander asked, turning to Cassander. "They swore to open the gates?"

"They swore it," Cassander insisted, staring Alexander in the eye. "They will have the gates open."

"These men who swore themselves to you," Andronicus said, no longer able to hold his silence, "did they also require payment?"

"Yes," Cassander said, sounding irritated. "They're mercenaries."

"And you would trust the word of a mercenary?" Andronicus asked.

"Your opinion was not asked for, Andronicus," Alexander said. "You're here because of your skill in killing, not for your command advice. Speaking of which, I don't believe I require the services of your protection with only Cassander here. You may wait outside. Both of you." Andronicus stood his ground for a moment, staring down the young king, then turned and left with Cleitus.

"You should have held your tongue," Cleitus said, scowling as they stood guard outside the tent.

"How could I?" Andronicus replied. "He's about to send his army—our army—into a damned ambush because he believes a group of mercenaries will open the gates for him."

"Parmenion tried to tell him as much," Cleitus said, "to no avail. What made you think you could get through to him?"

"Anything Parmenion says will be challenged by Hephaestion and will be lost on Alexander," Andronicus said, keeping his voice low. "Calas told him not to trust them, but he made no stand. Someone had to tell the boy straight."

"A lot of good it did," Cleitus grunted. "Got the both of us kicked out into the cold."

"I had to say something," Andronicus said, sighing as he rubbed his cold hands together.

"You didn't *have* to," Cleitus replied bitterly. "You *wanted* to."

"You would just sit by silently as he leads us into an ambush?" Andronicus asked. "You know as well as any that those mercenaries will betray him."

"Of course I do," Cleitus said, "but that doesn't mean I'm going to challenge the king's command. The boy thinks he can buy the mercenaries' loyalty. Let him learn the lesson the hard way."

"For him to learn that lesson hundreds of men need to die," Andronicus pointed out. "Not all lessons need to be learned in such a manner. The boy needs to listen to his advisors."

"Oh, he does," Cleitus said. "All three of them, because they only tell him what he wants to hear."

"He needs to listen to more than just his friends," Andronicus sighed. "He acts as though his generals want to see him fail, as if he can only achieve greatness by defeating the Persians without the help of others."

"Then he should be dead right now," Cleitus said. "He has no trouble taking help on the battlefield, but when it comes to the strategy of the same battle, he only listens to his little friends."

"So, what do you suggest we do?" Andronicus asked. "It's not as though he doesn't have the men to help him. Parmenion is the best commander I have ever seen, and yet the boy still sees him as his father's man."

"He still sees me as his father's man," Cleitus said. "He probably sees you that way as well. The only ones he thinks are truly his are those three damned boys."

"We can't get the king to listen to Parmenion," Andronicus said thoughtfully, "but perhaps the boys can."

Cleitus laughed. "Good luck getting Hephaestion to agree with Parmenion on anything."

"What about Cassander?" Andronicus suggested. "He's a smart boy, and he's always listened to me. Perhaps I can get him to make Alexander see the truth."

"Ha!" Cleitus barked. "Good luck to you."

5

Andronicus found Cassander sitting by the fire with Ptolemy. He sat down across from the boys. Cassander looked up hopefully, but his face fell when he saw Andronicus's demeanor.

"You have to know this is going to backfire," Andronicus said. "Aristotle and I taught you boys better than to believe this stupid plan of yours will actually work."

"You didn't speak to them, Andronicus," Cassander said, meeting Andronicus's eye. "I did, and I believe them."

"Of course you believe them," Andronicus said, trying not to shout. "You paid them a small fortune. They were going to tell you anything you wanted to hear."

"They have no loyalty to Memnon," Cassander insisted. "They said they would join us once the city is taken."

"They're Memnon's men, you fools," Andronicus said through clenched teeth. "They're going to betray you, and your men will die."

"You have too little faith in us, Andronicus," Cassander said, "and too little faith in the king. Just because he came up with this plan doesn't mean it won't work."

Andronicus sighed. "I do trust you, because I

know you. I don't trust a mercenary, any mercenary, and I would never bet my life on their word. It's a foolish risk, and unnecessary."

"The king has already made up his mind," Ptolemy said. "The attack will take place at dawn with or without the mercenaries' help."

Andronicus knew there was nothing he could say that would change the boys' minds. All that was left to do was protect the king in battle and pray that the mercenaries would keep their word.

Chapter 46
A Risky Ploy

1

Alexander sent his army forward just before dawn. Andronicus rode his horse not far behind the king, but most of the men were on foot. As the sun crested the horizon, and light spread across the land, the army reached the city gates. To Andronicus's surprise the large iron gate on the north side of the city stood open as they approached it, just as Cassander had promised.

When Alexander saw the open gate, he galloped to the head of the column, and Andronicus and Cleitus followed. Alexander clapped Hephaestion on the back, a big smile on his face. Then the two of them rode forward, ahead of the army. Cleitus called out as softly as he could for them to wait.

The boys either didn't hear the warning or didn't heed it. Either way, they continued to ride toward the open gate. When they were about twenty feet away, Andronicus heard a shout come from inside the city walls. A second later the heavy iron gate plummeted down and crashed into the dirt with a loud heavy thump. At the same time, archers appeared all across the wall.

Andronicus and Cleitus charged their horses at full gallop and reached the king just as the arrows began falling. Andronicus leapt off his horse, and tackled Alexander off Bucephalas. They landed hard in the dirt, and he pulled his shield over their heads. As

Andronicus felt the arrows crash against his shield, trying to cover Alexander's legs with his own, he was reminded of Thermopylae, though there were far fewer arrows than there had been on that day.

As he lay in the dirt, covering the king's head, he felt an arrow pierce his lower back. He hadn't been shot by an arrow since he was younger than Alexander, but he remembered the feeling well enough. His whole back tightened up, and a jolt of pain went up his left side and down his leg. Andronicus clenched his eyes tight and gritted his teeth as he waited for the rest of the army to reach them and provide them cover.

Seconds later, though it felt much longer to Andronicus, the army rushed past them. A dozen hands picked Andronicus up off the king and lifted the king to his feet. Andronicus looked behind him and saw the arrow sticking out of his back, not far from his spine. He reached back and took hold of it and felt pain shoot up his left side. He could feel it wasn't too deep, but the head had caught in his flesh. Andronicus picked a clean arrow up out of the ground and put it between his teeth. With one strong pull he wrenched the arrow out of his back, feeling his flesh burn.

It felt much worse going out than it had going in, and it brought Andronicus down to one knee. The battle had commenced all around him, and no one seemed to notice him kneeling in the dirt. A few arrows still fell around him, but the battle had mostly moved up to the wall. Andronicus tore off a long piece of cloth from his shirt and wrapped it around his torso as tightly as he could. He looked back again and saw a dark red stain moving across the cloth. He kept his left hand firmly pressed against the wound and stood up.

Once on his feet, he looked around, and saw that Alexander was gone. The Greek mercenaries inside the city had ambushed them perfectly, and everywhere Andronicus looked he saw Macedonians falling. He looked around wildly for the king and finally spotted him over by the wall, back atop Bucephalas and surrounded by his friends.

Andronicus began limping toward the king

when he heard horns sound behind him. He looked back and saw the siege towers they had assembled being pushed toward the walls. In front of the first tower, sitting on his horse with his sword raised, was Parmenion, a fierce look of determination on his face. As the tower got closer to the walls Andronicus saw Philotas standing on top of the tower, ready to lead the charge onto the wall. Andronicus had never seen a siege tower in person before, though he had read about them, and he couldn't believe something so big could have wheels and move.

"To me!" Alexander shouted over the din of battle. "Bring the towers to me!" Alexander was fighting not far from the gate, and the tower had been headed well to the right of there, but they turned in response to the king's call. A moment later the tower turned back to its initial course, and Andronicus saw Parmenion shouting at the men behind him. He also saw Calas riding with a group of guards toward Alexander.

Andronicus pushed past soldiers to where Calas was meeting the king. When he reached them, he saw Cleitus still on his horse, blood covering the left side of his face.

"What are they doing?" Alexander shouted as Calas reached them. "I told them to come to me."

"This is not a good position to lay the siege, my king," Calas replied, trying to reason with the boy. "Parmenion is right to stay his course. The walls there are lower and farther from their catapults. Perhaps the second tower can press here."

"Parmenion and his sons are trying to steal my glory again!" Alexander shouted. "They will not have my victory. Guards, with me to the tower!" With that Alexander charged back toward the tower. Andronicus jumped onto the back of Cleitus's horse, wincing at the pain in his back. The king led a small charge through his own ranks to get to the tower, arrows raining down all the while. Alexander reached the first tower just before it made contact with the city walls.

"You try to take my glory from me, Parmenion?" Alexander shouted as soon as he was close enough to hear. Parmenion turned around and looked at the king as if he couldn't believe his ears.

"Glory be damned!" Parmenion shouted back. "You can't have the towers hit the walls there; it has to be here. If you want to lead the charge, so be it. That is your kingly right." Alexander looked like he wanted to shout something else at Parmenion, but instead he turned and made for the base of the tower. Soldiers quickly moved aside as the king and his men entered the tower. Andronicus and Cleitus pushed their way through as well. Andronicus looked up at the giant wooden structure and was astonished. The tower was a hundred feet tall and as wide as a small house. There were ladders on all four walls, going all the way to the top, with two platforms in between. The soldiers standing in wait quickly moved aside for the king and his men.

Before Alexander could reach the top of the tower, however, the siege gate fell. Andronicus heard a battle cry, and knew it must be Philotas and his men. A second later everyone rushed forward, and Alexander was pushed out of sight. Andronicus pushed forward and up, climbing ladder after ladder until he reached the siege gate on top. He limped across, onto the wall and found a bloody battle well underway.

Andronicus looked to his right and saw Alexander slashing at a man clutching a bloody wound. Hephaestion and Cassander were on either side of him, slashing at the few Persians in front of them. Cleitus was right behind the king, ready to save him if need be. Andronicus looked to his left and saw Philotas leading three other men against a wave of mercenaries. One of Philotas's men was cut down and fell off the wall with a terrible scream.

Andronicus hurried over to aid Philotas, his lower back still burning badly. Just as Andronicus reached them, another one of the Macedonians took a spear to the gut and fell to the ground below. Andronicus stepped into his place beside Philotas and his last man. Even with an arrow wound in his back, Andronicus made quick work of the mercenaries, cutting them down one by one.

Philotas cut down nearly as many men as Andronicus. They kept pushing forward, side by side, until they reached one of the wall's towers. They stepped inside and felt rocks being hurled down on them. Andronicus rushed forward, taking a large rock to the side of his face, and drove his sword into one of the men who was throwing rocks. He turned to see Philotas standing over the other man.

Just then Alexander and his entourage rushed past Andronicus and Philotas, leading the charge out of the tower, and into the city. Cleitus shot Andronicus a furious look as he passed, and Andronicus knew what Cleitus was thinking. Andronicus went down the winding stairs and emerged into the city itself.

A contingent of Greek mercenaries was defending the gate, and Alexander was pushing his men toward them. Andronicus limped over to them and fell in beside Cleitus. They pushed forward, fighting enemy Greeks and Persians. Finally, they broke through the mercenaries' defenses, and Hephaestion ran up and began opening the gate. A second later four other men fell in beside him, and together they lifted the heavy iron gate. Once the gate was opened, the Macedonian army poured into the city.

As the army rushed in, Andronicus heard horns blowing from deeper inside the city. He turned to see the mercenary infantry charging toward the Macedonian army. Andronicus watched from twenty feet away as the two infantry lines crashed into each other. The king and his men were not far from the front, and he limped toward them.

The fighting was hectic and clustered together. Andronicus tried his best to push through the crowd. After struggling for several minutes, he gave up and joined a group of Macedonians who were pushing ahead of the others. With his help they were able to punch a hole in the mercenary line, and soon after that the Macedonians began swarming.

As the Macedonians pushed farther into the city, the mercenaries fell back. The Macedonians chased them, and minutes later Andronicus saw smoke billowing up from farther in the city. The main battle ended and became a scattering of smaller fights. As Alexander ordered his army into the city, Andronicus made his way to where the king and several of the generals stood.

"Alexander!" Calas shouted. "They have set the city on fire. We have to pull our men back."

"No, we must push forward!" Alexander shouted back, a mad look in his eyes. "They try to burn the city to keep it from me. We can stop them. Send the army forward. Have the fires put out!"

"Alexander, Calas is right," Cassander said, holding a wound in his side. "With this wind the fire will burn through the city in hours. We should pull out and wait until it runs its course."

"I will not let that cowardly traitor Memnon take my victory from me!" Alexander shouted. "I have taken the great city of Halicarnassus, and it will be mine!"

Alexander set off, shouting orders at his men as he went. Cassander turned to Calas with an apologetic look, and Calas gave him an understanding nod. Just then Philotas came running up with a group of blood-soaked soldiers behind him.

"What is he doing?" Philotas shouted. "We have to retreat. The city is going to burn."

"Alexander wishes to save the city," Cassander said, not meeting Philotas's eye. Philotas looked like he wanted to shout at Cassander, but instead he turned and stormed off with his men behind him. Cassander looked over at Andronicus, appearing as if he might cry, then turned and rode after Alexander.

2

The Macedonians managed to get the fire out not long after dark. Much of the city was burned away, but there was still enough to salvage. More than two hundred soldiers died getting the fire out, and twice as many were badly burnt. While the army was working to stop the fire, Memnon managed to escape the city with a large number of his mercenaries.

Alexander held a grand feast once the city was

his, in one of the smaller palaces that hadn't burned. He honored all those who had died, both in battle and by fire. The former leaders of the city were brought before Alexander, where he had them swear fealty to him. Once that was over with, the noblemen of Halicarnassus began presenting Alexander with gifts. The ceremonies went on for hours.

Andronicus sat on a chair in the corner on Alexander's right side, trying not to irritate the fresh wound in his back. Cleitus sat next to him, scowling as usual, and never taking his eye off the king. Alexander's friends all sat around him, laughing and drinking wine. Even some of the other generals joined in on the celebration. Andronicus did notice that Parmenion sat well away from the king, his sons beside him.

"Parmenion and the king grow further apart every day," Andronicus said, nodding toward the sulking general.

"That's because Parmenion knows what he's doing," Cleitus grunted. "Parmenion has been right time and time again, and the king rushes into battle like a fool, and with a fool's luck he defeats his enemy. Or rather, we defeat his enemies, and he claims the glory."

"Do you really think he's as bad as all that?" Andronicus asked. "He does fight with courage."

"Courage?" Cleitus said with a laugh. "Is that what you see? I see a foolish boy rushing into battle in search of nothing but glory. I see a boy who, without me, would have fallen in battle long ago, and without you, would have fallen this very day. I see a boy who has taken what his father gave him and is now presenting it as his own."

Andronicus thought about that as they fell silent again. He watched as Alexander and his young friends roared with laughter, splashing wine all over their clothes and the fine cushions they sat on. Finally, Andronicus got up and limped over to Parmenion's table. Parmenion and his sons greeted Andronicus as he approached, and he took a seat with them.

"A fine celebration, wouldn't you agree?"

Parmenion asked, his voice dripping with sarcasm.

"The king sits there as if he did not get hundreds of men needlessly killed and a whole city burnt to the ground," Philotas said, fuming with anger.

"Hold your tongue," Parmenion snapped. "It is never wise to disagree with a king."

"You need not fear me reporting you," Andronicus said. "You were right today."

"It is not just that he marched us right into an ambush," Parmenion said, "but now he tells the story as if he had intended to do so. And the worst of it is, he claims he led the charge on the wall."

"I was there," Andronicus said. "I know Philotas led the charge."

"Andronicus fought beside me on the wall, Father," Philotas agreed. "Many more of my men would have fallen if not for him."

"You have my thanks, Andronicus," Parmenion said, giving him a solemn nod. "And it is good to know that others amongst the king's inner circle know he's not Achilles reborn."

"I'm not sure I'm a part of his inner circle anymore," Andronicus said with a sigh.

"No?" Parmenion said, taken aback. "What happened? I thought that boy looked up to you."

"Perhaps he did," Andronicus said. "But I think I've told him the truth one too many times. I see now that he's not the kind of king who wants to be told hard truths."

"And yet they still must be spoken," Parmenion said. "He may be the king, but he's still a boy, and it's our responsibility to talk sense into him, even if he doesn't listen."

"We should not be talking like this here," Nikanor said, gesturing over to where the king was. Andronicus looked over and saw Hephaestion staring at them. Andronicus knew how much Hephaestion hated Parmenion, and he wondered if he had just made a mistake by speaking with him so publicly.

"You're right," Parmenion said to his younger son. "You should go, Andronicus. We can speak more later."

Andronicus nodded, then returned to where Cleitus stood, barely visible in a dark shadowy corner.

"You make friends with the general?" Cleitus asked.

"We see eye to eye," Andronicus replied, "as you would, I think."

"Of course we would," Cleitus said. "But I'm not about to congratulate him in front of the king's little friends. Did you see the way Hephaestion was glaring at you? That was foolish of you. Those boys will be watching you even more carefully now."

"I'm not worried about those boys," Andronicus said.

"You should be. You may be the best fighter here, Andronicus, but that boy is king, and he has an army. He has already shown us what happens to those who pose a threat to him."

"I'll be more cautious," Andronicus said, but inside he was already wondering if that were true. Could Alexander have him killed? Would he?

3

Andronicus stood in the corner with Cleitus, barely listening as Alexander and his generals yelled at each other. Memnon had managed to escape the city with a large number of his men as well as a large number of Persians, and now it was time for blame to go around. Somehow the mercenaries had reached their fleet and set sail into the Aegean. The early reports said that Memnon was heading toward the Greek islands.

"We must turn back to defend Greece," Parmenion urged. "If Memnon reaches the mainland, he will burn Athens to the ground."

"If Memnon reaches the mainland with an army he won't have to burn Athens," Calas interjected, "they will join him, as will most of the other cities. While you march east to face Darius, you'll lose your entire empire to Memnon."

"Memnon will not reach the mainland," Alexander said confidently.

"What will stop him?" Parmenion asked.

"Demosthenes swore an oath to me," Alexander replied, "as did the leaders of all the other Greek cities."

"Except for Sparta," Ptolemy added.

"And then there's Sparta," Alexander said with a sneer. "Andronicus," he said, startling Andronicus to attention, "you are from Sparta. Do you believe your people will let Memnon, a foreign invader, take Greece for himself?"

"They let your father take Greece for himself," Andronicus said, "and he was more foreign than Memnon. As long as Memnon is wise enough not to attack any Spartan lands, they will leave him be."

"Andronicus is right," Parmenion agreed. "The Spartans will not come to your aid. And if by chance they are brought to war, they could just as likely take Greece for themselves while it's so attainable."

"No," Andronicus said, shaking his head. "You are right that the Spartans will not help you, but they would not take Greece for themselves."

"And why wouldn't they?" Philotas asked.

"Sparta doesn't want to rule Greece," Andronicus said. "It never has. If Sparta wanted Greece, it would have taken it a thousand years ago. No, the Spartans are content to live in Sparta, forever."

"You think it is so easy to conquer Greece?" Alexander asked, a snide look on his face.

"Of course not," Andronicus said, meeting the king's gaze. "I'm sure your father had much difficulty with it."

A shocked murmur erupted from the men standing around the room. Alexander turned bright red, and looked like he wanted to attack Andronicus. Hephaestion got to his feet, a look of pure hate on his face.

"Alexander conquered Greece," Hephaestion said. "He rode south and fought the Thessalians, and he went to Corinth, and took oaths from every city."

"Very well," Andronicus said. "Alexander did what no man since Agamemnon has done; he conquered all of Greece. Well, almost all of Greece,"

Andronicus added with a sneer. "But if he doesn't do something about Memnon, he'll lose it all."

"Andronicus speaks the truth, my king," Parmenion said, knowing the dangerous waters he was in, "about Memnon of course," he added.

"I don't fear Memnon of Rhodes," Alexander seethed. "He will not reach Greece, and if he does the Spartans will defeat him. And as my Spartan friend here so wisely told us, the Spartans don't want Greece."

With that Alexander rose from his chair and left, his friends close behind. Cleitus followed them, leaving Andronicus standing there with the remaining generals.

"That was very foolish of you," Calas said once they were gone. "He could have had you killed for that."

"He could have tried," Andronicus grunted.

"He will not kill Andronicus," Parmenion said, sitting down where the king had been. "He knows how valuable he is in battle."

"What are we going to do about Memnon, Father?" Philotas asked, bringing them all back to the issue at hand.

"He must be stopped," Calas said. "The king may not believe he's a threat, but he is."

"Yes," Parmenion agreed, staring into the fire, "a grave threat."

"We should send a host of men to defend the shores," Philotas suggested.

"The king would never allow it," Calas replied, shaking his head. "He has decided Memnon is no threat to him, so he will not allow us to take men now."

"Then how do we stop him?" Philotas asked. "We can't just let him sail right into Greece."

"What if we stopped only Memnon?" Nikanor suggested quietly.

"What? Speak up, son," Parmenion said, turning to his younger son.

"I said what if we could find a way to stop only Memnon? If Memnon fell, his mercenaries would leave, wouldn't they?"

"You mean assassinate him?" Philotas asked, sounding a bit surprised that his younger brother was suggesting such a thing.

"Yes," Nikanor answered. "Why not? Alexander assassinated everyone else who posed a threat to him. Why not one more? Memnon is a traitor after all."

"Alexander would find out and know it was us who had it done," Parmenion said, shaking his head.

"What if we could make it look like an accident?" Nikanor said, thinking aloud.

"How would you do that?" Philotas asked.

"There are ways to do such a thing," Andronicus said, drawing all eyes to him.

"Could you do this thing, Andronicus?" Parmenion asked in a cautious tone.

"I doubt the king would excuse my absence," Andronicus replied.

"What if, when the army moves on, you fake an illness?" Philotas suggested, his eyes glittering with the possibility. "Tell him you'll ride at great haste and return to the army as soon as you're better. Then get to Memnon and back as fast as you can."

Everyone looked at Andronicus, waiting for his answer. He stood in silence for a moment, thinking. If he killed Memnon, he would likely save Alexander's empire. But Alexander would either not notice, or find a way to take the credit for himself.

"You must do this, Andronicus," Calas urged. "Not for Alexander but for Macedonia—and Greece," he added, remembering Andronicus was Spartan.

"Memnon will burn countless villages to the ground," Parmenion said. "The big cities will not burn, but the villages will. He has already shown his affinity for arson."

In the end that was what convinced him. Andronicus had no desire to help Alexander or save his empire. What made him agree was the memory of the burnt Helot woman, who had cursed him for letting her people burn. That face still haunted him, and this seemed as good a way for redemption as any.

Andronicus waited until the night before the army set out from Halicarnassus. He unfurled his cloak, revealing the old wooden box. He hadn't opened it in decades, and he had no idea how all the drugs and poisons had reacted over the years. He opened it carefully, keeping his head as far away as possible while making sure not to let anything spill inside. After examining the various powders, he found the little purple berries from deep in the jungle. They were as dried as anything he had ever eaten, but as long as they didn't kill him, it didn't matter.

He recalled the day he and Chaka had first found them in the jungle and eaten them. They had tasted delicious, and they had both eaten a dozen or so of the berries before they got sick. It was possibly the sickest Andronicus had ever been in his life. In his mind, he could still remember Chaka's wails of pain.

He took out three of the little berries and popped them into his mouth. They still had a hint of their delicious taste, but they were hard and chewy. It only took about thirty minutes before Andronicus was retching his guts out. He called for one of the slaves to bring water to him. Not long after that, Cassander came to see him. At first he looked suspicious, but once he saw Andronicus for himself, that all fell away.

"You look terrible," Cassander said, keeping his distance, "what happened?"

"I don't know," Andronicus panted, wiping his mouth. "I must have eaten something."

"You know we're leaving tomorrow," Cassander said, "marching east into Persia."

"I know, damn it," Andronicus said through the pain. "Tell the king I will ride as soon as I'm able and be with you when you face Darius."

"He will not be happy," Cassander warned.

"Well, what would you have me do, boy?" Andronicus barked. "Look at me."

Cassander nodded slowly as he looked at Andronicus's pale green face. "Very well," he said. "I'll tell the king." He started to leave and then turned back, tears forming in his eyes. "Andronicus," he whispered, and Andronicus looked up from his sick pail. "I'm sorry," Cassander said, trying to hold back his tears. "You were right, about the mercenaries. It was a trap."

"Of course it was," Andronicus said. "You should have been more cautious."

"I know," Cassander agreed. "I should have listened to you. We all should have."

"I know you boys think the men who served Alexander's father are still his men," Andronicus said, trying not to get sick again while he spoke, "but you have to know that we want the same thing as you. No one wants to see Alexander fail. Not Parmenion, not his sons, and not me."

"I know," Cassander said, sniffling. "I will not doubt you again. I promise."

"Or Parmenion," Andronicus insisted, and Cassander slowly nodded. "Good," Andronicus said. "Then go take care of the king. I'll join you as soon as I'm able."

Cassander left Andronicus alone to ride out the rest of his sickness. Having only eaten three of the berries this time, the pain only lasted a day. By the time Andronicus felt better, Alexander and his army had already left the city. As soon as he could walk, Andronicus went straight to the docks. He found the ship Parmenion had told him about and was welcomed aboard quietly and without question.

Andronicus was given a cot down below, and went to rest. As the ship rocked in the water, he realized he hadn't been on a ship since before he had left Greece, unless he counted the drunken haze he had been in when he crossed the Hellespont years ago. He still feared the sea, and he wondered if he always would.

The ship sailed north up the coast, stopping only occasionally at random ports along the way.

Memnon was still commanding a sizable force, and it was not hard to track his movements. He took his remaining Greek and Persian mercenaries north and stopped at the island of Lesbos. Memnon docked his fleet at the port, and his small army entered the city.

It was not difficult for the captain of Andronicus's ship to get them into port. They flew the colors of the Greek rebels, and since they were Greek as well, they blended in perfectly. When they were docked, Andronicus thanked the captain and paid him for his discretion. He had to pay bribes to three different guards on his way up through the port, but he made it through.

Once inside the city, Andronicus entered a lively tavern, filled with drunken Greek mercenaries. Men were stumbling all over the place, making a terrible racket. It seemed like all the whores in Lesbos had come to please the mercenaries. As soon as Andronicus sat down, a beautiful young girl plopped herself in his lap. She ground her hips on him, and Andronicus had to clutch the table to keep his balance. It had been far too long since he had been with a woman, and his carnal desires leapt to the fore.

The young girl leaned in and kissed Andronicus long and hard on the mouth. When she pulled off him, a jug of wine was thrust into his hand. Andronicus sat there for a long moment, just staring down at the jug. In that moment he wanted nothing more than to drink the jug in a single gulp and then take the girl to a more private place and have his way with her.

He thought about how far he had come since his last drink. Wine had led him straight into the ground and nowhere else. He had spent more than a decade in a drunken haze of misery. Since then he had watched a prince become a king and followed him into battle. Andronicus thought about all he had done for Alexander and all that Alexander had not done for him.

In a greater sense, he was tired of being the boy's servant. It had been over a year since the king had actually heeded his advice. Andronicus had become nothing more than a glorified bodyguard, and now he was going to be an assassin. Not an executioner, as he had been when he had slain the prince and his men, but an actual assassin. He was fed up with the king's foolishness.

Thinking dark thoughts, Andronicus brought

the jug to his lips. The wine tasted better than it ever had in his entire life. He finished off half of the jug before putting it down. The lovely girl on his lap laughed and wiped some wine off his chin. He spent a while longer in the tavern, drinking wine, laughing with the other Greek men, and enjoying the feel of a woman's body against his. Before taking her upstairs, he at least managed to get a good amount of information about Memnon's plans for Greece.

Chapter 47
And This One is for You
1

Andronicus awoke the following morning with an all too familiar pounding in his head. He sat up slowly, shielding his eyes from the bright light coming in through the window. He looked down and saw the girl from the night before sleeping soundly next to him, the sheets barely covering her naked body. Andronicus took a moment to admire her beauty, trying to ignore the headache that came after a night of drinking. A voice in the back of his head reminded him that a good drink in the morning could help with that, but he ignored it. He had slipped up, but he had no intention of falling back into his old ways. It had simply been a night away from the war.

Without waking the girl, he dressed and left the room. The city was filled with the defeated soldiers of the recent battle, mercenaries mostly but some Persians as well. No one seemed to think anything of Andronicus as he walked through the streets. A few people looked at him as he passed, but no one looked at him like he was one of the enemy. Many of them even gave him a nod. It was certainly much easier to infiltrate his own people than it had been with Africans, Egyptians, or Persians.

Andronicus knew that Memnon was holed up in the temple of Aphrodite, the largest in the city. It had not been hard to get information out of the men in the tavern once the wine began to flow. He was sure that Memnon would be surrounded by his close confidants and most likely a large number of guards as well.

Andronicus knew he could likely take them on under normal circumstances, but the wound in his back was still fresh and made it nearly impossible to turn his torso to the left. He didn't know how much it would hinder his fighting, but he thought it better not to find out.

He reminded himself that he was not there to murder the man or slaughter his guards; that would be a failure to their cause. He had to find a way to poison Memnon. He already had the perfect poison in mind, one that Glick had been most fond of. It would make a man die of what would appear to be a regular sickness three days after taking it. Andronicus had to sneak into the temple, find a way to get the poison to Memnon, make sure he took it, and then leave the city.

He waited until after dark and then made his way up to the temple. Two guards were standing in front of the door that Andronicus meant to enter. He approached them with his hands outstretched, making sure not to look threatening.

"Hold it there, soldier," the guard on the left said. "What's your business here?"

"I need to see Memnon immediately," Andronicus replied, sounding urgent. "I have something he needs to see."

"No one said anything about this," the other guard said, his eyes narrowing with suspicion. "What do you need to show him?"

"Something very important; trust me." Andronicus knew he had their interest now.

"Come on then," the first guard said. "Tell us. We cannot let you in the temple unless we know what your business is."

"Very well then," Andronicus said, sounding annoyed, "but if you tell anyone about this, you'll have to answer to Memnon himself."

Andronicus reached into the pouch at his side and pulled out a large diamond. He still had most of the stones that he had been given back in Africa, and this seemed like a good way to infiltrate the temple without killing anyone. The two guards' mouths dropped open as they saw the gem, and their eyes grew wide. The man on the left even set his spear aside, leaning it against the wall, and came closer for a better look. The other guard leaned in as well, holding his spear loosely at his side.

Andronicus knew that he could have both men dead in the dirt within mere seconds. He could probably even hide the bodies before anyone saw and still be able to sneak in. The dumb expressions on their faces as they stared at the diamond made him want to do it. Instead, he closed his fist around the stone. The two men snapped out of their trance and looked up angrily.

"Now, as you can see," Andronicus said, "I have to speak with Memnon at once. He needs to see this."

"Where did you get it?" the unarmed guard asked.

"That is no business of yours," Andronicus replied. "This is for Memnon's ears only. Now get out of my way, so I can report to him."

"Yes, sir. Sorry, sir," the other guard apologized, mistaking Andronicus's forceful tone for authority. They stepped aside, and Andronicus entered the temple, putting the diamond back in his pocket. He pitied Memnon for having such simple and gullible guards.

Once inside the temple, Andronicus made his way through the halls easily. He had never been in this particular temple, but he had spent enough time in enough Greek temples to know where he needed to go. He made his way to where he thought the dining hall would be, and sure enough, he found it a minute later. Inside were more than three dozen of Memnon's Greek mercenaries eating breakfast.

Andronicus had no intention of fighting his way out, so he slipped away from the hall, but not before checking for Memnon. He had only seen him from afar, on the battlefield at Granicus, but he knew well enough what the man looked like. Andronicus didn't see him in the hall, so he went looking for the library in the hopes that Memnon would be there going over his war plans.

Andronicus walked the longer way through the temple, making sure to avoid any unnecessary run-ins with Memnon's soldiers. Somehow he managed to find the library without being stopped. He looked inside, and as he had expected, Memnon sat at a large table with maps and scrolls laid out in front of him. At least six other men were in the room that Andronicus could see. Four of them were wearing white robes and appeared to be unarmed. They were all leaning over the table, staring at a large piece of parchment. The other two men were standing guard by the door, dressed in Athenian armor.

Andronicus guessed that two more guards were standing beside the door he was peeking through, likely just feet away from him. He kept his hand on the hilt of his sword, ready to fight if he had to as he tried to eavesdrop. The men weren't speaking very loudly, and it was hard to make out what they were saying. Andronicus closed his eyes and focused on the voices.

When he was in the jungle, he used to try and pick out just one sound to listen to. There would always be birds calling, monkeys howling, bugs chirping, rain falling, and sometimes even predators roaring, and Andronicus loved to try and find just one. He would pick out one of the birds or monkeys and then focus all of his thoughts on that one sound, then slowly block out the rest. It was hard to do, and it didn't always work, but he had spent many years in the jungle, and he had gotten quite good at the game.

Now he focused on the voices inside the room. There was a thick door between him and them and several fires crackling inside, but slowly the voices became clearer. At first he could only make out a few words: Athens, Sparta, march, capital, king, away. Andronicus focused harder, clearing his mind of everything but the voices.

"Sparta will never fight. If they wanted Greece, they would have taken it long ago," a deep, heavy voice said. "No, we'll have to find another way."

"The Spartans are insulted by the boy-king.

They will help us just to spite him," another voice said, this one higher and older.

"It doesn't matter," a third, much gruffer voice said. It sounded tough and mean, a fighter's voice rather than a politician's. "Even if Sparta doesn't help, we still have Athens, Corinth, and Thebes. That's enough to take the capital while the boy marches his army deeper into Asia." Andronicus couldn't be sure, but he thought that voice belonged to Memnon.

"These cities have pledged themselves to aid you?" the second voice asked.

"Yes," Memnon replied. "They have given me their word that if I march on Pella, they will send aid."

"And you really think you can take Pella with less than a thousand mercenaries? You forget, Memnon, that these men have no loyalty. If the fighting is not going their way, they will turn and run." This was a new voice, younger than the others but strong and bold.

"They are loyal to me," Memnon said angrily. "As long as I lead the charge, my men will not flee. Besides, the capital is guarded by less than a thousand men, commanded only by Antipater. That old oaf won't be able to hold the city against me for long."

"So, when do we sail to Macedonia?" the deep voice asked.

"We'll stay here until week's end, and then we'll sail up the coast and make our way across the Aegean, burning as many of their ships and ports as we can."

The men continued talking, but Andronicus was no longer listening, he had heard all he needed to hear. Parmenion had been absolutely right. While Alexander marched on Persia, Memnon was going to take Macedonia away from him. Andronicus knew that Alexander would not turn back; he would say that Memnon could have Macedonia for the time being and that when he returned he would execute him and all his men, but Andronicus knew better.

What Alexander would either fail to see, or choose to ignore, was that if Memnon took Macedonia, the army he now led would turn on him. The Greeks and mercenaries marching in Alexander's army would never follow him if a Greek took Macedonia from him. The army would turn on itself, and thousands would die for nothing. They would return to Greece to fight over it once again, and thousands more would die. And when the fighting finally ended, and someone would again be ruler of Macedonia and Greece, the Persians would come for their revenge.

Allowing Memnon to go free, as Alexander had chosen to do, would lead to the end of it all. Andronicus knew he had to kill Memnon. The man had said himself that so long as he led his men into battle, they would not flee. If he died, his men would not be able to take the capital from Cassander's father, and the other Greek cities would not dare break their pact with Alexander. The fate of Alexander's conquest, the fate of all of Greece and perhaps even the world, now relied on Andronicus stopping Memnon.

Andronicus had to laugh at himself. Aristotle would hate this. He had always said that Andronicus had a great worldly purpose, that he was meant to change the world. Andronicus had no doubt that Aristotle did not have political assassination in mind when he had said it, but it seemed that was the way it would have to be. Andronicus supposed that was the only way he really could change the world. Killing was the one thing he had always been good at, the thing he had been born and raised to do. He was a killer, and that was how he would change the course of history, by killing.

3

Andronicus crept away from the library toward the priests' quarters. He went down several halls until he saw a priest entering a small room. Andronicus was sure the priests in this temple treated their living quarters the same way the priests everywhere else did, with total privacy. When the man entered his room and shut the door, Andronicus approached.

He paused for a moment staring at the door, his knife in hand, ready to use on the unsuspecting priest. He knew the safest thing to do was to kill the man. His body would not be found for days, and by then Memnon would be dead and Andronicus long gone. If he left the man alive, he could alert someone before Andronicus escaped. He had known hundreds of priests in his life, and he disliked most of them—pompous, holy pretenders for the most part. But he had also liked many of them. Some priests, like Imhotep, were simply interested in learning and teaching others. Andronicus didn't know what kind of man this priest was, but in the end he decided to put his knife away.

He knocked on the door. A moment later the man opened it, looking thoroughly shocked to have a visitor at such an hour. Without a word, Andronicus punched the man in the face. He let out a comical grunt and then fell to the floor in a heap. Andronicus felt bad, but at least he was leaving the man alive. He dragged the priest inside and shut the door behind him.

Andronicus picked up one of the priest's dirty brown robes and ripped a piece off. He bent over the man and tied his hand's firmly behind his back. He hoped the cloth would hold, but he knew the man would likely be out for a while. Andronicus also knew he would be found before he starved, and he would live. Andronicus took another one of the robes from the priest's table and took off his armor.

Once he was properly dressed as a priest and completely unarmed, he took out the small piece of cloth he had folded up earlier. Inside was the poison he intended to give to Memnon. He tucked the cloth into his robe and then stepped out of the room and started toward the kitchen.

4

Andronicus kept his head down, avoiding eye contact with the other priests. To the soldiers he would look like just another priest, but most of the priests would surely identify him as an imposter. When he stepped into the kitchen, most of the soldiers were gone, though a few were talking loudly at one of the tables. At another table a few priests were eating quietly. Besides that, two other priests were by the food.

Andronicus was about to turn around and find another way when a fight broke out amongst the drunken soldiers. One man insulted another, and soon four of them were tussling over the table. The priests got up and either fled or went over to try and break up the fight. Andronicus seized the moment and stepped inside the room, walking over to where the jugs were.

Moving quickly, Andronicus picked up two of the jugs and brought them to his nose, then turned to leave with them. As he had hoped, one was water, and the other wine. As the fight wound down, Andronicus slipped out the other door. He didn't know if anyone had seen him come or go, but he didn't wait to find out.

He made his way back to the library. When he reached it, he peered in the side of the doorframe again, and saw Memnon still bent over the table. Two of his fellows had gone, and one was sleeping in his seat, leaving only Memnon and one other. Andronicus couldn't see any of the guards, but had no doubt that they were still there. Knowing what he had to do, he set one jug down and carefully took the cloth from his robe, hiding it in his hand.

He cleared his throat loudly and then knocked the other jug against the door. A second later the door opened, and an angry looking soldier appeared. Another soldier was to his right, and two more standing beside the door across the room. The first man just stared at him without saying anything.

Andronicus gave the man what he hoped was a priestly looking smile and held up the jugs. "Water and wine for the generals," he said in a meek voice. The man looked down at the two jugs and then back up at Andronicus's innocent smile. He nodded and reluctantly stepped aside. Andronicus hurried in and walked over to Memnon.

"Water or wine, my lord?" Andronicus asked, holding both jugs up.

"Wine," Memnon grunted, looking up from a map and rubbing his eyes. "The hour grows late, and we are almost finished here. Perhaps I shall go and visit one of the famous brothels here. I hear they are quite intriguing."

"They are at that, my lord," Andronicus said with a smile, thinking of the girl from the night before. He set down the jug of water and reached for Memnon's cup. He purposefully knocked the cup over, spilling a bit of water onto Memnon's lap. Memnon stood in anger and looked like he was going to hit Andronicus, but stopped short when he saw Andronicus's face. Andronicus tried to look like a meek little priest, but he knew that when Memnon had moved to strike him, his true self had shown for a second.

Memnon slowly sat down, staring at Andronicus, who bent down to pick the cup up off the floor. As he did, he opened the cloth and emptied the powder into the cup.

"My deepest apologies, my lord," Andronicus said as he stood up with the cup in his hand and the cloth back up his sleeve. Memnon gave him an odd look, staring into Andronicus' eyes. Andronicus did his best to look frightened, and after a moment Memnon looked away. Andronicus quickly poured wine into Memnon's cup, watching as the red liquid washed the grey powder away. When he handed the cup to Memnon, there was no trace of the added ingredient.

Andronicus retreated toward the door. Just before he left, he saw Memnon take a long swig from the cup. When he brought the cup down he smacked his lips in satisfaction and then went back to his work. Andronicus left, satisfied that he had achieved his result. He made his way through the halls and back to the room where he had left the unconscious priest.

The man was still out cold with a nice bruise forming around his eye. Andronicus quickly changed out of the priest's robes and back into his armor. He untied the priest's hands and slipped out of the room, then made his way to the exit. He didn't encounter anyone on his way out, and when he walked out the door, the guards didn't so much as say a word to him.

Once out of the temple, Andronicus considered going back to the brothel and spending another night with the girl he had been with, but then thought better of it.

When he arrived at the docks he found his ship waiting for him. The whole crew was on board, ready to go. Less than an hour later they were at sea, the lights of the city glimmering behind them in the dark night.

The weeklong sea voyage was the same as it always was for Andronicus. Every night he was haunted by dreams of a terrible storm and a great ship with sails one hundred feet high. Sometimes he would see the man behind the great wheel, roaring and waving a long sword over his head. Sometimes he would look down and see things moving in the water. He had no doubt the dream was a vision and that one day he would be in that storm, with that man, and those large grey creatures.

Every day he would wake and immediately go check the water. There were no storms or monsters from the depths, just the clear open sea, as beautiful as ever. The entire voyage back to Halicarnassus was calm and peaceful. When they returned to the city, Andronicus thanked the captain and gave him a small diamond on top of what Parmenion had already paid him. The captain actually fell to his knees in thanks. Andronicus made sure the man knew never to speak of any of it, and the man vehemently agreed.

Once back in Halicarnassus, Andronicus made his way to the large temple. The Macedonian army was long gone, but Andronicus knew that captains would still be posted in the temple. When he arrived he asked if there was any news of the rebel mercenaries. They told him that to everyone's complete surprise, Memnon of Rhodes had fallen ill and died just three days earlier. Andronicus feigned a stunned reaction, then redirected the conversation to the king's movements. The army had been marching east since Andronicus left, and he would have to hurry to catch up.

Chapter 48
The Legend of the Knot

1

Andronicus finally caught up with the army in the mountains between Phaselis and Termessos. There had been no real battles during his absence, and the army was in high enough spirits when he found them. The first thing Andronicus did was to go to the king. Alexander gave him a quick greeting and then carried on his way. Andronicus didn't mind. He was pleased to find Cleitus stalking the king, as always.

"I hear Memnon of Rhodes died in his sleep of a strange sickness," Cleitus said under his breath as they walked a ways behind the king.

"I heard the same," Andronicus replied.

"You'll have to tell me how you managed that sometime," Cleitus said with a cold smile.

"If I told you that, I'd have to tell you everything," Andronicus replied with a sly smile, and fell back to talk to Parmenion.

"Andronicus," Parmenion said, smiling when he saw him, "good to have you back. I heard you had a terrible illness."

"That I did," Andronicus replied, nodding.

"But you're better now?"

"The illness is gone," Andronicus said, looking Parmenion in the eye. "It will not be a threat again."

"And the other mercenaries?" Parmenion whispered, leaning over on his horse, so no one else could hear. "Have they fled?"

"From what I hear the mercenaries have all fled, and the Persians have sailed for Egypt."

Parmenion nodded, looking thoroughly relieved, then filled Andronicus in on what the army had been up to in his absence. There had been no battles, and each city had fallen without resistance, so it seemed Andronicus hadn't missed much.

2

When the army reached Termessos, Alexander had his men surround the small city. He seemed ready and even eager for another siege, but when the people of Termessos offered their surrender, he accepted it peacefully. They spent nine days in the city and then continued on toward Gordium. There was an ancient prophecy about the land of Gordium, which Alexander had practically become obsessed with since hearing of it.

The legend had started in ancient times. A noble people called the Phrygians had been without a home or a king. They had settled in the old city of Telmissus, where a beautiful oracle told them that the next man to enter the city by ox should be named king. That same day a man named Gordius came to Telmissus driving an old oxcart, and he was named king.

Gordius proved to be a great king, bringing peace and prosperity to the Phrygians. To express their thankfulness to the gods, Gordius's son tied that same oxcart to a sturdy wooden post. It was said that the boy tied the rope with many different knots, all tangled together, and tied it so tight that no man could ever untie it. Many men tried their hand at untying the knot, but they all failed. Everyone who looked upon it agreed that the knot was impossible to untie.

Years later, well after Gordius and his sons had all died, the Phrygians were again without a king. Another oracle came to what was now the city of Gordium. The oracle examined the old knot and proclaimed that the man who could untie the great knot would become the ruler of Asia. According to legend the knot was still there, holding an ancient oxcart to an ancient post.

Alexander believed he was destined to unite Asia and conquer the known world. To be the one to untie the knot and fulfill the ancient prophecy would be everything he dreamed of.

Andronicus didn't know what to make of the legend; it sounded like many legends he had heard over his lifetime, none of which ever came true. What he didn't like was the way Alexander seemed to obsess over it. The young king clearly believed that if he could untie the knot, he would be the ruler of Asia and would win every battle for the rest of his life.

As soon as the army reached Gordium, Alexander went straight for the knot. Andronicus followed, along with Cleitus, curious about it himself. He was a bit surprised when they found an actual decrepit old oxcart, half of it having deteriorated over time, tied to an old weathered wooden post by what had to be the biggest, most ridiculous knot Andronicus had ever seen. He stared at the knot in astonishment, guessing that it was about twice the size of a cat.

Alexander tried to untie it right away. Hephaestion and Cassander and Ptolemy all stood behind him with confident smiles on their faces. Andronicus wanted to burst out laughing, but he held it in. The idea of Alexander—or anyone, for that matter—ever finding a way to untie that knot was truly comical. Andronicus whispered as much to Cleitus, who chuckled quietly, and they walked away shaking their heads.

3

Two days later Alexander was still trying to undo the knot. The army had settled into Gordium and was simply awaiting the king's orders to continue. Andronicus returned periodically to see if Alexander had made any progress. After two days of tireless working, Alexander had not changed the knot so much as an inch. Whoever had tied the knot had done a tremendous job.

Many of Alexander's generals stood scattered about, watching in boredom as the king struggled to loosen the rope. Andronicus made his way over to where Parmenion and his sons were standing. Parmenion looked like he had about a thousand things to say to the king, but he knew he couldn't say any of them.

"Has the king made any progress?" Andronicus asked sarcastically. Parmenion let out a snort, and his sons both laughed. Andronicus saw Hephaestion shoot them a nasty look as he heard their laughter, and a moment later he went to whisper something in Alexander's ear.

"Quiet," Parmenion hissed to his sons. They all fell silent, but Alexander looked over at them anyway. Andronicus could see the sleep deprivation in the king's face, and knew he would not last much longer with the knot.

"Do you find this amusing, Philotas?" Alexander shouted.

"As a matter of fact, I do," Philotas replied, surprising everyone. Parmenion shook his head slowly, wincing at his son's brashness. "No one will ever untie that thing," Philotas continued. "Look at it." There was a soft pattering of laughter from many of the other men standing about. Alexander looked around furiously, silencing them all.

"The man who unties this knot is destined to rule Asia!" Alexander shouted. "Do you not believe I'm destined to rule Asia, Parmenion? Clearly, your son does not."

"You can rule Asia without that knot, Alexander," Parmenion said, as if speaking to a child. "Let us leave this place and continue on our course."

"I will untie this cursed knot!" Alexander shouted. "It's my destiny!"

Then, to everyone's surprise, Alexander drew his sword, and brought it down on the knot as hard as he could. The steel cut through the ancient rope, and the Gordian knot fell to the dirt, nothing but a mess of tangled rope. Alexander stood over the rope, panting heavily. Everyone else was dead silent, staring at him.

"You are cursed!" an old man shouted from somewhere in the distance. "You have desecrated an offering to the gods. You will be damned for this Alexander king!"

"Seize that man," Hephaestion shouted, and two soldiers quickly silenced the man. Alexander stood there staring down at the knot, his face pale and shocked.

"The man who unties the knot will be the ruler of Asia!" Cassander shouted, and everyone turned to look at him. "And here the knot lies. It is no longer tied, is it? Alexander bested the Gordian knot, and he *is* destined to rule all of Asia!"

There was a murmuring from the crowd, but Hephaestion and Ptolemy quickly joined in, declaring Alexander the prophesized ruler of Asia. Alexander looked up from the knot as if hearing what Cassander was saying for the first time. When the words registered, his expression changed from one of panic and fear to pride. Andronicus turned to Parmenion, who let out another snort of laughter and then turned to leave, his sons close behind him.

Word spread through the army about how King Alexander had outsmarted the knot. Instead of spending hours trying to untie it, he had simply looked at it, laughed, and cut it in half with his sword. Andronicus couldn't believe how fast the false story spread, until even those who had been there told it that way.

4

With Alexander having bested the Gordian knot and officially proclaimed himself ruler of all Asia, the army set out again. They moved east at first and then turned south. The army moved down through the mountains as fast as Alexander could make them go. As they traveled, Alexander continued receiving reports on what King Darius was doing and eventually he had to call another war council.

Andronicus stood in his usual place beside Cleitus, behind the rest of the generals. Alexander had not invited all of his generals and captains, as he had in the past, choosing only to have his top generals and closest advisors present. Once everyone was seated, Hephaestion rose and explained the situation to the other generals.

"Darius has been amassing a new army in Babylon. We have heard varying reports on its size, but it seems that he has at least two hundred thousand men."

"How can that be?" Calas asked, sounding shocked. "Thousands died at Granicus, and we have taken more than a dozen of his cities. How can he have found so many men so quickly?"

"The Persian Empire is vast, Calas," Parmenion

said with a sigh. "I feared this would happen, but it doesn't mean the end."

"Of course it doesn't mean the end," Alexander said, glaring at Parmenion. "We will fight Darius, and we will defeat him. It doesn't matter how many farmers he has marching behind him."

Parmenion nodded. "I agree. Our men are true soldiers. We can defeat the Persians again, but we must not let them reach the sea."

"We have heard some reports that Darius's army has already left Babylon and is marching toward Issus," Cassander said, sounding worried.

"It doesn't matter," Alexander said. "His empire lies to the east, not the west, and he doesn't have enough ships to sail his entire army across the Aegean."

"He won't need to sail his men anywhere," Parmenion said. "If Darius's army reaches the sea, they'll have enough aid and supplies from their fleet to be insurmountable. We can't let the Persian army reach their fleet, or we may very well be defeated in battle."

Everyone was silent for a long while, processing Parmenion's words. Finally Alexander looked up at him and nodded slowly. "How do we stop them from reaching the sea?" he asked, looking Parmenion in the eye. "I'm already driving the army as hard as I can. I don't think they can go any faster without becoming too weak to fight."

"You speak truly, my king, and wisely," Parmenion said with a pleased smile, "but you don't need to drive your whole army to Issus before Darius. You just have to make sure he doesn't reach it before you. Send me instead. I'll take two thousand men and hold the coast until you and the rest of the army arrive."

"You believe you can hold the coast with just two thousand men?" Hephaestion asked, sounding skeptical.

"Not indefinitely," Parmenion replied, "but I believe I can hold out until you arrive, if you make haste."

"We shall make haste," Alexander said, getting to his feet. "Set out at dawn with the best horses we have, Parmenion. We will reach you in time to face Darius. I swear it."

"Very good, my king," Parmenion said with a bow. "May I take my sons with me in this venture?"

"Nikanor may accompany you, but I need Philotas here with me to lead the infantry."

"Very well then. When we meet again, it will be time for the great battle. Be ready, my friends."

Parmenion turned and left the council to ready his men. There was a moment of silence after Parmenion left as everyone contemplated the scope of the upcoming battle. They had fought the Persians three times already and won all three times. The battle at Granicus River had been the biggest so far, and they had slaughtered the Persians. But somehow this battle already had a different feel. Perhaps it was because they would be facing Darius himself this time, not one of his generals. Maybe it was because the army they would be facing this time was made up of men from farther east than any Greek man had ever gone and were unknown to them. Perhaps it was because at Granicus they had faced forty thousand, a mixture of Greek mercenaries and Persian soldiers, and now they would be facing more than two hundred thousand men from a land they knew nothing of. Whatever the reason, everyone could tell this would be a battle for the ages.

Even Andronicus felt anxious at the idea of fighting such a massive force. He had been in enough battles, both as a young man and an old, to know that a battle of this scale could go on for a day or more, and tens of thousands would die, perhaps even hundreds of thousands. He had to wonder if this was going to be the biggest battle in history. It was said that Agamemnon had led a million Greeks into battle at Troy, but that could simply be legend. When Andronicus had fought at Plataea as a boy, they had called that the biggest battle ever on Greek soil, and this battle would be twice the size of that at least.

The meeting went on a little while longer,

though Andronicus had stopped listening. His mind was going over every bit of his history with the Persians. It had not just been a lifetime in the making. The Persians had killed his father, killed his king, and friends. The Persians had been the great enemy his whole life. From start to finish they had been the people he was meant to defeat.

Part of him knew that wasn't true though. He had gone nearly a hundred years without so much as thinking of the Persians, except in remembering the battles he had fought. They had not been his enemy when he and Chaka were walking across Swimha or through the jungle. He had not cared to fight Persians when he met them in Egypt; he had hardly cared at all. But now, being back in a primarily Greek army, marching into Persia, preparing to fight them in the biggest battle between their two people, they were the great enemy once again. He felt torn between the idea that he should not be there and the need to finish what he had begun so long ago.

Chapter 49
Remember, Remember
1

The battle did not take place in the city of Issus but rather a day's march to the south of it. Alexander had marched his army north at great haste, trying to reach Parmenion before the Persians. At the same time Darius brought his entire army from the east in an attempt to beat Parmenion and cut off the Macedonians from the sea. Alexander knew that if Darius's army reached the sea first, the Persians could steal his ships and get behind his army. So far Parmenion had been able to hold the coast with his small force, but Darius had brought his entire army into Issus with him. As Alexander marched his army up into the lands around Issus, Darius left the city and marched south to meet the Macedonians head on.

Up to that point Alexander had yet to face Darius in the field of battle, or his full army. At Granicus, Memnon had led the Persians, and none of the sieges they had won on the coastal cities were big battles. Knowing that Alexander was getting close to taking Asia Minor away from him, Darius had finally come to face the young king himself. Alexander and Darius raced their massive armies toward the sea and reached each other just south of Issus, on the fifth of November.

The two armies met at the River Pinarus, not long after daybreak. Just like at Granicus, the two armies formed lines on either side of the river. The Pinarus river was much smaller than the Granicus and was likely only a foot or two deep. Andronicus thought it looked more like a creek than a river, and he knew it wouldn't slow the fighting much.

Darius set most of his infantry at the center, facing the Greek infantry. Alexander had his forces set up much as they had been at Granicus. Parmenion led the infantry while Alexander rode Bucephalas on the far right, leading his royal companion cavalry.

Alexander had named a number of commanders for the battle. Among the cavalry commanders were Hephaestion, Cassander, and Ptolemy as well as Cretarus, a new captain who had proved himself at Halicarnassus. Leading the Thessalian cavalry on the far left were a few men Andronicus barely knew. It seemed Alexander was having a change in leadership amongst his generals. Andronicus noted that Calas had been demoted and now sat behind Cretarus rather than leading the men himself.

The battlefield was not gigantic, even though the two armies were. On the Greeks' left, the cavalry was lined up all the way to the sea. The land fell off into high cliffs over the ocean, and Andronicus knew many men would be going over those cliffs before the day was over. Darius had placed a large cavalry force next to the cliffs, facing down Cretarus and the Thessalian cavalry. On the far-right side of the Greek lines, beside Alexander and his royal companion cavalry, were high hills. Both armies had men placed well up the side of the hill, all the way up to where it became a mountain.

Between the hills and the cliffs, the small

Pinarus River snaked its way through the two armies. The cavalries on both sides would have to deal with the cliffs and hills alike, but between them stood over fifty thousand foot soldiers. The Macedonian infantry led by Parmenion was over twenty thousand strong. Andronicus didn't know how big the Persian infantry was, but it was much larger than the Macedonian infantry.

In the center of his army, about thirty lines deep, was Darius himself. He certainly didn't look like a soldier, even though he was dressed in gallant battle attire. He was sitting on a big white horse covered in bright robes. He also was wearing bright orange-and-red robes as well as golden armor. On his head was a bright Persian headdress, leaving only his face uncovered. He had a long black beard that fell past his breastplate, but he was too far away for Andronicus to get a proper look at his face.

Darius was the second Persian king that Andronicus had seen, but this man did not remind him at all of Xerxes. Leonidas had beaten Xerxes back at every stop, repelling his slaves and his elites alike. Andronicus had seen the anger and frustration on that king's face even as a boy. Darius did not appear to be a fool like Xerxes though. Xerxes had believed that the sheer size of his army would win him the war. He had only beaten Leonidas because of a betrayal. Darius seemed like much more of a proper battle commander.

Looking at both armies facing each other, Andronicus felt that it would be a great and terrible battle. Granicus had been a great battle, the biggest he had ever been in, but this one would be bigger. Both armies had been massive at Granicus, but then the Persians had been led by Memnon, and much of their army had been mercenaries. Now these were true Persians, led by their own king, who was not far from the front. Andronicus knew that neither army would flee easily, and he expected a tremendous amount of carnage come nightfall.

As was typical before a battle, there was a long, tense moment of silence as the two armies stood across from each other. The men on both sides stared into the eyes of the men that they would either kill or be killed by. Andronicus took out his old wooden comb from a lifetime ago. Some of the men around him gave him odd looks as he flicked at his hair with the comb, but he didn't care. It was an ancient Spartan battle custom, and he was still a Spartan warrior.

The moment lasted for a long minute. The only sound came from the carrion birds flying overhead, eagerly anticipating what was coming. Andronicus took the moment to size up the Persian line. He spotted two scared-looking men standing next to each other and decided to break the line there.

Alexander rode Bucephalas a few steps forward and then turned to face his men. He was wearing his usual shining golden armor and the tremendous red plume atop his helm. He opened his mouth and was about to give his speech when a horn sounded from the Persian line. More horns answered, and then before Alexander could rouse his men with strong words, the Persian center charged.

Andronicus watched from afar as Parmenion and his sons charged as well. The two lines met in the river, and within seconds it became a wild mess of fighting. Alexander raised his sword above his head and let out a mighty war cry. Then he charged Bucephalas at the Persian line, his cavalry right behind him.

Andronicus charged his own horse toward the two men he had picked out. As expected, they practically fainted when he fell upon them. His horse rammed into both men, either killing them or rendering them unconscious, and Andronicus swung his sword down at a man behind them.

Alexander and his cavalry pushed forward against the Persian line but held back their full might until Parmenion gave the signal. They cut through the Persian lines one by one, until some of the men in the rear began fleeing up into the hills. Andronicus cut his way through the Persians, the old fire taking hold of him. He felt his blood pumping as he swung his sword at one man after another. It felt different than it had when he was a boy, more satisfying. He let the old fire burn hot as he plunged into the depths of battle.

At one point he found himself standing over a litter of dead Persians, and he took a moment to look around. All he could see were men fighting. The noise had become a raucous clamor, a mixture of clanging metal, screaming men, and braying horses. Andronicus rode partway up the hill. He looked back over the tremendous battle and saw a hectic fight raging on in the middle, wild and chaotic. Straining his eyes toward the far side of the fighting, he saw that Cretarus's cavalry was falling back in the face of the Persian attack, putting more pressure on Parmenion's infantry.

At that moment Alexander shouted and then charged Bucephalas toward the center of the battle. Andronicus quickly fell in behind the king and rode toward the brunt of the fighting. The royal cavalry rode through the scattered Persian left flank easily, but before they reached Darius and his men, the Persian lines reformed and shifted a large part of their force to the left to face Alexander's charge, slowing the royal cavalry to a standstill.

Alexander and his cavalry fell into another bloody fight. Andronicus slashed down on either side of him at the Persians below. As he was pulling his sword from a dead man's skull, he felt a sharp pain in his right calf. A second later his horse reared, and then he was falling sideways. His horse collapsed with a terrible screech, its entire weight pressing down on Andronicus's leg. As soon as he hit the dirt, a sword came swinging down at him. Andronicus quickly raised his own sword and deflected the heavy blow.

His leg was pinned under his horse, which was now dead, and he struggled to fight off his attacker. The Persian soldier kicked at him and swung his sword in a series of wild, aimless blows. Andronicus deflected a few of them and then slashed his sword across the man's ankle. When he fell to one knee, Andronicus thrust his sword up into the man's chest.

Once the man was dead, Andronicus struggled to free his leg from his horse. When he finally did, he saw that his leg was covered in blood, a deep gash running across the back of his calf. He realized the spear that had killed his horse had also cut the back of his leg.

Wincing in pain, he tried to stand. He couldn't put his full weight on that leg, but he could still hobble. He was on flat ground and couldn't see anything more than five feet away. All Andronicus knew of the battle's progression was what was right in front of him. He didn't know if the Macedonians were winning or losing, but he knew that men around him were falling.

Andronicus limped painfully toward a Macedonian soldier fighting off three Persians. As he did, one of them shoved a spear into the soldier's back. Andronicus got there just as the man fell to the ground. The three men looked up just as Andronicus arrived, which was far too late. Before they knew what was happening, he decapitated one man and gutted another. The third man raised his sword, but Andronicus quickly drove his own sword through the man's chest.

When they were down, Andronicus moved swiftly from one Persian to the next, killing them easily despite his wounded leg. As he fought his way through the messy battle, he saw a gigantic Persian man not far away, cutting down Macedonians two at a time. The man stood more than a foot taller than everyone else, and he was swinging the longest sword Andronicus had ever seen. As he watched, the man took off the heads of two Macedonians with one swing and another a second later. He was easily the biggest man Andronicus had ever seen. Chaka may have been taller, but this man's chest was as big as a horse's, and his arms were bigger than most men's legs. He didn't even bother wearing any armor, and his huge muscled chest was bare, with blood splashed across it.

The beast took down two more Macedonians as Andronicus cut down a Persian. The giant was pushing through their ranks, and the men were beginning to flee from him. Andronicus cut down the man nearest him and started toward the giant. As he limped over, cutting down two more, the gargantuan man finally took notice of him. He shoved two of his own men out of his way and then stepped toward Andronicus.

Andronicus looked up into the man's eyes as he charged and saw a blind rage he had seen in many eyes before.

Andronicus meant to leap to the side, but he winced in pain as his wounded calf tore open. The giant swung his great sword down in a long arching blow, and Andronicus jumped to the side at the last second, howling as the pain in his leg exploded. Before he could raise his sword, an arm the size of a log came flying at him. The blow hit him square in the chest. For a moment he felt weightless as he flew through the air. Then he hit the ground with a hard thump.

Andronicus tried to inhale and felt his lungs close up tight. He coughed and sputtered for air and then looked up just in time to see the giant charging him again. Still gagging and choking, Andronicus reached for his sword and scrambled back to his feet. His head swam as he struggled to breathe. The giant's curved sword came swinging down at him again, and he leapt to the side this time.

As Andronicus struggled to his feet again, another Persian soldier stumbled into him. The man had a panicked look in his eyes, and he took a wild, aimless swing at Andronicus. He ducked the blow with ease and brought his sword up through the fool's chest. As he pulled his sword free, the giant swung his sword down at him again. This time Andronicus threw the body of the man he had just killed at the giant, and watched as the great sword cut through the dead man's shoulder and halfway down his body, nearly cleaving him in two.

Andronicus lunged forward and drove his sword into the giant's chest as the big man was pulling his sword free. Andronicus's sword sank all the way to the hilt, just below the huge man's ribs, but the giant still didn't fall. Instead he grabbed Andronicus by the neck and lifted him into the air, and he felt his sword slip out of his grip. The giant's strong hand squeezed around his throat, and Andronicus began to choke.

Thinking quickly, he reached behind his back, pulled out his bronze knife, and drove it into the man's chest. The giant's chest was huge, and the knife wasn't long enough to pierce him deep, but Andronicus pulled it out and stabbed the giant again and again. Each time he drove his knife into the man's chest, the hand around his throat loosened a little until finally the giant let him go. Andronicus collapsed to the ground, gagging and choking for air. The monstrous soldier fell to his knees, bringing his hands up to the many stab wounds Andronicus had inflicted. He gave Andronicus a final look of hate and then fell forward onto his face.

Once Andronicus could breathe, he got back to his feet, his leg burning with pain. He stumbled over to the huge man's body and pulled his sword free. With the big man down, he went back to striking down clumsy Persian soldiers. A few Macedonians fell in behind him once they saw his skill, and he moved slowly toward the center. They pressed forward, looking for the king and his men.

At some point Andronicus came across Ptolemy. He had his left arm pressed firmly against his side, and Andronicus saw that the whole left side of his torso was red. He looked down and saw that Ptolemy had a deep gash in the side of his midriff. Even though he looked badly wounded, he was still shouting commands to his men.

"Ptolemy!" Andronicus yelled over the chaos, his voice easily audible even with the clamor all around them. "The king! Where is the king?"

"He was going after Darius!" Ptolemy replied. "Last I saw he was still riding Bucephalas!"

"The left side isn't holding!" Andronicus cried. "We have to go to Parmenion! The king must give the order!"

"Right!" Ptolemy said, his brow furrowed in thought. "This way!"

Ptolemy led the charge toward where the king was meant to be. Andronicus fell in behind the boy he had trained and tried to keep up despite his wounded leg. They moved slowly through the Persian line. Everyone in their unit was hurt badly, but they carried on. Andronicus fought beside Ptolemy, making sure the boy did not fall.

Then, out of nowhere, Alexander appeared

atop Bucephalas. Hephaestion was right beside him, as was Cleitus. The king had that mad look in his mismatched eyes again. Alexander was swinging his sword down at the men around him, but he was clearly moving in the direction of Darius. As the king pushed forward, Cassander appeared on foot. He was also wounded. There was a dark cut across his cheek, and half his face was covered in blood.

"Andronicus!" Cassander shouted, "the king is going after Darius!"

"No!" Andronicus replied. "We must give aid to Parmenion! Cretarus's cavalry has failed! Parmenion is surrounded!" Andronicus saw Cassander's face as he registered the dilemma. The king would want to chase down Darius. If he killed the Persian king, he would win the war. However, if Parmenion's infantry fell, Alexander would lose the war anyway. The Persians would circle around the royal cavalry's back and surround them. Cassander nodded hurriedly, and then they set off toward where Alexander was leading his charge.

It was hard to catch up to him, as Alexander was still on his horse, but they managed it. Cassander shouted up to the king, telling him what Andronicus had told him while Andronicus turned to fight the nearest Persians. When he turned back to look at the king, he saw him shouting angrily at Cassander. Andronicus limped over toward the king.

"We must turn back, Alexander!" Cassander was shouting urgently. "If Parmenion falls we'll all die!"

"Parmenion will not fall!" Alexander insisted. "I will kill Darius myself! There he is. I can end it all this day!"

"Even if you kill him, Alexander, you will lose your army!" Hephaestion said. Andronicus was surprised to see Hephaestion disagreeing with the king, but was glad to see him speaking wisely.

"I won't turn back now!" Alexander shouted, his face contorted with rage. "I will kill Darius! I will have my glory!"

"You can still kill him, Alexander!" Hephaestion replied. "But today we must aid Parmenion!"

"Damn that cursed old man!" Alexander shouted, sounding like a boy throwing a tantrum. "Once again he takes my glory from me. Very well, to Parmenion!"

Alexander led a massive charge toward the center of the battle while Darius turned to flee. The Macedonians reached the center, surrounding the Persian infantry. The Persian men who saw their king retreating quickly followed suit. More and more Persians fled as they realized the battle was lost, and within a matter of minutes, it was all over.

Thousands of Persians fled back to the city of Issus, with others running into the hills. Alexander mustered all the cavalry he could and led a massive charge against the retreating men. Andronicus stayed behind and went looking for Parmenion.

2

When Andronicus found Parmenion, he was lying in the dirt with his sons beside him. Andronicus limped over to them and fell to his knees. Right away he could see that Parmenion was badly wounded. There was a hole in the bottom of his breastplate, above his stomach, where a spear had pierced him. Philotas was hurriedly trying to undo his father's armor while Nikanor stood above them, crying silently.

"How bad is it?" Andronicus asked the old general.

"It's not good," Parmenion wheezed, "but I have seen men survive much worse."

"As have I," Andronicus said, nodding in agreement. "You must seal the wound, boy, before he bleeds out."

Philotas nodded, then pulled his father's armor off and tore his shirt away, revealing the wound. It was not as bad as it had looked initially. The wound itself was only an inch and a half across and likely only three or so inches deep.

"You must thank the man who made your armor, my friend," Andronicus said with a smile. "He saved your life."

"That I shall," Parmenion said with a pained

smile. "Now then, the battle."

"The battle is over, Father," Philotas said as he patched up the wound. "We can discuss it later."

"Nonsense," Parmenion grunted. "Tell me what happened."

"You did it once again, my friend," Andronicus said. "Cretarus's cavalry fell back, and for a time you were surrounded."

"That much I know," Parmenion said, coughing. "You should have seen my sons, Andronicus. They fought almost as well as you."

"I'm injured, and they're not," Andronicus said, looking over at Philotas. "It seems they fought better than me this day."

"And what of the king?" Parmenion asked, still smiling.

"Chasing down the fleeing Persians as we speak," Andronicus replied with a sigh. "He loses himself in the heat of battle."

"I know," Parmenion said, nodding. "I have not seen it myself, not in him at least, but I have seen it in other men."

"It's not a shameful thing," Andronicus said. "I have felt it many times myself, but I'm not in command. A man in command of a battle can't lose his head."

"It seems to have turned out fine." Parmenion sighed as Philotas finished tying a corset around him.

"It was a close thing, my friend," Andronicus said. "When Darius fled, Alexander would have pushed after him and left you here to die. Hephaestion had to talk sense to him, if you could believe it."

Parmenion looked at Andronicus for a moment and then burst out laughing, which quickly turned into coughing. Philotas looked up at Andronicus in surprise, not knowing what was so funny. Andronicus didn't know either, but he could see that Parmenion was going to tear his bandage.

"You find humor in that?" Andronicus asked.

"The king would have left us," Parmenion said as his laughter died down, "but Hephaestion spoke sense to him. That means Hephaestion saved our lives."

Andronicus joined in the laughter this time. Hephaestion had seemingly hated and opposed Parmenion at every turn. He had even threatened the man on several occasions. Now it seemed Parmenion owed Hephaestion a debt of thanks.

Chapter 50
The King of Asia
1

When the battle was done, and the fighting had died down, the Macedonian army moved into the city of Issus. Alexander and his cavalry had taken the city without resistance, and the rest of the army followed. That night Alexander held a huge celebration in the great halls of Issus. The Persian army had not been completely destroyed, but it was a great victory nonetheless.

Darius had escaped, to Alexander's fury, taking at least half of his army with him. It was estimated that more than thirty thousand Persians had fallen on the field of battle, and the road from the Pinarus River back to Issus was littered with the corpses of the men Alexander and his cavalry had run down. The thousands of Persian soldiers who had made it back to Issus were executed there.

While Alexander and his generals held a great feast, the Persian soldiers were being slaughtered outside. The battle had been a bloody one, and many of the men celebrating with the king were bandaged. Ptolemy sat close to the king, bent over in his chair, favoring the wound in his side. Parmenion sat with his sons, a thick bandage wrapped around his chest. Cassander had an absurdly large bandage wrapped around his head, making him look ridiculous, and Andronicus was sure the boy would wear the scar the rest of his life.

Andronicus himself had a bandage wrapped tightly around his right calf. The spear had cut right through his muscle at least an inch deep, maybe more. During the battle he had barely felt the pain, even though he had practically been running on it. Now, sitting around with nothing to do, his leg hurt like hell. He wondered where it would fall on his list of injuries. The lion's claws tearing his shoulder had been bad, as had the arrows he had taken in battle, but the worst pain he had ever felt still had to be when he had torn apart his shoulder. That one still pained him from time to time.

Cleitus ambled drunkenly over to where Andronicus was sitting and collapsed into a chair beside him. He had a bandage on his left forearm, but other than that he appeared to be unscathed. His dark eyes were hazy and unclear, and Andronicus could tell he had been drinking for a while. Cleitus offered his jug to Andronicus, who shook his head.

"Why the hell not?" Cleitus slurred. "We're celebrating a great victory, a victory in which you were wounded." He pointed down to Andronicus's leg.

"I don't partake in wine anymore," Andronicus said. He could hear how pompous he sounded, and he hated it. He thought about the night not too long ago when he had partaken. He also remembered the girl's lovely figure and the way she had felt lying next to him. He had to ask himself if Cleitus wasn't right. Why shouldn't he have a drink? It wasn't as if he didn't want one.

He thought about it for a long time while Cleitus continued drinking beside him. He told himself that he had stopped drinking because it had gotten to be a problem. The only reason it had become such a problem was because he had been alone. It had been the loneliness, and the sense of meaninglessness that had driven him to drink so much. Now that he was amongst a great army, surrounded by people he considered friends, there was no reason why he shouldn't be able to celebrate with the men.

"On second thought, I think I will have some," Andronicus said after his long inner debate. Cleitus gave him a dark drunken smile, one that likely would've given small children nightmares, then handed him the jug. Andronicus brought it to his lips and tasted the delicious wine. He had forgotten how good it tasted. He finished it off in one long swig. Cleitus roared with laughter and clapped Andronicus on the back.

"That's more like it, brother!" Cleitus said. "You're not with the priests anymore. You're a soldier again, and soldiers drink."

"That we do," Andronicus agreed as he set the empty jug down. He could already feel the wine making its way to his head. Cleitus hailed a slave boy, who brought over more wine, then turned back to Andronicus. The two men spent the next few hours drinking and laughing. Philotas joined them, and the three of them got good and drunk together.

2

Alexander decided to have his official ceremonies that night rather than waiting. Everyone in attendance was terribly drunk, Andronicus and the king included. Alexander declared that since he had defeated Darius in battle, and Darius had openly retreated, he had forfeited his empire to Alexander. Alexander had himself named the king of Asia in front of all his generals and noblemen.

Darius's women were all in attendance as well, though they weren't drunk. Darius and his men had fled in such haste that he had left his wife, his mother, and his daughters behind in Issus. Philotas said Alexander had wanted to execute them, but he was talked out of it. Andronicus didn't believe that. Whatever Alexander was, he was not a butcher of defenseless women. They watched along with everyone else as Hephaestion anointed Alexander king of Asia.

Once the ceremony was over, everyone went back to drinking. Andronicus returned to his conversation with Cleitus and Philotas. They were discussing the battle and the aftermath. Calas, who had fought with Alexander since before he was king, had died in the fighting. He had been demoted just before the battle and fought behind Cretarus, who had also fallen. They all agreed that the command should have been given to Calas and that he may well have led his part of the cavalry into victory.

"He leans on his old generals less and less," Cleitus whispered drunkenly.

"My father is one of the only real generals left who fought beside King Philip," Philotas agreed.

"He has no trust in his father's men," Andronicus said, sighing as he took another long drink. "You and I included, Cleitus."

"How many times have we saved his damned life?" Cleitus said. "And yet he always turns to his little friends for advice."

"He is still young and vain," Andronicus said, trying to defend the king despite agreeing with Cleitus.

"How long can his age be used as an excuse for poor leadership?" Philotas asked. "Alexander is twenty-one years old, old enough to know that his father's men don't want to see him fail."

"I fear the boy still listens to his mother too much," Andronicus said. "He still receives letters from her every month."

"That woman is a witch," Cleitus growled, looking at Andronicus with his dark eyes. "She has what she wanted. Her husband is dead, and her son is king, but she still wants to punish anyone who followed Philip, and now she does it through the king."

3

Besides leaving his family behind, Darius also left behind a great deal of his fortune when he fled from Issus. After the ceremonies concluded, Alexander demanded to be taken to the great hall in which Darius housed his many treasures. Alexander and a dozen other drunk generals stumbled down to the hall, making a terrible racket. Parmenion had not wanted to come, and Cleitus had passed out drunk an hour earlier, but Andronicus and Philotas accompanied the king and his cohort.

When they reached the great hall, Andronicus was stunned. He knew that the Persians housed great treasures in Issus, but he was unprepared for the sheer size and range of it all. The generals all fell upon the treasures like children. Cassander went for a pile of rubies, and Ptolemy found a golden chalice, encrusted with gems. Hephaestion found a glorious crown that made Alexander's own crown look foolish, and he quickly put it on Alexander's head. Philotas found a beautiful staff that he began turning over in his hands.

Andronicus walked down a row of magnificent wonders. There were gems and diamonds, though none as big as the biggest he still had. He also saw a pile of bright ornate rugs that all looked spectacularly beautiful. Then Andronicus came across a barrel filled with swords. There had to be at least two dozen hilts sticking up from it. Andronicus examined them all. Most of them were from the Persian Empire, although some of them were of Greek making.

Andronicus lifted one especially fine-looking Greek sword out of the barrel and felt his heart skip. He immediately recognized the mark on the base of the blade, just above the hilt. It was the same mark that was on his own sword, the mark of Karpos of Sparta. Andronicus knew that Karpos's swords had been lost to Xerxes, but he never thought he would see another one again. Andronicus quickly looked through the other swords and found three more with the same mark. As he stared down at the swords, which looked so much like his own, he wondered whom they might have belonged to. Any one of them could have belonged to Leonidas himself, or Diokles or Gaios.

All the generals were taking small treasures for themselves, and Alexander wasn't making any objections, so Andronicus decided he would keep the blades. He didn't know if there were any other Karpos blades left out there, but he hoped there were at least two still with their owners. He didn't know why or for whom he took the blades, but he did, and no one noticed except Philotas.

As Andronicus was leaving the hall, he noticed Alexander admiring a shining ring. For some reason Andronicus stopped what he was doing and put the swords down. He walked over to the king as if he were in a trance. With each step the ring seemed to shine brighter. Andronicus felt like he was in a dream, his entire body buzzing. At first he didn't recognize it, and then he couldn't mistake it. It was a feeling he had been chasing for a very long time.

When Andronicus reached the king, he looked into his eyes and felt a shiver go through his bones. Alexander's eyes were shining. His head was cocked at its usual angle, but his eyes were neither blue nor brown. They burned with a pure white fire. Andronicus turned his head toward the ring, and then the light fell on his eyes as well. For a moment everything turned bright, brighter than the sun itself, and deep in the depths of the light, there were shadows. Andronicus knew the shadows were trying to tell him something, but he couldn't quite make them out.

Andronicus focused all his energy on the shadows, and thought he could almost make out the shape of a man. He felt himself begin to sway, and then suddenly he could smell Swimha, the grass, the dirt, the Swihmehe themselves. Andronicus felt warmth wrap around him like a blanket, and then he hit the floor, his head knocking against the stone. Then everything went dark.

4

When Andronicus awoke he was lying on his back in what felt like a bed. His head was pounding like a drum, but that could easily be from all the wine. He slowly opened his eyes, and saw a stone ceiling above him. He turned over and saw Philotas slumped in a chair in the corner, snoring loudly. Andronicus tried to speak, but nothing came out. His neck felt bruised from where he had been choked in the battle. He let out a deep cough and tried again.

"Philotas," he croaked. Philotas snapped awake and sat up.

"Andronicus," he said as he rubbed his eyes. "We were worried about you. You took a hard fall there."

"What happened?" Andronicus asked, sitting up.

"You got good and drunk, that's what happened," Philotas said with a laugh. "Then you fell over like a tree and knocked your head on the floor.

Right in front of the king, I might add."

"The ring," Andronicus said, holding his pounding head as he tried to concentrate. "There was a ring."

"What ring?" Philotas asked. Andronicus looked the boy in the eye, and could tell he had no idea what he was talking about.

"The king was looking at a ring," he said, trying to remember everything. "A shining ring."

"I'm sure he was," Philotas said, shrugging. "There were more treasures down there than I could even imagine. I mean, you saw it all."

"I need to see that ring," Andronicus said.

"Why?" Philotas asked, giving Andronicus an odd look. "If the king really was admiring it, I'm sure he took it for his own. He took nearly everything for himself. I got your swords though; I saw you carrying them."

"What?" Andronicus asked, thinking of nothing but the light from the ring.

"Those swords you had," Philotas said, "from Sparta. They're beautiful, a fine bounty. What will you do with them?"

"You can have one," Andronicus said offhandedly, still thinking about the ring. "I suppose I'll give one to Cleitus as well."

"That is truly a fine gift," Philotas said. "Thank you, Andronicus."

"You're welcome," Andronicus said, meeting Philotas's eye for a moment before returning to his thoughts.

"What will you do with the other two" Philotas asked, looking over at where the swords rested against the wall.

"The other two I'll keep," Andronicus grunted. He strained to remember what the ring had looked like, but all he saw was a blinding light. He had been terribly drunk. Perhaps he had imagined it or dreamed it. He would have to ask Alexander about it. There had to be some rational explanation, because what he was thinking seemed impossible.

Andronicus gulped down a few jugs of water in hopes of drowning out his headache. It helped a little, but mostly it just made him have to pee. He left Philotas alone to admire his new sword and went to find the king. Instead he found Cleitus sitting on a barrel, guarding the king's door, apparently also still feeling the pain from the night before. Cleitus looked up when he heard Andronicus coming and chuckled when he saw who it was. He got to his feet with a wince.

"I had no idea you could drink like that, brother," Cleitus said, laughing as he clapped Andronicus on the back. "You drink almost as well as you fight."

"I've had nearly as much practice," Andronicus said, his head still pounding away. Cleitus chuckled again, then sat back down on his barrel.

"I need to speak with the king," Andronicus said, trying to sound urgent while still whispering.

Cleitus laughed. "I don't think the king will be seeing anyone today. He didn't drink quite as much as you, but he drank more than his fill."

"It's important," Andronicus said, looking Cleitus in the eye. "I have to ask him something."

"Ask him what?" Cleitus asked, the humor gone from his face in a second.

"I have to ask him about something I saw last night," Andronicus said. "One of Darius's treasures."

"Forget it," Cleitus said with a wave of his hand, "the boy took the lot of it for himself. You're lucky Philotas grabbed those swords for you."

"I don't need to have it," Andronicus said, trying to get his urgency across without having to answer any serious questions. "I just need to ask him a few questions about something I saw."

"What did you see?" Cleitus asked, his interrogation voice coming out.

"I saw the king holding a ring," Andronicus replied, meeting Cleitus's dark stare. "I need to ask him about it."

"What about it?" Cleitus asked.

"I need to ask if he saw the same thing I did," Andronicus answered, getting a bit impatient.

"What did you see?" Cleitus asked. "Why is this ring so important to you?"

"I'm afraid that needs to stay between me and the king," Andronicus replied, frowning at his friend and comrade.

"Then I'm afraid I can't let you see the king," Cleitus said, getting to his feet.

"You tried that once already, brother," Andronicus said, facing down Cleitus, "the day we met. Or have you forgotten?"

"I forget nothing," Cleitus replied. The two men began circling each other, and both drew their swords. "I haven't forgotten the cut you have on that leg either."

"You think it's enough?" Andronicus asked, giving his sword an easy twirl. It was as if his mind had lost control, and some other thing was driving him.

"I like my chances," Cleitus growled, mimicking the motion.

"You shouldn't," Andronicus whispered. He was about to strike out at his close friend when the door opened behind them, snapping them both out of the trance. Andronicus turned and saw Hephaestion standing there, looking both surprised and curious.

"Everything alright out here?" Hephaestion asked, looking at the two men holding their swords.

"Fine," Andronicus replied as he put his sword away. Cleitus did the same, and they looked at each other for a moment. Andronicus could tell that Cleitus was as confused as he was. Cleitus was his closest friend in the army, and they both disliked the king. Why on earth would Cleitus have tried to fight him over seeing the king, and why would he have tried to fight Cleitus for doing his job? Andronicus felt the hairs on his neck stand on end. He knew he needed to talk to Alexander.

"Hephaestion," Andronicus said, giving the boy the most serious look he could muster, "I need to ask the king something, right away."

"What is it?" Hephaestion asked hesitantly.

"The ring," Andronicus said, "the one he was looking at when I fainted, I need to ask him about it."

"What ring?" Hephaestion asked. Andronicus stared deep into the boy's brown eyes. He had lived long enough to see the truth in a man's eyes, and yet he couldn't tell if the boy was lying. There had been a ring. He had seen it; he was sure of it. Yet he had been terribly drunk, and he had knocked his head rather hard. Andronicus considered the possibility that he had dreamed it, and knew it could have been.

"I don't want it for myself," Andronicus said, trying to keep his voice steady. "I just need to ask him a question."

"I told you," Hephaestion said, "I don't know what you're talking about."

Andronicus lunged forward before Hephaestion could react and pinned the boy against the wall, his forearm pressing into his throat. Hephaestion tried to call out, but Andronicus pressed harder, and he simply let out a small cough.

"Andronicus," Cleitus said, stepping up next to him, ready to act if Andronicus didn't let the boy go. "Enough. Release him."

"I am not playing with you, boy," Andronicus growled. "I'm going to ask Alexander about that ring, and he's going to answer me." He let Hephaestion go, and the boy fell to his knees, coughing. Cleitus grabbed Andronicus by the shoulder, and gave him a grave look, as if to say, "That was terribly stupid," but he kept his mouth shut.

"The king has taken the treasure as his own," Hephaestion said as he got to his feet, still coughing.

"I told you, boy," Andronicus said, his tone causing Hephaestion to take a step back, "I don't want it for myself. I just need to ask him a question."

"Fine then," Hephaestion said, keeping his distance from Andronicus. "Ask him your question. There was no ring anyway. Cleitus, you go too."

"Fine." Andronicus nodded, knowing he wouldn't get a better offer.

Andronicus walked into the large, illustrious

room, with Cleitus right behind him. It was truly a room for a king. The floor was made of white marble, and billowing curtains of every color were spread about the room. Many of the treasures from the night before were lying about on the floor. Alexander was lying naked in a massive bed along with two nude Persian girls and one nude Persian man, and they were all asleep.

"My king," Andronicus said, waking them all from their sleep. The Persians who had been lying with Alexander saw the two men standing there in armor and hurried out of the room without even trying to get their clothes.

"What is the meaning of this?" Alexander asked groggily as he sat up to find his bed empty. "You scared off my guests."

"Apologies, my king," Andronicus said, "but I must ask you something of great importance."

"What is it?" Alexander said, appearing to be nursing a headache of his own.

"About the ring," Andronicus said, staring into the king's peculiar eyes. They were the same blue and brown they had always been, but he felt like they had been different. *In the dream,* his mind finished for him. It couldn't have been a dream though; it had felt too real. He reminded himself that it wouldn't be the first time he had such a dream. Perhaps the ring had been part of a vision; perhaps it was something yet to come.

"What ring?" Alexander asked, sounding perfectly sincere. Andronicus just stood there, probably looking like a fool, trying to remember if it had been real or not. Cleitus stood by eyeing Andronicus carefully. The king sat in his massive bed, waiting to know why he had been woken. Eventually, his patience ran out.

"When was the last time you drank, Andronicus?" Alexander asked, rubbing his eyes.

"It's been a few years," Andronicus said, choosing not to tell Alexander about the night he had spent in Lesbos.

"And how much would you say you had to

drink last night?" Alexander asked, crawling across the bed to get some water.

"A good deal, my king," Andronicus admitted, asking himself if it had really just been a dream.

"Then do you not think it's possible you dreamed about this ring?" Alexander asked, sounding just like Aristotle. "Or perhaps you did see a ring down there. I know there were many. What made this ring so special?"

"I thought I saw something," Andronicus said, looking down at the floor.

"What do you think you saw?" Alexander asked after downing a cup of water and getting out of bed. He walked over to where his robes were and began dressing.

Andronicus's head was still pounding, but he tried to remember. It had not felt like a dream; he knew that much. All he could remember was the king holding up a shining ring. It had been bright, too bright, brighter than almost anything Andronicus had ever seen, save for one. The ring had shone with the same kind of light he had only seen once in his life, in a deep cave in the heart of a mountain.

"You were holding a ring," Andronicus said, meeting the king's eyes, "it was shining."

"Is that all?" Alexander asked, sounding annoyed again. "You saw me holding a shiny ring? Andronicus, there must have been a thousand rings in that room. Take your pick. You're welcome to have one. You've earned as much."

"It wasn't just any ring," Andronicus said, knowing how foolish he sounded. "It wasn't shiny, it was shining, with a light."

"You said I was holding it up, did you not?" Alexander asked.

"Yes," Andronicus replied, nodding slowly.

"Then it must have been reflecting the fire light," Alexander said. "It's actually quite interesting," he continued excitedly. "Aristotle taught me all about it, the light from the fire actually"

"I know how reflection works boy," Andronicus said, angry with himself rather than the king.

"Apologies, my king," he said quickly. "It was a long night, and I must have been drunker than I thought."

"Think nothing of it," Alexander said, waving his hand. "We all have those kinds of nights. Now then, you ought to get that leg of yours checked out."

"Yes," Andronicus agreed. "You're right. Thank you, Alexander, for your understanding."

6

"What's this ring about?" Cleitus asked once they were back in Andronicus's room, away from curious ears. "And what was all that about a light?"

Andronicus sighed. "It's a long story. A very long story."

"I'm a patient man," Cleitus said, sitting down. "I would like to hear this very long story."

"I can't," Andronicus said, sitting as well. "I'm sorry, but I can't tell you."

"You can't tell me?" Cleitus said, clearly offended. "I have fought beside you in battle. You would trust me with your life but not with this tale?" He made a fair point, and he wouldn't be the first man to whom Andronicus had told the truth. He trusted Cleitus as much as any man in the Macedonian army, but he still hesitated telling any man the truth. It was too dangerous.

"I know," Andronicus said, "and I do trust you, but I'm afraid this story is my life."

"Then trust me with your life, brother," Cleitus urged. "What are you afraid of? That I'll tell the king?"

"That you won't believe it, for one thing," Andronicus said, "and that you'll think I'm crazy."

"I already know you're crazy," Cleitus said. "That doesn't bother me. Is this story true?"

Andronicus nodded. "Every word of it."

"Then I'll believe it," Cleitus said. "You think you can get a lie past me?"

"If anyone can, it would be me," Andronicus said, laughing. "If I tell you this story you might know why."

"Enough preamble," Cleitus grunted. "Get on with it."

"Very well." Andronicus sighed, deciding to tell Cleitus the truth. "You probably won't believe me at first, so let me finish before you ask any questions." Cleitus nodded curtly, awaiting Andronicus's tale.

"I was born Andronicus, son of Aristocles, in the kingdom of Sparta, in the year 496 BC, though I have lived under other names in my lifetime." Cleitus stared at him intently for a long moment, and Andronicus stayed silent, giving his friend time to find the truth in his eyes. Finally, Cleitus sat back, looking at Andronicus with a mixture of awe and respect.

"I was trained to be a Spartan warrior from the age of six, until the day I marched off to war when I was sixteen," Andronicus continued. "I was one of three recruits to join King Leonidas's army, marching to defend against Xerxes's invasion . . ."

Cleitus didn't say a word as Andronicus talked. He just stared wide-eyed as Andronicus continued his tale.

7

Andronicus told Cleitus his entire life's story, right up to the ring he had thought he had seen the night before. Cleitus never interrupted once, and it still took all day to tell the whole tale. When Andronicus was finally finished, he waited anxiously for his friend to say something. Cleitus just sat there with a puzzled look on his face that Andronicus had never seen there before, as if he was deep in thought.

"So, how old are you now?" Cleitus asked finally, looking at Andronicus in awe.

"I'm one hundred and sixty-three," Andronicus replied. "This month I'll be one hundred and sixty-four."

"And this ring," Cleitus said, looking like he was thinking thoughts too complex for him, "you think it had the same kind of stone as the ones you touched?"

"I don't know," Andronicus said. "That's why I wanted to see it again. I'm sure if I see it when I'm not dead drunk, I'll be able to tell right away."

"Is it possible that you dreamed it?" Cleitus

asked. "Or that it was simply a reflection from a fire?"

Andronicus sighed. "I don't know. I guess so. It wouldn't be the first time I've had dreams that are more like visions."

"I don't think the king was lying," Cleitus said. "I saw his eyes, and they said that he doesn't remember this ring."

"I know," Andronicus agreed, knowing it was true. He had seen Alexander's eyes as well. The boy had not been lying; he truly knew nothing of the ring. It was beginning to seem more and more like it really had been a dream.

"What's it like?" Cleitus asked.

"What's what like?" Andronicus asked, looking up curiously.

"Being that old," Cleitus replied. "Not getting older, living on and on like that."

Andronicus thought about it for a moment. "It's awful," he replied after reflecting on his terribly long life. "It's awful, and it's endless."

Chapter 51
Technological Warfare
1

When Alexander and his army left Issus a week later, he let Darius's mother and daughters stay behind and keep their titles and authority in the city, under his rule, of course. Many members of the Macedonian Army thought that was bordering on treason, to let the family of the Persian king keep not only their lives but also their dignity and wealth, but a good deal of the men saw it as a kingly act, and the beginning of a great peace between Macedonia and Persia.

Andronicus wasn't sure where he stood on the matter. In truth he had given it little thought. Since the night of the battle, when he had either seen or dreamed of the ring, he had thought of little else.

Most of the women and children from Issus had been enslaved, and all the soldiers were slaughtered. A small Macedonian contingent stayed behind in the city to keep the king's peace, and the rest marched south.

Alexander only managed to march his army for three and a half days before he found a piece of land on which he wanted to build. He had the army set up camp with the nearby mountains as cover and began making plans for a new Alexandria. The next day most of the soldiers were put to work like common builders. Thousands of slaves were brought down from Issus and from the sea, and the building of a new city was quickly underway.

Andronicus had no interest in the building of a city. Normally, he would have been a great help to the king; he had studied architecture in Athens and Memphis, and he knew much of the inner workings of an immobile society, from Greek cities to African villages. Instead his thoughts were haunted by the memory of the ring he might have imagined. He had not had another drink since that night, but the memory had not cleared itself.

While Alexander went about building himself a city, and his army and slaves carried out the work, Andronicus stayed in his tent. He spent his waking hours trying to clear his thoughts, to find the truth of that night. He spent his sleeping hours desperately trying to dream of the ring again. If he could see it in a dream, he might be able to know if it had been a dream the first time as well.

No matter how much he focused his thoughts on it, no dream of the ring ever came. Instead he had the same old dreams he always had: the white mountain in the clouds, the terrible storm at sea aboard the great ship, the fire in the woods. Most often he would have the dream where he stood at the base of a great coliseum filled with cheering people. They were all fascinating dreams, ones he believed he would live one day, like he had dreamed of and then lived through the jungle and the desert, but they were not what he wanted to see.

The mysterious ring consumed his thoughts, to no avail. No matter how much time he spent thinking about it, he still wasn't even sure if it had been real. All he could remember was seeing Alexander holding a ring, and he could vaguely remember looking into Alexander's eyes and being frightened. For some reason when he concentrated hard enough on it, he felt like he could smell things that weren't there, like dirt and grass and animals.

2

The massive Macedonian army stayed put for two weeks while the king oversaw the beginnings of his new city. When Alexander was finally ready to move on, the army packed up and continued south along the coast while the slaves stayed behind to build the city, with enough soldiers to oversee them. The small coastal towns south of Issus all surrendered to Alexander without a fight. The news that Alexander had defeated Darius in battle had spread quickly, and none of the Persians wanted to engage in a fight from which their own king had fled.

The army made its way south, down the coast, without confrontation, until they reached the city of Tyre. The city was smaller than Issus and Halicarnassus, but it was much better fortified. Tyre was built on an island less than a mile from the mainland, too far to attack from the land. It had high stone walls, perfect for defending from a naval attack, and a vast navy as well. Darius had taken his army inland, to the east, and Tyre was the last coastal city held by the Persians. If the Macedonians took the city, the Persians would finally be cut off from their navy completely, and Alexander would be free to chase Darius all the way across Asia without worrying about the security of Greece.

Alexander had his army set up camp on the mainland, across from Tyre. While the army encamped on the beach, the king held a war council with his generals, and to Andronicus's surprise, he was asked to attend. It had been nearly a year since he had been invited into the king's war councils, and he didn't quite know what to make of it.

Andronicus arrived early and made sure to place himself next to Cleitus, in the rear of the great tent, where he could observe the meeting.

As all the generals filed in, Andronicus realized how much Alexander's new regime had taken over. Most of the generals around the table looked to be not much older than the king himself. There were less than a half dozen who had fought with King Philip and nearly two dozen new younger captains. Alexander had surrounded himself with people who would nod blindly whenever he spoke. The only people in the room who would dare speak the truth to the king were all across from Alexander while his friends sat at his side.

"Men," Hephaestion said once everyone had taken their seats, "as you know, the city of Tyre is the last true coastal threat to our invasion. Once we take it, Darius will be completely cut off from his navy."

"How do you hope to take this city?" Antigenes, one of the few older generals left, asked, making sure not to sound insulting. "It's as well fortified as any city I've ever seen."

"Truly," Cassander agreed, rising from his seat next to the king. "The only way to attack the city is a siege from the sea, and we don't have the ships to undertake such an endeavor."

"There must be a way," Alexander said from his great throne, looking out at his generals. "We have ten times as many men, we have enough siege weapons to take a city twice that size, and we have them cut off from the mainland."

"If the city was closer to the mainland, perhaps we could lay a siege, but this city was planned well, my king," Parmenion said from his place directly across from Alexander. "There is no way to get our men close enough."

"Why not?" Cassander asked, "We don't have to get all the way up to their walls, just close enough to attack."

"What are you suggesting?" Alexander asked.

"Building some kind of dock," Cassander replied, "big enough to bring our siege weapons closer to the city."

"We don't need to build a dock," Ptolemy pointed out excitedly. "There's a strip of land leading right up to the city. The water is only five feet deep, we could build a land bridge all the way up to their walls."

"Could this be done?" Alexander asked, looking at Parmenion.

"Aye," Parmenion agreed, nodding slowly. "I dare say it might, my king."

"Have men begin laying the foundations immediately," Hephaestion said to someone behind him, who promptly left the tent. The meeting droned on a while longer, but the plan to build a bridge was the only matter of importance.

3

The causeway, the land bridge, the dock, it took on many names, and it took many months to build. If it had been made of wood, it would have been done much faster, but that was not Alexander's way. The king made sure his causeway was built of stone, and was sturdy enough to guarantee the security of anyone who walked along it. The first three hundred yards were built easily enough, over the course of several months, and then they fell within range of the archers lining the walls of Tyre, as well as the Tyrian navy not far off the coast.

Rather than trying to build any farther under the rain of fire, Alexander had two great siege towers constructed at the end of the bridge. The towers took another three months to build. Nearly fifty men died from arrows as they built the towers, and twice as many were wounded, but when the towers were finished, they were truly something to behold. Each tower stood 150 feet high with great catapults on top, and heavy ballistae at their base. The towers were made of strong wood, but to ensure they could not be burnt by the flaming arrows raining down from the walls, Parmenion had the men cover the front of each tower in rawhide.

Once the great towers were completed, they began bombarding the eastern wall of Tyre around the clock. The large catapults atop the towers threw huge flaming rocks, while the ballistae fired giant flaming spears. After one day of the barrage, the arrows stopped coming from the walls. By the third day, the walls appeared to be abandoned, and the Tyrian navy had moved to the far side of the city. Alexander was sure that victory was in hand.

4

On the fourth day of the bombardment, there had been no sign of the Tyrians for a day and a half. Andronicus stood on the stone causeway not far from where the two great siege towers were launching their constant onslaught on the city walls. Cleitus stood beside him, and the two men watched in silence as the great towers barraged the city. It truly was something to behold, a true spectacle of technological warfare.

All of a Sudden, a horn blew from the top of the left tower. Both men looked up and saw a lookout pointing out to sea. They turned to see a ship sailing around the city walls. It was a fairly large ship, likely some kind of transport vessel, and it was moving fast. Andronicus saw only one man aboard, steering her straight toward the towers. The entire deck of the ship, save for where the lone man stood, was aflame. The ship's nose stuck absurdly high out of the water, as if it were weighted down in the back. As the burning ship sailed closer to the bridge, Andronicus saw what looked like barrel drums hanging from the mast, which was also aflame.

The men in the towers shot hundreds of arrows down at the ship as it approached, but there was no one to hit. The man who had been steering jumped off the stern and swam back toward the city. Before the ship reached the bridge, men inside the towers began jumping out into the water.

Andronicus and Cleitus watched helplessly as the burning ship crashed into the left tower. There was a horrible splintering of wood from the ship and the tower, followed by a massive explosion. Andronicus actually saw the first barrel fall, and saw the fiery blast that erupted from the base of the tower. The first explosion was followed by a second, much bigger one, and Andronicus and Cleitus were both knocked onto their backs. Wood and splinters rained down all around them, much of it aflame.

Andronicus looked up just as the left tower collapsed onto the burning ship. As the giant burning tower crumbled into the water, Andronicus could hear the screams of the men inside. The right tower was also aflame, and flaming men were leaping out into the water, thrashing about as the flames charred their skin.

Andronicus got to his feet, as did Cleitus, and they ran toward the burning tower. When they got there, they saw that the tower's base was fully engulfed. Huge, billowing flames roared all around the tower, and there was no way to get to the men trapped inside. The top of the tower was on fire as well, but Andronicus saw men leaping off the tower into the water far below.

Another horn blew out, this time from behind Andronicus. He whipped around to see the entire Tyrian navy sailing straight at them. There were at least two dozen ships, none of them empty or burning. Each ship carried at least a hundred men, ready to fight. Andronicus looked back and saw most of the men on the causeway already running for shore. All the way up the stone bridge however, was nearly all of the Macedonian army's siege equipment.

Andronicus turned to Cleitus, and they drew their swords simultaneously as the first ships made contact with the bridge. Persians and Tyrians alike stormed onto the causeway, engaging the few Macedonians who had remained to fight. Andronicus and Cleitus ran past the first bunch of men unnoticed and made it about fifty feet before a dozen men jumped from the nearest ship and ran toward them.

Shouts were everywhere, and up and down the causeway the wooden siege weapons were being set ablaze. The two skilled warriors fought the group of Tyrians until only two were left, both of whom promptly leapt into the water to escape their wrath. There were almost no Macedonians left on the bridge, and most of the Tyrians were busy destroying the siege weapons, so Andronicus and Cleitus were able to make their way quickly down the bridge, stopping to fight only when necessary.

They both had to kill many Tyrians, but eventually they made it back to the shore. As soon as they felt the sand beneath their feet, Alexander ran up to them. Andronicus and Cleitus fell to their knees, coughing profusely from all the smoke they had inhaled. They were both covered in blood and soot, but neither was badly wounded.

"What happened?" Alexander shouted, getting down next to them.

"The Tyrians," Andronicus said between coughs, sending dark phlegm across the sand. "They sent . . . a burning ship." Andronicus collapsed into a fit of coughing, and someone handed him a jug of water.

"What do you mean?" Alexander sounded as if he could not fathom that he had been beaten. "How could one ship have set fire to those towers? It's not possible."

"Oil drums," Cleitus answered, having finally stopped coughing. "They hung oil drums from the mast and set the deck ablaze."

"They even weighted down the rear of the ship, so the bow stuck up in the air," Andronicus added once he had regained his composure. "When it hit the tower, the whole thing burst into flames."

"I saw the explosion," Cassander said, approaching them. "I've never seen anything like it."

"Are the towers truly lost?" Alexander asked, sounding both remorseful and furious.

"Yes, my king," Hephaestion replied.

"And the siege weapons?"

"Gone, my king," Hephaestion said.

"All of them?" Alexander asked, looking ill.

"I'm afraid so," Cassander said.

"Have the men retake the bridge and put out the fires," Alexander said as he glared down the causeway, "and tell the generals I'm convening a war council immediately."

5

"I'm afraid the city is lost, my king,"

Parmenion said to Alexander, surrounded by the same members of the war council from six months earlier. "The towers were an excellent idea, and the causeway still stands strong," he added, trying to be optimistic, "but we have lost nearly all of our siege weapons. We simply cannot continue to lay siege to this city. We must abandon it before we lose any more men."

"I believe Parmenion is right, Alexander," Cassander said. "There's just no way we can continue, and every day we spend waiting to take this city, Darius grows stronger."

"I will not abandon the siege," Alexander said, glaring around at his doubting followers. "I have never lost a battle in my life. I have defeated the likes of Memnon and Darius both. I will not be beaten by a bunch of fishermen."

Andronicus had to stifle a laugh at the king's words. He spoke as if he had been fighting for years. The part about beating Memnon left a particularly sour taste in his mouth. He had been both clever and creative in killing Memnon, and Alexander took credit for it as if it were his own doing.

"The towers were truly magnificent, Alexander," Antigenes said, "but we can't rebuild them. It would take too much time, and the wreckage is still lying at the edge of the causeway."

"When we first reached this city, you told me that it could only be taken by sea," Alexander said, eyeing each member of his council in turn.

"That we did, my king," Parmenion agreed. "I wish it had not proven to be true, but it has. The city simply can't be taken by land."

"Then let us take it by sea," Alexander said, rising to his feet, "as we should have from the start."

"Alexander, we don't have enough ships to lay siege to a city that size," Parmenion said, sounding like he was trying hard not to yell, "especially not with the Tyrian navy resting offshore."

"What if we did have the ships?" Alexander asked, looking at them all for answers.

"What are you talking about?" Antigenes asked.

"When we last convened over our plans for the attack of Tyre, a full accounting of our new assets from our recently conquered cities had not yet been taken."

"What are you saying?" Cassander asked.

"It turns out there were over thirty ships at the port of Issus," Alexander said with a sly smile, "and twenty more at Sidon and two dozen more from the rest of the little towns we took. In addition, Ionia has sent me twenty ships at my urgent request."

"And there are the Cyprians as well," Ptolemy added with a big grin. Everyone eyed him curiously as he continued. "The king of Cyprus sent us a message. He wishes to join our cause, and he's sending one hundred and twenty ships at once."

"Why have you not told us this until now?" Parmenion demanded. "Why did we build those damned towers if you knew you had so many ships on the way?"

"How I choose to run my war is my own business, Parmenion," Alexander said sternly. "You would do well to remember it."

"And you would do well to remember that you are still a boy," Parmenion shot back, "and that I was leading your father's armies before you were born."

"My father is dead, old man," Alexander said, giving Parmenion a frightening looking glare with his mismatched eyes. "I am the king now, and there's no one here to protect you. The only reason you're still alive is because of your skill in commanding battles."

"And the only reason you're alive is because your father made sure to hire men who could protect you," Parmenion spat back. "If all you had was your friends to protect you, you would have died back in Greece."

"You go too far, old man," Alexander shouted, slamming his hands on the table and jumping to his feet. Parmenion rose as well, as did his sons. A second later Alexander and his friends had their swords drawn, and Parmenion and his sons had their swords drawn as well. For a moment it looked as though the leaders of the greatest empire on earth were going to attack each other like wild animals. Andronicus and

Cleitus moved in quickly, as did a dozen other clear-headed men, and they managed to separate everyone who meant to fight.

Andronicus dragged Parmenion out of the tent, with Cleitus dragging Philotas right behind him. Once they were outside, Parmenion began to calm down, but Philotas looked like he wanted to go back in and kill every man inside. Andronicus stepped between him and the tent and glared at the boy until he put his sword down and walked over to his father.

"You can't speak to the king like that," Andronicus said once everyone had calmed down. "He'll have you killed."

"Let him kill me then," Parmenion said. "The way he runs this army I'll be dead soon anyway."

"How can you defend him?" Philotas asked, turning on Andronicus. "You were on that bridge. You could have been killed. He knew the whole time that he had two hundred ships on the way, and he still had those idiotic towers built!"

Andronicus didn't say anything. There was nothing he could say. Philotas was right, Alexander had almost gotten him killed. He had gotten some three hundred men killed in those towers, and he had known he had a whole navy sailing this way. There was no reason to continue the siege from the bridge except for arrogance, or possibly impatience, and both were inexcusable reasons in Andronicus's mind.

"I don't think I can follow that boy any longer, Andronicus," Parmenion said. "My sons must stay to fight, but I am old and tired, and I don't owe him anything."

"You're not old, my friend, believe me," Andronicus said, thinking of his own age. "And one thing the king said in there holds true. You're still the best battle commander we have, and we will need you when we meet the Persians again. We've nearly got them beat, but there's at least one more real battle to come before Darius falls. You know that, and if you're not there to command the infantry, we'll likely fail, and you know that too."

"Andronicus is right, Father," Philotas agreed.

"Alexander may not ever give you the glory you deserve, but it's still you who held the lines at Granicus and Issus. You must see this thing through, as must we all."

"As must we all," Andronicus agreed "until the Persians are done. Then let the boy do whatever he wants with his army. Our job is to make sure a Persian army never dares set foot on Greek soil again, and we're going to see it through."

"Fine then." Parmenion sighed reluctantly, sounding old. "I'll stay until Darius is dead, and then I'm going back to Greece, where I belong."

6

Within two weeks of the disastrous defeat on the bridge, all of Alexander's new ships arrived and surrounded the city of Tyre. Over two hundred ships closed in on the city, trapping the Tyrian navy at port. The siege began from the sea, with Nikanor and Cassander in command. Andronicus watched from the shore along with the king and most of the army. The Tyrians fought bravely, much more so than any other city had thus far, but they were outnumbered four to one. Every day the Tyrians lost at least three ships, and the Macedonians pushed farther in.

Nikanor had five ships armed with battering rams, and he sailed them toward the walls, only to find there were stone pillars beneath the water. The Tyrians had set them there hundreds of years before, specifically to defend against such an attack. Nikanor had the men tie massive ropes around two of the underwater pillars and then attached them to five of the largest ships. They destroyed the bows of two ships in the process, but eventually they managed to tip the pillars over, and the battering ships were able to sail right up to the wall.

Once the ships were anchored against the south side of the city walls, huge battering rams swung from the masts of the ships, pounding at the high stone wall. They worked steadily at breaking through the stone for two days before the Tyrians made one final attempt to fight back. Their entire navy, less than twenty ships by that time, sailed out to fight the Macedonians one last time. Most of the ships were brought down before they even managed to reach the Macedonians, and the few that weren't didn't last long before they were taken.

Once the Tyrians' navy was destroyed and their walls breached, Cassander's men were able to take the city easily. The Macedonians lost only four hundred men over the five-month siege, and yet it had been the closest they had come to being defeated. Most of the Tyrian soldiers were slaughtered right away. As for the ones who had been on top of the wall, some two thousand in total, Alexander had them crucified on the beach for all to see. The rest of the people of Tyre were sold into slavery. Alexander only left about three thousand people from the city there. He brought in thousands of slaves from other cities and had them begin building him a new arsenal of siege weapons to replace the ones that had been burnt.

The army moved into the city, but only stayed for three days before leaving. They had spent more than five months trying to take the city, and everyone was eager to get back to the real task at hand. They moved south after Tyre, to the southernmost reaches of the Persian Empire. There were no towns or cities that could put up any kind of resistance until they reached Egypt. Andronicus wasn't sure how he felt about returning to Egypt, or the circumstances under which he was returning, and he hoped there would be no one left there who might remember him.

Chapter 52
Full Circle
1

It was exactly forty years since Andronicus had last been in Egypt. Back then he had been fleeing Memphis as a fugitive suspected of witchcraft. Now he was a member of a royal guard to an emperor intending to take Egypt as his own. It felt odd to be back, almost as if he still wasn't welcome. The army marched along the coast from Asia Minor into Egypt, taking all the villages and towns by the sea as they went. Andronicus had been much further inland when he left Egypt, but the land still had a familiarity to it.

When he first heard the language again, for the first time in decades, he couldn't make out the words. It took him a while before he could understand the language again. It made him wonder if he would be able to speak Swihmehe if he had to. He thought that he had spoken it often enough with Chaka to always remember it, but he wasn't sure anymore. It made him curious, the way his mind took time to remember a language he had spoken for more than twenty years.

Most of the towns along the Egyptian coast accepted Alexander as nothing short of a liberator. It seemed that the Egyptian people had not grown to love Darius as their ruler, and were more than ready to give Alexander a chance. The only city in Egypt to try and repel Alexander was the ancient city of Gaza. It had high stone walls and was positioned well by the sea.

The siege weapons that would have been used to bombard the city walls and give the army entry had all been burned at Tyre, and the new ones Alexander had ordered built, weren't ready yet. While the bulk of the army encamped surrounding the city, Alexander had a large group of soldiers begin building a dirt mound on the south side of the wall. At the same time he ordered a siege tower be raised.

Within two weeks the dirt mounds had risen twenty feet, and a sturdy siege tower stood atop them. The Gazans had barely put up any resistance to the construction occurring outside their walls. Then one day they launched a small attack, hurling stones and arrows down from the walls, catching everyone by surprise.

Alexander was overseeing the building at the time and was struck by a stone. He received a small gash on his shoulder and a dent in his armor, and he was livid. The next day more siege weapons arrived from Tyre, and Alexander was able to take the city before nightfall. He likely would have been more merciful to them if he hadn't been injured, but the fact that he had been hit in full sight of his men meant he had to react. He had every man over the age of sixteen executed, and then sold the women and children into slavery. Many thought it was too harsh a punishment, but none would dare say it in front of the king or his men.

2

After leaving Gaza, Alexander marched his army straight to Memphis, Andronicus's former home. When they first came in view of the great city, Andronicus felt a rush of emotions. He had spent over twenty years there, the first years after Chaka died. In many ways his time in Memphis was one of the major turning points in his long life. He knew that likely no one would be left to recognize him, and even if they did, they would be called crazy if they told anyone. Believing a man accused of being a sorcerer had returned after forty years, looking exactly the same as when he left sounded insane, even though it was true.

The Macedonian army entered the city to a spectacular celebration from the Egyptian people. Andronicus recognized it at once; he had seen such celebrations in Memphis on two occasions, both after the naming of a new pharaoh. The Egyptians treated Alexander and his generals and noblemen to a great feast. While everyone else enjoyed the food and wine and the many glorious things about Egypt, Andronicus walked through the streets alone toward the old temple he had once called home.

The bald priest who greeted him at the door saw his armor and hurriedly let him in. The priest led Andronicus to the great library, where he had spent so much of his time. Andronicus walked down the aisles of scrolls, looking for the ones he had read. To his surprise he had only read about half of the things he saw, and he had to wonder if what he had been looking for was still there in that great room.

"You are with the great king Alexander's army, yes?" a voice asked from behind Andronicus. He turned to see an older bald priest standing there. The man looked intelligent, and he reminded Andronicus of Horus, the high priest when he first arrived in Egypt. This priest, however, was eyeing Andronicus like he was a rabid dog.

"I'm with myself, friend," Andronicus answered in perfect Egyptian, causing the priest to do a rather comical double take, "but I did come here with the king's army."

"How is it you have come to speak our language so quickly?" the priest asked more politely, approaching Andronicus.

"I lived in this city once," Andronicus said, looking up at the shelves and shelves of scrolls, "a long time ago."

"Oh, really," the priest said, sounding a bit suspicious now. "We have not had many Greeks living here until quite recently. What was it that brought you to our city?"

"A series of accidents, really," Andronicus said, more to himself than to the priest, "a series of accidents and deaths."

"Deaths, whose deaths?" the priest asked, feigning concern.

"A great many people," Andronicus said, finally looking over at the priest.

The man's inquisitive expression quickly turned to apprehension. He looked away from Andronicus's stern gaze and fumbled with his collar for a moment. "My apologies, my lord," he said with a bow. "I didn't mean to impose. I only want to make sure this library is protected."

"You have nothing to worry about from me," Andronicus said. "I've probably spent more time in this room than any of you."

The priest gave him an odd look, and looked like he was about to contradict Andronicus but thought better of it. Instead he nodded and gave another bow, then turned and left Andronicus alone again.

Andronicus knew he couldn't stay in the temple much longer. Soon enough he would have the high priest and half a dozen others following him around making sure he wasn't a threat to the library.

He was about to leave the temple, but then he decided to go and see his old room first. It wasn't hard to find. Nothing had changed about the temple save for the people, and he had walked those halls for twenty-six years. When he came to his old door, he found it shut, a faint flicker of a light coming from underneath. He considered knocking, disturbing whomever was in his room, but what would he say? That he had lived there once, and it had been his room? What if the man living there now had been there for the last twenty years? Then what would he say?

In the end he merely put his hand on the door. He felt a sense of peace, of connecting pieces of a giant puzzle as he held his hand on the door that had once been his own. The wood felt old, like him, except that it was beginning to rot, and he still showed no signs of anything like that. When he finally removed his hand from the door, it was like letting go of that piece of his life, and he left with no regrets.

3

Despite his best efforts, Andronicus couldn't stay away from the library. He had spent so many years there, and yet there were hundreds of scrolls he hadn't read. While Alexander and his generals dealt with the regime change of the Egyptian people, Andronicus sat in the old library, reading the old language he hadn't seen in years. The priests came and went, eyeing him oddly, but not really paying him any mind. Andronicus was reading an ancient scroll that told of the evacuation of Troy when he heard someone walk up behind him.

"Is it really you?" a croaky old voice asked. Andronicus turned around to see a short, fat old man standing there with wide teary eyes. Andronicus stood up, wondering what this old fool wanted, and then abruptly sat back down. He hadn't recognized him at first, but he knew this fat old priest, or at least he once had.

"Im?" Andronicus said, staring into the old man's eyes as he finally recognized his old friend. "Is that you?"

"I always knew you would come back," Imhotep said, stepping forward and hugging Andronicus. Andronicus hugged him back, not believing his eyes. He hadn't even considered that Imhotep could still be alive.

"How?" was all Andronicus managed to ask. "How are you still here? I mean, how are you still alive? You must be a hundred years old."

"What, you're the only one who gets to live to one hundred?" Imhotep said with a short laugh. Andronicus couldn't believe that his fat little friend had grown so old. He looked much older than he had forty years earlier, but not as old as he really was. It reminded him of the way Chaka had stopped aging, and his mind began racing with new questions.

"No, I just . . . I had no idea you were still here. I thought everyone I knew here would be dead."

"Well, everyone else is," Imhotep said sadly. "I watched them all go, one by one, and now it's just me—and you," he added with a laugh.

"What happened to you after I left?" Andronicus asked, fearing the answer. Imhotep sighed, then turned away for a moment.

"It was very hard for the first few years," he said, sitting on the bench across from Andronicus. "The other priests thought I had helped you, but they couldn't prove it." Imhotep broke into a big grin. "But as the priests from those days died off, one by one, and new young priests came in, I gained a bit of clout." His grin stretched even wider, and he rocked merrily from side to side. "I was the high priest for twenty-two years, but they made me step down when I turned ninety-five."

"You look good for your age," Andronicus said.

"Ha!" Imhotep barked. "I look like an old frog. You look good for your age. How old are you now, one hundred and sixty?"

"One hundred and sixty four," Andronicus said with a faint smile.

"And what about you then?" Imhotep asked excitedly. "I've been right here where you left me, reading all these scrolls, but what about you? Where have you been since you left?"

"I went back to Sparta first," Andronicus said, shaking his head sadly in response to Imhotep's excited look. "There was nothing for me there, but I stayed a long time anyway. I went into a dark place for many years." Andronicus lowered his eyes. He wasn't sure how much he really wanted to tell his old friend, who clearly still looked up to him very much. "It got to where I was drunk all day," Andronicus continued, causing Imhotep to frown. "When I left Sparta, I went to Athens. I met some very smart people there. That was a better time than Sparta was, but I was still lost. Then a friend of mine, a man named Aristotle, he helped me get me back on my way and helped me get in with King Alexander."

"What is your job in the king's army?" Imhotep asked.

"I'm one of the king's bodyguards. I also helped teach him how to fight when he was a boy."

Imhotep laughed. "I should have known. Is he a good king then? Like they say."

"He can be," Andronicus sighed, thinking about Alexander. "He's still too young to be king, but there's no helping that."

Imhotep laughed. "Sure there is. You're doing it."

Andronicus eyed him curiously. "What are you talking about?"

"If the king is too young, then he needs to get older," Imhotep said, barely containing his smile. "That's your job, isn't it?" Imhotep erupted into a fit of giggles and began rocking back and forth.

"Aye, I suppose that's true." Andronicus smiled, amused at the jolly old man his friend had become.

"When are you leaving again?" Imhotep asked, his laughter fading.

Andronicus shrugged. "I don't know, not long probably. We still need to finish off the Persians, and Alexander won't want to wait long."

The two old friends continued chatting for a

long time. Eventually Imhotep had to go to bed. He left Andronicus in the library, amazed that he was still alive and also extremely curious as to how. He knew that normal people could live to be that old, but Andronicus was certain he had affected him somehow.

4

Memphis was one of the oldest and biggest cities in the world. It had been the capital of the Egyptian Empire since time out of mind. Yet it wasn't enough for Alexander. Not a week after arriving in Memphis, the king, now the pharaoh as well, proclaimed that he would build Egypt a new city. Of course he named it Alexandria, as he named all of his cities, yet he promised before the gods that this Alexandria would be the greatest of them all.

He had the finest minds from all over his empire sail to Memphis to aid in the construction. Among these minds was, of course, Aristotle. He arrived a week after the army and was greeted and feasted by the king personally. Later that night, after the king had gone off to have his fun, Andronicus took Aristotle to the great temple. The bald priest who manned the door at the temple had gotten used to Andronicus's visits over the past week and greeted them cordially despite the late hour.

Andronicus led Aristotle to the great library, and the two men fell upon the scrolls like children. The high priest arrived to see who was in his library so late at night. Aristotle introduced himself, and it turned out the high priest had heard of him. Aristotle had to listen politely to the man until he finally left them alone. Once the high priest was gone, they spent the next two hours walking down the aisles, pointing out some of the most important and influential texts in the world.

"You spent how many years here?" Aristotle asked as he sat down, looking up at the high shelves.

"Just over twenty-five years," Andronicus answered. "The longest I've ever stayed anywhere."

"Really?" Aristotle seemed surprised. "Not even in your youth? Your true youth, I mean."

"Technically, I lived in Sparta from when I was born until I left at age twenty-nine," Andronicus replied, "but I spent a year and a half away at war when I was sixteen."

"And you never left Memphis during your stay here?" Aristotle asked.

Andronicus shook his head. "No. I didn't leave until they were literally ready to kill me. I think I was scared of moving on without Chaka."

"That's when you started drinking, is it not?" Aristotle asked.

"Yes," Andronicus replied, "and then I spent who knows how many years drinking myself into madness. If you hadn't saved me, I would be passed out in some ditch right now, stinking of wine and piss."

"I merely helped you on your journey," Aristotle insisted. "You saved yourself."

"I wouldn't have," Andronicus said seriously, "not without you to remind me."

"Remind you of what?" Aristotle asked, raising an inquisitive brow.

"Of what I'm meant to do," Andronicus said, meeting Aristotle's gaze. It was the first time he had ever actually said the words, and as soon as he did, he knew they were the truth.

"You mean change the world?" Aristotle asked, looking surprised.

"No," Andronicus said, shaking his head. "Maybe someday it will be my duty to change things, but that's not what I have to do now."

"What are you meant to do then?" Aristotle asked, puzzled and yet clearly intrigued.

"Find them," Andronicus whispered.

"What was that?" Aristotle asked, leaning forward.

"I have to find them," Andronicus said, looking up at the high shelves. Repeating Chaka's last words filled him with sorrow and remorse, but also with determination, the kind he hadn't felt in a long time.

"Find who?" Aristotle asked.

"The answers," Andronicus said, a single tear rolling down his face. He quickly wiped it away. "To my questions. I suppose I never mentioned them before. I don't like talking about it much; they're just too bizarre, but I still think about them."

"What are your questions?" Aristotle asked, leaning forward on his elbows.

"What were those rocks?" Andronicus asked, turning back to Aristotle. "What did they show me? How did I wake up in Africa? Why did I wake up in Africa? Where is my brother? Where are my friends? Are they still alive like I am? How am I still alive? Why am I still young? Why do people who get close to me stay young? Where are those rocks now? What do the dreams mean? What does any of it mean?"

With each question Andronicus' voice became louder and more powerful, until he was practically shouting. He slowly rose to his feet, and proclaimed his questions to the library itself. When he was done, he looked down at Aristotle, panting slightly.

"Gods," Aristotle said, "I've studied and ratified some of the most progressive ideas in the world. I've spoken at great length with most of the greatest minds alive today, and I've never heard anything like that. I wish you had told me about your questions years ago, I could have tried to help you figure some of them out."

"I was lost," Andronicus said, feeling a new kind of energy coursing through his body, "first in books, then in wine, and now in war, but I'm done with all that. It's time for me to get back to work."

"You mean you're going to leave Alexander's army?" Aristotle asked, sounding shocked.

"Not yet," Andronicus replied. "I still have at least one more battle to fight beside the king."

"You mean you have to see the Persian king fall first?" Aristotle asked, sitting back in his chair.

"I didn't join the army to follow a boy or to make the Macedonians the rulers of the world," Andronicus said. "I joined to fight the Persians, to finish something I started a long time ago. When Darius is dead, and his empire has crumbled, I will leave Alexander."

"Where will you go?"

"East, I suppose," Andronicus answered after a moment's thought. "The Gauls and the Celts lie to the north and west, and I've already been south. No one knows what lies to the far east, and I would very much like to know."

"I wish I could be waiting for you when you return, to hear all about it, but I fear I will likely be long dead when you find your way back to Greece."

"You never know," Andronicus said with a wan smile, though he knew it was probably true. Seeing Imhotep again gave him hope, but he knew it could be a very long time before he returned to Greece. It dawned on him then that this could very well be the last time he ever saw Aristotle. He had been a truly great friend and had helped Andronicus when he needed it most. He was almost certainly the smartest man Andronicus had ever met, and he had to wonder if he always would be.

"Promise me something," Aristotle said, meeting Andronicus's eyes again. "Promise me that someday, after you've answered some of your questions, that you'll make your mark on the world."

"I've already made my mark on the world, friend," Andronicus said, thinking of Memnon and Amyntas.

"You know what I mean," Aristotle insisted. "Promise me that someday you'll use your gift for something good."

"OK," Andronicus said after a long pause. "Someday."

The two men sat in silence for a long time, looking up at all the old scrolls, some of them thousands of years old. When they finally left the great temple and they made their way back to where the noblemen were staying, the sun was beginning to rise. Andronicus said his final farewell to Aristotle. The two men embraced, and Aristotle began to cry.

"You've been given a gift, Andronicus of Sparta," Aristotle said through his tears, "not a curse. You have a long journey ahead of you, and at the end of it, you'll see."

"See what?" Andronicus asked, desperate for

the answer, any answer.

"I have no idea," Aristotle said with a laugh. "Maybe nothing, maybe everything. I'm afraid it's not for me to know."

"Goodbye, my friend," Andronicus said as they released each other. "I hope I'll see you again someday, in this world or another."

"I would offer to wait for you," Aristotle said with a smile, "but I think it might be a very long time."

5

Before the army left the city, Andronicus went to see Imhotep one last time. He found him in the library, humming to himself while reading an old scroll. Andronicus sat across from him, and Imhotep broke into a big grin when he looked up.

"Andronicus," he said, setting the scroll aside, "I still can't believe you're here. You know, you really do look exactly the same. It's only your eyes; they look older."

"We're setting out tomorrow morning, Im," Andronicus said. "I don't think I'll be coming back this way for a very long time. I think this will be the last time I see you, old friend."

"I know," Imhotep said, still smiling brightly. "I'm just happy I got to see you again. I always knew you were telling the truth, but it's one thing to hear it and another to see it."

"The same goes for you," Andronicus said, laughing. "I can't believe you're still alive. If I had known I would have come back sooner."

"You were where you were meant to be," Imhotep said, rocking back and forth again, "and I've been right where I was meant to be."

"I'm glad things turned out so well for you," Andronicus said, smiling.

"I don't mean I was meant to be here for me," Imhotep said, still rocking lightly. "I mean I was meant to be here for you."

"What do you mean?" Andronicus asked, eyeing his old friend.

"I never stopped the search, you know,"

Imhotep said. "I've read every scroll in this room."

"You read all of these?" Andronicus asked, looking around in surprise.

"Every single one," Im said, chuckling. "And I found it."

"You found what?" Andronicus asked, feeling his heart race as he leaned forward.

"I found the man with the marks on his arms," Imhotep said, "the one who was looking for Troy."

"What do you mean you found him?" Andronicus asked, barely able to contain himself. "Where is he? Who is he? Is he still out there?"

Imhotep shook his head. "I don't know, but I know he made it to Troy. He lived there for at least twenty years, like you did here. He was a priest, and then one day he vanished and was never seen again."

"How do you know this?" Andronicus asked.

"Here," Imhotep said, bringing out an ancient scroll. "I hid it away years ago in case you ever came back." He handed it to Andronicus, who took it with trembling hands. He thought about opening it and reading it right then but decided not to. He looked up at Imhotep, who was beaming again and still rocking gently.

"You are a true friend, Im," Andronicus said, fighting back tears.

"And you are the greatest friend I've ever had," Imhotep said. "Now don't you forget about me when you turn one thousand." He broke into a fit of giggles, and Andronicus chuckled as well. They sat a while longer, reminiscing about the old days, until Imhotep got tired and went off to bed. Andronicus bade him a final farewell and then left the temple for the last time. He was eager to read the scroll that Im had given him but decided to let it wait. He needed to stay focused on the Persians, at least until the war was done. Andronicus knew that day was fast approaching. The scroll could wait until then.

Chapter 53
The Battle of the Kings of Asia
1

Alexander insisted on building his new city from the ground up, making it truly his own. After a week of conferring with his engineers and architects, it was decided that the best possible place for the massive new city would be on the site of a small fishing village north of Memphis. Alexander could have had the villagers killed, and no one would have dared speak against it, but instead he let them live and gave them each gold enough to buy a new home in his new city of Alexandria. It was unusual for Alexander to be so merciful, but Andronicus just chalked it up to a byproduct of having his old teacher around.

The old village was destroyed, and the construction of a grand new city began. Egypt already had thousands of slaves ready to work, but Alexander had tens of thousands more shipped in to commence work on his newest Alexandria. Alexander left a man named Dinocrates as the head architect of the city while he prepared his army to move east again. Three thousand soldiers stayed behind to keep the peace in Egypt, and the rest of the army moved on, heading east, after Darius and the last of the Persian army.

2

The army marched out of Egypt and into Mesopotamia. When Andronicus had last traveled through the lands east of Egypt, he had done so mostly at night, far from roads or towns. Now, riding at the head of a great army, he was able to properly take in the land for the first time. There was the occasional mountain, but for the most part it was just desert. It was not nearly as arid as the heart of the Great Desert, but it was still terribly dry.

It took months for the army to make its way gradually east, and each day dozens of men fell from heatstroke. They had clear supply lines running from both Gaza and Tyre, but there still wasn't enough water for the nearly fifty thousand men. As they neared the ancient city of Babylon, where Darius was waiting with his army, Alexander called together another war council of all his generals.

A great tent was erected in the sand, with a throne for Alexander at its head. Dozens of men attended the meeting, far more than any other council Alexander had ever held. Everyone from the members of the old guard and their kin to newer largely unknown captains who had proven themselves recently in combat, and, of course, the members of Alexander's close inner circle were in attendance. Andronicus took his usual spot in a shadowy corner beside Cleitus.

"Generals," Alexander called out, silencing the room at once, "captains, noblemen of Macedonia, you all know why I have called this council."

"You have decided to accept Darius's sue for peace!" Antigenes shouted, and everyone broke into raucous laughter.

"So, you know that Darius has sued for peace?" Alexander said once the laughter died down. "Do you all know what he has offered in return for my surrender?"

"No," many voices called out together.

"Then I shall tell you," Alexander shouted to a chorus of cheers and stomping feet. "After we crushed him at Issus, Darius sent word to me demanding that I release all the slaves I took, leave his lands, and pay him a tribute for the men I killed." Alexander paused for a moment while his audience shouted obscenities at the notion of surrender.

"Then," Alexander continued, "he sent another envoy after we took Tyre from him. He did not demand so much that time." Another wave of laughter rippled through the crowd. "He offered me all the land west of the Halys River, a ransom for all the slaves we took, and a marriage to his eldest daughter." Again the room erupted into booming laughter. Andronicus couldn't help but join in. The idea that the Persian king had offered his own daughter to Alexander showed how desperate he was to avoid another battle.

"Not long after we left Alexandria, Darius sent me a third offer," Alexander said with a smile. "This time, he offered me all the lands west of the

Euphrates. He also said I may retain my title as king of Asia Minor and that we may be corulers of a great empire. He also offered me thirty thousand pieces of silver and the hand of any or all of his daughters. What do you think I should say to the great king Darius?" Alexander asked, basking in the shouts of fury from his men.

"You should accept!" a voice shouted, cutting through the racket and causing everyone to fall silent. Everyone looked over to see Parmenion standing across from the king, a dire expression on his face, and his sons at his side.

"What was that, old man?" Alexander asked, the laughter leaving his face. "I thought you just said I should accept Darius's offer of peace."

"That's exactly what I said," Parmenion replied, staring at the king.

"Traitor!" someone called out.

"Coward!" another voice shouted. The next second a cascade of insults pummeled Parmenion from all sides.

"Enough!" Alexander shouted, silencing the room. "Why would I ever accept his offer?"

"So we can go home to Greece where we belong," Parmenion said. "No more men need to die. You've beaten him, Alexander, we don't need to go any further."

"Are you truly so afraid, Parmenion?" Hephaestion sneered from beside Alexander. "You who would claim credit for defeating Darius at Issus?"

"I would never claim credit for any battle," Parmenion said. "The victory lies with all who fought and died. Thousands of Greek men have already died for your cause, Alexander, and you have won. Turn back, and let your men live in peace and prosperity." There was a soft murmur of agreement as many of the men considered Parmenion's words.

"What if we do make peace with the Persians" Alexander asked, "and we live without ever fighting them again? And then one hundred years go by, and then two hundred, and suddenly the Persians have forgotten our peace. Then an army of Persians will once again set foot on Greek soil. On that day it would be your fault Greek women and children would be raped and slaughtered." Another murmur of agreement met this, and a few men stomped their feet or pounded on the table. "No," Alexander continued once the din died down, "we must go on and finish them, so they will never again come to our lands. There can be only one king of Asia, Parmenion. I defeated the great king, I liberated the great cities of Issus and Memphis, and I broke the ancient knot at Gordium. I am destined to be the king of Asia, and I will not stop until Darius is dead."

"You would let thousands die, so that you can call yourself king?" Parmenion asked, eyeing Alexander with something like disgust. "Darius has gathered his entire army, more than one hundred thousand men, and he has offered you half of his empire. How can you not accept?"

"Were I you, Parmenion, I would gladly accept," Alexander said, eyeing his leading general with little regard, "but I am not you, and you are not me. I am Alexander, the great king of Macedonia and Asia and the pharaoh of Egypt. And you are Parmenion, a bitter old man who would rather die in his bed than on the field of battle."

"Of course I would rather die in my bed than in battle," Parmenion spat. "I'm not a child." With that he turned and stormed out, shoving men out of his way. Nikanor and some of his other followers left with him, but Philotas stayed behind to listen.

"Well, generals," Alexander said once Parmenion was gone, "Parmenion thinks we should accept Darius's sue for peace. What say all of you?"

His question was met by a loud "nay," but Andronicus noticed many men sitting silently who had been shouting before. He could tell that Parmenion's words had resonated with many of them, especially the members of the old guard.

"Now, we took Persian captives not two days ago," Alexander continued. "They told us that Darius is camped not far from here, at Gaugamela. I mean to meet Darius in the open this time, no more rivers, or mountains, or cliffs, just us and them."

A much softer chorus of agreement greeted this announcement. It seemed no one was overly eager to meet the Persians in an open field. The Persians still had them outnumbered at least two to one, and there were rumors throughout the army that Darius was going to use his warrior elephants in this battle. Andronicus had never seen such a thing in person, and he shuddered at the thought.

3

The Macedonian army arrived at Gaugamela to find the Persian army already spread out in formation across the better part of a mile. Horns blew, and the Macedonians quickly fell into their own battle lines, the same formation they had used in all of their major battles thus far. Alexander set up on the far right with his royal companion cavalry, and Parmenion set up in the middle, with the infantry. It seemed no matter how much Parmenion infuriated the king, Alexander still knew the value of having the older general on the field. A second cavalry was set up on the far left of the Macedonian lines, with Ptolemy back in command this time. Cretarus's failure to hold the left at Issus had nearly lost the battle, and Alexander knew he needed someone he truly trusted to lead the left now.

When the entire Macedonian army was in position, spread out over a quarter mile, they were still dwarfed by the Persians. On either side of the Macedonian lines, the Persian lines extended for another two hundred yards. They had their cavalry units set up on their outer flanks as well, with a strong infantry center.

Darius sat upon his white horse with his bright ornate robes, deep in the center of the infantry lines, surrounded by his Persian noblemen.

Twenty rows into the Persian infantry lines were two long rows of chariots. Farther back from them, near the rear of the army, was a single row of bull elephants, each with a giant basket attached to its back.

Andronicus had never seen elephant soldiers

before, though he had heard of them. It made him sad for the people he had once loved. He knew what seeing elephants put to such use would have meant to Chaka and his people, and it filled him with sorrow and rage. More than anything it infuriated him to know that the elephants would have to be put to death in the most violent ways. The image of the massive dead elephant he and Chaka had once come across and burned flashed across Andronicus's mind.

Not far from the front of the Persian lines, Andronicus saw the Persian elites. They were now called the Persian Immortals rather than elites, though he knew personally they were not immortal. They were dressed in the same grandiose attire they had been on the first day Andronicus had seen them at Thermopylae. He also saw a great number of Greeks standing in Darius's army, and told himself to kill them first. The idea of any Greek man standing with the Persians in such an important battle was utterly despicable to Andronicus.

The two armies stood facing each other for over twenty minutes, both waiting for the other to attack. Darius had made the first move at Issus, and it seemed he would not make the same mistake again. It was the Macedonians who were marching into their territory, so this time they would have to make the first move. There was an awkward moment of silence as the men looked around at each other, waiting for the inevitable slaughter to commence. Tension rippled throughout the Macedonian ranks, and Andronicus knew what had to be done. He rode forward, until he was just behind the king.

"Darius will not attack first this time. You'll have to make the first move," Andronicus said to Alexander, then leaned closer. "The men are tense, Alexander, you should speak to them, if you have the words."

Alexander nodded slowly. Andronicus saw what he had seen before in the king's blue eye, that spark of kingliness. Alexander rode forward a few paces and then turned to speak to his cavalry and the infantry men close enough to hear. He stayed silent for a moment, gazing out on his army. He had his head cocked at its usual inquisitive angle, and he looked kinglier in that moment than he had ever looked before.

"Macedonians!" Alexander shouted, his voice carrying well down the ranks. "Greeks, Thracians, we have fought each other before, and we may yet fight each other again." There was dead silence as Alexander's voice carried down the lines of men. "But we have a greater enemy this day! Today we fight the men who have haunted our lives for more than a hundred years! The Persians are a great and storied people, just as we are. They could have been a great ally to Greece and Macedonia. We could have lived in peace with these people, and the west and the east would have been one. King Xerxes had different plans than that! He wished for Greece to belong to him and not to Greeks. Xerxes underestimated Greece. He underestimated King Leonidas and his brave three hundred. For one hundred years the Persians have tried to take our lands, to burn our homes and rape our women. Today it's our turn! Today we have the chance to destroy the Persian Empire! Today we have a chance to change the course of history forever! No longer shall Macedonia be a secondary nation! Today we shall have the greatest glory there is! Now! Together! We fight!"

Bucephalas reared up, as Andronicus had seen him do before, but this time he appeared to be taller than a horse could possibly be. Alexander rose high above his men as they went into a wild frenzy, roaring at the top of their lungs, banging their spears on their shields, and stomping their feet. Andronicus felt chills move across his skin as he looked up at Alexander in a whole new light. Those had not just been inspiring words; it was as if he had taken the very thoughts from Andronicus's head. He had just been thinking about his history with the Persians, and Alexander had spoken of nearly all of it. Andronicus thrust his spear into the air and let out his own battle cry that rang out across the land, louder than any other.

The Persians looked shaken. It was unlikely

that most of them understood a word of what Alexander had said, but it was impossible for them to mistake the reaction. The Macedonians' frenzied battle cries rang loud and true and did not cease even after Alexander called for the first charge. He waved his sword three times, and Parmenion marched his lines forward.

Ten thousand men marched forward in close formation toward the awaiting Persians. They had stopped shouting, but the uproar behind them drove them on. Alexander and his cavalry watched from the far right as Parmenion led his men straight into the Persian lines. As soon as the armies met, the screams and shouting began. Andronicus could hear it even over the roaring of the Macedonians.

Horns bellowed, from the far side of the battle, and Andronicus saw the banners of the Persian cavalry charging into Parmenion's lines. At that moment Alexander called out and reared Bucephalas once more. As Bucephalas landed, he charged to the right, away from the battle and parallel to the Persian line. The royal cavalry quickly followed suit. They galloped past the end of the Persian lines and kept going. Once they had run more than a hundred yards beyond the Persian line, Alexander turned Bucephalas, and the cavalry turned left with him. As the cavalry came around behind the Persian lines, the Persian cavalry galloped out to meet them.

The Persians had meant to draw Alexander in, but his quick maneuvering forced them to come to him. As the two cavalries charged toward each other, well away from the rest of the battle, the Macedonians let out their war cries again. Andronicus was in the front line, and he felt the force of the two groups of horses colliding. In an instant, dozens of men and horses died all around him. For a moment there was only chaos, and then it became a fight.

Andronicus found himself facing a Persian rider on horseback, and quickly brought his sword down over the man's head. He felt the familiar feeling of bones cracking under his blade and saw blood spurt from the rider's skull as he turned to face the next man. The two cavalry forces fought each other to a standstill. It took less than ten minutes in total, and the companion cavalry lost nearly one hundred men, but the Persians lost the fight. A few of them turned and fled back to the greater Persian force, and Alexander quickly rallied his men.

"Now!" Alexander shouted. "To Darius! Break through their infantry lines!" He charged, and his cavalry followed. Andronicus spurred his own horse toward the awaiting Persian lines.

As they charged toward the Persian infantry, another cavalry troupe came galloping at them from their right. Before they could reach the infantry, they were met by the Persians' second cavalry wave.

The two cavalries collided with terrible force. Bodies went flying as the horses collided with each other. Andronicus was thrown forward as his horse crashed into another. When he sat back up, he swung his sword at two Persian riders, killing them both before they could even sit up. He turned around and began fighting another Persian rider.

The two cavalry units fought each other in brutal fashion. It looked as if the Persian cavalry was about to fall back again, but then the Persian infantry came charging in. Suddenly, there were men all around Andronicus, and he began slashing down at them with his sword. He looked around briefly and saw most of the Macedonian cavalry doing the same, but far too many were falling. Andronicus shouted and continued slashing wildly at the men around him. He had no idea how many men he killed, but eventually a spear found its way into his horse's side.

The beast let out a terrible screech, and Andronicus flung himself off, not intending to get trapped under this one. He landed on top of a Persian elite and drove his sword into the man's chest. He leapt to his feet, and began fighting the Persians all around him. He was vastly outnumbered, and he had no idea where the rest of the men were, but he kept fighting. He lost himself in the battle like he never had before. His mind went blank, and all he could see was red as he killed as many men as he could.

When he returned to reality, the Persian infantry was running back toward their center, apparently to fight off Parmenion's infantry. Andronicus looked around and saw more Greeks still standing than he had expected. Cleitus was not far away, limping over to where the king sat atop Bucephalas, surrounded by his men. Andronicus started walking over to them, only to feel a sharp pain in his side. He looked down and saw a dark red gash just below his armor, above his right hip.

After taking a moment to inspect his wound, Andronicus limped over to where the king was amassing his forces. Alexander was shouting orders, but his men could barely hear him. Once most of the remaining cavalry were together again, many of them no longer on horseback, Alexander called for another charge into the Persian infantry while most of the Persian force was busy in the center of the battle.

Andronicus and Cleitus both managed to mount unmanned horses and followed the king back into battle. They met the Persian lines for a third time. Again Andronicus found himself sliding into the din of battle. He ignored the pain in his side and cut through the Persians with terrible precision. As he slashed down at them, he heard an old familiar noise, though he had never heard it in battle before.

He looked up and saw an elephant pushing its way violently through the battle, trampling Persians and Macedonians alike. The men sitting in the basket on the elephant's back were shooting arrows down into the battle while one of them whipped the mad elephant. Andronicus looked into the poor beast's eyes and saw nothing but fear and panic. Ignoring the rest of the battle, Andronicus pulled a spear from a dead man's back and took aim. It was hard with an injured side, but he threw the spear and watched it fly straight into the neck of the man whipping the elephant.

As soon as the man tumbled down from the elephant's back, the great beast rose onto its hind legs, sending the men in the basket tumbling down into the battle. When it crashed back down to the ground with a mighty thump, men started slashing at it with spears and swords. The beast whipped its head around, sending several men flying with the force of its tusks, and then it charged forward. Everyone got out of the way as the elephant trudged through the hectic battle.

Andronicus watched for a moment as the elephant ran away from the battle, free at last. Then out of nowhere he felt something bash against his helmet. He hit the ground with a smack that knocked the wind out of him. Andronicus looked up, blood pouring down the left side of his face, and saw a Persian nobleman reaching back to strike at him again. Andronicus stabbed his sword up through the man's throat and pulled him to the ground as he brought himself up. Coughing, he reached up and touched the side of his face, feeling warm blood covering his cheek.

Before he could patch the wound, the battle found him again. Two Persian elites came running at him, and he clashed swords with them both. The cut on his face hurt, but the wound in his hip made it difficult to fight. Andronicus stabbed at one of them and missed. The other one stepped forward and raised his sword above his head. Andronicus tried to block it, but he was too late. The man had him beat. All he had to do was bring the sword down, and that would be the end. It was the end Andronicus had always told himself he wanted, to die fighting the Persians in battle, but at that moment he found he wanted to live. As he watched the sword come down at him, he wanted nothing more than to stay alive.

Just before the sword struck, he closed his eyes. In that instant he didn't see his mother, or his father, or brother, or his wife. He didn't see Aristotle or Alexander. He didn't see Chaka. In that instant what he saw was the shining rocks, and the light they had shown him. They had shown him so many things, things that had not yet happened but were still to come.

Instead of feeling a blade cut through his head, Andronicus felt a warm spray of blood hit his face. He opened his eyes and saw the Persian elite who would have killed him standing above him with a spear sticking out of his chest. He gave Andronicus a look of pure shock and then fell to the ground. The other elite shouted and tried to strike at Andronicus, but Andronicus parried the man's blow and then slashed at his leg. When the man fell to one knee Andronicus drove his sword through his chest.

Andronicus looked up to see who had saved him and saw Cassander on his horse. The boy gave Andronicus a quick nod before returning to the fray. There was no time to take in the moment, as another elite came charging in, and Andronicus began fighting the man. While he fought with the man, he heard someone shouting orders nearby and thought it might be Hephaestion.

Andronicus's sword found flesh, and he brought it down again quickly, killing his opponent. He looked up and saw that most of the Persians had begun fleeing. Dead bodies were strewn everywhere, more than he had ever seen before. Thousands of Persians were fleeing to the east, including most of their cavalry.

In the center of the battle, where the fighting was the thickest, the battle was still raging. Thousands of Persians still pressed against the Macedonian infantry, and the battle was not yet won. Andronicus looked around until he finally saw Alexander. He was still atop Bucephalas and had a good number of men around him. Andronicus started limping toward him until he heard the king shouting at his men.

"Darius tries to run from me again!" Alexander said. "We have to chase him! We have to kill him now!"

"Parmenion needs us, Alexander!" Hephaestion cried. "If they push back our infantry, they could still win this, even without their king!"

"He's right, Alexander!" Cassander shouted. "If we go after Darius, we could lose everything!"

"I won't let Parmenion take this from me again!" Alexander said, spit flying from his mouth. "I will kill Darius this day!"

"Then you'll lose this battle!" Hephaestion shouted back, trying to break through to the king.

Alexander looked at him and slowly seemed to come back to reality. He looked around and saw the battle raging behind him. Raising his sword and shouting as loud as he could, Alexander called for another charge, back to Parmenion. The cavalry charged into the Persian rear and began cutting through.

Andronicus stayed behind; the battle was won, and he could barely walk on his injured hip. He stumbled over to a dead horse and sat on the beast's belly. He looked at the wound on his hip and saw that it was still leaking blood. He took a handful of dirt, closed his eyes, clenched his teeth, and shoved it into the wound.

When he looked back down, the wound was no longer bleeding, but it looked much worse. He brought his hand up to his face, and winced as his fingers touched the wound above his eye. The fine helmet Alexander had given him had surely saved his life, but the sword had still cut him deeply. He was sure he would have the scars to remember this battle for a long time.

4

The battle lasted another hour. Andronicus watched from afar as Alexander's cavalry rode to the aid of Parmenion and the infantry. By the time the greater Persian force had surrendered, tens of thousands lay dead on the battlefield. Darius was long gone. He had fled to the east, to escape Alexander's wrath, and he had a good head start. As soon as the Macedonian infantry was secured, Alexander mustered all the cavalry he could and rode after Darius, but everyone knew it would likely be fruitless.

While the victorious king and his men chased down the fallen king, Parmenion took command of the army. First they rounded up every remaining Persian soldier and took them prisoner. While a large group stayed behind to try and save as many of the wounded as possible, Parmenion marched most of the army on to Babylon. Andronicus fell in line with Parmenion and his sons. For a long time, none of them said anything.

"Do you think it's done, Father?" Nikanor

asked, finally breaking the silence. "Do you think the Persians are defeated?"

"There will be more fighting," Parmenion said in a raspy voice, and Andronicus could tell he was utterly worn out from the battle, though he was still able to lead. "Not all of the cities will yield without a fight, and Darius may try to amass an army one last time, but yes, the Persians are defeated. Alexander has won Asia, just as he wanted."

"Then will you return home, Father?" Nikanor asked, giving his father a concerned look.

"I . . . I should stay," Parmenion said, looking at his son. "There will be more fighting, and the king and his friends don't know how to command an infantry of this size."

"But I do," Philotas said. "Nikanor is right. You should return home, to mother. I'll command the infantry in your place. I'm ready for it."

"I know you are," Parmenion said, his eyes welling up with tears as he looked at his eldest son. "Perhaps you boys are right. I almost died today. I should retire while I still can. Ah, look, there she is boys, Babylon."

As they rode around a corner, the massive city came into view. They all fell silent as they gazed at the ancient and storied city. Some said it was the biggest city in the world, and Andronicus could believe it. The Euphrates river flowed right through the middle of Babylon, and there appeared to be some kind of levy system at the base of the walls. The walls themselves were as high as any Andronicus had ever seen, and there were buildings inside the city that stood even taller than the walls.

Andronicus knew that the Babylonians had been their own kingdom for more than a thousand years, and had once been one of the strongest dynasties in the world. Babylonia had been its own nation until the Persian king Cyrus the Great conquered much of the known world. In its two hundred years under Persian control, the city had only flourished, and it was said that over two hundred thousand people were living inside its walls. Now

Babylon would begin a new age, under King Alexander, as would the rest of the east.

Andronicus wondered, and not for the first time, what would become of the world once Alexander had conquered the Persians. The two largest and greatest empires in the world would have to become one. People from more than a hundred cities with a hundred histories and a hundred religions would have to learn to live together. It seemed impossible, and Andronicus had mixed feelings about leaving the world he knew at such a time.

He knew he could do the world good by staying with Alexander. He could help the king rule his people the way he should, but Andronicus also knew things wouldn't go that way. Alexander had gotten a taste for conquering, and he would not be satisfied to just rule his empire. Eventually, it would all come crumbling down. It was inevitable, and Andronicus didn't want to be there when it happened. For whatever reason, he felt his destiny lay to the east, and that's where he meant to go.

Chapter 54
Babylon
1

The army stayed in Babylon for three weeks, giving most of the men time to heal from their wounds. More than five thousand Greeks and Macedonians had died in the battle, and twice as many had been badly wounded. Andronicus was among the wounded, and he knew he wouldn't be ready for battle again for months. He still didn't know if a sword or a spear had pierced his hip, but whichever it had been, it had pierced deep. He also now had a dark red gash going over his left eye and down his cheek.

When the cavalry returned from their failed pursuit of Darius, Andronicus sought out Cassander immediately. The young man looked haggard and tired and was still covered in dried blood and dirt from head to toe. He looked like he wanted nothing more than to find a bed and sleep for a week, but Andronicus pulled him aside and made him listen.

"You saved my life, boy," Andronicus said, meeting Cassander's exhausted eyes.

"It was nothing," Cassander said, trying to shrug it off, but Andronicus grabbed his shoulder and held him there.

"It was not nothing," he said. "I think that was the closest I have ever come to dying. You can't possibly know what that means."

"I owed you one," Cassander said with a sigh. "You saved me at Granicus. Besides, in a way you saved yourself by teaching me how to fight."

"Still," Andronicus said, reaching behind his back and pulling out one of the old Spartan swords, "I want you to have this. You've earned it."

"Thank you." Cassander looked surprised as he took the blade, admiring its fine edge. "I'm sure this will come in handy when we meet the Persians again."

"Again?" Andronicus said, looking up from the blade. "It isn't over then?"

Cassander shook his head. "Darius got away, along with at least twenty thousand of his men. We'll have to fight them once more at least."

"Do you think Alexander will stop?" Andronicus asked. "When Darius is dead, do you think he'll just pack up, and take his army back home?"

"Of course," Cassander replied, taken aback. "Once Darius falls, the Persian Empire will belong to Alexander. Why would he stay?"

"Oh, I don't think he would stay," Andronicus said. "Not in any of these cities, no matter how old or grand they are. I think he'll want to keep going."

"Going where?" Cassander asked.

"As far as he can. He has gained a hunger for conquering lands. I don't think he'll be satisfied with just the Persian Empire. I don't know where Alexander will go, but I know it won't be home."

2

The Persians had suffered much worse casualties than the Macedonians. No one was sure of the exact numbers, but the consensus was that this was now the deadliest battle in history. At least twenty thousand Persians had died in the fighting, possibly as many as five thousand more. Another ten thousand Persians had either died or been executed since the end of the battle, and that number was sure to grow. Alexander and his cavalry had chased Darius for three days before they turned back, and killed hundreds more of his men who fell behind. In total the Persian army lost some fifty thousand men at the battle of Gaugamela, and their king had fled in disgrace.

Alexander was eager to resume the chase and kill Darius once and for all, but Parmenion and the other generals advised him to stay, so he and his men could regain their strength. Alexander wouldn't listen though. It seemed that having to go back to help Parmenion again during the battle had been the last straw for Alexander. Less than a week after taking Babylon, Alexander held a council of his generals. He arrived late, walked straight to his throne, and sat down, glaring at Parmenion.

"What do you have to say for yourself?" Alexander asked, his voice cold.

"What are you talking about?" Parmenion asked, getting to his feet. "I have done nothing wrong."

"Nothing wrong?" Alexander laughed. "Because of you Darius is still alive."

"My infantry has held the center in every one of your battles," Parmenion said, shaking with anger. "While you parade your cavalry about, me and my men have done the real fighting."

"Then why did I have to bring my cavalry back to save you, again?" Alexander asked, rising to his feet. "I could have killed Darius. I could have ended this war but for you."

"You arrogant little fool," Parmenion sneered.

"Hold your tongue, old man!" Hephaestion yelled, stepping forward and drawing his sword. Philotas rose and drew his sword as well. Andronicus and Cleitus both stepped forward, but they held still, waiting to see what would happen.

"I have let you live this long because of your skill on the battlefield," Alexander said, "but you have proven you can no longer lead men in battle. For your help in my earlier battles, I'll let you live, but you are done here."

Parmenion glared at the king for a moment, clearly wanting to say more, but instead he drew his sword and threw it down on the table.

"Fine then," Parmenion said hoarsely. "My sons and I will go back to Macedonia, where we belong."

"Your sons will remain in my army," Alexander said. "I'm still in need of good captains, and they have proven to be that."

"Philotas will stay and command the infantry in my stead, but Nikanor comes with me," Parmenion said, glaring at Alexander.

"Your sons will do as their king commands," Hephaestion sneered, "or they will be executed for treason."

Philotas turned and whispered something into his father's ear. Parmenion gave him a worried look, then nodded and turned back to Alexander. Alexander had sat back down in his throne and was looking down at Parmenion with nothing but contempt in his mismatched eyes. Parmenion looked around at all of the other generals standing around the room. Some of them he had fought with for twenty years. All of them knew how much he had done for them.

"What will happen when he's done with Darius?" Parmenion asked the room. "When the Persians have fallen, and Asia is his, do you think he'll let you go home?"

"What are you talking about?" Alexander asked, sitting forward with a concerned look on his face.

"I'm talking about you, Alexander." Parmenion turned to face the king. "I don't think you will ever see Macedonia again."

"You dare threaten the king?" Hephaestion shouted, taking a step toward Parmenion, and being met by Philotas.

"I'm not threatening anyone," Parmenion said, his eyes still fixed on Alexander. "Tell us, when Darius falls, and his empire is yours, what will you do with your army? Will you return home?"

Everyone in the room turned to look at Alexander. He stayed silent for a moment, keeping them all waiting.

"I'll keep going east," Alexander said in a tone that offered no room for question. "I'll take my army to the farthest reaches of the known world and beyond."

"You have beaten the Persians because you knew the Persians," Parmenion replied with a sad shake of his head, "Greeks fought them for two hundred years before you, and learned their ways. Whether you care to admit it or not, the plans for this invasion were not laid by you." Alexander looked like he wanted to shout at Parmenion, but he stayed silent. "If you take your army east of Persia, you will be facing the unknown in every possible way. No one knows who or what lies there. The odds of you or any of your men ever returning home would be slim, Alexander. You don't even know what you would be fighting for. Why not let your men return home, victorious, to their families?" There was a soft murmur from the crowd, but Alexander looked unperturbed.

"Leave, Parmenion," he said. His voice was cool, but Andronicus saw his knuckles turning white as he gripped the sides of his throne. "You have no place in my army. Go back to your home in disgrace, for you are a coward. I don't need you, and I never have. I'll win my battles on my own from now on."

"Gods pity you, Alexander," Parmenion said hoarsely, sounding more like an old man than a battle commander. "I know I do."

"Get out!" Alexander shouted, pointing to the door. Parmenion turned and left before Alexander could change his mind.

Once he was gone, Cassander called the meeting to other business while Alexander sat fuming in his throne. Andronicus slipped out the door and ran after Parmenion, knowing he would be out of the city as fast as he could.

He sprinted to the stables and caught Parmenion just as he was mounting his horse.

Andronicus ran over to him, trying to catch his breath. Parmenion looked down at him from his horse, and Andronicus didn't know what to say. He knew he was never going to see Parmenion again. Parmenion would go back to Macedonia, and Andronicus meant to go east, and he knew he likely would not return west for a long time.

"You're a good man, Andronicus," Parmenion said, "and the best fighter I have ever seen. Look after my sons for me."

"I'm going to leave the army as well," Andronicus said, not quite sure why he was telling Parmenion. "I mean to leave as soon as the Persians are finished."

"Where will you go?"

"East, just like Alexander said. Farther east than any man has gone."

"Alexander is going east, so why leave the army?" Parmenion's cohort was clearly ready to leave, but he looked genuinely interested in Andronicus's answer.

"He will be marching with fifty thousand men," Andronicus said, "and you just reminded every general and captain in that room that he has no plans to bring them home. Alexander will be dealing with all of that, and I'll be alone. I think I'll make it farther than him."

Parmenion chuckled. "That you will. I'm glad you were with us, Andronicus of Sparta. Good luck in your travels."

"Farewell, Parmenion," Andronicus said, knowing it truly was goodbye. "Enjoy your retirement. You've earned it."

Parmenion and his dozen guards rode off down the street. Andronicus watched them go until they were out of sight. He knew that Parmenion would do well for himself back in Pella, but he was worried about Philotas. Philotas had little love for the king, and with his father gone, he would have to be the one to oppose Alexander when it was needed. Andronicus wasn't sure Philotas had the same temperament as his father, and he had to wonder how long Philotas would follow Alexander's orders.

Two weeks after Parmenion left, the army set out again, marching east toward the city of Susa. It was a slow march, with many of the men still wounded, and it took two months to reach Susa. When they arrived they found the city nearly deserted. All of the Persian soldiers and noblemen had fled to the east with Darius. Only the slaves and lowborn were left in the city, and they accepted Alexander graciously.

The ones who had fled had apparently not had time to take their wealth with them. When Alexander's soldiers stormed the palaces, they found all kinds of treasures. Alexander had it all collected and brought to him. After inspecting the great wealth of Susa, he had it sent back to the great library he was building in Alexandria. Andronicus inspected the treasure himself before it left. He spent hours looking through it all, searching for a ring. While he found many rings and other gems and precious stones, none of them were what he was looking for.

Chapter 55
The Persian Gates
1

From Susa, Alexander took his army down the Persian royal road toward Persepolis. It had become the new capital of Darius's flickering empire, and was the last major city that the Persians held. It was said that Darius was amassing a final army there and would try to give Alexander at least one more fight before surrendering. Alexander marched at the head of an army that was now less than twenty thousand strong. Between the casualties of war, the men who were still too wounded to travel, and the men who had to stay behind in each city, Alexander had lost more than half of the men he had started out with.

As they marched east to Persepolis, and winter came on, the dry flat desert turned into a snowy mountainous place. Hills rose around the royal road until the road became an actual valley. At first there was room enough on the road to march three phalanxes side by side, but as they marched onward, the valley grew steadily narrower. Less than a week after entering the valley, the army was attacked by wild hill tribes. Alexander had the army stop and sent two hundred men to seek out the mountain men and kill them.

By the time they managed to track them all down, the mountain men were willing to barter with Alexander, but he had them killed instead. Once the wild tribesmen were dead, the army resumed its march. Persepolis was less than three weeks away, and the entire army was inwardly preparing themselves for another battle with the Persians.

2

On January tenth, 330 BC, the Macedonian army was crossing the narrowest part of the valley leading into Persepolis. The narrow pass was called the Persian Gates, and it was said one could only pass through with the permission of the Persian king. The pass was less than fifty feet across, with high rocky mountains on either side. Andronicus rode beside Cleitus, not far from where Alexander rode with his friends. Philotas had taken his father's place at the head of the infantry, and Nikanor had been demoted to captain, though he didn't seem to mind.

The sun was high overhead, and a brisk wind blew through the mountainous gates. Most of the companion cavalry rode at the head of the army, with Alexander and the generals behind them. Behind the cavalry marched Philotas's infantry, in columns of one hundred men. The only noise was that of feet crunching snow and kicking rocks. Occasionally, a horse would whinny, but the exhausted men mostly stayed quiet as they trudged through the snowy mountain pass.

Andronicus thought he heard a shout from high above and looked up. The sun was right above him, and he had to squint as he searched for the source of the noise. He couldn't see anything. He turned to see Cleitus looking up as well and knew he had heard it too. Andronicus looked ahead and saw that Alexander and the others had not heard it. He opened his mouth to call out to the king when a thunderous crash rang out above him.

Everyone below the noise flinched instinctively. Andronicus looked up again in time to see a giant boulder, bigger than a horse, tumbling down the mountainside. He shouted, as did several others, but it was too late. The boulder came crashing down onto a group of men on horseback. It broke apart as it did, sending rocks flying everywhere. At least a dozen men were killed in the initial impact, and two dozen more were hit by the rocks.

Before they had time to react, rocks began falling down all around them. Andronicus looked up again, and this time he saw men standing high in the hills, throwing rocks down at them. For a moment he thought it was the hill tribes again, foolishly making another attempt against the massive army. Then arrows began to fall, and he knew it was the Persians. He saw archers all along the left mountain, firing down at them.

Andronicus leapt off his horse and grabbed his shield. He dropped down behind the horse and covered his head from the attack. All around him were shouting, panicked voices. He saw bodies everywhere, some with arrows sticking out of them, others with terribly mangled wounds from the rocks. Cleitus appeared beside him and pointed toward the king. Andronicus nodded, and they started toward Alexander, their shields covering their heads. As they walked, Andronicus saw a man with a shield covering his head get hit by a rock nearly as big as his shield. The man crumpled to the ground under the force of it, his neck clearly broken.

When they reached the king, he had four men standing over him with great bronze shields. Hephaestion and Cassander and the other generals were scattered about, all cowering under their own shields.

"Alexander!" Andronicus shouted. "We have to pull back now! They're going to cut our army in half from up there!"

"Sound the retreat!" Alexander shouted from under his bodyguards. "Get us out of here!"

"Sound the retreat!" Andronicus bellowed. His voice echoed twice off the high mountains, and then it was back to the shouting, and the clanging of rocks and arrows. A moment later horns began blowing, sounding the retreat. Alexander and his generals got up and began making their way back through the tight pass. They made it about a hundred feet before there was no more room to retreat. Thousands of men were still marching in, blocking their escape.

Andronicus looked behind him and saw hundreds of bodies lining the floor of the pass. All they could do was stay under cover, and wait for the army to back out. They had moved out of range of the rock throwers, but the arrows still rained down around them. Alexander had men covering him, but everyone else was left to their own defense. It took nearly an hour before they were all able to retreat, and by then hundreds more had died. By the time the entire army was out of the ambush, thousands were dead. They didn't have an exact number because they had to leave them all behind.

3

The Macedonian army encamped two miles from where they had been ambushed, where the pass was much wider. The first thing Alexander did was place two hundred archers in the hills on either side of them. Dozens of scouts were sent ahead, but only a few returned. They reported that the Persians had set up a camp not far from the site of the ambush, and they still held the hills. That night Alexander held an impromptu war council.

"We have to march around," Cassander said. "We cannot make another attempt at the gates. It's too dangerous."

"It would take more than a year to march all the way around," Hephaestion pointed out, "and by then Darius will have raised an army big enough to defeat us."

"You saw what those rocks did," Cassander

replied. "The Persians hold those hills. It would be madness to try and cross through that pass."

"Hephaestion is right," Alexander agreed. "We can't take the time to march around. Darius is afraid. We can't give him time to settle."

"I will not march my infantry through those hills again," Philotas said, sounding every bit like his father's son. "I lost more than two thousand men in that pass."

"You mean Alexander lost two thousand men," Hephaestion said. "Those were not your men, Philotas. They were not your father's men either. They were the king's men."

"Then the king can march them through those hills himself," Philotas said, "because I won't." Hephaestion looked like he was going to say something else when the king spoke up.

"Philotas is right too, Hephaestion," Alexander said, remaining surprisingly calm. "We can't try to take the pass that way. But we can't go around the mountains either."

"Then what do you suggest we do?" Cassander asked.

"We find another way through the hills," Alexander said. "Xerxes was once in this very same predicament, was he not? He had a bigger army than Darius or I ever had. Leonidas had him blocked at Thermopylae. Andronicus," Alexander said, turning to face him. "You're a Spartan. Do you believe that Leonidas and his men could have held that pass against the Persians?"

The question caught Andronicus completely off guard. Instantly he saw the faces of all the men who had fought at Thermopylae. Obviously, Alexander had no idea Andronicus had actually been there; he was just asking because he was Spartan. Andronicus took a moment to think about it. He was sure that Leonidas would have held the pass had they not been routed; Diokles alone would have taken hundreds down with him.

"We—," Andronicus stopped short, realizing his slip. "*They* would have held that pass until every one of those Persians was dead."

"But they did not, did they?" Alexander asked, turning to his generals.

"No, they did not," Andronicus said softly, thinking of his long-dead brethren.

"Because Xerxes found a way around," Alexander said, "just as we will."

"You think there's a way to get behind them?" Cassander asked.

"There must be," Alexander said. "These mountains are endless. There must be some small pass, some trail up the mountain."

"And how are we going to find this pass?" Hephaestion asked.

"How many Persian slaves do we have with us right now?" Alexander asked. For a moment no one answered, and then someone in the back called out that there were just under one thousand.

"Good," Alexander said, nodding. "Tell them that the man who helps me across these mountains will not only be freed, but will be made a nobleman and given a palace back in Babylon.

"That's a good idea," Cassander said, nodding in agreement. "We'll have it done immediately."

4

Alexander was right; the slaves told of a number of different trails in the hills. Alexander had scouts check them all out and found one that would be perfect. He took one thousand handpicked men and started up the path. Andronicus stayed behind with the infantry, knowing there could be a tight battle in the pass.

Between the rocks, the snow, and the wind, it was extremely slow going up the mountain path. It took Alexander and his men several weeks to make their way around the Persians. Once they were close to the Persian camp, Alexander split his force in two, with himself leading one around to the far mountain and Cassander leading the other force against the archers. When they were finally in position, the Persians still had not found them out.

At dawn on February the twenty sixth, Alexander and Cassander and their men ambushed the Persians, catching them completely unawares. It didn't take long to take the hills, and once they did, Macedonian horns blew. The Macedonian infantry, still some ten thousand strong, began marching through the pass again, Andronicus among them.

They hurried down the valley until they reached the place they had been ambushed before. The valley floor was still littered with rotting corpses and now carrion birds as well. The smell was awful, and everyone had to cover their faces. Andronicus looked up at the hills they had been fired upon from and saw Macedonians roaring loudly. With the hills safe, the large infantry force easily made its way through the Persian gates. On the other side they found the Persians fleeing back to Persepolis.

While Alexander brought his men down from the hills as fast as possible, Philotas called the infantry into a charge. They ran after the fleeing Persians. Persepolis was only six miles away, and the Macedonians chased the Persians all the way there. When the Persians reached the city walls, they began piling up against the city gate. Andronicus strained his eyes and could see that the gate was still shut.

The Persians were abandoning their own men to die rather than fight. The men who were banging on the walls, trying to get in, slowly realized they would not and turned to face the Macedonians. Many of the Persians tried to run, but many more turned to face their deaths with honor. They charged back at the Macedonians, and a small fight ensued. The Persians fell quickly, but they took some Macedonians with them.

By the time Alexander and the other generals arrived, the city was surrounded. Siege equipment began rolling in, and less than an hour after surrounding the city, the people surrendered. The city gates opened, and horns of retreat blew throughout Persepolis. The Macedonians marched into the city, and by nightfall it was done. Alexander went straight to the treasury and began inspecting his newest fortune.

Chapter 56
Betrayal

1

The army settled into Persepolis, with no immediate plans to move on. They had lost nearly three quarters of the men they had set out from Greece with, and everyone knew they needed time to regroup. Darius was on the run again, without much of an army, and Alexander knew he didn't have to worry about the Persians for the time being. The Macedonians settled in well enough; they all seemed happy just to have a place to stay for a while. For two months there was peace in the city, between the Greeks and the Persians.

The only person who seemed genuinely displeased was Philotas. Ever since his father's departure from the army, Philotas had been growing progressively angrier with Alexander. Andronicus and Cleitus did their best to keep him away from the king, but they knew they could not stop him indefinitely.

One night Andronicus came across Philotas with a group of Persians he didn't recognize. They were standing in an alleyway not far from the palace, and everyone but Philotas left in a hurry when they saw Andronicus, but not before he saw their faces.

"You keep strange company these days, Philotas," Andronicus said as the other men scurried away. "I'm not sure your father would approve."

"He may not approve of the means," Philotas replied, "but he'll approve of the ends."

"What end is that?" Andronicus asked.

"I think you know already," Philotas answered, meeting Andronicus's eye.

"You mean to kill the king," Andronicus said, not asking but stating it as a fact.

"The war is won," Philotas said, trying to keep his voice down. "He's going to march us halfway across the world, chasing ghosts and dreams."

"Then return to Greece, as your father did," Andronicus said. "Let Alexander march his army into the unknown."

"My father did not leave," Philotas said, his voice bitter. "He was exiled like some kind of criminal. My father won those battles, not Alexander. None of this would have been possible without my father."

"I know," Andronicus agreed, "and so do the men. Who cares what the king thinks?"

"Everyone," Philotas said seriously. "The men may know the truth now, but what about twenty years from now, or fifty, or one hundred? Do you really think my father will be given the credit he deserves? No, they will say that Alexander the Great did it all by himself."

"And you think that gives you the right to kill him? Because he stole your father's glory?"

"I don't care about rights," Philotas said. "I don't care if I'm wrong either. I'm going to kill that boy, like I should have done years ago."

"I'm one of Alexander's sworn guards," Andronicus pointed out, eyeing Philotas carefully. "It's my sacred duty to protect the king's life."

"Are you going to stop me then?" Philotas asked, meeting Andronicus's stare. "Are you going to tell my plan to the king, and let him execute me? Do you think he'll stop there?"

"No," Andronicus replied, "if you're caught, he'll kill your father, your brother, and anyone else who is close to you. Is killing him truly worth all that?"

"I won't be caught," Philotas said, "not unless you tell him."

"Philotas," Andronicus said, "you must reconsider. Your father made me promise to look out for you. I can't let you do this."

"I'm not asking your permission, Andronicus," Philotas said, "nor my father's. I'll do it myself."

With that Philotas turned and walked away, leaving Andronicus terribly conflicted. On one hand he agreed with Philotas. Alexander had gotten out of control; he was marching his army much farther than they needed to go. The Persians were defeated, and they would never threaten Greece again. On the other hand, Andronicus was sworn to protect Alexander, and even if he wasn't, he didn't believe Alexander deserved to be killed. He realized then that he had made promises to both Philip and Parmenion, to keep their sons safe. Now it seemed like he had a horrible choice to make. If he let Philotas go through with his plan, the army, and the empire at large, could fall into chaos. Everything they had fought so hard for could be taken back. But if he tried to stop Philotas, Alexander would find out and have him executed. In the end Andronicus decided to take the news to Cleitus, so he could have some help with the decision.

2

"You're sure of this?" Cleitus asked once Andronicus had informed him of the situation. His expression was as icy as usual, and Andronicus had no idea what he thought about Philotas's plan.

"He all but said it aloud," Andronicus replied. "If we don't stop him, he'll make an attempt on the king's life before the week is over."

"Do you know how he plans to do it?" Cleitus asked, still showing no sign of what he was thinking.

"No, but he was with a group of Persians I have never seen before. I don't think he'll make the attempt himself. But it's still his plan."

"Why are you here, Andronicus?" Cleitus asked, finally looking up. "You have no love for Alexander. You told me yourself you planned on leaving the army anyway. Why tell me of Philotas's plot?"

"I swore an oath to protect Alexander," Andronicus admitted, looking down, "just as you did. I thought at the very least you deserved to know."

"What did you think I would say?" Cleitus asked. "That I would gladly stand aside and let another king die at my feet? You know I must stop this."

"I didn't know what you would say," Andronicus said. "I didn't know what I would say." He took a long pause, and then went on, "I may not love Alexander, but he is still a king, and he doesn't deserve to be killed by his own men."

"You know we have to tell him then."

Andronicus nodded slowly, already feeling the betrayal of what he was doing.

"Philotas will be executed," Cleitus added, "probably by one of us."

"Let me talk to him one last time," Andronicus said, not yet ready to give the boy up so easily. "Let me try to convince him to leave."

Cleitus didn't say anything; he just stared at Andronicus with his cold dark scowl. Andronicus could tell that Cleitus thought it wouldn't work, but he still had to try. Finally Cleitus gave him a distinct nod and rose to his feet. He stared at Andronicus a moment longer, then turned and left. Andronicus felt more conflicted than he had in a great many years. He knew Philotas would not listen to reason, and even if he did, Cleitus might still tell the king anyway, but he had to try. He owed it to Philotas and to Parmenion for all they had done for him in battle.

He could ask Philotas to come with him. Andronicus was already planning to leave the army soon anyway. He had thought he would have to go alone, but maybe he wouldn't have to. Chaka had saved his life a thousand times over during their long years of travel. Philotas would never be the friend Chaka was, but he was an excellent fighter and good enough company. Andronicus decided he would rather take the boy with him than let him die at Alexander's order.

3

Andronicus looked for Philotas everywhere, but he couldn't find him. He checked in the brothels and inns and in the stables and the granaries. He even checked in dark alleys and corners. He looked throughout the city of Persepolis but couldn't find Philotas anywhere. Eventually, after hours of searching, Andronicus returned to the palace. As he neared it, he heard whispers of something going on. He picked up his pace, and when he entered the massive stone building, the guards told him to go to the great hall.

When he arrived he found a full court in

attendance, with Alexander sitting at its head. He was surrounded by his friends, with a full audience of generals, captains, and noblemen spread out around him, chattering quietly. In the middle of the hall, kneeling in front of Alexander, was Philotas. Andronicus looked at Cleitus, who shook his head warily as if to say it wasn't him who had told. As Andronicus walked farther into the room, he saw that Philotas was bleeding badly from a cut on his arm, and his nose and mouth were covered in blood.

"You have been accused of conspiring to kill the king," Hephaestion said, silencing the room. "How do you respond?"

"I am innocent," Philotas said, "just as my father was when you exiled him."

"Your father was not exiled," Cassander pointed out. "He was relieved of his command. He went back to Greece of his own accord, and he retains his lordship and his wealth."

"Parmenion is not on trial today," Alexander snapped. "Do you deny paying these men to have me poisoned, Philotas?"

A door burst open, and three Persian men were dragged in and thrown to the ground next to Philotas. Andronicus recognized them as the men Philotas had been speaking with earlier. All three men began begging for their lives with terrible attempts at speaking Greek. Cleitus stepped forward, and struck one of them hard in the face, knocking him onto his back. The other two instantly fell silent and cowered away from Cleitus, who towered over them.

"I have never seen these men in my life," Philotas said, glaring up at the king with hate in his eyes.

"So you do deny it then?" Alexander asked.

"I deny it!" Philotas declared, so everyone could hear. "I deny any part in this madness. I am the general of your infantry, as my father was before me. I am of noble Macedonian blood. You have no right to put me on trial. You have no proof of any of this!"

"Alexander is the king!" Hephaestion shouted. "He has every right, and we do have proof."

The door opened again, and this time a Persian man came walking in with two guards escorting him rather than dragging him. Andronicus recognized him as the last of the men Philotas had been conspiring with, only now he was dressed in much nicer attire. He stood before the king, a little ways from where Philotas and the other men were kneeling.

"Do you know this man, Philotas?" Alexander asked in a cold, flat voice.

"No," Philotas said hoarsely, though Andronicus could see the fear in his eyes. "I have never seen him before."

"He tells a different story," Alexander said. "He says you know him well. He says that you paid him one hundred gold coins to have me poisoned."

"Lies!" Philotas shouted. "Lies from the mouth of a Persian savage. You trust these beasts too much, Alexander. Would you truly believe him over your own general?"

"Tell me, Philotas," Alexander continued, ignoring the outburst, "do you think one hundred gold coins is enough to pay for the murder of a king?" Philotas didn't answer; he just glared up at Alexander in anger.

"The problem with paying assassins to kill a king, Philotas, is that the king will always have more money than you," Alexander pointed out with a dry smile. "This wise man came and told me about your plot and asked to be paid two hundred gold coins."

"Lies," Philotas said again, with no real vigor this time. "I had no part in this."

"And yet all four of these men have told us that you paid them one hundred gold coins to have me murdered," Alexander said.

"You would believe these men? Over me?" Philotas said. "I have fought alongside you since before you were king. You defeated these men in battle. Why do you listen to them?"

"Each one of them was found with a pouch containing exactly one hundred gold coins," Hephaestion said. "Macedonian gold coins."

Philotas seemed to deflate, as if he knew he

had lost. His body drooped a bit, but he never took his eyes off Alexander.

"You will make a fine example to all would-be assassins, Philotas," Alexander said, looking down on him with a triumphant smile. "Yours will be a lesson in caution. You see, if you were not so sloppy and foolish, you might have been able to kill me yourself, but instead you trusted these men."

"You have been found guilty of treason, Philotas, son of Parmenion," Hephaestion proclaimed. "What have you to say for yourself?"

"You are a bastard, Alexander," Philotas said through clenched teeth, hate dripping off him. "Your father would weep if he could see what has become of his empire. You can kill me now for trying to save my own people, but someday you will answer for your actions as well."

"I am the king," Alexander said. "I answer to no one."

"In life, perhaps not," Philotas snarled, "but you will die one day, Alexander, and when you do, you will have to answer to the gods for all that you have done."

"What have I done?" Alexander shouted, rising to his feet, "I have led my people into war, into victory. I am the first Greek man to conquer the Persians. Tell me, Philotas, what crimes will I answer to the gods for?"

"You crucified thousands of men," Philotas seethed, "for defending their homes against you. You turned your back on your generals because they were a threat to your personal glory. Some even say that you killed your own father."

"Enough!" Alexander shouted. "Kill him! Kill them all!"

Cleitus shot Andronicus one last solemn look and then drew his sword. The Persian men began begging again, dropping to their hands and knees, but Philotas slowly rose to his feet. His hands were tied behind his back, but he stood tall, facing Cleitus. In his final moments he held his head high and never took his eyes off Alexander. Andronicus could see that

Philotas had no remorse for what he had done, even as he faced his death. There was no sadness in his eyes, or regret, only hate.

Andronicus wanted to shout for them to stop it, to save his friend, but he knew there was nothing he could do. He watched helplessly as Cleitus raised his sword and then swung it hard at Philotas.

Philotas never flinched or made a sound. The sword hit his neck and cut through his flesh with a sickening squelch. Andronicus watched in horror as Philotas's head flipped through the air twice and then crashed against the floor with a dull thud. A second later his body collapsed beside it, and blood began pouring from his neck onto the marble floor. Three soldiers stepped forward and drove spears through the backs of the begging Persians. They all cried out, and everyone in the room watched in a mixture of fascination and revulsion as they died slowly.

"As for you, my friend," Alexander said, turning to face the man who had betrayed the others, "allow me to show you how we reward men such as you."

The man bowed low, clearly expecting some sort of gift. Instead Cleitus stepped in and brought his sword hilt down on the man's head. He fell to the floor and looked up in surprise. Even as Cleitus brought his sword back up, the man didn't seem to understand what was happening. Cleitus brought his sword down again, killing the man, and then turned to face the king.

Alexander looked out over his many generals and captains. They all looked terrified. Philotas had been the ranking general among them, and his head now lay on the floor. Alexander and Hephaestion both had a triumphant look about them, the same kind they got after a victorious battle, and even Ptolemy looked pleased. Only Cassander seemed saddened by what had happened. He stared down at Philotas with pity, and regret, and Andronicus could tell he would not have chosen to execute him.

"Hephaestion," Alexander said, "send word back to Greece. Have Parmenion executed as well."

"Alexander," Andronicus said, finally stepping forward. He had not saved Philotas, but Philotas had at least been guilty of the crime for which he had been killed. Andronicus knew full well that Parmenion had no knowledge of his son's plot, and had he known he surely would have counseled him not to go through with it. Andronicus could not stand by and let his friend die for his son's crime. "Parmenion had no knowledge of this, and he's still one of the most respected men in Macedonia. You can't have him killed for his son's treason."

"How do you know if Parmenion knew of this or not?" Hephaestion asked. "He had no more love for the king than his traitor son; he surely could have known. He could even have sent the gold to pay the assassins."

"Do you have any evidence at all to suggest that he did?" Andronicus demanded. "I know you boys have never liked Parmenion, but that doesn't give you the right to kill him."

"I'm the king!" Alexander shouted, slamming his fists against the arms of his throne. "I'll do as I please! I don't care if Parmenion knew of this treason or not. When he hears that I had his eldest son executed, he'll move against me. I must have him killed before he becomes a threat to me. You taught me that, Andronicus, or do you not remember?"

"Parmenion fought for you and your father," Andronicus urged. "He is a good man. When he learns of his son's treason, he'll understand why you killed him. He won't move against you. You don't have to kill him, Alexander."

"I've made up my mind," Alexander said, sitting back with a smug look. "Parmenion dies, as does Nikanor. You are all dismissed."

Everyone left the room in a hurry, not wanting to stare at Philotas's dead corpse any longer. Andronicus stayed behind, however, glaring at the young king and his friends.

"You should not contradict me in front of my men," Alexander said once it was only Andronicus and the boys.

"You once held great councils," Andronicus said, meeting Alexander's mismatched eyes. "You asked the advice of your generals and leaned on them when you needed help. Now you threaten me for trying to help you see reason?"

"I'm no longer a boy, Andronicus," Alexander said. "I don't need your help or your advice. I have defeated the Persians. I no longer need anyone's advice."

"Philotas was wrong," Andronicus said. "Your father would not be the one to weep. Aristotle would weep if he could see you now. He taught you to have compassion and wisdom. You have betrayed his every teaching. You once wanted to be a great king, Alexander."

"I am a great king!" Alexander shouted. "I have won every battle. I have defeated the Persians! I have liberated Greece, Thrace, Egypt, Persia, and Mesopotamia! I am the greatest king to ever live!"

Andronicus looked at Alexander with pity for a moment longer and then turned to leave. In his mind's eye he could see the face of Leonidas, a king he had considered to be truly great. He wondered if Leonidas had ever had to point out that he was king, or call himself the greatest king ever, and was quite sure he never had. As he walked away from the palace, he wondered what would become of the blade he had given to Philotas and guessed Alexander would take it for his own.

Chapter 57
Moving On
1

Everything changed after Philotas's execution. Alexander largely withdrew to his palace. He still had his friends with him, but the rest of the generals were no longer welcome except during feasts, which became much more seldom. Andronicus was once again not allowed in the king's close company. He didn't know what his position in the army was now, but he didn't intend to stay long enough to find out. He wanted to try to convince Cleitus to go with him, but he knew he would leave soon either way.

A few weeks after Philotas's death, a massive fire broke out in the palace at Persepolis. Andronicus wasn't there when it started, but he watched as it burned the immense Persian palace as well as a number of other buildings surrounding it to the ground. In the end nearly half the city burned down. Rumors spread about how the fire started, and most said that Alexander himself had started it.

Some said he burned the temple down as revenge for Xerxes burning down Athens 150 years earlier. Andronicus remembered that fire well. He had seen the burnt ruins of Athens after Xerxes was finished with it. He had also seen Athens a century after the fire, and it had become a far greater city than it had been prior to its burning. Andronicus doubted that there were any Athenians who still held any anger over the long past act.

The other rumor, whispered much more quietly, in far darker corners of the city, was that Alexander had started the fire in a drunken mistake. Whether he actually started the fire, or had simply ordered it, the accounts all seemed to say that he had been terribly drunk, and almost as soon as the fire started, he ordered it stopped, but it was too late.

2

A month after the fire, the army finally set out again. Andronicus no longer wanted any part in it, but they were marching in the same direction he was intending to go, so he thought he would stay with them a little while longer and try to get Cleitus to join him. He knew he could travel alone this time if he had to; it had been more than fifty years since Chaka died, and he felt ready to travel on his own now. Having Cleitus accompany him would simply be easier and smarter. As a strong, experienced fighter, he would be invaluable in their travels. He wasn't the cheeriest company, but Chaka hadn't really been either.

Andronicus talked to Cleitus about it as often as he could without anyone overhearing, but Cleitus refused to go with him. Andronicus could tell he wanted to go; he certainly didn't want to stay to protect Alexander. It seemed the only thing stopping Cleitus was the oath he had taken. Or perhaps it was the guilt of letting Philip die and the need to keep his son alive. Whatever the reason, Cleitus was unwilling to leave the king's army, so Andronicus would have to go it alone.

3

While Alexander and his army had been resting in Persepolis, burning palaces and executing generals, Darius had been on the run with his dwindling forces. He had fled through Media and into Parthia, and there he had been betrayed. Word came back to Alexander that Darius had been taken captive by his own men. Alexander pushed his army south, hoping to catch the Persians while their leadership was in such flux.

The Macedonians caught up to the Persians in the Bactrian desert. The Persians were caught unawares and fled at the sight of the Macedonian army. Before they reached the barren hills, someone stabbed King Darius and left him lying in an oxcart. When Alexander was told, he hurried over to where Darius lay dying. Andronicus was still in the king's guard, so he followed.

No one had bothered to take Darius out of the cart, and he lay in a growing pool of his own blood. He looked ghastly. Andronicus had only ever seen the man from afar during battles, but he could still tell that the old king was at his weakest. His cheeks were so thin that the bones stood out clearly around his jaw. His hair and beard, which had probably been trimmed and manicured his whole life, were messy and unkempt. He appeared to be on the verge of dying, but he looked up when Alexander walked up to him.

"So," Darius said, coughing harshly, "you're the boy-king who has beaten me." He spoke in a much better Greek accent than any other Persian Andronicus had ever heard, and he guessed Darius must have been well educated.

"I am," Alexander said proudly, looking down at his dying nemesis. The rest of the Persians had fled in fear and disgrace, and this was undoubtedly the end of the Persian war.

"Are you going to enslave my people?" Darius asked, struggling to hold his head up.

"Your soldiers will be given a choice," Alexander said. "They can fight for me or be enslaved. As for the women and children, they will be free so long as they obey the laws of my kingdom."

"Thank you." Darius coughed again, and let his head slump against his chest. "For my people, for my family, thank you, Alexander King. You are an honorable man."

Darius's voice trailed off, and his head slumped even more. There was a moment of silence as Alexander and his generals stood around the oxcart, gazing down at the fallen king. His eyes were still open, but they could all see that he was dead.

"Someone get him out of there," Alexander commanded. "Wrap his body. He'll be buried in Babylon alongside his ancestors."

"You would give him a royal funeral?" Hephaestion asked angrily. "Thousands of our men died fighting him."

"He is still a king," Alexander said sadly, "even if he was betrayed by his men. Besides, he's now my predecessor. He deserves to be buried with the rest of the dead kings of Persia."

"You are king of Asia now," Cassander pointed out. "There is no one left to dispute your claim."

"I'm king of Persia now," Alexander corrected. "There is still much of Asia left to be conquered."

4

Andronicus had known Alexander wouldn't stop at Persia. Parmenion had warned them all that Alexander would keep pushing them further after Darius fell, and he had been right. Alexander kept his army moving deeper and deeper into the Persian outlands, toward lands controlled by wild tribes. Andronicus wanted no more part in it. It was not that he didn't want to see the lands Alexander would be marching through; he just didn't want to do it with an army. He would go east as well, but he would go on his own. The Persians were finally done, and it was time for Andronicus to leave.

He packed his things and left them at the edge of the small city they were camped in, along with two horses, just in case Cleitus changed his mind. He had packed all his worldly possessions for the journey: his old Spartan cloak and sword, along with the last Karpos blade he had found, his special box of poisons and powders, one sack of gold, and a smaller sack full of diamonds. He still had his comb from when he was a boy, and the small piece of fabric that had been Manyara's. He hadn't worn it in many years, but he tied it around his wrist now. He picked up Chaka's jaguar tooth necklace, the one he had been so proud of, and threw it over his neck.

Wearing his Spartan and African attire, Andronicus made his way to the great tent where Alexander would be. When he entered the tent, he found the place stinking of smoke and wine. Alexander was with his friends, as always. They all had half-naked Persian girls on their laps, and they were all drunk. Andronicus saw Cleitus sitting at a table not far from the king, downing a jug of wine. He made his way over to Cleitus and sat beside him, facing the king.

"What in hells is that around your neck?" Cleitus barked, eyeing the necklace.

"The claws of a spotted jungle cat," Andronicus replied. "It belonged to my old friend, Chaka."

"The African one?" Cleitus asked, louder than Andronicus would have liked. "The one who went with you before?"

"Yes," Andronicus said. "These claws are from a great cat he killed in the jungle; he made this necklace himself."

"So why are you wearing it?" Cleitus asked as he took another drink. "And why are you wearing that cloak? The king won't like that."

"I'm done with the king," Andronicus said. "I'm setting out tonight. Are you sure you won't come with me?"

Cleitus didn't answer for a moment, and

Andronicus could tell he was actually considering it. He looked over at the king, laughing and spilling wine all over himself, and then back to Andronicus, with his heavy red cloak and ornate claw necklace.

"I swore an oath," Cleitus said, finally meeting Andronicus's eyes.

"You swore an oath to Parmenion as well," Andronicus pointed out, "and to Philip. You have lived your whole life in the service of other men. Come with me, brother. See the world. Be your own man." Andronicus grasped Cleitus's arm, shaking him.

"If I go with you, I'll just be in your service instead of his," Cleitus said, shaking him off and taking another long swig of wine.

"No," Andronicus insisted, "you'll be free. We'll see the world and meet people we have never even heard of before. Whatever happens to us, it'll be better than what would become of us here, with him."

Cleitus looked at the king for a moment, not saying a word, and then turned back to Andronicus. The cold emptiness that usually rested in Cleitus's eyes was gone, replaced by something Andronicus had never seen there before. It took him a moment to recognize it, but once he did it was unmistakable. Cleitus looked excited, even hopeful. Andronicus thought that he might have actually convinced him; Cleitus might come with him. Now all they had to do was tell Alexander. Andronicus rose and turned to face the king.

"Alexander," Andronicus said as he approached. Alexander and his friends looked up from their women and stared at Andronicus. He had no doubt that he looked a bit ridiculous with his cloak, armor, and necklace, but he didn't care.

"Yes?" Alexander said, frowning at the necklace.

"I'm leaving," Andronicus said. "I thought you deserved to know."

"Leaving?" Alexander slurred drunkenly. "And where are you going, Andronicus of Sparta?"

"East," Andronicus replied, "into the unknown."

"We're all going east," Cassander pointed out,

also sounding very drunk. "Why not stay with us?"

"I'm afraid my time in this army has come to an end," Andronicus said as politely as he could. "I thank you for everything you have done for me, Alexander. And you boys," Andronicus added, turning to the others, "you're the best friends a king could ever ask for. Keep him safe."

Cassander met Andronicus's eyes as he realized he was being serious and nodded slowly. Ptolemy looked shocked and frightened, glancing back and forth from Andronicus to Alexander. Hephaestion looked confused, but he gave Andronicus a curt nod nonetheless. Alexander, however, looked furious.

"I have not released you from your oath," he said, reaching for his chalice.

"I never made an oath to you, Alexander," Andronicus said. "I made oaths to your father and to Aristotle, and to Parmenion as well, but never to you."

"You dare speak that traitor's name in my presence?" Alexander said, rising to his feet.

"Parmenion was no traitor," Andronicus replied, meeting the king's eyes, "but that doesn't matter now. He's dead and so are his sons."

"That's right, they're dead," Alexander sneered. "You would do well to remember what happens to those who betray me. Now return to your chambers, and speak no more of leaving my army."

"I am leaving, Alexander," Andronicus said, staring into the king's hazy, discolored eyes. "This is goodbye."

"I'm leaving as well," a voice shouted from behind Andronicus. Everyone turned to see who had spoken, and everyone was surprised to see Cleitus the Black step up next to Andronicus.

"You can't leave, Cleitus," Alexander said. "He may not have sworn an oath to me, but you did. And I don't release you from your oath."

"I'm not asking your permission," Cleitus said, clearly as drunk as the king, "I'm telling you. I'm leaving with Andronicus."

"To break an oath to your king is treason," Hephaestion pointed out, rising to his feet.

"Are you going to have me executed, boy?" Cleitus growled. "In case you haven't noticed, both of your executioners are leaving. You'll have to do your own killing from now on."

"You think you're the only man who knows how to kill?" Alexander asked bitterly. "Every single man in this room has killed for me before, and every single man in this room will kill for me again."

"Perhaps," Cleitus said, his face returning to its dark scowl, "perhaps not."

"You think my men would betray me?" Alexander asked. "Just as Darius's men did to him? If I give the order, my men will cut you down right here and now."

"They could try," Andronicus said, placing his hand on the hilt of his sword.

"Enough!" Alexander shouted. "You don't threaten the king! Kill them!"

There was a tense moment of silence as everyone in the room looked from Andronicus, to Cleitus, to the king. When no one moved, Alexander looked around in anger.

"You have been given an order by your king!" he shouted. "Kill these traitors at once!" No one moved. Not even Hephaestion.

"You see, boy," Cleitus said, "you have lost the respect of your own men. You made promises to them, to let them go home. You're going to make them fight and die for lands no one has ever even been to. You care for no one but yourself. Andronicus and I have saved your life countless times, and you would have us killed? I pity you, Alexander, and I hope you get what you deserve."

Cleitus turned to leave. Andronicus gave Alexander one last look of pity. The king looked mad with hatred, his hair askew and his eyes filled with a wild fire. Andronicus looked over at Cassander, who nodded slowly again, and then he turned to leave. The two men walked through the tent, past rows of silent men, all staring at them in awe. Everyone seemed amazed that they were just walking away from the king like that.

Just as they were approaching the mouth of the tent, Andronicus heard Cleitus let out a sudden gasp.

Andronicus turned just as Cleitus fell to his knees. A blade was sticking out of his chest, covered in blood. Andronicus looked back and saw a spear sticking out of Cleitus's back. Cleitus looked up at him with shock and fear in his eyes. Andronicus had never seen fear in Cleitus's eyes, but it was there at the end. He opened his mouth and looked like he was trying to say something, then fell forward into the dirt. Andronicus stared down at his dead friend a moment longer and then turned back to face the king.

Alexander was on his feet, already holding another spear. He still had a wild look about him, but Andronicus thought he could also see regret. Alexander slowly set the spear down. He looked terribly conflicted, like he hadn't meant to do it. Andronicus didn't care, not anymore. He had sworn to protect Alexander, and he had sworn to leave in peace, but now all he saw was red, and the old fire and fury of battle engulfed him. Andronicus drew his sword and started walking toward Alexander with a look so terrifying that men scurried away like mice.

"Andronicus wait!" Cassander shouted, trying to stop what had already begun. Two soldiers stepped toward Andronicus, but Andronicus's sword whipped out, catching the light for an instant, and before either of them could even draw, they were both on the ground, clutching at fatal wounds. Men began shouting, and women started screaming. Many people got up and tried to flee, and several soldiers jumped up and charged Andronicus.

None of them stood a chance against him, even with his recent wounds. He cut down the men he had fought beside for years with terrible ease. He let out a cry as he drove his blade through one man's armored chest, and everyone around him scurried back from the force of his call. He had already killed a dozen men, and the rest of them stayed back, none of them wanting to face him. At least twenty soldiers surrounded Andronicus, all pointing spears at him, but they kept their distance. Behind them was Alexander, standing behind a group of guards. Hephaestion was next to him, his sword drawn as well, a confused and worried look on his face. Cassander was nowhere to be seen.

"He saved your life!" Andronicus shouted, his voice reverberating off the tent walls. "You would be dead if not for that man!"

"He betrayed me," Alexander said, sounding more like a scared child than a king. "He swore an oath."

"You'll die for this," Andronicus seethed through clenched teeth. "If I have to kill every last one of you, I will see you dead for this."

"Take him!" Alexander shouted to his men in a high, scared voice. "Alive if possible. I would make an example of those who threaten me."

"Then come fight me yourself, coward!" Andronicus shouted. "You hide behind your guards, you stabbed a man in the back. You have no honor left to you!"

Andronicus turned to face the men surrounding him and raised his sword. He stepped forward to begin the killing again, and then he felt something hit him in the back of the head. Whatever it was, it was heavy. He fell down to one knee and reached back to feel the back of his head. His hand came away wet with blood, and he turned to see who had hit him. To his surprise he saw Cassander standing there with another hand-sized rock. Andronicus opened his mouth to speak, and then he felt something else hit his head, and everything went black.

5

When Andronicus came to, he was being dragged across a rough stone floor. He felt strong hands around his arms, pulling him, and his knees were scraping across the stones. Andronicus slowly lifted his head and opened his eyes and saw that he was surrounded by soldiers with drawn swords. He looked down and saw that his sword was not at his side. He noticed he was still wearing Chaka's necklace, and then he realized he wasn't wearing his cloak anymore.

He kicked his feet up, trying to get his legs under him, and felt someone hit him hard in the back. He let out a grunt and fell back to the ground. A second later the hands were lifting him up and dragging him again. He tried to stop them, and again someone hit him hard in the back.

"Stop trying to resist," Hephaestion said from behind him. "You're being taken to the cells to await your sentencing for attempting to kill the king."

"And what of the king's sentencing?" Andronicus asked, coughing as they dragged him along the floor. "What happens to him for killing Cleitus?"

"Alexander is the king," Hephaestion said. "He can kill whomever he likes."

"And what about when he wants to kill you?" Andronicus said, wincing as his knees were knocked about on the hard stones.

"If Alexander ever wants to kill me," Hephaestion began, then paused for a moment, "then I suppose I'll die." Andronicus had to admire the boy's loyalty. No matter what else Alexander was, he had the full love and loyalty of his true friends.

They turned a corner, and Andronicus saw a row of dark cells going down a long dark corridor. A huge bearded man was standing at the mouth of the tunnel. He had a massive belly, and when he stood up he towered over the other men. The huge man looked at Hephaestion as if he were used to receiving prisoners at odd hours, and Andronicus wondered how many men Alexander had locked up down here.

"This one is dangerous," Hephaestion said. "You'll want to keep him away from the others."

"Put him in with the crazy one then," the huge man said in a deep, booming voice, "the last cell on the left."

The two men who had been dragging him pulled his arms, and he began to slide across the stone floor again. He looked at the cells as they passed and saw each one of them filled with dozens of men, Persians and Greeks alike by the looks of them.

As they neared the end of the cells, Andronicus tried to resist again. He heard the whip crack a split second before it struck his back. It stung like nothing he had ever felt, and he was sure it had been the huge man who had whipped him. As they pulled him up to the cell, he felt blood dripping down his back.

Someone swung the cell's heavy iron door open, and the two men threw Andronicus onto his belly in the dark, musty cell. Before he could move, the door slammed behind him. He pushed himself onto his hands and knees and then stood up. He turned to see Hephaestion, Cassander, and a half dozen soldiers staring at him. The robust prison guard had already ambled back to his post. Hephaestion looked like he wanted to say something, and Andronicus could tell he did not want to have to lock him up.

"You should not have tried to attack him," Hephaestion said finally, looking like he was close to tears.

"We didn't try to attack him," Andronicus said through panting breaths. "We tried to leave. He killed Cleitus for nothing but his own jealousy, and you know it."

Hephaestion looked down at his feet. He didn't bother trying to contradict Andronicus; he knew it was true.

"He should not have killed Cleitus," Hephaestion said, a pained look on his face. "But it's done now, and you know what he has to do to you."

"Then why wait?" Andronicus said, gripping the bars of the cell. "If he has to kill me then get it over with. I've been waiting to die for years."

"He wants to make an example out of you," Hephaestion answered apologetically. "He says he needs to show the rest of the army how traitors and deserters are treated."

"He's going to kill me in front of his army?" Andronicus asked, glaring at Hephaestion. "Will he at least do it himself?"

"Yes." Hephaestion nodded slowly. "I think that's why he's doing it, to show he doesn't need you or Cleitus. I'm sorry, Andronicus, I never wanted this to happen."

Hephaestion turned and walked away, and the soldiers followed him. Only Cassander stayed behind. The young man looked like he had been through more that night than Andronicus. Andronicus glared menacingly at him. He was the one who had thrown the rock at him. Once the others were all gone, Cassander stepped forward.

"Promise me you won't go after him," he said, staring Andronicus in the eye.

"What?" Andronicus said, genuinely taken aback.

"If I help you," Cassander whispered, "if I get you out of here, promise me you'll just leave. Promise me you won't go after Alexander."

Andronicus thought about it for a moment, not wanting to let Alexander get away with what he had done, but he saw no other choice.

"If you get me out of here, I promise I won't go after Alexander," Andronicus said, meeting Cassander's eye. He seemed convinced, and he nodded slowly.

"OK. I'll be back later tonight. Be ready to leave."

"My things are packed and waiting for me at the edge of the camp," Andronicus replied, "along with two horses."

Andronicus could see that Cassander had taken the implication. He didn't say anything for a moment, seeming to consider it, then slowly shook his head.

"I can't," he said. "He's my best friend Andronicus. He's been my best friend since I was five years old. You may see him as a spoiled, angry, selfish boy who doesn't deserve to be king. I see a man who has taken care of his friends since day one, never failing. I see a man who was made king before his twentieth birthday, and handed an empire on the cusp of a great invasion. He took his father's place, and he defeated the Persian Empire." Cassander paused for a moment, giving Andronicus an earnest look. "I know he didn't do it on his own, and I know he takes too much of the credit for himself, but he's still a boy. I'm still a boy. We weren't supposed to have to do all of this so young. We were supposed to have more time."

Andronicus felt guilt begin to mix with the anger he felt toward Alexander. Cassander was right; whatever else Alexander was, he was still just a boy. He had been given more responsibility at a younger age than any man in history. He took the credit for his victories because he still felt the need to live up to his father's image, and his wicked mother's aspirations.

"Alexander is not perfect," Cassander continued. "He may not be the great king you want him to be, but he still can be. We're still young, and the war is over. He still has a lifetime to be a great king, and I'm going to be there with him the whole time. So is Hephaestion, and so is Ptolemy. We'll never give up on him."

Andronicus nodded slowly. "You have my word," he said, meeting Cassander's eye. "I'll leave peacefully."

"Good. I'll come back later this evening," Cassander said, turning to leave, then coming back. "Oh, by the way, watch out for that man in your cell. I heard he has killed other prisoners."

Cassander left, leaving Andronicus alone in the cell except for a dark shape huddled against one of the walls. Andronicus turned to face whoever it was, waiting to see if he would attack him, but the shape didn't move. After a few minutes Andronicus decided the man wasn't an immediate threat. He sat against the wall opposite him, keeping his eyes fixed on the man.

6

Andronicus waited hours for Cassander to return. The only light came from a torch burning on the wall outside the cell, and the light barely reached him. The huddled mass against the far wall still hadn't moved or made a sound, and he wasn't even sure if the person was alive.

There was a sudden noise somewhere down the tunnel, and Andronicus leapt to his feet. He pressed his face against the cell bars and strained his eyes to see down the dark tunnel. He thought he saw something move, and then he felt strong hands grab his neck.

In an instant his cellmate had him down on the floor and began punching his face. Andronicus kicked up with his knee and caught the man in the gut. He guffawed and bent down, and Andronicus quickly pushed him off and sprang to his feet. He faced the man as he also got to his feet. The man glared at Andronicus, and Andronicus felt all the wind leave his body. He knew the face of the man across from him. It was haggard, scarred, and bearded, but the face was not a day older than the last time he had seen it, over a hundred years earlier. It was a face he had seen every day for years, a face he had grown up with. A face he had thought he had forgotten, but there could be no mistaking it. The man standing before him with his fists clenched was . . .

"Lycus," Andronicus said, his voice a breathy whisper. "Lycus," he repeated, not knowing what else to say. Lycus just glared at him with a mad look in his eyes that Andronicus didn't remember being there before. He was staring at Andronicus like he didn't believe he was real. Andronicus wasn't fully sure that Lycus was real himself. He had taken a hard hit to the head, and it could be some kind of trick of the mind. The man clenched his fists again, and Andronicus noticed that he was missing two fingers on his left hand. It looked like an old injury. There was a scar on his face that hadn't been there before either. Then Andronicus saw his ear. His left ear was missing its bottom half, just as Lycus's was, from the battle of Plataea.

"Lycus, it's me, Andronicus," he said, beginning to grasp what this meant. "We found each other," he said, feeling a flood of emotions.

Lycus's lips began to move, but Andronicus couldn't hear what he was saying. He had a wild look in his eyes, but Andronicus could tell there was recognition there as well. Andronicus realized then that this might be a very different person than the one he had known 130 years ago. As Andronicus looked him over, he noticed that Lycus was in much better shape than he was, the kind of shape Andronicus had been in during his traveling years with Chaka. He wondered if Lycus had been in many fights in recent years.

"Lycus, it's me, Andronicus," he said again, trying to sound as composed as he could. "We're still alive because of those rocks."

"It's the only way," Lycus said and then launched himself forward. Andronicus was caught off guard and he fell backward as Lycus fell on top of him. Andronicus tried to fight him off, but Lycus was stronger, and he wrapped his hands around Andronicus's neck, not having any difficulty without two of his fingers. Andronicus tried to kick up with his knee again, but this time Lycus was ready for it. As Andronicus struggled against his old friend's strong arms, he felt the urgent need to breathe. He grabbed at Lycus's head just as he felt himself beginning to lose consciousness.

Chapter 58
Out of the Blue
1

Lycus gradually felt himself coming out of the shadows. At first he was standing side by side with Andronicus and Niko, swords in hand, facing down the Persians at Thermopylae. Then, gradually, everything began to fade, and his head began pounding. Lycus felt himself come out of the dream into a world of ringing pain. He was lying on his back, a bright light above him. He tried to open his eyes, but the immense brightness forced them shut again. Lycus slowly lifted himself up, keeping his eyes clenched tight. It took a long time, but eventually he was able to open them.

Once his eyes were open, he only became more confused. Nothing looked familiar. He tried to remember how he had gotten there, but all he could recall was a storm and a mountain. Everything beyond that was cloudy, like he had been drinking too much, but he knew he hadn't.

He was in a desert of some kind, but not the same one he had been in. The place he was in now was drier and hotter, and there were no hills or mountains anywhere, except on the distant horizon. Lycus looked around to see where the others had gone, but he couldn't see anyone or anything. All around him was a dry red wasteland as far as he could see. Again he tried to remember how he had gotten to this dry, desolate place.

It was still blurry, covered in dark, moving shadows, but slowly he began to remember bits and pieces. The harder he concentrated, the more his head hurt, but he also started putting things together. They had climbed the mountain. Andronicus had sent them up the hill to find a cave, which he thought was a foolish idea. The storm had thickened, and they found a cave. The memory of Androcles finding the cave slowly came back, and Lycus felt an icy chill despite the immense heat.

He had never trusted Androcles, ever since they were children. He had hated Andronicus when they were young, but over the years they had become close friends. Once they went to war together, it was like they were brothers. Andronicus and Niko had been the best friends Lycus ever had, and even Euthymius, Andronicus' kind-hearted but weak friend. But he had never taken to Androcles, even after they had gone to war together. There was something about him that Lycus didn't trust.

It made Lycus shiver to remember how Androcles had mysteriously found the hidden cave in the middle of the storm. It was inconceivable. The cave had been so well covered that it would have been nearly impossible to find even without a storm.

He tried to remember what had happened after they entered the cave. His head was pounding harder than ever, and he felt like he might vomit. He ignored his headache and pushed harder. He knew the memories were there, and he was determined to bring them out. His head felt like it was splitting, sending him to his knees, but he persisted.

After they found the cave, they had gone down a path. The others had said they felt some kind of force pulling them farther down, but Lycus had felt nothing. He had followed them down into the depths of the mountain because he didn't want to be left alone. He followed them down the long tunnel, farther than he would have guessed possible. Then something had happened.

Lycus felt his stomach turn as his head pounded relentlessly, and he heaved whatever was in his stomach into the dirt. When he was done he wiped his mouth, and forced himself back to the memories, ignoring the horrible ringing in his ears and the pounding splitting through his head.

They had been walking through the dark cave. The others were all walking so fast, as if they could see in the dark, but Lycus bumped into rocks around every turn. He opened his eyes and looked down, and saw several fresh cuts and bruises on his legs and a few small dents in his armor. He closed his eyes again and tried to remember what had happened next.

They had found another cave, deep in the heart of the mountain. They had come to a sort of room, and there had been a pool. The pool had been glowing, and Lycus saw a bright light coming from its bottom. He had walked toward the pool, along with the others. They had walked into the water. Then he remembered the smoke. He had seen dark shapes moving in the water. He tried to remember what he had seen in the shadows and felt a cold chill run through his body. For a moment the shadows started to take shape, and then a cold black darkness fell upon everything. In the heart of the darkness, Lycus saw two small red dots, like eyes.

His stomach turned again, and he retched, harder than before. He continued heaving long after his stomach was empty. When he was finally done he fell back into the dirt, panting heavily. He knew what had happened next; he didn't need to push himself. They had all reached down and touched the glowing rocks. Somehow it wasn't hard to remember reaching down toward the light, but even thinking about the shadows made Lycus feel sick.

When he regained his breath, he stood up and scanned his surroundings. Nearly all of the horizon was nothing but endless red dirt. Only one direction held any hope of life, with several dead-looking trees and a mountain range in the far distance. Lycus looked around again for his friends once more before setting off toward the far off mountains. He wanted to shout for the others, but the thought of shouting made his head hurt and his stomach churn, so he stayed quiet.

2

Lycus walked all day, not stopping once. There was no water to be found in the dry red dirt, but he knew there might be some farther ahead.

When night fell and the stars came out, he continued to walk. It was light enough to see, and there was certainly nothing to bump into. As he walked through the night, he looked up at the stars. He had always loved looking at the stars. It was the only thing that old fool Philander had ever taught him that he actually cared about. He knew all of the constellations by heart, but he didn't recognize any of the stars above him now. They were as bright as he'd ever seen them, and there seemed to be more than usual, but none of them were familiar. The moon was resting just above the hills in the distance, and it looked right, although maybe a bit bigger than normal. He didn't know what it meant, but he knew he had to find water. He continued walking toward the hills, but now he scanned the sky as well, looking for any familiar stars. It was as though he had woken up in a completely different world.

3

By the time he reached the hills, Lycus felt like he might collapse at any moment. He had resorted to dragging his armor behind him in the dirt, and his whole body was covered in burnt cracked skin. His mouth was so dry that his lips cut his tongue. He knew he needed water soon, or he would die.

When Lycus finally reached the hills, he began walking alongside the range. Eventually, he found a cactus. He hobbled over to it like a drunkard, thanking the gods he despised. He cut off an arm from the cactus, pulled out the thorns with trembling hands, and took a bite, feeling the liquid fill his mouth. It tasted better than anything he'd ever eaten. He spent the rest of the day sitting next to the cactus, cutting off pieces and eating them.

That night he got little sleep. He hadn't been sleeping much since he had woken up in this horrible wasteland. He had feared since the first day that he might be dead and that this was Hades' house. It wasn't what they told the children, but it seemed more like what hell would be like, if it really did exist. He still had not seen another living being since waking up, not even a bird. He wondered how he had died, and guessed it must have been the rocks. There was something about them, something dark.

As he lay there staring up at the night sky, he thought he could see two red stars amongst all the white ones, like a pair of haunting eyes. He closed his eyes and rolled over. It took a long time to fall asleep, and he was filled with dark thoughts the whole time, but eventually he did fall asleep, only to find the eyes waiting for him in his dreams.

4

Lycus cut off as much of the cactus as he could and then moved on. He walked alongside the hills for days, hoping he would come across something living. The days turned to weeks, with nothing changing at all. Finally he gave in and climbed the hills. When he reached the top, he saw the same thing on the other side that was behind him: endless desert.

Far in the distance was another cactus, so Lycus started toward it. It took another week to get to that cactus, and he spent the night beside it before moving on again. He walked through the endless wasteland for months, living from one cactus to the next. He began to see birds at some point, but he couldn't remember when. They were not beautiful birds or seabirds but carrion birds, the kind that always showed up after a great battle to feast on the flesh of the dead.

They began to circle Lycus as he walked, and

he was sure they were waiting for him to fall. He became more sure with every day that he was indeed dead. He didn't know why he still had to eat and drink or piss and shit or even sleep, but he was convinced this was the underworld. He wondered where the others had gone and if it was only him walking through the endless heat, or if they were out there somewhere as well.

5

Lycus walked and walked, with no company except for the buzzards circling high above him. Occasionally, one of them would land too close to him, and he would take careful aim with his sword and kill them from ten yards away. He had always been the best at throwing his sword, even at their first test, when they were boys. He had killed the deer by throwing his sword. He had nothing to start a fire with, so he tore the raw meat off the bone with his teeth, the same way they would have done to him.

For months the only food he had was cacti and raw bird meat. Then, finally, months after he had woken in the desert, he began to see life again. It started with a few scarce trees, followed by all kinds of grass—tall grass and short grass, green grass and yellow grass. With the grass came animals, and fire. The first night that he roasted a rabbit over a fire and ate the cooked meat, he almost thought he was alive again. That night he slept better than he had since the incident, and he didn't dream at all of the red eyes in the dark.

6

Once he came to more fruitful lands, Lycus began seeing things he had never dreamed of. Animals began to roam the land again, though not ones he had ever seen before, for the most part. Each new animal he saw looked stranger and more alien than the last. There were all sorts of different rodents that didn't look at all like the squirrels or rabbits back home. They looked strange and even a bit frightening, but they tasted quite good.

In addition to his sword, Lycus picked out a stick and sharpened it into a spear. Once he had the spear, hunting the little creatures became far too easy. Some of them would even come up to him, as if they had never seen a human before, and then he would promptly skewer them and roast them. The farther he walked, and the more strange things he saw, the more questions he had. He still thought that he was in some kind of hell, a terrible version of the afterlife that no one living could have ever imagined. He wondered where the others were—where all the other people were. No matter where he was, whether he was alive or not, he would have thought there would be other people. Never in his wildest dreams had he imagined hell to be like this.

7

It wasn't until a few weeks after he left the desert behind that Lycus came across the hoppers. When he saw the first one, he thought he was going mad, and then four more hopped out to join it. Lycus stared at them, dumbfounded. He had never seen anything like them. He watched as the strange creatures hopped about on their big hind legs and picked at the grass with their small front legs.

They were mostly brown, some dirtier than others, and had thick fuzzy fur. They stood on their hind legs, which were bent slightly to accommodate their absurdly large feet. Their front legs were small and practically useless except for picking at the grass they ate. Their bodies were big and muscular, and their tails were long and thick. Their heads looked a bit like a giant rabbit, only longer, and they had big ears that stood high above their heads. One of them had a pouch in its stomach, and the face of a much smaller hopper was sticking out of it.

Lycus watched in fascination as the creatures hopped about on their huge feet. One of them got near where another was eating. It lifted its head and let out a long, odd noise that sounded a bit like a goat. Then the first one let out the same noise, and the two beasts faced each other. Lycus leaned forward in anticipation as the two hoppers circled each other. He had no idea how they would fight without front legs or sharp teeth, but he was eager to find out.

The first hopper leaned back and then launched itself forward. Lycus couldn't believe how far the thing jumped. It flew at least twelve feet through the air toward its foe. The second hopper leaned back on its tail and then jumped and kicked out with both feet at the flying one. The second hopper caught the first one hard in the stomach with both feet. The contact forced them both backwards, though the one who had been kicked fell hard to the ground, and didn't get up for a long time.

Lycus spent the rest of the day watching the hoppers go about their routine. There wasn't any more fighting between them, but Lycus didn't care; they were the most fascinating creatures he had ever seen. It made him wonder again if he might still be alive. He still felt alive, the same as he always had, though he supposed he wouldn't know what not being alive felt like. All he knew for certain was that he was no longer anywhere near Greece, and that he would likely never see his home again.

8

The weeks went on, and on, and on, and Lycus continued walking aimlessly through the strange wilderness. He continued to see new bizarre animals, disfigured rodents, giant rabbits, and all manner of birds. The hoppers seemed to be everywhere he went since leaving the dry wastelands behind. He waited for months before finally killing one and eating it. It tasted far better than the rodents and birds, and he decided he would have to eat them more often.

After many months of walking, how many Lycus had no idea, he reached a giant swamp. The red dirt and yellow grass ended abruptly, and the murky green water began. Trees and grass were growing out of the water, so it couldn't be too deep, but he didn't want to cross it. The water stretched out of sight, and he had no idea if there would be dry land on the other side, or how far away that land might be.

He decided to walk alongside the swamp and try to find a way around it, but when he saw no sign of the swamp ending, he decided to take his chances.

When Lycus stepped into the water, just as he had guessed, it was only about three feet deep. As he waded through the murky water, he saw things moving around him. He realized he had no idea what kind of creatures might be in these waters, and he drew his sword as a precaution.

Lycus walked through the swamp all day, occasionally finding dry land on which to rest. When the sun began to set, he made his way over to a piece of dry land about ten feet wide. He set his cloak and armor on the ground and then used his spear to fish. He had felt them swimming around him all day, and he knew it wouldn't take long to catch one. He stood on the patch of dirt waiting for just the right fish. Finally, he saw a nice fat one swimming by, and he plunged his spear into the water. He hit his mark, as he almost always did, and pulled the spear out of the water. However, just then, something huge came splashing out of the swamp.

Lycus leapt backward and watched in amazement as a man-sized lizard reared up out of the water and opened the biggest mouth he had ever seen. The long sharp-toothed mouth snapped down on the end of his spear, which snapped in two. The creature fell back into the water with the fish and then disappeared.

Lycus looked at the broken end of his spear in anger; it had taken him weeks to find the perfect stick.

For a moment Lycus began to worry about how he would get food without the spear, and then he realized he had a much more pressing concern. The giant lizard looked to be nearly as big as he was, and its mouth was big enough to take his leg off. He worried about how he would get out of the swamp without having to battle the creature. Then he began to wonder if there were more of them out there.

He stayed up the whole night, waiting to see if the beast would return for him, but it never did. In the morning he packed up his things, realizing he would have to go through miles of water in any direction. After wondering if he should retrace his steps back to the grassland, he decided to keep going through the swamp in hopes of finding the other side.

He still didn't know what he was searching for. He was all but certain he was dead and that this world was some kind of terrible afterlife. He supposed what he was really looking for was other people. If he could find other people, he could ask them where he was or if he was still alive. Maybe he could even ask them how to get back to Greece, if that was even possible. Even if they couldn't help him, it would be nice to hear another human voice beside his own, and the ones that sometimes spoke in his head.

9

The swamp went on farther than Lycus could have imagined, and it was indeed filled with more of the giant reptilian beasts. The more of them he saw, the more he respected their predatory instincts. He watched the beasts take down every other kind of animal except for him. After two full weeks of wading through waist-high water, being watched by the beasts, he was sure they were ready to attack him.

He knew how they liked to hunt; he had been observing it, preparing himself for the inevitable. They liked to stay perfectly still, like a log floating on the water. Once their prey got close enough, they would lash out as fast as anything Lycus had ever seen. Once they got their powerful jaws around their prey, it was always over. They didn't have long legs, and they couldn't swim very fast, but they could whip their bodies around lightning fast.

The first time one of them got too close to him, he drew his sword, and brought it down hard on the beast's head. To his shock and alarm, his blade made only a slight nick in the creature's scaly hide before it bounced off. The beast jerked around angrily in response to the blow. Lycus swung again, but it barely made a mark. The beast opened its wide mouth and hissed at him.

Lycus pulled the spear out from behind his

back. He had sharpened it into a new point, though it was now a foot shorter than before. While the beast's mouth was wide open, Lycus flung his spear into the beast's mouth. The sharpened stick plunged through the beast's inner flesh, and it began writhing in pain. Lycus quickly pulled the spear back before it could be snapped again. The injured monster swam away, leaving a trail of red in the water. Lycus saw several of its companions follow it, and knew they would finish the job for him.

After that he made sure to keep the spear in hand at all times while he was in the water. The whole procedure repeated itself twice over the next week. One of the giant lizards would swim too close to him, and he would slash at it with his sword until it opened its mouth to hiss at him, and then he would plunge his spear into its open mouth. After he replicated the technique on the third one in as many days, he lost respect for the predatory beasts. He knew all they had to do was attack his legs under the water, and they would surely cripple him, but they never did. Instead they would always approach him on the surface.

10

After nearly a month of wading through the dense swamplands, walking on land as often as he could, Lycus finally grew tired of eating practically nothing but fish, with the occasional bird or frog. He decided he wanted to know what the giant lizards tasted like. They were clearly the alpha predators of these lands, and nothing ever ate them except for each other. But he had lived in the swamp for over a month, and killed half a dozen of them already, so in a sense, that made him the new alpha predator. The only thing left to make it official was to eat one of them.

He waited until he found a large piece of dry land. He had seen them crawl out of the water before, but he was sure that once on dry land, he would be able to kill one and keep his kill away from the others. First he caught a half dozen fish. Then he laid them out about six feet away from the water.

Eventually, one of the large scaly beasts crawled out of the water. It was about eight feet long; not small by any means, but far from the biggest he had seen. Part of him wished a bigger one had come for his trap. As far as he could tell, there was no one to show his kill to either way, but he still wanted to kill the biggest one he could find. It wasn't just for himself; it was for the beasts, to show them he was the alpha predator now, not them.

As the scaly monster moved gradually toward the dead fish, Lycus crept out of his hiding place in the grass. He knew he had only two options at attacking the beast. He could spear it in its open mouth, as he had to the others, and risk it slithering back into the water, or he could go for the harder kill. The lizards had big black eyes on the sides of their narrow faces, and Lycus was sure that if he drove his spear through its eye, he could likely kill it in one blow, but to get close enough to attempt such a tactic would put him at risk of being attacked by the beast as well.

He had ample time to consider the two options, as the beast lumbered its way across the land. It looked a bit odd, lifting its heavy scaled body up with such small weak looking legs. As the over-sized lizard finally approached the fish, Lycus crept forward to make his move, and the beast froze. Lycus froze as well, keeping as still as he could, but he could tell he had been discovered. Realizing he would have to go with the first option, he crept around to face the thing head on.

It opened its mouth wide and hissed at him, and Lycus slowly moved in. It whipped its head around, causing Lycus to freeze again, and then it was still. He crept around to face the beast, his spear at the ready. If he could get his spear in at the right angle, he could drive it deep enough to kill the beast in one blow. When he was about four feet from the thing, it began to close its mouth, and then it opened it wide again and let out another gurgling hiss.

Lycus seized the moment and plunged his spear into the scaly creature's waiting mouth. Before the beast could snap its powerful jaws shut, the wood plunged through its inner flesh. It let out a terrible mangled hiss, and its mouth fell shut. Lycus pulled his spear free, and the beast collapsed to the ground. He had done it; he had killed the beast with one fluid motion.

Feeling as proud of himself as he ever had, Lycus dragged the heavy corpse over to where he had set up camp. He had all the makings of a fire laid out and ready to go, and he quickly set it ablaze before beginning to skin the beast. He knew there would be no way of cutting through the thick, scaly hide on top, so he flipped the beast over. Its stomach was yellow and softer, though still covered in rough hide. Lycus took his old dagger out and plunged it into the beast's belly. The blade cut through the flesh easily enough, and he split its stomach all the way open.

Lycus spent over an hour butchering the beast. First he removed all the needless organs and tossed them back into the water for the others. Then he took all the good meat out. He threw some over the fire and set the rest aside on a clear patch of grass. He wasn't sure what to do with all the rough hide, but he knew it could be useful. He thought about trying to make some kind of leg armor for himself out of the stuff but guessed it would take too long.

As Lycus worked, he heard something move in the water behind him. He turned around and saw a monstrously huge lizard crawling out of the water. It dwarfed all the others and looked big enough to eat a horse. Lycus jumped to his feet as the gargantuan beast opened its monstrous mouth. It was big enough to eat him whole, and some of its teeth looked to be nearly four inches long.

The beast pulled its gigantic body out of the water and crawled toward Lycus and the carcass. When it was fully out of the water Lycus couldn't believe its size. It was easily the biggest creature he had ever seen, more than twice the size of the others, and he had to wonder how many of them were this one's children. Then he realized the one he had killed could be this one's child, and he prepared to fight the monster. He picked up his sword with his left hand and braced his right hand to plunge the spear again. He knew that the same tactic he had used on the smaller one would not work on this colossal beast, but he didn't know what else to do.

As the monstrous beast dragged its gigantic belly across the dirt, Lycus backed away, not yet ready to make his move. He heard a noise behind him and turned his head to see two more of the creatures in the water behind him, though they were both of normal size. For a moment he thought about trying to run from the beast, but then he pictured himself trying to fight the thing in the water, and he quickly put that idea out of mind.

There was no more land behind Lycus, and the gargantuan beast was still closing in on him. He set his feet firmly in the dirt and readied himself for the fight of his life. He reminded himself that he had practically asked for this a few hours ago, and he let out a laugh. He had wanted to fight the biggest of them, to prove that he was the alpha predator in the swamp, and now he had that chance. He just hadn't expected the biggest one to be quite so big.

It stopped moving when it was about five feet away from him, and he took a deep breath and steeled his nerves. There was a moment of serene peace as he stared into the big black eyes of the king of these lands. He could tell from the way it looked at him that this one had seen men before, and killed them. Lycus wondered how long this thing had been there, killing and eating anything it wanted. It gave him a sort of thrill to know he would either dethrone the beast or die fighting a truly worthy opponent.

The second the beast moved, Lycus plunged his spear into the gigantic mouth. He felt it cut through flesh, and then the powerful jaws slammed shut. The spear splintered like a twig, and Lycus fell backward onto his butt. He tried to push himself up, but the beast was on him in a second. It whipped its massive head around, opening its mouth wide. Lycus tried to roll out of the way. He almost made it, but the beast caught him as he turned over. It closed its mouth over his leg, and for an instant he felt pain shoot up his entire left side.

Without thinking, he shoved his sword between the beast's jaws. He stabbed at the inside of its mouth, and it opened for a split second. Lycus quickly pulled his leg free and began crawling away. He looked down to see his leg bleeding from about twenty different holes, but he ignored it. The beast turned to face him and opened its giant mouth again, now showing a good amount of blood. Lycus hoped the blood was from the creature, but he knew most of it was probably his.

He tried to get to his feet, but the pain in his leg caused him to fall back down. The beast let out a terrible noise as it crawled toward him. It wasn't like the hissing noise that the others made. It was deeper, more guttural, almost like a roar. Lycus grabbed a nearby stick with his left hand, and prepared for the final attack. When the beast was nearly upon him, he rolled to the side. The giant mouth whipped around, and Lycus flung the stick at it.

The gigantic mouth snapped shut on the stick, catching the side of Lycus's hand with it. He watched more than felt as two of his fingers disappeared into the beast's mouth. When he pulled his hand away, his fingers were gone, replaced by a bloody mangled mess. He looked back up at the monster and saw that its mouth was still closed. Not taking time to worry about his hand, Lycus lunged toward the beast and flung his sword at it, letting out a loud battle cry. The giant mouth opened again, and the head turned just in time for Lycus's sword to find the beast's cold black eye. The blade sunk in deep, just as he had known it would, and he pushed it in with all his weight. The gargantuan beast let out a final sickening sort of hissing gurgling croak and then collapsed in a massive heap.

Lycus leapt to his feet and pulled his sword free from the beast's eye. He was prepared to keep fighting, but the beast wasn't moving. He kicked it with his foot, and it didn't budge. Not wanting to take any chances, Lycus walked around the gigantic beast, barely aware of the pain in his leg and hand, and plunged his sword into its other eye. Once he was absolutely sure it was dead, he fell to his knees and looked down at his trembling hand.

The two small fingers of his left hand were completely gone, along with a good portion of the hand below them. An alarming amount of blood was gushing from where they used to be, and he felt himself beginning to get light headed. Knowing he could not afford to pass out, he ran over to his little camp, no longer feeling the pain in his leg at all, and tore a long strip off his cloak, wrapping it around his mangled hand.

Once he had the bleeding in his hand under control, he realized his leg was also losing a tremendous amount of blood. The holes he was bleeding from on his leg were too big and too numerous for him to simply patch up; he knew he would have to seal them. He took a moment to ready himself as he set his sword in the fire, wishing he could have a drink of wine. Before he went to work on his leg, he took a moment to look at the beast he had killed. It had given him one hell of a fight, but he had defeated it. Feeling an immense sense of pride wash over him, he reluctantly returned his attention to his leg.

There were at least twenty holes in his leg leaking blood, none very wide, but some of them much deeper than others. He pulled his blade from the fire and shuddered at the thought of pressing the red-hot metal to his flesh, but knew he had no other choice. He started with the deepest hole, which had a steady stream of blood coming from it. He bit down hard on a stick and then took three deep breaths as he pressed the scalding metal to his leg. His eyes filled with tears, and he screamed around the stick. When he pulled the blade away, he looked down to see that the wound had indeed sealed shut, though it was now surrounded by a terrible burn.

He repeated the awful procedure four more times on the worst of the puncture holes and then decided to let the rest heal on their own. He realized he would not be leaving the little patch of land for some time.

Once he was finally done with his leg wounds, he looked at his hand again. It had stopped bleeding, but it looked awful, and he knew he would never be able to fight the same again.

Sitting there trying to ignore the pain, Lycus looked over at the dead beast again. Blood was leaking from both of its gouged-out eyes. Lycus stared into the red eyes for a long time, mesmerized by them. They weren't the same red eyes from his dreams, but somehow he felt like they were connected. He didn't know what the red eyes were, or if they were even real, but he felt like this monster had been some kind of test, and he had passed.

11

Lycus stayed put for a while after his dire battle with the monstrous lizard. The piece of land he was on was bigger than he had initially thought, and had enough trees to keep him warm for weeks. As for food, he wouldn't have to worry for a long time; the dead lizard's monstrous corpse wasn't going anywhere. The first night he feasted on a piece of its flesh, he felt like the king of the swamp. He had dethroned the great beast, and now these wretched lands were his.

The other lizards stayed away from him, not just that first night but every night after. They didn't even try to come for their colossal leader. Lycus could tell they were somewhat intelligent beasts, and it made him feel all the prouder for killing the best of them.

For the first two days he ate the meat from the smaller one he had killed, not bothering to do all the work of cutting into the big one.

When he had finished the smaller one, he tried to push the big one onto its back, but he couldn't budge it. He tried to tell himself that it was because of his injured leg and hand, but he knew it wasn't true. He had no idea just how much the thing weighed, but he guessed no man in the world could move it on his own.

It was long, arduous work cutting through the scaly hide with his sword, but Lycus did it. It smelled a bit foul after sitting in the sun for days, but Lycus didn't care. He threw the meat over a fire and roasted it until it was black and crispy, just how he liked it. It tasted fine to him, and his stomach accepted the meat graciously.

As he sat alone on the little island in the endless swamp, he thought again about his predicament. He still didn't know what this world was or what would happen to him if he died here, but he didn't want to find out. He had thought he was dead, but now he wasn't sure. He didn't know why he thought he might still be alive; perhaps because of the constant pain in his disfigured hand. He wondered, not for the first time, where Andronicus was and if he was alone in some foreign land as well.

If the others were out there somewhere, only Andronicus would survive; he was sure of that. Theodotus was a godly man, an honorable man, and a fool. If he was anywhere like where Lycus was, his gods wouldn't save him. Theo could never kill one of the biters, let alone the biggest one. Euthymius was kind, and wise, but he was also weak. Lycus had always thought he was going to get Andronicus killed, but he never had. Euthymius did his part when the time for fighting came, but Lycus could tell how much he hated it. Alone in the wilderness, without Andronicus there to urge him on, Thymi would surely die. Androcles perhaps could make it, the crazy bastard. He had his brother's grit, and he was a good enough fighter to take care of himself, but he was crazy. Lycus had always known he was crazy, but after the storm, the way he had led them straight to the cave and then to the glowing rocks, there was no denying it. It was Androcles's fault he was in this mess, whatever this mess was.

Lycus knew far too little about what was happening, and it made him angry, angry and scared, though he would never admit the latter to himself. He had told the others they shouldn't go up the mountain or down into the cave, but no one had listened. Niko would have listened. Niko would have made sure they stayed together, and would have definitely been able to make it out here. He thought about the faces of Niko's boys and knew he had to get back to Greece. He had made a promise. Niko hadn't asked the others, he hadn't asked Andronicus, he had asked Lycus. His dying words had been to tell Lycus to watch over his boys, and Lycus had promised to do so. He had a duty to his friend to try and make it back.

12

Lycus stayed on his little swamp island for two months while his leg and hand slowly healed, well after the monstrous beast he had killed began to rot. He ate its flesh right up until the point he began heaving it back up, and then he went back to catching fish. By then he had fashioned a new spear, though it was not as good as the old one. He stayed on the island, eating fish and letting his hand and leg heal, until there was no wood left to burn. His leg was mostly healed by then. Rough scars ran up his left leg, some of them surrounded by ugly burnt skin, but they were healed enough for him to move through the water again.

His hand was another story; the skin had begun to grow back around all the dead tissue, but it was still an ugly mess, and he didn't want to risk putting it in the water in case it got infected. So, he tore off another piece of his cloak and wrapped it around his hand. Then he rolled up his cloak, strapped on his armor, and picked up his sword and spear. He looked over at the decaying corpse of the beast that had taken his fingers. It seemed an awful shame that such a mighty creature should lie rotting in the sun. Lycus knew he would never forget the monster, but he wanted to take something of it with him, something to remind himself of what he had done, something more than the scars.

Turning his head away as the stench hit his nose, he tried to hoist the beast's mouth open, but it was too heavy. Some of the bigger teeth were visible outside the mouth though. Finding the largest one, he carefully removed it. When he was done, he held the tooth up to get a better look at it. It was at least five inches long and as sharp as his blade. He wondered if this tooth had given him one of the holes in his leg, and he liked the idea. With a final look at the rotting remains of his greatest opponent, he waded back into the swamp.

13

It took Lycus another two months before he finally found his way out of the swamplands. When he finally found solid ground again, he was a little alarmed to see that it looked exactly like the land before he had entered the swamp, complete with hoppers. He hoped he hadn't made a big circle somehow, but at the moment, he had more pressing concerns.

After more than a month of wading through waist-high water every day, some of the wounds on his leg had begun to take on a bad color. A week after that they also began to smell. By the time he made it out of the swamp, he knew at least three of the wounds on his leg were terribly infected. Back home there were medicines that could help the infection go away, and he suspected there were probably herbs nearby that could help him, but he didn't know which ones they were. He cursed himself for not listening more when Philander had taught them about herbs and medicines.

The only way he knew of to get rid of the infection was the soldier's way. Once again he dipped his sword into a fire and waited until it got red-hot. Before he performed the procedure, he inspected the wounds carefully, locating all of the infected tissue. At that moment he would have given the rest of his left hand for a jug of wine. He took the blade out of the fire, took a long deep breath, then held it against his infected wounds.

He felt every bit of the pain as the blade cut away at his decaying wound. Blood ran down his leg, and he could smell his flesh burning, but he kept going. It was hard to see as tears spilled down his face, but he didn't slow down. When he was done with the first one, he took a moment to breathe and cry. He had always thought crying was a shameful act, but there was no one around to see, and it hurt so damn bad he didn't care.

Before moving on to the second infected wound, he placed the blade back in the fire. When it was glowing red again, he readied himself to repeat the procedure, twice. The second scab proved easier to clean than the first, though it was still total agony. When he was done, he didn't bother to take another rest. He gave the final infected wound a quick once over and then sent his blade in. At one point as he cut through his own flesh, he thought he was going to pass out, but he pushed through it.

When all three wounds had been cut and seared, he tied a piece of cloth around each one. He was so exhausted he didn't bother to eat or make a fire; he simply laid down in the dirt. As he lay there, trying to fall asleep, he couldn't get the smell of his own burning flesh out of his nose. When he finally did fall asleep, he immediately fell into a strange dream, one so vivid it felt like reality.

He was in a dark room, and someone was standing in front of him. As he stared at the shadowy figure, it turned into Andronicus. Lycus rushed forward to greet his friend, and then the figure opened its eyes. The eyes were red, blood red, and it was no longer Andronicus standing before him. The face began changing before his eyes. He watched as it grew long and misshapen, and fangs appeared between its dark lips. The face became alien and monstrous, and then it spoke, and everything went cold and black.

Lycus awoke with a jolt, the echo of something awful ringing in his ears. For a moment after he sat up he thought he could hear some kind of inhuman whispering, and he felt his stomach turn over. He vomited into the dirt and then got up and walked away from it. He looked down at his leg in the moonlight and saw that some of the red lines coming out of the infected areas were shrinking. He wasn't quite sure what he had been dreaming of, but it made him feel cold to think about it. He tried to fall asleep again later that night, but every time he got close, he would hear an awful hissing voice, and he would quickly sit up to find nothing but the empty wilderness around him.

Chapter 59
Into the Black
1

Once his leg had healed again, Lycus began walking alongside the water. He didn't know what he was looking for or what he would do if he came to the end of the swamp. Part of him just wanted to stay there because he still felt like it was his. The great biter had undoubtedly been the ultimate ruler of the swamplands for a long time, and he had defeated it in combat. No matter what anyone might say, in his mind that made the swamplands his.

He stayed beside the swamplands for months. He couldn't believe how big the swamp was, and it made him wonder if he had truly met the greatest of the biters, or if there was an even larger one out there. He thought about it a lot and decided he would rather not find out. Eventually, he knew he had to leave the swamplands behind and trek across the grasslands. A low mountain range was not far away, disappearing from sight in the distance, so he figured he would follow that.

Once the swamp was behind him, his diet returned to rodents, birds, and the occasional hopper. He didn't like killing the hoppers when he didn't have to; he certainly enjoyed their company much more than the other animals. Sometimes they would hop along with him for miles, lending him silent company. As the months went on, and on, he stopped killing the hoppers altogether. They were the only real company he had, other than the rodents and the carrion birds. And the voices.

He didn't like thinking about the voices. They annoyed him, and confused him, but more than anything they scared him. He knew that men weren't supposed to hear voices in their heads. He had seen men back home who had gone mad, men who couldn't handle war or had been at the drink too long, and he had no intention of going crazy like them. It was only a matter of time before he would find other people, and then he could finally get some answers. Until then he just had to try and keep his wits about him.

At first it had only been his voice occasionally saying something to him. Then at some point he began to speak with that voice in his head. No one else was around, and there was nothing to do but walk, so it didn't seem odd to Lycus that he should talk to himself in his head. In fact, it almost seemed necessary to stay sane. It was a little more troubling when new voices joined the conversation, voices he didn't recognize at all. At first he didn't respond to them out of fear of what they might mean. He felt like if he began to converse with them, he might really be going insane.

After months and months of listening to the strange voices speak to him, he finally spoke back. To his complete surprise, the voices responded. He began to engage in conversation with them. After a while he didn't care if it meant he was crazy; he just liked having people to talk to. There were more than a dozen voices, some old and some young, some mean and some kind. Even some women's voices spoke with him, and he wished that he could see them and be with them. He didn't care if the voices sometimes said things that didn't make sense, he just liked having company again.

2

One day Lycus was walking through a forest of thin trees. He wasn't sure how long it had been since he had left the swamp behind; he had stopped counting days a long time ago. The most alarming part of his situation was becoming more evident and worrisome as time went on. He had not cut his hair or shaved his beard once since awaking in the desert, and it didn't seem any longer than it had been the day he had awoken. Back in Greece he had needed to cut his hair four times a year, and it still grew long and thick. Now he hadn't cut it in more than a year at least, and it hadn't grown at all.

He checked his appearance whenever he came across a pool of water, waiting to see some kind of change, but it never came. His hair was too long to notice any kind of growth, but his beard seemed a bit rougher than it had been months ago. He wasn't sure what that meant. If his hair wasn't growing at all, it would all but confirm that he was dead and in some kind of hellish afterworld. If his hair grew normally, he could be much more confident that he was still somewhere in the world and alive. Having it grow at such a painfully slow rate just confused the hell out of him.

As Lycus walked through the trees, thinking about his life and his friends, he heard a hooting noise behind him. He didn't recognize the noise, and he had become quite familiar with the noises and habits of all the creatures around him. He crept over to the nearest tree and peered around it, looking for the source of the odd noise. He heard rustling, and then saw what looked like a person dart from one tree to another.

Lycus shook his head and rubbed his eyes, then peered out into the trees again. His mind had to be playing tricks on him again; it had been happening more often lately, but it had never shown him an actual person before. He knew he really had seen something this time. He told himself it must have been a hopper, but then he saw it again. This time there was no mistaking that it was a man, a dark-skinned man holding a spear. The man jumped out from behind his tree and ran over to another, closer to Lycus.

The initial shock and joy of seeing another human was quickly followed by the realization that the man was almost definitely not alone. Lycus became keenly aware of the fact that he was standing completely in the open from all sides except the one from which the man was approaching. He looked around but didn't see anything but trees. He slipped his cloak off his back and placed it on the ground. His armor was hanging loosely on his shoulders, and he carefully tightened it, then unsheathed his sword. He gripped his spear awkwardly with his left hand. He still hadn't quite learned how to use that hand properly for most things yet.

Lycus got low to the ground and listened

carefully. He waited for nearly a minute, keeping totally still, and then he heard a rustling to his left. He turned to see a man darting from one tree to another, alarmingly close to him. Lycus crept toward the tree. When he was about five feet away from it, he heard a loud whoop from somewhere behind him.

The man behind the tree jumped out, holding a spear in both hands. He clearly wasn't expecting to find Lycus so close to him, and he jabbed clumsily at him with the spear. Lycus easily sidestepped the attack and drove his sword forward instinctively. It caught the man in the left side of his chest, right where his heart was. Lycus withdrew his sword as the man collapsed, and turned around to see three more men charging out of the trees. He tried to hold his hand out and tell them it was an accident, but they didn't seem to care.

The first man to reach him was clearly enraged by the death of his comrade. Lycus easily ducked the wild swing of his spear. He stepped forward and drove his sword through the man's bare chest without thinking. The other two stopped running and looked at each other, and then back at Lycus. He could tell they had never seen anyone like him before. Both men had dark brown skin, much darker than the Persians, and they wore nothing but thin loincloths around their waists. Ashes covered their faces, chests, and arms, and Lycus guessed that the men were the hunters of their people. He also guessed they had never fought other people before, and certainly not a Spartan warrior.

The two men looked hesitantly from each other to Lycus to their dead comrades on the ground. Lycus could see they had no desire to fight him but that they didn't know what to do. He slowly raised his left hand in peace, keeping his right hand ready with the sword. The men looked at his mangled hand in fascination, and one of them spoke. Lycus had no idea what the man said; it didn't sound like any language he had ever heard.

"Lycus," he said, pointing to himself with his left hand. The men looked at him in fear and confusion. He knew they were terrified of him and he was worried they would make a rash move and make him kill them. He took a small step toward them, but they both scurried back, stabbing at the air in front of him with their spears. He wondered what the men were hunting, and decided it had to be the hoppers. Knowing that these pathetic little men were killing his only friends filled Lycus with a sudden inexplicable rage.

Without waiting for the foolish terrified men to make a mistake, Lycus stepped forward. He ducked one spear easily and sidestepped the other. His sword slashed out and caught the one on the left in the throat. In the same motion, Lycus drove his spear through the second man's chest and out his back. The moment of rage over the hoppers ended as they fell, and he looked down and saw the dead men at his feet.

Lycus dropped his sword and backed away in horror. He had not meant to kill them. He had tried to reason with them, and then something had happened to him. It was like something else had made him move. He thought about how many of the hoppers he had killed and how recently he had stopped killing them, and couldn't believe he had just killed the poor men for such a simple crime.

Lycus stayed there all night, sitting with the corpses of the first humans he had seen since waking up. He knew a village or town of some kind had to be nearby. He wondered if he could go to them without them discovering what he had done. Even if he could keep the murders from them, they would surely speak the same gibberish language the hunters had spoken. He wouldn't be able to talk to them, and it would almost surely end with him having to kill more people. He spent the whole night trying to decide what to do while also trying to ignore the voices whispering to him to go and find the others and kill them.

3

In the end he didn't go looking for the village. Instead, he kept going in the direction he had been walking. The forests, and the grasslands, and hills, and mountains, it all went on and on, one taking the place of the other over and over again. Lycus tried not to listen to the voices in his mind, but there was nothing else to listen to. No matter how hard he tried to ignore them, they were the only sound in the world beside the wind, the rain, and the occasional bird call.

He followed the mountains, hoping they would lead him to more people, but instead they led him to the sea. When he first saw the sea, he was filled with more hope and joy than he had been since waking in the desert. He ran down to the sand, right into the waves. It felt amazing to be back in the water, not murky swamp water but the crystal-blue waters of the sea. He spent the night on the beach, listening to the waves crash, relishing the sound of something other than the voices.

The next day he began walking along the beach. He didn't know what was across the sea, but he knew that Greece lay next to the sea, and if he followed the beach long enough, perhaps he would find his way back home. He still didn't know how long he had been wandering, where he was, or if there was anyone else out there, but being near the water gave him hope that he might actually be able to find something, anything.

4

Lycus walked alongside the ocean day after day, and month after month. The months turned to years, which began piling on top of each other. Lycus had no idea how long it had been; there was no way to know. He had lost count of the days so long ago he could barely remember counting days at all. The stars were all different than the ones he had known growing up, and he didn't know how to judge time by these new ones. The one way he should be able to tell time, by his physical appearance, was impossible.

Somehow he had stopped growing older. The same way his hair had all but stopped growing, so had the rest of him. It made him both scared and curious to think about how it all worked. Something had happened, something terrible, he knew that much. When he tried to think about that fateful day in the cave, all he could remember was a murky pool of light filled with dark shadows, and it always ended with the red eyes opening.

He didn't dream of the twisted face and the horrible eyes very often, but every time he did he would awake covered in cold sweat, gasping for air. He could never quite remember what the face looked like, but he usually heard odd noises for a few seconds after he awoke. Most nights he dreamed of battle, either with the Persians or with the monstrous biter he had killed. Those dreams he could take, even when they ended with his fingers being bitten off. The only dreams that truly terrified him were the ones with the face and the eyes.

During the day, Lycus simply walked, and walked, and walked. He tried to stay close enough to the sea that he could hear the crashing of the waves, but after a while even that was not enough to drown out the awful voices. They constantly whispered in his ear, telling him nonsense mostly, things he didn't understand, and didn't want to. When he could understand them, they were usually talking about killing. He didn't know where the voices had come from or why they spoke to him, but he didn't like them; they felt like something alien trying to ruin his mind.

Over time Lycus began to talk out loud to himself to drown out the whispers, but also because it was nice to hear a voice, even if it was his own. He wanted nothing more than to see another person again. He promised himself not to kill the next person he met, no matter what they did. He could beat them up if he had to and even take them with him as a sort of pet; he just wanted someone else to listen to besides himself. The voices shouted that he could always listen to them, and he let out a dry chuckle.

5

The land and the sea went on together forever. Lycus walked not far from the sea, waiting to see other people, but they never came. The years went by unnoticed as he kept on walking. A thousand times Lycus thought about killing himself, about ending the terrible charade of a life he was now living. He still didn't know what kind of world this was or what it meant, but as time went on, he began to believe it was a test of some kind. His friends had to be out there as well in their own empty world, just like him. He didn't know if he would ever see any of them again, but he could still beat them. Maybe the last one standing would get to go home. If he could just keep going and outlive Andronicus and the others, he could go back to the real world, where there was wine to drink and real people to talk to.

The only problem with his plan was that it didn't seem like he could die from old age here, which meant neither could the others in their worlds. He would have to either wait endlessly until they all died; the thought of being alone with the voices for decades made Lycus shiver; or he could try and find his way to them, wherever they were. He tried to tell himself that when he found them, they could figure out what had happened together, but another part of him said he had to kill them, that he had to be the last one standing if he hoped to return home.

6

It was many years before Lycus came across humans again, though time had ceased to operate in a linear fashion for him long ago. He was walking along the edge of a high cliff, about six miles inland from the sea, when he saw five people walking across the plain down below. Lycus hid behind a rock and watched them from afar, then decided to follow them, creeping down the hillside.

When the sun began to set, the men set up camp. Two of them built a fire while the other three went hunting. Naturally, Lycus followed the hunters. He watched as they killed two large tree-dwelling rodents; they were far from the tastiest meat available, but they were the easiest to catch. Lycus pitied the fools. What kind of hunters went after the easiest kill when better meat was available? He had seen a group of hoppers earlier in the day and knew the men must have as well. He hoped they hadn't killed the hoppers for the same silly reasons he used to, but the voices confirmed what he already knew, that the men were either too afraid or too lazy to kill one of the hoppers. Either way, they weren't who Lycus was looking for.

He followed them back to the camp and watched as they skinned their kills. They were terribly sloppy about it, and they let plenty of good meat go to waste. Lycus watched with growing contempt as the men roasted the meat for a short while and then handed it out to each other, hardly cooked. He saw their looks of disgust as they chewed the meat, and wondered why they hadn't taken the time to kill something better. *Because they're too weak,* a voice whispered to him, and he smirked in agreement.

He waited until after they had all fallen asleep and then snuck into their camp. Not one of them so much as turned as he stepped over them.

They're weak and stupid, the voice whispered again.

They don't deserve to live, another voice added.

You killed the great king biter, the first voice said. *They can't even kill anything better than a stinking tree squirrel.*

You should kill them, Lycus, an oddly familiar voice chimed in. *Then you can be king of these lands just like you were in the swamp.*

Lycus drew his sword and stood over one of the sleeping men, staring down at his dark, strange-looking face. Lycus felt a mixture of emotions. Part of him was screaming not to do it, not to let it happen again. He could still save the person that he was. He tried to stop and think, but the voices would not stop whispering in his ear. They kept telling him to kill the men, that they didn't deserve to live. In a kind of trance, he raised his sword above the man's chest, and readied himself to plunge it into the man's heart.

Wait! one of the voices shouted. Lycus stopped, and cocked his head slightly, waiting to hear what the voice had to say. *If you kill them here, it won't make any difference,* the voice said. *Follow them back to their village. Kill them all, and then you can truly rule these lands.*

Lycus thought for a moment, his sword hovering over the sleeping man. It would be pointless to kill only these five men. He knew there must be more of them somewhere. Either he should let them go or kill them all.

Or you can try to find a way to communicate with them, a voice somewhere in the back of his head said, but it was quickly drowned out by all the other voices.

He lowered his hand, staring down at the strange face below him. It had been so long since he had seen a human that he had nearly forgotten what they looked like, and this man looked much different than what he remembered from back home or even from Persia. These men had the same dark skin as the last men he had seen years ago, and he wondered if there were any people like him anywhere.

There is no one like you, Lycus, a voice said. *You can live forever remember.*

He supposed that was true, but what if these men stayed young as well. What if everyone in this awful hell just lived on and on until they were killed?

You can be the winner then. You can kill them all.

He decided to follow the men back to their people. He didn't know what he was going to find when he got there, or even what he wanted to find. Part of him still wanted to try to talk to them. He was sure if he tried hard enough he could get them to understand him, at least a little. If he could talk to them, maybe he could get some answers.

They would try to kill you, Lycus.

But why would they try and kill him if he didn't pose a threat?

They hate you, Lycus. They know you killed those men in the forest.

He knew that couldn't be true; that had been too long ago and too far away.

They hate all Spartans. They will try to kill you.

Lycus shook his head and tried to turn the

voices off. Then he crept away from the men and found a bush he could hide behind not too far away. As Lycus drifted off to sleep, the dream began.

He was following the hunters back to their village. It was still dark. They were walking ahead of him, but he couldn't see their faces. Even when they turned to talk to each other in their terrible hissing language, he couldn't quite see them. When Lycus looked up at the sky, he saw the full moon, only it was an awful shade of red that he had never seen before. It looked like it was filled with blood. He kept following the hunters, but he couldn't stop looking at the moon.

Then a village appeared in front of them. The huts were made out of brown clay, and a huge fire was burning in the middle of the village. People were dancing around the fire, stomping their feet and waving their hands. Some of them were wearing masks, and the others were somehow all facing away from him. Between the fire and the moon, everything was stained red. Lycus thought it was like the way the world looked when he had blood in his eyes.

As the hunters approached the fire, everyone stopped dancing and they all turned to face the biggest hut together. Everyone was facing away from Lycus as the five hunters walked up to the hut. A dark figure stepped out of the shadows inside the hut, and everyone dropped to their knees and bowed their heads all the way down to the ground. Even the hunters bowed as the dark figure slowly rose above them. Lycus watched as the figure rose to its full height, which seemed impossibly tall. The man was wearing a strange mask, just like the others. Then his head slowly turned to face Lycus.

"We've been waiting for you," the shadowy figure said in a strangled hissing voice, sending an icy chill through Lycus's bones. Slowly, all the people lifted their heads and stood up. The leader grasped his mask with both hands, and Lycus noticed his hands didn't look at all human. The fingers were long and twisted, like talons, and the cracked, scaly skin was a dark shade of red. The monstrous hands pulled the mask away from the thing's head, and there it was. The dark red eyes opened wide, and the long, terrible face twisted into an evil grin. "We have been waiting for you for so very long, Lycus."

The people slowly turned toward him, and he could finally see their faces. They weren't the dark human faces he had seen the night before; they were the monstrous faces from the blackness, red and twisted and snarling.

They began walking toward him. He tried to turn to run, but he couldn't tear his eyes away from the red eyes staring at him, into him. He tried to scream as their twisted claws reached out for him, but nothing came out. Just before they ripped him open, he saw the leader's fanged mouth curl into an awful twisted smile, "I told you to kill them, Lycus." Then their talons were clawing at his skin, ripping him open.

7

Lycus awoke with a start and reached for his sword. His heart was racing, and his body was covered in cold sweat. He heard voices speaking in some strange language and tried to tell them to be quiet. Then he realized they weren't in his head.

He sprang to his feet and peered around the bush. The hunters were chatting and eating their breakfast. The awful dream slowly returned to him, and he looked over to make sure the men's faces were human. They were. Whatever they were saying, it wasn't in that awful hissing language, but in whatever strange but still human language they spoke.

Lycus tried to figure out what the dream could have meant. It was the first time he had been able to understand the monster with the red eyes, and it hadn't been alone this time. There had been a whole village of the awful twisted faces. And what was the red moon about? The end of the dream came back to him, and he shivered. It was as if he could still feel where the claws had cut him in the dream. Part of him wanted to flee, to leave the hunters and go on his way. Perhaps the dream had been an omen of sorts, telling him to stay away.

He found himself wishing one of the voices

would tell him what to do, but they were all silent. All he could hear was the strange foreign language of the brown men as they ate their breakfast. Lycus sat silently in the bushes, watching the men and waiting for them to go home. After twenty minutes or more, the men stood up and began walking again. Lycus didn't just follow them, he stalked them like a predator. They never left his sight, and yet they were completely unaware of his presence.

The hunters spent the whole day walking. They talked nonstop, laughing often, and occasionally yelling at each other. Lycus had no idea what they were saying, and he didn't care. He didn't want to know what the strange men were saying; he wanted his voices to speak up. They hadn't said a word since he had woken up from the dream, and he was beginning to wonder why. It was by far the longest they had stayed silent in many years.

Lycus stopped short, letting the men drift out of sight in the distance for a moment. He realized he had just thought of the voices as *his* voices. All day every day for as long as he could remember he wished they would be quiet, and now that they actually were, it gave him an odd sense of loneliness, even though actual living humans were not far away from him. He began walking again, catching up to the men a few minutes later. As the sun began to set, and the light faded from the land, the moon rose over the far-off hills. It was big and full, but it was the same color it usually was.

They kept walking through the forest for hours as the moon slowly rose. As it got higher and higher, it began to change color. To Lycus's astonishment and horror, the moon began to slowly turn red. At first he thought it was just another trick of his mind, but as it rose higher into the sky, it just got redder, until he could no longer deny it. It sent shivers down his spine. He looked at the men's faces again, making sure they were still human.

They were walking through a thin forest of tall trees when Lycus began to hear strange noises in the distance. At first he couldn't figure out what it was, and then it couldn't be mistaken. As they got closer it became obvious that the village was not far ahead, and some kind of celebration was taking place. He heard shouts and whoops and the crackling of a huge fire.

When the hunters emerged from the trees a loud cheer erupted from the village. Lycus hid behind a tree and watched. As the hunters walked up, Lycus crept closer. A chill shot up his spine, and he felt the hairs on his neck and arms stand on end. The village looked exactly as it had in his dream. The huts were the same ugly brown mud color. The giant fire in the center of the village crackled loudly, and the people were dancing around it. Some of the men were wearing the same masks he had seen in his dream. He looked up to the sky and saw the moon was nearly as red as it had been in his dream.

He didn't know what any of it meant, but it made him more scared than he had been in a long time, perhaps ever. The hunters walked through the crowd, right up to the biggest hut beside the fire. Lycus quickly glanced at a few faces to make sure they were still human. Everyone stopped dancing as a figure stepped out of the hut. Lycus held his breath as the man slowly stood up. He was wearing one of the masks, just like in the dream, but he was of normal height, short even. Lycus was desperate to know what it meant. Why had he seen this place so clearly in his dream, and why had they all been monsters? And what the hell was that red moon about? He closed his eyes and begged the voices to tell him what to do.

I already told you, a familiar voice said. *You have to kill them, Lycus. You have to kill them all.*

Lycus let out a long sigh. He didn't want to kill them; they were the only people he had seen for so long. As he watched, he saw a number of bare-breasted women dancing around the fire and felt the old carnal urges stir. He didn't want to have to kill any of them; he wanted to join them. As he crouched in the bushes, watching silently, the leader reached up and took off his mask. Lycus half expected to see the twisted face and the red eyes, but it was just an old man. He had grey hair and a kind face.

"I don't want to kill them," Lycus whispered to the darkness. There was no response. He waited for a long time as the celebration resumed, hoping for the voice to tell him why he had to kill them. Slowly he began to realize the voice was not going to answer him; none of them were. They had given him an order, and now they wouldn't speak to him unless he carried it out.

He wondered for a moment if he really wanted the voices back. The whole time they spoke to him he wished they would be quiet. The people out there were real. They could actually speak with him, and they had women and maybe even wine.

Lycus almost went out to talk to them, but he didn't. In a way he was scared of not having the voices. They had been speaking for so long that he thought he might go mad if they weren't there to talk to him. The idea that the voices were a sign that he had already gone mad long ago didn't occur to him. Lycus wondered what would happen if he just left without speaking to the people or killing them, if he just kept on walking like he had been doing for so long. Somehow he knew the voices would stay quiet if he did that, if he betrayed them.

Lycus found himself having to make the most terrible decision he had ever made. He was a warrior and a hunter. Killing people was not a problem for him, but to kill innocent women and children was more dishonorable than he cared to think about. Everything he had believed in his whole life, everything he had always fought for, told him he couldn't do it, that he shouldn't even be thinking about it, but the idea of being alone in the dark without anyone or anything to talk to was terrifying.

If you kill them, Lycus, I'll show you how to get home.

"You know how to get back to Greece?" Lycus whispered, feeling his hopes rise for the first time in years. For some reason he looked up at the red moon. He didn't know why, but it felt like it was speaking to him.

Of course I do, Lycus. Greece is across the sea, and I'll tell you how to get there. All you have to do is kill them.

"Why do I have to kill them?" Lycus asked again, desperate for any answer. He didn't even care if it was good, any reason would do, but no answer came. The voice stayed silent, not indulging in his meaningless questions.

"What if I just kill the men?" Lycus suggested to the haunting red moon above him. "I could kill every man and let the women and the children live." The voice didn't respond, as he knew it wouldn't. He knew the voice wasn't going to say anything else until it was done. It had given him an order, and it had even offered him a reward; he couldn't hope for anything else. He looked out at the villagers, laughing and smiling, most of them still dancing about joyously. He thought about Greece for a moment, about actually going back home, and felt a desperate longing to return there.

Kill them, Lycus, the voice said so softly that Lycus almost couldn't make out the words. *Kill them, and I will take you home.*

"Promise me," Lycus whispered in the faint red glow of the fire and the moon, staring out at the only people he had seen in so many years, "promise me I'll make it back to Greece."

I promise, the voice replied, and Lycus nodded slowly. He took a moment to mentally prepare for what he was about to do. Thinking cold, dark thoughts, he drew his sword and stepped out from behind the bushes.

At first no one noticed him walking up to the village with a dark, blank look on his face, his sword in hand, and then a woman screamed. Most of the people noticed him just as he was reaching them. Several men ran toward him, some of them grabbing spears, and began shouting in their foreign tongue.

Lycus wasted no time in doing what he had been bidden. As soon as the men reached him, he swung his sword through the air. At first there was a stunned silence as he cut down the first of them, as if none of them had ever seen such carnage. Then the screaming began in earnest. The women and children ran away in terror, but most of the men ran at him; he had to give them credit for that.

Lycus cut through the villagers as if he had last been at war just yesterday. He felt the old muscles stretch out as he swung his sword in wide arcing blows, killing them one by one, and relished the old feeling. None of them put up any real fight, not even the ones with the spears. He simply sidestepped their clumsy terrified blows. It didn't take long for him to kill all of the men. He knew most of the women and children had hidden in the huts, so he stepped toward the nearest one. He poked his head inside, saw it was empty, and moved on to the next one.

Lycus went from hut to hut. The ones that were empty, he passed by. The ones with terrified people in them, he stopped only long enough to kill them all and then kept going.

When he came to the big hut, he found the village leader sobbing and begging in his language, but Lycus took off his head in a single blow. The man's cold dead eyes stared up at him from the ground, as if they were seeing through Lycus. He picked up the severed head and cut out the eyes. Then he walked outside and held the head up for the moon to see.

The blood-red moon seemed to stare down at the bloody red eyes of the dead head, and Lycus smiled in hypnotized fascination. When he threw the head back into the dirt, its dark red eyes stared up at him, and he smiled as he resumed his work.

When every last villager was dead, Lycus stood over their bodies, breathing in the stench of flesh and blood. For a moment, as the haze of battle fell off of him, and the realization of what he had just done sank in, he thought about killing himself too. It only seemed right; he had just betrayed everything he had ever tried to stand for. He looked down at his blood-soaked sword and thought about plunging it into his own chest. He actually lifted the blade, and then all the familiar voices came flooding back.

We're proud of you, Lycus. We knew you could

do it. We're so glad to be back. We'll never leave you again.

Lycus let out a long sigh as he listened to the old voices soothe him. He walked over to a log by the huge fire and sat down. For the next hour he just sat there, staring up at the moon as it slowly lost its red hue, speaking with his voices, seemingly unperturbed by all the corpses around him.

Sometime later, maybe minutes, maybe hours, he walked over to one of the empty huts and lay down on a cot inside. That night he dreamed of the battle of Plataea, his finest hour, and yet for some reason the faces of the men he was killing, which should have been Persian, were much darker, and some of them were far too young.

8

Lycus moved on from the decimated village and returned to his endless journey as if nothing had happened. The voices certainly acted as if nothing had. They never said anything about that night, the dream, or the moon. They also didn't say anything about returning to Greece. The voices would go on and on about nonsense, things he didn't understand in the slightest, or care to, but if he asked anything about going home or how to get to Greece, they would go silent for hours. Sometimes he would ask the question just so he could have a few hours of silence and enjoy the peaceful landscape around him.

There were no other people, at all. He wondered if he had killed the only people in this world, and had mixed feelings on the matter. The thought of ending a people altogether made him feel ill with guilt and remorse. At the same time, another part of him relished the idea that he was the decider of fates, like a god. Mostly, he just felt betrayed. He hadn't wanted to kill those people, but the voices had told him they would show him the way back to Greece. He had held up his end of the bargain, killing everyone in the village, but the voices wouldn't tell him how to go home.

The animals stayed away from him, even the

hoppers. Where they had once hopped along with him for days at a time, they would now scurry off at the sight of him. He wondered if they somehow knew what he had done, or if they could simply sense what kind of a predator he was. He had no doubt that he was the ultimate alpha of these lands now; he had killed the king biter and all of the other people. If he wasn't the king of this place, then no one was.

Lycus walked on, and on, and on, waiting for some kind of sign, but none ever came. He walked along the mountains and the beaches. He walked through the plains and the swamps. The voices told him all manner of things but never how to get home, as they had promised. Over the years his hair slowly grew long again, and his beard grew thick and bushy. Sometimes he wondered just how long it had been since he had touched those cursed stones. If someone told him it had been seventy-eight years since that fateful day, he might even believe them.

9

Lycus kept walking and waiting for a sign. His days consisted of endless walking, hunting, and talking to his voices. He had grown so accustomed to their presence that he had a different relationship with each one. The days all blended together so seamlessly that Lycus never knew where he was, though the lands looked somewhat familiar. At some point he reached the swamplands again. He made his way through and around them, killing more of the biters but never finding one anywhere close to the old king.

When he left the swamp again, he crossed mountains and plains, forests and rivers. The metal straps on his armor had begun to rust sometime along his travels, and it only grew worse, until one day he cut himself setting it down. It left a nasty cut along his already disfigured hand. Two days later Lycus lay in the dirt, sweating like a stuck pig and wondering if he was finally going to die. He had lost his fingers, had two dozen holes in his leg, he had made it through war with man and beast alike, and now it seemed like he was going to die from a cut on his hand.

The voices never stopped talking, and Lycus began to see things. It felt like one of his dreams, but he knew he was awake. First his old friends were there, as were the men he had served with. Diokles came by and roared laughter at the sight of Lycus lying helpless in the dirt. Other people came too, but Lycus didn't know them. He wondered if they were his voices, and he tried to talk to them, but they only stared at him, like all the rest. People kept coming, and the voices kept talking, and Lycus's fever grew worse.

On the third day, Lycus was sure he would die. He felt hotter than he would have imagined possible, and yet every time the wind hit his sweat-drenched body, it felt like icy needles stabbing at his skin. His whole body was trembling, and his entire field of vision had gone hazy. He couldn't make out the trees just ten feet away. He was drifting in and out of consciousness when a new figure approached him.

Lycus lifted his head and saw that the figure was very tall and covered in heavy black robes. Lycus couldn't make out the face or anything else, just the big black robes. The figure reached behind its back and then bent down. Lycus caught a whiff of a foul stench, and then there was a bowl in front of his face. Lycus looked up, trying to see the man's face, but all he could see was an empty black hole under a heavy hood. Just before the bowl touched his lips, Lycus thought he saw red scaly hands pushing it forward.

Lycus was too weak to resist, so he let the figure pour the contents of the bowl down his throat. He drank it, knowing things couldn't get any worse than they already were. When he had swallowed it all, the figure got up and turned. Lycus called out to him, and the effort of shouting brought on a fit of coughing, which caused him to pass out seconds later.

When Lycus woke up, he felt better than he had in days. He even felt strong enough to get up and search for food. The cut on his hand still looked nasty, but not as bad as before. Lycus didn't know what to make of any of it. He remembered the tall figure giving him the bowl, but he couldn't figure out how it was possible. There was no one else out here, he knew there wasn't. The only people he had seen since he arrived were all dead, and even if they weren't, he hadn't seen anything like the black robes the man had been wearing. They looked like the kind of thing one could only get in Greece, or perhaps Egypt.

Lycus wondered if the monster from his dreams had come to save him. That led to a slew of new and terrifying possibilities. He had been waiting for a sign, and perhaps this had been it. He hadn't learned anything about how to get home; all he had learned was that the monster was more real than he had thought. The monster still terrified him, but now he had to wonder why it had saved him, if that was indeed what had happened. No matter how much he thought about it or consulted his voices, he didn't have any answers.

The only thing to do was keep going. He stayed put for a few more days until he felt ready to go on, and then he resumed his march. As Lycus walked along the mountain range, he knew he had walked along it before, but he kept going, hoping and waiting for a sign.

10

And then one day it finally happened. Lycus was walking through a wide open plain listening to an irritating debate on the intricacies of skinning a hopper going on in his head. Then, without warning, a voice shouted, *Stop!* It was so clear and so loud that Lycus actually dropped to the ground and drew his sword, looking around for the source of the noise. It took him a moment to realize it was actually one of his voices in his head. The other voices had all ceased their endless chattering, and Lycus waited to hear the voice again.

He waited hours for further instruction. He sat down right where the voice had told him to stop, and waited. After several hours of him just sitting silently in the dirt, the animals began to come out again. They still kept their distance, but they at least showed themselves. Lycus smiled to himself, knowing that once the voice spoke again, he would have an easy dinner.

It wasn't until the sun had nearly set that the voice finally did speak again. The first time the voice had shouted at him so loud he had thought it actually was out loud. This time the voice came in with the breeze, as a whisper, as if it really were someone else's voice. He was sitting in the dirt, staring at a hopper he intended to eat, when a breeze blew over him. It was a hot day, and the cool breeze felt good against his burnt skin. Then he heard it, a single word. *North.*

Lycus didn't need to ask any questions; that was enough for him. He still didn't know where he was or which way Greece was, but he knew which way north was. The sun rises in the east and falls in the west, and north falls in between; that much he knew. If the voice said to go north, that's exactly what he would do. He had been walking aimlessly for decades, with no real idea of where he was going. Just the thought of having somewhere to go made him excited.

He got to his feet and started walking north without even stopping to eat. Lycus walked through the entire night, letting the stars guide his way. He still didn't know them by name, but he had become more familiar with the stars here than he had ever been with the stars above Greece. Even when the sun began to rise, he still didn't feel tired. Having a sense of purpose again had filled him with a sort of liveliness he had not felt in many years. Part of him told him that the voice could have lied, that there may be nothing to the north but more hills and plains, but the voice had made him a promise. He had massacred an entire village for that promise, and the voices had to honor their agreement, or Lycus would just have to kill them too.

11

Lycus walked north for days, and then for weeks, until he finally reached the sea. When he could walk no farther north, he looked around, half expecting to find someone there waiting for him. There was a low hill off to his right and some trees to his left, but other than that there was nothing awaiting him. For a moment he felt his rage boil over, and he began shouting at the voices.

"You promised me!" Lycus screamed to the open sea. "You promised to take me back to Greece!" Lycus fell to his knees, tears of rage spilling down his cheeks. "I killed those people for you," he whispered. "I gave up my honor. I killed those children." Lycus began to weep. It was the first time in his extraordinarily long life that he had ever wept. He had cried before, either from pain or rage, but he had never truly wept. In that brief moment, he knew he had gone mad long ago. He knew there was no life for him back in Greece or anywhere else. He was a monster, and a danger to everything around him.

Lycus pulled his sword out and stared down at it as he thought of all the terrible things he had done, all of them with that blade. After a long time, he stood up and turned to face the setting sun. He looked out over the sea and the clouds above and felt a moment of true peace. He knew exactly what he was supposed to do, not because any voice had told him but because somehow he just knew. Holding his head high, Lycus raised his sword to his chest, the blade resting just over his heart. The voices had all gone silent, and he was alone as he prepared to end the nightmare. He closed his eyes and took a long inhale, gripping the sword tight.

Stop! a voice shouted so loud that Lycus flinched in surprise, causing the sword to poke a small hole in his chest. A single droplet of blood ran down his chest like a red tear.

"You lied to me," Lycus whispered, staring out at the sea.

I didn't, the voice replied. *I told you that Greece is north, and it is, across the sea.*

"Egypt is across the sea from Greece," Lycus said, "not this cursed land. You lie again."

There is much land between here and Greece, and much sea. I can show you the way.

"How can you know the way?" Lycus asked the empty beach. "You're not even real; you're just in my head."

The voice didn't respond. Lycus couldn't tell if it was because he had correctly accused the voice of being a part of him or because the monster had taken offense. He waited nervously for the voice to speak again. His sword was resting at his side now, and he seemed to have completely forgotten what he had almost done. In that moment he had no idea if the voice was in his head or if it really was the voice of the monster from his dreams, and he didn't know which one scared him more.

He knew that the voices he usually heard were of his own making. They sounded like him, and they only knew as much as he did. The only voice that seemed foreign was the one giving him the instructions. In his heart he hoped it wasn't part of him, that he hadn't made himself murder those people as some sort of sick joke. But the alternative was even worse. If the voice was real and not just his own madness driving him on, that meant the monster was real too.

At that moment, as if it were a sign sent by the gods, a big black raven came falling out of the sky. Lycus watched the bird tumble through the air until it smacked down into the water with a splash. It surfaced a moment later, floating. Then, to Lycus's utter amazement, a hawk plummeted out of the sky faster than any bird he had ever seen. It swooped over the water, and with flawless grace and precision, it grabbed the dead raven in its talons and flew away with it. The hawk must have killed the raven high in the air and then dove down to retrieve its kill, but the way it appeared to Lycus was the only sign he needed. In that moment he had no doubt that the monster was real and had just shown itself to him once again.

He didn't need to wait for further instruction; he knew what he had to do. If the voice said Greece was across the sea, he would cross the sea. He had no boat, and had never built one in his life, but he was confident he would get the job done. Feeling hopeful and alive again, he started toward the trees in the distance, seeking the perfect one for his boat.

12

It took many months before Lycus had a boat that he felt confident would carry him across the sea. At first he tried to build a boat out of different pieces of wood, but he could never get them to float properly. He knew that if he had nails he could build a boat much easier, but there was nothing strong enough to use as proper nails. After much trial and error, he realized that his boat would need to be made from one single piece of wood.

He searched for weeks before he found the perfect tree. The tree he chose was much taller and wider than the others. He tied a flat, sharpened rock to the end of a strong stick to make an axe and then used it to cut the tree down. It took three weeks with the makeshift axe, but he brought the tree down. Once it was lying on the ground, he began carving out his boat. It was long, tedious work, but Lycus didn't mind. He felt like he had a purpose again, and it wasn't as if he didn't have company; his voices spoke to him the whole time.

When the boat was done, he dragged it to the sea and went out for the first time. He spent the next week paddling up and down the coast with an oar he had made from the same tree. After making sure his boat and paddle would both hold up, he prepared to depart. He loaded the boat with his sword, his cloak, the axe and spear he had made, and as much fruit and dried meat as he could. Then he laid his cloak over it to shield it from the sun.

Before he left, he spent a final night by the sea, thinking about the strange land he had lived in for so long and how he was finally going to leave it behind. Thinking of his time since he had woken in the desert wasn't easy. The early days had been brighter than the later ones, and the early days had been awfully dark. The only real thing of importance that he had done there was kill. He had killed people and animals alike, including the great king biter. He looked at the old scar on his hand, where his fingers had once been, and smiled fondly. Lycus didn't know what lay ahead, but he felt ready.

13

The wooden boat glided gently across the sparkling blue water, the sea flat and unmoving. He didn't know how long he had before the wind and waves returned or how far he had to go to reach land again, but he meant to get as far as he could as fast as he could. He hadn't used his upper body so much in all his life, and by midday his arms felt like they would fall off, but he kept paddling. He would take turns paddling on one side and then the other, trying to balance out the workload.

He stopped twice to eat and drink a bit of water. He had filled three large gourds with fresh water, but by the end of the first day, he knew that wouldn't be enough. When night fell, and the stars came out, Lycus could tell he was still heading north. He still didn't know if land was directly north of him, but he believed the voice would tell him if he needed to change course. After a full day's worth of paddling through the open sea, Lycus finally laid down in his boat.

He was as tired as he had ever been, and his arms were like jelly, but he felt good. It felt better than he would have ever believed to be gone from the hell in which he had been living. No matter what happened or where he went, at least he wouldn't have to die in that hell, which he had been so sure he would. As he lay there staring up at the thousands of stars above, he heard a strange noise. It took him a while to recognize it; he hadn't been at sea in so long. Finally he remembered Captain Sophos telling him and Niko about whales and their songs, so very long ago. He lay there listening to the songs of the great beasts below him as he drifted off to sleep.

In his dream he was also at sea, only on a huge ship rather than his little boat. He looked around and saw men hustling across the ship, apparently preparing for something. The ship was bigger than any he had ever seen, and built differently too. He noticed a staircase at the back of the ship, leading to a huge deck above the rest of the ship. Lycus made his way to the staircase, staying out of the way of the hurrying men. He walked up the stairs, and at the top he found a huge wheel attached to the ship's mast. Lycus had never seen anything like it. A man was turning the wheel to the left, and the ship was turning slightly. Lycus realized the giant wheel was some kind of rudder, and was amazed at the ingenuity of it all.

Lycus turned to look out at the sea, and then he understood why all the men were in such a hurry. Four gigantic ships were sailing toward them. They all had three huge masts that rose high into the sky and white billowing sails so big they could cover a house. On the decks of all four ships were men holding sticks. Lycus wondered why the men were not better armed; they were clearly readying for an attack. Lycus turned back to the ship he was on and saw all of the men standing still, looking up at him. For a second he didn't know what was happening, and he prepared himself for the men to turn into monsters and kill him. However, as he stood there staring down at them, he realized the men were waiting for him. It slowly dawned on him that he was the captain of the ship.

Before he could utter a word, a tremendous boom sounded from one of the other ships. Lycus turned, expecting to see the ship going up in flames, but instead he saw a white plume of smoke rising from some strange thing on the ship's deck. Then the blasts began in earnest. As one blast followed another, Lycus didn't know what they were or how it was happening, but his ship was being destroyed. Whatever those blasts were, they were somehow hitting his ship instead of theirs.

Lycus turned to shout to his men, but they were all dead. The deck was covered in blood and fire, and death. The ship gave an awful lurch, and then it was sinking. Lycus jumped off the deck into the water below. As he swam through the blood-filled water, he felt something brush past his leg. It was slimy and inhuman. Lycus ducked his head underwater and opened his eyes and saw a huge grey beast gliding just beneath the water's surface. As he watched, the beast opened its mouth and began tearing a man apart.

Lycus popped his head back up, gulping for air, and then he saw a huge mouth full of rows of sharp teeth coming at him. The teeth clamped down on him, and he let out a terrible scream as his flesh tore away.

14

Lycus lurched forward as he awoke from the dream, as he so often did. He looked around and saw that he was still in the open sea, though there were no great warships in sight. Lycus thought about the dream as he began paddling again. He didn't know why some of his dreams were so much more vivid than others, and so strange. Just thinking about the gigantic ships from his dream made him shiver. He knew there were no such ships in the world, and he wondered where they came from.

He spent the whole day paddling, drinking as seldom as possible. By sundown he was completely dehydrated and beginning to see things in the water. He couldn't tell if it was the monsters from his dream, fish, or just something his mind was showing him. When the sun was gone, and the stars came out again, he saw that he was still heading north. He wondered how far he had traveled in the two days at sea and how much farther there was to go. He looked down at the gourds of water and saw that one of them was nearly empty.

After eating one of the small purple fruit he had grown quite fond of, he lay down to sleep again. This time he had more normal dreams, at least for him. He dreamed he was a child again, out in the woods on his first test. Andronicus was there, and so was Niko. In the dream Lycus tried to talk to Niko, but every time Niko would turn his back to him and walk away. Then the wolves came, just like they had in real life, and he fought them, with Andronicus at his side.

When Lycus woke, he raised his head and felt the wind hit his face. He sat up and saw that the wind had begun to blow to the east. The wind wasn't too strong, but Lycus could feel it pushing his boat as he began to paddle. That day he probably went half as far as he had the two days before, but he was twice as tired. His arms and chest felt like they were on fire. As the sun went down, Lycus saw a storm front approaching from the west, and he knew he would get no sleep that night.

Lycus spent his third night at sea battling the waves. The storm was not terrible, but Lycus's boat was tiny. The wind howled around him, and the waves just kept coming. Lycus would maneuver his small craft up one high wave and then come crashing down the other side, only to find another wave waiting for him. It was the longest night of his life, fighting off wave after wave until well after dawn. At some point in the night it began to rain, though only for a little while. Lycus made sure to fill his gourds to the brim again and drank as much as he could.

When the clouds finally parted, the sun was nearly right above him. Not long after the sun came out, the wind died down, and the waves dissipated with it. Lycus had to fight off the waves for another two hours before he could finally rest. When he finally put his paddle down on his lap and rested his arms at his sides, he felt dizziness wash over him. He looked at the sky to make sure another storm wasn't coming and then passed out in his boat.

15

Lycus opened his eyes slowly, and saw the clear blue sky above. A bird called somewhere nearby, and another one was flying overhead. Lycus tried to sit up, but his body was too sore. He tried to grasp the sides of his boat, but he couldn't lift his arms. That was when he noticed his boat wasn't rocking at all. Even when the sea was flat, the boat had swayed slightly, but it wasn't now. Feeling a burst of excitement, he lifted himself up, ignoring the pain in his torso.

When he sat up, he was greeted by the most wonderful sight he had ever seen. His boat had washed up on shore, and there could be no doubt that he was on an island. Twenty feet up from the water was a thick jungle. High above the trees in the distance was a tall mountain, covered in more lush trees.

Lycus lifted himself out of his little boat and flopped onto the sand. It felt amazing to be back on dry land, and he realized only then just how scared he had been during the storm.

Now that he had made it across the sea, he supposed he needed new directions. He would have to wait for the stars to come out to be sure, but he thought the mountain lay to the north. He thought about going that way and felt a sort of jealousy and anger. It took him a minute to understand what it was about. He didn't want to leave his little boat behind. He had spent a year carving the thing, and it had brought him across the sea, through a storm, and kept him alive. He couldn't just leave it behind for someone else to steal; it was his. The voices all seemed to agree, but none of them said anything about which way he should go.

Lycus decided to wait for a sign, like he had gotten before. He didn't know what kind of sign it would be, but he had faith now, for the first time in years, perhaps for the first time in his life. He didn't know what the monster wanted, or if it really was a monster. All he knew was that it would show him the way, and he would listen. Perhaps that was how Androcles had felt when they found that cave. Lycus didn't know what to expect or what he would have to do, but he was committed to following the voice.

He spent the day scouting the nearby jungle and found some fruit to eat. He also found some dry wood and brought it back with him to the beach, and built a fire. The jungle was filled with the same kind of ugly tree rodents that had been back in the land he had come from, and he killed two of them easily.

As he sat by his fire, skinning the second rodent as the first roasted on a spike, he heard a bird screech. He looked up, and saw a hawk flying by high above him. It had something in its talons, and droplets of blood fell off it as it flew by. The hawk screeched again and then flew off to the west, down the coastline, and Lycus knew that was where he had to go. He finished his supper and slept by the fire that night. In the morning Lycus got back in his boat and started paddling west up the coast. He didn't know how far he had to go or what he would have to do, but if he followed the voices and signs, he knew they would get him home.

Chapter 60
The Best of Us
1

Everything was white. It was the brightest thing Andronicus had ever seen, and it was all around him. It encompassed every part of his being. The light was everywhere, and it was everything. It was all he was, and all he wasn't, all he was meant to be, and all that he would become. The light was so powerful that it seemed there could be nothing else, and yet deep within the light, there were shadows, and slowly they began to take shape. At first it was just moving images and blurry lines, but then the shadows twisted and pulled and stretched themselves into shapes. They became trees and bushes and then an entire forest. As the shadows cleared, and color came into the world, the forest slowly came into focus.

"This," a child's voice said from the shadows, "just sitting around in the forest, with nothing to do but watch the trees and the birds and the sky."

Andronicus was sitting against a tree in the middle of a forest he recognized from a lifetime ago. He looked over at his oldest friend sitting next to him and felt his own lips moving, but he couldn't hear what he was saying.

"Yes." Thymi looked over at Andronicus with a smile. "I would much rather sit in the forest all day than be a great warrior." Thymi laughed cheerily, and then everything began to fade away and take on new shapes.

When the shadows cleared again, Andronicus was at a table, and all around him sat his old friends: Lycus, Thymi, Theo, and Niko. Androcles was standing off to the side though, staring silently at them. They were all laughing and drinking, enjoying their youth and their health. Andronicus tried to speak, to shout to them, to tell them not to leave. He thought he could do it, keep them from going into the cave. Maybe he could even keep Niko from dying, but nothing came out.

Andronicus jumped to his feet, and they all looked up at him. Then they began to fade away into nothingness too. Only Androcles remained. Andronicus looked at his little brother, standing in the fading room, staring back at him. He tried to run to him, but he couldn't. Andronicus reached out his hand, but Androcles just stared back. Just as the room was falling into total blackness, Andronicus heard his brother's voice. "Find them, Dron. It has to be you. You have to be ready for when he comes."

A strong breeze blew through the open plain, sweeping Andronicus's long hair back from his face. He was back in Swimha. He closed his eyes and breathed in the rich air of the plains, feeling the sun's warmth on his face. When he opened his eyes, Manyara was there. She was walking toward him from far away. Holding her hand was a little boy. He had dark skin, though not as dark as the Swihmehe, and he had shining green eyes.

Andronicus ran to them with his arms outstretched, tears falling down his face. The little boy broke into a big grin, and he ran ahead of his mother, his little arms outstretched toward his father. Andronicus ran, and ran, and ran, but they never got any closer. He tried to shout to them, but nothing came out. The boy stopped running, and Manyara took him by the hand again. Andronicus stared at her soft brown eyes. There was so much he wanted to say to her, so much he wanted to tell her. More than anything he wanted to tell her how sorry he was. He tried to say it with his eyes, and he thought he saw her smile before she faded away with the dirt and the grass and the little boy.

He was in the jungle then, kneeling by a pool of water, staring into the yellow eyes of a big black cat. The cat stared back at him, unblinking. Andronicus didn't try to speak or move; he just knelt there with the beast. Before the jungle faded away, he thought he saw something deep in the heart of the cat's yellow orbs.

A heavy breeze hit Andronicus's face again, this time bringing a gust of sand with it. Andronicus raised an arm to shield his eyes and saw Chaka doing the same beside him. They were in the desert where Chaka had died, but he still looked healthy and young. Andronicus wanted to speak, but he knew he could not. Instead he reached out his hand, and Chaka did the same. He held Chaka's hand for a moment. Chaka smiled and pulled his hand away. When another breeze blew, it took Chaka with it. As he faded away, he spoke his last words once again. "Find them."

Then Andronicus was in a dimly lit room. Cleitus was sitting across from him, taking a drink from a jug. Andronicus felt the anger and guilt come flooding back as he saw his newly dead friend. Alexander had killed him, but it had been Andronicus's fault. He tried to say this, to say anything, but he could not. Cleitus was looking at the fire, not meeting Andronicus's eye. Finally he looked over, the shadows falling across his dark face.

"I thought you were a fighter," Cleitus said, "the best. So, fight."

The last thing Andronicus heard was a voice he didn't recognize.

"Get up," the voice said. It sounded familiar and yet foreign at the same time. "Get up and fight. It has to be you, Andronicus. It has always been you."

Andronicus's eyes snapped open, and the world around him came crashing back as his body flooded with adrenaline. The hands around his neck were strong, and they were squeezing hard, but Andronicus's entire body was coursing with energy. He brought his right fist up, and hit Lycus in the face. He didn't let go, but Andronicus felt his grip loosen slightly. Andronicus punched him again and again, feeling Lycus's hands loosen further. Then he hit Lycus in the ribs and shoved him off.

They rolled over, and Andronicus began pummeling Lycus's face with blows. Lycus took it for a moment and then kicked with his left foot, catching Andronicus in the gut. Andronicus let out a huff of air as Lycus lurched forward. He hit Andronicus square in the nose, breaking it. Then he reached for Andronicus's eyes, his thumbs pressing into them as a look of fiery hatred gripped his face.

Andronicus let out a mangled scream as he felt Lycus's thumbs push against his eyes. He grasped Lycus' arms and dug into his flesh with his fingers. He felt blood run down his hands, and then Lycus' thumbs were gone. Andronicus tried to open his eyes, only to see a blur before Lycus hit him in the face again. Andronicus stumbled back, and Lycus jumped on him, sending them both to the floor.

They scrambled to their feet and dove at each other like lions, clawing at each other's eyes and pummeling each other in the face. They were both shouting and grunting as they hit each other. Andronicus had no time to think or to register the fact that he was trying to kill one of the men he had spent most of his life trying to find. All he could do was try and protect himself from the vicious monster trying to kill him. Andronicus didn't know what had happened to Lycus or what had driven him so mad, but he knew they were past the point of stopping. The fight they were in seemed like it could only end in death.

As they fought each other, they both let out the frustrations of one hundred painful years. They had both spent so much time thinking about what they would say to one another when they finally found each other, but now there were no words.

At one point in the fight, Andronicus took a step backward and tried to reason with his old friend. "Lycus, stop this madness," Andronicus said through panting breaths. His voice sounded thick and nasally from all the blood in his mouth and nose. "You know it's me."

"I have to," Lycus replied, glaring at him with pure hatred, "It won't be you."

Andronicus remembered the voices from the dream. They had all said it had to be him, and he wondered what kind of voices Lycus might have heard.

"I have no idea what you're talking about," Andronicus said, holding his hands out and trying to keep Lycus from leaping at him again. He still couldn't see clearly, and he felt blood running from his right eye.

"That's why it will be me," Lycus said, diving forward again. This time Andronicus was prepared, even with his bad sight. He drove his knee up into Lycus's gut, then brought his elbow down hard on the back of Lycus's head. Lycus fell to his knees, momentarily bringing his hands down to catch himself, and Andronicus slammed his fist down on the back of his head. Andronicus felt his hand break against the back of Lycus' skull, but he brought it down again and again. When Lycus fell onto his face, Andronicus turned him onto his back. Blood covered most of Lycus' face, and his eyes were only half open, but Andronicus began punching him over and over with both hands, ignoring the pain, ignoring his thoughts, ignoring everything but killing the man beneath him.

Somehow he managed to stop himself before Lycus was dead. Puffing with exertion, he looked down at the broken, mangled mess of his old friend's face. Andronicus fell back onto his butt, staring in horror at what he had done. Lycus had attacked him, but Lycus was clearly mad. Andronicus had let the old fire take hold of him and knew he may have killed one of his only true friends, and one of his only sources for answers.

He got up to see if Lycus was still breathing when a huge hand grabbed the back of his neck. The powerful hand picked him up and threw him across the room like a toy. Andronicus scrambled to his feet and looked up, only to see the giant prison guard standing over him, whip in hand. He had a menacing smile on his face, and he brought the whip back over his head in a flash. Andronicus brought his hands up and felt the whip crack against them a second later, and then across his face. The newly drawn blood joined the rest already running down his face as Andronicus prepared to be whipped again.

This time he turned his head away and waited for the whip to crack against his back, but it never came. Instead there was a muffled grunt. Andronicus looked up and saw the huge jailer looming over him, with a look of total shock on his face, and the shining tip of a sword sticking out of his barrel chest. The huge man fell to his knees with a thud. As he toppled over, Andronicus saw Cassander standing behind him, looking terrified.

"What happened here?" Cassander asked, looking from Andronicus's bloody face to the even bloodier face of Lycus, lying on the ground floor.

"Lycus happened," Andronicus said, slowly getting to his feet.

"Wait, you know this man?" Cassander asked, astonished.

"I knew him," Andronicus said as he walked over to Lycus, "but that was long ago. I fear the man he is now is not the man I once knew."

"And that's why you did that to him?" Cassander asked, looking at Andronicus hesitantly.

"He tried to kill me," Andronicus said, kneeling next to him. "I don't know why he did it, but I had to defend myself." Andronicus placed a hand on Lycus's chest. His chest was still rising slowly, and Andronicus could feel his heart pumping.

"Is he alive?" Cassander asked.

Andronicus nodded, standing up again.

"What are you going to do with him?"

"What do you mean?" Andronicus asked, not having had a second to think about it.

"I mean you can't take him with you," Cassander said, causing Andronicus to remember his plan. He was supposed to leave the city tonight, or else Alexander would kill him. All that seemed like it had happened a hundred years ago, and his days with Lycus in their youth seemed like just yesterday. Andronicus stared down at his old friend. Under all the blood and scars it was still Lycus, the same man he had once called a brother.

8

"Andronicus," Cassander said, snapping him out of it, "we have to leave now. Everyone in this prison heard you two fighting, and more guards will be here any second."

"What will they do to him?" Andronicus asked, gesturing toward Lycus.

"I don't know," Cassander said, sounding impatient. "They might kill him. They might keep him in prison. I don't know. But I do know that if we don't leave now, they're going to kill you, and probably me too."

Andronicus knew Cassander was right. They had to leave; they should have left already, but he couldn't just leave Lycus. He may have lost his mind, but perhaps he could be brought back. Andronicus felt torn by the weight of the decision and the pressure of time. He could save Lycus, or at least he could try. He could carry him out on his back, and when they got clear of the city, he could tie him up. When he woke up, Andronicus would force him to talk.

"Andronicus," Cassander said, "it's time. I'm going."

"Help me lift him up," Andronicus said, bending down to pick up Lycus.

"You can't be serious," Cassander said. "He tried to kill you!"

"I can't just leave him here," Andronicus insisted. "Now help me with him."

"You're going to get us both killed," Cassander said, but he bent down and helped pull Lycus onto Andronicus's back.

Andronicus stood, picking Lycus up with him. They left the cell, with Andronicus carrying Lycus the same way he had once carried Chaka. They ran past cell after cell, some men shouting at them, some cheering them on, and others cursing them. When they reached the end of the long tunnel and emerged into the starlight, Andronicus heard soldiers coming around the nearest building.

"Here," Cassander whispered, handing Andronicus his sword and cloak. "Now go. I'll distract them." Andronicus gave Cassander a last look of thanks, then nodded at the boy. Cassander had saved his life many times, and he would likely never see him again. Cassander still looked impatient, but he nodded back, and gave Andronicus a smile, before turning to meet the guards.

Andronicus ran in the opposite direction of the soldiers, and around another building. He heard Cassander hailing them, but he didn't wait around to listen. Andronicus ran through the dark city streets, with Lycus slung over his shoulder. He knew he was almost to the edge of the city, where his things were stashed and his horses tethered. The second horse had originally been for Cleitus, and then he had offered it to Cassander, but never in his wildest dreams would he have guessed it would be for Lycus.

Then, out of nowhere, eight fingers dug into his sides, and Andronicus fell to the ground, sending Lycus into the dirt. In a flash Lycus was on his feet, and then he was gone. Andronicus looked around, but he was nowhere to be seen. He ran to the nearest alleyway, but Lycus wasn't there. He stayed there for a moment, looking around and wondering what to do, and then he heard voices shouting nearby, followed by footsteps.

Andronicus ran away from the shouts, toward the edge of the city, ignoring all the broken bones Lycus had given him. Finally he reached the place where his horses were tethered. He looked around again for Lycus, hoping he might still be nearby.

"Lycus," he whispered as loudly as he dared, "if you're out there, come with me." There was no answer. Andronicus waited a minute longer, hoping Lycus might turn up, but he didn't. Finally Andronicus mounted his horse.

As he rode away, a rush of thoughts flooded his head. Seeing Lycus again had answered many of his questions, but it had also raised quite a few new ones. As Andronicus rode away from the city, and the army, and Alexander, and the life he had been living for the last ten years, he thought about the others.

He had always wondered where they were, what had happened to them, if they were still out there. He had wondered if they were still young like him and if they had been sent to strange far-off lands. He had wondered what might have become of them if they were out there. But he had never really expected to see any of them again. When he saw Lycus' face, it was like seeing Zeus himself. He now had answers, and new questions as well.

He was sure that Thymi and Theo were out there somewhere, and so was Androcles. He remembered the odd visions he had seen when Lycus was strangling him. They had been so much like his visions of the future, but they had been his past. He remembered seeing what his son would have looked like, and wept for what could have been. Mostly the visions had just been memories, but not Androcles. His brother had spoken to him. Andronicus tried to remember what he had said. He had said find them. Chaka had said find them. And now he knew who "them" meant. Lycus was lost, but he was still alive, and the others had to be out there somewhere.

Andronicus looked up at the bright starry sky above and he made a promise, not to Androcles, or Chaka, or Manyara. His promise was not to the gods, or even to the light. Andronicus made a promise to himself. He promised he would find them, no matter how long it might take.

41348917R00449